In the past three yea   _imes_ _.stselling author
Shei. iyn Kenyon has ci..   .. #1 spot sixteen times. This
extraordinary bestseller continues to top every genre she
writes. With more than 25 million copies of her books in
print in over 100 countries, her current series include: The
Dark-Hunters, The League, Chronicles of Nick, and Belador.
Since 2004, she has placed more than 50 novels on the _New
York Times_ list in all formats including manga. The pre-
eminent voice in paranormal fiction, with more than twenty
years of publishing credits in all genres, Kenyon not only
helped to pioneer, but define the current paranormal trend
that has captivated the world.

Visit Sherrilyn Kenyon's websites:
www.darkhunter.com | www.sherrilynkenyon.co.uk

www.facebook.com/AuthorSherrilynKenyon |
www.twitter.com/KenyonSherrilyn

Praise for Sherrilyn Kenyon:

'A publishing phenomenon…[Sherrilyn Kenyon] is the
reigning queen of the wildly successful paranormal scene'
Publishers Weekly

'Kenyon's writing is brisk, ironic and relentlessly
imaginative. These are not your mother's vampire novels'
Boston Globe

'Whether writing as Sherrilyn Kenyon or Kinley
MacGregor, this author delivers great romantic fantasy!'
New York Times bestselling author Elizabeth Lowell

D0755669

30130505501327

Acheron

SHERRILYN KENYON

piatkus

PIATKUS

First published in the US in 2008 by St. Martin's Press, New York
First published in Great Britain in 2008 by Piatkus Books
This paperback edition published in 2012 by Piatkus

Copyright © 2008 by Sherrilyn Kenyon

The moral right of the author has been asserted.

*All characters and events in this publication, other than those
clearly in the public domain, are fictitious and any resemblance
to real persons, living or dead, is purely coincidental.*

All rights reserved.
No part of this publication may be reproduced, stored in a retrieval system, or
transmitted in any form or by any means, without the prior permission in writing
of the publisher, nor be otherwise circulated in any form of binding or cover
other than that in which it is published and without a similar condition including
this condition being imposed on the subsequent purchaser.

A CIP catalogue record for this book
is available from the British Library.

ISBN 978-0-7499-56561
Printed and bound by Clays Ltd, St Ives plc

Papers used by Piatkus are from well-managed forests
and other responsible sources.

MIX
Paper from
responsible sources
FSC® C104740

Piatkus
An imprint of
Little, Brown Book Group
100 Victoria Embankment
London EC4Y 0DY

An Hachette UK Company
www.hachette.co.uk

www.piatkus.co.uk

For my husband, who is my eye in the storm. Hand in hand, we've weathered many typhoons, and together we're still here. Thank you for being my light in the darkness and for showing me what loyalty and love are all about. You are the gentle wind that allows me to soar to the highest level. Thank you.

And for my children, who never shirk at eating more pizza. You guys are the greatest.

Acknowledgments

To the entire staff at St. Martin's for being so great, especially Monique and Matthew, who didn't faint at the length of this book. No author could ask for a better team. Thank you for all the hard work.

To Dianna Love, for keeping me sane through the long days of writing and the delirium that often ensues. Not to mention for being my intrepid tour buddy. Alethea Kontis, for babysitting me on the lockdown weekends and keeping me fed. Kim, Loretta and Tish, for all the verbal support. Pam and Kim, for being my comic relief. Steven, for writing Ash's song and for being the best little brother ever. Jack, Carl, Aimee, Ed, Alex, Soteria, Bryan, Judy and all the support staff who keep the site running so that I can work. Not to mention Zenobia, who is the greatest lithromancer.

Thank you to Pam Gardner, for her winning bid to be the best friend in the book, and Jessica Hayes, who also won this spot in the acknowledgments. Between the two of you alone, we raised over $4000 to help Autism and Diabetes Research. Thank you, ladies!

And to the readers, who love the series and characters as much as I do. For all of you who call Dark-Hunter.com home and who venture to the MySpace pages and Yearof Acheron.com site. And for the RBL women who've been with me from the very beginning—even before there was a Dark-Hunter series. Thank you all. You guys rock!

Last, but not least, Merrilee, for all the hard work you do on my behalf and for making the Dark-Hunter series manga! At last, my lifelong dream is a reality.

AUTHOR'S NOTE

First, let me say that I'm more than aware of the fact that the ancient calendar differed dramatically from our own. But since I'm dealing with a time of unrecorded history, I used our calendar for the dates to allow the reader to have an idea of when things were taking place. I hope those of you who are sticklers for such things will understand why it was necessary.

That being said, I've also taken license with how things were in the ancient world at the beginning. I've structured the world of ancient Greece and Atlantis around a later time period and given them more technological advances than what the historical record shows for the true time of when the book is set.

In my world, they had a lot of nifty toys until Atlantis sank into the ocean and Apollymi's wrath sent mankind back into the Stone Age. This is also dealt with and explained in more detail in the latter part of the book.

It's so strange now to have this tale written. I can still remember the first time I sat down to write a Dark-Hunter novel. Ash was one of the original characters, but back in the day, he was actually the leader of the Daimons and not the Dark-Hunters.

He's changed a lot over the years, but the one thing that hasn't ever changed is my love for him.

For my loyal readers, I want to warn you that the first half of this book is very different from the previous ones. Ash's human life is grim and it's harsh. I promised you the whole sordid truth of it, and that's exactly what I've written. I've pulled no punches.

As a survivor of childhood abuse myself, I know the strength it takes to try and silence the voices in your head and heart that haunt you long after you've broken free. It's not an easy thing to do, and just when you think you've buried those demons, they come back for you with a vengeance.

It takes a lot of strength and courage to trust a stranger when you've been harmed by the very people who were supposed to protect you. But the one thing I've learned is that it can be done. That all of us are worthy and that we all matter. As to this, I can never thank my husband enough for being the man he appeared to be both inside and out. Thank you, baby, for saving me, and for showing me that there are people in the world like you.

As my friend Tish taught me to say: *Digmus Sum*. Thank you, Tish.

So if you're looking for the humor of my previous books, it picks up when we go from Ash's past to present day New Orleans. I assure you all the sarcasm and bantering that the series is known for is alive and well.

But to understand Ash's present personality and mind-set, I think it's imperative to know his past.

And so here it is. Unvarnished and whole. This is the steel that was forged by the fires of hell.

As we leave behind this arc in the series, we will pick up with Stryker's tale, *One Silent Night,* in November, which starts us on the next arc: Jaden's, and it picks up right where this tale ends. The Dark-Hunter world is evolving, but Ash and the others will still be back and will still hold their places in this elaborate universe.

Part I

May 9, 9548 BC

"Kill that baby!"

Archon's angry decree rang in Apollymi's ears as she flew through the marbled halls of Katoteros. There was a fierce wind blowing down the hallway, plastering her black gown against her pregnant body and whipping her white blond hair out in spiraling tendrils. Four of her demons ran behind her, protecting her from the other gods who were more than eager to carry out Archon's orders. She and her Charonte demons had already blasted half of her pantheon back. And she was ready to kill the rest.

They would not take her child!

Betrayal burned deep inside her heart. Since the moment of their union, she'd been true to her husband. Even when she'd learned Archon had been faithless to her, she'd still loved him and welcomed his bastards into her home.

Now he wanted the life of her unborn child.

How could he do this? For centuries she'd been trying to conceive Archon's son—it was all she'd ever wanted.

A babe of her own.

Now due to the prophecy of three small girls—Archon's jealous bastards, her child was to be sacrificed and killed. Because of what? Words those little brats had whispered?

Never.

This was her baby. Hers! And she would kill every Atlantean god in existence to keep him.

"Basi!" She shouted for her niece.

Basi flashed into the hallway before her and staggered until she braced herself against the wall. As the goddess of excess, she was seldom sober—which fit Apollymi's plan perfectly.

3

Basi hiccupped and giggled. "Did you need me, Auntie? By the way, why is everyone so upset? Did I miss something important?"

Apollymi grabbed her by the wrist and then teleported them out of Katoteros where the Atlantean gods made their home down to the hell realm of Kalosis where her brother ruled.

She'd been born here in this dank, forbidden place. This was the only realm that truly scared Archon. Even with all his power, he knew the dark was where Apollymi reigned supreme. Here, with her powers fortified, she could destroy him.

As the goddess of death, destruction and war, Apollymi kept a room in her brother's opulent ebony palace to remind her of her station.

That was where she took Basi now.

Apollymi locked the doors and windows to her room before she summoned her two most trustworthy demon protectors. "Xiamara, Xedrix, I need you."

The demons who resided on her as tattooed marks pulled themselves off her body and manifested before her.

In her current incarnation, Xiamara's everchanging skin tone was red, marbled with white. Long black hair framed a pixieish face where large red eyes glowed with concern. Xiamara's son Xedrix shared her features, but his skin was marbled with red and orange, something it often did when he was nervous. "What do you need, akra?" Xiamara asked, addressing her with the Atlantean term for lady and master.

Apollymi had no idea why Xiamara insisted on calling her akra when they were more like sisters than master and servant. "Guard this room from everyone. I don't care if Archon himself demands entry, you kill him. Do you understand?"

"Your will is ours, akra. No one will disturb you."

"Do their horns have to match their wings?" Basi asked as she spun around the bedpost while eyeing the demons. "I mean really. You'd think to be so colorful, they'd have more variety. I think Xedrix would look better if his were orange."

Apollymi ignored her. She didn't have time for Basi's stupidity. Not if she were to save her son's life.

She wanted this child and she was willing to do anything for him.

Anything.

Her heart hammering, she pulled her Atlantean dagger from her dresser drawer and held it in her hands. The gold hilt was cold against her skin. Black roses and bones were entwined and engraved down the steel blade that glowed in the dim light. It was a dagger meant for ending life.

Today it would be used to give it.

She winced at the thought of what was to come, but there was no other way to save him. Closing her eyes and gripping the cold dagger, she tried not to weep, but one tear slid from the corner of her eye.

Enough! She roared at herself as she angrily wiped it away. This was a time for action, not emotions. Her son needed her.

Her hand trembling from fury and fear, she went to the bed and lay down. She pulled her gown up, exposing her belly. She ran her hand over her distended stomach where her son was waiting, protected and yet in danger. Never again would she be this close to him. Never again would she feel him kick and turn in restlessness as she smiled in tender patience. She was about to separate them even though it wasn't time yet for Apostolos to be born.

But she had no choice.

"Be strong for me, my son," she whispered before she sliced open her stomach to expose him.

"Oh, how disgusting!" Basi whined. "I'm—"

"Don't you move!" Apollymi roared. "You leave this room and I'll rip out your heart."

Eyes wide, Basi froze.

As if knowing what had happened, Xiamara appeared by her side. The red-and-white-skinned demon was the most beautiful and loyal of all of Apollymi's army. In silent understanding, Xiamara lifted the baby out of her and helped Apollymi seal herself shut.

The demon removed the blood red scarf from around her

neck and wrapped Apostolos in it before she held him out to Apollymi and bowed low.

Apollymi pushed the physical pain aside as she took her son into her arms and held him for the very first time. Joy spread through her as she realized he was whole and alive. He was so tiny, so frail. Perfect and beautiful.

Most of all, he was hers and she loved him with every part of herself.

"Live for me, Apostolos," she said, her tears finally flowing. They fell like ice down her cold cheeks, glittering in the darkness. "When the time is right, you'll return here and claim your rightful place as king of the gods. I'll make sure of it." She placed her lips to his blue forehead.

He opened his eyes then to look at her. Mercurial and silver, just like hers, they swirled. And they held within them a wisdom far beyond even hers. It would be by those eyes that mankind would recognize his divinity and treat him accordingly. He brushed her cheek with one tiny fist as if he understood what was meant for him.

She sobbed at the contact. Gods, it wasn't fair! He was her baby. She'd waited a lifetime for this and now . . .

"Damn you, Archon, damn you! I will never forgive you for this."

She held her son close and never wanted to let him go.

But she must.

"Basi?" she snapped at her niece who was still swinging around the bedpost.

"Mmm?"

"Take him. Put him in the belly of a pregnant queen. Do you understand?"

She let go and righted herself. "Um, I can do that. What about the queen's brat?"

"Merge Apostolos's life force with that of the queen's child. Let her know by oracle that if my child dies, so does hers." That would protect him more than anything else.

But there was one more thing to be done. Apollymi jerked the white sfora from her neck and held it to Apostolos's chest. If anyone suspected he was her son or any god detected his presence in the human realm, they would kill him instantly.

His powers would have to be bound and locked away until he was old enough and strong enough to fight back. She placed the orb to his chest and watched as his godhood slid from him to the sfora. His tiny body turned from blue to the pale skin of humanity.

Now he would be safe. Not even the gods would know what she'd done.

Clutching the sfora tight in her hand, she kissed his brow one more time before she held him out to her niece. "Take him. And don't betray me, Basi. If you do, Archon will be the least of your fears. So help me, I won't rest until I bathe in your entrails."

Basi's brown eyes widened. "Baby in belly. Human realm. Don't tell anyone and don't mess up. Got it." She vanished, instantly.

Apollymi sat there, looking at the spot where they'd been. Her heart screamed out, wanting her baby returned.

If only . . .

"Xiamara, follow her and make sure she does as she was ordered."

The demon bowed before she vanished.

Her heart broken, Apollymi remained in her bloodied bed. She wanted to weep and to scream, but why bother? It would do no good. Her tears and pleas wouldn't prevent Archon from killing her child. His brats had him convinced that Apostolos would destroy their pantheon and replace Archon as the king of the gods.

So be it.

Her body aching, she pushed herself from the bed. "Xedrix?"

Xiamara's son appeared before her. "Yes, akra?"

"Fetch me a stone from the sea, please."

He appeared confused by her order, but he quickly complied.

When he returned, she wrapped the rock in swaddling. Weak from her son's birth and her own anger and fear, she leaned against Xedrix and held his arm. "Take me to Archon."

"Are you sure, akra?"

She nodded.

The demon helped her back to Katoteros. They appeared in the center of the hall where Archon stood with his daughters Chara and Agapa—ironically the goddesses of joy and love. The two of them had been born parthenogenically the first time Archon had looked at Apollymi. Together the goddesses had sprang out of his chest. His love for Apollymi had been legendary. Until he'd destroyed it by asking for the one thing she'd never give him.

The life of her son.

Archon's features were perfectly formed. Tall and muscular, he stood with his blond hair shining in the dim light. Truly, he was the most beautiful of all gods. Too bad that beauty was only superficial.

His blue eyes narrowed at the bundle in her arms.

"It's about time you came to your senses. Give me that child."

She moved away from Xedrix and placed the stone baby in her husband's arms.

Archon glowered at her. "What is this?"

"That is what you deserve, you bastard, and it is all you'll ever get from me."

By the light in his eyes, she knew he wanted to strike her. He didn't dare. They both knew who the stronger god was and it wasn't him. He ruled only because she stood at his side. To rise against her would be the last mistake he'd ever make.

By Chthonian law, one god was forbidden from ever killing another. To do so would bring their wrath down on the foolish god who'd angered them. The punishment for such actions was swift, brutal and irreversible.

Right now, Apollymi was embracing her rational thought over her turbulent emotions by a narrow margin. For Archon to strike her would push her over the edge and he knew it. It would make her forget to be afraid of the Chthonians and then she'd unleash the whole of her fury against him. She would no longer care who was punished and who died . . . not even herself.

Patience to the spider . . . She reminded herself of her mother's most favored saying.

8

She would bide her time until Apostolos grew into his own. Then he would rule in Archon's place and show the king of the gods what it meant to be all powerful.

For her son's sake, she wouldn't upset the capricious Chthonians who might very well side with Archon and kill her child. They alone could permanently strip her powers and destroy Apostolos. After all, Archon and his lover Themis's three bastard daughters had been given the power of fate over everyone and everything. And out of their stupidity and fear, the Greek Fates had accidentally cursed her son.

That alone was enough to make her want to kill her husband who stared at her with a confused frown.

"You would damn us all for one child?" Archon asked.

"You would damn my baby for three half-Greek bastards?"

His nostrils flared. "For once be reasonable. The girls didn't realize they were condemning him when they spoke. They're still learning their powers. They were afraid that he'd supplant them in our affections. It's why they were holding hands when they spoke their fears. And because of that, their word is law and it can't be undone. If he lives, we die."

"Then we die, because he *will* live. I've made sure of it."

Archon bellowed before he threw the swaddled stone through the wall. He reached for Agapa and Chara and began chanting.

Apollymi's eyes flared red at what they were doing. It was an imprisonment spell.

For her.

And because they united their powers, they would be able to bring her to heel.

Even so, she laughed. But most of all, she took note of every god who joined in to help her husband bind her. "You will all regret what you've done here this day. When Apostolos returns, you will all pay dearly."

Xedrix put himself between her and the others. Apollymi placed one hand on his shoulder to keep him from attacking. "They're not going to hurt us, Xedrix. They can't."

"No," Archon said bitterly, "but you will remain locked in Kalosis until either you reveal Apostolos's location or he dies. Only then will you be returned to Katoteros."

Apollymi laughed. "My son, at his maturity, will have the power to come to me. When he releases me, the world as you know it will die. And I will take you all down. *All* of you."

Archon shook his head. "We will find him. We will kill him."

"You will fail and I'll dance on your grave."

The Diary of Ryssa,
Princess of Didymos

June 23, 9548 BC

My mother, Queen Aara, was lying on her gilded bed, her body covered in sweat, her face ashen as an attendant brushed her damp, blond hair from her pale blue eyes. Even through the pain, I'd never known my mother to appear more joy-filled than she did that day and I wondered if she'd been this happy at my own birth.

The room was crowded with court officials and my father, the king, stood to the side of the bed with his Head of State. The long, glass windows were open, letting the fresh sea air offer relief to the heat of the summer day.

"It is another beautiful boy," the midwife happily proclaimed, wrapping the newborn infant in a blanket.

"By sweet Artemis's hand, Aara, you've done me proud!" my father said as a loud jubilant shout ran through the room's occupants. "Twin boys to rule over our twin isles!"

At only seven years of age, I jumped up and down in glee. At long last, and after my mother's numerous miscarriages and stillbirths, I had not one brother, but two.

Laughing, my mother cuddled the second-born infant to her pale breast while an additional midwife cleaned the firstborn.

I snuck through the crowd to watch the firstborn baby with the midwife. Tiny and beautiful, he squirmed and struggled to breathe through his newborn lungs. He had finally taken a deep, clear breath when I heard the cry of alarm from the woman who held him.

"Zeus have mercy, the eldest is malformed, majesties!"

My mother looked up, her brow creased by worry. "How so?"

The midwife carried him over to her.

I was terrified that something was wrong. The babe looked fine to me.

I waited while the baby reached for the brother who had shared the womb with him for these months past. It was as if he sought comfort from his twin.

Instead, my mother pulled his brother away, out of his sight and reach. "It cannot be," my mother sobbed. "He is blind."

"Not blind, majesty," the eldest wisewoman said as she stepped forward, through the crowd. Her white robes were heavily embroidered with gold threads and she wore an ornate gold crown over her faded gray hair. "He was sent to you by the gods."

My father, the king, narrowed his eyes angrily at my mother. "You were unfaithful?" he accused her.

"Nay, never."

"Then how is it he came from your loins? All of us here witnessed it."

The room as a whole looked to the wisewoman who stared blankly at the tiny, helpless baby who cried out for someone to hold him and offer him solace. Warmth.

But no one did.

"He will be a destroyer, this child," the wisewoman said, her ancient voice loud and ringing so that all could hear her proclamation. "His touch will bring death to many. Not even the gods themselves will be safe from his wrath."

I gasped, not really understanding the significance of her words.

How could a mere baby hurt anyone? He was tiny. Helpless.

"Then kill him now." My father ordered a guard to draw his sword and slay the infant.

"Nay!" the wisewoman said, halting the guard before he could carry out the king's will. "Kill this infant and your other son dies as well. Their life forces are combined. 'Tis the will of the gods that you should raise him to manhood."

The elder twin sobbed.

I sobbed, too, not understanding their hatred of a simple baby.

14

"I will not raise a monster," my father snarled.

"You have no choice." The wisewoman took the baby from the midwife and offered it to my mother.

Frowning, I saw a note of satisfaction in the midwife's eyes before the beautiful blond woman made her way through the crowd to vanish from the room.

"He was born of your body, Majesty," the wisewoman said, drawing my attention back toward her and my mother. "He is your son."

The baby squalled even louder, reaching again for my mother. *His* mother. She cringed away from him, clutching her second-born even tighter than before. "I will not suckle it. I will not touch it. Get it away from my sight."

The wisewoman took the child to my father. "And what of you, Majesty? Will you not acknowledge him?"

"Never. That child is no son of mine."

The wisewoman took a deep breath and presented the infant to the room. Her grip was loose with no love or compassion evident in her touch.

"Then he will be called Acheron for the River of Woe. Like the river of the Underworld, his journey shall be dark, long and enduring. He will be able to give life and to take it. He will walk through his life alone and abandoned—ever seeking kindness and ever finding cruelty."

The wisewoman looked down at the infant in her hands and uttered the simple truth that would haunt the boy for the rest of his existence. "May the gods have mercy on you, little one. No one else ever will."

August 30, 9541 BC

"Why do they hate me so, Ryssa?"

I paused at my loom to look up at Acheron's timid approach. At age seven, he was an incredibly handsome boy. His golden hair gleamed in the room as if it had been touched by the gods who seemed to have abandoned him. "No one hates you, akribos."

But in my heart I knew the truth.

And so did he.

He came closer to me and I saw the red, angry handprint on his face. There were no tears in his swirling silver eyes. He'd grown so used to being hit that it no longer seemed to bother him.

At least nowhere other than in his heart.

"What happened?" I asked.

He looked away.

I left my loom and crossed the short distance to his side. Kneeling in front of him, I gently brushed the blond hair away from his swollen cheek. "Tell me."

"She hugged Styxx."

I knew without asking who *she* was. He'd been with our mother. I'd never understood how she could be so loving to me and Styxx and yet so cruel to Acheron. "And?"

"I wanted a hug, too."

Then I saw it. The telltale signs of a boy who wanted nothing more than his mother's love. The shallow trembling of his lips, the slight watering of his eyes.

"Why is it that I look exactly like Styxx and yet I'm unnatural while he is not? I don't understand why I'm a monster. I don't feel like one to me."

I couldn't explain it to him, for I, unlike the others, had

16

never seen the difference myself. How I wished Acheron knew the mother I did.

But they all called him a monster.

I saw only a little boy. A small child who wanted nothing more than to be accepted by a family that wanted to disown him. Why couldn't my parents look at him and see what a kind, gentle soul he was? Quiet and respectful, he never sought to harm anyone or anything. We played together and we laughed. Most of all, I held him while he cried.

I took his little hand into mine. A soft hand. A boy's hand. There was no malice in it. No murder.

Acheron had always been a tender child. While Styxx sought to whine and complain over every minor thing, to take my toys and those of any other child near him, Acheron had sought only to make peace. To comfort those around him.

He seemed older than a child of seven. There were times when he seemed even older than I.

His eyes were strange. Their silver, swirling color betrayed the birthright that linked him to the gods. But surely that should make him special not horrendous.

I offered him a smile that I hoped would ease some of his pain. "One day, Acheron, the world will know just what a special boy you are. The day will come when no one will fear you. You shall see."

I moved to hug him, but he pulled back. He was used to people hurting him and even though he knew I wouldn't, he was still reluctant to accept my comfort.

As I stood, the door to my sitting room opened. A large number of guards came inside.

Scared of the sight, I stepped back not knowing what they wanted. Acheron clenched his small fists in the skirt of my blue gown as he huddled behind my right leg.

My father and uncle walked through the men until they stood before me. The two of them were virtually identical in looks. They had the same blue eyes, the same wavy blond hair and fair skin. Though my uncle was three years younger than my father, one would never guess to look at them. They could easily pass as twins.

"I told you he would be with her," my father said to Uncle Estes. "He's corrupting her again."

"Don't worry," Estes said. "I shall take care of the matter. You'll never again have to worry about him."

"What do you mean?" I asked, terrified of their dire tone. Did they intend to kill Acheron?

"Never you mind," my father snapped at me. I'd never heard such a harsh tone from him before. It made my blood run cold.

He grabbed Acheron and shoved him toward my uncle.

Acheron looked panicked. He reached for me, but my uncle took him roughly by his arm and jerked him away.

"Ryssa!" Acheron called.

"No!" I shouted, trying to help him.

My father pulled me back and held me. "He is going to a better place."

"Where?"

"Atlantis."

I watched in horror as Acheron was taken away, screaming for me to save him.

Atlantis was a long way from here. Too far, and up until a very short time ago, we'd been at war with them. I'd heard nothing but terrible things about that place and everyone who lived there.

I looked up at my father, sobbing. "He'll be afraid."

"His kind are never afraid."

Acheron's screams and pleas denied those words.

My father might be a powerful king, but he was wrong. I knew the fear inside Acheron's heart.

And I knew the fear of my own.

Would I ever see my brother again?

November 3, 9532 BC

It has been nine years since I last saw my brother, Acheron. Nine years and not a day had gone by without my wondering what he was doing. How he was being treated.

Whenever Estes visited, I always took him aside and asked about Acheron.

"He's fine and healthy, Ryssa. I cherish him as an addition to my household. He has everything he requires. I shall be glad to tell him that you asked after his welfare."

Still, something inside me was never quite content with those words. I'd petitioned father repeatedly to send for Acheron. To at least bring him home for a holiday. As a prince, he should never have been sent away. Yet there he stayed in a country that was constantly on the brink of war with ours. Even though Estes was an ambassador, it didn't change the fact that if we went to war, Acheron, as a Greek Prince, would be killed.

And Father refused every request I made.

I'd been writing to Acheron for years and normally he wrote back religiously. His letters were always brief with only a handful of details, but even so I cherished every one.

So when a letter had come to me a few weeks ago, I'd thought nothing unusual about it.

Not until I read it.

> Greetings most esteemed and exalted Princess Ryssa.
>
> Forgive me for my forwardness. Forgive me my impertinence. I found one of your letters written to Acheron and have, at great peril to myself, decided to write to you. I cannot tell you what harms befall him, but if you truly love your brother as you say you do, then I would ask you to come and see him.

I'd told no one about the letter. It hadn't even been signed. For all I knew it was a hoax.

Yet I couldn't shake the feeling that it wasn't, that Acheron needed me.

For days I debated about going until I could stand it no more.

Taking my personal guard Boraxis with me for protection, I snuck out of the palace and told my maids to tell my Father I was visiting my aunt in Athens. Boraxis thought I was a great fool for traveling all the way to Atlantis for a letter that the author hadn't even signed, but I didn't care.

If Acheron needed me, then I would be there.

However that courage faltered days later as I found myself outside my uncle's home in the capital city of Atlantis. The large gleaming red building was even more intimidating than our palace at Didymos. It was as if it had been designed for no other purpose than to inspire fear and awe. Of course, as our ambassador, it would benefit Estes to impress our enemies so.

Far more advanced than my Greek homeland, the island kingdom of Atlantis glistened and glowed. There was more activity from the people around me than I'd ever seen before. It was truly a bustling metropolis.

Swallowing the fear I felt, I looked at Boraxis. Taller than most men, with coarse black hair he wore braided down his back, he was large and burly. Lethal. And he was loyal to me to a fault, even though he was a servant. He'd been protecting me since I was a child and I knew I could rely on him.

He would never allow me to be harmed.

Reminding myself of that, I walked up the marble stairs, toward the golden entrance. A servant opened the door even before I reached it.

"My lady," he said diplomatically, "may I help you?"

"I've come to see Acheron."

He inclined his head and told me to follow him inside. I found it odd that the servant didn't ask me for my name or business with my brother. At home, no one was allowed near any of the royal family without a thorough screening.

To admit someone unknown into our private residence was a crime punishable by death. Yet this man thought nothing of leading us through Uncle's home.

Once we reached another hall, the older man in front of me turned back to look at Boraxis. "Will your guard be joining you for your time with Acheron?"

I frowned at the odd question. "I suppose not."

Boraxis sucked his breath in sharply. There was worry in his deep brown eyes. "Princess . . ."

I put my hand on his arm. "I should be fine. Wait here and I'll return quickly."

He didn't look pleased by my decision and honestly neither was I, but surely no harm would come to me in my uncle's home. So I left him there and continued down the hallway.

And as we walked, what struck me most about my uncle's home was how eerily silent it was. Not even a whisper could be heard. No one laughed. No one spoke.

Only our footsteps echoed down the long, dark corridor. Black marble stretched as far as I could see, reflecting our images back at us as we made our way through the opulence of carved naked statuary and exotic plants and flowers.

The servant led me to a room on the far side of the house and opened the door.

I stepped inside and hesitated as I realized it was Acheron's bedroom. How very strange for him to admit me here without knowing I was Acheron's sister. Then again, perhaps he did. That would explain much.

Aye, that must be it. He must have realized I looked a great deal like my brothers. Except for Acheron's divine silver eyes, we had identical coloring.

Relaxing, I glanced about. It was an exceptionally large room with an oversized hearth. There were two settees before the stone hearth with an odd, pole structure between them. It reminded me of the punishment block, but that made no sense. Perhaps it was something unique to Atlantis. I'd heard all my life that the people here had bizarre customs.

The bed itself was rather small for a room this size, with four tall posts intricately carved into the design of a bird.

On each post, the bird's head was turned upside down so that the beaks curled outward like hooks to hold bed curtains back, yet there were no bed curtains there.

Like the foyer leading to the room, the walls were a shiny black marble that reflected my image back to me perfectly. And as I looked about, I realized there were no windows in this room at all. Nor was there a balcony. The only light came from wall sconces scattered about. It made the room very dark and sinister.

How very strange . . .

Three servants were making Acheron's bed and a fourth woman oversaw them. The overseer was a frail woman, slight of stature who appeared around the age of forty or so.

"It's not time," she said to the man who had led me through the house. "He's still preparing himself."

The man curled his lip at her. "Would you have me tell Gerikos that I kept a client waiting while Acheron dawdles?"

"But he hasn't had time to eat yet," the woman insisted. "He's been working all morning without a single rest."

"Fetch him."

I frowned at their whispered words and behavior. Something was very wrong here. Why would my brother, a prince, be working?

The woman turned toward a door on the far side of the room.

"Wait," I said, stopping her. "I'll get him. Where is he?"

The woman passed a fearful look to the man.

"It's her time with him," the man said firmly. "Let the lady do as she wishes."

The older woman stood back and opened the door to an antechamber. As I stepped through, I heard her and the man gather the servants and leave.

Again, how very peculiar . . .

Hesitantly, I stepped into the room expecting to find Styxx's twin brother. An arrogant youth who thought he knew everything about the world. An insulting, boastful man-child who was sullen and spoiled who would wonder why I was bothering him with so foolish a quest.

I was completely unprepared for what I found.

Acheron sat in a large, bathing pond alone. He had his flawless bare back to me and was bent over with his blond head against the rim as if he were too tired to sit up while he bathed himself. His long hair hung just past his shoulders and was damp, but not wet.

My heart pounding, I moved forward and noticed a strong scent of oranges in the air. A small tray of bread and cheese was set on the floor beside him, untouched.

"Acheron?" I whispered.

He froze for a moment, then rinsed his face in the water. He left the tub and quickly toweled himself dry as if completely unabashed by the fact that I had intruded on his bath.

There was an air of power that surrounded him as he toweled himself with short, quick strokes, then tossed the towel toward a small stack of them.

For an instant, I was captured by the youthful, masculine beauty of him. By the fact that he made no move to dress or cover himself. All that adorned him were gold bands. He had a thin one around his neck that held a small pendant of some sort. Thicker bands encircled each of his biceps at the top of his arm and at the crook of his elbow with another band around both wrists. A chain of smaller circles connected each band down the length of his arms. And a band of gold with a small circle attached was worn around each ankle.

As he approached me, I was stunned by what I saw. He was Styxx's twin in physical looks and yet I saw few similarities between them.

Styxx moved fast. Mercurially.

Acheron was slow. Methodical. He was like a sultry shadow whose every movement was a poetic symphony of muscle, sinew and grace.

He was thinner than Styxx. Much thinner, as if he didn't get enough food to eat. Even so, his muscles were extremely well shaped and honed to perfection.

He still had those eerie silver eyes, but I only glimpsed them briefly before he averted his gaze to the floor at my feet.

There was also something else. An air of hopeless resignation surrounded him. It was one I'd seen countless times from the peasants and beggars who came to collect alms from the palace back gate.

"Forgive me, my lady," he said softly, his voice strangely seductive and quiet as he spoke between clenched teeth. "I didn't know you'd come."

His chains jingling softly in the quietness, he moved behind me like a sleek, seductive wraith. He reached around my neck and unfastened my cloak.

Stunned by his actions, I didn't think to protest when he removed the garment and dropped it to the floor. It wasn't until he brushed my hair back from my neck and moved to kiss the bared flesh that I bolted from him.

"What are you doing?" I asked.

He looked as puzzled as I felt, but still he kept his gaze locked on the floor before me. "I wasn't prepped on what you paid for, my lady," he said quietly. "I assumed from your looks that you wanted me gentle. Am I wrong?"

I was completely baffled by his words as well as the fact that he continued to keep his jaw locked. Why did he speak that way? "Paid for what? Acheron, it is I. Ryssa."

He frowned as if he had no memory of my name. He reached for me again.

I stepped away and grabbed my cloak up from the floor. "I'm your sister, Acheron. Do you not know me?"

His eyes flashed angrily as he met my gaze for an instant. "I have no sister."

My thoughts whirled as I tried to make sense of this. This wasn't the boy who wrote letters to me virtually every day, the boy who told me of his days of leisure.

"How can you say that after all the gifts and letters I've sent you?"

His face relaxed as if he finally understood. "Ah, this a game you wish to play with me, my lady. You wish me to be your brother."

I glared at him in frustration. "No, Acheron, this isn't a game. You *are* my brother and I write to you almost every day and you, in turn, write to me."

I could sense he wanted to look at me and yet he didn't.

"I'm illiterate, my lady. I won't be able to play your game that way."

The door behind me swung open. A short, round man wearing a long Atlantean formesta robe came through it. He was reading from a parchment and not paying attention to us.

"Acheron, why aren't you in your . . ." his voice trailed off as he looked up to see me.

His gaze narrowed dangerously.

"What is this?" he growled. He turned angry eyes to Acheron who took two steps back. "Are you taking clients without notifying me?"

I saw the fear on Acheron's face.

"No, despotis," Acheron said using the Atlantean term for master. "I would never do such."

Fury curled the man's lips. He grabbed Acheron by the hair and forced him to his knees on the hard, stone floor. "What is she doing here then? Are you giving yourself away for free?"

"No, despotis," Acheron said, clenching his fists as if trying not to reach up and touch the man who was wrenching his hair. "Please. I swear I've done nothing wrong."

"Let him go!" I grabbed the man's hand and tried to force him away from my brother. "How dare you assault a prince! I shall have your head for this!"

The man laughed in my face. "He's no prince. Are you, Acheron?"

"No, despotis. I am nothing."

The man called for his guards to escort me out.

They came immediately into the room to take me.

"I will not go," I told him. I spun on the guards and gave them my haughtiest glare. "I am the Princess Ryssa of the House of Arikles of Didymos. I demand to see my Uncle Estes. Right. Now."

For the first time, I saw reservation enter the man's eyes. "Forgive me, Princess," he said, his tone less than apologetic. "I will have you taken to your uncle's greeting room."

He nodded to the guards.

Appalled by his arrogance, I turned to leave. In the black marble, I saw him whisper something to Acheron.

Acheron's face paled. "Idikos promised I wouldn't have to see him anymore."

The man yanked on Acheron's hair. "You will do as you're told. Now get up and prepare yourself."

The guards closed the door and forced me from the room. They led me back through the house until we came to a small greeting room that was bare save for three small settees.

I didn't know or understand what was going on here. Had anyone ever touched me or Styxx the way that man had touched Acheron, my father would have had them instantly killed.

No one was allowed to speak to us with anything less than respect and reverence.

"Where's my uncle?" I asked the guards as they started to withdraw.

"He's in town, Highness. He'll be back shortly."

"Send for him. Now."

The guard inclined his head to me, then closed the door.

I'd only been there a short time when a secret door opened beside the hearth. It was the overseer who'd been in Acheron's room when I first arrived, the older woman who'd been concerned for his welfare.

"Your highness?" she asked hesitantly. "Is it really you?"

It was then I realized who she must be. "You're the one who wrote asking me to visit?"

She nodded.

I breathed in relief. Finally someone who could explain. "What's going on here?"

The woman drew a deep, ragged breath as if what she was about to say hurt her deeply. "They sell your brother, my lady. They do things to him that no one should have to suffer."

My stomach shrank at her words. "What do you mean?"

She twisted her hands in the sleeve of her dress. "How old are you, my lady?"

"Three and twenty."

"Are you a maiden?"

I was offended that she would dare ask such an intimate question. "That is not your concern."

26

"Forgive me, my lady. I meant no offense. I'm merely trying to see if you will understand what they do to him. Do you know what a tsoulus is?"

"Of course, I . . ." Absolute horror consumed me. It was an Atlantean term that had no real Greek translation, but I knew the word. They were young men and women trained as sexual slaves for the wealthy and noble. Unlike prostitutes and others of that ilk, they were very carefully trained and sequestered from an early age.

The same age my brother had been when they took him away from home.

"Acheron is a tsoulus?"

She nodded.

My head reeled. This couldn't be. "You lie."

She shook her head no. "It's why I told you to come, my lady. I knew you wouldn't believe it unless you saw it for yourself."

And I still didn't believe it. It wasn't possible. "My uncle would never allow such."

"Your uncle is the one who sells him. What do you think paid for this house?"

I felt sick with the news and still part of me denied what was truly obvious. "I don't believe you."

"Then come, if you dare, and see for yourself."

I didn't want to and yet I followed her into the back passageways of the house. We walked endlessly until we reached the antechamber where Acheron had been bathing.

She held her finger to her lips to caution me to silence.

It was then I heard them. I might be virgin, but I wasn't naive. I had overheard others copulating at the parties my father forbade me to attend.

But worse than the sounds of pleasure were the cries of pain I heard from my brother. The man was hurting Acheron and he was taking great pleasure in the pain he caused him.

I started for the door only to find the woman in my way.

She spoke in a low, deadly tone. "Stop them, my lady, and your brother will suffer in ways you cannot imagine."

Her whispered words went through me. My soul screamed out for me to stop this. But the woman had been

27

right about everything so far. She knew my brother and uncle far better than I did.

The last thing I wanted was to see him hurt more.

Finally, after what seemed to be an eternity, there was silence.

I heard heavy footsteps cross the bedchamber, then the door opened and closed.

Stunned, I couldn't breathe. I couldn't move.

The maid opened the door to his room to show Acheron chained to the bed by those circles. The ones at his wrists and ankles had been slid onto the bird beaks that decorated the four posts.

And I'd stupidly thought them to be hooks for bed curtains.

"I wasn't prepped on what you paid for, my lady. I assumed from your looks that you wanted me gentle. Am I wrong?"

Those words tore through me as I watched the woman unfasten him.

I couldn't take my eyes off the sight of him lying there, naked. Injured. Bleeding.

My brother.

Tears filled my eyes as I remembered him the last time I'd seen him. His plump face had been hurt, but not like this. Now his lips were split, his left eye swelling, his nose bloodied. There were red handprints and bruises forming over most of his body.

No one deserved this.

I took a step forward at the same time the far door opened. The overseer motioned me out of the room.

Terrified, I rushed to the shadows where I could hear but not be seen.

A curse rang out. "What has happened here?" I recognized Uncle Estes's voice.

"I'm fine, Idikos," Acheron said, his voice thick and pain-filled. It sounded as if he left the bed and stumbled.

I expected my uncle to be angry at the man who'd hurt Acheron. He wasn't. His wrath was for my brother.

"You're worthless," Estes snarled. "Look at you. You're not worth a lead sola like this."

28

"I'm fine, Idikos," Acheron insisted in a voice so obsequious it turned my stomach. "I can clean my—"

"Fetch the block and scold," Estes said, interrupting him.

I heard Acheron's protest, but instead of words, his voice was muffled as if something prevented him from speaking.

I wanted the courage to barge into the room and tell them to stop, but I couldn't seem to make my feet obey me. I was too horrified to move.

I listened as chains clinked and then I heard the sound of wood striking flesh.

Acheron cried out, a muffled sound of pain.

The beating dragged on and on until Acheron was finally silent. I sank to the floor, weeping for him. I held my fist to my mouth, silencing my tears as I tried to think of what I should do. How I could stop this?

Who in the world would ever believe me? Estes was my father's most beloved brother. There was no way he'd take my word over his. None.

"Put him in the box," Estes said.

"For how long?" another man's voice asked.

I heard Estes's disgusted sigh. "Even with his ability to heal quickly, it'll be at least a day before he's well enough to entertain again. Find Ores and make him pay us for our losses. Cancel Acheron's appointments and leave him in there until tomorrow morning."

"What about food?" the female overseer asked.

Estes snarled, "If he can't work, he can't eat. He hasn't earned his food this day."

I heard a door open and close.

"Now, where is my niece?"

"She's in the greeting room," the man said.

"She wasn't there when I came in."

"She said she was going into town," the overseer quickly supplied. "She'll be back shortly, I'm sure."

"Let me know the instant she returns," Estes snarled. "Tell her Acheron is away, visiting friends."

The men left the room.

I sat there on the floor, staring at the bathing pond. Staring at the mirrored walls of this room.

How many clients had my brother entertained? How many days had he lived with what I'd just witnessed?

He'd been gone for nine years. Surely it hadn't always been like this for him. Had it?

The very thought sickened me.

The overseer returned. I saw the horror in her eyes and wondered if I held the same look in mine.

"How long have they done this to him?" I asked.

"I've worked here for almost a year, my lady. It's been going on since before I came."

I tried to think of what I should do. I was a woman. Nothing in this world of male power. My uncle wouldn't listen to me. For that matter, my father wouldn't listen to me.

He would never believe his brother could do such a thing. Just as I couldn't believe the uncle whom I had always loved and adored could do such a thing.

Yet there was no denying this.

How could Estes come to our palace and sup with me and Styxx, knowing that while he was here at home, he was selling a boy who was identical to Styxx in every way, but for his eyes?

It didn't make sense.

The only thing I knew was that I couldn't leave Acheron here. Not like this.

"Can you get my guard to this room without being seen?" I asked her.

The maid nodded.

She left me and I waited in my corner too afraid to move.

When she returned with Boraxis, I finally found the courage to stand.

Boraxis frowned as he helped me to my feet. "Are you all right, my lady?"

I nodded numbly. "Where is Acheron?" I asked the maid.

She led me into his bedchamber.

Again I saw the bed that was still mussed and bloodied. Averting my gaze, I followed her to a door.

When she opened it, Acheron was inside, kneeling on a hard pad that had rough bumps on it so that it would bite into his knees, causing him pain. The inner room was so tiny, that I knew it had been built for no other purpose than to be a punishment for him. He was naked, his body bruised and bloodied. His wristbands had been joined together behind his back, but what captured my attention most was the bottoms of his feet.

They were blackened by bruises.

Now I understood the sound I'd heard. What better place to punish someone when you didn't want their body damaged? No one would see the bottoms of his feet.

As gently as we could, the overseer and I took him from the room. There was a strange strap buckled around his head. As the maid removed it, I realized it held a large barbed ball underneath his tongue. There was fresh blood leaking from the corners of his mouth.

I cringed as she pulled it away and he hissed in pain.

"Put me back," he said between his clenched teeth as the maid freed his hands.

"No," I told him. "I'm getting you out of here."

Still he kept his teeth firmly clenched. "I'm forbidden to leave, my lady. Ever. Please, you must put me back. It's only worse when I fight them."

My heart broke at his words. What had they done to him that he was too terrified to even attempt to leave?

He tried to return to his torture room, but I cut him off and forced him back.

"I won't let them hurt you anymore, Acheron. I swear it. I'm taking you home."

He looked at me as if the word was alien to him. "I *have* to stay here," he insisted. "It's not safe for me outside."

I ignored him and turned toward the maid. "Where are his clothes?"

"He doesn't have any, my lady. He doesn't need any for what they use him for."

I winced at her words.

"So be it." I wrapped him in my cloak and with Boraxis's help, we took him from the house even while Acheron protested every step of the way. My legs and hands were shaking in fear that we would be discovered any moment by Estes or one of his servants.

31

Luckily the maid knew every back way through the house and out to the street.

Somehow, we made it to a rented enclosed herio behind the house. Boraxis got up on top to ride with the driver while Acheron and I rode inside. Alone.

Together.

I didn't really breathe again until Estes's house had faded and we were outside the city walls, across the bridge and on the road that would eventually take us to the docks.

Acheron sat in the corner, looking outside through the small windows and saying nothing.

His eyes were dead. Lifeless. As if he'd seen one horror too many.

"Do you need a doctor?" I asked.

He shook his head no.

I wanted to soothe and comfort him, but wasn't sure if anything on this earth could do that.

We rode in complete silence until we reached a small village. The driver changed horses while we entered a small home to wait. I rented a room from an older woman so that we could wash and rest in peace.

Boraxis somehow found or bought Acheron clothes. They were somewhat small for him and rough in texture, but he didn't complain. He merely took them and dressed himself inside the rented room.

I noticed Acheron had a limp as he came out of the room to where I waited in the narrow hallway. My heart ached at the thought of his walking on his bruised feet and yet he still said no words of complaint.

"Come, Acheron, we should eat while we can."

Panic flared in his eyes. It was instantly followed by a look of resignation.

"What's wrong?" I asked.

He didn't respond. He merely pulled the cowl of his cloak over his head as if to shield himself from the world. With his head held low and his arms wrapped around himself, he followed me to the small dining room below.

I headed for a table in the back, near the hearth.

"Who do I have to pay for the food?" Acheron asked quietly, his face completely shielded by his cowl.

I looked up at him with a frown. "You have money?"

He looked as baffled by my question as I was by his.

"If he can't work, he can't eat. He hasn't earned his food this day." My stomach shrank as I remembered what Estes had said. Tears choked me.

He thought I wanted him to . . .

"I will pay for our food, Acheron, with money."

The relief on his face tugged even more at my heart.

I sat down. Acheron moved around the table and knelt on the floor to my right, just behind me.

I scowled at him over my shoulder. "What are you doing?"

"Forgive me, my lady. I meant no offense to you." He scooted back on his knees several more inches.

Completely flabbergasted, I turned around to stare at him. "Why are you on the floor?"

He looked immediately disappointed. "I shall wait for you in the room."

He moved to leave.

"Wait," I said, taking his arm. "Aren't you hungry? I was told you hadn't eaten."

"I am hungry," he said simply from between his clenched teeth.

"Then sit."

Again he knelt on the floor.

What was he doing? "Acheron, why are you on the floor and not sitting at the table with me?"

His look was empty, unassuming. "Whores don't sit at tables with decent people."

His voice was steady as if he were merely repeating something that had been said so often it no longer had any meaning to him.

But the words cut through me.

"You're not a whore, Acheron."

He didn't argue verbally, but I could see the denial in his pale, swirling eyes.

I reached out to touch his face. He stiffened ever so slightly.

I dropped my hand. "Come," I said softly. "Sit at the table with me."

33

He did as I told him, but looked terribly uncomfortable, as if he feared someone would wrench him up by his hair at any moment. Over and over, he pulled at the cowl as if to protect himself.

It was then I realized the second way to punish someone when you didn't want any visible marks. The head. How many times had they wrenched his hair?

A servant came to take our orders.

"What would you like, Acheron?"

"My will is your will, Idika."

Idika. An Atlantean word that a slave used for his owner.

"Have you no preference?"

He shook his head.

I ordered our food and watched him. He kept his gaze on the floor, his arms locked around his body.

When he moved to cough, I caught sight of something strange in his mouth.

"What is that?" I asked.

He glanced up at me, then looked down. "What is what, Idika?" he asked, again with his jaw clenched.

"I'm your sister, Acheron, you may call me Ryssa."

He didn't respond.

Sighing, I returned to my original question. "What is in your mouth? Let me see your tongue."

He obligingly parted his lips. The entire line down the center of his tongue was pierced and studded with small gold balls that shimmered in the light. I'd never seen anything like it in my life.

"What is that?" I asked, frowning.

Acheron closed his mouth and by the way he moved his lips and jaw, I could tell he was rubbing the balls against the roof of his mouth. "Erotiki sfairi."

"I don't understand that term."

"Sex balls, Idika. It makes my licks more stimulating to those I service."

I couldn't have been more surprised had he slapped me. He was nonchalant about something that was taboo in the world I knew.

"Do they hurt?" I couldn't believe I was asking this question.

34

He shook his head. "I just have to be careful not to let them strike my teeth lest they break them."

So that was why he kept his jaw clenched when he spoke.

"It's a wonder you can speak at all."

"No one pays a whore to use his tongue to speak, Idika."

"You are not a whore!" Several heads turned, making me realize I had spoken louder than I meant to.

My cheeks burned, but there was no embarrassment on Acheron's face. He merely accepted it as if he were nothing more and deserved nothing better.

"You are a prince, Acheron. A prince."

"Then why did you throw me out?"

His question startled me. Not just the words themselves, but the heartfelt pain in his voice as he spoke them.

"What do you mean?"

"Idikos told me what was said by all of you."

Idikos. The masculine form of the word a slave used for his owner.

"Do you mean Estes?"

He nodded.

"He is your uncle, not your idikos."

"One doesn't argue with a whip or scold, my lady. At least not for long."

I swallowed at his words. No, I guess they didn't. "What did he tell you?"

"The king wanted me dead. I live only because the son he loves will die if I die."

"That's not true. Father said he sent you away because he was afraid someone would try to hurt you. You are his heir."

Acheron kept his gaze on the floor. "Idikos says that I am an embarrassment to my family. Unfit to be with any of you. That's why the king sent me away and told everyone I was dead. I'm only good for one thing."

I didn't need him to tell me what that one thing was. "He lied to you." My heart broke with the weight of the truth. "Just as he's been lying to me and to Father. He told us that you were healthy and happy. Well-schooled."

He laughed bitterly at that. "I am well-schooled, Idika. Believe me, I'm the best at what they trained me to do."

How could he find humor in that?

I looked away from him as the servant brought food to us. As I started to eat, I noticed Acheron hadn't moved. He stared at the food before him with hunger in his eyes.

"Eat," I told him.

"You haven't given me my portion, my lady."

"What do you mean?"

"You eat, and if I please you while you dine, you will determine how much food I'm to have."

"Please me how . . . no wait. Don't answer that. I'm not sure I want to know." I sighed, then gestured to his platter and cup. "All of that is yours. You may eat as much or as little as you like."

He looked at it hesitantly, then glanced to the floor behind me.

It was then I understood why he'd knelt there. "You normally eat on the floor, don't you?"

Like a dog or rodent.

He nodded. "If I'm particularly pleasing," he said softly. "Idikos will sometimes feed me from his hand."

My appetite left me at his words.

"Eat in peace, little brother," I said, my voice cracking from my unshed tears. "Eat as much as you want."

I sipped my wine, trying to settle my stomach and watched him eat his food. He had perfect manners and again it struck me how slowly he ate. How meticulously he moved.

Every gesture was beautiful. Precise.

And it was designed to seduce.

He moved like a whore.

Closing my eyes, I wanted to scream at the injustice of this. He was firstborn. He was the one who should be heir to the throne and here he was . . .

How could they have done this to him?

And why?

Because his eyes were different? Because those eyes made people uncomfortable?

There was nothing threatening about this boy. He wasn't like Styxx, who'd been known to have people locked up and beaten just because they offended him. One poor peasant had

36

been beaten because he'd come to the palace without shoes on his feet. Shoes he couldn't afford.

Acheron didn't play pranks on me, or laugh at others. He didn't judge anyone or make them feel small.

Rather, he merely sat there silently eating.

A family came in and sat at the table beside us. Acheron paused as he noticed the boy and girl. The boy was a few years younger than he and the girl probably his age.

By the look on his face, I could tell he hadn't seen a family sit down together before. He studied them curiously.

"May I speak, my lady?"

"Of course."

"Do you and Styxx sit down and eat with your parents like that?"

"They are your parents too."

He returned to his food without commenting.

"Yes," I said. "We sometimes dine with them like that." But Acheron never had. Even when he'd been at home with us, he'd been banned from the family table.

After that, he didn't speak. Nor did he look at the family. He merely ate with those impeccable manners of his.

I choked down a few bites, but found I wasn't very hungry after all.

I took us back to our quarters to wait for the driver to finish his rest and feeding the horses. It was nearing dusk and I wasn't sure if we would continue to travel through the evening or not.

I sat down on the small chair and closed my eyes to rest. It had been a long day. I'd only arrived in Atlantis that morning and hadn't anticipated so quick a return. Not to mention the undue stress of stealing my brother away from my uncle. At the moment, all I wanted was to sleep.

I felt Acheron in front of me.

Opening my eyes, I saw him naked again save for his bands.

I frowned at him. "What are you doing?"

"I owe you for my food and clothes, my lady." He knelt down at my feet and lifted the hem of my himation.

I bolted upright and grabbed his hand. "You don't touch family like that, Acheron. It's wrong."

Confusion creased his brow.

And then I knew the most horrid of truths. "Estes . . . does he . . . Do you . . ." I couldn't bring myself to say the words.

"I pay him every night for being kind enough to shelter me."

I'd never wanted to cry so much in my life and yet I found my eyes strangely dry—even as anger and disgust welled inside me over what had been done to my brother. Oh, if I could only lay hands to my uncle . . . "Put your clothes on, Acheron. I have no need of you to pay me for anything."

He left me and did as I asked.

For the rest of the evening, I watched him while he sat silently in the corner without moving even a single muscle. Obviously he'd been trained to do that, too. I walked my mind through the horrors of the day's revelations.

Through the horror that must have been his life.

My poor Acheron.

I told him how glad father would be to welcome him home. How happy mother would be to see him again.

I told him stories of our palace and of how grand his room would be.

He listened silently while his eyes told me he didn't believe a single word I spoke.

Whores don't live in palaces.

I could hear his thoughts plainly.

And honestly, I was beginning to doubt those words myself.

November 4, 9532 BC

Acheron remained so silent for the rest of our journey to the docks that I began to worry. He didn't look well. In fact, he was prone to break into a sweat and shake for no apparent reason. There was an awful ashen cast to his skin.

Whenever I asked if something was the matter, he would only say that it sometimes happened to him.

As we were around more people, he became more nervous.

"Estes won't find you," I told him, hoping to alleviate his fear.

It didn't work. If anything, he grew more apprehensive.

Boraxis returned with our tokens for the journey across the Aegean that would take us home to Didymos. I knew I wouldn't truly stop being scared until the boat sailed.

At any moment, I was afraid my uncle would find us and take Acheron back.

It was just after midday that they allowed us to board the ship. Boraxis led the way with me in the middle and Acheron following.

The first mate took the tokens from Boraxis and gave him directions for our quarters, but as we walked past, he stopped Acheron.

"Lower your cowl."

I saw the panic in Acheron's eyes before he complied. As soon as the material was lowered, I felt a strange almost wave-like sensation sweep through those who were near us. All eyes turned toward my brother.

The first mate shook his head and tsked at me. "My lady, we don't allow slaves to travel on the main decks."

I gave him a withering stare. "He's not a slave."

The first mate actually laughed at that. He reached to the band around Acheron's throat and pulled at his pendant that held the symbol of a fiery sun.

Acheron didn't move or speak. He merely kept his gaze lowered.

The first mate looked back at me. "I can appreciate your wanting to keep your tsoulus with you, my lady, but he'll have to travel below deck with the other slaves."

It'd never occurred to me to have Acheron's bands removed. In Greece, our slaves wore no gold whatsoever, so it hadn't dawned on me that his would betray him.

"Nexus," the first mate called to another sailor. "Escort this one below deck."

Acheron's panicked gaze held mine. "Please, Idika, don't send me there. Alone. You can't."

"I'll pay more," I told the sailor.

"I'm sorry, my lady. It's our strictest policy. The other passengers would be extremely upset if we broke the rules for you."

I felt horrible for him. "It'll be all right, Acheron. It's only a few days and we'll be home."

My words only appeared to scare him more. But he said nothing else as Nexus came forward to lead him away from me.

Acheron replaced his cowl and glanced about nervously.

"He'll be fine, Your Highness," Boraxis assured me. "His quarters won't be refined, but they'll be serviceable and clean."

And Boraxis would know. He had once been a slave before my father freed him.

"Thank you, Boraxis."

My heart heavy, I went to my quarters and wondered what Acheron would do for the next four days.

November 8, 9532 BC

I waited on the deck with bated breath for Acheron's return. Over the last four days I'd tried my best to see him, but no one would allow it. Apparently the regular passengers weren't allowed below decks anymore than the slaves were allowed above.

Almost everyone was gone now, even the sailors, while Boraxis and I waited.

At last, I saw Acheron appear. As he had on the day they'd taken him below, he had his cowl pulled low, his head bent down.

Not even a single glimpse of his body or face could be seen.

"There you are!" I said in joy at seeing him again.

He said nothing in return.

When I tried to embrace him, he shrugged me away. When I tried to meet his gaze, he moved past me.

His actions irritated me. Was this the thanks I received for saving him from the madness of my uncle's home? Surely as bare as the slaves' quarters had been, they were preferable to being mauled by others.

"Don't be so petulant, Acheron. I had no choice."

Still he spoke no words.

I wanted to shake him. This was the first time his behavior reminded me of Styxx. "What is wrong with you? Answer me!"

"I want to go home."

I was completely flabbergasted that his whispered request was tinged with anger.

"Are you mad? Why would you ever want to return to Atlantis?"

He didn't respond.

Sighing in frustration, I led him from the deck. Once we were on the docks, Boraxis went to procure us a closed herio for the journey home.

Still Acheron remained silent. He didn't look around or show any interest at all in the fact that he was safe from Estes's clutches.

"We're in Greece now. Not too far from home."

When he made no response, I sighed and was grateful to see a herio drawing near us. Maybe that would cheer his malaise.

As it stopped before us, a nobleman hailed me.

"My lord?" I asked as he drew near. He wasn't much older than I. His clothes and bearing said that he was extremely well to do, though I didn't recognize him as an aristocrat or dignitary.

He barely looked at me. It was Acheron who held his attention, Acheron who shrank away from the man. "Is he yours, my lady?"

I hesitated at answering that. "Why do you wish to know?"

"I want to buy him. Name your price and I'll pay it."

Anger cut through me. "He's not for sale."

The man finally met my gaze. I swear I saw madness in his blue eyes. "I'll pay anything you wish for him."

Boraxis rejoined us and frowned a stern warning at the man. "Get in the herio, Acheron."

Acheron didn't speak as he quickly climbed inside.

When I tried to join him, the man actually stopped me. "Please, my lady. I have to have him. I'll give you anything you wish."

Boraxis forced the man aside.

I climbed into the herio all the while the man continued to try to bribe me.

"I can't believe this," I mumbled. "Does this happen often?"

"Yes." Acheron's response was barely more than a whisper.

Boraxis secured our door. "I shall ride with the driver, my lady." He handed me a wineskin and what felt like bread wrapped in cloth. "If you need anything, call for me."

"Thank you, Boraxis."

He nodded, then climbed up on the seat outside.

Having eaten a large breakfast on the ship, I wasn't hungry. I could feel Acheron's stare, but he still kept himself covered by his cloak. "Would you care for a bite?" I asked, handing the food to Acheron.

As the herio started forward, he tore into the cloth like a starved animal. It wasn't until he moved to eat that I finally saw a glimpse of his forearm.

There was blood encrusted around the gold band on his wrist. But he didn't seem to notice as he shoved chunks of bread into his mouth.

"Are you all right, Acheron?"

He only continued to eat ravenously.

When the bread was gone, he attacked the wineskin with the same fervor. It was several minutes before he lowered the skin and let out what sounded like a relieved breath.

I reached for his injured arm.

He didn't move as I sat forward and pulled the band back to uncover a nasty wound there. As I looked at his bloodied wrist, I noticed more bruises on his forearm.

And then I saw his face.

I gasped in alarm. Before I could think of what I was doing, I jerked the cowl down. His skin was still that dull, ashen gray, his hair lank and matted.

But it was his face that held me transfixed. Dark purple circles ran underneath both eyes as if he hadn't slept at all. His lips were chapped, raw and bleeding. Both of his cheeks were bruised as if someone had slapped him repeatedly. One eye was red from broken blood vessels.

His clothes were torn and dirty.

"What happened to you?"

He gave me a true, insolent glare that cut through me. "I'm a trained tsoulus, Idika, that you left unprotected for four days. What do you think they did to me?"

Horrified, I called for Boraxis as Acheron replaced his cowl.

The herio stopped immediately. Boraxis came down and opened the door. "Yes, Highness?"

"Take me back to the ship."

43

"May I ask why, Highness?"

"They . . . they . . ." I couldn't even bring myself to say it. "I want everyone who touched Acheron to be put into chains!"

Boraxis frowned.

I pulled the cowl down again and showed Boraxis Acheron's battered face. "Look what they did to him."

Acheron met Boraxis's gaze and something strange passed between them.

"Highness," Boraxis said in a low, calm tone, "I'll take you back if you wish it, but only Acheron's rightful owner can demand restitution for his damage."

I ground my teeth at him. "He is not a slave."

"He's marked as a slave, Highness. That's all that matters."

"So that gives them the right to abuse him?"

"And again, Highness, I repeat, only his rightful owner can demand restitution. All the law will give you for what they did is financial compensation for his use. No free man will be punished for using a slave."

"A slave can be beaten for hurting him like this! And I want it so."

"Highness, a slave wouldn't have dared touch him like that."

I gulped. "What are you saying?"

Boraxis looked past me to Acheron. "Acheron? Who hurt you?"

"The sailors, and when they were done with me, they sold me to noblemen they brought below the decks."

Boraxis returned his gaze to mine. "You are a noblewoman and I your servant. No one will care what we think any more than they will care what was done to a slave."

Then an awful fear went through me. "Did you know they'd do this to him?"

"No, Highness. I assumed he'd be left alone with the other slaves. Had I any inkling they would have harmed him, I would have warned you."

I believed him.

Even so, I'd never been so angry in all my life. If we were in my father's kingdom . . .

But we weren't. Boraxis was right. Here, outside my father's realm, I had no voice.

Sick over the matter, I nodded. "Find us someplace where we can have his bands removed, Boraxis."

"You can't remove them," Acheron said in a panicked voice. "It is a death sentence to any tsoulus for anyone other than their idikos to remove their bands."

"You're not a slave and I will not have you marked as one!"

He shrank away from me.

Sighing, I looked back at Boraxis. "Acheron needs more food and someplace safe to rest and bathe. He could also use fresh clothes."

"I'll ask the driver for such a place, Highness."

I nodded at him. He left us and climbed back up. It was a few seconds later that we started forward again.

"No one is going to hurt you anymore, Acheron."

Tears gathered in his eyes before he pulled the cowl back up to shield his face from me.

"Speak to me, little brother. Tell me what thoughts you have."

"My will is your will, Idika."

"Stop calling me that! I am Ryssa. I'm not your owner."

And again he had no response to that.

Aggravated, I left him to himself while we traveled for the next hour until Boraxis found us a large hostel where I could rent Acheron a room so that he could bathe and rest.

A short time later, Boraxis brought a smith to the room.

I knocked on Acheron's door, then pushed it open to find him lying naked on his bed. I motioned Boraxis and the smith to stay in the hall while I entered.

"Acheron," I said softly, reaching to shake him awake.

I paused as I saw the myriad of scrapes and bruises that marred his perfect skin. There were places where entire handprints were still visible from his abuse. Gods, the horror he must have faced alone in the belly of the ship.

My stomach churned at the sight of my failure to protect him. How could I be so worthless? I pulled a blanket over him before I shook him very gently and promised myself that he wouldn't be hurt like this again.

45

He came awake as if terrified.

"All's well," I assured him.

He looked about as if not quite sure he should believe me.

"Boraxis?" I called.

He entered with the smith behind him. As soon as Acheron saw the tools in the smith's hands, he panicked and tried to run.

"Stop him."

Boraxis did. He grabbed him and held Acheron down on the floor while the smith brought a large pair of clips forward to snip through the bands.

Acheron screamed and fought as if we were cutting off his limbs.

"Please, stop!" he begged hoarsely. "Please!"

His pleas tore through me, but this was what must be done. I didn't want anyone else to mistake him for a slave. "It's all right, Acheron. You're free."

Still he fought until the last band had been removed. Then he lay without moving, his eyes dazed.

"Keep the gold," I told the smith, who then thanked me and left.

I looked at Boraxis, stunned by Acheron's actions. "Why would he not want them removed?"

"You took his registration shield. If a slaver finds him now, he doesn't have to be returned to his owner. Anyone can claim him."

I growled at words I didn't want to hear. "He's not a slave."

"He's branded as such on his hand, Princess. If anyone sees that mark, they'll know he's not freeborn."

I frowned. "What brand?"

Boraxis held Acheron's right hand up to show me a jagged brand in his palm that looked like an X through a pyramid. How odd that I hadn't noticed it before. But it made no difference to me.

"No one will know."

"The smith knows, Highness. For that reason, I would suggest we leave here as quickly as possible and reach your father's kingdom before we're stopped again."

My jaw slackened. "You're not serious?"

By his face, I could tell that he was. "Please, Highness. Listen to me in this. The last thing I want is to see either one of you harmed. We need to leave."

"Why didn't you tell me about the brand before the smith removed his bands?"

"Highness, I'm a freed slave. It's not in my nature to question my betters. I love and serve you and should the gods decree, I'd give my life for yours."

He was right. I'd seen my father and Styxx beat many a servant for hesitating after they'd given the servant an order.

Nodding, I went to Acheron who still hadn't moved. "Come, Acheron, we must hurry."

He looked at me then with his eyes filled with despair. "Idikos will punish me harshly for this. Have you any idea what you've done?"

"Estes is not going to hurt you ever again. I'm your sister and my word to you, you are safe."

He shook his head in denial. "He will find me. He always does."

"How many times have you escaped?"

"Enough to know it's not worth it."

"This time, it will be." At least that's what I was hoping. And by all the gods, I intended to make it so. No one deserved to live in fear. No one deserved to be mocked and abused. Especially not a boy who had been born a prince.

But even as I promised myself I'd protect him, a part of me wondered if I could.

Like Acheron and Boraxis, I, too, was prisoner to my station. And even against my will, my wings were often clipped.

November 15, 9532 BC

It had been eleven days since we'd left Atlantis. Eleven days I'd traveled with my brother who didn't know laughter or smiles. Or even how to form an opinion of his own. Whenever I asked, his response was always the same. "Your will is my will, Idika."

It was enough to make me scream.

The last part of our trip was again by ship, but this time we purchased a private vessel to take us to the island where our father ruled as king. I didn't want to take any more chances with Acheron or his safety. And the longer I was with him, the more I understood. He held an unnatural sexual magnetism.

Everyone who saw him wanted to touch him. To possess him. It was why he kept himself completely covered whenever we ventured into public. Why he cringed whenever someone neared him. Not even I was fully immune to whatever that unholy draw was and it sickened me that I could feel that way toward my own brother. The worst part was, I could tell when he knew my thoughts. He would tense as if bracing himself for my attack.

But I would never hurt him or touch him in such a manner. Still, he didn't trust me and honestly I couldn't blame him for it given his experiences.

He said Estes protected him. I knew the truth. There was no protection in what our uncle did, he only controlled how many people attacked Acheron at once.

May the gods punish Estes for it.

How could I have been so blind to such a monster all these years?

How could my father ever allow this? I preferred to think

he didn't know anything about it. It was the only way I could live. And I hoped with every part of myself that I never laid eyes on my uncle again.

It was our fifth day into the journey that Boraxis finally explained to me why Acheron was so pale and given to attacks of extreme sweating and vomiting.

It was the drugs Estes had used to control him. The orange scent I'd smelled was from the aphrodisiac they used to make him crave sex and the other was an inhaled substance to make him more pliant and accepting of what was done to him.

Acheron was so weak now that it frightened me. We needed to find a physician who could help. Boraxis kept telling me the best thing would be to buy our own supply of the drugs and keep him on them. But I couldn't do that to my own brother. He needed to live his life free of such things.

Surely he wouldn't continue to be ill from them. They had to pass out of his system eventually. Yet every day he seemed to grow weaker and weaker.

And now at last, we were home.

The palace loomed before us as we approached in a covered chariot. I didn't dare travel with Acheron in the open where any stray breeze might blow his cowl back and expose him. People could become quite violent at the sight of him and we'd already had to have Boraxis get rough with several of the more persistent.

I swallowed as we entered the palace gates and drew near the entrance. After all my bravado of telling Acheron how welcomed he would be by his family, I felt my courage wavering.

What if he was right? What if Father didn't care? For all I knew, Father was aware of what Estes was doing to him. He might even condone it. The very thought made me ill, but it was something I had to prepare myself for. It was possible.

Acheron had been hurt so much already that I was afraid of hurting him anymore. Trust was a fragile thing and he was only now beginning to trust me. I didn't want anything to damage that.

Or him.

So I took him through the side entrance and led him to my chambers where no one would disturb him.

"I'm going to Father. You wait here and I'll be back very soon."

Acheron didn't speak. He was shaking uncontrollably again. Instead, he nodded before he went to a corner and sat down on the floor with his back against the wall. He was so well covered that he looked like a sack of grain on the floor.

I picked up a clay urn from beside my hearth and placed it beside him. "Should you get sick."

Again, he didn't respond in any way.

Saddened by that, I turned to Boraxis. "Stay with him and make sure no one disturbs him."

"Yes, Your Highness."

Hoping for the best, I left them in my chambers and went to speak to Father alone.

I found him in the outer courtyard with Styxx. The two of them were reclining on cushioned chairs while they ate a light repast of honey and bread as Father instructed Styxx on matters of state. They were surrounded by servants who were attending their every need. How lush a sight they made.

Styxx's blond hair gleamed in the sunlight. His skin glistened with vitality. There was no grayish cast to it from his being forced to take drugs so that others could abuse him. Even from my distance, I could see his arrogance as he ordered everyone around.

I thought of Acheron and wanted to scream at the injustice.

"Hey, it's lamb-head," Styxx said as he saw me. The little ogre had always mocked my curly blond hair. "Where have you been?"

"Away," I told him. The troll didn't need to know my business. "Father, might I have a word alone with you?"

He cast a smug glance toward Styxx. "Anything you have to say to me can be said in front of your brother. One day Styxx will be your king, and you will be answerable to him."

The thought made my blood run cold.

"That's right," Styxx said snidely. "That means you have to kiss my feet just like everyone else."

Father laughed at him. "You're such a scamp."

I bit my lip to keep my silence. How could he not see what a spoiled, obnoxious little troll Styxx was? But then Father had always been blind to Styxx's apish ways.

"So why are you here, kitten?" Father asked. "Do you wish a new trinket or clothes?" The man had always indulged me. At least on anything that didn't involve Acheron.

"No. I want to bring Acheron home."

Father sputtered at my request. "Now see here, what has gotten into your head? I've told you repeatedly how I feel. That monster doesn't belong here."

Styxx curled his lips. "Why would you want him here? He's a danger to all of us."

"A danger how?" But then this was so familiar an argument, I could answer with their excuses before they did.

My father curled his lip. "You don't know what a demigod is capable of. He could kill your brother while he sleeps. Kill me. Kill all of us."

How could he say that? Acheron had never once made any attack on me. He didn't even raise his voice. "Why do you not fear for Estes?"

"Estes keeps him under control."

With drugs. So Father had known about that part of it. It was all I could do to keep my anger from showing. And it made me wonder what else he knew about Acheron's treatment.

"Acheron belongs here, with us."

Father came to his feet. "You are a woman, Ryssa, and a young one at that. Your mind is best occupied with fashion and decorating. Planning your dress for a party. Acheron doesn't belong in this family. He never will. Now go find your mother and gossip. Styxx and I have important matters to discuss."

Like which of the serving maids Styxx would bed next . . . Matters so much more important than his eldest son's life.

I glared at him. "Matters more important than your own son?"

"He is not my son!"

I shook my head, unable to believe his denial. So Acheron had been right all along. Father had intentionally sent him away and he would never allow him to return. Why had I not seen the truth earlier? Because I loved my father. To me, he'd always been kind and adoring.

At least now I knew the truth.

Now I saw him for what he really was. Heartless.

"So that whole story you told me about protecting Acheron was wrong?"

"What are you talking about?"

He didn't even remember his own lies. "You told me when they took Acheron away that you were doing it to protect him. You said that two heirs shouldn't be raised together as it would be an added target for enemies. You said you would bring Acheron home when he was old enough. You never intended to return him here, did you?"

"Leave us!"

I did. The sight of him and Styxx truly sickened me just then. And with every step that took me away from my father, I lost respect for a man I had once adored.

How could he do this? How could he not care? How could the same man who coddled me and Styxx turn his back on his heir?

I returned to my chambers to find Acheron sitting on the balcony. He had his legs bent, his chin resting on his knees, and his arms were crossed around them.

He was sweating again. His eyes were hollow and empty. He looked so ill and frail. How could my father fear a boy who wouldn't even meet someone's gaze?

I knelt beside him and reached to touch him. He tensed as he always did.

Acheron didn't like to be touched. No doubt he'd suffered enough touching to last his lifetime.

"Father isn't here," I lied even though I choked on the words.

How could I tell this boy the truth? I'd begged for his trust, only to find out that I was a fool.

How could I tell him that if it were up to his father, he would again be sent to Estes to be prostituted to anyone who was willing to pay for him?

I couldn't let him know the truth any more than I could let him go back to Atlantis.

"I'm going to take you to the summer palace to wait on him."

He didn't question me, which let guilt roost in my heart. But what did it matter? I was going to take him someplace safe. Secure. Someplace where no one would hurt him or shame him.

I stood up and motioned for him to follow me and he followed without question.

We moved down the back hallways the way we'd entered the palace—like petty, fearful thieves instead of the heir and princess of this land. Acheron didn't know we were being secretive or that I was terrified of what would happen if anyone saw us.

Luckily they didn't and in no time we were gone again. But in my heart, I kept wondering how long I could stay away before Father dragged me home.

What would happen to Acheron then?

November 18, 9532 BC

The summer palace was completely empty this time of year. Only a small handful of servants were in residence. Petra our cook, her child and her husband who was also the groundskeeper. A housekeeper and overseer finished out the small number.

Luckily, they were all loyal to me and would never tell my father that I was staying here with a guest who bore a striking resemblance to the heir. I didn't explain Acheron's existence and they didn't ask. They merely accepted it and made a room ready for him that was only two doors down from my own.

Acheron was extremely hesitant as he entered the room. By the way he looked around, I could tell he was thinking back to his old room where uncle had sold him to others.

"May I speak, Idika?"

I hated whenever he called me that. "I've told you repeatedly that you don't have to ask me to speak, Acheron. Say whatever is on your mind." Uncle had beaten him so often for speaking out of turn that he couldn't seem to break the habit.

"Who will I be sharing this room with?"

My heart wept at his whispered question. He still had a hard time believing that he didn't have to use his body to pay for every kindness or staple. "It's your room, Acheron. You share it with no one."

The relief in those silver eyes made my throat tighten.

"Thank you, idika."

I wasn't sure what to despise more, his insistence on calling me his owner or that he thanked me for not selling him.

Sighing, I patted him gently on the arm. "I'll have some of Styxx's clothes brought in for you to wear."

He turned away before he spoke again. "He'll be angry should he learn I've touched them."

"He won't be angry, Acheron. Believe me."

"As you wish, idika."

I ground my teeth at his subservience. While Styxx went so far as to be obnoxiously domineering, often making people redo tasks just for the feeling of power he had over them, Acheron accepted anything done to him without complaint.

Wishing there was something I could do to make him feel safe and more comfortable, I left him in his room and went to rest in mine. I just needed a small break from the stress of worrying about him. The servants here were mostly elderly and the one thing I'd noticed was that older people seemed more immune to whatever it was Acheron possessed. Or if not immune, they were less likely to act upon it.

Not to mention, the staff would realize he was family and that alone would keep them away from him.

I hoped.

Weary, I went over to my desk and wrote a quick note to Father to let him know that I needed some time away from Didymos. He was used to my travels as I often visited my widowed aunt in Athens or would come here to the summer palace so that I could just be alone. Like Acheron, I valued my solitude. So long as I had Boraxis with me and kept my father notified of my well-being and whereabouts, my father was indulgent of my impulsive trips.

The only place he'd forbidden me to visit had been Atlantis—now I knew why. And to think, I'd honestly believed him when he'd told me it was too far and dangerous a trip for a girl my age to make without proper escort. Little had I suspected it was to protect his brother and his licentiousness.

I'd just finished writing the note telling my father I was in Athens, when I stood up and paused. My attention was caught by movement outside my window, in the garden. At first, I couldn't believe what I saw.

It was Acheron.

How unlike him to do anything without express permission. He would barely move unless he was told to do so. I had to blink twice just to make sure I wasn't dreaming. But no, it was definitely he . . .

Even though it was a mild winter, it was cold enough to need a cloak outside. Yet there he stood, barefoot, walking in the grass by the fountain. He had his head bent low and appeared to be curling his toes in the grass. It looked as if he was enjoying the sensation, but since he never smiled, it was hard to tell.

What on earth was he doing?

I grabbed my cloak and headed outside to check on him.

As soon as he saw my approach, he shrank from me until he was up against the far stone wall. With no place else to go, he sank to his knees and held his arm up as if to protect his head and face. "Forgive me, Idika. Please, I-I-I meant no offense."

I knelt beside him and took his face in my hands to soothe him. He tensed so much at my touch that it was a wonder he wasn't brittle from it. "Acheron, it's all right. No one's angry at you. You've done nothing wrong. Shh . . ."

He swallowed as his fright turned to confusion. Dear gods, what had they done to him that he should tremble so when he'd done nothing to warrant it?

"I was only curious why you were out here without your shoes on. It's cold and I didn't want you to catch a fever."

My concern baffled him as much as his fear baffled me.

He gestured toward his room that held a small terrace which, like mine, opened out onto the garden. The door was still ajar. "I didn't see anyone here so I thought it safe. I just wanted to feel the grass. I-I meant no harm, Idika. I was going to return to my room as soon as I finished. I swear it."

"I know," I said, stroking his face again before I released him. He relaxed a tiny degree now that I didn't touch him. "It really is all right. I'm not upset at you. But I don't understand why you'd want to feel the grass as cold as it is. It's all dried up this time of year."

He brushed his hand over it. "Does it not always feel like this?"

I frowned at his question. "You've never touched grass before?"

"I think I did when I was small. But I don't remember." He brushed his hand over it again in a gentle action that wrung my heart. "I only wanted to touch it once. I won't leave my room again, Idika. I should have asked permission first. Forgive me." He hung his head down.

I wanted to reach out and touch him again, but I knew how much he hated that. "You don't have to ask my permission, Acheron. You may come here anytime you wish. You're free now."

He looked at his branded palm that held his slave's mark, then clenched it into a fist. "Idikos said that the king made him promise I would never leave the house."

I gaped at his disclosure. "You've been locked in your room since you arrived at Atlantis?"

"Not always. When idikos returns from a trip, I greet him in the receiving room. I'm always the first one he wants to see. Then sometimes idikos chains me in his office by my ankles or to his bed. And at night I go to the dining hall and to the ballroom when we have parties."

And every night he slept in Estes's bed. He'd already told me that much.

"But you've never been outside?"

He glanced at me, then averted his gaze. It was what Estes had taught him to do since so many people were put off by his swirling silver eyes. "I'm allowed to sit on the balcony between clients so that my skin isn't so pale. Meara will even let me eat out there sometimes."

I'd learned from him that Meara was the maid who'd written to me and who'd helped him escape. She'd been the kindest of his keepers and the only one who'd made sure that he ate and was comfortable . . . when not entertaining. The other thing I'd learned from him was that Estes used food to control him.

Acheron ate only when he was pleasing to others. How much he was allowed depended on how many clients he'd seen that day and how happy they'd been with him.

The very thought sickened me.

"You love Meara, don't you?"

"She's always kind to me. Even when I'm bad, she doesn't hurt me."

Bad. Defined by Estes as anytime a client was rough with Acheron and left a mark on his body. Acheron was charged with pleasing them in any way they wanted and yet if they wanted to be rough and he allowed it, he was punished for it. If he didn't allow them to hurt him, they were displeased and Estes punished him twice as hard for not giving them what they paid for. Acheron couldn't win this battle.

I clenched my hands into fists to keep from reaching out to touch him. I just wanted to gather him into my arms and hold him until the nightmare that had been his life was completely erased from his memory.

But how? How could I make him understand that he was safe now? That no one would ever touch him without his explicit invitation? That he was free to make his own decisions and that no one would beat him for voicing his opinion?

Or for walking outside to feel the grass on his feet?

It would take time. "I'm going back to my room." I pointed to the doors that opened into my chambers. "You can stay out here as long as you like. When you're hungry, tell Petra, the tall older woman you met on our arrival, and she'll make you whatever you wish. If you need me, don't hesitate to come to my room. The day is yours, little brother. All I ask is that you please put on your shoes so that you won't fall ill."

He nodded and didn't move until I'd put enough distance between us that he was sure I couldn't strike him. I wanted to weep over that.

But there was nothing to be done except to show him that I meant what I said. His life was now his own.

Withdrawing, I returned to my room where I watched him as he put on the shoes he must have been holding under his cloak. Then he explored the small garden for hours. He must have touched everything that was there, feeling the texture and smelling it.

It wasn't until the sun had begun to set that he made his way back to his room. I waited a few minutes before I went to the kitchen and had Petra take him a tray of food.

"Highness?" she asked as I started to leave.

"Yes, Petra?"

"Our guest . . . is he all right?"

"He's fine. He's just bashful and quiet."

She nodded before she made his tray and left with it. Her daughter, whose name I couldn't recall, smiled at me from the corner where she played by the fire.

"Your friend seems lost, Highness. Like the puppy I found last summer. At first he was scared to let anyone near him, but I kept talking to him and leaving him food." She pointed to the dog that was sleeping a few feet from her. "Now he's the best dog in the world. He never leaves my side."

"Everything in the world needs kindness, child."

She nodded, then went back to playing.

I watched her for a moment as old memories surged. Acheron had never been given toys even before Estes had taken him away. Back then, I would share mine with him, but they were all he'd ever had.

The girl was right. My brother was sadly lost. I just hoped that in time he would become as comfortable here as the dog obviously was. That he would learn to feel welcome in a world that so obviously hated him.

November 19, 9532 BC

I'd slept late today without meaning to. It was almost the noon hour before I awoke. And what awakened me was the most startling thing of all.

It was the sound of a child's laughter.

I got up and pulled my red woolen cloak around me before I walked to the window so that I could look outside.

There in the garden was Acheron with the cook's young daughter. They sat on a cloth with bread, meat, olives and figs while they talked and played a dice game. I couldn't hear what was being said, but the little girl would squeal with laughter every so often.

When the girl decided to stand, she reached out and touched Acheron's shoulder. He didn't cringe at all. To my amazement, he actually picked her up and set her on her feet so that she could run inside.

For the first time since I'd found him, he was relaxed. He ate without fear and his features weren't pinched. He glanced about openly and would actually look the girl in the face.

The girl returned with her doll which she handed to Acheron. He took it and pretended to feed it an olive. The girl squealed in delight.

Enchanted by their play, I headed outside to join them. As soon as Acheron saw me, the light went out of his eyes. I watched as he literally pulled back into himself and became instantly afraid.

"You should go, Maia," he whispered to the girl.

"But I like playing with you, Acheron. You don't get angry at me for being silly or asking questions."

"She can stay," I added quickly. "I didn't mean to disturb the two of you."

Acheron kept his gaze locked on the ground.

I sighed before I glanced to the girl. "Maia, would you fetch me a cup of wine from the kitchen?"

"Yes, Highness. I'll be right back."

As soon as she was gone, I turned to Acheron who was withdrawn and fearful again. "Have you been around many children?"

He shook his head. "It's forbidden."

"But you seem so at ease with Maia. Why?"

He wrapped his cloak tighter around himself before he spoke. "She wants nothing from me other than a playmate. To her, I'm no different than any other adult. She doesn't mind my eyes and she isn't aware that I'm unnatural."

"You're not unnatural, Acheron."

He looked up at me with those eerie eyes. "You feel the pull of me. You haven't acted on it yet, but you feel it just like everyone else. Your heart quickens when you watch me move. Your throat goes dry as your eyes dilate. I know the physical signs. I've seen them too many times not to."

It was true and I hated the fact that he could see inside me so easily. "I would never touch you like that."

A tic started in his jaw before he looked away. "Gerikos and others have said that, too. And when they can no longer resist it, they hate me and punish me as if I have control over it. As if I make them want me." This time when he met my gaze, I saw the anger that burned deep inside him. "Sooner or later everyone who's around me fucks me, Idika. Everyone."

His anger ignited my own. "And I will *never* touch you like that, Acheron."

The doubt in those eyes burned through me.

"What of Meara?" I asked, trying to show him that not everyone was an animal out to mount him. "She never touched you like that, now, did she?"

The look he gave me told me the answer. My stomach shrank.

"She was kinder than most."

No wonder he didn't trust me. How in the name of Olympus could I ever convince him that I wasn't like that

61

when everyone else had used him? Yes, I felt that unnatural allure he spoke of. But I wasn't an animal unable to control my urges. It sickened me that others had so little control that they would have used him so.

"I will prove myself to you, Acheron. You can trust me. I promise."

Before he could respond, Maia returned with my wine. I offered her a kind smile before I took it from her. "You two play. I need to go bathe and dress."

After rising to my feet, I headed toward my room. At the door I paused to look back at them.

Acheron was rolling the dice while Maia held her doll. He was right, there was an unnatural something about him that called out to my body. Even when he was unhealthy in his appearance, he was beautiful. Compelling.

He looked up at me and I quickly glanced away before I entered my room.

"You're my brother, Acheron," I whispered. "I won't hurt you." It was a promise not only to him, but to myself as well.

December 15, 9532 BC

The mild winter continued. Warm enough some days even to venture outside without cloaks.

Over a month had passed since I escaped with Acheron. My letters sent to my father with false locations helped to keep us safe. As did the men and women I bribed to give false sightings of us in other cities. I just hoped he continued to buy into my ruse until spring when it would be safe for us to travel.

The drugs were gone from Acheron's body now and I scarcely recognized the boy I'd found chained to a bed.

His hair shiny and gold, he had gained weight and could easily be mistaken for Styxx now. All except those swirling silver eyes, and his quiet, introverted personality. There was no boisterous swagger, no annoying bragging.

Acheron was thoughtful and respectful. Grateful for any kindness shown to him. He could sit for hours and not move or speak. His favorite activity appeared to be just sitting on the balcony that looked out over the sea, watching the waves crash into the shore, watching the sun rise and set with a fascination that amazed me.

Or playing games of chase and dice with Maia. The two of them shared a bond that warmed my heart. Acheron never hurt her or raised his voice. He very seldom even touched her. And when it came to her incessant questions, he had more patience than anyone I'd ever seen. Even Petra commented on it and how grateful she was that Maia had found a willing playmate.

Earlier today, we'd been out in the orchard, trying to find fresh apples even though it was past season. Acheron had finally admitted to a preference for the fruit—it'd taken me weeks of trying before he would admit a preference for anything.

"Do you think Father will come soon?" he asked.

I swallowed in fear. I don't know why I'd kept up the lie. Except that the truth of Father's feelings was something I didn't think he needed to know. It was easier to tell him that his family loved him—that they all felt toward him as I did.

"Perhaps."

"I would like to meet him," he said as he peeled an apple with his knife. It was the only one we'd found and though it wasn't quite fresh, Acheron didn't seem to mind. "But it's Styxx I'd like to meet most. I can only vaguely recall him from before."

From before. That was the only way he'd refer to the time in Atlantis.

He'd ceased speaking of himself as a whore, said nothing of torture or abuse, not even when I asked him for details. His eyes would become haunted and he would hang his head low. So I learned not to ask, not to remind him of anything about his years spent with our uncle.

The only telltale sign of his time there was still the way he moved. Slowly, seductively. He had been so thoroughly trained as a prostitute that even here, he couldn't shake those movements.

The only other reminder of his past were the balls in his tongue that he refused to remove and the brand on his palm.

"It hurt too much to have it pierced," he'd told me when I'd asked about the balls. "My tongue was so swollen that I couldn't eat for days. I don't want to have to experience that again."

"But you won't, Acheron. I told you, I won't let them return you there."

He'd looked at me with the same indulgence he'd given Maia when she told him that horses could fly—like a parent who didn't want to spoil the child's delusion with the truth.

So the balls remained.

But then so did Acheron.

January 20, 9531 BC

I sat for hours today, watching Acheron. He'd awakened early as he often did and walked down to the beach. It was so cold that I feared he'd become ill, but I didn't want to infringe on his freedom. He'd lived so long with rules dictating his every movement and opinion that I never wanted to impose any limitation on him.

Sometimes the mind's health was even more important than that of the body. And I believed he needed his freedom more than he needed to be protected from a small fever.

I kept to the shadows, just wanting to observe. He walked for almost an hour in the freezing surf. I had no idea how he withstood the coldness of it, yet he seemed to derive pleasure from the pain.

Whenever one of the sea animals from the water washed ashore, he took great care to get it back into the water and send it on its way.

After a while, he climbed up the craggy rocks where he sat with his legs bent and his chin resting on his knees. He looked out across the sea as if waiting for something. The wind blew his fair hair out and around him, his clothes rippled from the force of it while the water plastered the light golden curls of his legs to his skin.

Still, he didn't move.

It was almost noon before he returned. He joined me in the dining hall for our midday meal. As we were being served, I saw the jagged cut he had on his left hand.

"Oh, Acheron!" I gasped, worried about the deep gash. I took his hand into mine so that I could examine it. "What happened?"

"I fell against the rocks."

"Why were you sitting up there?"

He pulled away, uncomfortable.

That only worried me more. "Acheron? What is it?"

He swallowed and dropped his gaze to the floor. "You will think me mad if I tell you."

"No, I won't. I would never think such a thing as that."

He looked even more uncomfortable before he spoke in a thin tone. "I hear voices sometimes, Ryssa. When I'm near the sea, they're louder."

"What voices?"

He closed his eyes and tried to withdraw.

I gently took his arm and kept him by my chair. "Acheron, tell me."

When he met my gaze, I saw the fear and anguish inside him. It was obvious this was something else that had caused him to be beaten in the past. "They're the voices of the Atlantean gods."

Shocked by his unexpected answer, I stared at him.

"They call to me. I can hear them even now like whispers in my head."

"What do they say?"

"They tell me to come home to the hall of the gods so that they can welcome me. All but one. Hers is stronger than the others and it tells me to stay away. She tells me that the others want me dead and that I shouldn't listen to their lies. That she'll come for me one day and take me home where I belong."

I frowned at his words. By his eyes, everyone knew Acheron was the son of some god. But to my knowledge no demigod had ever heard voices of the other gods. At least not like this.

"Mother says that you must be a son of Zeus," I told him. "She says that he must have visited her one night, disguised as Father, and that she didn't know he'd been in her bed until you were born. So why would you hear the voices of the Atlantean gods when we're Greek and your father is either Zeus or a Greek king?"

"I don't know. Idikos drugs me whenever I hear them until I'm too dizzy and numb to notice anymore. He says it's a figment of my mind. He says . . ." His face stricken, he looked away.

"He says what?"

"That the gods have all cursed me. It's their will that I serve as I do. It's why I was born so unnaturally and why everyone wants to sleep with me. The gods all hate me and they want to punish me for my birth."

"The gods don't hate you, Acheron. How could they?"

He wrenched his arm from my grasp and gave me a look so insolent that I was shocked by it. Never had he shown this much spirit. "If they don't hate me, then why am I like this? Why has my father denied me? Why would my mother never even look at me? Why have I been kept as an animal whose only role in life is to serve as my master bids me? Why can't people look at me without attacking me?"

I cupped his face in my hands, grateful that he no longer tensed when I touched him. "That has nothing to do with the gods. Only other people's stupidity. Has it never occurred to you that the gods sent me to free you because they didn't want to see you suffer anymore?"

His gaze fell. "I can't hope for that, Ryssa."

"Why not?"

"Because hope scares me. What if this is all I am? A whore to be bartered and sold. The gods make kings and they make whores. It's obvious which role they chose for me."

I winced at his words. Honestly, I preferred the weeks when he refused to mention being a whore. I hated the reminders of what had been done to him against his will, especially those wretched balls in his tongue that flashed every time he spoke.

"You are not cursed!"

"Then why when I tried to gouge out my eyes would they not stay out?"

Paralyzed by those words, I couldn't breathe for several seconds. "What?"

"I've tried three times to gouge out my eyes so that they couldn't offend others, and each time they returned to my skull by themselves. If I'm not cursed, why would they do that?" He lifted his hand to show me that cut that had already started to mend. "Injuries that take weeks for others to heal, heal in days if not hours on me."

Tears stung my eyes at the pain in his deep voice. I didn't know what to say to that. "You get sick. I've seen it."

"Not for long. Not like a normal person and I can go three weeks without a single morsel of food or drop of water and not die." The fact that he knew how long he could go without nourishment told me it'd been done to him. But even though he could go that long and not die, he starved just like the rest of us. I knew that too from being with him.

I closed my hand around his. "I don't know the will of the gods, Acheron, no one does. But I refuse to believe that it's their will to hurt you so. You were a precious gift that was scorned by the very ones who should have cherished you. That is a human tragedy that shouldn't be laid at the feet of divinity. The priests often say that the gifts of the gods are sometimes hard to accept or identify, but I know in my heart that you are special. That you are a gift to humanity. Never doubt that you were placed here with some higher purpose and that purpose was not with malice or to be abused."

I swallowed before I kissed his injured hand. "I love you, little brother. And I see in you nothing but goodness, intelligence, compassion and warmth. One day I hope you'll see it too."

He placed his other hand on mine. "I wish I could, Ryssa. But all I see is a whore who's tired of being used."

February 15, 9531 BC

Time has flown by as I've watched Acheron grow from a timid, frightened boy into a man who is more confident to voice his own opinions. He no longer cringes or holds his head down. When I speak to him, he now meets my gaze levelly. Truly his transformation has been the most beautiful thing I've ever witnessed.

I'm not sure if I've had the most impact on that, or if it was Maia who finally reached him and brought out this new side. The two of them are inseparable.

Today they were in the kitchen while Petra was cooking. I stood in the doorway watching them closely.

"You have to pound the bread like this." Maia chopped at it with her tiny hands as she knelt on a tall stool so that she could reach the table. "Pretend it's somebody you don't like," she whispered loudly as if imparting a great secret to him.

Acheron's expression glowed with warmth. "I didn't think there was anyone you didn't like."

"Well, I don't, but there's probably someone you don't like."

I didn't miss the torment in his eyes as he averted his gaze. I wondered who topped his list. Our father or our uncle?

"We need more milk."

Acheron dutifully handed it to her.

Petra glanced over, smiled and shook her head at them as Maia added much more salt than was needed.

Maia wiped her runny nose before she put her hands back in the dough. I cringed, making a mental note not to eat any of the bread they were cooking, but Acheron wouldn't be so squeamish. He'd even eaten a bite of a mud pie several days ago to make Maia happy.

"Now we have to shape it into loaves. Let's do little ones because those are my favorite."

Acheron dutifully complied.

The dog started barking.

"Shh!" Maia said as she tore a part of the dough and handed it to Acheron so that he could make a loaf. "We're working."

The dog jumped up and pushed Maia who lost her balance. Acheron caught her against him at the same time the dog jumped at his leg, unbalancing him. One instant, they were upright, the next they were on the floor with Acheron on his back and Maia on his chest. The dog barked and danced around them, bumping into the table.

The bowl of flour they'd been using tumbled over the edge and landed on top of them. I covered my mouth as I looked at them, saturated with dough, flour and milk. All that was visible were startled wide eyes.

Maia squealed in laughter and to my utter amazement, Acheron laughed, too.

The sound of it, combined with an honest smile from him, stunned me. He was absolutely beautiful when he smiled . . . even when he was covered in flour and dough.

His eyes were bright as he wiped the flour from his face and helped Maia clear some off her cheeks.

Petra let out a sound of disgust as she shooed the dog out of the kitchen. "You two look like shades out to scare me to an early death. What a mess!"

"We'll clean it, Petra, I promise," Acheron said as he set Maia on her feet. "You're not hurt are you?"

Maia shook her head. "But I fear our loaves are all a ruin." Her tone was dire indeed.

"True. But we can always make more."

"But they won't be as good."

I bit back a laugh. Yes, it was true, the swipe of Maia's runny nose had been the perfect spice necessary to all good bread. Without that, I was sure the next batch would be nowhere near as good. However, I kept that comment to myself while Acheron comforted the poor child.

70

Acheron took Maia outside so that the two of them could shake the flour out of their clothes and hair while Petra set about cleaning up the kitchen. Within a few minutes, they were back to help.

I watched in awe that a prince would be so considerate. But Acheron never flinched at helping Petra whenever he and Maia were in the kitchen with her. It was just his nature.

And he always doted on Maia like a patient older brother.

"Acheron?" Maia asked as he set out a new bowl for her. "Why do you have those gold things in your tongue?"

He glanced away. "They were put there when I wasn't much older than you."

"Why?"

He feigned a menacing face. "So that I could scare little girls who annoyed me."

She giggled as he gently tickled her. "I don't think you could ever scare anyone. You're too nice for that."

He didn't comment as he helped her measure out the flour.

Maia scratched her head as she watched him with innocent curiosity. "Do the balls ever hurt?"

"No."

"Oh." She cocked her head to study his lips. "Do you ever take them out?"

"Maia," Petra said gently as she returned to the lamb she was seasoning, "I don't think Acheron really wants to talk about them."

"Why not? I think they're pretty. Can I have some?"

"No," Acheron and Petra said simultaneously.

Maia huffed. "Well I don't see why not. Princess Ryssa has small silver balls in her ears and Acheron's are very pretty too."

Acheron tweaked the end of her nose. "They hurt when they're put in, akribos. It's a pain you never want to know and it's why I don't take them out. I don't want anyone to hurt me like that again."

"Oh. Is that like the burn on your hand that you told me about?"

Petra turned toward them. "What burn on his hand?"

"The one Acheron did when he was young. It's very pretty, too, like a pyramid. He said he got it because he didn't listen to his mother. He said it's why I should always listen to you when you tell me what to do."

A dawning light came into Petra's eyes. Acheron didn't miss it. Lowering his head submissively, he mumbled an apology to Maia before he left.

I followed him. "Acheron?"

He paused to turn back toward me. "Yes?"

"She didn't mean anything by her questions."

"I know," he breathed. "But it doesn't make it any less painful, does it?"

I wanted so desperately to hold him. If only he'd allow it. But only Maia in her innocence was able to reach out to him. "You can take the balls out and we can disguise your hand. No one would ever know then."

"*I* would still know." He laughed bitterly. "You can't undo the past, Ryssa. Marks on my body or not, it's always there and it's always brutal." His eyes seared me and in them I saw an anguish no boy so young should ever know. "Because of the way I heal, have you any idea how many times and how deep they had to burn my hand in order to scar it?"

Nausea welled up inside of me. It was something I'd never considered. "Your past is over, Acheron. All that remains are the two parts you won't let go of."

He shook his head in denial before he waved his arm toward the palace. "This . . . this is all a dream and I know it. One day, all too soon, I'm going to wake up and it'll be over. I'm going to be right back where I was. Doing things I don't want to do. Being groped and shoved around and beaten. There's no need to pretend otherwise."

How could I make him feel safe and secure? "Why won't you take my word and believe me? The past is over. You have a new future now. Boraxis is on his way to Sumer to deliver my letter to my best friend. Once I have her word, we'll have a safe place where you can go and no one will ever harm you again."

His expression was bleak and cold. "I don't know how to trust, Ryssa. Not you or anyone else. People are unpredictable. The gods more so. Things happen that are out of our control. I want to believe you, I do. But all I hear are the gods' voices, and yours. And then I see things . . . things I don't want to see."

"What kinds of things?"

He turned away and headed for his room.

I ran after him and pulled him to a stop. "Tell me. What do you see?"

"I see myself begging for a mercy that never comes. I see myself cast out into the streets with no place to rest and no one around me willing to help without exacting a payment I don't want to make."

Gods, how I wanted to make him trust in me and the future I was going to make sure he had. "This isn't a dream, Acheron. It's real and I'm not going to let you return to Atlantis. We will find you a home that is safe."

He looked away, his eyes stormy. "Why hasn't Father come? If he loves me as you say, why hasn't he come in all these months to see me? And why are you trying to find me another home?"

"He's busy." I couldn't bear even now to tell him the harsh truth.

"You keep saying that and I try to believe you. But do you know what I remember of him?"

I was almost afraid to ask. "What?"

"I see him holding you away from me while Idikos jerked me out of the room. I've never forgotten the hatred that burned in Father's eyes as he glared at me. I had nightmares for years over that look. And now you tell me that he's forgotten it." A muscle worked in his jaw. "Should I really believe you?"

No, he shouldn't. I was lying, but I couldn't ever let him know the truth. "One day you're going to believe in me, Acheron."

"I hope so, Ryssa. I really do. I want to believe desperately, but I can't afford to be disappointed again. I'm tired of it."

I watched as he turned away and left me standing

there. He was so beautiful. Tall. Proud. In spite of everything, he still maintained a dignity I couldn't fathom.

"I love you, Acheron," I whispered, wishing that I wasn't the only one in my family who felt that way toward him.

Why couldn't they see what I did?

And inside was the pain that knew just how right Acheron was. Sooner or later, our father would come. Should that day happen, Father would never forgive me for taking Acheron out of Atlantis. He would never forgive me for the lying letters I'd written about my whereabouts or the people I'd had Boraxis pay on his journey to fool him. I had no doubt that by now both Father and Estes were looking for us while Boraxis scouted a safe haven for Acheron in another country or kingdom.

But I was doing what I thought best for my brother. All I could hope for was that I could guarantee his freedom and happiness—to keep my promises to him. Once he was safely away, I'd return to Didymos and face my father and his wrath.

For Acheron, I would do anything, even jeopardize my own freedom. I only hoped that Boraxis returned before my father thought to search for us here.

May the gods have mercy on us both should that happen.

March 18, 9531 BC

The warmer weather arrived miraculously as Persephone must have returned to her mother's bosom. All my life, I've favored springtime. The rebirth of the land and the beauty. In particular, our island was lovely as the workers come to plant seeds and sing.

But this year, I felt dread as I awaited word of Boraxis. He'd sent a missive only a few days ago, that there might be a place in the Kiza kingdom for Acheron. They have a queen who was rumored to be elderly and kind. Her own sons were dead, and perhaps she might welcome an exiled prince.

I hoped with all my heart that this would be so.

And as each day passes, I fear that Father will extend his search to our oasis. But I am ever hopeful that he might instead find me a husband, and we will be able to bring Acheron into our household so that I can protect him. Then he would be forever beyond my father or uncle's touch.

I won't think of that for now.

The best part of being here has been that the servants have all accepted Acheron and his quirks, and we've formed a very close family of sorts. In Acheron, I've found the brother I've always wanted. Where Styxx is petulant, Acheron has finally learned to laugh without fear of drawing unwanted notice.

Today, I found him with Maia out in the garden. She'd been drawing letters in the dirt with a stick and teaching them to Acheron.

It was then I remembered what he'd told me in Atlantis about being illiterate—the shame that confession had caused him.

"May I help?" I asked as I approached them.

Maia leaned toward Acheron and spoke in that typically loud whisper of hers that was as charming as it was sweet. "She'll make a much better teacher than me. She knows *all* the letters and how they make words. I only know a few."

Acheron smiled at me. "Would you please?"

His request shocked me to my core. He'd never asked for anything before.

"Absolutely." Taking the stick from Maia, I began lessons for both of them so that they could read.

Acheron was a clever student and absorbed everything I showed him with an aptitude that was absolutely miraculous. "Are Atlantean letters different than the Greek?" he asked as I made my way through the alphabet.

"A few are. They have several vowel diphthongs that we lack."

Maia frowned. "Is their language like our Greek?"

I smiled at her innocent question. "Their language can be very similar to ours. So much so that sometimes you can understand it without knowing the meaning of the words. But it is a separate language. I personally know very little, but Acheron speaks it fluently."

Her face brightened as she turned to face him. "Can you teach it to me?"

Reservation glowed deep in his eyes. "If you like. But it's not a pretty language."

I completely disagreed. Unlike Greek, there was a melodic lilting quality to the Atlantean language that made it seem as if they sang whenever they spoke. It was a joy to hear, but then given Acheron's experiences in Atlantis I could well understand his sentiment about the ugliness of the people and their language.

Acheron turned his attention back to me. "Do the Atlanteans and Greeks share gods too?"

Maia laughed. "Don't you know about the gods, Acheron?"

He shook his head. "I only know the name Zeus because many use it to swear by and someone named Archon and Apollymi."

I frowned at the names of the king and queen of the Atlantean pantheon. "How do you know their names?"

76

He didn't respond, but the look on his face made me suspect that they must be some of the ones he could hear in his head.

"Well," I said, trying to lighten the sudden malaise, "Zeus is the king of the Olympian gods and his queen is Hera."

"I like Artemis," Maia spoke up. "She's the goddess of the hunt and of childbirth. She's the one who saved my mother's life when I was born and we were so ill. The midwife swore that we'd both die, but my father sacrificed and made offerings to Artemis and she saved us both."

Acheron smiled. "She must be a great goddess indeed and I owe her much that she allowed you to be born."

Maia beamed in happy satisfaction.

Over the course of the afternoon, I ran through a quick lesson of the Greek gods, but unlike the writing, Acheron had a hard time grasping all the names and their titles. It was as if they were so alien to him that he couldn't tell one from another. He constantly confused them.

We spent many hours there until Maia fell to sleep sitting beside Acheron.

His features softened as he looked down at her and cradled her in his arms. "She does this a lot. She'll be chatting away one moment and then fall sound asleep the next. I've never seen anything quite like it."

I smiled as warmth seeped through me. He looked so sweet holding her like a protective father. Given the brutality of his past, his ability to still feel compassion and to show tenderness never ceased to amaze me. "You love her, don't you?"

His expression was one of pure horror and then blatant rage. "I would *never* touch her that way."

His rancor baffled me until it dawned on me why he was so angry. In his world, love was a physical act and not an emotion. The very thought made my heart ache. "Love doesn't have to be sexual, Acheron. In its purest form it has nothing to do with a physical act."

Confusion lined his brow. "How do you mean?"

I gestured toward the girl he held so protectively in the shelter of his muscular arms. "When you look at Maia, your heart softens, doesn't it?"

He nodded.

"You look at her and all you want to do is keep her safe from harm and take care of her."

"Yes."

I smiled at him. "You want nothing from her except to make her happy."

He cocked his head curiously as he studied my face. "How do you know that?"

"Because that's how I feel about you, little brother. The love you have for her is the same as what I feel whenever I think of you. If you ever needed me, there's no hardship I wouldn't endure to be by your side as quickly as I could."

He swallowed as a haunted look came into his swirling silver eyes. "You love me?"

"With every part of my heart. I would do anything to keep you safe."

For the first time since he'd come here I felt as if I'd finally reached him. And then the most miraculous thing of all happened.

Acheron took my hand. "Then I love you, Ryssa."

Tears clouded my eyes as emotions choked me. "I love you too, akribos. And I don't want you ever to doubt that."

"I won't." He squeezed my hand. "Thank you for coming to get me."

No words had ever meant more to me nor touched me so deeply. My throat was so tight that I couldn't even speak as he let go of my hand to rise with Maia in his arms so that he could take her to her mother. I watched him walk away and hoped with every part of my soul that he would always feel that way toward me. I could stand anything except my brother's hatred.

March 19, 9531 BC

Today I decided to teach Acheron how to read from some of the scrolls I kept in my room. We'd barely begun when I noticed something very different about him.

The balls in his tongue were gone.

"You took them out," I breathed, unable to believe what I was seeing.

His expression was a cross between sheepishness and pride. "I made myself trust you. You say that I'm safe here and that no one is going to take me away again. I want to believe that. So I took them out and am going to trust in the gods that they'll keep me with you."

I cupped his face in my hands, delighted even more that he didn't stiffen, and pulled him into my arms so that I could hug him close. "You're safe here, little brother. I swear it."

For the first time, he wrapped his arms around me and hugged me back.

Never had anything touched me more.

I heard someone clearing their throat. Pulling back, I found Petra in the doorway with wine and cheese. "I thought the two of you would like a snack."

I nodded before I pulled away. "That would be wonderful. Thank you."

She inclined her head to me before she placed the tray on a small side table.

Acheron watched until after she'd left us alone before he spoke. "Do you ever think about getting married, Ryssa?"

I hesitated before I poured our cups. "I do sometimes and I wonder why Father hasn't procured me a husband. Most princesses are married long before they reach my age. But

Father says he can't find anyone he deems worthy." I smiled. "Truthfully, I'm not in any great hurry. I've seen too many of my friends married to ogres, so if Father wishes to take more time to find me a gentle husband, I can certainly wait. Why do you ask?"

"I was thinking of Petra and her husband. Have you ever noticed the way they laugh whenever they're together? And when they're apart, there's a sadness to them. It's as if they can't bear to be parted even for a few minutes."

I nodded. "They share a great love of one another. It's a pity not all married couples are like that."

"Are our parents like that?"

I glanced away as my memories brought images of the way my parents had been before Styxx and Acheron's births. In those days, they'd loved each other passionately. Seldom had they parted and my father had doted on my mother with a love that appeared unending.

Then their sons had been born. Since that fateful day, my father couldn't stand to be near my mother. He blamed her for Acheron.

"You whored yourself to a god. Don't deny it. There's no other way he could have come from your womb."

The more my mother protested her innocence, the more my father seemed to hate her. Finally she claimed that Zeus had tricked her and that she'd had no idea of his presence in her bed.

Instead of drawing my father closer, her confession had alienated him even more and now he avoided all contact with her.

"No, Acheron," I said quietly before taking a cup to him. "They seldom even see one another unless it's for a state function. Father keeps company with Styxx and his senators while Mother spends a great deal of time lost in her cups." And I hated that. At one time my mother had been wonderful. Now she was a bitter drunkard.

He looked stricken as if he understood why. "Do you think that a woman could ever love me?"

"Of course. Why would you doubt it?"

He swallowed before he answered in a tone so low I barely heard it. "How could anyone ever love me? Idikos

80

says that I only bring shame to all decent people. I'm a fatherless bastard and a worthless whore. Surely no decent woman would ever have something like me."

"That is absolutely not true," I said vehemently. "You are worth this entire world and I assure you that you will find a woman out there, besides me, who sees just how wonderful you really are."

He swallowed hard. "If I'm ever so fortunate, I swear she'll never doubt my affection for her."

"You *will* be that fortunate."

He smiled at me, but it was hollow and the doubt in his eyes was enough to bring tears to mine.

Clearing my throat, I sought to distract him. "Now let's learn your letters, shall we?"

He returned to the scrolls and for hours I watched as he applied himself with a fervor I'd never seen. And every time he spoke without those balls on his tongue, my heart soared. This was a great victory, and one day soon I would win this war and his past would be put to rest.

May 9, 9531 BC

I was alone in my room when Maia pushed open the door.
  "Is Acheron ill?"

I put down my quill to frown at her. "I haven't seen him today. Why do you ask?"

She scratched her nose and looked completely perplexed. "I went to get him so that we could bake today, but he didn't appear well. He said his head was hurting and he was rather sharp with me. Acheron is never sharp with me. Then when I took him some wine for his head, his room was empty. Should I be worried?"

"No, akribos," I said, feigning a smile I didn't feel. "You run to the kitchen and I'll check on him."

"Thank you, Princess." She returned my smile before she skipped out of the room.

Worried about him myself, I opened the doors that led into the courtyard. Acheron had been spending a lot of time out there with the grass and flowers. But he wasn't there now.

My next stop was the orchards. Again, he wasn't to be found.

After a quick search of the house, I was truly becoming concerned. He never strayed very far on his own. And it was truly rare for him to avoid Maia.

Unreasoning panic set in as I headed out of the house to search the grounds again.

Where could he be?

If he were Styxx, I'd most likely find him cavorting with a maid in the privacy of his room. But I knew Acheron would never do such a thing.

Then it dawned on me.

82

The sea . . .

He hadn't gone there since the wintertime, but I could think of no other place that hadn't been searched. It was the only place he could be. Whispering a quick prayer to the gods that I was right, I made my way down to the beach, toward the rocks where he used to sit.

He wasn't there either.

But as I climbed up, I caught sight of him lying on his back on the sand with the waves rushing over him. My breath caught. He didn't appear to be moving at all.

Soaking wet, he lay in the surf with his eyes closed.

Terrified of the sight, I scrambled down and rushed to his side. Even before I reached him, I could see the pallor of his beautiful face.

"Acheron!" I shouted with fearful tears in my eyes. I was terrified he was dead.

To my instant relief, he opened his eyes to meet my gaze. Still he didn't move.

"What are you doing?" I asked as I sank to my knees beside him. My gown was completely wet and ruined now, but I didn't care. My vanity didn't matter at all. Only my brother did.

He clenched his eyes shut before he spoke in a tone so quiet I could barely hear it over the surf. "The pain isn't so bad if I lie here."

"What pain?"

He reached out to take my hand. His own trembled to such an extent that it returned my fear to me tenfold. "The voices in my head. They're always excruciating on this day, every year."

"I don't understand."

"They keep saying that it's the anniversary of my birth and that I should come to them. But Apollymi is screaming at me to hide and not listen. The louder she shouts, the louder they shout. It's. Unbearable. I just want them to go away. I'm going mad, aren't I?"

Clutching his hand, I wiped his wet hair from his brow and realized that he hadn't shaved. A full day's growth of beard stubbled his chin and cheeks—something he never allowed. Acheron was always impeccably groomed and dressed. "Today isn't the anniversary of your birth. You were born in June."

"I know, but they scream just the same. I fell trying to reach the rocks and discovered that in the sea the voices are muffled."

That made no sense to me. "Why would that help?"

"I don't know. But it does."

A wave rushed to shore, completely covering him. He didn't move at all even though it knocked me sideways. I straightened myself and watched as he coughed up water. Still he made no move to leave the sea.

"You'll catch a chill lying here."

"I don't care. I would rather be sick than hear them yelling at me so loudly."

Desperate to help soothe him, I moved to his head and sat crosslegged on the ground before I pulled his head into my lap. "Is this any better?"

He nodded as he again laced his fingers with mine and led my hand to his heart where he held it. By the tight grip, I knew his head was still aching unmercifully.

We didn't speak for hours as he lay there with my hand on his chest. My legs lost all feeling, but I didn't care. We were gone so long from the house that Petra came out to check on me. She was as confused by Acheron's explanation as I was, but she dutifully left us alone and brought food and wine.

Acheron was in too much pain to eat even though I forced him to nibble at some of the bread.

By nightfall, the voices quieted enough that he was able to push himself up. He was unsteady on his feet.

"Are you all right?" I asked in concern.

"Just a little dizzy from the voices. But they're not so loud now." He draped one arm over my shoulders and together we made our way back to his room.

I had Petra draw him a hot bath while I wrapped a towel around him. He was still pale, his features pinched.

Maia came running in with two glasses of warmed milk. "I was worried about you, Acheron," she admonished.

"I'm sorry, bit. I didn't mean to concern you."

"Are you feeling better?"

He nodded.

"Maia," Petra said from the doorway. "Come away so that Acheron may bathe in peace."

"I put some sugar in the milk," Maia confided before she obeyed her mother. "Hope you feel better soon."

Charmed by her actions, I followed her.

"Ryssa?"

I paused at the door to look back at Acheron who was still wrapped in the towel. "Yes?"

"Thank you for being worried about me and for staying with me today. Now get yourself dried off before you catch a chill."

"Yes, sir," I said with a smile.

I left and closed the door before I made my way to my own room. The doors were still open so I shut them. As I did so, the strangest thing happened.

I heard a vague whisper on the wind.

"Apostolos."

Frowning, I looked about, but couldn't see anyone. Where on earth had the voice come from? More than that, I didn't know anyone named Apostolos.

I shook my head to clear it. "Now I'm hearing Acheron's voices."

It was strange to be sure.

But even as I dismissed it, there was a part of me that wondered about it. Most of all, I wondered if it might be yet another threat to my brother.

Only time would tell.

June 23, 9531 BC

At last word came. The Queen of Kiza had agreed to take Acheron in. The messenger had arrived yesterday with word that Boraxis was on his way here to escort Acheron to safety. He should arrive in another three days.

Elated, I planned to tell Acheron tonight during the surprise celebration for the anniversary of his birth.

My brother was going to be safe. Forever.

Happily we were out in the orchard today. In truth, we'd spent the entire morning there, laughing and sampling the gardener's prized fruit. The orchard was so beautiful. Peaceful. The leaves were a bright, breathtaking green that was punctuated by the golden apples that burst with sweet, succulent taste. Even the old, stone walls were tranquil, draped with flowering vines.

No wonder Acheron preferred it to any other place at the palace. The summer air was fresh and warm and I could have spent hours watching the way Acheron enjoyed the simplest of things such as the sensation of sunlight on his skin. Grass beneath his bare feet.

Of course, his life had held far too little of either one. How I wish I could have given him another life. A better one. The life he deserved where no one had ever hurt him for things he couldn't help. Where people could see in him all the beauty that I saw and understand what a truly gentle soul he possessed.

As I watched him inhale the scent of an apple before he added it to the bunch he'd picked, I was struck by how much he'd changed these last few months.

For once, he reminded me of a youthful seventeen-year-old boy and not a jaded, used-up old man. He'd learned to trust me. To trust in the fact that here he was safe and secure. That no one feared him or was out to seduce him. He could be himself without being obsequious or afraid of being grabbed or hurt. And I prayed he found the same peace in Kiza.

Oh, the pain I felt whenever I thought about his life in Atlantis. How could our uncle have treated him that way? Even now I could see Acheron held in chains. See the shallow emptiness that had been there in his eyes the first time he'd looked at me when he had no idea who I was.

Who *he* was.

I might have failed him earlier, but I vowed I would not fail him again. Here, he knew peace and happiness. I would try my best to always keep him far away from the world that couldn't understand or abide him.

While he picked the apples, he reminded me of a squirrel as he jumped from tree to tree, gathering his treasure. He was such a handsome boy. In my heart I knew that he and Styxx were twins, and yet as I watched him, I was struck by their differences.

Acheron moved much more gracefully. Fluidly. He was leaner, his hair a tad more golden, his muscles more defined. His skin softer.

And those eyes . . .

They were beguiling and terrifying.

After he was done, he brought his treasure to me and laid it out in a circle so that I could choose which apples I wanted first. He was always considerate that way. Thinking of others before himself.

"Do you think Father will come and visit soon?" he asked as he lay on his side, watching me eat my apple.

I could sense that he was probing me to see if I were lying. His silvery, swirling eyes were so disturbing whenever he held that gimlet stare. No wonder Uncle beat him for looking at people. It was disconcerting and even frightening to be under such bold scrutiny.

But he didn't deserve to be hit for something he couldn't help.

"I'm thinking you and I should take a trip in a few days to visit a queen."

87

He looked away, disappointed, as he toyed with his own apple.

Wanting to soothe and reassure him, I reached out to brush his golden hair out of his eyes.

"Is that the tenderness of true affection you spoke of?" he asked me in a hesitant voice. "The one where people who love you, touch you without asking for anything in return?"

"Yes," I answered.

He smiled at me, openly and honestly like a child. "I think I like it."

Then I heard something that made my heart stop beating.

There were several footsteps drawing near. I knew there shouldn't be any such sound in our temporary paradise. Petra and Maia were busy in the kitchen. Petra's husband had gone to town and the rest were busy with their duties.

Only one person would come with someone else.

I knew it was Father the instant Acheron sat up, his face overjoyed.

I closed my eyes and ached in terror as I forced myself to stand and turn around to confront him. His face angry, Father stood between the old stone columns that marked the opening of the orchard with Styxx by his side.

My blood froze in my veins.

I wanted to tell Acheron to run and hide, but it was too late. They were already too close.

Just three more days and he would have been safely away from here. I wanted to weep.

"Father," I said quietly. "Why are you here?"

"Where have you been?" he demanded as he moved forward. "I have searched and searched until it dawned on me to come here."

"I told you, I wanted time—"

"Father?" Acheron's excited voice filled my ears. This was the first time the boy had seen him since Father had sent him away.

Horrified, I watched him run to embrace his father. Unlike Acheron, I knew what reception he'd receive.

Not one ever to disappoint me, Father shoved him away ruthlessly and raked him with a repugnant grimace.

Acheron frowned in confusion as he looked to me for an explanation.

I couldn't speak. How could I tell him that I'd lied to him when all I had wanted was to make his life better?

"How dare you steal him from Atlantis!" Father snarled.

I opened my mouth to explain, but was distracted by the way the twins studied each other. I was entranced by their mutual curiosity. Even though each of them knew the other existed, they hadn't been together in over a decade. Neither of them really remembered what it was like to see and interact with the other one.

Joy was etched on Acheron's face. I could tell he wanted to embrace Styxx, but after Father's reception was hesitant.

Styxx looked less than enthusiastic. He stared at Acheron as if he were a bad dream made real.

"Guards!" Father shouted.

"What are you doing?" I asked, unable to comprehend why my father would summon guards for his own son.

"I'm sending him back where he belongs."

Acheron's jaw went slack as he turned toward me with terrified eyes.

My heart thumped wildly in fear of his being taken back to Atlantis. "You can't do that."

Father turned on me with a glare so hateful it actually made me take a step back in fear. "Have you lost your mind, woman? Why would you coddle such a monster?"

"Father, please," Acheron begged, falling down on his knees before him. He wrapped his arms around Father's ankle in the most obsequious pose I'd seen since we left Atlantis. "Please don't send me back. I'll do anything you ask. I swear it. I'll be good. I won't look at anyone. I won't hurt anyone." Acheron kissed his feet reverently.

"I am not your father, maggot," Father said cruelly as he kicked Acheron away. He glared at me with venom. "I told you, he doesn't belong with this family. Why would you defy me so?"

"He's your son," I said through my own tears of anger and frustration. "How can you deny him? It's your face he has. Styxx's face. How can you love one and not the other?"

89

Father reached down and gripped Acheron's jaw tightly in his hand. I could tell his fingers bit into Acheron's cheeks as he pulled him roughly to his feet so that Acheron could face me. "Those are not *my* eyes. Those are not the eyes of a human!"

"Styxx," I said, knowing if I could win him to my cause, he could sway Father's opinion of Acheron. "He's your brother. Look at him."

Styxx shook his head. "I have no brother."

Father shoved Acheron back.

Acheron stood there quietly, his eyes dazed by the reality of the moment. By his face I could tell he was reliving every nightmare he'd experienced in Atlantis. Every degradation.

I watched as he wilted right before my eyes.

Gone was the boy who'd finally, after months of tender coercion, learned to smile and to trust, and in his place was the defeated, hopeless shell I'd found.

His eyes were hollow now, empty. I'd lied to him and he knew it. He'd trusted in me and now that fragile bond was severed.

Acheron hung his head down and wrapped his arms around himself as if that could protect him from the brutality of a world that despised him.

When the guards entered the orchard and my father told them to take him back to Atlantis, Acheron followed them without a word or a fight. He was once again unassuming and opinionless. He no longer had a will of his own or even a voice. He was what he'd been.

With a few harsh words, Father had undone all my months of careful nurturing.

I glared at my father, hating him for what he was doing. "Estes abuses him, Father. Constantly. He sells Acheron to—"

My father slapped me for those words. "That is my brother you speak of. How dare you!"

My face stung, but I didn't care. I couldn't stand by quietly and let them shatter the soul of an innocent boy who should be coddled, not thrown away like he was nothing. "And that is my brother you cast off. How dare *you*!"

I didn't wait to see what else he would say. I ran after Acheron who'd already been ushered away by the guards.

He was waiting at the front entranceway of the palace for horses to be brought to them. His head was bent so low that he reminded me of a turtle who only wanted to crawl back into its shell so that no one could see him. His grip on his arms was so tight that his knuckles were white.

He stood like a statue.

"Acheron?"

He refused to look at me.

"Acheron, please. I didn't know they'd come today. I thought we were safe."

"You lied to me," he said simply as he stared blankly at the floor. "You told me my father loved me. That no one was ever going to make me leave here. You swore that to me."

Tears fell from my eyes. "I know, Acheron."

He looked at me then, his silvery eyes tormented. "You made me trust you."

Shamed to my soul, I tried to think of something to say to him. But nothing substantial would come. "I'm so sorry." It was a lame apology even to my own ears.

He shook his head. "I was never to set foot out of my chambers without escort. Never was I to leave the household. Idikos will punish me for leaving. He'll . . ." Horror filled his eyes as he tightened his grip on himself even more.

I couldn't even begin to imagine what was waiting for him in Atlantis.

The horses were brought forward.

When Acheron spoke, his words were a soft, heart-wrenching whisper. "I wish you'd left me as I was."

He was right, and deep in my heart I knew it. All I'd done in my stupidity was to hurt him more. I had shown him a better life, one where he was respected and given choices.

Now he would have no say in anything about his life. He would be less than nothing in Atlantis.

I sobbed as a guard grabbed him roughly by his arm and forced him into a chariot. Acheron never looked back at me. I realized he must truly hate me for what I'd done to him and I couldn't blame him for it.

Heartsick, I stood there and watched as they rode away.

"Acheron!" Maia screamed as she came tearing out of the doorway.

Only then did he look back. His face was stoic, but I saw the tears in his eyes as he waved good-bye to her.

Falling to my knees, I pulled Maia into my arms as she sobbed with the heartfelt sadness that haunted me as well.

Acheron was gone and there was no hope of my ever freeing him again. Father would make sure of that.

Then I remembered the words the old priestess had uttered the day of his birth.

May the gods have mercy on you, little one. No one else ever will.

I knew just how right she'd been. Acheron was right, the gods had cursed him.

Otherwise we would have had our three days . . .

June 23, 9530 BC

It has been one year since I last saw Acheron. Maia and I sat in the orchard of the summer palace for hours this afternoon thinking about him. Wondering what he was doing. How he fared. I told Maia that I was sure he was fine, but in my heart I knew the truth. He was anything other than fine. There was no telling what was being done to him while the two of us sat nibbling on olives and cheese while playing in the warm sun.

I'd sent numerous letters to Acheron in Atlantis to no avail. No one would tell me anything of him. The maid who'd originally contacted me had died under suspicious circumstances—that much I'd overheard in a conversation between my father and my uncle not long after Acheron had returned to Atlantis.

Estes hasn't spoke to me since.

I'd attempted to ask my uncle on his last visit about Acheron. He brushed me aside with a bitter dismissal. He knows I know what he's doing and he will no longer acknowledge me in the least.

I'm dead to my uncle. Not that it really matters to me at this point. He died to me the moment I saw my brother tied to a bed because of Estes's greed.

But it made me wonder how Acheron felt about me. If he even thought about me anymore. Did he hate me over what had happened? Or was he so drugged now that he no longer even recalled my name?

There was no telling.

I had no hope of saving him again. Because of what I'd done, Father now keeps me under extreme guard at all times. I no longer have the freedom to travel without his express permission. Boraxis was reassigned to cleaning out the stables and replaced with another guard who refuses to even speak to me.

Even Styxx barely acknowledges my presence.

"How can you let your own twin suffer so?" I'd asked him barely a week after Acheron had been taken.

"Estes would never do such a thing. It's another of your lies designed to make us free Acheron. You should be grateful I'm not king yet. I'd have you whipped for such treachery."

I'd wanted to choke him for his obstinacy.

Even more upsetting were the rumors I'd heard of political trouble between Greece and Atlantis. Our truce seemed to be threatened. What would happen to Acheron should war resume? Even though Father and Styxx denied it, Acheron was still a Greek prince. He could easily be taken prisoner and executed . . .

I wondered if Father had considered the fact that if Acheron were killed, he'd lose his precious Styxx in the process. Most likely, he'd forgotten that bit of prophecy.

But I remembered and I ached for a brother I doubted I'd ever see again.

Acheron was lost to me now.

If only I could see him one last time . . .

September 21, 9530 BC

Estes died two days ago while he was staying with us on Didymos. Styxx and my father were naturally heartbroken. But I wasn't so stricken. While a part of me was saddened by his untimely death, another part rejoiced. Though Estes had been rather young to have had the seizure that claimed his life, I couldn't help but wonder if it hadn't been sent by the gods to punish him for what he'd done to Acheron. Perhaps it was uncharitable of me to think that. Still, I couldn't help but wonder.

We were headed now for Atlantis to collect Acheron and bring him home at long last.

Home where he belongs.

Because of the impending war with Atlantis, Father intended to close Estes's house and sell it. I couldn't be more thrilled by the prospect. And I was sure that Acheron would be even more so. No doubt he wanted to see it kept even less than I did.

Before we'd left home, a suite had been prepared for Acheron at the palace. I couldn't wait to see him again. What I could almost find humorous was that, after avoiding me for so long, Father and Styxx allowed me to accompany them. Of course that was only so that I could keep Acheron away from them. But I didn't care so long as I saw him again.

Just a few days more and we'd reach Atlantis. This time, when I collected Acheron, he would stay where he was safe.

September 26, 9530 BC

I was excited beyond excited when I saw Estes's house again. Not much had changed since my last visit. Even the same servant opened the door. He seemed surprised to see the three of us, especially my father.

"I've come to collect Acheron," my father announced. "Show me to him."

Without a word, the gloomy old man led us down the same hallway I'd traveled once before. Down to the room that had haunted my nightmares and thoughts.

My happiness died as we reached it and reality came crashing down on me.

Nothing had changed.

Nothing.

I knew it before the servant opened the door.

When it swung open my worst fears were confirmed with crystal clarity.

"What is this?" my father roared.

I covered my mouth with my hand as I saw Acheron on his bed with a man and a woman—all of them were completely naked and writhing entwined on the linen sheets. I was horrified by the sight of what they were doing to Acheron. Of what he was doing to them.

In all my life, I'd never seen such depravity.

The man pulled back from Acheron with a feral curse. "What is the meaning of this?" he demanded in an equally imperious tone. I could tell by his bearing that he was an Atlantean of wealth and power. "How dare you interrupt us!"

Acheron gave one last playful thrust and lick to the woman's body before he rolled over onto his back. He lay unabashedly naked on the bed, smirking.

"Prince Ydorus," Acheron said to the angry man addressing my father. "Meet King Xerxes of Didymos."

That took some of the bluster out of the prince, but not much.

"Leave us," my father demanded.

Offended, the prince gathered his clothes and his companion and did as my father ordered.

Acheron wiped his mouth on the sheet. His skin once more had that sickly, gray cast to it. He was even thinner than he'd been the last time I'd seen him in this room, his features gaunt. He was again adorned with the gold bands on his neck, arms, wrists and ankles.

Worst of all, I saw the balls on his tongue flash in the light as he spoke. No longer did he clench his teeth as if embarrassed by what he was. Now it was as if he took pride in it.

"So what brings you here, Majesty?" Acheron asked, his tone mocking and cold. "Do you wish to spend time with me, too?"

It was then I realized the hurt boy I'd saved was gone. The man on the bed was bitter. Angry. Defiant.

This wasn't the youth who'd fearfully snuck out of his room so that he could feel the grass on his feet.

This was a man who had been used one time too many. And he wanted the world to know exactly how much he hated it and everyone who was part of it.

"Get up," my father snarled. "Cover yourself."

One corner of Acheron's mouth quirked up in a mocking expression. "Why? People pay five hundred gold pieces an hour to see me naked. You should be honored you get to look for free."

Father strode over, grabbed him roughly by his arm and pulled him from the bed.

Acheron covered Father's hand with his own and tsked at him. "It's a thousand gold pieces an hour if you want to bruise me."

Bile rose in my throat.

Father backhanded Acheron so hard he fell to the floor where he sprawled naked on his back.

Laughing, Acheron licked at the blood on his lips before

he wiped it away on the back of his scarred hand. "It's fifteen hundred to make me bleed."

My father curled his lips. "You're disgusting."

With a wry grin, Acheron rolled to his side and gracefully pushed himself up from the floor. "Careful, Father, you might actually hurt my feelings." He walked around my father like a proud, stalking lion, looking him up and down. "Oh wait, I forgot. Whores don't have feelings. We have no dignity for you to offend."

"I am not your father."

"Yes, I know the story well. It was beaten into me years ago. You're not my father and Estes isn't my uncle. It saves his reputation if everyone thinks I'm some poor waif he found on the streets and gave shelter to. It's fine to sell a homeless beggar, a worthless bastard. But the aristocracy frowns on those who sell their blood relatives."

Father backhanded him again.

Acheron laughed, unfazed by the fact that his nose was now bleeding along with his lips. "If you really want to hurt me, I'll ring for the whips. But if you continue to strike my face, you'll make Estes unbelievably angry. He doesn't like anyone to mar my beauty."

"Estes is dead," my father roared.

Acheron froze in place, then blinked as if he couldn't believe what he'd heard. "Estes is dead?" he repeated hollowly.

My father sneered at him. "Yes. Would that it were you in his place."

Acheron took a deep breath and the relief in his eyes was tangible.

I could almost hear his thoughts in my head.

It's over. It's finally over.

Acheron's obvious relief made my father furious. "How dare you have no tears for him! He sheltered and protected you."

Acheron looked at him drily. "Believe me, I've paid him well for his shelter and concern. Every night when he took me to his bed. Every day when he sold me to whomever paid his price."

"You lie!"

"I'm a whore, Father, not a liar."

Father attacked him then. He beat and kicked furiously at Acheron who didn't bother to fight or protect himself. No doubt he'd been trained to take that too. I ran to Acheron, trying to shield him.

Styxx pulled Father back. "Please, Father," he said. "Calm down! The last thing you need is to tax your heart. I don't want to see you die as Estes did."

Acheron lay on the floor once more. His face, covered in blood and bruises, had already started to swell.

"Don't," he said, pushing me away. He spat the blood from his mouth to the floor where it landed in a stark red splatter.

"Get out," Father snarled at him. "I don't ever want to see you again."

Acheron laughed at that and cast a look to Styxx. "Rather difficult for that, isn't it?"

Father started for him again, but Styxx put himself between them.

"Guards!" Styxx shouted.

They appeared instantly.

Styxx indicated Acheron with a jerk of his chin. "Put this trash on the street where it belongs."

Acheron pushed himself to his feet. "I don't need their help. I can walk out the door on my own."

"You need clothes and money," I told him.

"He deserves nothing," my father said. "Nothing but our scorn."

Acheron's battered face was completely stoic. "Then I am rich indeed from the abundance of that which you've shown me." At the door, he paused to smirk one last time at our father. "You know, it took me a long time to realize why you hate me so much." His gaze went to Styxx. "But then it's not me you really hate, is it? What you truly despise is how badly you want to fuck your own son."

My father bellowed in anger.

With his head held high, Acheron left the room.

"How could you?" I asked Father. "I told you years ago what Estes was doing with him and you denied it. How can you blame him for this?"

My father snarled at me. "Estes didn't do this. Acheron did it himself. Estes told me of the way he parades himself around. The way he tempts everyone. He's a destroyer just as they said at his birth. He will not rest until he ruins every person he's around."

I was appalled. How could a man renowned for his practical sense be so blind and stupid?

"He's just a confused boy, Father. He needs a family."

As always, Father ignored me.

Disgusted by him and Styxx, I rushed from the room, after Acheron.

I caught up to him as he was leaving the house and pulled him to a stop. The torment and pain in his silver eyes cut through me. There was no pleading from him this time. No asking me why. As with everything else, he merely accepted this as his due.

"Where are you going?" I asked.

"Does it matter?"

It did to me. But I knew he wouldn't answer.

I pulled my cloak off and wrapped it around his shoulders so that at least his nudity would be covered. I raised the cowl to shield his head and beauty, knowing it would be modest protection from the world around him.

He placed his hands over mine, then lifted my right hand to his bloodied lips and kissed the knuckles.

Without another word, he turned and left.

I stood in the doorway watching him as he walked through the crowded street and realized that he was wrong. He did have dignity. He walked down the street with all the proud bearing of a king.

May 17, 9529 BC

I was in the market square today, shopping with my maid Sera when I saw an exceptionally tall man pass by me. At first I thought it was Styxx, especially when a sudden gust of wind blew the cowl off of his head and I saw his incredibly handsome face.

But as I started to call out to him, I noticed that he wore the scarlet chiton of a prostitute—it was forbidden by law for prostitutes to appear in public wearing anything else and their heads must always be kept covered. If a practicing prostitute was caught mixing with people without that mode of dress to warn "decent" people what they were, they could be executed on sight.

Acheron quickly covered his head again as he moved through the crowd.

He looked much better than he had the last time I'd seen him. His skin was golden and tanned, and he was no longer painfully thin. His chiton covered one shoulder, leaving the other bare. An engraved golden cuff encircled his left biceps over an arm that finally had serious muscle to it.

My word, he was without a doubt the most handsome of men—even if he was my brother. I'd have to be blind not to notice.

Leaving Sera to browse over cloth, I followed after him, so grateful to find him alive and well.

But it broke my heart that he was still selling himself.

He met an attractive older woman at one of the booths who held a ring up to him.

"Does this fit?" she asked.

He handed it back to her. "I don't want a ring, Catera. But I thank you for the thought."

She returned the ring to the vendor, then ran her hand up and down his bare arm in an intimate caress.

A lover's caress.

He didn't react to it at all.

"My precious Acheron," she said with a laugh. "You're so unlike my other employees. You take only what you earn and nothing more and you tip every servant at the stew which is why they're so kind to you. I don't think I'll ever understand you." She took his hand and led him through the booths. "A word of wisdom to you, akribos, you need to learn to accept gifts."

He scoffed at her words. "There's no such thing as a gift. If I were to take that from you, sooner or later you would ask a favor from me in return. Nothing in life is ever truly given without expectation."

Catera tsked at him. "You are far too young to be so jaded. Whatever did they do to you to make you so suspicious?"

He didn't say anything.

But in my heart, I knew the horrors of his past. Knew what had stolen his trust. No doubt I was one of the key factors that had turned him into this bitter stranger I barely recognized.

As they walked, the woman chatted endlessly, trying to entice him to notice other trinkets and such. He would only look at them silently, then turn away.

I stayed back, making sure they didn't notice me. Not that it was difficult. Acheron kept his eyes cast down as if unwilling to look at anyone around him while Catera saw only him.

A man came up to them and pulled her aside.

Acheron wandered a few booths over while they spoke. It hurt me to watch him. To see the way the vendors curled their lips at his approach. The way "decent" people averted their eyes or looked scornfully at his clothes.

But even more horrifying than that was the way their expressions shifted the moment they saw his face. The blazing hot lust was undeniable. The intensity of it frightening.

Little did they know that but for an accident of birth and my father's unfounded hatred, Acheron would have been their future king.

It made me seethe and at the same time, there was nothing I could do to help.

How I hated being born a woman in a world where women were barely one step up from dirt.

Catera returned to his side.

Acheron glanced to the man who was still watching them. The man's eyes were hungry.

Acheron's were empty. "He wanted to purchase me." It was a statement of fact as if he were more than used to it.

She laughed at that. "They all want to purchase you, akribos. If I ever wanted to sell you as a slave, no doubt I would be richer than Midas."

A shadowed pain darkened his eyes at her words. "I should go back and prepare myself for—"

"No," she said, cutting him off. "This day is yours to do with as you please. You work too hard. You can't stay inside all the time."

His jaw flexed at her words. "I don't like being around people."

"And yet you don't mind having sex with them. I don't understand you."

He started away from her.

"Acheron," she said, pulling him to a stop. "I'm sorry. I just . . ." She paused and rubbed his hand. "You can't continue on the way you do. No one sees clients from waking to sleeping, day after day without stop. Don't get me wrong, I enjoy the money you make for me, but at the rate you're going, you'll end up dead before you're one-and-twenty."

He gave a short, bitter laugh. "I told you, it's what I'm used to."

"And I told you that I wouldn't let you be hurt at my house. I take care of my people, especially those who are as popular as you are." She pressed a small purse into his hand. "Take the rest of the day and enjoy it. Go to a play. Go get drunk. Go enjoy being young while you can and I'll see you this evening."

The woman walked away from him.

Acheron gripped the purse in his hand before he tucked it inside his robes, then he headed in the opposite direction.

Torn, I stood there debating whom to follow.

I sent my bodyguard after the woman. I knew I couldn't meet with her openly lest someone see us together and report it to my father. So I had him invite her into a small hostel.

I paid the owner to let me into a small room in the back where I could speak to Catera without being seen.

A few minutes later, my bodyguard appeared with Catera by his side. He left us alone and went to stand guard outside the door.

"My lady," Catera said, shifting uneasily. "What can I do for you?"

"Please be seated." I indicated the chair in front of me.

Obviously nervous, she took a seat.

I softened my expression, hoping to calm her nerves. "I wanted to ask you about . . ." I hesitated at saying "my brother." Such knowledge might hurt him. "Acheron," I finished. "Where did you find him?"

She smiled knowingly. "He is handsome, is he not? But alas, he's not for sale. If my lady is interested in purchasing his services—"

"No!" I said, shocked at her suggestion. But then I realized it wasn't out of character for her to think that. "He . . . He reminds me of someone."

She nodded. "Yes, he's almost identical in looks to Prince Styxx. A lot of my clientele thinks so as well. It's been very lucrative for him."

Little did she know it was the most destructive part about my brother. "Where did you find him?" I repeated.

"Why do you want to know?"

I didn't dare tell her the truth. "Please," I said quietly. "I can pay you whatever you wish, I just need a few questions about him answered." I pressed a dozen gold solas into her hand.

She tucked them away. "I know not where he comes from. He refuses to speak of it. But by his accent, I assume he's Atlantean in origin."

"He came to you?"

She nodded. "He showed up at my back door several months ago. Dressed in rags and barefoot, he looked like any other beggar except that he was freshly washed and his clothes looked as if he had tried to keep them laundered. He was pale, thin and so weak from hunger that he could barely stand."

I was horrified by what she described.

"He said he was looking for work and wanted to know if I had anything he could do. I told him that I wasn't hiring, but he'd heard from another brothel that I was looking for a new prostitute. It was all I could do not to laugh at him. I couldn't imagine anyone paying for such a pitiful creature. My first impulse was to throw him out."

"Why didn't you?"

"I can't explain it. Even though he was ragged in appearance, there was something undeniable about him. Something compelling that sent heat over me. It made me want to touch him even though he was skinny and frail. Then he said the most unbelievable thing of all. He told me that if I would give him five minutes, he would give me three orgasms."

I gasped at her words.

She laughed at my expression. "I was surprised, too. I've been around plenty of boastful men in my time that such a claim was hardly unheard of. But I was a bit intrigued to hear that out of the mouth of someone so young. At first I thought he was like many of the young men who come to me, most of them with little to no experience, who think prostitution is an easy way to make money. They have no idea just how hard it is physically. How taxing it is spiritually. I figured he was from a farm and had come to the city to try and make it rich."

I swallowed in dread before I spoke. "You made him prove his words?"

She laughed. "My lady, at my age, I'm lucky to get three orgasms in a year. So I told him if he was as good as he said then I would hire him. What I found out was that even half-dead from starvation he was better than he claimed. I've been with the best and his skills are completely unrivaled."

My stomach clenched at her words. I knew only too well just how much practice he'd had. "So you took him in."

She nodded. "It's a decision I haven't regretted. I had no idea just how handsome he would turn out to be once he had a few meals in him and some rest. Nor that he would be so strikingly similar to Prince Styxx. I kept him for three weeks before I let him work. From the first night he was taking clients, he was so popular that we had to start a waiting list.

"If you're interested in purchasing an hour with him, I can put you on the list, but as it stands, it'll be at least ten weeks before there's an opening."

I sat there stunned by her words. Stunned by what had become of the small boy I used to hold on my knee and bounce while he laughed.

What had they done to him? How could this be his life? It wasn't fair and it made me want to cry.

"Is there any way I might speak to him privately?"

Catera looked skeptical at the suggestion. "He prefers not to speak with his clients."

"I don't want to be a client," I told her sternly. "I happen to know him personally."

She arched a brow at that. "A friend?"

"Something like that," I said, unwilling to let her know the truth of our relationship. I pulled out more money and handed it to her. "Please. I will pay you anything if you can give me just a handful of minutes alone with him."

She debated for several heartbeats before she answered. "Very well, if you can come by my stew tonight—"

"I can't be seen by anyone in such a place."

"I understand, but I doubt he'll go out to meet you. He refuses to see anyone off the premises. Today is the first day since his arrival that I've been able to get him outside at all.

"But," she said thoughtfully, "if you can come by right at dawn, there's seldom anyone around. We're cleaning up from the night and all our clients are gone. I could let you in to see him then."

Relieved, I smiled. "Thank you. I'll see you at dawn."

May 18, 9529 BC

The morning was cold as if it were as afraid as I was. Alone, I snuck from the palace and crept silently through the city, following Catera's directions until I found her stew.

As she predicted, there was no one around.

She let me inside through her back door, then led me quietly through the house to a room in the far back. I kept my head and face well covered and did my best not to look at the poor souls we passed.

She opened a door.

I stepped inside hesitantly, expecting to see Acheron. He wasn't there. Instead, I heard water splashing in the room set off to the side and knew he must be bathing.

The musty scent of sex hung heavy in the room and I tried not to look at the freshly made bed. I closed my eyes as I thought of Styxx and the way he lived his life in comfort and peace while Acheron was forced to this.

I couldn't imagine the degradation that Acheron must suffer every day. The pain.

He entered the room completely naked, toweling his hair dry. He pulled up short as he caught sight of me standing just inside the threshold.

"Forgive me, my lady," he said in that sultry, smooth voice of his that held just a hint of an Atlantean accent. I was grateful that at least the balls were no longer lining his tongue. "I thought I was through for the night."

I lowered my cowl.

Recognizing me instantly, he narrowed his gaze. "Well, if it isn't Sister Ryssa. Tell me, are you here to save me or to fuck me? Oh wait, I forgot. When you save me, you do fuck me, don't you?"

Tears pricked my eyes at his hostile disdain. But then who could blame him for it? "You don't have to be so crude."

"You'll excuse me if my manners are lacking. Being a whore, I'm not very well versed in how decent people speak. The only time any of them converse with me is to give me instruction on how to better screw them." He dropped the towel on the bed and moved to a chair by the window.

Ignoring me, he sat down and opened a box on the table. I watched in silence as he placed several strange weeds and flowers in a flagon. He lit them, then closed the lid. Picking up a small clay bowl, he held it to his face, covering his mouth and nose, and inhaled it.

"What are you doing?"

He took several breaths before he pulled the clay bowl away from his mouth. "I'm using Xechnobia." At my frown, he explained it to me. "It's a drug, Ryssa."

"Are you sick?"

He laughed at that, then inhaled more of it. "That's a matter of opinion," he said after a small pause. A tic started in his jaw as he watched me closely. "I use it so that I can forget how many pairs of hands I've had on me in one day. It allows me to sleep in peace."

I'd heard of such things, but in my world they didn't exist. No doubt it was Estes who'd shown him the drug. I wanted to weep at what had become of the Acheron who used to bake bread and play games with Maia.

"So why are you here, Princess?" he asked.

"I wanted to see you."

"Why?"

"I was worried about you. I saw you yesterday in the market and wanted to see how you were doing."

Acheron added more herbs to the pot, then blew on them to stir the embers around them. "I'm well. Now you can go home and sleep in wealth and good conscience." The mocking sarcasm of his tone stung me soul-deep.

I shook my head as tears gathered in my eyes. "How can you do this to yourself?"

He arched a mocking brow. "I'm a trained dog, Ryssa. I'm only doing what I was well taught to do."

"This is so demeaning. How could you have gone back to this?"

His eyes stormy, I saw the rage he bore me. "Gone back to this? Why, big sister, you speak as if *this* is a bad thing. For me it's paradise. I only have to fuck ten to twelve people a night, generally only one at a time. I'm finally allowed to eat at a table, not off the floor or someone's lap. No one makes me beg for food or punishes me the few days a year when I'm sick and can't screw. If anyone hurts or beats me, Catera bans them from her stew. She even pays me for my work and I get a day off once a week. Best of all, when I go to sleep, I go to bed alone. I've never had it so good."

I wanted to scream at the horror he described. The fact that I knew it was the truth only hurt me more. "And so you're content to live like this?"

He set the clay pot down on the table and pierced me with his mercurial gaze. "What do you honestly think, Princess?"

"I think you're worth more than this."

"Well, aren't you special to be able to see me as something more than a whore? Let me educate you on what the rest of the world sees. I left Atlantis and was sick for weeks from the drugs Estes had forced down my throat."

I remembered well how ill he'd been when I had rescued him.

"I had nothing but the himation you gave me. No money, no clothes. Nothing."

"So you went back to whoring?"

"What choice did I have? I traveled far and wide, while trying to find work doing anything else, but no one would hire me to work. When people see me, they only want one thing from me and I happen to be very good at it. Tell me, Princess, if Father threw you out tomorrow, naked on the streets, what would you do? What do you know how to do?"

I lifted my chin. "I could find something."

"I defy you to try it, Princess." He gestured toward the door behind me. "Go ahead. I don't even know how to sweep a floor. All I know how to do is use my body to please others. I was sick and alone with no references, friends, family or money. I was so weak from hunger that even a beggar stole your himation from me while I lay on the ground, wanting to die and unable to stop him from taking it. So don't come here now with your disdainful eyes and look at me like I'm beneath you. I don't need your charity and I don't need your pity. I know exactly what you see when you look at me."

"Do you really?"

He stood up and spread his arms wide, showing me his perfect naked body. "I see it clearly on your face. What you see is the pathetic little boy who kissed his father's feet and begged him not to send him back to whoring. You see the whore who pleasured a prince and was then thrown from his home."

I shook my head in denial. "No, Acheron. What I see is the little boy who used to run up to me and ask why his parents didn't love him. The same little golden-haired cherub who chased sunbeams in my room and laughed when they filled his palm. You are my brother and I will never see anything bad about you."

The anger on his face intensified to the point I actually thought he might strike me. "Get out."

Covering my head, I turned and left.

I waited for him to stop me. He didn't.

And with every step I took, I cried harder for what I'd found this morning. My precious Acheron was gone and in his place was a man who wanted nothing to do with me.

The worst part was, I couldn't even blame him for it. This was all so unfair. He should be in his royal apartments with servants at his beck and call.

Instead he was locked into a nightmare that neither of us could release him from. Surely this wouldn't be his life. Surely Acheron was meant for more than this.

Yet how could I deny what I saw? He was right. People only wanted one thing from him. And unless Father was willing to protect him, Catera was better than nothing.

My little brother *was* a whore. It was time that I realized the truth.

August 23, 9529 BC

The day had dawned with the most wretched of meetings. I'd been told that my father and his senators had decided to try and placate the god Apollo with a human sacrifice.

Me.

Ever since war had broken out between Greece and Atlantis, the Greek kings had been trying to think of some way to stave it off. But the Apollites who ruled Atlantis hated us and were determined to make the whole of Greece nothing more than an Atlantean province.

Afraid of being slaves to the superior technology of the Atlanteans, the Greek city-states had been fighting with everything we had.

Unfortunately, it didn't seem to be enough. Apollo favored the Atlanteans and the Apollites he'd created who shared Atlantis with them. So much so that as long as they fought during the light of day, they were invincible.

The Greek kings were at their end. So the priests and oracles had gathered to see what, if anything, could return Apollo's favor to the people who'd originally worshiped him.

"The god can only be distracted and tamed by the most beautiful of all princesses," the oracle of Delphi had proclaimed to them all.

Some lunatic had then named me as said princess.

That man, I could kill.

"Father, please," I begged, following in the wake of him and Styxx. They were headed toward the Senate room and had no time for me. Not that that was unusual.

"Enough, Ryssa," he said sternly. "The decision is made. You are to be offered to Apollo. We need him on our side if

111

we're to win this war against the Atlanteans. So long as he continues to favor and aid them, we will never stand a chance. If you are his lover, he will look more kindly toward our people and might be swayed to our cause."

It stuck in my craw that I was to be bartered and sold without so much as . . .

I stumbled as I thought of Acheron. I finally understood exactly how he felt. Understood what it was like to have no say in what was done to my body.

It was an awfully sick feeling. No wonder he'd thrown me out of his room. No doubt in my innocence I'd seemed quite sanctimonious about something I had no understanding of.

However, I wasn't through with them. Determined, I followed Father and Styxx into the back corridor.

As we approached the main hall, the sound of a small group of senators conversing out in the atrium stopped me dead in my tracks.

"He looks just like Styxx."

My father and Styxx paused as they heard them, too.

"What say you?" another voice asked.

"It's true," the first senator said. "They couldn't look more alike had they been born twins. The only difference is their eye color."

"His eyes are eerie," a third senator interrupted. "You can tell he's the son of some god, but he won't say which one."

"And he's in a stew you say?"

"Yes," the second man said. "I'm telling you, Krontes, you have to visit him. Pretending he's Styxx has helped me immensely in dealing with the royal prick. Spend an hour with Acheron on his knees and the next time you see Styxx, you'll have a whole new perspective."

They laughed.

I felt the blood drain from my face as Father and Styxx's turned red with fury.

"You should have been at our banquet last night," the first man said. "We dressed him in royal robes and passed him around like a bitch in heat."

I felt suddenly sick.

Father charged into the group, calling for his guards to arrest them for defaming Styxx in such a way.

Styxx defamed.

Hysterical laughter welled up inside me as I doubled over in pain. Zeus forbid Styxx ever be insulted. It didn't matter that it was Acheron who was being degraded and made to serve them.

Acheron never mattered.

At least not to anyone but me.

June 23, 9529 BC

It was dawn when I left the palace alone. It was a foolish quest I was about, but I couldn't stop myself. Today Acheron turned nineteen.

In my heart I knew no one had ever given him a present for the anniversary of his birth. I wondered if he even knew the exact day when he'd come into this world. And I thought about the celebration I had planned that our father had ruined by returning him to Atlantis.

I clutched his gift under my himation as I walked through the abandoned streets to the stew I had gone to before.

I knocked on the back door and asked for Catera. After a brief wait, she appeared with a frown.

"My lady? Why are you here?"

I smiled gently at her. "I wanted to see Acheron again. Just for a few minutes."

Sadness darkened her eyes. "I wish I could help you, my lady, but he's no longer here."

Cold dread seized my heart. "What? Where did he go?"

"I know not where he was taken."

"Taken?" I whispered the word cautiously, hoping she didn't mean what I thought she did.

Unfortunately, she did. "He was arrested several weeks ago. The king's guards came in early one afternoon. They broke through the front door and demanded to be shown the royal imposter. Acheron was pulled from his bed while he still slept and bound into chains, then they dragged him out of here and I haven't heard anything since."

My fingers numb, I felt my gift fall to the floor as I stood there too stunned to move.

My father had taken him?

Of course he had. I should have realized that myself. No doubt he'd sent his men the same day he'd overheard the senators talking. What kind of fool was I not to check on that?

But then I'd been too busy thinking about my impending doom with Apollo. Shame on me for not putting Acheron first. There was no telling what they had done to him.

My only comfort was the knowledge that father couldn't kill him. Not without killing Styxx too.

Catera picked up my wrapped present and handed it back to me.

I thanked her out of habit and left.

Acheron had to be somewhere in the palace. No matter what it took, I was going to find him and get him out.

June 23, 9529 BC

It was midday before I finally found Acheron's where-abouts. I knew better than to ask my father for his location—that would only invite his anger toward me, and learn me nothing I didn't already know, so I resorted to bribing the palace guards.

Even that was easier said than done since most of them knew nothing at all and those who did were too afraid of my father's wrath to speak of it.

But at last, I had the answer. My brother had been taken to the lowest part of the palace, beneath the foundation where they kept the worst sort of criminals: rapists, murderers, traitors . . .

And one young prince whose father hated him for no reason other than he'd been born.

I didn't want to go down there where you could hear the cries and moans of the damned, where you could smell their rotting flesh and torture. It was only the knowledge that Acheron was there that made me find the courage I needed to visit.

I was quite sure that if he'd been given a choice he wouldn't have been there either.

I walked down the twisting corridors, pulling my cloak ever closer to me for warmth. It was so damp and cold here. Dark. Unforgiving. Not even my torch could banish the dankness.

As I passed the cells, those who could see the light called out for my mercy. However it wasn't my mercy they needed to be free. It was my father's.

Unfortunately, he had none to spare.

The captain of the guards led me to a small door at the

very end of the corridor, but he refused to open it. I could hear the sound of water dripping from inside, but nothing else. There was a fetid stench permeating the air and choking me. I had no idea what caused it. Truly this was a frightening place.

"Just hand over the key to me. I swear no one will ever know."

The guard's face paled. "I cannot, Your Highness. His majesty made it clear that anyone who opens this door will be sentenced to death. I have children to feed."

I understood his fear and had no doubt whatsoever that my father would indeed kill him for the affront. The gods knew, he'd killed men for far less. So I thanked him and waited for him to leave me alone before I knelt on the cold, damp floor and opened the small trap door that had been designed to pass food from the hallway into the cell.

"Acheron?" I called. "Are you in there?"

I lay flat on the filthy floor to peer through the small opening, but could see nothing. Not a single bit of flesh or clothing or light.

Finally, I heard something rustle ever so slightly.

"Ryssa?" His voice was weak and scratchy, but it filled me with joy.

He was alive.

I reached my hand through the opening as an offering to him. "It is I, akribos."

I felt his hand take mine. It shook ever so slightly. His fingers were thin, skeletal, his grip gentle.

"You shouldn't be here," he said in that raspy tone. "No one is allowed to speak to me."

I closed my eyes at his words and drew a ragged breath. I wanted to ask him if he were well, but I knew better. How could he be all right living in a small cell like an animal?

I tightened my grip on his hand. "How long have you been here?"

"I don't know. There's no way to judge day from night."

"Have you no window?"

He laughed bitterly at that. "No, Ryssa. I have no window."

I wanted to weep for him.

He released my hand. "You need to go, Princess. You don't belong down here in this place."

"Neither do you." I tried to reach him, but felt nothing save the dirt floor. "Acheron?"

He didn't answer.

"Acheron, please. I just need to hear the sound of your voice. I need to know that you're all right."

Silence answered me.

I lay there for a long time with my hand still in his cell, hoping he would retake it. He didn't. While I waited, I kept talking to him even though he refused to speak to me. Not that I blamed him.

He had every right to be angry and sullen. I couldn't imagine the horror of them dragging him through the streets to lock him in this place.

And for what?

Some imagined slight my father felt? Some need Styxx had to assuage *his* dignity? It disgusted me.

I didn't leave until a servant brought his dinner. A bowl of thin soup and fetid water. I stared at it in horror.

Tonight Styxx would dine on his favorite foods and eat until he was full and content while nobles would gather to wish him well and dote upon his every whim. Father would heap presents upon him and shower him with love and good wishes.

And here Acheron would sit in a filthy cell. Alone. Hungry. In chains.

My eyes full of tears, I watched the servant close the door and leave us.

"Happy birthday, Acheron," I breathed, knowing he couldn't hear me.

October 22, 9529 BC

For the last few months, I'd been preparing for my union with Apollo. During the morning hours before the palace began stirring with activity, I'd made it a point of visiting with Acheron at his cell. He seldom spoke, but every so often I would get a word or two out of him.

I cherished every one of them.

I only wished he'd participate more in our discussions. Sad to say that at times I was rather curt with him, even angry. I made such an effort, and risked much to see him and bring him tidbits of bread and sweets. The very least he could do was be semi-cordial to me.

But apparently, that was asking too much.

It was afternoon and I'd been meeting with Father, Styxx and the High Priest in Father's study to discuss what I would have to wear for the ceremony that would bind me to Apollo.

Originally the council had wanted to offer me to the god completely naked. Luckily the priest had talked them out of it and now there was much debate over the right gown and jewelry.

As the scribe took notes, Styxx fell suddenly ill. Too weak to stand, he collapsed on the floor where he lay like a small child, trembling. Every heartbeat seemed to make him paler. Weaker.

Terrified, I watched as Father picked him up in his arms and carried him to his room. I followed them, scared of what might have possessed him. Though we fought much, I did in fact love my brother and the last thing I wanted was to see him hurt.

Father laid him on the bed and called for a physician. I

moved forward, trying to help, but there was really nothing I could do. Styxx couldn't even speak. He breathed as if his throat was parched and his lungs were damaged. He stared at me, his own eyes filled with terror at what was happening to him.

Praying for him, I took his hand into mine and held him the way I'd often done Acheron. It was rare for Styxx to tolerate my touch which told me just how ill he was.

By the time the physicians arrived, Styxx had grown ghostly pale and gaunt.

I moved away so that they could examine him and while they worked, I watched fretfully.

"What is it?" my father asked, his voice fraught with concern.

The physicians appeared baffled. "I've never seen anything like it, Sire."

"What?" I asked, my voice breaking.

The head physician sighed. "It's as if he's about to die from thirst and starvation though I know he's never missed a single meal. From the looks of him, I doubt he'll live out the day. It doesn't make sense. How could a prince have these symptoms?"

My heart stilled at his words and instantly I knew the source of Styxx's illness. "Acheron," I said to my father. "He's dying."

My father didn't hear me. He was too busy yelling at the physician to heal his heir.

"Father!" I shouted, shaking his arm to get his attention on me. "Styxx is dying because *Acheron* is dying. Do you not recall what the wisewoman said when they were born? If Acheron dies, so does Styxx. Acheron is the one who is starving to death in his prison cell. If we heal him, Styxx will live."

His face furious, he called for his guards and ordered them to bring Acheron to the throne room.

I ran after them as they walked the breadth of the palace and went to the below-ground cells to retrieve him. As always, it was dank and smelly. I hated this place and it bothered me much that Acheron had been confined here these many months.

My heart pounding, I stood back as they opened the cell door. Finally I would see him again.

They stepped back, showing me Acheron.

Never in my life had I cursed aloud, but I cursed foully when I saw how they'd kept my brother.

The room was so small that he'd been forced to sit doubled over inside it. It was even smaller than the one Estes had used in Atlantis to punish him. Acheron was literally curled into a ball. There was no light whatsoever inside it.

My brother had lived in total darkness and filth for almost a year now. Unable to move or stretch, or to even relieve himself. Not even animals were treated this poorly. Why had Acheron never told me what lay on his side of the door?

The guard tried to pull him out. Too weak to protest, Acheron spilled across the hallway floor. The stench of him and the room was so rancid that it made my stomach lurch. I was forced to pinch my nose closed so as not to vomit.

Acheron lay on his back, his breathing shallow and faint. He was so thin that he didn't look real lying there. I could see every single bone in his body. A thick beard covered his face and his hair hung around him like a frail spiderweb. He looked like an old man, not a boy of nineteen.

I knelt beside him and pulled his head into my lap. "Acheron?"

He didn't respond. Like Styxx, he was too weak to do anything more than stare blankly at me.

"Take him upstairs to my room," I ordered the guard.

He curled his lip in repugnance. "My lady, he is foul."

"You take him to my bed or I will see you beaten for your insolence."

Indecision played across his face for several minutes before he complied. I ordered another guard to fetch food and drink while I followed them.

Every step seemed to take too long. I couldn't believe the shell of a human in the guard's arms was the same handsome boy who'd chased Maia in our garden. How could my father have done this to him?

How could Acheron have done this to himself?

121

Entering my room, the guard placed him on my bed, then left immediately. I sent my maids for water and linen so that we could bathe some of the filth from him.

It was so horrible to be near him like this. He smelled so bad, looked so weak . . . How could anyone suffer such a tragedy? And I felt completely helpless.

Using my sheet, I tried to wipe some of the dirt from his face.

My maids returned at the same time food was brought.

I cradled Acheron's head as I carefully fed him small pieces of bread. But he didn't seem to want to chew. I didn't know if he was too weak or too far gone to even know it was bread in his mouth.

"My lady," Kassandra said, "you'll ruin your clothes touching him like that."

"I don't care." And I didn't. All that mattered to me was saving his life. I dripped wine slowly into his mouth. "Eat, Acheron," I breathed.

Weakly, he turned his head away from me. "Please," he begged, his voice a ragged, hoarse whisper. "Let me die."

Tears choked me as I realized he must have done this on purpose. No doubt he'd been going without food, praying for death to come and free him from that hole where he'd been trapped.

The kindest thing I could do would be to let him go.

But I couldn't. I wouldn't just lose him, I'd lose Styxx as well and I loved both my brothers.

"Stay with me, Acheron," I whispered.

But he didn't do it for me. Instead, he fought for death and the days passed as I watched my father's physicians violently force feed him while he tried to spit the food out. They were merciless in their attention.

They kept him tied to my bed and pried his lips apart so that they could pour milk, wine and honey down his throat. He would try to spit the food and drink out only to have them beat him and hold his mouth and nose shut until he swallowed it.

He cursed them and he cursed me.

I couldn't blame him.

Every day was a nightmare for him while Styxx grew

stronger in comfort with everyone lavishing praise on him and serving his every need. Meanwhile bruises marred Acheron's skin, especially his jaw where they continually pried it apart. The physicians demanded that he be "fed" at least every two hours.

Every time the guards and servants appeared for those feedings, he'd stiffen and cast me the most condemning of glares.

As he grew stronger, the fights became worse until he finally stopped fighting at all. The hateful angry glares were replaced by a hopeless resignation that hurt me even more. Still they left him tied down and I realized that I hadn't really changed his position. Only his location was different.

My brother's reality was ever the same.

November 1, 9529 BC

Today Father had Acheron moved to a new room down the hall from mine. Once more, he was tied spread eagle on the bed, but at least this time he was clothed. The feedings continued, but now they only occurred five times a day.

I made a point of seeing Acheron every chance I could and every time I saw him my heart broke more.

Acheron never moved or spoke to me during my visits. He lay there, staring at the ceiling as if he were immune to what was happening around him.

"I wished you'd speak to me, Acheron."

He acted as if I weren't even there.

"You have to know that I love you. I don't want to see you like this. Please, little brother. Could you at least look at me?"

He didn't even blink.

His lack of response angered me and a part of me wanted to lash out verbally against him. But I held my tongue. He'd been abused enough by the insults of my father and the guards and servants who fed him.

There was nothing more I could do. Ill from the knowledge, I left him and continued my preparations for Apollo.

November 20, 9529 BC

Acheron continued to lie unmoving on his bed. He stared at the ceiling as always, ignoring me while I tried to talk to him.

"I wish you'd speak to me, Acheron. I miss the way we used to talk together. You were my best friend. The only person I could ever talk to whom I knew wouldn't tell every word I said to Father."

Again, there was no response.

What would it take to make him acknowledge me? Surely he couldn't continue to lie in bed like that. Then again, given the fact that he'd been sitting in a tiny hole these months past, he'd probably grown more than accustomed to not moving.

My heart aching for him, I started away from the bed when I noticed something odd. Frowning, I headed to the bedpost where his ankle was secured by a metal shackle. It took me a second to realize what I was looking at. Fresh and dried blood coated the metal.

I cringed as I saw his raw and bleeding skin that was mostly hidden from my view by the cuffs. So Acheron wasn't always inert like this. From the wounds that marked each arm and leg, I could tell he'd been fighting fiercely for his freedom whenever he was alone.

As I saw the blood, my own vision turned red. I'd had enough of this abuse.

My fury smoldering, I left his room to find our father.

After a quick search, I learned he was out in the training area watching as Styxx practiced his sword fighting.

"Father?"

He gave me an agitated stare that I'd dare to interrupt his encouragements to Styxx. "Is there a problem?"

125

"There is indeed. I want Acheron freed. I demand it."

He sneered at my request. "Why? What would he do with it?"

I wanted him to understand what he was doing to someone who'd never caused him harm. Someone who was his own flesh and blood. "You can't leave him tied like a beast, Father. It's cruel. He can't even attend his basic needs."

"Nor can he shame us."

"Shame us how?"

"Women," he snarled. "You're ever blind. Can you not see him for what he is?"

I knew exactly who and what my brother was. "He's a boy, Father."

"He's a whore." There was more venom in those words than in the snake pit where my father threw his enemies.

It made my ire seethe. "He was a tortured slave you turned out into the street. What was he supposed to do?"

He answered me with a feral snarl.

But I refused to back down. "I won't have this, Father. I won't stand for it another minute. So help me, if you don't let him out of those shackles, I will shear the hair from my head and scar my face to the point that neither Apollo nor anyone else will have use for me."

"You wouldn't dare."

For the first time in my life, I stared at him as an equal. There was no doubt inside me that I could carry out the threat. "For Acheron's life, I would. He deserves better than to be kept as he is."

"He deserves nothing."

"Then you can find another woman to whore for Apollo."

His eyes darkened in such a way that I was sure he'd strike me for my boldness.

But ultimately, I won this battle.

That very afternoon Acheron was freed from his bed. He lay there as the restraints were opened and I saw the suspicion in his eyes. He was waiting for something worse to happen.

Once the shackles were gone, I ordered the guards to leave the room. Acheron didn't move until we were alone.

Slowly, angrily, he pushed himself up to glare at me. He was unsteady, his muscles weak from lack of use.

His long blond hair was matted and greasy. His skin sickly pale from the darkness that had been his home. A thick beard covered his cheeks. There were deep circles underneath his eyes, but he was no longer so gaunt—the atrocious feedings had added enough weight to him that he at least appeared human.

"You can't leave this room," I warned him. "Father was explicit in his terms that you're only allowed freedom in here so long as you stay hidden."

Acheron froze at my words and gave me a piercingly cold stare.

"At least you're no longer tied down."

He didn't speak to me. He never did anymore. But his swirling silver eyes spoke volumes. They told of the pain and agony that made up his life. They accused and they ached.

"My rooms are two doors down should you—"

"I can't leave," he snarled. "Isn't that what you just said?"

I opened my mouth, then paused. He was right. I'd already forgotten it. "I shall come visit you, then."

"Don't bother."

"Acheron—"

He interrupted my words with a cutting glare. "Do you remember what you said to me on your last visit to my cell?"

I struggled to recall it. I'd been angry at him for not speaking to me, but that was all I remembered. "No."

"Go die for all I care. I can't be bothered with you anymore."

I winced at words I should never have spoken. They cut me soul deep which was nothing compared to how they must have felt to him. If only I'd known the misery he was in . . . "I was angry."

He curled his lips. "And I was too weak to answer. It's hard to speak when you go days with nothing but darkness and rats for company. But then you don't know what it's like to have rats and fleas bite you, do you? What it's like to sit in your own shit."

127

"Acheron—"

His nostrils flared. "Leave me, Ryssa. I don't need your charity. I don't need anything from you."

"But . . ."

He shoved me from the room and slammed the door shut in my face.

I stared at it until a movement beside me caught my notice. Acheron's guards. He had two of them to make sure he didn't breach Father's mandate.

So this was his fate. I'd only changed the location of his prison. He still had no freedom.

I ached deep inside my soul for him. He was alive, but to what purpose? Perhaps it would have been kinder to let him die after all. But how could I have done that? He was my brother and I did love him even when he hated me.

Ill, I turned and went back to my chambers, but there was no peace there. I'd been uncharitable to Acheron, unkind. Thoughtless. No wonder he didn't want to speak to me.

But I couldn't leave it at this. I would give him time. Perhaps he'd come around eventually.

At least, I hoped deep inside that he could find it within himself to forgive me for being like everyone else. For hurting him when I should have been fighting for him.

December 1, 9529 BC

As the days passed by, I learned more things about Father's mandates for Acheron's treatment. No one was allowed into Acheron's room, except for me whom he refused to see, and everything he touched was to be shattered and burned.

Everything.

His dishes, his sheets. Even his clothes. It was Father's public humiliation for Acheron.

It sickened me.

Until the day I made the most frightening discovery of all.

I'd gone with several friends to see a play in the middle of the day. It wasn't something I normally did, but Zateria had a desperate crush on one of the actors and had insisted I judge him for myself.

We'd been laughing among ourselves when I happened to notice someone who was sitting two rows down from us in the peasant section. He sat alone with a peplos shielding him. He had the hood pulled up over his head so that I could tell nothing about his features and yet something seemed oddly familiar about him.

It wasn't until the play ended and the man got up that I realized why he was familiar.

It was Acheron.

He pulled the cowl down lower, but I'd already glimpsed the beauty of his face and I knew Styxx would never deign to come to something as common as a midday play. Even if he had, he'd *never* be in that section of seats.

I excused myself from my friends to go after him.

"Acheron?"

He hesitated an instant before he pulled the cowl lower and continued on his way.

Rushing to catch up, I pulled him to a stop.

He looked at me coldly. "Are you going to tell him?"

"No," I breathed, knowing the him he meant was our father. "Why would I?"

He started away, but I stopped him again.

His expression was exasperated. "What, Ryssa?"

"How did you come to be here? The guards—"

"I bribed them," he said in a clipped tone.

"With what? You have no money."

The look he gave me answered that question plainly. I was nauseated with the mere thought of what he'd used to get out of the palace.

He narrowed his eyes at me. "Don't look so horrified, Ryssa. I've been bartered for much less than an afternoon of freedom. At least they're gentle with me."

Tears stung my eyes. "You can't keep doing this."

"Why not? It's all anyone wants me for."

"That's not true."

"No?"

I watched as he angrily lowered his cowl. I could feel the ripple that went through everyone around us as people caught sight of him.

The sudden silence was deafening. It was tangible and there was no mistaking the attention that was immediately focused on him.

Solely him.

Women's heads came together as they giggled and tried to remain inconspicuous in their ogling. Men weren't so subtle. There was no denying the fact that every one of them stared at him with longing. With desire.

I was no more immune to his unnatural allure than they were, but mine was tempered by the fact that we were family.

"Do you really want to know why your father hates me?"

I shook my head. I knew the answer. Acheron had said it the day Father had banished him. Because he, too, was attracted to Acheron and he despised the boy for it.

Acheron pushed past me, out of the stadium. With every step he took, he was dogged by offers and invitations. Even once he'd replaced his cowl, people didn't stop calling out and pursuing him through the street.

I hurried after him.

"Don't be like that," a man said as he trailed behind Acheron. "I would make you a most beneficial mentor."

"I have no need of a mentor," Acheron said as he continued walking.

The man grabbed him roughly. "What do you want?"

"I want to be left alone."

The man lowered Acheron's cowl. "Tell me your price. I'll pay anything to have you."

That hollow, empty stare came into Acheron's eyes as he shoved the man away from him.

"What is this?"

My blood went cold as I recognized the hostile, demanding voice of my father. I'd been so intent on Acheron and the unknown man that I had failed to realize Father and his entourage were traveling past.

Now Father's full attention was riveted on Acheron whose face had turned to stone.

Father roughly snatched the cowl back over Acheron's head and shoved him toward his guards who were ordered to take him into custody. Acheron was escorted back to the palace where Father had him beaten for his disobedience.

I tried to mitigate the punishment, but Father wouldn't listen. They dragged Acheron into the courtyard that was reserved for punishment outside my father's throne room. The guards stripped Acheron bare and delivered sixty-five strokes to his back. I couldn't watch, but I heard every whistle of the whip as it traveled through the air and every lash that cut through his flesh.

Acheron would grunt and several times I heard him fall, only to have my father order the guards to make him stand again. Never once did he cry out.

When it was finally over, I turned to see Acheron leaning against the post, bleeding, his hands still securely tied. The guards threw a coarse blanket over him before his ropes were cut and he was dragged back to his room and locked inside.

All I could do was hold Acheron afterward. For once, he didn't turn me away. He lay with his head in my lap as he used to do when we were children. When he would beg me to tell him why his parents hated him so.

I waited for someone to come and tend his ravaged back. No one did.

It was only later that I learned Father had forbidden it. So I sat with Acheron for hours, holding his head as he quietly wept from the pain.

But whether he cried from the throbbing wounds of his back or the deeper ache in his heart, I didn't know. Gods, how I wanted to take him back to that day in the orchard when it'd been just the three of us playing and laughing. Away to some place where he could be free and lackadaisical, where he'd be a normal boy of nineteen as he should have been.

When he finally fell to sleep, I continued to brush my hand through his golden hair as I stared at the ragged welts on his back. I couldn't imagine a pain so severe.

"I love you, Acheron," I whispered, wishing my love was enough to spare him from this.

December 10, 9529 BC

After that day, I never spoke again of the fact I knew Acheron continued to slip out of the palace to go to plays. Many days I followed him just to make sure no one bothered him. That no one knew what it was he did.

He kept to the shadows, his identity and beauty carefully guarded. His head was always hung low, his gaze on the ground as he passed through the unsuspecting crowds.

Acheron risked much to go. We both knew it. I'd asked him once why he dared so much and he'd told me simply that it was all that comforted him.

He liked to watch the characters in the plays. Liked to pretend he was one of them. How could I fault him for that when so little brought joy to his life?

As my union with Apollo drew critically near, I spent more and more time in Acheron's chambers. He alone didn't treat the event as some magical moment that I should be anticipating with relish and enthusiasm.

He saw it for the horror it was.

I too was being whored. Only Father saw my whoredom as noble and wonderful.

"Will it hurt much when he takes me?" I asked Acheron as we sat on his balcony that overlooked the sea below.

I was on the ground while Acheron sat up on the banister as he always did. He balanced precariously over the edge of it which dropped down to the raging sea.

I was terrified of heights, but he seemed oblivious to the danger.

"It depends on Apollo and his mood. It always depends on your lovers and how much force they use. How much pleasure they take from causing you pain."

That didn't comfort me since I couldn't control someone else's mood. "Was it painful your first time?"

He nodded subtly, his eyes blank. "At least you won't have an audience when he violates you."

"Did you?"

He didn't answer, but then he didn't have to. His expression told me that he had.

My heart aching for him and the horror he must have known, I looked down at the cord I was twisting in my hands. "Do you think Apollo will hurt me?"

"I don't know, Ryssa." His tone showed his impatience. He always hated talking about intercourse. Then again, he hated talking, period.

But I had to know what was coming and no one else would speak to me of such things. I met his swirling gaze. "Just how painful can it be?"

He glanced away, out toward the sea. "Try not to think about it. Just close your eyes and imagine that you're a bird. Imagine that you live high up in the clouds and that there's nothing that can touch you there. You're free to fly anywhere you want to go."

"Is that what you do?"

"Sometimes."

"And others?"

He didn't respond.

So we sat there in silence, listening to the waves below crash against the rocks. For the first time, I finally understood some of his pain. His humiliation. I wanted no part in my future and yet I had no choice.

As I listened to the waves, it reminded me of the time we'd spent alone when he was younger. Of the hours he used to spend on the rocks, listening to the sea and the voices that called out to him. "Do you still hear the gods' voices, Acheron?"

He nodded.

"Do you hear them now?"

"Yes."

Years ago, he'd told me they were the gods calling out to him. Telling him to come home. "Do you ever think of doing what they say?"

He shook his head. "I never want to go back to Atlantis. I hate it there."

I could well understand that and it made me wonder how much more he must hate it here. Sorrow always followed him and it was never his fault. How awful not to be able to show your own face for fear of people assaulting you. Everywhere he went, everyone who came near wanted him with a desperation that made no sense.

Even I desired him. I was only grateful that he couldn't feel those impure thoughts that came to me at the worst possible times.

But unlike the other people in his life, I would never act on them. He was my brother and I only wanted to protect him. Unlike the rest of my family, he saw the real me and loved me in spite of my faults. Just I as loved him in spite of his.

"Will you go with me tomorrow to the temple?" I asked quietly.

He looked startled by the question.

"Please, Acheron. I'm so scared of what they're planning. I don't want to be the mistress of a god. I've never been touched by any man. Never been kissed. I don't think I have the courage for this."

"It's not hard, Ryssa. Just lie there and act as if you like it."

"And if I don't?"

"You pretend you do. He'll be so intent on his own pleasure that he'll never even notice if you're grimacing or crying. Just tell him how skilled he is and how good it feels. That's all that matters."

I reached up from my place on the ground and took his hand in mine. I stared at the strength of his tanned tendons. He'd been through so much. Truly, I had no right to complain or bemoan my fate. No one had ever been there to comfort him through the terrors of his life.

But I wasn't as strong as Acheron. I couldn't do this alone. I wanted . . . no, I *needed* someone to be there. Someone I could trust to tell me the truth and to see tomorrow for the horror that it was. "Please come with me."

There was still reservation in his eyes. He didn't want to do this, but he nodded anyway.

Grateful, I kissed his hand and held it tightly in mine. He alone understood my fears. Knew what it felt like to be sold against his will.

In this we were kindred spirits.

December 11, 9529 BC

I'd tried my best to sleep, but it was fitful at best. This was to be the worst day of my life. Today, my own father would tie me to a god . . .

When it was time to leave for the temple, I found Acheron in the hallway outside my room wearing the bland colored peplos he used to visit the plays. As always, it was pulled up over his head to shield him from others.

It was good of him to come with me when I knew he didn't want to. I wanted to hold his hand for courage, but didn't dare for fear of drawing attention to him. The last thing I wanted was for him to be hurt again because of me.

Without a word, he followed me and my maidservants as we left the palace. I thought Father would meet me outside, but I was told he was already at the temple.

I hesitated there in the street as my courage fled and left me on trembling legs.

Turning back, I met Acheron's gaze. "Should I run?"

"They always brought me back whenever I tried and made me very sorry for the attempt."

My stomach cramped even more as I remembered the time I'd taken him from Atlantis. He'd told me then that he would be punished for my actions, but not once had he ever told me how. "What did Uncle do to you after I took you from—"

He placed his hand over my lips and shook his head. "You don't ever want to know."

I stared up into his silver eyes and saw the pain that was there and it was then I fully understood why he hadn't left behind the life our uncle had taught him. I remembered what he'd said to me at the brothel.

Without skills there was nothing either one of us could do. No way to support ourselves.

"I tried to find honorable work . . ."

His words haunted me now.

Acheron was right. They would find me and they would punish me.

Taking a deep breath for courage, I turned and headed toward the temple district.

There was a crowd waiting for me there to cheer the fact that I was being sold against my will to a god. Six young girls stood with baskets of white and red rose petals in their hands. They scattered them before my feet as they led me toward Apollo's temple.

At the door, I met my father. He smiled at me until his gaze went past my shoulder to see my tall "guard."

A snarl curved his lips. "What is he doing here?"

"I asked him to come."

Father shoved Acheron back. "He's not allowed here. He's unclean."

"I want him here."

"No!"

I looked back to see Acheron lift his chin as if the words didn't hurt him, but I saw the pain in his gaze.

"I shall wait outside for you, Ryssa."

Father made a disgusted noise and I knew it was only fear of making a scene before Apollo that kept him from doing anything. However, there would be punishment for Acheron later. Of that I had no doubt.

I held my hand out to my brother, but Father shoved me toward the door. Tears gathered in my eyes as I choked. I wanted to call Acheron to my side, but couldn't get my voice to cooperate.

Acheron drifted away, into the crowd.

I wanted to see him. I needed his strength, but there was nothing I could do.

Against my will, they drew me into the temple and to a destiny I wanted no part in . . .

Acheron

9529 BC–7382 BC

December 11, 9529 BC

Acheron turned away from Apollo's temple. Impotent anger roiled through him. He was so tired of being reminded of his place in this world.

Being reminded he was nothing.

No doubt his father would punish him later for this. Not that he cared.

He no longer felt physical pain like the rest of the world. Too many days of being used and abused had left him hollow and unable to feel much of anything except hatred and anger.

Those two emotions burned inside him constantly.

He'd been made a whore against his will and now it was held against him as if he'd had a choice in the matter. As if he enjoyed being groped and fought over.

So be it.

Seeking some sort of vengeance on the ones who had cursed him to this fate, he found himself heading into the temple across the street from Apollo's.

It was empty. Most likely the occupants and caretakers were all across the street to witness his sister's sacrifice.

Fucking pigs.

There was nothing people loved more than to watch someone else being humiliated, especially royalty. It gave them a sense of power. A sense of superiority. But in the back of their minds, they all knew the truth. They were just grateful it wasn't them being degraded.

He walked down the center aisle that was framed by huge columns that stretched up toward the heavens. Columns that led toward the statue of a woman. He'd never been inside a temple before. Whores weren't allowed since

141

the gods had abandoned them and mankind had damned them.

Defiantly, he lowered his cowl as he stared up at the carved image of the goddess. Made of solid gold, she was beautiful. Her peplos seemed to be rippling from an unseen wind and she held a bow in one hand with a quiver of arrows on her back. Her left hand rested on a tall poised deer that was brushing up against her leg.

He stared at the writing on the tablet at her feet, but couldn't read it.

He vaguely recalled Ryssa trying to teach him to read all those years ago when she'd rescued him. He hadn't seen a scroll or word since.

As he traced the first letter of the goddess's name, he thought he recognized it.

It was an A. Ryssa had told him his own name began with that letter.

He ran through his mind his limited knowledge of the gods and what he knew of them as he tried to think of one whose name sounded similar to his.

"You must be Athena," he said out loud. It would make sense since Athena was goddess of war and held a bow in her hand.

"I beg your pardon? *Athena?!*"

He turned sharply at the angry voice behind him. The woman was incredibly voluptuous with long, curling auburn hair and dark green eyes. Her beauty was natural and piercing. If he were capable of being sexually attracted to anyone, he might even have desired her. But honestly, he'd screwed so many people that he could live the rest of his life without another body under, over or near him.

Dressed in a white flowing gown, she stood with her hands on her curvy hips. "Are you blind? Or just stupid?"

He snarled at the insults. "I am neither."

She approached him with a narrowed gaze before she gestured toward the statue behind him. "Then how is it you don't know the image of Artemis when you see her?"

Acheron rolled his eyes at the mention of Apollo's twin sister. He should have known since the temples were so close together. "Is she as worthless as her brother?"

The woman's mouth fell open. She appeared shocked by his question. "I beg your pardon?"

Anger burned through him as he saw the tributes laid out on the altar before the imperial goddess. He flung his arm against them, sending them flying. Platters crashed to the floor while bits of flowers, toys and other offerings scattered and rolled over the marble. "Why do they bother when no one on Olympus hears them and if they do it's obvious they don't care?"

"Are you mad?"

"Yes, I am," he said from between clenched teeth. "Mad at this world where we are nothing to the gods. Mad at the Fates who put us here for no purpose except to toy with us for their petty amusement. I wish all of the gods were dead and gone."

The woman snarled, rushing at him. Acheron caught her hand before she could slap him.

She shrieked and something slammed into him, knocking him straight to the ground. Pain spread through his body.

An unseen force picked him up from the floor and flung him against the wall. The breath left him as he was pinned to the wall, a good ten feet above the ground.

The woman glared at him. "I should kill you."

"Please do so."

Artemis withheld the final god bolt that would have sent this human straight to Tartarus where he belonged, and let him fall to the ground. She'd never met anyone who didn't know her on sight. Never met anyone who couldn't feel her unearthly presence and god powers and yet this human seemed immune to them.

She watched as he pushed himself to his feet and stood defiantly before her. He was a handsome young man. She'd give him that. His face was flawless in its beauty. Dark blond brows slashed over swirling silver eyes that were searing with their hatred. No one had ever dared give her such a look.

His long blond wavy hair framed his features to perfection. It appeared softer than down and was every bit as inviting.

And his body . . . It was lean and well muscled. Tanned. Gorgeous. There was something about it that made her mouth water for a taste of him. Never in her life had she felt such an incredible pull toward any man.

More than that, he was taller than she, a mortal rarity that she appreciated.

"Have you any idea who I am?" she asked him.

"Judging from your anger and what you just did to me, I would assume you're Artemis."

So, he wasn't stupid after all.

"Then bow down and apologize."

Instead, he offered her an intense look that caused her stomach to flutter. He walked toward her with an arrogant swagger that made his entire body ripple like a panther's. A foreign aching need pounded through her. She didn't understand what she felt, but whatever it was, it left her breathless and weak.

He laid his warm hand against her cheek as he stared down at her face with those beguiling eyes that seemed to hypnotize her. "So, you're a goddess," he said, his voice thick as he boldly examined her. His pupils dilated . . .

Her stomach tightened even more. His nearness was searing. His eyes riveting.

She'd never felt anything like this.

Before she realized what he intended, he pulled her into his arms and kissed her.

Artemis couldn't breathe as she tasted him. Part of her was outraged that he would dare such, but another, alien part of her was thrilled by the unexpected sensation of his lips on hers. Of his tongue exploring her mouth.

His arms surrounded her as he pulled her closer to him.

Her head spun as he pulled back slightly and trailed his lips from her mouth to her neck. Chills swept over her, and at the same time an incredible heat built inside her. All she wanted was to pull him closer . . .

To feel every inch of his body.

He made an appreciative noise against her skin that made her ache. "You do taste divine."

He dropped to his knees before her.

"What are you doing?" she asked as he lifted one of her feet into his hands. She didn't understand what was going on. It was as if she had no control of herself.

This . . . creature compelled her in a way that was wholly unnatural.

He looked up at her and her stomach felt as if it were turning over. "Kissing your feet, goddess. Isn't that what I'm supposed to do?"

Well, yes, but as he nibbled her instep she couldn't suppress a deep moan of pleasure. Artemis leaned back against the wall as his mouth worked magic on the sensitive tendons of her foot.

She'd never known such a rich, deep burn deep in her blood. And he didn't stop with her feet, he trailed his lips up her leg, to the back of her knee.

Artemis struggled to breathe.

Then he moved his mouth higher.

"What are you doing now?" she gasped as his warm breath fell against her buttocks.

"I'm kissing your ass. Isn't that people are supposed to do?"

"Not like that."

She groaned as he nibbled her high on her buttocks. She should stop him. He had no right to touch her like this and yet she didn't want this to end. It felt too good.

He nudged her legs farther apart.

With a mind of their own, her legs obeyed him. Artemis looked down to see him with his eyes closed as he tormented her with pleasure.

She felt his hands on her as he touched her where no man had ever touched her before. His fingers ran down her cleft, making her burn even more before he took her into his mouth.

Reaching down, she buried her hand in his hair as he tasted her.

Her senses went wild as she surrendered herself to him and the licks he gave that sent her careening to an unimaginable height. Every one sent a white hot shiver through her. Her throat went dry an instant before her body burst apart.

Artemis cried out as she experienced her first orgasm.

Terrified and embarrassed, she vanished.

Acheron sat on the floor in stunned disbelief. The taste and smell of Artemis permeated his senses. His body burned with aching need.

He'd never really tasted desire before. His body had always reacted to being stimulated by others or by drugs, but he'd never really wanted to touch someone.

Until now.

Now he wanted a woman . . . no, he wanted a goddess and that made no sense to him.

He laughed bitterly. "The least you could have done was kill me, Artemis," he shouted. That had been his only intent when he'd first approached her.

But the moment he'd touched her, he'd felt real desire.

Unable to fathom that, he wiped his mouth and pushed himself to his feet. Turning around, he looked up at her statue which bore no resemblance to her whatsoever. He gave her a sarcastic salute.

His body strangely hungry, he left the temple and made the long walk back to the palace alone. And with every step he took, his anger built even higher than it'd been before.

It was eerily silent as he walked through the marbled corridors of his father's home with no destination in mind. Everyone had gone to see Ryssa's sacrifice. He wondered idly if it would work. If Apollo's favor could be swayed from the Atlanteans to the Greeks.

Not that he cared. Neither the Atlanteans nor the Apollites had been any kinder to him than the Greeks had been.

All any of them wanted to do was fuck him.

Sighing, he found himself in his father's large and impressive throne room—his first time walking into it, since the previous times he'd been bound in chains and dragged through the doors.

His gaze narrowed as he saw the two gilded thrones at the far end. Thrones that should have been his mother's and father's, but since his mother had been banished for his birth, Styxx had occupied her place. Too bad the old bitch had died in her isolation. She would have loved to see her precious Styxx become King.

Styxx. His baby brother.

Acheron cursed. If not for his eyes, he would have been the one to sit to the right hand of his father.

No one would dare mock him then. No one would ever have forced him to his knees to . . .

He snarled at the memories.

It was so unfair.

He'd never asked for this life. Never asked to be born. Never asked to be a demigod.

He heard Estes's voice in his head. *"Look at him. Son to an Olympian. How much will you pay for a taste of a Greek god?"*

Acheron didn't even know who his father was. His mother had always protested her innocence over his birth and no god had ever stepped forward to acknowledge him.

Angered by that fact, he crossed the room to sit on his father's throne. The man would die to see him perched on it and that gave him an instant moment of gratification. His father would have it burned.

Perhaps he should let his father find him here. It would serve the king right to know a whore had fouled his beloved throne.

A whore . . . he flinched with the thought.

By birthright, this should have all been his. Closing his eyes, Acheron tried to imagine what the world would have been like had he possessed blue eyes like Styxx.

People would respect him.

Respect.

The word hung like a phantom in his mind. That was the only thing he'd ever craved.

"Don't you want to be loved?"

He opened his eyes to see Artemis standing in the center of the room, studying him.

"Everyone claims they love me." At least while they screwed him. Unfortunately, that affection ended the minute they came. "I've had more than my share of other people's love. I'd rather do without it for a while."

She frowned. It was a delicate expression that he found oddly sweet. "You're a strange human."

He scoffed at that. "I'm a demigod. Can't you tell?"

Her frown deepened as she drew near him. "Whose issue are you?"

"They tell me Zeus."

She shook her head at that. "You're no son of an Olympian. I would know it if you were. We can always sense our own."

Her words went through his heart like a knife. "Then whose son am I?"

She cupped his chin in her warm, soft hand so that he looked up at her as she stared into his freakish eyes. Eyes he'd hated all his life. Eyes that betrayed him.

"You're human."

"But my eyes . . ."

"They are strange, but birth defects are common among your kind. There are no god powers inside you. Nothing to mark you as divinity. You're human."

Acheron closed his eyes as pain assailed him. So he was his father's son after all.

It was the last thing he'd wanted to hear. A birth defect. A simple accident of birth had deprived him of everything. He wanted to scream out in anger.

"Why are you here?" he asked, opening his eyes to find Artemis still staring at him.

She ignored his question. "Why do you not fear me?"

"Should I?"

"I could kill you."

"I asked you to, but you didn't."

She cocked her head as if he baffled her completely. "You're very handsome for a human."

"I know."

Artemis scowled at his words. They weren't said arrogantly. Instead, he'd said them angrily as if his beauty bothered him. He was so unlike any human she'd ever met.

If she didn't know better, she would believe his claim of divinity. There was something unnatural about the desire he created in her.

But gods and their issue had an essence that was unmistakable. All she felt inside this human was hatred, despair. He hurt so badly that it was almost painful for her to be near him.

"Why are you so sad?"

"You would never understand."

Most likely not. Sadness wasn't something she normally felt. As for despair . . .

It was completely alien to her.

In all eternity, she'd never wanted to comfort a human. Today, she did and she didn't know why.

"Do you ever smile?" she asked him.

He shook his head.

"Never?"

"No. All it does is draw people toward me. Make them want me more."

"But I thought all humans longed to be desired."

Again he scoffed. "Do you know the Atlantean term *tsoulus*?"

"Sex-slave?"

He gave her a blank stare.

Artemis gasped as she caught his meaning. "You're one of them?"

"I was."

Her vision darkened with the knowledge. "And you dared to touch me?"

"So will you kill me now?"

That made her anger falter under another wave of confusion. Who was this man who braved more than any before him? "If you wish to die so much, why not kill yourself?"

His lip curled as his eyes flared with fury. "Every time I've ever tried, I was brought back and punished for it. It appears the gods don't want me dead so I figure if one of you kills me, then I'll finally be at peace."

"Then it's not fated for you to die."

He came to his feet with a snarl so feral that Artemis actually took a step back in fear.

"Don't you dare say their name to me. I refuse to believe this was my fate. I was not meant to be this. I was never meant to be . . ." The pain in his eyes tore through her. "This can't be all I was born for."

"It's the fate of mankind to suffer. Why should you be different?"

Acheron couldn't breathe as her words tore through him. Over and over in his mind he saw himself and his past. Saw the horrors and degradations he'd suffered.

But the most horrifying thoughts were those of the future. Forever alone with nothing but scorn and abuse for company. Being forced to eat against his will, or worse, traded like nothing more than a sack of wheat.

Too angry to speak, he stormed from the room and headed to his "prison." Granted it was better than the hole his father had thrown him into initially, but it was still a prison.

It was all he would ever know and if his father had his way, he'd be kept shut in here for the rest of his life.

At least there were no guards outside it today. Even they had been given a day of freedom. A day to do as they pleased.

"Why did you leave?"

He drew up short as Artemis appeared before him. "Why are you following me?"

"You make me curious."

"Curious about what?"

"About you."

He laughed bitterly at that. Even a goddess was no better than the humans who hounded him. "Do you want me naked so you can explore me?"

Her cheeks darkened, but even so he saw the heated look in her eyes.

He also noticed she didn't contradict him. So be it.

Artemis watched as her newfound human slowly released the pin for his peplos. She should stop him, she knew it and yet she couldn't bring herself to say the words.

She trembled from expectation of what he might look like naked. No wonder her brother spent so much time with human females. If they were half this evocative . . .

He dropped his peplos to the floor.

Her thoughts scattering, she swallowed as she saw his nudity. He was even more handsome than she'd suspected.

His skin was tawny, inviting, and stretched over a body that was finely honed and well muscled.

Against her will, her gaze dropped down to the part of him that was uniquely male. He was very well endowed and as she stared at him, his shaft grew larger, thicker as it slowly lifted to curve against his body. His balls tightened.

She'd never seen a man like this. Rife with desire. So bold and uninhibited by fear of her.

He closed the distance between them. "Don't you want to touch me?"

Yes she did, but she couldn't move. Couldn't breathe. She felt the heat from his body, the stirring of his breath against her face.

His nearness was intoxicating.

He took her hand into his and led it toward his erection. His grip was tight as he brushed her palm against the tip of his cock. He was so soft, and yet hard.

She swallowed as he slowly slid her fingers down the length of him until he rubbed her hand against the soft sac. She bit her lip while he rubbed himself against her palm. His body was so different from hers. So incredible and beguiling.

He released her hand.

Her first instinct was to withdraw, but she wasn't one for timidity. Instead, she ran the back of her fingers underneath his sac, letting his balls sag around them. His body felt so strange to her.

She lifted her hand up in silent exploration over his stomach to his chest.

He didn't move to touch her. He just stared at her silently while she explored every inch of his body. His eerie silver eyes were incredible. She'd never seen anything like them. Never felt anything better than his masculine skin beneath her hand.

Oh, but he was luscious.

"Do you want me to fuck you?"

She shivered at a question that should have offended her to the core of her being. At the deep accent of his voice. She wanted him with a madness that was consuming.

If only she could.

"No," she said quietly. She looked up at him. His gaze was searing. "I want you to do to me what you did earlier. Make me feel that again."

He took her hand and led her toward a bed where they could be alone. Undisturbed.

She shouldn't be doing this. She was a virgin goddess. Untouched by man or god.

At least until today.

No one had ever kissed her before. No one had ever breached her. She'd been known to kill men just because

151

they had seen her naked and yet for this one, she was willing to let him seduce her.

She didn't know why any more than she understood the compulsion inside her to be with him.

He just made her feel oddly happy. Warm. Decadent. Desirable.

Acheron laid her back against the mattress. She was nervous—it was something he was used to with women who lacked experience. Even so, she was beautiful. Her auburn hair fanned out over his pillows, making him even harder for her. It wasn't something he was used to feeling.

The scent of roses clung to her skin. He kissed her lightly on the lips while he grazed his hand up her leg, lifting the hem of her gown. She stiffened a bit, but quickly relaxed. She was shy.

Not wanting to embarrass her, he left her lips to crawl down her body.

Artemis was uncertain as she watched him vanish beneath the folds of her white gown. Even so, she could feel him moving. Feel his whiskers scraping against her thigh as he trailed a hot line of kisses up the inside of her thigh until he reached the part of her that ached for him.

She moaned the instant his lips and tongue found that spot. Biting the heel of her hand, she surrendered herself to the pleasure he gave her. It was blinding and exhilarating. No wonder the other gods and humans risked so much for this.

And this time, when she came, she fully understood what was happening to her body. At least she did until he made her do it again and again.

Acheron growled at the taste of Artemis. At the sound of her cries filling his ears. He loved the way she purred. The sensation of her hand in his hair, stroking him.

She slapped her other hand against the mattress beside her. "You have to stop. Please. I can't take any more."

He gave one last, long lick before he pulled away. "Are you sure?"

She nodded.

Reluctantly, he did as she asked and moved to stretch out beside her even though his own body was far from sated.

Artemis draped herself across his chest, listening to his ragged breathing. He was still hard and stiff.

"Does it hurt you to stay like this?" she asked, brushing her hand over his cock.

He drew a sharp breath as if her caress pained him. "Yes."

"Can you not pleasure yourself?"

"I can." He studied her face. "Would you like to watch?"

Before she could answer, his hand enclosed around hers, holding her palm against him.

Acheron closed his eyes at the heat of her hand against his cock. Sex meant nothing to him. It never had. It was just something that was expected of him.

He'd masturbated before crowds and with lovers more times than he could even recall. For some reason, it seemed to give other people pleasure to see him come. He barely felt the momentary release of hormones anymore. It was a piercing pleasure, quickly gone.

He'd long ago learned to want something more than this.

But it wasn't meant to be and he didn't know what it was he craved anyway. Artemis was here because, like many others before her, she was curious about his body. She might come back to visit him. She might not.

There was a time when he would have been beaten had a lover not returned for him.

Back in Atlantis, everything had hinged on his ability to make people crave him. How much sleep he was allowed. How much food.

How much dignity.

If his lovers didn't feel well sated after leaving him, he was beaten for it.

Now his father would beat him if he ever learned of this. The king demanded celibacy from a man who had never known it. But in truth, he liked being with Artemis. Her touch was gentle. Her skin creamy and soft.

Sucking his breath in, he imagined what it would feel like to slide himself inside her body. No, better yet, he imagined what it would be like to have her hold him cradled against her as if he mattered. The very thought of someone caring about him, *really* caring about him was almost enough to make him smile. But he knew better.

What he had was a stupid dream that had been fed by Ryssa and Maia at a time when he'd been gullible. Those illusions were long shattered.

Artemis was a goddess. He was lucky she would even deign to be in the same room with him. He would please her because that was what they'd trained him to do.

There could never be any kind of relationship between them. No doubt she'd vanish as soon as this was over. He'd be alone again.

Nothing in his life ever really changed.

Artemis watched Acheron's face while he used her hand to stroke him. It was odd to touch a man like this and she wondered what thoughts were in his head. Normally she could hear mortal thoughts when she wanted to, but for once she couldn't.

How very strange . . .

He stiffened ever so slightly before his hot seed shot through her fingers. Instead of crying out as she'd done, he merely sighed raggedly, then released her.

She ran her hand through his warm moisture, studying it. "So this is what makes women pregnant."

"In most cases."

"In most?"

He shrugged. "Mine is harmless enough."

"How so?"

"I was sterilized at puberty, Goddess. My kind always are. No one wants to be made pregnant by a whore."

Artemis arched her brows at his disclosure. "Humans can do such a thing?"

"No, but the Atlanteans can. They taught the procedure to the Apollites."

She studied his fluid again. " 'Tis a shame they did that to you," Artemis said quietly. "You are far too beautiful to be made sterile. Shall I fix you?"

"No. There's no reason to. I told you, no one would ever welcome a child conceived from me."

It was the pain in his silvery eyes as he spoke that brought an unfamiliar ache to her chest.

Her poor human.

He looked spectacular lying back against the white

154

linens that only emphasized the wide expanse of tawny masculine skin. Every muscle of his body was a study in perfection. He was so inviting. Warm. And he was completely unabashed about his nude sexuality. About what they'd done. He wasn't cocky or arrogant that he had touched her.

He treated her like she was . . .

Human.

Most of her family couldn't stand her. Humans feared her. Even her handmaidens laughed among themselves, but kept their guard up whenever she drew near.

But this man . . .

He was different. He held no fear of anything or anyone. Like a powerful, untamed beast, he was defiant and bold. Unyielding in her presence. He was docile now, but the power of him was undeniable. It was frightening even to her.

"Have you any friends?" she asked.

He shook his head.

"Why not?"

"I suppose I'm not worthy of any."

Artemis frowned at his reasoning. "It can't be that. I haven't any either and I am more than worthy. Perhaps there is a flaw to us." She paused as she thought about that. "No, that can't be right either. I have no flaws and yet I'm as alone as you are."

Never before had Artemis realized just how alone she really was. Her twin brother had friends. He had lovers. Apollo was the closest thing to a friend she'd ever known, but even he was reserved around her. Apollo never invited her to do things with him unless it involved destruction or punishment. He didn't laugh with her or ask her to go out carousing or gaming.

For the first time in her life, she realized just how lonely she was.

"Will you be my friend?"

Acheron was utterly stunned by her unexpected question. "You would befriend me?"

She cocked her head as she watched him with a small puckering of her divine brow. She was shimmery and

155

ethereal—far beyond the reach of something like him. "Well, yes. I mean, we can't let others know it, but I like what you have shown me. I wish to learn more about this world and about you." She smiled warmly at him as if she were truly sincere with her offer. It reminded him how rare such a thing as sincerity was. And friendship . . .

It was an elusive dream he dare not allow himself. People like him didn't have friendship. Any more than they had love or kindness. Yet he found a foreign part of himself aching for want of it.

Aching for want of her.

"So, are we friends? I promise you, you'll never regret it."

This had to be the strangest moment of his life and given the oddity of his existence, that said a lot. How could a whore be the friend of a goddess?

Acheron pulled the blanket from the bed and wiped himself clean. "I think you would regret being my friend."

She shrugged. "I doubt that. You're human. You'll only be alive . . . what? Another twenty or so years? That is so little time that it hardly matters and I doubt I shall be your friend once you grow old and unattractive. Besides regret isn't something an Olympian feels."

She smiled as she traced his lips. "Kiss me. Kiss me and let me know that we are friends."

It was a ludicrous thought and yet he found himself doing just as she asked.

Friends.

The two of them. He wanted to laugh at the thought. Instead, he closed his eyes and breathed her in. Her hands were sublime in his hair. And as they kissed, he wanted her friendship with a desperation that made him ache. His only hope was that he'd be worthy of it.

December 13, 9529 BC

"What are you doing?"

Acheron opened his eyes to find Artemis standing on his balcony a few feet away from him. Even though it was freezing cold, he was sitting on the railing, leaning back against a column while he listened to the turbulent sea below. "I was getting some fresh air. What are *you* doing?"

She pushed her lower lip out into a becoming pout. "I was bored."

That amused him. "How can a god be bored?"

She shrugged. "There's not that much for me to do really. My brother is off with your sister. Zeus is holding council and I'm never invited to those. Hades is with Persephone. My koris are bathing and cavorting with each other and ignoring me. So I'm bored. I thought you might have some idea of something we could do together."

Acheron let out a long, tired breath. He knew where this was headed and yet he was still compelled to ask the rhetorical question. "May I at least go inside where it's warm before I remove my clothes?"

She frowned. "Is that what humans do when they're bored?"

"It's what they do with me."

"And you enjoy that?"

"Not really," he answered honestly.

"Oh." She paused a second before she continued. "Well then, what do you do for fun?"

"I go to plays."

Crossing her arms, she approached him. "That's those made up stories where they have people pretending to be other people, right?"

He nodded.

By her face he could tell that she had no understanding of why he might find that entertaining. "And you like that better than being naked?"

He'd never really thought of it quite that way before, but . . . "Yes. It makes me forget who I am for a while."

She looked even more puzzled. "You like to forget yourself?"

"Yes."

"But isn't that confusing for you?"

Not half as confusing as this conversation. "No."

Artemis tapped her fingers against her upper arm. "I guess if I weren't a god I wouldn't like remembering who I am either. I can see why people would feel that way. So, is there a play we can go to now?"

"There's one every afternoon in town."

"Then we should go," she said firmly.

He snorted, wishing everything was as easy as she seemed to think it was. "I can't leave."

"Why not?"

He glanced to his closed bedroom doors that had been slammed and locked since the last time he'd been thrown in here and left to rot. Oh wait, that would have been yesterday. "My previous guards were beheaded for allowing me to leave. The new set is much more cautious. If I try to speak to them, they draw their swords and push me back into my room, then lock the doors."

She shrugged. "They're no problem for me. I can take you into town."

Acheron swung his legs down from the railing as hope swelled inside him. He hated being trapped like a rabid animal. He always had. All he'd been doing for the last two days was dreaming of escaping this place if only for a brief time. But the only two ways to leave his room were through the doors behind Artemis or jumping from the stone balcony that dropped a hundred feet to the rocks below. "Really?"

She nodded. "If you'd like to go, yes."

It felt as if something in his chest was lifted at her words. He could actually kiss her for this. "I'll get my cloak."

Artemis followed her new friend into his room and watched as he pulled a cloak from beneath his straw mattress. "Why do you keep your cloak under your bed?"

He shook it out as he answered. "I have to hide my cloak or else the maids will burn it."

"Why?"

He gave her a blank look. "I told you I'm not supposed to leave here."

She didn't understand that. Why would they keep him locked inside this small room? "Did you do something wrong to be imprisoned?"

"My only crime was being born to parents who have no use for me. My father doesn't want anyone to know his eldest son is deformed so here I'm to stay until I die of old age."

A foreign pain fluttered in her stomach as she felt sad for him. There were times when she felt imprisoned, too, though no one had ever made her feel freakish by any means.

She looked down at his muscular legs. "Is that why your feet are bare?"

He nodded as he wrapped the cloak around his body and raised the cowl over his head. "I'm ready."

"What about your shoes?"

He looked baffled by her question. "I haven't any. I told you, I'm forbidden to leave."

Now that she thought about it, she realized he hadn't been wearing any shoes in her temple either. "Won't your feet be cold?"

"I'm used to it."

She curled her toes in her shoes as she considered walking over winter stones barefoot. It would be a miserable feeling that not even a human should bear. Shaking her head, she manifested a pair of warm leather shoes on his feet. "There now, much better."

Acheron looked down in amazement at the dark brown shoes lined in fur. They felt so strange against his skin. But they were incredibly warm and soft. "Thank you."

She smiled at him as if the shoes pleased her as much as they did him. "You're welcome."

The next thing he knew, they were in the center of town. Acheron gaped at the sight of them standing by a well. No one in the busy crowd seemed to notice the fact that they'd just appeared out of nowhere. He immediately drew his cowl lower over his face to make sure he was shielded from those around them.

"What are you doing?" Artemis asked.

"I don't want anyone to see me."

"Oh, that's a good idea." An instant later, she wore a richly woven cloak that was pulled up around her face in a way identical to his. "How do I look?"

Before he could prevent it, a smile curved his lips at her innocent question. He quickly banished it. He knew better than to smile. It always got him into trouble. "You're beautiful."

"Why does saying that make you uncomfortable?"

Acheron clenched his teeth at the simple truth that had haunted him the whole of his life. "People destroy beauty when they find it."

She cocked her head. "How so?"

"By nature, people are petty and jealous. They envy what they lack and because they don't know how to acquire something, they try to destroy anyone who has it. Beauty is one of those things they hate most in others."

"Do you really believe that?"

"I've been attacked enough to know it for a fact. Whatever people can't possess, they try to ruin."

Artemis was stunned by his cynicism. She'd heard such comments from some of the gods. Her father, Zeus, was always making similar statements. But for such a young human . . .

Acheron was strangely astute at times. She could almost believe his claim of divinity, but she knew better. He was just a little more perceptive than most humans.

"Where do we go?" she asked, changing the subject.

"The common gate is over here." He led her toward a small door where a group of unwashed and filthy humans gathered.

Curling her lip in repugnance, she pulled him to a stop. "Should we be going through the *common* gate with *common* people?"

"It costs to go through the others."

How could that possibly be a problem? "Don't you have any money?"

He frowned at her. "No."

Sighing, she manifested a small purse and held it out to him. "Here. Get us decent seats. I'm a goddess. I don't sit with *common* people."

He hesitated before he obeyed her. *Hesitated*. No one did that. Yet he seemed oblivious to the fact that she was divinity. On one level it insulted her that he could be so cavalier and on another it intrigued her. She liked the feeling of being nothing more than a woman with a man.

Especially one so incredibly handsome.

But he did need to respect her godhood. She was, after all, the daughter of Zeus. She could kill him if she chose to.

Then why didn't you? His dare echoed in her head and she again saw him so proud and defiant in her temple. He was definitely an odd human.

And she liked that second only to his beauty.

Artemis stayed by his side as he purchased their seats and led her to an area that was sectioned off from the peasants. The seats here were less crowded and filled with nobles and the families of senators. Acheron paid more money to buy her a stuffed pillow that he set down on the stone for her comfort.

"Aren't you getting one for yourself?" she asked as she took a seat on it.

"I don't need one." He returned the purse to her.

Wrinkling her nose, she stared at the hard stone where he sat oblivious to the cold. "Aren't you uncomfortable?"

"Not really. I'm used to it."

He was used to a lot of things that weren't natural. Something odd went through her chest. It actually bothered her that he was abusing himself. He shouldn't have to do without things and most definitely not while he was with her. Snapping her fingers, she created a pillow underneath him.

He looked up with a startled expression that was almost comical.

"You shouldn't have to sit on cold stone, Acheron."

Acheron touched the padded blue cushion beneath him in disbelief. Only Ryssa had ever cared about his comfort.

161

Well, and at times Catera. But Catera's care had come from a desire to make more money from him. Artemis had no reason to care whether or not he was bruised or cold. He was nothing to her and yet she'd done something truly kind for him. It made him want to smile, but he didn't trust her fully yet. He'd been fooled too many times by people's kindness that had been motivated only by their selfishness.

His chest tightened as his memories surged and he recalled the time he'd been homeless after his father had cast him out of Estes's house.

"I'll give you work, boy . . ."

He squeezed his eyes shut in an effort to banish the horror that followed his blind trust. Truthfully, he hated people. They were users and they were cruel to others.

All of them were cruel to him.

"Wine for my lord and lady?"

It took Acheron a moment to realize the old vendor was speaking to him. Stunned by the show of respect, he couldn't formulate an answer.

"Yes," Artemis said imperiously. She handed him coin and he in turn gave her two goblets of wine.

The vendor bowed low before them. "Thank you, my lady. My lord. I hope you enjoy the show."

Acheron couldn't speak as he took the cup from Artemis's hand. No one had treated him with such regard since the time he'd spent with Ryssa and Maia at the summer palace. And no one had *ever* bowed to him before.

No one.

His throat tight, he slowly sipped the wine.

Artemis paused to study him. "Is something the matter?"

Acheron shook his head, unable to believe that he was actually seated next to a goddess. In public. Wearing clothes. What a strange turn of events.

Artemis dipped her head, trying to meet his gaze.

Out of habit, Acheron averted his eyes.

"Why don't you look at me?" Artemis asked.

"I do look at you."

"No, you don't. You always avert your gaze whenever someone comes near."

162

"I see you though. I learned how to see without looking directly at things a long time ago."

"I don't understand."

Acheron sighed as he turned the cup in his hands. "My eyes make people uncomfortable so I try to keep them hidden as best I can. It prevents people from becoming angry at me."

"People get angry at you for looking at them?"

Acheron nodded.

"What does that feel like?"

He swallowed at the memories that cut him all the way to his soul. "It hurts."

"Then you should tell them not to do it."

If only it were so easy. "I'm not a god, Artemis. No one listens to me when I speak."

"I listen."

She seemed to, and that meant a lot to him. "You're unique."

"True. Perhaps you should spend more time around the gods."

He snorted at the very idea. "I hate the gods, remember?"

"You don't hate me, do you?"

"No."

Artemis smiled. His words relieved her and she wasn't sure why. Intrigued by him, she reached over to touch his back. The moment she did, he sucked his breath in sharply between his teeth and pulled away. "What's the matter?"

"My back's still tender."

"Tender from what?"

Somehow he managed to give her an insolently droll stare without looking directly at her. "I told you I was forbidden to leave my room. My trip to your temple cost me."

"Cost you what?"

He sighed as the play started. "Let's watch the play, please."

Turning her attention to the actors, she listened as they told some insipid story that held no real interest for her. The human beside her . . . that was another matter. He intrigued her greatly.

Anytime she'd ever approached a human of any stature, he or she would grovel and beg for her approval. Even

163

royalty. Or they'd stare at her as if she were sublime, which, of course, she was. But this one didn't do any of that. He seemed blind to the fact that she could kill him with a glance. Even now he was ignoring her completely.

How very strange.

"Why does that group keep singing?"

"It's the chorus," he whispered, his attention firmly on the actors below them.

"They're key-off."

He frowned at her. "Key-off?"

"Their tune . . . it's not right."

"Off-key," he corrected as he turned away from her again. "No, they're not. They sound fine."

She arched a brow at his peeved tone. "Are you arguing with me?"

"I'm not trying to argue with you, Goddess. I'm trying to hear what the actors are saying. Shh."

No . . . no, he hadn't really shushed her! Anger whipped through her. "Excuse me? Acheron? Shh?"

For once he met her gaze and there was no mistaking the agitation in those swirling silver eyes. "I'm not the one talking, Artemis." He turned back toward the stage.

Aggravated at him, she snatched the cowl from his head to get his full attention. The instant she did, she realized she'd made a mistake. Every person near them was suddenly fascinated by Acheron whose face had lost all color.

Without a word to her, he covered himself and rushed for the exit. Several of the people around her headed after him.

Curious, she followed up the stairs and out of the stadium to find Acheron as he was becoming surrounded by people. He appeared panicked as he tried to push his way through the crowd that continued to try and talk to him.

One of the men grabbed him roughly by the arm.

"Let me go," Acheron snarled, shoving at the stranger.

The man tightened his grip so much that Acheron flinched from it.

Enraged over the abuse of her friend, Artemis sank her nails into the hand of the man who then grimaced in pain. He let go of Acheron and the moment he did, she took Acheron's hand and teleported him back to his room.

164

She expected his gratitude.

He gave her none of that. Instead, he turned on her with fury pouring out of his entire being. "How dare you do that to me!"

"I saved you."

His intolerant gaze was as accusatory as his tone even though he kept it at her feet. "You exposed me!"

She didn't understand why he was blaming her for something that wasn't her fault. "You were ignoring me."

"I was trying to watch the play. That was why we were there, wasn't it?"

"No. We were there to keep me from being bored. Remember? I was getting bored again."

That didn't placate him in the least. If anything, it seemed to anger him more. "Then you can go be bored somewhere else."

Artemis was aghast. "Are you throwing me out of your room?"

"Yes."

Rage clouded her vision. No one had ever taken such a tone with her. "Who do you think you are?"

"The one who almost got attacked because you're thoughtless."

"I am not thoughtless."

He gestured to the door behind her. "Just go. I don't like being around people. I'd rather be alone."

She frowned at him. "You are really, truly angry at me, aren't you?"

He actually rolled his eyes as if he were exasperated with her. Shocked, Artemis gaped at him. "Human beings don't get angry at me."

"This one does. Now please leave."

She should and yet she couldn't make herself go. She was too compelled by this man who should be infuriating her and yet she wasn't really angry. A part of her was even tempted to apologize to him. But goddesses didn't do that to humans.

"Why did those people surround you like that?" she asked, wanting to understand him and his unwarranted hostility toward her.

"You're the goddess. You tell me."

"People don't normally do that to others of their kind without a reason. Were you perchance cursed?"

He laughed bitterly. "Obviously so."

"What did you do?"

"I was born. Apparently that's all the gods need to ruin someone." He snatched the shoes off his feet and held them out to her. "Take your shoes and go."

"I gave those to you."

"I don't want your gift."

"Why not?"

His gaze was on the floor, but there was no missing the fury and contempt. "Because you'll make me pay for it eventually and I'm tired of paying for things." He dropped the shoes and turned to walk out onto his balcony.

Ignoring the shoes, Artemis followed him. "We were having fun. I liked it until you angered me."

He dropped his gaze to the floor as all the anger evaporated from his face. "Forgive me, my lady. I didn't mean to offend you." He sank to his knees in front of her.

"What are you doing?"

"My will is yours, akra."

Artemis yanked his cloak off. He didn't flinch or move. He merely stayed there like a mindless supplicant. "Why are you behaving like this?"

He kept his gaze on the ground. "It's what you want, isn't it? A servant to entertain you?"

Yes, but she didn't want that from him. "I have servants. I thought we were friends."

"I don't know how to be a friend. I only know how to be a slave or a lover."

Artemis opened her mouth to speak, but before she could, the door behind her swung open. She made herself instantly invisible as she stepped back into the shadows.

Two guards came in.

The moment Acheron saw them, he rose to his feet and backed up on the balcony as they made their way toward him. His face went cold and stoic.

Without a word, they grabbed him roughly and pulled him to the hallway. Wondering about their intent, she followed them, making sure to keep herself hidden.

Acheron was taken to the throne room where she'd popped in on him two days ago. The guards forced him to his knees before the thrones that were occupied by an elder human and a young man who was identical in looks to Acheron. Only he didn't have Acheron's silver eyes and he lacked the same compelling nature. The one on the throne was the same as any human and she took an instant dislike to him.

"As per your instructions, he hasn't left his room, Sire," the guard on the left of Acheron said firmly. "We've made sure of it."

The king's blue eyes were piercing. "You weren't in the square earlier, teritos?"

Artemis's eyes widened at the word that meant slug.

Acheron gave the king a defiant glare. "Why would I have been in the square, Father?"

The king curled his lip. "Thirty-six lashes for his insolence, then return him to his room."

Acheron closed his eyes as the guards grabbed him by the hair and hauled him through a set of double doors that opened into a small courtyard. Scowling, she watched as they stripped him bare, then tied him to a post. His perfectly formed back was covered with dark bruises, red welts and cuts. No wonder he'd recoiled in pain when she'd touched him. It had to hurt fiercely.

Unable to detect her presence, the younger guard walked to her side and pulled a whip from the holder before he returned to Acheron.

Acheron stiffened and braced himself against the post as if he knew what would happen next.

The whip whistled through the air, then tore through his bruised back.

Gasping, Acheron gripped the post so tight that every muscle in his arms and legs was taut and outlined. It was as if he were trying to merge himself with the post . . .

Mesmerized by the sight, she watched as lash after lash rained down on his back. Never once did he cry out or beg for mercy. The most he would do was gasp or curse them and their parentage.

When it was over, the guards freed him. His face ashen,

Acheron picked his chiton up from the ground where the guards had thrown it but didn't have time to dress before they dragged him back to his room and threw him inside. The doors rattled as the guards slammed them shut with an echoing clatter.

Artemis walked through the locked doors to find Acheron lying on the floor where he'd landed. His bloodied blond hair was tangled and fanned out behind him while blood seeped from the wounds on his back. He made no move to cover himself or to cry. He merely lay there staring into space.

"Acheron?"

He didn't speak to her.

She materialized in front of him, then knelt by his side. "Why were you beaten?"

He drew a ragged breath as he tightened his grip on the wadded up chiton. "Stop asking me questions I don't feel like answering."

Her heart hammering, she reached out to one of the bleeding welts that curved over his right shoulder. He hissed in response to her touch. Withdrawing her hand, she frowned. His warm, sticky blood coated her fingertips. She drew back, staring at his naked body. For the first time, she felt a wave of guilt stir in her breast.

His punishment was her fault. Had she not taken him out of his room, they wouldn't have done this to him. Part of her was even angry that he'd been injured.

"I don't like you like this," she whispered.

"Just please leave me alone."

But she couldn't. Wanting to comfort him, she placed her hand on his shoulder and closed her eyes before she healed him.

Acheron panted as a searing pain tore through his battered body. A second later, all the pain was gone. He tensed, expecting it to return.

It didn't.

"Is that better?"

He stared at the goddess in disbelief. "What did you do?"

"I'm a goddess of healing so I healed you."

Rolling onto his back, he was amazed that the pain didn't return. For the last two days, he'd been beaten at various intervals because he'd dared walk to the temple with Ryssa. Honestly, he'd begun to fear that his skin would never heal completely.

But Artemis had helped him. "Thank you."

The goddess smiled at him as she brushed his hair back from his face. "I didn't mean for you to get hurt."

Acheron covered her hand with his before he kissed her palm that tasted like roses and honey. To his complete shock, he felt his body stirring. For that alone, he expected Artemis to jump on top of him.

Instead she watched his cock as he hardened even more. "Does it always do that?"

"No." He rarely got hard unless it was required of him or he was drugged.

Her brow drew tight as she touched his chest. He was used to people being curious about him. Since the assumption went that he was the son of a god, everyone wanted to touch him, to explore his body.

Yet she was hesitant. Her hand drifted over his abdomen lightly as if she were afraid to touch the part of him she was staring at.

"I won't do anything you don't want me to," he told her quietly.

Her eyes flashed. "Of course not. I'd kill you if you did."

No one had been quite so blunt before, but that threat had always hung over his head. He'd had plenty of clients after leaving Atlantis who'd threatened him for numerous reasons. Mostly political or possessive. They were afraid he'd tell on them for what they wanted to do to their Prince Styxx or they didn't want to share him with anyone else.

Three times he'd almost been killed.

He didn't know why people reacted to him the way they did. He'd never understood it. Artemis, even with her divinity, didn't seem any different than anyone else.

Except her touch set him on fire.

Acheron closed his eyes as her hand lightly brushed the tip of his cock. The need inside him for her was unexpected and shocking. He should be angry at her for what she'd done to him and yet he couldn't find any anger inside himself right now. Only a desire to please her that he didn't comprehend.

A noise sounded out in the hallway.

Artemis pulled back with a sharp intake of breath. "We could be seen."

The next thing he knew, they were inside a bright, white marble bedroom. Acheron shot to his feet as he turned around slowly, trying to understand where he was.

There was an incredibly large bed against one wall. The sheets and curtains were as white as everything else. The only color to be found was gold trim.

"Where am I?"

"Mount Olympus."

His jaw went slack. "How?"

"I brought you to my temple. Don't worry. No one ever enters my bedchambers. These are sacred to me."

Artemis approached him with a smile on her face. She rubbed her cheek against his an instant before a red chiton appeared on his body. "We can be alone here."

Acheron couldn't even form a coherent thought as he looked at the splendor surrounding him. The ceiling over his head was solid gold and carved with brilliant forest scenes. How could this be? How could a whore be in the bedroom of a goddess renowned for her virginity? The mere thought was laughable.

Yet here he stood . . .

Artemis took him by the hand and led him toward her balcony that let out onto a garden resplendent with flowers. The riot of color was almost as beautiful as the goddess beside him.

"What do you think of it?" Artemis asked.

"It's wondrous."

She smiled. "I thought you'd like it."

He frowned at her. "How could you be bored here?"

She looked away and swallowed. A deep sadness darkened her green eyes. "It gets lonely. There's seldom anyone who wants to talk to me. Sometimes I walk in the woods and the deer come to me, but they don't really have much to say."

He let out an awed breath at the incredible scene. "I could happily lose myself in those woods and never speak to a soul again as long as I live."

"But you'll only live a few more years. You've no idea what eternity feels like. Time has no meaning. It merely stretches out and hangs on ever the same."

"I don't know. I think I should like forever . . . If I could live it on my own terms."

She smiled at him. "I could see you as you are now a thousand years in the future." Her eyes lit up. "Oh wait, there's something I have to share with you."

Acheron cocked his head in consternation as she snapped her fingers and a peculiar brown package appeared in her palm. She held it out to him.

"What is it?"

"Chocolate," she said breathlessly. "Hershey's. You must try it."

He took it from her and held it to his nose. It smelled sweet, but he wasn't sure about the taste. As he started to take a bite, Artemis jerked it out of his hand.

"You have to unwrap it first, silly." Laughing, she tore the brown paper and an odd silver material from it before she broke a piece off and gave it to him.

Gingerly, Acheron took a bite. The minute it melted on his tongue, he was in heaven. "This is delicious."

She handed him the bar again. "I know. It comes from the future—we're not supposed to go there, but I can't help it. There are just some things I can't wait for and chocolate is one of them."

He licked the brown smear from his fingertips. "Could you take me to the future?"

She shook her head quickly. "My father would kill me if I took a mortal there."

"One god can't kill another."

"Yes, they can. Believe me. They're not supposed to, but it doesn't always stop them."

Acheron took another bite as he considered her words. He would love to travel away from this time. To a place where no one knew him or his brother. Where he was free of his past and able to make a life without everyone trying to possess him.

That would be perfection. But he'd learned the hard way that such a place didn't exist.

Artemis took the bar from him and bit off a piece. A bit of it melted on her chin.

Acheron reached out to wipe it away.

"How do you do that?" she asked him.

"Do what?"

"Touch me without fear? All humans tremble before the gods, but not you. Why is that?"

He shrugged. "Probably because I'm not afraid of dying."

"You're not?"

"No. I'm afraid of reliving my past. At least with death, I'd know that it's all behind me. It would be a relief, I think."

She shook her head. "You're a strange man, Acheron. Unlike any I've ever known." Walking backwards, she took his hand and pulled him into her bedroom.

Acheron went willingly.

Artemis didn't speak as she knelt on the bed, then turned to face him. She gathered him into her arms for an incredibly hot kiss.

Closing his eyes, Acheron breathed her in as her tongue danced with his. How odd . . . when he held her, he didn't feel like a whore. Maybe because she wasn't asking for anything more than his company. No one was being paid. Neither of them wanted anything except a respite from their solitude.

Was this what it felt like to be normal? He'd always wondered.

Artemis pulled back to stare up at him. "Promise me you'll never betray me, Acheron."

"I would never do anything to hurt you."

Her smile blinded him before she pulled him onto the bed and rolled him over onto his back. She straddled his hips before she brushed the hair away from his neck.

"You are so handsome," she whispered.

Acheron didn't comment. She hypnotized him with those flashing green eyes and skin so smooth and soft it haunted him. At least until he saw a flash of fang.

An instant later a blinding pain tore through his neck. He tried to move, but he couldn't. Not a single muscle.

His heart pounded until the pain gave way to an unimaginable pleasure. Only when the pleasure replaced the pain could he move. He cupped her head to his neck as she continued to suck and lick until his body exploded into the most intense orgasm he'd ever known.

No sooner had he felt it than his eyelids sank down as if lead weights were pulling them. He tried to fight the darkness, but he couldn't.

Artemis moved back and licked the blood from her lips as she felt Acheron pass out. She'd never tasted human blood before . . . it was incredible. No wonder her brother sought it out so often. There was a vitality to it that immortals lacked. It was so intoxicating that it took all her strength not to drink more. But that might kill him.

It was the last thing she wanted. Acheron fascinated her. He didn't flinch or fawn. Even though he was a mortal, he met her as an equal.

Delighted with her newest pet, she lay down by his side and snuggled up against him.

This was definitely the beginning of a great friendship . . .

December 14, 9529 BC

Acheron woke up to a pounding ache in his head. Opening his eyes, he found himself naked in his bed. It wasn't until he moved and felt no pain that he remembered everything that had happened the day before.

Everything.

His breath catching, he reached to his neck to find a small trace of dried blood where Artemis had bitten him. But that was the only mark on his body. All signs of his beatings were gone.

What was a little bite when compared to that?

He glanced around his room. "How did I get here?" He couldn't remember that part. The last thing in his memory was Artemis biting him in her bed and a sense of exhaustion overtaking him.

Someone knocked on his door before pushing it open. He knew before he saw the small blond woman coming inside that it was Ryssa. No one else knocked on his doors.

He quickly brushed the blood away and covered his neck with his hair before she drew close enough to see it.

Her cheeks were flushed and her body was obscured by thick purple robes. It was the first time he'd seen her since Apollo had claimed her.

Before he could speak, she threw herself into his arms and wept.

Acheron held her close as he rocked her. "What happened? Did he hurt you?"

"He was gentle," she said between sobs. "But he scared me and it hurt occasionally." Her grip on him tightened. "How do you stand it?"

There had been many times when he'd wondered the same thing himself. "It'll be all right, Ryssa."

"Will it?" She pulled back to stare at him as if she was trying to see whether or not she should believe him. "What if he wants me back?"

Acheron cupped her face in his hands. "You'll endure it and you'll survive."

Ryssa ground her teeth at words she knew Acheron understood all too well. "I don't want to go back to him. I feel so naked and exposed even though he wasn't particularly mean or unkind. But you were right. He didn't care what I thought or felt. All that mattered was *his* pleasure." She shook her head as she held a new understanding of her brother that she'd never had before.

Her shame was but one instance. Acheron's was many. It was awful to be at someone else's mercy. To have no say in what was done to your body. She felt so used . . .

"I want to run away from this."

He took her hand into his. "I know. But you'll be all right. Really. You will get used to it."

It didn't feel that way. She was terribly sore and still bleeding from Apollo's intrusion into her body. He'd taken care of her and yet he'd been callous, too. The last thing she wanted was to be at his mercy again.

"Ryssa!"

She jumped at her father's shout.

Acheron tensed. "You should go."

She didn't want to but she was afraid of getting Acheron into trouble. Sniffing back her tears, she pulled away and saw the raw sympathy in his swirling silver eyes. "I love you, Acheron."

Acheron cherished those words. Ryssa was the only person who'd ever loved him. At times he hated that love because it made her do things to hurt him, but unlike with others he knew her actions were motivated out of kindness.

She scooted from his bed and ran across the room, to the hallway.

He heard their father's angry curse through the walls. "What were you doing in there?"

Acheron winced. At least Ryssa didn't have to fear being beaten. To his knowledge their father had never once struck her.

"You are the mistress of a god now. You're not to keep company with the likes of him ever again. Do you understand? What would Apollo think? He'd throw you out and spit on you."

He couldn't hear Ryssa's soft reply.

But his father's words tore through him. So he wasn't worthy of being in Ryssa's presence, but he could keep company with Artemis. He wondered how his father would deal with that knowledge. If it would make his father look at him with something other than derision in his eyes.

Most likely not.

His doors swung open so forcefully they echoed. The king strode into the room with fury punctuating every step. Acheron looked away and forced all emotion from his face . . .

Fuck it. If his father wanted to hate him, let him. He was tired of hiding and cringing. Beatings and insults he could take.

His nostrils flaring, Acheron met his father's angry glare without flinching. "Good morning, Father."

He backhanded him so hard, Acheron tasted blood as pain erupted through his skull. Gasping, he shook his head to clear it, then he met the king's furious glower.

"I am not your father."

Acheron wiped the blood away with the back of his hand. "Is there something I can help you with?"

"Father, please," Ryssa begged, running across the room. She took his arm before he could advance on Acheron again. "I went to him on my arrival. Acheron did nothing wrong. It's my fault, not his."

The king leveled one bony finger in a condemning gesture at Acheron. "You are to stay away from my daughter. Do you hear me? If I catch you near her again, I'll make you wish you'd never been born."

Acheron laughed bitterly. "That would be different from a normal day, how?"

Ryssa put herself in front of their father as he started for Acheron. "Stop it, Father. Please. You had questions about

Apollo. Should we not focus on that?"

He cast a superior, condemning sneer at Acheron. "You're not worth my time."

With that, he hauled Ryssa out of the room. "Seal his door shut. He can go without food this day."

Acheron leaned back against the wall and shook his head. If his father wanted to control him with food, he should have spent more time with Estes. That bastard had known how to hold food over him.

His gut tightened at the memory of his begging Estes for even a drop of water to slake his thirst.

"You've earned nothing and nothing is what you'll have . . . Now get on your knees and please me, then we'll see if you're worthy of salt."

Squeezing his eyes shut, he forced the images away. He hated begging and crawling. But the only thing that would make it go away was the memory of the goddess who'd claimed him.

"Artemis?" he whispered her name in fear that someone might actually hear him call her. Honestly he expected her to ignore him as everyone else did.

She didn't.

She appeared before him. Acheron's jaw opened ever so slightly in shock. Her long red hair appeared to glisten in the dim light. Her eyes were vibrant and warm and welcoming. There was nothing about her demeanor that condemned or mocked him. "How do you feel?" she asked.

"Better with you here."

A small smile toyed at the edges of her lips. "Really?"

He nodded.

Her smile widened as she approached his bed and crawled across him.

Acheron closed his eyes as the sweet smell of her skin filled his head. He wanted to bury his face in her hair and just inhale it. Straddling his hips, she brushed the hair back from his neck before she fingered the skin she'd bitten.

"You're very strong for a human."

"They trained me for stamina."

Ignoring his comment, she frowned. "You're still not looking at me."

"I see you, Artemis." And he did. He saw every single line of her face, every curve of her luscious body.

She took his face in her hands and turned his chin until he was facing her squarely. Still Acheron kept his gaze on her knees that poked out from underneath her dress. "Look at me."

Acheron wanted to run. He'd spent his entire life never looking directly at anyone except for those times when he wanted them to see his defiance. And any time he dared that, he'd been brutalized for it.

"Acheron . . . Look. At. Me."

Bracing himself for her attack, he obeyed. His heart stilled as every part of his body tensed in expectation of being hurt.

Artemis sat back on his groin with a pleased expression. "There now. That wasn't so hard was it?"

Harder than she could ever imagine, but as each second passed and she didn't slap him for looking at her, he relaxed a bit more.

She smiled. "I like your eyes. They're strange, but very pretty."

Pretty? His eyes? They were disgusting. Everyone, including Ryssa, was afraid of them. "You don't mind my looking at you?"

"Not at all. At least this way I know you're paying attention to me. I don't like the way your eyes dance around the room as if you're distracted."

That was a first for him. "How could anything ever distract me while you're with me? I assure you, whenever you're around, all I see is you."

She beamed in satisfaction. "Now why did you call me?"

"I'm not sure. Truthfully, I didn't think you'd come. I only whispered your name, hoping you might answer."

"You're such a silly human. Are you stuck inside again today?"

He nodded.

"We can't have that. Come." The word had barely left her lips before they were once more in her bedroom.

Acheron was again dressed in red, which was odd given that everything else was white or gold. "Why do you always put me in crimson?"

She bit her lip as she walked around him, dragging her finger over his body. "I like the way you look in it." She paused before him so that she could lift herself on her toes and kiss him.

Acheron gave her what she wanted. It was always in his training to please whoever he was with. To take nothing for himself. His needs never mattered. He was only a tool to be used and then forgotten.

But with Artemis he didn't feel like that. As with Ryssa, she made him feel like he was a person—that he could have his own thoughts and it wasn't wrong. He could look at her and she didn't curse him.

Artemis sighed as Acheron pulled her close. She loved the way he held her. The way his muscles rippled around her body. He was so handsome and strong. So seductive. All she wanted was to be alone with him like this. To feel his heart beating against her breasts.

His breath mixed with hers. She could feel her teeth growing as her hunger for him increased even more . . .

She pulled back and met his gaze so that he could see the real her. He didn't even blink at her fangs. Instead, he tilted his head and offered her what she wanted most. No one had ever been so accommodating before. Normally she fed from her brother or one of her maidens. But they didn't care for it.

Her heart racing, she brushed her hands over his neck before she sank her teeth deep.

Acheron hissed as pain spread through his body. But it was quickly replaced by a pleasure so profound that it made his cock harden. Weakened by it, he staggered back. Artemis followed, gripping him even tighter.

His head swam as everything around him became sharp and clear. He felt her breath on his skin, heard her blood pumping through her veins. Every part of him seemed alive. So strong and yet so weak. He staggered again, falling against the wall behind him.

"Acheron?"

179

He heard her voice, but he couldn't respond to it.

Artemis licked the blood from her lips as she saw the bluish tint to his skin. His breathing was so shallow that she half expected him to die. "Acheron?"

His eyes were half open. There was no recognition in his gaze that he saw or heard her.

Afraid she might have hurt him, she transported him to her bed and laid him down gently. She took his hand into hers and rubbed it. "Acheron, please say something."

He whispered something in Atlantean, but she couldn't understand it. With one last expulsion of breath, he passed out. Artemis jerked back as his entire body flashed to a vibrant blue while his lips, nails and hair turned black. An instant later, he appeared normal.

What on Olympus? Never had she seen such. Had her feeding caused it?

Swallowing, she crawled closer to him and poked him with one finger. He was completely unconscious.

Manifesting a warm fur, she covered him and watched as he drew shallow breaths. While he slept, she traced the shape of his lips, the length of his nose. His features were sharp and flawless. Like his body. She didn't understand why he compelled her so. Afraid of being dominated, she'd asked her father when she was a child to make her immune to love and to give her eternal virginity. Zeus had granted that request. Yet as she looked at Acheron resting, she wondered at the emotions she felt for him. They were unlike anything she'd ever felt before.

She liked the way he talked to her. The way he held her and made her scream in pleasure with his touches and licks. Most of all, she loved the way he tasted when she fed from him.

He's just a pet.

Yes, that was it. She didn't have any real feelings for him. He was merely like the deer that lived in her forest. Beautiful to watch and to touch. They licked and brushed up against her, too. And like them she was sure he'd come to bore her in time. Everything did.

But for now she intended to enjoy her pet for as long as possible.

Acheron *woke up* starving. The hunger pain was so fierce that at first he thought he was again in the dark hole underneath his father's palace. But as he opened his eyes and saw the gold ceiling above him, he remembered being with Artemis.

He sat up slowly to find himself alone in her bed. There were voices outside. He started to get up and head toward them, then thought better of it. Artemis had left him here for a reason. No good could come of his opening those doors.

So he sat in bed, his stomach aching while he listened to words that had no real form. They were muffled through the gold and stone. He had no idea what time it was or how long he'd slept.

It seemed like forever before Artemis appeared. She drew up short and smiled. "You're awake."

He nodded. "I didn't want to disturb you. You sounded busy."

She closed the distance between them to cup his cheek. "Are you hungry?"

"Starving."

She spread her arm out and a table covered with food appeared beside the bed.

Acheron gaped at the feast.

"If you'd like something else, tell me."

"No, this is wonderful." He left the bed to tear into a loaf of bread. His eyes widened at the taste of it. Coated in honey and warm, it was the best he'd ever had.

Artemis poured him a cup of wine. "Goodness, you were hungry."

He took the cup gratefully then drank deep of the rich flavor. "Thank you, Artie."

She arched a brow at his unintended nickname. "Artie?"

Acheron cringed as he realized his slip of the tongue. "Artemis. I meant to say Artemis."

She nuzzled him. "I think I like Artie. No one's ever called me that before."

Acheron leaned his head down to kiss her hand.

Artemis couldn't breathe as that simple touch electrified her. What was it about this man that set fire to her entire being? She wanted to hold and protect him. More than that, she wanted to devour every inch of his lush body.

Closing her eyes, she leaned into him and inhaled that intoxicating scent that was all male and all him. "Eat, Acheron," she whispered. "I don't want you to be hungry."

He stepped away from her and she felt the sudden cold left in the wake of his heat like a punch against her stomach. She watched as he dipped the bread in a small dish of honey before he took a bite and smiled a smile so handsome it made her heart lift.

He dipped another piece, then turned toward her. "Would you like some?"

She nodded. He held it for her to take a bite. Artemis opened her mouth. As he set the bread on her tongue, she licked his fingers that were delicious. Salty and sweet, they whetted her appetite for more.

His eyes darkened, causing a wave of desire to flare deep inside her. He dipped his fingertip in the honey, then outlined her lips before he pulled her close for a blistering kiss. The taste of him combined with honey was more than she could stand.

Pulling him toward the bed, she lay down and tugged his hand until he was on top of her.

Acheron growled at the sight of Artemis underneath him. "You are so incredibly beautiful."

Artemis couldn't respond verbally. She was completely captivated by the look of tenderness on his face. No one had ever looked at her like this. And when he buried his lips against her throat all rational thought was lost to the fire inside her.

She'd never been completely naked with anyone. But as he unfastened her gown, she didn't protest. With an excruciating slowness, he slid the cloth down her body until she was bare to him. He made no move to remove his own clothes.

Instead, he lifted her foot to nibble her instep. Biting her lip at the exquisite torture, she watched him as he worked his way up her body.

He paused as he gently licked the inside of her thigh. "Do you want me to stop?"

Artemis shook her head. "I love for you to touch me."

His look scorched her before he nudged her thighs farther apart and touched the part of her that ached the most for him. She sank her fingers in his hair and fisted her hands.

Acheron pulled back with a hiss as if she'd hurt him.

She frowned. "Is something wrong?"

"Please don't grab and pull my hair. I hate it when people do that."

"Why?"

"It makes me feel like I'm garbage."

There was no missing the raw pain in his voice. "I don't understand."

"People snatch at my hair to control me or to hold me down at their feet. They yank it while they violate and humiliate me. I don't like it."

Artemis stroked his cheek, wanting to soothe him. "I'm sorry, Acheron. I didn't know. Is there anything else you don't like?"

Acheron froze at her question. No lover had ever asked him that question before. He still couldn't believe he'd told her that he didn't like having his hair touched. It wasn't something he'd normally do, but since she'd asked, he felt compelled to tell her. "I don't like anyone breathing on the back of my neck. It reminds me of being a slave with no will of my own and it makes my skin crawl."

"Then I shall never do that to you."

Those words touched him so deep inside that it brought tears to his eyes. He swallowed the lump in his throat before he nuzzled her. There was nothing he wouldn't do to please his goddess. Artemis was all that was kind. He couldn't imagine why she wanted to befriend something as low as an ex-slave, but he was grateful to be with her.

Wanting to please her not because he had to but because he wanted it, he took his time teasing her body until she screamed out his name. True to her words, she didn't grab his hair as she came. She sank her nails into his shoulders.

Grateful that she'd kept her word, he crawled up her body and pulled her into his arms.

Artemis sighed as she lay against him. He was still fully clothed. "Why do you never take anything for yourself?"

"I don't find real pleasure in sex."

She frowned at him. "How can you not enjoy it?"

He couldn't even begin to explain to her that nothing about sex made him feel good. He liked to touch her, but he didn't have the same reaction to her touch that she had to his. Orgasms were pleasurable no doubt. He just didn't care whether or not he had one.

"I enjoy it," he lied. It would make her feel good to hear that. He would keep the truth of it buried inside him. Honestly he loved being with her. When they were together he felt like a man with no past. She saw him as her friend and if a goddess liked him he couldn't be as repugnant as his father and brother made him out to be.

She rubbed herself against his body.

Acheron closed his eyes and savored the sensation of her warm body next to his. "I wish I could stay here with you forever."

"If you were female you could, but only my brother is allowed in my temple. No other male."

"But I'm here now."

"I know and it's our secret. You can never tell anyone."

"I won't."

She lifted herself up to give him a stern frown. "I mean it, Acheron. Not even in your sleep are you to breathe a word about me."

"Trust me, Artie, keeping secrets is the one thing I learned early in my life. I know when to keep my mouth shut. Besides no one really talks to me anyway."

"Good. Now it's time for you to go home."

One minute he was in her temple beside her, the next he was in his bed naked again. He realized too late that he hadn't really eaten anything. Damn. But at least it was dark outside. He'd missed most of the day. So long as his father hadn't sent guards to beat him no one would know of his visit to Olympus.

Sighing, Acheron draped one arm over his eyes. Maybe

184

he could just sleep until Artemis came for him again.

But even as the thought occurred to him he knew this couldn't last. A whore didn't befriend a goddess. It was impossible. Sooner or later Artemis would be like everyone else.

Yet deep in his heart was a tiny splash of hope that maybe, just maybe, Artemis because of her godhood would be different.

"I would sell my soul to keep and protect you, Artie," he breathed, wondering if she could hear him. If only he were born of the gods too . . .

He shook his head at the harsh reality he knew all too well. "And if wishes were horses, I'd have been run over in childhood."

No, this was all they could ever have. All he could do was make sure that no one learned the truth. May the gods help him if anyone ever did.

Acheron sat on the railing of his balcony, missing Artemis. She was off at a festival that was being held in her honor and she wanted to spy on the people there in person. She was odd that way and liked to see people worshiping her while she pretended to be mortal.

He found it strangely endearing and had to admit that these last few weeks had been the best of his life.

Artemis was the only person who'd ever allowed him to be himself. If he didn't like something, he could tell her and she'd promise not to let it happen again.

She never broke her word to him. That more than anything was a dream come true. And because they spent so much time together, and Acheron wasn't causing trouble or sneaking out through his guards, his father had left him alone. He couldn't remember a time in his life, except for the months with Ryssa, when he'd gone this long without being hit or beaten.

The reprieve was divine.

Suddenly the doors to his room were shoved open.

His gut tightened. Afraid it was his father coming for him, he gripped the stone beneath him.

It wasn't. Ryssa strode into the room with the brightest smile he'd ever seen on her face. "Good day, little brother."

"Good day," he greeted hesitantly in return, wondering at her mood and the fact that she'd left the doors behind her wide open. "Is something wrong?"

Maybe his father had finally died. It was the best he could hope for. Stopping just before him, she pulled a small purse out from behind her back and held it out toward him. "You're free."

His father *must* be dead!

Acheron swung his legs down. "What do you mean?"

"I've discovered one of the benefits to sleeping with Apollo. Father listens to me now. Your guards are gone and you'll have a monthly stipend to spend however you wish." She placed the purse in his hand. "I've also procured for you a reserved spot at the stadium for any and all plays. No one but you will be allowed to sit there. Ever."

He couldn't believe what he was hearing. "What are the conditions?"

Her smile faded so that she could grind her teeth in aggravation. "Typical comment of Father's. You're not allowed to shame him or the family. He wouldn't elaborate, but so long as you don't cavort with anyone I think you'll be fine."

Acheron scoffed at the mere idea. "I have no plans to cavort with anyone." At least not publicly. He'd grown tired of *that* long ago. He didn't like being a spectacle.

She leaned forward. "Would you like to go to a play with me?"

"What about Apollo?"

"He's off with his sister. I have most of the day to myself." She held her hand out to him. "What say you, little brother? Shall we celebrate your freedom?"

Acheron gave her a real smile—something he almost never did. "Thank you, Ryssa. You've no idea how much this means to me."

"I think I have an idea."

Acheron went to retrieve his cloak from under the mattress . . . and the shoes Artemis had given him. He held the shoes for a moment, missing the goddess even more than before. How he wished he could celebrate with her, but that would have to wait.

After dressing himself quickly, he followed Ryssa out of the room. In the hallway, he hesitated as he looked around the bright walls. With the exception of Ryssa's offering to Apollo, he'd never left his room through the doors without having to bribe his guards with sex.

The degree to which his life had changed hit him full force. No longer a slave. No longer a prisoner. He was free now.

Acheron lifted his head proudly with the knowledge that he had money and he hadn't had to screw anyone to get it. More than that, he had a friend and a lover who treated him like he mattered.

For the first time in his life, he felt like a human being and not a possession or an object. It was a damn good feeling and he didn't want it to end.

Ryssa took his hand in hers and led him through the hallways, out the front door as if she wasn't ashamed in the least to be seen in his company. But as they moved among people, Acheron remembered one thing that hadn't changed.

Other people's reactions to his beauty. He pulled the cowl low over his face and kept his eyes on the ground at Ryssa's feet. He'd spent so much time with Artemis lately that he'd all but forgotten about his eyes and how much they repulsed regular people.

As they walked through the town square, he paused. There was a group of children with a teacher standing in front of a temple. A boy around the age of seven was reading the text that was written at the feet of the god.

" 'In all things moderation. The key to the future is understanding the past.' "

"Acheron?"

He blinked at Ryssa's voice and turned away to see her staring up at him with a frown. "Do all children know how to read?"

She glanced at the students. "Not all. Those are senators' sons. They come out here to learn about the pantheon and to see how the priests serve the gods while their fathers make the laws to govern people."

Acheron stared at the words that held no meaning to him. He was too ashamed to admit to Ryssa that he remembered almost nothing of his lessons with her and Maia. "All noblemen can read though, can't they?"

She tugged at his hand without answering. "We're going to be late to the play."

Acheron turned and followed her. "Have you any word about Maia?"

Ryssa smiled. "She married last year and is expecting her first child."

The news hit him hard. He didn't like the thought of a man hurting the girl he'd been so fond of. He hoped whoever she'd married treated her with the regard she deserved. "Isn't she too young for that?"

"Not really. Most girls wed at her age. I was a rare exception, but Father refused all suitors who asked for my hand."

"Why?"

"I honestly don't know. He would never explain himself to me. I suppose I should be grateful to Apollo. If not for him, I'm sure I would have lived my life as a spinster."

He could think of many things worse than that. But his sister was allowed her delusions he supposed. "Does Apollo make you happy now?"

"He's gentle most of the time." There was a sadness in her beautiful blue eyes that belied her words.

"But?"

She touched her neck in a nervous gesture that made him frown in understanding. "I'm not allowed to talk about what we do when we're together."

So Apollo fed from her in the same manner Artemis drank from him. It made him wonder if all the gods did that or was it something unique between Artemis and Apollo. "You deserve to be happy, Ryssa. More than anyone I know."

She smiled at him. "Not true. You're the one who deserves happiness. I could just choke Father for his blindness."

"I don't mind it so much anymore," he said honestly. "I'd much rather be ignored than abused."

She shook her head before she bypassed the crowd to show him where the proprietor had made a special entrance to the royal seats reserved for them.

Acheron hesitated. They were separated from the crowd by a cord and each of the ten seats was covered with a cushion. But what he didn't like was the fact that the area stood out and others kept glancing over at them. He hated people to focus their attention on him.

But he didn't want to insult Ryssa's gift. Pulling his cloak tighter, he followed her to the seats.

189

Neither of them spoke while the actors came out to perform. Acheron watched them as he thought about the children they'd seen on their way here. He wanted to read the way they did. Artemis deserved a consort who was literate.

Maybe if he could read, she might not have to hide their friendship . . .

Artemis *felt her* brother's presence behind her like a physical touch. As twins, the two of them shared a special bond.

And a special hatred.

She wasn't sure when they'd become friendly enemies, but it was a cold fact. Though there was nothing they wouldn't do for each other, they could barely stand to be in the same room.

Hatred aside, she couldn't deny that Apollo was one of the more handsome gods. His shining blond hair was cropped short and the strong lean lines of his face were set off by the small goatee. His blue eyes were riveting with intelligence, power and a hint of cruelty.

He arched a brow at her. "I'm surprised to see you here."

"I could say the same for you. It's about time you crawled out of your human pet's bed. I was beginning to think she was the one controlling *you.*"

His look turned arctic. "And what has been keeping you so occupied? Father said you haven't been to the Olympian hall in weeks."

She shrugged. "It's boring there."

"That's never stopped you before."

She rolled her eyes at him. "Do you mind? I'm trying to watch the humans worship me."

Before she could move away, Apollo took her arm and pulled her closer to him so that he could whisper in her ear. "You haven't come to me to feed in a while. Who have you been taking your nourishment from?"

"What do you care?"

He gripped her neck as his canine teeth elongated. "There's only so long you can feed from a human before you hunger for something a little more substantial." He dipped his head toward her neck.

Artemis stepped away from him. "I'm not interested."

Apollo's eyes flamed red. "You do remember what happened to the last man you trifled with?"

She cringed at the reminder. Orion. Artemis had taken a fancy to the man but before she could even approach him, Apollo had jealously tricked her into killing him with one of her arrows. Then her brother had placed his image in the stars to always remind her that Apollo was the only male she could feed from.

"I didn't trifle with Orion."

He forced her to face him. "You need to feed."

Yes, but she didn't want to feed from her brother. She wanted Acheron.

Apollo pulled her into the shadows of his temple while the humans were gathered outside of hers to pay tribute. She didn't want to follow him. But if she didn't, he'd know she'd been with someone else and may Zeus help Acheron then. Her brother would tear him apart.

Her heart aching, she tried not to cringe as Apollo jerked her against him and offered her his neck. She took it and in her mind she pretended he was Acheron. Even so, she could taste the difference between them. Apollo's blood lacked the spirit. There was no racing inside her as she tasted him. No fire that wanted her to hold him close.

It was just blood.

When she'd taken enough to placate him, she pulled back and licked her lips.

Apollo attacked her then. His teeth tore through the tendons of her neck, leaving it throbbing. She wanted to slap him for it and many times in the past she had. Damn Hera for this curse. The jealous bitch had tried to kill both of them at birth and because Artemis had helped her mother deliver Apollo, this was her punishment. There was nothing worse than being forced to feed on your own kind. It was a lesson she and Apollo had known the whole of their lives.

Her head light, she tried to think clearly. Apollo was taking too much blood. It was something he always did when he was angry at her.

191

Grinding her teeth, she kneed him hard in the groin. He jerked back with a curse, tearing at her neck. Her curse joined his as she covered the gaping wound with her hand. "You're such a bastard."

He grabbed her upper arm, blistering it with his grip. "Remember what I told you. I catch you with a mortal man and I will kill him."

Artemis snatched her arm free. "Go play with your humans and leave me alone."

Her joy in the festival completely squelched, she transported herself back to her temple. But it was so lonely here. Her koris were gone for the day.

She looked at her bed and imagined the sight of Acheron there, his smile warming her while he pleased her with kisses and gentle caresses.

Needing him desperately, she flashed to his room. The instant she saw him sitting cross-legged on the floor with his back to her, her heart lightened. Without thought or hesitation, she ran to him and embraced him.

Acheron was startled as Artemis threw herself against his back and wrapped her arms around him in a tight hold. Even so the scent of her filled his head.

"I missed you today," she whispered in his ear, sending chills over his entire body.

"I missed you too."

Her grip tightened before she released him and placed her chin on his shoulder. "What are you doing?"

Acheron snatched the scroll up from the floor and folded it so that she couldn't see what he was about. "Nothing."

"You're doing something . . ." She grabbed the scroll from him before he could stop her and opened it. She frowned at his childish marks. "What's this?"

He felt heat sting his face at having been caught. "I was trying to teach myself to write."

"Why?"

"I don't know how and I wish to learn."

She lowered the scroll to stare in disbelief. "Can't you read?"

Acheron hung his head as shame poured through him. "No."

Artemis lifted his chin in a gentle caress until he met her gaze. The kindness in her eyes warmed him completely. "You can now."

Acheron gasped as a slight pain went through him. She handed him the scroll back.

"Write your name."

Baffled by what had just happened to him, he picked up the quill and knew how to draw the letters. He wrote his name flawlessly. "I don't understand."

"I'm a goddess, Acheron. And I don't want you to hang your head in shame. Does this please you?"

"More than anything."

Her smile dazzled him. "Come with me. I'm in the mood to hunt."

"I don't know how to hunt."

"You will."

True to her words as soon as they were in the woods, she gave him a bow and arrow and just like with the writing, he knew exactly what to do.

How wondrous to be able to do something without all the years of learning it. But in truth, there was something more he wanted than literacy and hunting. "Can you teach me to fight?"

Artemis turned on him with a stunned expression. "What?"

"I want to know how to fight."

She scowled, then asked the one question that she never failed to voice. "Why?"

"I'm tired of being hit. I want to know how to defend myself."

Artemis was stunned by his unexpected request. An image of Apollo knocking her around went through her head so sharply that she flinched. Like most men she'd known, Apollo was such a controlling bastard. The last thing she wanted was to make herself vulnerable to Acheron. Teaching a man to fight could never lead to anything good. "I don't think so. I won't let anyone hurt you, Acheron. I'm all the protection you need."

"What if you grow bored with me?"

She cupped his cheek in her hand. "How could I ever be bored with you?"

Acheron offered her a smile that didn't reach his eyes. "I really wish you'd teach me."

His insistence set her hackles rising. "I said no," she snapped.

Acheron paused at the hostility in her tone. He knew that anger and what it stemmed from. "Who hits you?"

Artemis lowered her bow. "I think there's deer over this way."

"Artie . . ." He pulled her to a stop. "I know the sound in your voice. I've had it too often in mine not to recognize what it means. Who has hurt you?"

She hesitated for so long that he didn't expect her to answer, but when she did her tone was so low that he barely heard it. "Other gods."

He was stunned by her confession. "Why?"

"Why does anyone hit?" Her eyes were furious again. "It makes them feel more powerful. I will not have you hit me. Ever."

"And I would never do so," he said, his voice rife with conviction. "I could no more do to another what has been done to me than cut my own heart out. I only wish to protect myself."

"And I told you. I will protect you."

He caressed her arm before he dropped his hand and stepped back. "Then I shall trust you, Artie. But I want you to know that I don't trust easily. Please don't be like everyone else and break your word to me. I hate being lied to."

She kissed him lightly on the cheek. "Let us hunt."

Acheron nodded before he nocked a new arrow and placated the only real friend he'd ever had. She didn't shun him and he didn't have to hide from her. What scared him, though, were the feelings inside him whenever she was near.

He was falling in love with a goddess and he knew just how stupid that was. Out of all the things he'd been, he'd never been a fool.

Until now.

She made him feel whole. Happy. And he never wanted these feelings to leave.

194

Pushing the thought away, he took aim at a buck. As he sighted it, Artemis ran at him and tickled him. The arrow flew wide of its mark, embedding itself in a tree where it disturbed a squirrel that actually threw a nut at him.

Acheron laughed before he narrowed his eyes on Artie. He tossed his bow aside then stalked toward her. "You have fouled my perfect shot. You're going to pay for that."

Artemis dropped her bow before she bolted.

He ran for her as she tried to disappear into the woods. Her laughter taunted him and made him smile all the more. He caught up to her right as she reached the small stream.

Wrapping his arms around her waist, he swung her around in his arms.

Artemis couldn't breathe as the full weight of Acheron slammed into her. The sight of his smile, the light in those magical eyes . . .

It made her want to shout out in ecstasy.

He twirled around with her while the birds sang a special melody for them. She was lost in this one time and place with him. This was what she'd always wanted. Always needed.

Acheron didn't care about her quirks or her moodiness. Nor did he flinch from feeding her. He took her as she was and held her regardless. Unlike her family he didn't belittle her or tell her that she lacked the followers he had. He didn't care about any of that.

She wanted to lose herself to this moment and to him for the rest of eternity.

"Make love to me, Acheron."

Acheron froze at her words as his smile faded. "What?" He set her back on the ground.

She brushed his beautiful hair back from his face. "I want to know you like a woman. I want to feel you inside me."

He released her and stepped back, his expression reserved. "I don't think so."

"Why not?"

He swallowed and she saw the fear in those silver eyes. "I don't want anything to change between us. I like being your friend, Artie."

"But you already touch me in places no one else has. Why wouldn't you want to be inside me?"

"You're a virgin."

"Only by a small technicality. Please, Acheron. I want to share myself with you."

Acheron looked away as his emotions burned through him. What she offered him was unimaginable. Yet he'd had numerous princesses and noblewomen come to him so that he could break their bodies in gently for intercourse with other men.

Parthenopaeus . . . Of the pierced maidenhead—that was how Estes and Catera had billed his services to his female clients. Acheron's reputation for gentleness had been legendary. The fact that he was extremely well-endowed and was still careful with them hadn't hurt him either.

Now a goddess offered herself to him. Any other man would leap at the chance. For that matter, any other man would already be naked.

But unlike the rest, he fully understood the intricacies of physical intimacy. Even though they asked and paid for it, some women cried at the loss of their innocence. Others cursed him and themselves. Some had even turned violent over the loss. A small handful rejoiced.

The problem was he didn't know which one Artemis would be.

"I don't want to hurt you."

She walked herself into his arms. "Please, Acheron . . . I want to feel you in me when I feed on you."

"I really don't think we should."

Her eyes snapped fury at him. "Fine. Go then. Get out of my sight."

"Artie . . ."

It was too late. He was back in his room. Alone. "I'm sorry," he whispered, hoping she could hear him.

If she heard, she gave him no clue.

You should have slept with her. Would it really have mattered? He'd slept with everyone else. But the others had just been bodies for him to please. Artemis was different.

He loved her.

196

No, it wasn't as simple as that. What he felt for her . . . it defied love. He needed her in a way he wouldn't have thought possible and now he'd angered her.

His heart heavy, he only hoped that he could find some way to win her back and make her forgive him.

January 26, 9528 BC

It had been two weeks since Acheron had last seen Artemis and with the passing of each day, he grew more despondent. She refused to answer his calls.

He didn't even bother going to plays. Nothing could alleviate the pain inside him that wanted to be with her. All he wanted was to see her again.

Tilting his head back, he guzzled the last of the wine in the bottle he'd been drinking from. Angry and hurt, he threw it over the banister to let it smash on the rocks below. He reached for a new bottle and tried to pull the cork from it. He was too drunk to manage it.

"Acheron?"

He froze at the sound of the one voice he'd been begging to hear. "Artie?" He attempted to push himself to his feet, but instead he fell back to the ground. Looking up, he saw her in the shadows of his room.

She stepped forward, her face pale and drawn. Her left eye was swollen and there was the faint outline of a bruise in the shape of someone's handprint.

Rage darkened his sight. "Who hit you!"

Artemis stepped back, afraid of the man before her. She'd never seen Acheron drunk, but whenever Apollo drank, he turned violent. "I'll come back—"

"No," he breathed, his voice a hoarse whisper. "Please don't leave." He reached his hand out to her.

Her first instinct to run, she swallowed and reminded herself that she was a goddess. He was human and therefore couldn't harm her. Her legs trembling in reservation, she reached out slowly and took his hand in hers.

198

Acheron held it to his cheek and closed his eyes as if he were content to die now, as if touching her was the greatest pleasure he could imagine. He buried his face against her skin and inhaled deeply. "I've missed you so . . ."

She'd missed him too. Every day she'd sworn she wasn't going to see him, but today . . .

After Apollo's attack, she needed to be held by someone she knew wouldn't hurt her. "You look terrible," she said, frowning at the thick, prickly beard that had grown over his face. "And you smell bad."

He laughed at her criticism. "It's your fault I look like this."

"How so?"

"I thought I'd lost you."

Those anguished words touched her so deeply that it brought tears to her eyes. Falling to her knees, she shook her head at him.

Before she could speak, he whispered in her ear. "I love you, Artie."

Her breath caught in her throat. "What did you say?"

"I love you." He leaned against her and wrapped his arm around her neck before he collapsed and passed out.

Artemis sat there, holding him as his words echoed all the way to her soul. Acheron loved her . . .

She looked down at his face that was still incredibly handsome even in its unkempt state. He loved her. That succeeded in making her cry in a way she hadn't cried since she was a child. And she hated the fact that he could make her do this. She hated the fact that those words meant so much to her when they should mean nothing at all.

But the truth was the truth and she couldn't deny it.

"I love you too," she whispered, knowing that she could never tell him that if he were awake. It would give him, a mortal, too much power over her.

But here in this moment, she could tell him a truth that she wanted to deny with every part of herself. How could a goddess be in love with a man? Especially her? She was supposed to be immune to it. But somehow this mortal had crept into her soul.

If only he were a god . . .

He wasn't and it wasn't meant to be. He was human and not just any human. He was a slave. A whore who'd been brutally used by everyone around him. They mocked him and they would mock her for being with him. She winced at the truth. She had enough trouble with her credibility where the other gods were concerned. Should they ever learn about this, they'd strip her powers from her and banish her to the human realm.

She couldn't allow that.

Not even for Acheron. It was more than she could give. More than she could bear. She'd seen how cruel mankind was to each other. The last thing she wanted was to be naked in this world and at the mercy of people who had no heart. Look what they'd done to Acheron. He couldn't even walk in public without someone hurting him.

Imagine what they'd do to her should they learn she'd been a goddess . . .

They'd tear her apart.

Sobbing, she held him close and took him away from this stupid, mean world.

In her own bed, she brushed her hand over him and cleaned him up so that he looked like the Acheron she loved. His hair was fresh and clean, his cheeks smooth and soft while he lay naked on her feathered mattress. Every muscle of his body was sharply sculpted. The lines of his abdomen . . .

How could any woman not love a face and body so perfect?

Wanting to be as close to him as possible, she removed her clothes, then crawled into bed to lie beside him. She manifested a fur to cover them as she snuggled close and listened to his breathing.

While he slept, she ran her hand over the muscles that covered his chest. His body was flawless. Lean and well muscled, he looked powerful even while he was unconscious. Heat poured through her as she fondled his nipple. It puckered in response to her touch, making her smile.

And she wondered what it would taste like . . . Acheron was always tasting her, but she'd never done that to him.

She was bashful about his body. But with him like this, she was emboldened.

Dipping her head down, she ran her tongue over the taut peak. Hmmm, he did taste good. His skin was salty and smelled of all Acheron. Her body aching, she moved slowly over his chest, sampling every inch of it.

It wasn't until she reached his stomach that she pulled back. His entire torso was bare except for a small patch of hair that ran from his navel down to the thicker patch at the center of his body. She buried her hand there, letting the coarse hair tease her fingers. Unlike the hair on his head, these were prickly and as she ran her hand through them, his cock began to harden.

Artemis touched him cautiously. She was fascinated by the part of him that was so different from her own body. At first she was able to move it at will, but before long he was so hard and stiff that all she could do was run her hand down the length of him and make his cock dance in response to her touch.

How odd . . .

Even stranger was the moisture that leaked from the tip. She glanced up to make sure he was still unconscious. Reassured, she bit her lip, then crawled closer. Her heart hammering in fear and curiosity, she dipped her head down for a taste.

Artemis groaned deep in her throat. There was nothing scary about this. Truly, nothing scary about Acheron in the least. Smiling, she pulled back to cup him in her hand.

He slept on, oblivious to the fact she was exploring him.

She moved back up his body to kiss those lips that had haunted her dreams these days past. She couldn't stand it anymore . . .

"Wake for me, Acheron."

Acheron was in a daze as he tried to focus his thoughts. But all he could see was Artemis. She was leaning over him, her green eyes scorching him with their heat.

"You take my breath away," he whispered.

She smiled ever so sweetly before she nipped his chin with her teeth.

He was already hard and aching for a taste of her. Was

this a dream? His head was so foggy that he couldn't tell. There was a haze over everything.

"Show your love to me," she breathed in his ear.

He wanted to and with her on him like this he couldn't remember his objections to it. Turning his face into hers, he kissed her deeply. He'd never wanted to make love to anyone before, but right now he wanted inside her with a madness so unexpected that it tore through him and left him weak.

His head spinning, he rolled over with her and dipped his head down to tease her right breast.

Artemis gasped at the sensation of his tongue stroking her. Her stomach contracted sharply with each delectable lick. And to her amazement, she actually came from it.

Gasping, she clutched his head to her and shook as wave after wave of pleasure swept through her. She'd had no idea that he could do *this*.

He growled unexpectedly, before he lowered himself down her body. He nudged her thighs apart to stare at her with a hunger so raw it sent a shiver over her.

"Touch me, Acheron. Show me what you can do."

He ran one long finger down her, making her shudder in response. An instant later he buried his mouth against her. She cried out as his tongue tormented her. It was unbearably pleasurable.

And she wanted more.

For the first time, he slid a finger inside her while he tasted her. The intrusion was startling at the same time it was incredibly pleasing. When he slid another finger inside, she tensed.

"What are you doing?"

He met her gaze before delivering another exquisite lick. "I'm getting your body ready for me so that I won't hurt you when I enter you." He pulled back. "Have you changed your mind?"

She shook her head. "I want you, Acheron."

He kissed his way slowly up her body while he continued to tease her with his hand.

Artemis clutched him as another orgasm tore through her. The moment it started, Acheron slid himself deep inside her body. He moved so quickly and smoothly that instead of hurting her, it increased her orgasm to a blinding level.

Her head lolled back and forth on the pillow as she tried to make sense of this. But there was no sense to it. And when Acheron started to slowly and deeply thrust against her, she moaned in ecstasy.

Acheron lost himself to the contented sighs Artemis made that matched his strokes. She held him in a way no one ever had before . . .

As if he meant something to her.

Tears pricked at the back of his eyes as he drove himself even deeper into her. No longer drunk, he was in bliss. All he could see was her beautiful face.

Her eyes darkened an instant before she brushed the hair back from his neck and sank her teeth into him. The moment she did, she came again.

The sensation of her drinking from him while her body clutched his drove him over the edge. Unable to stand it, he too came in a blinding wave of ecstasy.

He collapsed on top of her while she fed. Between his orgasm and blood loss, he was weak and sated. She rolled him over onto his back so that she could drink even more.

At the moment Acheron would have given her anything she asked of him. Even his life.

Artemis pulled back as her leg touched something wet on the bed. Glancing down, she saw her blood mixed with his seed on her mattress. The reality of what she'd just done slammed into her with a force so sharp it shattered all her happiness.

She was virgin no more.

If Apollo or the others found out . . .

She'd be ruined. Ridiculed. Humiliated.

What had she done?

You've been defiled by a human whore . . .

His eyes half-hooded, Acheron reached for her. She pulled back as her heart slammed against her breast. This was terrible. Awful. Terrified over what she'd allowed him to do, she left the bed, feeling sick.

Acheron followed her. "Artemis?"

"Don't touch me!" she snarled as he tried to hold her. She pushed him back.

"Did I hurt you?"

The concern in his voice left a ragged hole in her heart. But it was nothing compared to the shame and fear she felt. "You've ruined me."

In that moment she hated him for what they'd done. How dare he make her want him like this. Make her forget who she was and why her virginity was so important.

Dear gods, what had she done?

She wanted to kill him and yet she couldn't. How could she hate him so badly and still crave him?

"Why did you touch me?"

He looked stunned by her question. "You asked me to."

"I didn't ask you to kiss me in my temple," she accused. "I'd never known a kiss before. And then you touched me . . ." She slapped him hard for the affront.

Acheron staggered back in shock as his cheek burned. Before he could recover himself, Artemis attacked him, slapping and punching. When that didn't seem to satisfy her, she flung him against the far wall and held him there with her god's powers.

I will protect you . . .

Her words rang in his ears as he stared down at her, waiting for her to finally kill him. Truthfully he'd rather be dead than feel the splintering in his heart over what she was doing.

She'd lied.

Suddenly, he slammed to the floor. That same invisible force rolled him over and held him against the marble as Artemis approached him with a feral glare. "So help me, you ever breathe a word of this to a single soul and I will see you killed so painfully that your screams for mercy will resonate throughout eternity."

Those words brought tears to his eyes as they reminded him of so many others who'd hated him because they craved being with him. How many dignitaries and nobles had come to him and then cursed him the moment after he'd pleasured them?

They lived in fear of a whore ruining their precious

reputations. They'd kicked him from their beds or knocked him to the ground, cursing him for their own lust as if he'd wanted it.

Why had he ever thought for one moment that Artemis would be any different?

In the end, he was what he was.

Nothing.

"Do you hear me?" Artemis snarled in his face.

"I hear you."

"I'll rip your tongue out."

He had to force himself not to laugh at a threat he'd cut his teeth on. But he knew the truth. His tongue had more value than anything else since it gave them the most pleasure. "Your will is my will, akra."

She grabbed him by the hair and pulled his head up to force him to look at her. "I am the goddess Artemis."

And he was Acheron Parthenopaeus. Cursed whore. Despised slave. Incapable of being loved by anyone.

How stupid of him to fall for her lies. To think for one minute that something like him could ever have had value to a goddess.

Artemis saw the hurt in his eyes and it ripped through her own heart. She didn't want to do this to him, but what choice did she have? He would be dead in a few decades, but her shame would be eternal if word of this ever reached the other gods.

Humans couldn't be trusted. Ever.

"Remember my wrath will be legion." She wrenched his hair in warning before she sent him back to his world.

Shattered, Acheron sat on the floor of his room. Numb by the rejection and attack, he crawled out to the balcony that overlooked the sea and laid his head against the stone railing. He heard the voices of the Atlanteans calling to him.

More than ever before he was tempted to go. What would it matter if they did kill him?

If he could make sure they wouldn't abuse him more, he'd go to them. But deep in his heart was the fear that they only summoned him so that they could torture him too. Bowing his head, he wept and as every tear fell he hated Artemis for it.

No one had made him cry like this in years. Not since the day Estes had sold his virginity to the highest bidder and then held a party for everyone to watch the brutal violation that had made him ache and bleed for days afterward. Even now the laughter and jeers haunted him.

Break the whore in for the rest of us . . .

Acheron pounded his fist against the stone, wanting the pain to erase the shame inside him. But there was no relief. No mercy. Nothing could take it away.

The whore was tired now. He was finally broken. And it wasn't by the hand of his master or a client.

It'd been by the hand of the only person he'd ever loved. Defeated and lost, Acheron lay down on the cold balcony and closed his eyes, praying for death to finally come and end this nightmare that was his life.

January 28, 9528 BC

Ryssa was in her father's throne room while he, Styxx and Apollo laughed together, ignoring her. Which was normal. But what she hated was the fact that Apollo wanted her by him any time he came here. He treated her like a possession whose only purpose was to smile and fawn over his presence. And it made her wonder if this was how Acheron had felt in Estes's home.

So what if the god was exceptionally handsome? She despised the way he dismissed her as if she were insignificant. The only thing worse than his treatment of her was her father's insistence that she was blessed to be in the god's presence.

If this was blessed, she'd hate to see cursed.

She turned her head as she caught a glimpse of a servant hesitating in the doorway. Pretty and timid, the girl was a year or two younger than Styxx. "Is something wrong, Hestia?" she asked the maid.

Hestia looked at the men fearfully before she made her way to Ryssa's side so that she could speak to her in a soft tone. "His Majesty wanted me to report if . . ." Hestia's gaze returned to the king before she finished the statement, "the royal prisoner stopped eating."

The royal prisoner. Acheron. Ryssa's heart pounded in fear. "Is he ill?"

She cleared her throat. "I know not, Your Highness. I haven't seen him in days. I leave food and when I return it's untouched. No one's slept in his bed."

"What?" her father's roar made both of them jump. "Guards! Follow me." He stormed from the room in the direction of her wing.

Terrified for her brother, Ryssa ran after him.

"What's going on?" Apollo asked Styxx as the two of them followed in her wake.

Styxx made a sound of disgust deep in the hollow of his throat. "It's Acheron. He's a worthless slave who used to be a tsoulus. Unfortunately his life is tied to mine so we have to keep him healthy. Although I feel fine so I'm sure he's only doing this for attention. May the gods forbid we ever be allowed to forget his presence here for one single day."

Ryssa ground her teeth. The last thing Acheron wanted was any attention from either Styxx or their father. But in Styxx's selfish mind he couldn't fathom Acheron wanting to hide from their glorious presences.

Her father stormed into Acheron's room, then drew up short. She entered behind him and paused to scan the empty interior. There was no sign of Acheron.

Her father turned on her with a furious glower. "I told you he couldn't be trusted."

Ryssa ignored him as she went to the one place her brother frequented. The balcony.

At first she didn't see him, but as she stepped forward under the awning that shielded her from the passing storm, she saw a figure out of her peripheral vision. It was Acheron sitting to the side with his knees bent and his arms folded over them. Completely naked, he stared into space as if unaware of the frigid cold and the rain that poured down on him. His hair was plastered to his head and at least two days' growth of beard dusted his cheeks.

Careful to stay out of the rain, she approached him slowly. "Acheron?"

He didn't respond. There was something about him that wasn't quite right. It was as if he'd died, but his soul hadn't left his body yet.

She knelt beside him. "Little brother?"

He turned those eyes on her with a fury she hadn't seen since the morning he'd thrown her out of his brothel. "Leave me," he growled in a tone so ferocious it honestly scared her.

From the corner of her eye, she saw her father's anger. "Don't you dare speak to her that way."

"Fuck you, you bastard."

Styxx growled low in his throat as he rushed Acheron.

Ryssa fell back as Acheron came to his feet and ran at Styxx with the same fury. She covered her mouth as the two of them clashed in the pouring rain. Never once had she seen Acheron strike another living soul. But he fought Styxx with everything he had.

Apollo snatched her back so that they didn't accidentally hit her.

Styxx had been trained to fight from the age of five by the best instructors her father could hire. And he beat Acheron down in the rain. Even so, Acheron fought as hard as he could.

But in the end he was no match for his twin. Styxx kicked him in the ribs. "You're pathetic."

Acheron rolled in the water and pushed himself up. As he went for Styxx again, Styxx knocked him back. The rain ran down his face, mixing with the blood that ran from his eye, nose and mouth. Still he ran at Styxx, over and over again as if he thought his sheer will alone would be enough to defeat his twin brother.

"Guards, take him," her father ordered.

Acheron tried to fight them as they came forward to subdue him, but he was already weakened by Styxx. They hauled him back into his room where her father waited.

Her father buried his hand in Acheron's wet hair and snatched his head back so that Acheron could see the full contempt the king bore his eldest son. "Beat him until there's no skin left on his back. If he passes out, wake him and beat him again."

Acheron laughed coldly. "I love you, too, Father."

Her father backhanded him. "Take him out of here."

"Father?" Apollo asked with an arch stare.

Her father scoffed. "He calls me that, but he's no son of mine. My former queen whored herself and begat that abomination."

Ryssa felt her tears fall at her father's condemnation. "He's human, Father."

They all laughed at her. Unable to stand their ridicule, she followed the guards to offer comfort to Acheron.

By the time she reached the courtyard where they beat him, he was already bloodied. But unlike the other times they'd punished him, he fought against his restraints.

"Hit me again!" he shrieked at the guard. "Harder!"

The unbridled rage in him shocked her completely. He was actually laughing at the guards as if he took pleasure in what they were doing.

Had he gone mad?

What had happened to him?

Acheron taunted them until he passed out from the beating. The guards exchanged a wary look between each other before the taller one reached for a bucket of water to revive him.

Ryssa placed her hand on his arm. "Please don't," she begged.

"Highness . . . your father will be angry if he learns we didn't carry out his orders."

"I won't tell if you don't. Please. He's been through enough."

The guard nodded, then went to cut him down. She saw the pity in both their eyes as they carried Acheron back to his room and, under her direction, placed him face down on his bed. They turned and left her alone with her brother who looked so pathetically vulnerable lying on the bed, bleeding.

Ryssa had no idea where Apollo and her brother and father had gone off to. Honestly, she didn't care. They could all rot for their cruelty.

Her hand shaking in pity for her brother, she brushed the hair back from Acheron's cheek. He was burning with a fever. "Don't worry, Acheron. I'll take care of you."

"Well, *that was* highly entertaining."

Artemis dragged her gaze away from her koris who were swimming in the fountain outside her temple to see her brother beside her. "What was?"

210

"My pet has an illegitimate brother they hate."

Her heart stilled at the mention of Acheron. "Really?" she said, hoping he didn't detect the catch in her voice.

He nodded before he took a seat next to her. "I've never seen anything quite like it. He was sitting naked in the rain completely quiet, not bothering a soul, and they beat the shit out of him, then had him hauled down for a whipping."

Artemis forced herself not to react to the news in the least little way. "Why?"

"No idea. But I swear the prince heir had a hard-on when he held him down on the ground and beat him."

Artemis looked away as she remembered how many times Apollo had treated her in a similar fashion. Strange that he didn't see his own actions mirrored by the humans. Her poor Acheron. She wanted to go to him, but didn't dare.

Apollo laughed. "I give the human credit though, he fought like a lion against them. Even dared them to hit him harder."

Tears gathered to choke her. Artemis blinked quickly to dispel them. "I'll never understand humans."

"That's why my Apollites will one day subjugate them. The humans are too flawed."

She shook her head at her brother's plan to overthrow the people her father had created. "Do the Greek humans know that you're not backing them in their war against the Atlanteans and Apollites?"

"Are you insane? Of course not. Let them offer their daughters to me and make sacrifices. What do I care?"

Artemis cocked a brow at that. "You care for your pet, don't you?"

He shrugged nonchalantly. "She amuses me for the time being. But there are many more exquisite women in the world. Besides she'll eventually age and I'll cast her off then."

"They do age too quickly." That was more for her benefit than his. Surely Acheron wouldn't appeal to her once his beauty faded.

Apollo didn't comment.

Artemis wondered at his presence in her temple garden. "Why aren't you with your pet?"

"She's with the slave, tending him. Once they beat him, she became too morose for my taste."

"And you tolerated that?"

He shrugged again. "I think her illegitimate brother must have given her tips on how to please me. She's been way too knowledgeable and compliant for a virgin. Styxx told me that they used to sell the bastard to humans for sex. Apparently it's a family tradition."

That news surprised her. Normally her brother shunned anyone who was unchaste. "Ryssa has had others?"

"No. I'd have killed her. When I'm not around, they keep her well guarded. But I find it fascinating that they offered her to me in such a manner. I would never do that with my daughter."

Artemis glanced to Satara, Apollo's young daughter who was dancing in the fountain with another of her koris. "No, you only gave your daughter to me to be a servant."

"I gave my daughter to you to feed you when I'm not around and to keep you away from the humans. She's never to be touched by any man."

"She's young still. What will happen when she grows older and decides to take a consort?"

Apollo's eyes flared with anger. "I'll kill them both."

Artemis was aghast at his words. "You would kill your own child?"

His look pierced her. "I'd kill my own twin should she whore herself for a man. Satara is one of many children I have. But none of them will shame me without feeling the full weight of my wrath."

"Even if she loved him?"

He curled his lip in disgust. "What are you? Aphrodite? Don't speak to me of love. You're a goddess. There is no love for us. Only lust which fades. A man can seek lovers, but for a woman to do such . . ."

Made her a whore. She knew her brother's stance on that.

As if she could hear his words about her, Satara paused in her play to look at her father.

"I'm off." Apollo vanished.

Artemis didn't miss the look of disappointment on Satara's face that her father hadn't bothered to speak to her. An instant later, she shoved the kori closest to her and stalked off.

Artemis shook her head. Apparently violence ran deep in their genes.

Her thoughts turned to Acheron and guilt slammed into her. What she'd done to him had been wrong and she knew it. But how could she face him after the way she'd acted?

You're a goddess. He should be grateful you even noticed him.

That was the way she'd been reared. Yet Acheron was different. He hadn't just been another human. They'd been friends.

And she'd hurt him out of fear. She'd done the very things to him that she'd sworn she'd never do. Things she knew hurt and humiliated him.

Why?

Closing her eyes, she could see him chasing her through the forest. Hear his laughter as he teased her.

No one else made her feel like that. No one.

And she'd ruined it by being stupid.

He's human, who cares? That would be Apollo's stance. If only she could share it. But deep in her heart she knew the truth. She missed him and she ached at the thought of his being hurt again by his father.

Don't even think it . . .

It was too late. She'd already flashed herself from her garden to his room. She hovered in the shadows where she saw his sister leaning over him.

"Please eat, Acheron," Ryssa whispered. "I don't want them to hurt you anymore. Father says that if you refuse any more meals he'll have them force feed you again." She held a piece of bread toward his mouth.

He turned his head away.

Artemis saw the raw pain on Ryssa's face.

"Fine. I won't have you hurt any more." The princess shoved the bread into her mouth and swallowed it whole. After that, she ate all of his food.

Her eyes filled with sorrow, Ryssa stood up. "I'll tell them that you ate it." When she reached for Acheron, he grabbed her hand and shoved it away from him.

Her face stricken, she sighed. "Sleep in peace, little brother. I'll make sure no one disturbs you."

Artemis didn't move until Ryssa had left them alone. Materializing into a solid form, she stepped out of the shadows.

Acheron curled his lip at her. "Leave."

"You shouldn't take that tone with me."

He laughed, then winced as if something pained him. "Do I look like I give a damn what you do to me? Get your ass out of here and leave me alone."

"Acheron—"

"Go!" he snapped, then hissed as if in severe pain. "You've already made it clear to me what I am to you. As you can see, I don't need you to beat me or hit me. There are plenty of others vying for that honor."

She knelt by the bed, her heart breaking at the bruises on his face . . . at the wounds marring his back. "I can heal you."

"I don't want your healing. I want nothing from you except your absence."

"Don't do this, Acheron."

Acheron cursed. "I'm through begging for mercy. No one heeds it when I do anyway. Better I should die on my feet with all the dignity a whore can manage than crawling on my belly like a worthless slave."

She shook her head as she tried to explain to him what had happened. "I was scared of what we'd done."

His look went through her like a dagger. "And I'm sick of being everyone's regret. My mother died in shame because she'd borne me. My father and brother despise me and my sister can barely look me in the eye. And you . . . you made me actually believe in something. I trusted in you and you lied to me."

"I know and I'm sorry." She placed her hand on his whiskered cheek, hoping to make him understand just how sincere she was. "I'm here now, not as a goddess, but as your friend. I miss you when you're not around."

Acheron wanted to shove her away, but the truth was he couldn't. No matter how much he needed to hate her, he didn't know how.

Her eyes tormented him before she closed them and healed his sore body.

He let out a tired breath as the pain faded and left him whole again. "Don't expect me to thank you."

"Don't be like this. I don't apologize to humans. Ever. Yet I've apologized to you . . ."

He understood what she was saying, but it didn't ease the pain inside his heart where she'd stabbed him. "I don't want your friendship anymore, Artie. You'll have to find another whore to entertain you."

Before he could even blink, she set upon him and shoved him back upon the bed. Acheron sucked his breath in sharply as she sank her teeth into his neck. This time there was no pleasure for him. Only pain wracked him with every drop she drained. Even worse, she kept him paralyzed so that he couldn't move or fight her.

It was an act of violation and he knew it. He'd had enough people attack him in a show of power to recognize it when it happened to him.

Beg me for mercy, whore. Tell me how much you enjoy it.

Acheron struggled to stay conscious as the voices from the past echoed in his head. The pain and frustration built inside him as impotent rage simmered deep.

Finally Artemis pulled away. By the bemused expression on her face he could tell she was surprised to see him still awake.

Acheron swallowed as he stared up at her with contempt. "Are we even now? Or do you want to rape my body as much as you've raped my soul?"

Pain sliced through him as all of his wounds and bruises from his beating returned. He cried out from the intensity of it as it increased even more than it had been before.

Artemis stood up to glare down at him. "You will not mock me, human. I've had enough of your ridicule." With that she vanished.

Acheron closed his eyes as relief coursed through him. Maybe now he'd be left alone.

But as he sought comfort in his mind, instead of the orchard he'd played in at the summer palace that one spring day, it was an image of Artemis that haunted him. An image of their brief friendship before she'd turned vicious.

He missed that respite.

"It's over," he breathed. He was through being her toy. His life had been controlled by others for far too long. It was time he stopped trying to please everyone else and learned to live for himself. He would never again allow anyone to have power over him.

Especially not the gods.

Acheron walked through the center of town on his way to the stadium to watch the latest play. Entering the market-place, he paused as he glimpsed a shadow from the corner of his eye. He turned quickly toward it only to see nothing. Unsure if it was Artemis following him, he ducked behind a small group of people.

He felt so hollow inside. So used. Honestly, he never wanted to see her again. The mere thought of her set his anger on fire and yet there was also a sadness so profound at the loss of what could have been between them that it almost brought him to his knees.

He didn't want to be used anymore. Not even for love.

Why not? You've been bartered for everything else.

He ground his teeth at a brutal truth he didn't want to think about.

"Grandma, he's cheating us."

The young boy's voice drew his attention to a table close by. An older woman was there with braided gray hair that was laced with black streaks. Her eyes were milky white and she stood with one hand on the boy's shoulder. No older than seven or eight, he had dark hair and a face so in-nocent it was touching. Though their clothes were thread-bare, they were both well washed and clean.

The vendor raised his hand in warning to the child as if he were about to hit him.

Backing up, the boy's face lost all color.

"Merus?" his grandmother breathed. "What's happening?"

"N-nothing, Grandma. I-I-I was mistaken."

Acheron didn't know why, but the boy's cowering went through him like a dagger. How dare the man take advantage of an old woman and her charge when it was so obvious that neither of them had much in this world.

Before he could think better of it, he stepped forward. "You need to give them what they've paid you for."

The man started to argue until he took in the full height of Acheron who stood more than a head taller than he. Though Acheron was lean, he was muscled enough to look intimidating. Luckily the vendor had no idea that Acheron knew nothing about fighting. The man's eyes also widened at the quality of the cloth he wore—a royal chiton Ryssa had insisted he wear whenever he ventured out to the plays.

"I wasn't cheating them, my lord."

Acheron looked down at the boy who gaped at his height. "What did you see, child?"

Merus swallowed before he crooked his finger at Acheron.

Softening his face so that he didn't scare the boy any more than he was already, Acheron bent down.

The boy whispered loudly in his ear. "He had his thumb on the scale. My ya ya told me to always tell her whenever they did that. She says it's cheating."

"So it is." Acheron patted him on the arm before he straightened to look at the vendor. "How much flour were you buying, Merus?"

"Three pounds."

"Then I shall watch as it's measured again."

The vendor's face turned bright red as he poured the flour out and showed him that it was indeed short of the mark. Cursing under his breath, the vendor added more until it reached the correct weight. There was malice in his gaze for Merus once he had the sack resealed and shoved it toward the boy.

"Merus?" Acheron said, keeping his gaze locked on the vendor who couldn't see his face.

The boy looked up at him. "Yes, my lord?"

"Should you ever find your ya ya cheated again or should anyone here ever hurt you, I want you to go to the palace and ask for Princess Ryssa. Tell her Acheron sent you and she'll make sure that you're treated fairly and that anyone who hurts you is punished for it."

His eyes lit up even as the vendor's darkened. "Thank you, my lord."

His grandmother placed a gentle hand on Acheron's forearm. "May the gods bless you for your kindness, my lord. Truly, you are an asset to this world. Thank you."

Her words touched his heart and brought a lump to his throat. If only they were true. But they weren't and the old woman would recoil in horror if she knew what she was touching the arm of. "May the gods be with you," he breathed quietly before he started away from them.

He hadn't gone far before Merus came running up to him.

"My lord?"

It was so strange to have someone address him like that. "Yes?"

"I know we're beneath you, my lord, but my ya ya wanted me to ask you if you'd take bread with us so that she can thank you for your kindness. I know she's blind, but she's a wonderful cook. We bake bread for the baker who sells it to the king and his court."

Acheron looked back to where the old woman stood proudly even though she couldn't see any of the activity bustling around her. *Beneath him* . . . If the child only knew what he really was, he'd be shunning him like everyone else.

They both would.

Still, Acheron hesitated. He should go before they learned the truth of him, but he didn't want to insult them and make them feel as low as people made him feel.

So instead he nodded. "I should like that very much, Merus. Thank you for asking."

The boy smiled, then led him back to where his grandmother waited at the edge of the market.

"He's with me, Ya Ya."

The kind lines of her face crinkled as she smiled and spoke in the opposite direction from where he stood. "Thank you, my lord. It might not be as fancy as you're used to, but I promise you you've never tasted better."

"We're over here, Ya Ya."

Her cheeks pinkened. "Forgive me, my lord. I fear I'm a little directionally inept."

"I don't mind." He took the packages from Merus that the boy was holding. "I'll carry these if you wish to help your ya ya home." He was amazed at how heavy the load was for the child.

Beaming, Merus took his grandmother's hand and led her through the crowd.

"My name is Eleni, my lord."

"Please, just call me Acheron. I live at the palace, but I'm no one of any importance."

"He looks important, Ya Ya. He's got very nice clothes and shoes, and he's really, really tall."

She tsked at her grandson. "It's not nice to contradict people, Merus. Remember what I've told you. Looks can often deceive you. A poor man can don the robes of a prince and a prince can be shoeless in the street. We judge people by what their actions are, not by the clothes they wear." Her smile was one of complete serenity. "And by Lord Acheron's actions today, we know him to be noble and kind."

Acheron paused as her words touched him deeply. Never in his life had he felt like anything other than a whore, yet here, with two people who were dressed in rags, he felt like a king. It was such a foreign sensation that he actually lifted his chin a degree.

Merus opened the door to a small house that was nestled among a row of them. Acheron had to almost bend double to fit through the short doorway as he followed the two of them inside. The main room was small and crowded, but it felt like home. There was an energy to the place that let him know Merus and Eleni were very happy here together.

However, it made him appreciate how much space he needed in order to move. The rafters were so low, he'd almost given himself a concussion two seconds after he'd entered.

"Are you all right, Lord Acheron?" Merus asked.

Acheron nodded without moving his hand away from his forehead that throbbed from its collision with the wood.

"What happened?" Eleni asked in a panicked tone.

"As I said, Lord Acheron is extremely tall. He banged his head on the ceiling."

Eleni's eyes widened. She approached him with her hand waving in front of her.

Acheron took her hand in his and put it on his shoulder so that she could tell just how tall he was.

"Oh, my gracious," she breathed. "You are huge. Like one of the gods."

Yet another thing that made him a freak to normal people—it'd also made Estes and Catera a lot of money since those who were shorter liked the feeling of power they had over someone his size.

Moving with a grace that was unfathomable to him, Eleni crossed the floor as if she could see every item in it and pulled out a chair for him. "Best you sit, my lord. I can only imagine how stifling our tiny home must seem to you."

"Not at all," he said honestly. Though he was fearful of colliding with more objects, he rather liked her peaceful home.

"Fetch us some milk, Merus."

The boy ran out the door.

Acheron watched as she went to her stove and stoked the fire there effortlessly. He was amazed at how she knew where everything was. There were no missteps or burns.

"My lord?" she asked as she pulled a knife from its holder. "May I ask you a prying question?"

"If you wish."

"Why are you so sad?"

He started to deny it, but why? She didn't know him and he didn't know her. Honestly, he was stunned that she could pick up on his mood without any visual clues. "How can you tell?"

"The sound of your voice when you speak. I hear the weight of sadness in it and a strong lilt of Atlantean."

She was unerringly astute as she cut, then placed bread on a stone trencher to warm. "Is it the loss of a person who saddens you?"

His gut knotted at the thought of Artemis. "A friend."

"Then I weep with you," she said, her tone comforting. "I've lost many friends over the years, and my children. Loss is always hard. But I have Merus and I take so much pride in his growth. He's such a fine boy. You've no idea how much a son means to his parents. I'm sure yours must smile every time they look upon you."

Unable to bear the wounds she opened, Acheron stood. "I should probably be going."

She looked stricken. "Did I say something wrong?"

"No." He didn't want her to feel bad when her intent had been to comfort him. It wasn't her fault that the only person who loved him was his sister and that his parents had both cursed him since the moment of his birth. "I was headed toward the stadium for a play when I stopped in the market. I should go before I miss anymore of it."

She took his hand in hers, then froze as her fingers touched his slave's brand. Her grip tightened. "You're a slave?"

He felt his face heat as humiliation washed over him. He wanted to curse at her accidental discovery. "I was. I'm sorry. I shouldn't have come here."

But she didn't release him. She covered his hand with her other one and offered him a smile of friendship. "Take your cloak off and sit, Acheron. You've done nothing to apologize for. I admire you all the more for stopping to help us. It's nothing for a nobleman to do so, yet they seldom bother to help those less fortunate. For a freedman to speak up in defense of another takes great courage and character. What you did is all the more noble and kind, and I would be honored to have you sit at my table with us."

Acheron couldn't breathe as emotions gathered to tighten his throat. He wasn't used to anyone complimenting him outside of a bed. "Thank you."

Smiling, she patted his hand before she let him go. "You know, my father used to tell me all the time when I was a child that when we first meet someone we never recall later what was said or what they wore. What we remember most is how that person made us feel. You made my grandson feel important by defending him and you've made me eternally grateful for that selfless act. Thank you, child."

And the two of them had given him dignity. She was right. He'd remember that always.

Merus returned with a clay jug, breathless. "I've plenty of milk, Ya Ya. Is the bread ready?"

"Almost, dearest." She took the milk from him and poured it into cups for them.

Merus brought a cup for Acheron and set it before him. "Have you fought many battles, my lord?"

He lowered his cowl to smile at the innocent question. "No, Merus. None, and please, just call me Acheron."

"It's all right, akribos," Eleni said gently. "Acheron doesn't like titles."

Merus got his own cup and then ran back to the table with it. He climbed up on the chair next to Acheron. "Can you fight with a sword?"

"Not at all."

"Oh . . ." he looked disappointed by that. "So what do you do?"

"Merus," his grandmother chided. "We don't interrogate our guests." She shook her head. "Forgive him, Acheron. He's only seven and still learning."

"He doesn't bother me. I'm nineteen and still learning."

Merus squealed with laughter.

Eleni brought the bread to the table and set it before Acheron along with a jar of honey and butter. "You have a most generous spirit. That is rare in this day and age."

Merus scratched his ear as if he was confused by his grandmother's words. "But what if he's not what he seems? You always tell me that people sometimes put on masks and we don't know what's inside them."

Eleni ruffled his hair. "You're right, scamp. We can never really see into the hearts of others. When I wasn't much older than you, my father used to charge my brothers for their room and board. Everyone thought he was mean to do such a thing to his own children. My brothers hated him for it."

"For being poor?" Acheron asked.

She shook her head. "No. My family actually had quite a bit of money because my father was a miser with every coin. People hated him for that too, yet what they didn't understand was that as a boy, he and his family been thrown out of their home for lack of coin. His baby sister, the one he loved more than anything, became ill from homelessness. She died of starvation in his arms and he swore then that no one he loved would ever die because of poverty again."

Acheron felt for the poor man. Having known such poverty himself, he could understand the man's reasoning. There was nothing worse than starving. Nothing worse than living on the street with no protection from the elements . . . or other people.

Merus cocked his head. "But why did he charge your brothers if he had plenty of money?"

Her features softened as she cupped his chubby face. "He was putting all that money aside for when my brothers were ready to wed."

"Why, Ya Ya?"

She still didn't lose patience with him. "Because you can't marry until you can afford a bride price and you must have a home to take your wife to. When my brothers found those wives, my father pulled out all the money they'd paid him over the years. He'd put it aside for them as savings so that each of my brothers had a small fortune to set up a household when they were old enough. In the end, he wasn't the mean person everyone thought him to be. What he did was for their benefit since it was money they would have squandered on foolishness. And it goes to show that we never know what's in the heart of people when we judge them. Actions that sometimes seem mean aren't. Rather they are done by the ones we love in order to protect us without our knowing it."

Merus held the plate of bread out to Acheron. "Ya Ya says that company gets first choice."

Acheron smiled before he took a piece and buttered it. "Thank you, Merus."

The boy served himself and then his grandmother. The normality of it all slammed into Acheron. Here he sat, with his head uncovered and neither of them reacted to him at all. There were no furtive, lustful glances that they were trying to conceal. No nervous movements.

224

He was just another person to them. Gods, how much that meant to him.

"You're right," he said after he swallowed his bread. "This is the best I've ever eaten."

Eleni lifted her chin in pride. "Thank you. I learned the art of it from my mother. She was the most skilled baker in all of Greece."

Acheron smiled. "Surely in all the world. I can't imagine anything better than this."

"Her pastries," Merus said around a mouthful of food. "They'll make you weep."

Acheron laughed. "I imagine a man would look rather strange weeping over food."

Merus smacked his lips. "Trust me, it's worth the humiliation."

Eleni ruffled his hair. "Eat up, child. You need to grow strong and tall, like Acheron."

Acheron didn't speak as he finished the bread. He delayed as long as he could, but all too soon he was done and it was time to leave.

"Thank you again," he said to them.

Eleni stood up with him. "Our pleasure, Acheron. Feel free to return anytime you'd like to try some of my pastries."

Merus grinned at him. "I'll have a hankie ready."

"I'm sure you will." Lifting his cowl, Acheron made sure to cover himself completely. "Good day to you."

"May the gods be with you."

If she only knew. Acheron carefully ducked out of the door and made his way back toward the hill where the palace was set. Strange, he'd set out to escape into the world of fantasy through the plot of a play and instead had his spirits lifted even higher by an unexpected encounter with real people. Eleni and Merus had given him more than an escape.

They'd given him normality. If only for a short while. And it meant everything to him. He felt better than he had in a long time.

At least until he returned home.

He hesitated in the foyer as he saw the large gathering of

nobles and senate members who were accompanied by their families. Not that it should be that much of a surprise, but no one had told him there was to be a party.

Had he known, he'd have stayed locked in his room. His experience with such events had never gone well. Of course, in the past, he'd been the main attraction/fascination for all the guests. A chill swept over him as he remembered the times he'd been paraded around and pawed at before someone in the group threw him to the ground . . .

Pulling his cowl lower, he kept to the shadows as he made his way to the stairs. With any luck no one would approach him.

Yet as he drew even to the ballroom, his father's voice stopped him dead.

"Thank you all for coming to celebrate with me. It's not every day that a king is so blessed."

Acheron crept closer to the doors to see his father on a dais. Ryssa stood to his left with Apollo by her side. The god's arm was wrapped possessively around her shoulders. Styxx was to his father's right. He held hands with a tall, beautiful dark-haired woman.

"Let us all raise our cups in honor of my only daughter, the human consort for the god Apollo who is now expecting his child and to my only son who will be marrying the Egyptian princess Nefertari. May the gods bless them both and may our lands forever flourish."

A bitter jealousy tore through him as he listened. It stung so deep in his heart that it was all he could do not to lower his cowl and call out to his father that he did indeed have another son. But to what purpose?

His father would only deny him and then have him beaten for the affront and embarrassment.

Anger overrode the jealousy as his father proudly kissed Ryssa and then Styxx.

"To my beloved children," he said to the crowd once more. "Long may they live."

A deafening shout rose up from everyone except Acheron who couldn't breathe from the weight of agony and rejection.

I am the eldest . . .

226

"You are a deformed whore and a slave." Estes's voice echoed from his past. *"You don't speak unless you're addressed. You are never to look anyone in the face. You should be grateful I even tolerate you in my house. Now get on your knees and please me."*

Acheron wanted to die as shame filled him. His father was right. There was nothing about him worth loving and definitely nothing that warranted any kind of pride. Hanging his head, he made his way up the stairs and to his bedroom.

His heart heavy, he lowered the cowl, grateful there was no mirror here to remind him of why he deserved nothing save the scorn of decent people.

"Acheron?"

He froze at the whisper behind him. "What do you want, Artemis?"

"I want my friend back."

Acheron closed his eyes against the tears that he hid inside himself. He wanted so desperately to have value to someone. Anyone. Not for what he earned for them, but because they cared for him.

Artemis moved to stand just behind him. So close he could feel her presence as if they were touching. "I've missed you."

He wanted to rail at her. To scream out how much he hated what she'd done to him.

To beg her not to ever hurt him again.

But what was the use? All humans were the playthings of the gods. He was only a little closer to one than the others.

"Am I forgiven then?" he asked, hating himself for the subservient question.

"Yes." She pressed herself to his back and wrapped her arms around him.

Grinding his teeth, he forced himself not to stiffen or shove her away. "Thank you."

Artemis wanted to weep at the joy she felt. She had her Acheron back . . . She couldn't believe how much she'd missed him. How afraid she'd been of his rejection.

Most of all, she wanted him to know how glad she was to have his friendship returned. "I promise, I will never hurt you again."

Acheron didn't believe that for one instant. She'd shattered his trust the moment she'd taken him by the hair, knowing how much he despised it. Knowing how demeaning that action was for him.

He'd have rather she just tossed coins in his face and walked out.

She pulled him against her and kissed him like a lover. He returned the kiss with all the passion of someone who'd been paid for it. How sad that she couldn't tell the difference between a kiss he felt and one that was born of obligation. Then again, he was the best whore money could buy.

When she moved back, he saw the joy in her gaze. How he wished he felt it too.

"You'll never again doubt my affection," she breathed against his lips.

Acheron didn't respond as she dropped to her knees in front of him. He frowned in confusion until she ran her hand down his cock before she guided the tip of it into her mouth. Gasping in shock and pleasure, he almost staggered back. No one had ever done this to him before.

His job was to please. It wasn't to have others, especially not a goddess, pleasure him. All the anger inside him evaporated under the assault of her tongue on his body. He'd never felt like this before . . . never dreamed of just how good this would be. Her hand stroked and cupped his sac while her warm breath scorched him. The love for her that he'd buried and denied came back with a fury so intense it sent him into an immediate orgasm.

Artemis pulled back, sputtering as she quickly covered him with the skirt of his chiton. "That is so disgusting. How can anyone enjoy *that*?"

Acheron couldn't answer as he clutched himself while his body continued to finish what she'd started.

She looked up at him with a hesitant smile as she licked her lips. "You enjoyed that, didn't you?"

"Yes," he said, his voice ragged.

"Am I forgiven?"

Acheron ran his thumb over her lower lip where a trace of his seed was left. Her gaze unwavering, she flicked her tongue over the pad of his finger to taste it. The sight of her doing that . . . the sensation of her hot tongue on his skin was the most incredible thing he'd ever experienced.

Drained and sated, all he could do was nod.

Her smiled widened as she stood up and pulled him in for another kiss. The next thing he knew, they were in her temple bedroom and he was completely naked. She nipped his lips, brushing her hands over his chest. "Make love to me, Acheron."

Her words sent a wash of frigid cold through him. "I don't want to be beaten today, Artie. I've suffered enough shame this afternoon."

Laughing, she pulled his head down so that she could kiss him roughly, nipping his skin until he feared he'd be bruised. "I won't beat you. Promise." She took his hand and led him to her bed. She rolled onto her back and jerked him over her naked body.

Still Acheron was uncertain.

Artemis rolled him over onto his back. She was relentless in her demands and his body did exactly what it'd been trained to do . . . it hardened for her.

Closing his eyes, he wished he'd been neutered as a child. His life would have been infinitely easier.

As she slid herself onto him, he wondered how it could be that a goddess couldn't tell what was inside him. That she had no idea how little he wanted this from her right now. Reserved and terrified of what abuse she'd deliver once she was finished, he pleased her as best he could.

By the time she was fully sated, his body was sore. Sliding off him, she sighed contentedly. She reached up toward his face and he turned his head quickly in expectation of a slap.

"What's wrong?"

He swallowed as she pulled a pillow over him and then tucked it under her head. "Nothing."

She propped herself up so that she could trace the lines of his face with her fingertips. "I think I shall keep you with me tonight."

Before he could answer a golden cuff surrounded his ankle. A chain at the end of it entwined itself around her bedpost. "What's that for?"

"To make sure you don't wander about while I sleep."

Acheron jerked his foot making the links jingle. It was all he could do to bury his anger and not shout in frustration. "I don't like this, Artemis. I'm not a dog to be chained outside your house because you're afraid I'll piss on your rug."

She tsked at him. "Don't be so contrary. It's for your own safety."

Brutally force feeding him had been for his own good too. He couldn't stand being chained down. More than anything else, it made him feel like a whore again. "Please don't do this to me. I promise I won't leave your bed while you sleep."

Artemis hesitated. She couldn't tell if he was still angry enough to strike back at her or not. For all she knew, he might march up to the hall of the gods just for spite.

Humans were treacherous that way.

But in the end, she decided to trust him. The chain fell away. "If you betray me, Acheron—"

"You'll make me suffer through all eternity. I know. I was listening to the threat the first time you uttered it."

"Good. Now be a good man and give me your neck."

He dutifully brushed his hair back, exposing the beauty of his tawny skin and the delectable curve of his throat.

Her mouth watering, she dipped her head down to taste him and this time she didn't withhold the pleasure of the bite. She let him feel it fully. Cradling her head against him, he came in her arms as she drank from him.

Satisfied, Artemis watched as his eyes fluttered closed. "You will be mine, Acheron, for as long as your beauty holds. I will share you with no one else. Ever."

She would sooner see him dead.

April 3, 9528 BC

Acheron was slowly learning to trust in Artemis again. Either that or he was just becoming a more obedient pet. There were times when he wasn't sure which category he fell into.

She came to him when she was bored or hungry and ignored him when she had other obligations.

But at least she'd kept her word not to hit him anymore. In fact he hadn't been hurt in weeks now since Artemis kept him out of his father's way, too.

He currently sat in her temple, on the white chaise that was set in the middle of her receiving room. One of her maids had called her away and she'd sealed him inside before she left. Bored out of his mind, he cast his gaze around the room until he spied a golden kithara lying on a cushion on the floor in a corner.

Mesmerized by it, he retrieved the instrument and held it reverently in his hands. He hadn't played music since he'd left Atlantis. Music had been one of many things he'd been taught and he'd had a natural aptitude.

The thing he'd always loved most had been the way the music made him feel. Like plays, he could lose himself to the song and notes.

He strummed the strings and cringed at how badly out of tune it was. But after a minute, he had it back to perfection. Content for once, he started playing.

Artemis paused before she materialized back into her temple. At first she thought it was her niece Satara playing the

231

kithara that she used to entertain Artemis and her koris. Until she heard the deep and beautiful male voice singing in a low perfect pitch. The song, so tender and heartfelt, brought tears to her eyes.

She'd never suspected that Acheron possessed such talent. Not even the muses could compete.

Solidifying in the room, she listened while he kept his back to her. "You're amazing," she breathed, moving to sit behind him.

He stopped instantly.

As he started to set it aside, she stopped him. "Please keep playing."

"I only like to play when I'm alone."

"Why?"

"Because it makes people want to fuck me."

She tsked at his contrariness. "You shouldn't use words like that around me, Acheron. I'm a goddess. You need to show me more respect."

"Forgive me, akra."

Artemis sat back with a sigh at his subservience. She hated whenever he took that tone. It was the fire and defiance in him that she craved. Whenever he relaxed, that was the side he showed her. But the moment she corrected him, he immediately fell into this role he wore right now.

And she despised it.

She pushed the instrument toward him. "Would you play for me? There's only the two of us and I should like to hear your voice."

He returned the kithara to his lap and idly strummed it.

She leaned against his back and held him while he played. "What other talents do you have that you've hidden from me?"

"I'm accomplished at anything that entertains others."

"Such as?"

"Musical instruments, song, strega, massage, dance and fucking."

"Acheron!" She hid her smile behind his shoulder. So he wasn't quite subservient after all.

"I was only answering your question."

Sure he was . . . Her Acheron could be quite a handful and in more ways than one. "Can you dance as well as you play?"

"Better."

She found that impossible to believe. "Show me."

"There will be no music if I stop playing to dance."

She pulled the kithara from his hands. "There will be." She used her powers to continue the song. "Now show me what you can do."

He stood up and turned to face her. Holding his hand out, he waited for her to take it before he pulled her to her feet. True to his words, he was an elegant dancer. He moved with a graceful beauty that was almost godlike.

The more they danced, the more she ached for a taste of him. Her body on fire, she jerked him into her arms, intent on stripping him naked.

"Artemis!" Apollo's call shook her.

Acheron saw the doors to Artemis's temple opening. The next thing he knew, he was falling onto the floor of his own bedroom. The stone slammed painfully into his body as he landed flat on his back. His breath rushed out of him in a loud *oof*.

"You could have put me on my feet or in the bed," he said from between clenched teeth.

A bright light flashed in the room an instant before the kithara landed on top of his stomach. Acheron cursed in pain. It'd been a nice thought of hers, but damn . . . for a goddess renowned for her aim in hunting, her aim in this left much to be desired.

He'd barely risen to his feet before his own doors swung open to show Ryssa.

"Where have you been?" she demanded in a tone he'd seldom heard her direct at him. It was anger mixed with worry.

He set the kithara on his bed before he answered. "I don't know what you mean."

"I've been looking for you. You were gone for hours."

It was strange how time on Olympus passed very differently from time here. To him, it seemed as if only minutes had passed. "I was nowhere important."

She narrowed her gaze on him as she drew near. It was a probing gaze as if she were trying to unravel a mystery. "There's something different about you."

"There's nothing different."

"Yes, there is. You don't cower as you used to. You look at me when I speak to you. There's a confidence and peace that wasn't there before. What has caused this change?"

"I have no idea what you're talking about."

Ryssa stepped closer to him, then froze. Her gaze fastened on his neck and before he could stop her, she reached out and brushed his hair back from his shoulder. She gasped. "You've been with Artemis."

Terror filled him, but he kept it from showing as he silently cursed. "I've been with no one."

"I'm not a fool, Acheron. I know the marks left by the gods." She looked at the kithara. "I know their gifts."

Damn it. He should have thought of that. But it was too late. All he could do was lie to her and hope she'd believe him. "I have been with no one."

"Why don't you tell Father?" She turned to leave.

Acheron grabbed her arm. "Listen to me, Ryssa. I've been with *no one*. I know nothing of what you speak. If you love me even a little, you'll forget this moment and pretend you've seen nothing . . . please."

She placed a tender hand to his cheek. "I love you, little brother. I would never betray you. If you don't want me to tell him, then I won't."

He moved her hand to his lips so that he could kiss it in gratitude. "Now what had you seeking me this day?"

"I wanted to go to the market, but didn't want to go with a servant. I thought you'd enjoy the excursion."

"Why didn't you ask me?"

Acheron looked past her to see Styxx standing outside the door with a livid expression.

Ryssa turned to frown at him. "I didn't think you'd like to go. It's rather common for you, isn't it?"

Styxx curled his lip. "You'd rather be with an abomination than me?"

"Acheron isn't an abomination."

234

There was no missing the hurt in Styxx's eyes and it stunned Acheron that his brother would feel that way given all the people who loved, respected and admired Styxx.

"Why do you always defend him?" Styxx asked her, his voice laden with pain and anger. "Every time we turn around, you've crawled off to be with him."

Ryssa was aghast. "Surely to the gods you're not jealous?"

"Of that maggot? Never!"

But he was. Even Acheron could see it plainly.

Styxx spun on his heel and stalked off. Ryssa ran after him and pulled him to a stop in the center of the hallway. Acheron went to the door to watch them.

"Styxx . . . what is wrong with you?"

"What's wrong? The fact that my sister parades herself around with a whore and degrades herself by begging for his comfort when she won't even acknowledge the brother who loves her."

"You've never wanted to be with me. All you've ever done is deride me and my actions as you are now."

He shook his head. "You remember nothing, do you?"

"Remember what?"

"Anytime Acheron and I were ever crossed you ran to him to cuddle him while you ignored me. Every time I ever reached for you, you couldn't be bothered with me. Acheron is all that's ever mattered to you."

Ryssa shook her head with the same disbelief that Acheron shared. "You cannot possibly be jealous of Acheron."

"Don't you dare laugh at me." His eyes narrowed dangerously. "I am prince and heir. I can have you killed, sister or not."

Acheron saw the tears in her eyes over that threat and fury took him. He left the door to defend his sister. "Don't you dare talk to her like that."

Styxx backhanded him so hard, his lip and nose exploded with blood. "Don't you ever address me again, you filthy whore. I wish to the gods that you knew the humiliation you've caused me. Whenever I walk into a room, I see the snide glares, hear the whispered comments and jeers about my *twin* and his unrivaled skills. Because of you, I never knew my mother. I barely know my sister. I hate you with a passion so fervent that I can imagine no greater pleasure than killing you. If only the gods would grant me that one desire."

"Styxx!" Ryssa snapped. "How dare you!"

He curled his lip at her. "Don't you dare chastise me. In the end you're both nothing but whores. You're beneath me." He stormed off.

Acheron's heart bled for his sister as he saw the tears begin to flow down her face. He pulled her into his arms. "You're not a whore, Ryssa."

"Am I not? Tell me, what's the difference between us?"

"You are loved and claimed by the one who takes you to his bed. Believe me, that's a big difference."

No, his sister was kind and gently born. She was a lady. Styxx was an ass. And the only shit in the family was clearly Acheron.

June 23, 9528 BC

"Happy birthday, Acheron."

Acheron rolled over at the sound of Ryssa's voice. Sore from a night spent with Artemis, he was slightly disoriented. He'd gone to bed on Olympus, but at some point Artemis must have returned him to his own room.

"Good morning, sister." She looked particularly radiant today. Her blond hair was swept up around her head in small braids that were held in place by the silver set of combs he'd bought for her a few weeks back when they'd gone to the market together. The light blue gown she wore made her eyes shine bright as she placed her hand against her stomach. Her pregnancy was just starting to show.

"Get up and dress. I had the cook prepare you a special breakfast celebration for just the two of us. The meal's already being brought out."

He looked past her, but saw nothing. "Where is it?"

"Downstairs."

Acheron shook his head. "I'm not allowed to eat in the dining room. You know that."

She waved his words away. "Father was up late with Styxx. They won't awaken for hours. I want to give this bit of normality to you, little brother. You deserve it. Now dress quickly and join me."

Acheron really didn't want to do this. In truth, he hated venturing into the lower rooms where his family had made it clear he wasn't welcome. But Ryssa had gone to trouble for him. The least he could do was humor her.

Leaving his bed, he dressed quickly and joined her in the hallway. She wrapped her arm around his and smiled. "This is the first time we've celebrated the anniversary of your birth together. You're now twenty and next year you'll reach your majority."

As if that would make a difference to him. "Is there a party planned for Styxx?"

She looked away with a troubled expression. "Yes. Tonight as there is every year."

"Then I shall make myself scarce."

The look in her eyes mirrored the grief he felt inside. But they both knew he would be as welcome at the party as a plague of frog turds. Without another word, she took him to the dining room where she'd laid out a grand buffet.

"I wasn't sure what you'd like so I had them prepare a little of everything." She picked up a platter and handed it to him before she kissed his cheek. "Happy birthday, little brother."

Nothing could have touched him more. "Thank you."

He followed her down the line as she explained the various dishes to him.

As Acheron reached for a piece of fruit, she took his hand and laughed. "We don't eat that. They're decoration." She thumped it with her hand. "See, it's plaster."

They laughed together at his ignorance.

"Oh, it does a father good to hear his children laughing with one another."

Acheron froze at the sound of their father entering the room behind him. Cold dread seeped through his entire being.

Ryssa covered her panic with a dazzling smile. "Good morning, Father. I was told you'd sleep late today."

"Too much to do in preparation of Styxx's celebration." He clapped an affectionate hand on Acheron's shoulder before he kissed his cheek.

Both savoring and cursing the embrace, Acheron closed his eyes and held his breath. His silver eyes would betray him. They always betrayed him.

"I'm surprised to see you up, scamp. I heard you'd taken three women to your bed last night. They pleasured you well, I trust."

Ryssa cleared her throat. "Father, could I have a word with you outside?"

"Absolutely."

Acheron let out a tiny breath in relief as his father stepped away from him. He set his plate down and took a step toward the door when the unthinkable happened.

Styxx entered the room with one of his friends. "What is this? What are you doing here?"

Their father turned back and cursed before he glared at Ryssa. "You deceived me?"

"Not exactly."

Rage contorted his face as he crossed the short distance and slapped Acheron so hard it unbalanced him. He fell to the floor, dazed by the blow that loosened his front teeth and shattered his nose.

"You dared defile my table!"

Ryssa stepped forward. "Father, please! I'm the one who brought him here. It was my idea."

Her turned on her with malice. "Don't you dare defend him. He knows better." He snatched Acheron up by his hair and shoved him against the wall. "I want everything he's touched burned. Now!" he roared at the servants. "And throw out all the food."

Acheron laughed. "It must really chafe your ass that you can't be rid of me so easily."

His father punched him hard in the stomach.

"Father, please," Styxx begged. "Remember your heart."

His father slung Acheron sideways, tearing out a handful of hair as he did so. "Get this filth out of my sight."

"Guards!" Styxx roared. "Take the bastard out and beat him."

Acheron straightened before he approached his twin. "Tell me something, brother. What angers you most about me? The fact I share your face or the fact I know *exactly* what your best friend wants to do to you . . . and how often?" He slid his gaze meaningfully to the man behind Styxx who looked away red-faced. Acheron smiled at him. "Good to see you again, Lord Dorus, especially clothed."

Styxx let out a shriek of pain an instant before he ran at Acheron who tried to defend himself. But it was useless. His brother spent hours a day training to be a fighter. The best he could do was cover his head and try to protect his face. Styxx rained blow after blow on his ribs until the guards finally pulled him off.

"I want him to feel every lash!"

Acheron spat blood at Styxx's feet. "Happy birthday to you too."

His ears clear of his pounding blood and Styxx's curses, he finally heard his sister's sobs as she begged their father for a mercy the king had no intention of giving.

One guard clenched his fist deep in Acheron's hair, then shoved him out of the room toward the courtyard that he knew intimately. They should just move his bed out here and save them all the effort.

Acheron ground his teeth as his hands were tied and his clothes stripped from his body. He cursed the gods after the first lash cut through the skin on his back. Damn them for this. It was bad enough they'd abandoned him, but by condemning him to have the ability to heal most wounds, it made his punishments all the worse. Instead of scar tissue forming a barrier for his abuse, new skin grew each time, which meant they were striking virgin flesh with every beating.

And it hurt . . .

He lost track of the lashes as he tried to focus on anything else. His sweat mixed with the blood pouring from the wounds on his face making them burn all the worse. Still they beat him.

"Enough."

Acheron frowned through the haze of pain as he recognized Styxx's voice. His breathing ragged, he couldn't fathom why Styxx would stop the punishment he'd called for.

Not until his brother came around so that they were eye to eye. The hatred in Styxx's gaze was piercing. "Leave us," he ordered the guards.

Acheron heard the door close. He opened his mouth to taunt his brother but before he could, Styxx slammed an iron bar across his ribs with enough force to lift him off his feet. All the breath rushed out of his lungs.

"You think you're so fucking clever," he sneered. "Let's see how clever you are now."

Styxx vanished out of his sight. He came back a moment later with a gleaming red poker. Panic set in. Acheron fought his restraints with every ounce of strength he had. But he was weakened by the beating and held down completely.

With a gleam of sadistic satisfaction, Styxx laid the poker across Acheron's face. Screaming, Acheron tried to move away, but all he could do was smell the burning of his flesh. Feel the deep, penetrating pain that washed over him.

Smiling, Styxx jerked it away and walked behind him again.

Hanging limply, Acheron could do nothing but cry from the agony of his face that continued to burn. When Styxx returned, he carried a fresh poker.

"Please, m-m-mercy," he begged. "Please don't . . . brother."

"We are not brothers, you bastard!" Styxx shouted before he laid the poker across Acheron's groin.

Acheron screamed out. Tears fell as he prayed for death to come and stop this torture.

"Where's your laughter now?" Styxx asked, tossing the poker aside. "Don't you ever mock me again, you fucking whore."

Acheron felt something cold and sharp pierce his side. Looking down, he saw the dagger in Styxx's hand that his brother had buried to the hilt. He tasted more blood in his mouth as he choked on it and the pain that seared him.

"Don't worry," Styxx said, jerking the dagger free. "You'll live." He brought the blade down across Acheron's unburned cheek, laying it open to the bone.

Styxx cut him down, then walked off without even a backward glance.

Acheron lay on the ground, his head swimming as unimaginable pain ripped through him. "Please gods," he whispered desperately. "Please let me die."

He expelled one deep breath and surrendered himself to the darkness.

Artemis *was trying* to be patient as she watched the offerings the humans brought to her altar. But they didn't interest her.

She hadn't seen Acheron in two days and this was the celebration of his birth—something she wouldn't have known had Apollo not told her about the party tonight. She didn't know why Acheron had failed to mention it, but then he was odd that way.

Apollo wasn't going to the party, but his pet was.

Which meant Artemis would be free to visit Acheron later.

Yet dutifully, she'd been at her temple all day long. The sun had set almost an hour ago and as the day turned to night, she was restless for it to end.

An old man came forward with a goat.

Oh, this was no use. What was she going to do with a goat? Snapping her fingers, she granted his wish even before she heard it.

She picked up the ring that she'd made for Acheron and left them where they were to keep making offerings she had no interest in. Unlike these other mewling, pathetic humans, her Acheron would please her.

Even when he didn't please her, he still did.

Smiling, she materialized on his balcony, expecting him to be at his usual perch.

It was empty. Frowning, she looked over the edge to see the nobles and dignitaries gathered for the festivities. Surely Acheron wasn't there. He didn't like such events.

Artemis stepped through the doors without opening them. Her frown melted as she saw Acheron already abed. Good. She could join him there.

But as she approached, she slowed her gait. His breathing was shallow and ragged. He lay with his back to her and as she drew closer, she saw the pink stains marring his sheets.

Blood. Acheron's blood.

It was so much more than she'd ever seen before.

Terrified, she moved around the bed to find him weeping soundlessly. But that wasn't what stunned her most. It was the sight of his beautiful face. Or what was left of it.

One side had a vicious gaping wound that exposed part of the bone and on the other was a burn that had left his eye partially closed, his flesh scorched and his mouth twisted.

"What happened?" she demanded as anger tore through her.

He didn't answer but the shame in his eyes, the pain, lacerated her heart. Kneeling on the floor, she laid her hand to his burned cheek.

"Kill me," he breathed. "Please."

That ragged plea brought tears to her eyes. Wanting to understand, she used her powers to see what had happened to him. As every scene of it played through her mind, her fury built.

How dare they do this to him!

She felt her teeth growing sharp as her need for vindication tripled.

Acheron screamed as Artemis healed his battered body. Whenever his injuries were bad, her cure was every bit as painful.

Once he was healed, Artemis gathered him into her arms and held him in a way no one had ever held him before—as though she cared. "I'm so sorry, Acheron. Why didn't you call for me?"

"You wouldn't have come."

"Yes, I would."

But he knew the truth. She'd never have risked being seen. "You're here now. That's enough for me."

She nodded as she brushed his hair back from his face. "And woe to those bastards for this. They won't do this to you and not suffer for it." Taking his hand, she pulled him from the bed.

When she started for the door, he froze. "What are you doing?"

"I'm going to make them pay."

"How?"

She laughed evilly. "Trust me, love. You'll enjoy it."

The next thing he knew they were in the ballroom, unseen by the revelers. Artemis walked over to Styxx who stood beside his betrothed, laughing smugly with a group of his friends who were mocking an unattractive young woman in the corner. The woman had tears in her eyes as she tried to ignore their laughter and brutal comments.

Artemis leaned forward to whisper into Styxx's ear. "You want to see humiliation, you little prick? You're about to get a handfirst lesson on it."

One second Styxx was smiling. The next he was vomiting all over Nefertari and his friends. In fact, he vomited so forcefully that he lost control of his bladder and wet himself. When he tried to run, he tripped and fell into the mess.

Acheron looked away, as disgusted by it as everyone else.

But Artemis wasn't through. Raising her hand, she opened the double doors that led to the gardens. A pack of angry dogs ran inside and set upon Styxx with a vengeance.

Their father ran to his heir who was on the ground, crying for help.

Artemis gave Acheron a crooked grin before everyone at the party, except Ryssa and the woman who'd been teased, became ill. The guards tried to protect Styxx from the dogs an instant before they unloaded their stomachs all over their prince.

Crossing the distance between them, Artemis clapped her hands together in satisfaction. "I don't know about you," she said with an evil glint in her green eyes, "but *I* feel better." She looked around proudly. "They'll be fine by morning, but none of them will be out of their beds much tomorrow. As for Styxx, he will feel the effects of his cruelty for at least a week."

Acheron wished he could take pleasure in the pain around him, but he didn't. No one deserved what she'd done tonight any more than he deserved what Styxx had done to him.

She cocked her head. "Aren't you happy?"

Acheron glanced at the poor wretches around him. "Thank you for avenging me. It means a lot, Artie. Truly. But having been on the receiving end of cruelty my entire life, I don't take pleasure in harming others, so, no, it doesn't make me happy to see them like this. Especially those who've never done me harm."

"You're a fool not to. Believe me. They wouldn't be so kind to you."

In his experience, she was right. Even so, he just couldn't bring himself to laugh at the humiliation they suffered.

Artemis let out a sound of disgust. "You are such a strange human." She cupped his cheek in her hand. "I warn you now though, if he ever scars your face again I'll unleash an agony on him that he'll *never* recover from."

The anger and sincerity of her gaze scorched him. Only Ryssa had ever been indignant over his punishments. The fact that Artemis cared went a long way in erasing the anger he'd harbored against the goddess.

In truth, she'd kept her word and had done nothing to hurt him.

Don't trust her.

But his heart wanted to believe that on some level she loved him—that she cared.

She raised up to kiss him. The instant their lips touched, she took him to her temple. Acheron felt a strange fissure go through him.

"What the . . . ?"

Artemis's eyes were glowing bright. "I've given you the power to fight to protect yourself. You were right. I can't always be there when you need me. But—" she placed her fingertip on his lips. "You can't use those skills on a god, only a human."

"Why would I want to attack a god?"

Artemis leaned her head against his shoulder and inhaled his masculine scent. She adored the innocence inside him that couldn't even conceive of hurting her. "Some men do."

"Men do a lot of things I don't agree with."

"And that's why I've given you the powers you need. I don't want you hurt like that ever again."

Acheron tried to fight the swell of love inside him. But he couldn't. Not when she gave him so much. Not when she touched him like this and made him feel decent and wanted.

Artemis squeezed him tightly, then pulled back to hand him a small box.

"What's this?"

"My gift to celebrate your birth. Open it."

Stunned, he gaped at her. Honestly, he couldn't fathom what he held in his hands. "You're giving me a present?"

"Of course."

But it couldn't be that simple. Nothing ever was. "What payment do you want?"

She scowled at him. "I want no payment, Acheron. It's a gift."

Still he shook his head in denial. "Nothing is ever freely given."

She closed his hand around it and caressed his fingers. "This is freely given to you, akribos. And I wish to see you open it."

Truly, he couldn't fathom this. Why would Artemis give him a present?

His heart pounding, he opened the box to find a ring inside. Picking it up, he saw a double bow and arrow on it, but when he moved the ring, it shifted to an image of Artemis with a deer.

She smiled happily. "It's an insignia ring. I give them to my followers whom I grant the ability to summon me. Most of them have to find a tree and perform a ritual and say the right words. But you, my Acheron, you may summon me at any time."

When he started to put it on his finger, she stopped him. "It should be worn over your heart." A gold chain appeared and as Artemis placed it around his neck, another thought occurred to him. It wasn't just over his heart . . . worn like this the ring was also out of sight.

At least she thought enough of you to give you a gift.

That was true.

She kissed his cheek, then manifested a sword in her hand. Handing it to him, she winked. "Show me what you do."

"What do you mean?"

She inclined her head to two shadow warriors behind him. "Fight them, Acheron. Whatever you need to defeat them will be yours."

Skeptical, he stepped away from her. But the moment they approached, his body knew instinctively how to fight.

Artemis smiled in satisfaction as she watched Acheron spar with the shades. She'd done a good deed for her human. And as she watched, heat invaded every part of her.

246

He moved like quicksilver. His muscles rippled and flexed, straining and defining with every blow he parried and delivered. Her hunger built and she wondered why his blood was so addictive . . . more so than even her brother's.

Why did she crave Acheron so?

Yet there was no denying his allure. Right now, she wanted to throw him on her bed and keep him there for the rest of eternity.

The smile he gave her as he finished off his sparring opponents made her melt.

"I told you," she said, approaching him.

Acheron held the sword in his fist with a confidence he'd never known outside of someone's bed. He couldn't believe that he finally knew how to fight as well as he knew how to use his body to please others. It was a heady concoction.

Power . . .

Grateful to Artemis, he tossed the sword aside and pulled her into his arms. Something strange rippled through him. It was like a part of him had been unleashed and it shook him to his foundations.

Artemis trembled as she saw his silver eyes flash red at the same time his lips turned black. It happened so fast that she wasn't sure she hadn't imagined it.

Then Acheron took possession of her mouth with a fury that was dizzying. She felt the power of him and it made her tremble. Her heart pounding, she surrendered herself to him. He pinned her to the wall behind her. His lips and tongue burned her, and let her know exactly how much he'd been withholding from her these months past.

This was a new side of her pet. And when he entered her, she almost passed out from the sheer pleasure of it.

He was as wild and untamed as a predator in the wild. The sound of his breath, punctuated by grunts of pleasure set fire to her soul. A laugh caught in her throat. Had she any idea he'd be like this, she would have given him this gift long ago.

Screaming out as her orgasm ripped through her, she dug her nails into his skin. But he didn't even pause as he delivered even deeper and harder strokes to her body. She wouldn't have thought it possible, but her pleasure increased as another orgasm exploded.

When he finally came, she was completely weak and sated. So much so that she realized she hadn't even fed from him.

Blessed Olympus, how could this be?

Effortlessly, Acheron swung her up in his arms and carried her back into her temple, to her bedroom.

"How can you even move after all that?" she asked breathlessly.

"Goddess, I could fly right now if you asked me to."

Laughing, Artemis lay weakly on her bed as her body still tingled from the memory of his.

Acheron lay beside her, then rained kisses over her lips and breasts.

She shook her head at him. "You are feisty this day."

Acheron paused at her words before he betrayed himself. He wasn't feisty. The truth was that her actions had made him fall in love with her all over again. He remembered now why he'd opened himself up to her. Artemis was kind when she chose to be.

If she didn't care for him, his wounds today wouldn't have mattered to her. Not even Estes had cared emotionally when he'd been harmed. Wounds only meant lost profits to him. But Artemis had been genuinely angry on his behalf.

He took her hand and led it to his lips so he could kiss the palm of her hand. "I am ever your servant, my goddess. I pledge myself to you forever."

She giggled. "My Acheron, you have no concept of forever."

"Then I pledge myself to you for the rest of my life."

She brushed the hair back from his face. "I accept that pledge . . . and that's the best one I've heard this day. Now come feed me. You've made me terribly hungry."

Acheron slid himself up her body and offered her his neck. At the twinge of pain, he remembered Styxx laying the brand over his skin.

Hissing, he pulled back instinctively. He felt his flesh tear as blood flowed freely from the wound. He tried to cover it, but the blood spurted between his fingers, coating them and staining the white linens under him.

Artemis sucked her breath in sharply as she realized what Acheron had done. His blood covered them both. She grabbed his neck and held him close while she healed the wound. He trembled against her.

"You should never do that, Acheron."

Now he'd be too weak for her. She bit back her anger. Normally she'd have punished him, but he'd been through enough. Cleaning him up, she laid him back against her bed to let him rest.

He tried to stay awake, but his eyes finally fluttered closed. Artemis stared at his naked beauty on her bed. His legs and arms were so long and graceful, so incredibly well formed. His stomach muscles were cut so deep that they looked chiseled. And as she remembered the way he'd made love to her, she grew hot all over again.

"You should always touch me like that."

If only he could hear her.

She reached to brush her hand through his hair and the instant her hand made contact, his hair turned jet black. She jerked back and watched as blue marbled itself over his skin.

Terrified, she scrambled from the bed. The number twenty-one wrote itself down his spine before the color faded and he returned to his normal state.

She frowned in confusion. Was this a reaction from her gift or her feeding from him? She'd never fed from a human before. Did they all do this?

Again she heard him whispering in Atlantean.

"It wasn't a happy anniversary. I want to come home now."

"Acheron?" She approached him slowly before she shook him awake.

He opened his eyes. Instead of silver, they were so black she couldn't even see the pupils. Then his eyes fluttered shut and he returned to sleep.

That was *not* normal. "What are you, Acheron?"

Every god power she possessed said he was human. But this wasn't typical of that species.

"Artemis!"

She jerked back and dressed herself as she heard Apollo's shout. Leaving Acheron to sleep in her bed, she materialized in the center of her greeting room where her brother stood with an angry sneer on his face.

"Is something wrong?"

"I. Need. Food."

She folded her arms over her chest. "Why are you so angry about it?"

"I wanted my human, but she's pregnant and can't suffer it."

"You have others."

"I don't want them." He grabbed her. The moment he did, he paused then smelled her hair. "You've been with a man?"

Her heart faltered. Unwilling to betray Acheron, she slapped Apollo's hand. "Why would you say such a thing?"

"There's a foreign scent on you. And it's masculine."

She rolled her eyes to cover the fear inside her. "I've been with humans all day, accepting their offerings. I must reek of their stench."

He fisted his hand in her hair. Artemis grimaced, finally understanding why Acheron found the gesture so offensive. Apollo wiped his finger behind her ear, then studied the digit. "Blood? Have you fed on another?"

She steeled herself and met his gaze levelly. "I didn't know when you'd be back and I was hungry."

His eyes sharpened. "Have you found yourself a male pet?"

She clawed at the hand he held in her hair. "You're my little brother, not my lover. Now release me or feel the full measure of my wrath."

He shoved her back. "You'd best remember who I am and who you are, sister." He curled his lip as if she suddenly disgusted him. "I'd rather feed from a servant."

Artemis didn't take another breath until he was gone. Her entire body was quaking from fear of his wrath.

The door to her room opened. She turned to see Acheron staring at her. He leaned against the door with one arm braced. The mixture of power and weakness was compelling. "I would fight him for you but for the dishonor you'd suffer."

Her heart was warmed by the thought. "You can never fight him, Acheron. You have no power to fight a god. He'd kill you and not blink." She closed the distance between them and wrapped her arm about his lean waist. "Come, my sweet. You need to rest."

But as she returned him to bed, the fear inside her built. Should Apollo ever learn about Acheron, no power on Olympus would be able to save his life.

August 25, 9528 BC

Acheron lay in his bed, missing Artemis. Holding her ring over his heart, he smiled at the memory of her last night. Over the past weeks she'd been so kind and giving to him. No one, not even his sister, had ever been more thoughtful.

Closing his eyes, he could see her running toward him in her garden, laughing. They spent hours hunting, in shooting practice or just lying together in her garden while he played for her and she read to him.

How he wished they could stay like that.

Unfortunately, she couldn't have the stain on her reputation and he understood it even though he hated it.

A knock sounded on his door.

Rolling over, he saw Ryssa push the door open. She closed the door carefully before rushing to him. She was amazingly agile given her distended stomach. "Are you coming?"

Now there was a question he wasn't used to hearing from his sister. "Where?"

"To Artemis's temple?"

Again, not a question he was used to hearing. "What are you talking about?"

"This is her feast day. There will be games and offerings in her temple all day long. Father's already sent his offering and is overseeing the others, but I thought you might be going too."

Not with his father. Was she insane? He'd been making it a point to avoid any contact whatsoever with him or Styxx.

Acheron shook his head. "I don't think I should."

She gaped at him. "Are you mad? Don't you think Artemis would be offended if someone close to her didn't show her *his* respect?"

252

Acheron frowned. Would she? Artemis could be temperamental that way.

I'll be in the temple all day, but I shall see you afterward. I wish I didn't have to wait so long to see you.

Could that have been a veiled invitation?

No, Artie was anything but subtle.

"I don't have an offering."

Ryssa shoved at his shoulder. "Make one of the heart. It won't matter to her what it is. But you have to show your appreciation of the gods, Acheron. It's unwise not to honor them, especially when one has been shown a degree of favoritism." She smiled at him. "Now get yourself dressed. I have to go and can't wait for you. But I'll watch for you at the temple—don't be long."

Acheron didn't move from bed until Ryssa had left him. He still wasn't sure this was the best idea. But so long as he kept his presence veiled, there shouldn't be any harm. He could just go, make an offering and leave.

No one, other than Artemis, would even know he'd been there. And if that would please her . . .

How could he not honor her on her feast day after all she'd given him? He wanted her to know how much he loved her. Wanted her to see that he was willing to risk his life for her.

The very thought of making her happy brought a smile to his face. Getting out of bed, he tried to think of what Artemis might enjoy. She liked to hear him play and she loved his body and blood. But those would make her angry should he make a public offering of them . . .

White rose petals—for her purity and grace. And pearls. The goddess loved pearls. She'd even taken him pearl diving.

That was it, it would make a perfect gift to show her how pure his love and admiration for her was.

He dressed quickly, then headed to the market to buy what he needed.

By noon, he was at her temple which was crowded with people. Nobles and officials had a separate entrance where their offerings were blessed by the priests. Even though he technically qualified, Acheron stayed in the common line. He didn't want to do anything to draw attention to himself or risk angering his father who sat on a throne just right of Artemis's statue, watching the people. Apollo, Styxx and Ryssa were with him.

Warily, Acheron kept glancing up, hoping to the gods that his father wouldn't see him. He would make his offering quickly and be gone.

No one would know.

Keeping his face covered, he handed his gifts to the priest so that he could place them on the altar.

"What is it you ask of the goddess, paidi?"

Acheron shook his head. "Nothing, papas. I only offer her my respect and love."

The priest nodded in approval before he took the small bowl of rose petals and pearls. As Acheron stepped away, someone in the crowd shoved him and he staggered into a woman holding a baby. She cried out as she lost her balance and her grip.

Acheron froze as he realized the baby would hit the floor unless he let go of his cloak to catch it. If he did that, he'd be exposed and as close as he was to his father, there was no way he'd escape notice.

But there was no choice.

He caught the infant to his chest as the mother fell. Reaching out to save herself, she grabbed his cloak and jerked it free.

Acheron winced as all attention turned to him. He'd always hated this attention and if he could, he'd make himself invisible. But there was no escaping this.

Roaring in anger, his father shot to his feet.

Sick to his stomach, Acheron helped the woman up and returned the baby to her.

She was sobbing in relief. "Thank you so much for your kindness. Bless you for saving my son."

"Take him!" his father ordered the guards.

Acheron met Ryssa's gaze and saw his own horror mirrored in his sister's face as the guards grabbed his arms and hauled him to their king. The thought of fighting crossed his mind, but what was the use? They were only doing what they were told. Besides the crowd around them was tight and innocent people would be hurt if he did.

He met his father's fury without flinching.

"How dare you defile this temple!" He turned to the guards. "Lock him in his quarters until I'm finished here."

Acheron smirked. Such a sweet promise from the lips of his father. He couldn't wait until nightfall.

For the first time, Acheron looked at Apollo whose derision for him was tangible. If the god only knew the truth . . .

Drawing a ragged breath, he watched the priests remove his offering from the altar as he was hauled from the temple.

Artemis *looked up* from her kithara as Apollo manifested in her greeting room. She'd been trying to play it the way Acheron did, but she had no talent for music. Her frustration was already taut and her brother's presence did little to alleviate that. "What are you doing here?"

He smirked. "Why weren't you at Didymos today?"

"You said you were going in my stead. I didn't see the point in both of us being there." But the truth was she didn't want to be around Acheron's family. They all disgusted her. Had she gone, Styxx would have had a lot more than just a stomach illness visited on him. Of course that might alert her brother about her feelings for Acheron so she thought it best that she just stay away from them. "Why? Did I miss something?"

He threw a beautiful strand of pearls at her. They were covered in white rose petals. Artemis frowned as she reached for them. "What is this?"

"The Prince Whore brought those to you."

Her heart ceased beating. "Excuse me?"

"It was entertaining really. He came in with the rest of the filth and after he handed those over by saying he asked nothing of you in return for his gift, he was exposed. Last I heard, they were going to make him pay for defiling you."

It took every piece of control she had not to betray their relationship. But in truth, her throat burned with tears for her Acheron . . . and bitter anger that they would hurt him again. She wanted to kiss the pearls that he'd given her because she knew that unlike the other tributes, his had truly come from his heart. More than that, she wanted to go to Acheron and help him.

If only she could.

Steadying herself, she threw the pearls down. "Why would you bring these to me?"

"I thought you should know that a whore breached your temple. Zeus knows, I wouldn't tolerate such a person in mine. Shall we go exact our own revenge on the whore?"

She returned to strumming her kithara. "He's not worth my time."

"Since when do you not have time for vengeance?"

"Since I'd rather stay here and play. Now go and visit one of your pets. I can't be bothered with you."

"Suit yourself."

Artemis didn't move until after he'd left her. The moment he did, she held her hand out for the pearls. They flew into her hand. Rubbing them against her heart, she went to see if she could help Acheron.

Acheron stood in the courtyard with his hands tied above his head. His lips and nose were already bleeding from the hits Styxx had gleefully rained down on him.

He spat blood on the ground before he narrowed a murderous glare at his brother. "Shouldn't you be at the temple still?"

Styxx backhanded him so hard his ears rang.

Acheron laughed at the pathetic slap. "You hit like an old woman."

Styxx stepped forward but was stopped by their father who entered through the doors. The look on his face was one of supreme disgust.

Acheron sighed. "I know I shouldn't have gone. Could we just start the beating, finish it and let me go back to my room?"

His father narrowed his eyes. "Why are so eager to be beaten?"

"It's the only attention I get from you, Father. As with Estes. So let the blows commence."

His father dug his fingers into his face as hatred blazed in his blue eyes. "I've told you not to mention my brother's name from your foul mouth." His gaze dipped down to the necklace Acheron wore.

Acheron held his breath as he realized he'd forgotten to remove Artemis's gift before he went to her temple. His heart stilled and for the first time he tasted fear as his father released his face and plucked it up to examine it.

"What's this?"

Acheron forced himself to remain calm and nonchalant. "A trinket I bought."

Styxx peered at it over his father's shoulder. "It's the same ring Artemis's priests wear to summon her." His features hardened. "You stole it!"

His father snatched it from his neck, causing the chain to cut into his skin before it broke. "Do you think the gods give a damn about you?"

Not as a rule, but Artemis did.

Styxx took the ring and grabbed a ladle of water. "We should teach the thief a lesson." Before Acheron could move, Styxx shoved the ring into Acheron's mouth and poured water into it, forcing him to swallow it.

Tears gathered in Acheron's eyes as the ring scraped his throat and burned. He choked on it and the water, but Styxx didn't let up until he was satisfied the ring was completely swallowed.

Acheron coughed and sputtered, trying to catch his breath.

Styxx wrenched his hair. "A whore has dishonored our beloved virgin goddess on her feast day. I think he should be publicly gelded."

Acheron's eyes widened at the punishment.

His father laughed approvingly before he cut him down. "It would please Artemis I think."

Acheron tried to run, but his father caught him and knocked him to the ground.

"Tell me why you came to the temple," his father demanded.

Acheron pushed himself up to find Ryssa joining them. His father struck him again and spun him around so that he could pin Acheron to the wall with his forearm held across Acheron's throat.

"Explain yourself, whore. What made you venture to the temple?"

Ryssa ran to Acheron. "Tell them. You must."

Fear gripped him as he shook his head at her.

"Tell us what?" the king demanded.

"Don't, Ryssa," Acheron whispered from his pinched throat as he tried to push his father's arm away. "I beg you. If you love me even a little, don't betray me."

"They're going to geld you. If they know the truth, they'll leave you alone."

"I don't care."

Ryssa pulled their father away from him. "Father stop! He's innocent. He's with Artemis. Tell him, Acheron! For the sake of the gods, tell him the truth so he'll stop this beating."

His father knocked him to the ground. He then kicked him onto his back and pressed his foot to Acheron's throat to the point bile rose to choke him. "What lies have you told her, maggot?"

Acheron tried to push the foot away, but his father pressed it even harder against his windpipe. Speaking was all but impossible. "Nothing, p-p-please . . ."

"Blasphemer." His father stepped back then and left Acheron to strangle as he tried desperately to breathe through his bruised esophagus. "Strip him and drag him to Artemis's temple. Let the goddess witness his punishment and if he really was with her, then I'm sure she'll come to his defense." He'd turned a smug look at Ryssa.

The guards moved forward, but Ryssa put herself in front of him. The only way to get to him would be to harm her and possibly the baby she carried. "Father, you can't."

"This doesn't concern you."

"If you hurt Acheron, Artemis will unleash untold horrors on you."

Their father laughed. "Are you insane?"

"No, Ryssa, please stop!" Acheron begged. "Don't!"

"Acheron is her consort."

Acheron couldn't breathe as those words rang in his ears . . . Ryssa had betrayed him. But in her world the gods protected their pets. She had no reason to think that Artemis wouldn't come to save him the way Apollo would save her. Too bad Artemis was not her brother. Closing his eyes, he wished himself dead.

When he opened them, he saw an outline of Artemis in the shadows. She was holding his pearls.

His father's laughter mixed with Styxx's. "You are Artemis's consort?"

Acheron couldn't respond as he saw the look of horror etched on Artemis's face. It faded beneath a look of anger so palpable it singed him.

His father sneered. "Do you really expect me to believe a goddess would have anything to do with you?"

Acheron couldn't speak. He couldn't even deny it. Artemis had frozen his vocal chords.

She thinks I told him . . .

Acheron shook his head at her, trying to make her understand that he hadn't told anyone.

His father seized him by the throat again. "Fine. Let's see what the goddess thinks of you." He turned to the guards. "Take him to Artemis's temple." He sneered at Acheron. "If you mean so much to the goddess, surely she'll come save you. If not, we'll show the world what we do to blasphemous whores. Beat him at the altar until Artemis shows herself."

"No!" Ryssa shrieked.

It was too late. Completely naked, Acheron was dragged unceremoniously out of the palace and through the crowded streets.

His body was bloody before he ever reached the temple. Everyone parted as the guards hauled him to the altar and strung him up between two columns.

"What is this?" the head priest demanded.

"By the king's orders, the blasphemer is to be punished until the goddess is appeased. He's to be beaten on her behalf until she shows herself to stop it."

Acheron met Artemis's gaze and the satisfaction in those green eyes scorched him.

"I told you what would happen if you betrayed me." Her voice whispered through his head.

He choked on his tears as the first lash sliced through his back. "I didn't betray you," he whispered. "I swear it."

Artemis moved forward and struck him across the face with the pearls he'd given her. "Beat him harder," she whispered to his punisher. "Make him feel every lash."

Acheron cried out as the lashes cut ever deeper.

The crowd cheered his beating. Repressed memories tore through him even sharper than the lashes. He was again in Estes's home, surrounded by people, pulling at him, grabbing him, calling for his submission and humiliation. How many times had he been jeered at? Laughed at and mocked?

"Beg me for mercy, whore . . ." His uncle's voice was loud and clear.

Acheron locked gaze with Artemis. How could she do this to him? How?

Artemis inwardly flinched at the torment and pain in those swirling silver eyes. They accused her as if she were in the wrong. She'd warned him what would happen if he told anyone. Did he think for one minute that she'd been joking?

"I gave you everything," she growled at him, making sure that only Acheron could see or hear her. "Everything!"

He lowered his head before he whispered in the lowest of tones. "I loved you."

Artemis shrieked in outrage that he'd dare say that to her after what he'd done this day. If anyone found out that she'd allowed him to touch her, she'd be ruined. Did he think his paltry love would ease her humiliation? Her ruination? Was it love to drag her down to be ridiculed alongside him?

"Hit harder!" she urged the guard. "I want his blood covering the floor of my temple."

That would teach him!

"You are nothing to me, human," she sneered in his ear. "Nothing."

Acheron let his tears flow as Artemis abandoned him. There was no need to beg for her forgiveness or mercy when it was obvious she had none where he was concerned. More than that, he felt her rip away his ability to fight. She took everything from him.

Unable to bear the pain, he surrendered himself to unconsciousness. But it was short-lived as they revived him to beat him more.

One his third session, he opened his eyes to find his father and Styxx standing in front of him. "Where's your goddess, maggot?"

He looked to Ryssa whose face was pale and drawn. He saw the guilt in her gaze as tears streamed down her cheeks.

"I have no goddess." He had no one and he knew it. "Just geld me and get it over with."

But they didn't. Instead they beat him until he lost count of the lashes. Drifting in and out of consciousness, he wasn't sure when the beating finally stopped. He could feel nothing but the searing pain on his back.

Still there was no mercy for him. They left him tied before the altar where the crowd could add their own blows to him in defense of their beloved goddess.

For three days, Acheron hung there with no food or comfort. The closest he had was to see Merus approach him.

The boy stopped before him with a frown. "I thought you were a nobleman. You lied to us." His eyes angry, he picked up a rock from the floor and threw it at Acheron. It caught him on the chest.

Leaning his head back, Acheron stared up at the gilded ceiling. "Why!" he shouted at the gods. Why had they done this to him? Why was this his fate?

He'd been born a prince. He should be honored as such and instead, he was nothing. Surely he must be cursed. There was no other reason for this life. No reason for his suffering. And in that instant he hated everything on this planet. Everyone.

With a battle cry born of desperation and torment, he fought against his chains. But there was no one to care and no way to break free. All he succeeded in doing was re-opening the wounds on his back and making new ones on his wrists. In the end, it only hurt him more.

So he stayed until the evening of the third day. The guards returned to free him, but before they did, his head was shaved and Artemis's double bow symbol was branded into his skull.

Acheron laughed at the irony. Her name had been branded into his heart before this and now he publicly wore the symbol of a goddess who would never again acknowledge him. The cruelty of it was unbearable.

Once they were finished, he was taken out to the street where a horse waited. His hands were tied in front of him so that the horse could drag him all the back to the palace. By the time he reached it, there was little to no skin left on his body.

Barely conscious, he was taken to his room and thrown inside it. Acheron took one step and fell to his knees. Too weak to move, he sprawled across the floor. But at least the stone was cool against his wounds, even though it made them throb.

There would be no Artemis to help him this time. No goddess to offer him succor or refuge.

"You are nothing to me, human." Those words would be forever etched in his heart.

So be it.

Closing his eyes, he had no hope for the future. No will to ever recover or move forward. His sister and his lover had shattered him for the last time. There were some betrayals no amount of apology could rectify and this time, Acheron had hit his limit.

There was nothing more they could do to hurt him. Soul sick, he crawled deep inside himself and swore that he'd never again open himself up to anyone.

September 2, 9528 BC

Artemis sat alone on her chaise, wanting to weep. Apollo had told every god on Olympus about Acheron and his claim to be her consort.

They'd all been laughing at her ever since.

"You should gut him on the floor of your temple," Zeus had said to her last night while she was visiting his hall.

Apollo had scoffed. "Can't. His life is tied to his twin brother and they both die which would ruin my fun for a while. But it's hysterical what lies these humans tell."

Aphrodite had rolled her eyes. "I can't imagine a whore thinking he could claim a relationship with Artemis of all the gods. Has anyone checked his mental state?"

"He's definitely insane," Apollo had said. "I knew it the first time I saw him."

After that, Artemis hadn't gone near any of the others. But even worse than their laughter was the sick lump in her stomach over the pain she knew Acheron was in.

He deserves it.

It was true. His betrayal deserved a painful death and yet all she wanted to do was hold him. She missed the way he made her feel. The taste of his lips . . .

When he was with her, she smiled all the time. There was something about him that made her happy. Nothing else really mattered except the two of them.

He betrayed you.

That was something she couldn't forgive. He'd made her a laughingstock. The only saving grace was the fact that none of the others believed his claims.

Yet even so, all she wanted was to go to him . . .

A*rtemis, I summon* you to human form." Ryssa held her breath inside Artemis's temple, afraid the goddess would ignore her. She glanced about, making sure again that she was all alone. "Goddess, please hear my call and come to me. I need to see you."

A shimmery haze appeared to the right of the altar. Ryssa smiled as the mist thickened to form an incredibly beautiful redhead. Artemis's features were very similar to Apollo's, except the goddess's face was more finely boned.

"What do you want, human?"

"I'm here on behalf of Acheron."

Artemis's eyes flamed with anger. "I know no one by that name." She began to fade.

"No please . . . It wasn't his fault. He didn't tell anyone. I did."

Artemis rematerialized as those words ripped through her. She glared at the petite blond beauty who carried her brother's child. "What?"

Ryssa took a step forward, her eyes shimmering with unshed tears. "Acheron has never once breathed a word about you to anyone, not even me. I saw the bite wound on his neck and I knew it had to be you. Please, if I was wrong, then forgive me. But if I'm right, I didn't want you to be angry at him for something he didn't do."

Artemis glared at her swollen stomach. "You better be glad you carry my brother's son. It's the only reason you're still alive. You ever link my name to Acheron's again and by the River Styx I will have your hide mounted on my temple wall."

Artemis flashed herself away, but she stopped herself before she returned to Olympus. In truth, her heart was singing over the fact that he hadn't betrayed her. Her Acheron had been true . . .

Relieved, she went to see him.

Naked, he was lying on the floor of his room in front of his bed. She frowned at the sight of his bald head and the savage wounds that were still carved all over his body. But the one that appeared most painful was her own symbol that was still raw on the back of his skull.

"Acheron?"

He opened his eyes, but didn't speak.

She reached to heal him. Before she could touch him, he caught her wrist in his hand. His grip surprised her. She wouldn't have thought he'd have such strength in this condition. "I want nothing from you."

"I thought you'd betrayed me."

"I don't break my word, Artemis. Ever."

"How was I to know?"

He laughed bitterly. "What? You think a few lashes are enough to break me? You're a goddess. How can you know so little?"

"You have no idea how hard it is to be a god. The sniveling voices that are always crying out for help for the smallest things. 'I want a new pair of shoes. I want more grain at harvest.' You learn to turn it off."

"Those things may be petty to you, but to some humans even something as innocuous as one moment of peace can make all the difference in a life. One smile. One tiny act of kindness. That's all it takes for us."

"Well, I'm here with my kindness."

Acheron scoffed. "I'm tired of being your pet, Artemis. I've nothing left inside to give you."

His anger ignited her own. "You are a human. You don't order me about."

Acheron sighed. She was right. Who was he, a worthless maggot, to say anything to her? Besides, he was in no condition to argue with anyone. "Forgive me, akra. I forgot my place."

She smiled and brushed a hand over his bald head. "That's the Acheron I know."

No, it wasn't. This was the Acheron who was bought and sold. The hollowed out shell who performed for the amusement of others, but who felt nothing inside. How pathetic that his heart meant so little to anyone, that she couldn't even recognize the fact that it was missing.

Releasing her hand, he lay still as she healed him. For once he tolerated the pain.

Once done, she sat back to look at her handiwork and then grimaced. "Oh, this baldness has to go. I like your hair too much."

It grew in perfectly and still Acheron didn't move.

In a tiff, Artemis folded her arms over her chest. "Can you not at least say thank you to me for healing you?"

Given the fact that she was the reason he was beaten so badly, the mere thought of thanking her stuck in his throat. But then he was used to such things as this. "Thank you, akra."

Like a child who was unaware she'd broken her favorite toy, she smiled in satisfaction. "We should hunt today."

Acheron didn't speak as she took him to her private forest and dressed him in red as if he was her doll and not a flesh and blood man. Her face was bright as she handed him a bow and quiver. He slung the quiver over his back without comment and followed her as she headed off in search of deer.

She chattered away about nothing in particular while he did as she asked, and tried his damnedest not to feel anything at all.

"You're being awfully quiet," she said once she realized he wasn't participating in her conversation.

"Forgive me, akra. What would you like me to say?"

"Whatever's on your mind."

"There's nothing on my mind."

She huffed at him. "Nothing? You have no thoughts whatsoever?"

He shook his head.

"How can this be?" She stuck her bottom lip out petulantly. "You're trying to punish me, aren't you?"

He kept all emotion out of his voice, especially the anger he bore her. "I would never seek to punish you, Goddess. It's not my place."

She grabbed him by his hair, making him grimace before she forced him to meet her gaze. "What is wrong with you?"

Acheron took a deep breath as he braced himself for what was to come. One thing he'd learned while living with his uncle, lust overrode anger. She might still beat him later, but if he pleased her enough the punishment wouldn't be as severe.

Stepping closer, he kissed her.

Sure enough, she loosened the grip in his hair and melted in his arms. Strange, he felt more like a whore in this moment than he'd ever felt before and he didn't understand why.

Perhaps because he shouldn't have to use his body to bargain with someone he'd given his heart to. Yet here he was, using his touch to lighten her anger . . . as always.

Disgusted with himself, he offered her his neck and died the death of a coward as she took it.

But what else could he do? It was either fuck or be beaten. Though to be honest, he could no longer tell which of the two was the most painful for him. One left scars on his body.

The other scarred his soul.

September 14, 9528 BC

Acheron sat on the railing of his balcony, drinking. He was mystified at how Artemis had managed to make him feel so unclean and yet as the days passed by he felt more and more like what his uncle had made him.

"Brother?"

He leaned his head back to see Ryssa approaching him. "Yes?"

"I'm sorry to bother you, but I'm in so much pain from the baby. Could you please do that thing you do that makes me feel better?"

He snorted at words that could so easily be misconstrued. Thank the gods his father hadn't heard it. "It's called a massage."

"Can you do it?"

"Sure." Like everything else, he'd been well schooled in every muscle of the human body and taught how to loosen and please it. Sliding off the railing, he had her sit down on the floor and lean forward so that he could ease the tension in her back.

"Mmm," she breathed. "That is the most magical thing you do."

Not really. He was just glad to be able to use it on someone who wasn't going to turn around and start humping him over it. "You're really tense."

"I can't get comfortable. I'm aching all over."

"Just breathe then. I'll get the knots out and you'll feel a lot better." He went down to the pressure point and dug his nail in.

Ryssa let out a satisfied moan. "How do you do that?"

"A lot of practice." And a lot of beatings anytime he'd messed up.

"I swear we should bronze your hands."

Most people felt that way, but for many other reasons.

She glanced at him over her shoulder. "Are you planning to stay hidden until your hair grows back?"

Acheron paused as pain cut through him at the reminder. The only time he had hair was whenever Artemis showed up—even though she was the cause of it she hated the sight of him like this. The moment she left him, his hair returned to its real state.

"I have no reason to leave. Period."

"I thought you enjoyed going to plays. Yet you haven't been in ever so long."

Not even they could ease the pain he felt inside. The betrayal. If anything, watching the plays made him even more morose. "I'd just rather stay in my room, Ryssa."

She opened her mouth to speak, but her words died underneath a sharp cry of pain.

"Ryssa?"

"It's the baby . . . he's coming!"

Acheron's heart pounded as he rose to his feet, then swept her up in his arms. He carried her to her room before he left to find her maids so that they could summon the midwives and his father.

"Acheron," she called as he started to withdraw. "Please, don't leave me. I'm scared. I know you can make the pain less. Please . . ."

"Father will beat me if I stay."

She screamed out as another contraction seized her.

Unable to leave her like that, he went to the bed and started massaging her again. "Breathe, Ryssa," he said in a calm tone, applying a counter pressure where she was tense.

"What is this?"

He cringed at his father's snarling voice. Ryssa turned to look at him. "Father, please. Acheron can help with the pain."

His father shoved him aside. "Get out."

Acheron didn't speak as he obeyed. He passed Styxx and a line of senators in the hallway who were coming in to witness the culmination of his sister's union with Apollo. Several of them sneered at him and made comments under their breath. A couple even made offers.

He ignored them and kept going to his room. Then he locked his doors to make sure no one followed him inside.

Wishing he could have helped his sister, he sat in his room and listened to her screams, sobs and cries that went on for hours. Gods, if this was childbirth it was a miracle any woman would endure it.

Why would they?

And yet having endured something so horrifically painful, how could a mother shun the very child she'd fought so hard, and suffered so long, to birth?

He struggled to recall his mother's face. All he could really remember was the look of hatred in her blue eyes. *"You're disgusting."* Every time he'd ever gone near her, she'd slapped him away.

But not all mothers were like that. He'd seen them in the market and in the stands during the plays. Mothers who held their children with love—like the one he'd stumbled into in Artemis's temple. Her baby had meant everything to her.

Acheron brushed the back of his fingers against his own cheek. Closing his eyes, he pretended it was a mother's gentle touch, that a woman was touching him so sweetly. Then he scoffed at his own stupidity. Who needed tenderness? All he had to do was walk near any human being and he'd have all the caresses he wanted.

But they were never loving and they never came without conditions and cost.

"It's a boy!" His father's shout was muffled through the walls and was followed by a massive shout that echoed.

Acheron smiled, happy for his sister. She'd given Apollo a son. Unlike their mother, she'd be honored for her labor.

Hours went by as he waited until he was sure everyone had left her.

Acheron headed to her room, but was stopped by the guards outside.

"We were told to keep you away. Under no circumstances are you allowed in to see the princess."

How stupid of him to think otherwise. Without a word, Acheron returned to his room. With nothing else to do, he took himself to bed.

"Acheron?"

He jerked awake at the whispered call. Opening his eyes, he found Ryssa kneeling beside him. "What are you doing here?"

"I heard them turn you away, so I waited until I was free to come to you." She held a small bundle up for his inspection. "Meet my son, Apollodorus."

A smile curved his lips as he saw the tiny infant. He had a wealth of black hair and deep blue eyes. "He's beautiful."

Ryssa returned his smile before she set the baby in his hands.

"I can't, Ryssa. I might hurt him."

"You're not going to hurt him, Acheron." She showed him how to support his head.

Amazed, Acheron couldn't believe the love he felt inside him that swelled up.

Ryssa smiled. "He likes you. He's been fussing all night with me and the nurses, but look how quiet he is for you."

It was true. The babe gave one tiny sigh, then went to sleep. Acheron laughed as he examined the tiny fingers that didn't even seem real. "Are you all right?"

"Sore and very tired. But I couldn't sleep until I saw you. I love you, Acheron."

"I love you, too." Reluctantly, he held Apollodorus out to her. "You'd best go before you're caught. Father would be extremely angry at us both."

Nodding, she took the baby and left him.

Still the scent of the baby stayed with him, as did the image of innocence. It was hard to believe he'd ever been so small and even harder to believe he'd survived given the animosity his family bore him.

As he tried to return to sleep he wondered what it would be like to have a woman hold a child of his with such love and pride. Imagine a woman's face so joyful because she'd borne a part of him . . .

But it would never happen. His uncle's physicians had seen to that. His cock jerked at the memory of their surgery.

It's for the best.

As bad as it was for the rest of the world to hate him, he could imagine nothing worse than to see his child despising him. To have his own child deny him.

Of course, if he had one, he would never give it cause to hate him. He'd hold it and love it no matter what.

Go to sleep, Acheron. Just forget everything.

Closing his eyes, he let out a tired breath and tried to sleep again.

"What are you doing?"

He opened his eyes to find Artemis in his bed, beside him. "I was trying to sleep."

"Ah . . . Did you hear about our nephew?"

"I did. Ryssa was just here with him."

She wrinkled her face up. "Don't you find babies nasty and disgusting?"

"No. I thought him beautiful."

She scoffed. "You would. I think they're smelly and fussing. Never content. Always demanding. Yuck, I can't imagine going through all that to have something so nasty clinging to me."

Acheron rolled his eyes as he imagined all the poor infants that were given to Artemis. Obviously she gave their care over to someone much more maternal. "I'm thinking the Greeks should have learned this about you before they declared you the goddess of childbirth."

"Well, that's because I helped my mother give birth to Apollo. That was different." She reached down to cup him softly in her hand. "What have I here?"

"If you don't know by now, Artie, no amount of explaining is going to help."

She laughed deep in her throat as his cock hardened even more. "I was hoping to find you still awake."

Acheron didn't comment as she dipped her head down to take him into her mouth. He stared up at the ceiling while she tongued him. It would probably be more pleasurable if he didn't have to make sure to keep himself in check. But he knew better than to come with her like this. She liked the taste of him, but she didn't like it when he released anywhere except inside her.

Even then she only tolerated it.

He jerked as she nipped him hard enough to hurt. She curled her fingers in the hair around his cock. Sighing, Acheron wished he could go back to the beginning of their relationship. Back to when this had meant so much more than just her sucking on him.

She gave one long lick before she pulled back. He expected her to return to his lips. Instead she sank her teeth into his upper thigh, barely two inches from his sac.

Yelping from the pain, he had to force himself not to push her away and hurt himself even more.

The pain quickly passed into a wave of extreme pleasure. But she didn't allow him to come yet. "I want you deep inside me, Acheron."

Rolling her over onto her stomach, he propped her hips up on his pillows and obliged her request. He held her hips in his hands and buried himself deep inside her. He thrust against her until she'd had enough orgasms that she begged him to stop. Rolling over onto her back, she laughed in satisfaction.

Artemis sighed contentedly until she realized he was still hard. "Why didn't you finish?"

Acheron shrugged. "You were done."

"But you weren't."

"I'll live."

She let out a sound of disgust. "Acheron? What is wrong with you lately?"

Acheron clenched his teeth, knowing better than to answer her question. She didn't want to hear anything other than how wonderful she was. "I don't want to fight, Artemis. What difference does it make? You were pleased, weren't you?"

"Yes."

"Then all is right in the world."

She propped herself up on one arm to stare down at him as he lay beside her. "I really don't understand you."

"I'm really not complicated." All he asked for was the two things she couldn't give him.

Love and respect.

She dragged one long nail around his neck. "Where's my ring that I gave you?"

Acheron flinched at the memory of being forced to swallow it. "It was lost."

"How could you be so callous?"

Him callous? At least he hadn't thrown her gift back in her face and then had her beaten for it. "Where are the pearls I gave you?"

Her face turned red. "Fine. I'll get you another one."

"Don't. I don't need one."

Her eyes darkened angrily. "Are you shunning my gift?"

As if he'd ever take another gift like that from her. He'd had enough abuse. "I'm not shunning anything. I just don't want to take a chance on shaming you. Given everything that has happened, I really don't think it's wise I have something that is so clearly yours."

"That's a good point." She smiled at him. "You are ever loyal to me, aren't you?"

"Yes."

She kissed his cheek. "I'd best go now. Goodnight."

After she was gone, Acheron rolled over onto his back. Closing his eyes, he let his thoughts drift. In his mind he pictured a woman with kind eyes. One who held his hand in public, who was proud to be with him.

He imagined how her hair might smell, how her eyes would light up every time she glanced at him. The smiles they would share. Then he imagined her kissing her way down his body, imagined her looking up at him as she went down on him.

His breathing ragged, he thrust himself against his hand, pretending it was her he made love to.

"I love you, Acheron . . ." He could hear her voice so sweet and calm . . . most of all, it would be sincere.

He gasped as his warm seed coated his hand and seeped between his fingers and not inside a woman who loved him.

Shuddering and only partially sated, he opened his eyes to the harsh reality of his life.

He was alone.

And no woman, mortal or otherwise, would ever willingly claim him.

October 23, 9528 BC

Acheron rolled over in bed, trying to sleep. Apollodorus was screaming so loudly that it echoed all the way down to *his* room. For hours the baby had cried.

He wasn't supposed to go near the infant, yet he couldn't stand the sound of so much anger and unhappiness. Unable to tolerate another minute of it, he got out of bed and dressed.

Quietly, he walked down the hallway to Ryssa's room, making sure no one saw him. He cracked open the door to find Ryssa and her nurse in the room, swapping the baby between them.

"Why is he doing this?" Ryssa asked in a voice that sounded as if she were about to cry herself.

"I don't know, Highness. Sometimes babies cry for no reason."

Ryssa shook her head at the baby the nurse was rocking in her arms. "Please, child, have mercy on your mother and rest. I can't take much more of it."

Acheron slipped into the room. "I'll take him."

The nurse's face paled as she turned away.

"It's all right, Delia. Let Acheron see if he can quiet him."

The nurse appeared dubious, but in the end she obeyed.

Acheron took his nephew and tucked him into the crook of his elbow. "Hello, little one. You're not going to fuss at me, are you?"

Apollodorus took a deep breath as if he were about to let loose another wail, then opened his eyes. He stared at Acheron for several heartbeats before he quietly cooed, then settled down to sleep.

275

"*That* is a miracle," the nurse breathed. "What did you do?"

Acheron shrugged as he placed Apollodorus on his shoulder.

Ryssa smiled. "That's it. I'm making you his nurse."

Acheron laughed at the thought of him as a nurse to anything. "Go to bed, sister, you look exhausted."

Nodding gratefully, she started off. The nurse held her hands up for the baby.

Acheron handed him back, but the instant Apollodorus left his arms, the baby woke up and screamed again.

Ryssa jumped. "For the love of the gods, let Acheron keep the boy. I can't take another hour of this."

The nurse obeyed instantly.

Again Apollodorus cuddled against Acheron and went to sleep.

"Where should I take him?" Acheron asked.

Ryssa paused. "You better not risk the nursery. Father or Styxx might venture there. Take him to your room." She looked at her nurse. "You go to the nursery and cover for us should they ask after him."

"Yes, Your Highness." She bowed and left them.

Ryssa patted his arm gratefully. "Wake me when he's ready to feed. In the meantime, I must sleep."

Acheron kissed her lightly on the cheek. "Rest. We'll be back when he needs you." He watched her climb into bed before he took his nephew down to his room.

"Well, it appears to be just the two of us, little one. What say you we get naked, drunk and find us some wenches?"

The baby actually smiled up at him as if he understood.

Acheron nodded. "So that's it, eh? Barely a month old and you're already lecherous. You are your father's son."

Sitting on the bed, he leaned his back against the headboard and lifted his knees so that he could lay Apollodorus against his legs to cradle him. Acheron tickled his belly, causing him to laugh and kick Acheron's stomach.

The tiny infant amazed him. He'd never really been around one before. Apollodorus took his finger into his tiny hand and led it to his mouth so that he could suckle Acheron's knuckle. The sensation of the toothless gums against his flesh was so strange, yet it pacified the baby even more.

How could anyone hate something so purely innocent? Something so helpless?

The thoughts chased themselves around his mind as he thought about his parents and tried to understand them. He could fathom some of his father's hatred now. It wasn't as though Acheron went out of his way to please the man.

But as a child . . .

How many times had he been slapped for nothing more than looking at someone? How many times had Estes tied his hands behind his back and put a scold in his mouth for asking a simple question?

But worse than his memories were the fears of someone hurting this babe in such a manner.

"I would kill anyone who hurt you like that, Apollodorus. I promise you, no one will ever make you cry."

The baby yawned and smiled before he closed his eyes. Still holding Acheron's finger, he fell asleep. Warmth spread through Acheron. There was no judgment or anger in the baby. He accepted him without malice.

Smiling, he placed the baby down on his bed to sleep more comfortably and covered him with a blanket.

Acheron lay for hours, watching him sleep in perfect repose. Exhausted himself, he finally nodded off.

"Acheron?"

Acheron woke up to find Ryssa standing in front of him. He was lying on his side with his hand still on Apollodorus's stomach. The baby had yet to waken, but by the rise and fall of the tiny chest, he knew the baby was fine.

"What time is it?"

"Midmorning." She looked incredulous. "How did you get him to sleep through the night?"

"I don't know. We were talking about wenching and he fell asleep."

She laughed. "No, you weren't. Were you?"

"I suggested it and he liked the thought. Unfortunately, he had no stamina for it."

She laughed again. "Don't you dare corrupt my baby, scamp."

Acheron withdrew his hand so that Ryssa could pick the baby up. Apollodorus opened his eyes and smiled at his mother before he put one fist in his mouth to slurp it.

"Whatever you did, bless you for it. It's the first good sleep I've had in months." She glanced to the door. "Now, let me run before Father learns we were here."

Please. That was the last thing he needed.

Stretching, Acheron sat up in bed. It was later than he normally rose. He preferred to get up before the rest of the household and tend his needs without fear of running into anyone.

That being said, it was late enough that everyone should now be about their business.

He grabbed his clothes and razor and headed down to the bathing room. Luckily the large room was empty. As always, he placed his razor by the basin on the wall and hung up his clothes.

Naked, he descended to the steps to take him into the heated water that felt incredible against his skin. The pool was waist deep unless he sat in it and as large as a dining table. Acheron went down on his knees and leaned back to wet his cropped hair so that he could wash it. Closing his eyes, he sighed contentedly. This was the best part of his day.

He rose up and reached for the soap, then froze as he realized he was no longer alone.

Nefertari was there, staring at him with a heated look he knew all too well.

Acheron withdrew his hand and stepped back in the pond. "Forgive me, my lady. I didn't mean to intrude on your time."

She watched him like a cat eyeing a mouse and when he reached for a towel, she stopped him. "How is it you're so much more handsome than your twin brother?" She pulled the pin from her gown and let it fall to her feet. Her nude body was beautiful, but he wanted no part of it.

Acheron bolted from the pool, but she blocked his way to the door. "I need to leave."

Laughing, she wrapped herself around him. "No, you don't." She nipped his chin with her teeth.

"I'm involved with someone."

"So am I."

Acheron tried to pry her loose but short of hurting her, there wasn't much he could do as she grabbed at him. Wrenching himself from her grasp, he started away only to step on the soap where he'd left it by the pool. He hit the ground hard enough to knock the breath out of him.

Nefertari was on him in an instant. "Make love to me, Acheron."

He rolled over with her, and just as he was rising, the door swung open.

The blood drained completely out his face as he saw Styxx and his entourage there. They drew up short, their eyes not missing a single detail.

Acheron cursed as he realized how damning this looked. How damning it was.

Nefertari started screaming and slapping at him. "Don't rape me. Please!"

Sick to his stomach, he rolled away from her. She scrambled away and rushed to Styxx where she cried as if her heart were broken. "Thank the gods that you came when you did. It was terrible."

Styxx handed her over to his guards.

Acheron rose slowly to his feet to face his twin whose fury was so great his cheeks were mottled with red. He knew better than to even try to explain. Styxx would never believe him.

So he let them take him. They hauled him down to the cells under the palace. Acheron grimaced as he was wedged into a hole that brought back "fond" memories. He wrapped his arms around himself, trying to banish the chill. But nothing could warm the one on his soul that dreaded what they were going to do to him after this.

"Artemis?" he breathed her name quietly.

He could feel her presence even though he couldn't see it. "What are you doing in here?"

"I've been accused of rape."

He felt a severe pressure on his neck as if she were choking him. "Did you?"

He coughed. "You know better."

The pressure withdrew. "Then why are you here?"

"They won't believe my innocence and I swear on my soul that I didn't touch her. I . . . I need your help."

"With what?"

He looked up to where there was only a shadowed image of her and spoke the one thing he wanted most in life. "Kill me."

"You know I won't do that."

"They're going to geld me, Artemis. Do you understand that?"

"I'll fix it."

Acheron laughed bitterly. "You'll fix it. That's your answer?"

"Well, what would you have me do?"

"Kill me!" he shouted.

"Don't be so melodramatic."

"Melodramatic? They're going to chain me down, cut open my scrotum and remove my testes and then crush the channel. All while I feel every move they make and I can assure you they won't be gentle. How the fuck is that melodramatic?"

She scoffed at his anger. "And I will repair you afterward. So there's nothing for you to worry about."

Aghast at her attitude and dismissal, he felt her withdraw from him. Wanting to kill all of them, he banged his head against the stone wall.

I should have fought them . . .

But honestly what good would it have done him? They would have outnumbered him and beat him down until there was nothing left to fight with. Then he would have been dragged in here anyway.

Repulsed by his life, he wasn't sure how much time had passed before the guards returned to get him. He was dragged out of the room and shackled, then taken to his father's throne room. Naked, Acheron was forced to his knees in front of Styxx, his father and Nefertari who was still weeping.

The king glared at him unmercifully. "I find myself in a dilemma. The crime you've committed is punishable by death. But since I can't do that, we've decided to castrate you. No doubt it's what we should have done at your birth."

Acheron laughed at the irony. "That would have been too merciful an act for you. Not to mention how angry your brother would have been had you neutered his favorite toy."

His father came off the throne with a violent shout.

Acheron didn't so much as flinch. "Don't be so angry, Father. It's not like you didn't know what Estes did to me. In fact his greatest dream was for you to die and leave Styxx with him too so that he could have us both in his bed at once."

His father's curses echoed in his ears as the man set on him with the wrath of the Furies. The first blow caught Acheron across his jaw. The next broke his nose and set it to throbbing viciously. Blow after blow rained down on him.

Acheron welcomed every one of them as he continued to taunt the king. At best his father would kill him. At the very least he'd be knocked senseless enough to not feel the full pain of what they were going to do to him.

"Father, please!" Styxx said, hauling him back. He turned on Acheron who was lying on his side. "You are nothing but filth." Styxx kicked his side so hard that he heard his ribs snapping. The force of it rolled him over onto his back. Styxx's next kick landed solidly between his legs.

Acheron cried out at the unbearable pain as his brother repeatedly kicked him there until he was sure he no longer needed gelding.

"Fetch the physician," his father roared. "Let's see this bastard finished."

Panting in an effort to get breath into his abused body, Acheron was placed on a cold slab of stone, his arms chained above his head while his legs were spread and chained. He leaned his head back and laughed at them. "If you're planning a party, Father, you need to chain me face down first."

"Gag that filth."

One of the guards shoved cloth into his mouth. Acheron saw the shadow of the physician coming forward. He tightened his grip on the chains, bracing himself for what was to come.

But no amount of preparation could reduce the pain of what they did to him. Acheron screamed out in agony until his throat was as raw and bleeding as the rest of his body.

By the time he was dumped back in his room, he was spiritually numb—if only the rest of him was too. Unable to stand, he crawled across the floor to the small table where he'd left a knife from his meal the night before. Reaching up, he took it in his trembling grasp.

He was so tired of begging and he was tired of being hurt. Unable to stand another day of it, he sliced open his wrists and watched as the blood poured out.

October 25, 9528 BC

Acheron cursed foully as he woke up in extreme pain. Why wasn't he dead? But then he knew. So long as his life was tied to Styxx's no one would have mercy on him. Ever. Overwhelmed by despair, he tried to move only to find himself chained again to his bed.

He cried out in frustrated fury before he banged his head against the straw mattress.

A movement to his right drew his gaze and he went cold at the sight of the small woman who stood there. It was Ryssa, dressed in purple and gold.

She came forward and the look of pity and guilt in her eyes was enough to bring tears to his own. "I didn't tell them," she whispered. "Styxx passed out and Father found you." Tears fell down her face. "I can't believe what they did to you. I know you didn't touch Nefertari. You would never have done such a thing to anyone and I've told them that repeatedly. They never hear a word I speak . . . I know it doesn't help, but Styxx broke off his engagement to her and sent her back to Egypt. I'm so sorry, Acheron." She laid her head against his and wept quietly in his ear.

Acheron kept his own tears inside. There was no need to cry. This was his life and no matter what he tried, it would never get better.

Besides Artemis would fix him . . .

He wanted to shout out in bitter frustration and anger at the goddess's cavalier attitude.

Ryssa stroked his cheek. "Will you not speak to me?"

"And say what, Ryssa? I think my actions speak loudly enough for even a deaf man to hear. But no one ever listens to me either."

She sniffed back her tears while she brushed tender fingers through his hair. "This is so unfair to you."

"Life isn't about being fair," he breathed. "It's not about justice. It's all about endurance and how much we can suffer through."

He was so tired now. But no one would let him sleep.

Through the walls he heard Apollodorus crying. "Your son needs you, Princess. You need to go to him."

"My brother needs me too."

He let out a tired sigh. "No, I don't. Trust me, I don't need anyone."

She pressed her lips to his cheek. "I love you, Acheron."

He didn't speak as she withdrew. Right now there was no kind of love inside him. Only anguish and despair and anger could be felt. Turning his head, he looked down at the stark white bandage on his wrist. They had it padded so that he couldn't reopen the wound to finish what he'd started.

So this was it then.

Closing his eyes, he thought of his future. Of nothing changing. Of living tied down and beaten . . . forever.

He bellowed at the weight of his hopelessness. Then he fought his restraints with everything he had. But it wasn't enough to break them.

He was never enough of anything.

Bellowing even louder, he took comfort in the throbbing pain of his wounds.

Ryssa came running into the room.

Acheron ignored her as he tried to break through the chains that held him down. "I've had enough and I want out!"

She gathered him in her arms to hold him. He tried to fight her, but he couldn't. "I know, Acheron. I know."

No, she didn't know. Thank the gods that she had no idea how fucking awful his life was. How much pain he lived with. How much rejection.

He slammed his head back into the headboard and finally let his tears fall. Even though he was a man, he felt like that same little boy who'd reached out for his mother's touch only to have her backhand him. "Get me drunk, Ryssa."

She pulled back. "What?"

"For the love of the gods, get me something to make it stop hurting so much. Alcohol or drugs, I don't care which. Just make it all go away . . . please."

Ryssa wanted to deny him. She didn't believe in running away from her problems, but as she looked at him and saw the blood seeping from the wounds of his body and the tears in his eyes, she couldn't turn aside this one request.

No one should suffer so much. No one.

Against her will, her gaze went to his groin. The blood there made her sick to her stomach. The cruelty of what they'd done to him had been beyond measure—the fact that both her father and Styxx took so much pleasure from their actions disgusted her on a level she'd never dreamed existed. She would never feel right about either one of them again. "I'll be right back."

She ran to her room and grabbed the one bottle of wine that she had. "Nera?" she said to her maid who was dusting the chairs. "Could you get more wine and bring it to me in Acheron's room?"

Confusion wrinkled the petite girl's brow, but she knew better than to question her mistress. "How much more, Princess?"

"As much as you can carry."

Ryssa headed back to his room with what she had. He lay spread out on the bed with only a thin sheet covering him. Dried blood and bruises marred most of his body and the pain in those silver eyes stole her breath.

Aching for him, she wiped the tears from his eyes before she lifted his head and helped him to drink.

"May the gods bless you for your kindness," he breathed as he finished it off.

Nera came in with more. Ryssa traded bottles with her, then tipped it to Acheron's lips. It wasn't until the third bottle that he was completely drunk.

"Acheron?" she asked, afraid she might have given him too much.

He let out a long breath before his tormented gaze captured hers. "Promise me something, Ryssa."

"Anything."

"Don't ever hate your son. Please." His silver eyes fluttered closed as he passed out.

Weeping, Ryssa held him close as she ached for him. She would kill anyone who ever hurt her son like this. Even her own father. But Acheron had never known such love, such care, and that broke her heart even more. "Sleep in peace, little brother. Sleep in peace."

Wiping away her tears, she left him alone and went to check on Apollodorus. For the rest of the day she held her son close, promising him that he would never be left alone in the world. That she would always love him and protect him from anyone out to do him harm.

If only their mother had made such a promise to Acheron.

October 27, 9528 BC

Acheron lay in bed with the tip of his nose itching so badly it actually overrode the rest of his pain. He'd sell his soul if only he could scratch it. A bright flash to his left drew his attention.

It was Artemis. Dressed in white, she was as beautiful as always and he hated her for it.

His stomach knotted in anger that she'd finally remembered him. "What are you doing here?"

"I was bored."

He scoffed at her petulance and the fact that she'd come to him now. "I'm afraid I can't entertain you anymore. I'm no longer capable of it."

She pulled the sheet off him and curled her lip at what they'd done to his groin. "Ew! What did they do?"

He closed his eyes as humiliation washed over him. "They emasculated me. Remember? I was even stupid enough to ask for your help."

"Oh, that." She snapped her fingers.

Acheron gasped as even more pain tore through his groin. It ached so badly it took his breath and brought tears to his eyes.

"See? You're all better."

His breathing ragged, he was still on fire.

"Your hair's longer."

Was that all she cared about? His hair was longer? It was a good thing he couldn't move, otherwise he might have gone for her throat over that comment.

"Why are you chained?"

If she asked one more stupid fucking question, he really was going to strangle her. "To keep me from trying to kill myself."

"Why would you do that?"

Acheron ground his teeth. What good would it do to even try to explain it? She couldn't care less. She hadn't cared less when he'd begged her to do it for him. Except for the fact that she'd be bored and might actually have to try and find another man to jump on top of. Gods forbid someone else's cock might actually satisfy her. "It seemed like a good idea at the time. Not so much presently."

She gave him an annoyed glare. "I shall have to get them to release you. I swear, you're more trouble than you're worth. Wait here."

As if he had a choice? "Don't worry," he called out after she'd vanished. "I can't even get up to piss."

And his nose was still itching.

It wasn't long before his father entered the room to glare at him in displeasure. What else was new?

As always, the king looked freshly groomed. His blond hair was perfectly combed and his white robes gleamed in the sunlight.

Acheron met his scowl unflinchingly. "Can I help you?"

His father's blue eyes lit with fury. "What more has to be done to teach you your place?"

His place? That should be as his father's heir. It should be one of a revered prince.

Instead, he was lying chained down on a bed, his nakedness only concealed by the bloodied sheet Artemis had tossed back on top of him so she wouldn't have to see the butcher's handiwork. He was filthy from lack of washing and no doubt his hair was as ragged as his beard.

Acheron looked away. "I know my place."

His father kicked the bed. So much for Artemis getting him freed.

"The maids are sick of cleaning up your filth, not that I blame them. For that reason, you're being set free. But if you do anything else stupid, I swear by all the gods that I'll chain you to a wall in the dungeon and leave you there to rot."

He'd already done that to him.

"Don't worry, Father. I'll stay out of your way."

"You better." He gestured for the guards behind him to remove the shackles.

Finally, Acheron could scratch his nose again. He'd barely finished it before Styxx entered the room and tossed a pale blue garment at him.

Acheron frowned until he realized it was one of Ryssa's gowns.

Styxx laughed. "I thought you might want something to match the new you."

His gaze turned red in anger.

Before he could think better of it, Acheron was off the bed. He tackled Styxx to the floor and pounded his head against the stone, wanting to shatter it like a melon. He got in a good six solid whacks until the guards pulled him off Styxx's stomach.

Acheron fought them with everything he had, but they held his arms twisted behind his back so that there wasn't much he could do except curse them. *Thank you, Artemis, for rescinding your gift.*

Styxx came off the floor with a furious curse of his own. He grabbed their father's sword and would have killed Acheron had their father not stopped him.

"Take him out and beat him," his father snarled.

"No!"

Acheron looked up to see Ryssa in the doorway.

His father's expression was one of complete disbelief. "What did you say?"

She folded her arms over her chest and stood strong and determined in the center of the opened doors. "You heard me, Father. I said no."

The king's face flushed with fury. "You do not tell me what to do, woman."

"You're right," she said calmly. "I can't order you about. I have no power over you, but as the mistress of Apollo, I do have some say in what he does and who he pacifies, especially in regards to my own family . . ." She glanced meaningfully from him to Styxx and back again. "I'm sick of Acheron's abuse. No more."

The king gestured to Styxx. "Look at your brother. He's bleeding."

She looked at Acheron and nodded. "He's bled more than his share."

"*Styxx* is bleeding."

Her gaze went to the gown on the floor. "And for his cruelty I'd say he received a light sentence."

Styxx glared at her. "One day, Ryssa, I will be your king. You'd do well to remember that."

She met his angry sneer levelly. "And I'm the mother of a demigod. You'd do well to remember that, brother."

Styxx shoved her aside as he walked out of the room. Their father shook his head. "Women," he snarled before he left them alone.

Ryssa moved forward and snatched the gown from the floor before she wadded it into a ball. "I would apologize for him, but there's no excuse to be found." She snorted. "I only wish I could have used that argument to save you earlier. Little do they know Apollo couldn't care less what I thought. But that will be our secret, won't it?"

Acheron shrugged as he moved to the bed and pulled the sheet around him to cover his nudity from his sister's gaze. "I'd only be shocked if Father showed me anything other than contempt."

She let out another long, sad breath. "Should I have a tray of food sent to the bathing room for you?"

He shook his head. "I have no intention of going there again."

"You have to bathe."

Not really. Maybe if he stank enough no one would bother him anymore. But he wasn't willing to argue with his sister. "You should go and rest while Apollodorus doesn't need you."

She gave him a gentle hug before she left.

Ryssa had barely closed the door before Artemis stepped out of the shadows.

She smiled at him. "Say thank you, Artemis."

"Only if I can say it through gritted teeth."

She gaped at him as if she couldn't believe his anger. "You're not grateful?"

Acheron threw his hands up in surrender. "I don't want to fight with you, Artie. Honestly. I just want to lick my wounds for a while."

She materialized at his back and pulled him against her.

"I'd rather lick them for you." She dipped her hand down to cup him.

Cringing over her caress, Acheron pulled her hand away from his groin. "Given that it's been less than a week since I had my nuts cut out, Artemis, I'm not in the mood."

She made a sound of disgust. "Don't be such a baby. You're intact now. Let's celebrate by putting them to use." She blew in his ear.

Acheron jerked away from her. Naturally, she followed him.

Just give her what she wants. Otherwise this would only continue to the point she'd get angry and probably attack him. *I would rather have my eyes gouged out.*

Of course, they'd only regrow which made him wonder if his balls wouldn't have done the same thing even without Artemis's help.

Honestly, there was no use in fighting this. It wasn't like he hadn't been forced to have sex with people he detested before. All an argument would do was delay the inevitable and get him hurt again.

You might as well get it over with as quickly as possible.

He turned to face her. "Where do you want me?"

The words had barely left his lips before he found himself on his back, in her bed with her naked on top of him.

"I've missed you, Acheron."

He cringed as she sank her teeth into his neck and then he did what he always did. He pleased her and took nothing for himself.

She didn't even notice except to say that she liked it when they weren't as messy as they were whenever he ejaculated. Now he lay holding her while she purred in satisfaction.

And Acheron was still empty inside.

Artemis sat up and wrapped a sheet around herself. "You better go back now. Hades is hosting a party in Zeus's temple tonight and I have to make an appearance."

He didn't even have time to open his lips before he was back in his room alone—like a discarded piece of furniture she was through with for the time being. He went to the washing bowl and poured a little water out of the pitcher to clean himself with and shave, then he dressed.

Soul sick, he considered going to a play, but why bother?

It would take much more than that to ease what was hurt inside him. And as he looked around his prison, his gaze was drawn to the wine that Ryssa had brought. Unfortunately it wasn't strong enough to fill the empty hole that burned.

Grabbing his coin purse and cloak, he left the palace and went to the street where all the stews in town were relegated. It didn't take long to find his old merchant. Short and plump, the man was bald with a mouth full of rotten teeth, and standing on a corner outside the worst brothel in town.

Euclid smiled the moment he saw him approach. "Acheron, it's been a long time."

"Greetings. You have any Morpheus Root?"

He licked his lips greedily. "Of course I do. How much do you want?"

"I'll take everything you have."

He arched a brow at that. "You got enough coin?"

Acheron held his purse out to him.

Impressed, Euclid pulled out a small wooden arc from the wheeled cart that to the uninitiated or naive appeared to hold only rags. He handed the arc to Acheron for his inspection. Acheron opened it and lifted the herbs to his nose. The pungent lavender wasn't enough to overwhelm the herb that would ease him.

Acheron closed it. "My thanks. I'll need the cord and pots for it as well."

Euclid handed them over in exchange for more coin. "I'll have more of it next week. Anytime you need some, let me know and if you haven't the coin for it, I'm sure the two of us could work something out." He dragged one dirty finger down the side of Acheron's face.

He didn't know why that offended him. After all it was a common practice for whores to barter their bodies for supplies, but for some reason it cut him deep. "Thanks, Euclid." Pulling his cowl lower, he made his way through the dark alleys back to the palace and his room.

There in the darkness, he opened the lid and mixed the herbs together. Strange how he could still recall the exact amounts to use.

"Inhale this, boy. It'll make it all so much more pleasant for you."

His gut tightened as he heard Estes's voice in his head. The first time he'd been given this, his uncle had held him on the ground and forced him to breathe it in. After that, Acheron had needed very little coaxing. His uncle had been right, it'd made everything much more tolerable since it took away all of his conscience and fight. It'd made him a mindless supplicant to whatever deviant act they wanted to perform on him.

He lit the herbs and blew on them ever so slightly to get them charred to the right amount so that the fumes would be potent enough. Closing his eyes, he picked up the clay mask and held it to his nose, then inhaled until everything that hurt stopped.

His head swimming, he stumbled to his bed and lay down so that he could watch the ceiling tilt and spin.

Apostolos? Where are you?

"Hello, voices," he breathed. They were always louder when he was high.

We want you to come home, Apostolos. Tell us where to find you.

He looked around the room and sighed. "I'm in a dark room."

Where?

Acheron laughed, then rolled over onto his stomach and groaned at the sensation of the coarse linen brushing against his body. He drew a ragged breath as his cock hardened. Artemis had thrown him out too soon. The drug was making him incredibly horny.

Then again, she didn't really care for the mess he made. Every time he came in her bed, she wrinkled up her nose distastefully. It was why it was easier for him to just screw her and please himself later when he was alone.

He sucked his breath in sharply as the sheet rubbed against his nipples. The pleasure was excruciating. But he refused to touch himself.

He didn't want release or any kind of pleasure. He just wanted peace.

More than that he wanted to be touched by someone who gave a fuck about him. And that certainly wasn't him.

November 12, 9528 BC

Acheron sat outside on his balcony, letting the chill winds freeze him as he realized his sister was in the window watching him. He motioned for her to come outside.

Her teeth started chattering immediately. "It's freezing out here."

"Feels good to me." He was actually sweating.

Ryssa narrowed her eyes suspiciously as she neared him. "What have you done?"

"I've done nothing. Absolutely nothing." He barely had the strength to eat.

She shook her head in anger. "You've been taking those drugs again, haven't you?"

Acheron looked away.

She gripped his face in her hand and forced him to look at her. "Why would you do such a thing?"

"Don't start on me, Ryssa."

"Acheron, please," she said, her voice strained as she released him. "You're killing yourself."

He wished. Glancing down, he turned his wrist out to look at the perfect unblemished skin. There was no trace of the cut that had severed his skin and veins. "I can't kill myself. The gods know I've tried. There's no way out for me so here I sit, biding my time until the gods end my life, while I try to stay out of everyone's way."

She brushed the hair back from his eyes. "You look terrible. When was the last time you bathed?"

He shoved her away, angry over the question. "The last time I bathed, I was accused of rape and then castrated. No offense, I'd rather smell."

She shook her head. "When was the last time you ate?"

294

"I don't know." He scratched at the beard on his cheeks. "What difference does it make? It's not like Father's going to let me starve to death. I'll eat when I have to. When they make me."

The next thing he knew, Ryssa reached up and grabbed his ear in a tight pinch. "You're going to eat right now."

"Hey!" Acheron snapped, but she refused to let go. With a determined grip, she pulled him from the railing and forced him to follow her to her room. She was so much smaller than him that he was bent almost double and had to struggle to keep up with her frenetic steps. "You do know that I'm bigger than you," he reminded her.

"Yes, but I'm meaner and madder." She snatched her hand away, making a lasting sting on his lobe.

Frowning, he rubbed his ear.

She pointed at her dressing table where a plate of fruit, bread and cheese rested. "Sit down and eat. Now!"

"Yes, Your Majesty." As Acheron reached for a bit of cheese, he caught his reflection. Sunken eyes, tinged by red stared out from an unkempt man. His beard was ragged, his cropped hair shaggy. He looked like an old man instead of a youth.

That was okay, he felt even older than he looked. Averting his gaze, he placed the cheese in his mouth while Ryssa poured him a goblet of wine.

She left him to walk over to the door that led to her maid's quarters. "Nera? Would you have them draw me a bath in my room? And find me a razor."

Acheron didn't speak as he ate. Honestly, he was starving. The maids hadn't been bringing food for him and he didn't dare go in search of it on his own given the way his father had reacted the last time he found him near the kitchen and dining room.

When Ryssa returned, she was holding Apollodorus. The baby smiled the moment he saw Acheron and reached for him.

Unable to deny him, Acheron took him into his arms. "Greetings, bit. How have you been?"

He squealed in response.

Acheron look up at Ryssa as she folded cloth for a diaper. "He's grown since I last saw him."

"Yes, he has."

Acheron glanced at the baby's thinning hair. "You're getting bald too."

Ryssa laughed suddenly. "You did the same thing. All of your black hair fell out and then it came back in blond."

Apollodorus reached out and tugged at his beard.

Acheron held the baby out to Ryssa. "I'm too dirty to hold him."

"He doesn't mind. He's just glad to see his uncle again. He's missed you."

He'd missed him too.

Acheron hugged the baby close even as he glared at his sister. "That's unfair, Ryssa. You know what would befall me if Father ever found me here. And if he ever saw me near Apollodorus . . ."

She placed her hand on his shoulder. "I know, Acheron."

The door opened to admit servants who brought in a large tub and hot water. Ryssa took the baby while Acheron ate more.

Once the bath was ready, she left him alone.

With more enthusiasm than he wanted, Acheron sank into the steaming hot water and sighed. It'd been so long since he last had a bath that he'd almost forgotten how good it felt. Even so, it wasn't worth the risk to him.

"I love you, Ryssa," he whispered. She was the only one who really cared about him. Artemis wanted to love him, but she was a goddess and hers was a selfish love—very much like Estes's. So long as he pleased her, she was kind. Granted she was more giving than Estes had ever been, but there were still limits on what she'd do.

What hurt most with Artemis was the memory of how they'd been in the beginning. He craved that innocence on his part. That feeling that he'd meant something to her . . .

Trying not to think about it, he reached for the razor to finally scrape his cheeks smooth. Once he was finished, he dragged himself out of the tub and reached for his clean clothes.

After he was dressed, he knocked on the door to the maid's room. "I'm finished. Thank you."

Ryssa joined him before she closed the door so the maid couldn't hear them. "Please don't take any more of your drugs, Acheron. I don't like what they do to you." The concern in her pale blue eyes scalded him.

"I'll wean myself."

"Promise?"

He nodded. "But only for you."

She smiled at him. "You look so much better. Anytime you want a bath, come here and I'll have one drawn for you." She lifted herself up on her tiptoes to hug him.

Acheron gave her a squeeze, then withdrew. He'd stayed here too long already. They both knew the risk was too great for him to be in her chambers while the rest of the household was awake.

Entering his room again, he stared at the arc of Morpheus Root on his table.

Throw it out.

No, he couldn't. He'd be sick again if he stopped cold. His existence was miserable enough without that. He'd do what he promised Ryssa. He'd wean himself back off it.

"Acheron?"

He tensed at Artemis's voice. How did she know the precise moment to come see him?

Then again, she was a goddess.

"Greetings, Artie."

She flashed in behind him and wrapped her arm around his waist. "Mmm, you smell good."

It was the bath mixed with the drugs. "I just bathed."

Pulling back, she scowled at him. "You look strange. Are you ill?"

"No."

"Then come. I'm in the mood to dance."

As if he had a choice? But he wasn't in the mood to be defiant. He was actually learning to avoid beatings and enjoying it.

Artemis took him to her temple. Acheron drew up short as he saw what she'd done to it. There were candles everywhere while the music played very low. A small feast had been laid out.

He frowned at her. "What is this?"

She offered him a tender smile. "It's been a while since we've been together. I wanted it to be special tonight. Do you like it?"

He was too surprised to even think. "You did this for me?"

"Well, I certainly didn't set romantic lighting for my brother or one of my koris." She went to the table and picked up a small box. "And I had Hephaestus make this for you."

Acheron was completely stunned as he stared at the box and what it signified. This was so out of character for her that for a moment he wondered if someone had knocked her in the head. "You have a gift for me?"

"Well, I wanted something to replace the ring. You can't take this back with you, but you can leave it here to use when you visit me."

Curious, he opened the box to find a set of gold vambraces.

Artemis squeezed his forearm. "It's for your wrists whenever we hunt. You never say anything, but I know the bowstring stings your wrist when you shoot. These will protect your skin and they'll make sure the arrow always flies true to its mark."

It was so incredibly thoughtful and reminded him of how easy it'd been to give his heart to her. Why couldn't she always be like this?

"Thank you, Artie."

"Does it make you happy?"

She was almost childlike in her effort to please him. Acheron brushed the hair back from her face so that he could kiss her cheek. "It makes me more than happy."

"Good. You've been so sad lately and I don't like it when you're sad."

Then why did she do the things she did that upset him? He didn't understand it, but she was trying now. He wasn't about to throw the past in her face.

He held his hand out to her. "Shall we dance?"

Smiling, she took his hand and allowed him to twirl her around. Her laughter filled his ears.

Acheron wanted desperately to feel her joy too. But there was nothing in him except a fleeting sense of relief that she wasn't throwing him down and jumping on top of him. Of course he was still buzzed from the remnants of the Morpheus Root he'd taken a couple of hours ago. It was the part where his body was calm and he could function without being horny or sick.

Artemis leaned her head against his chest and sighed while they swayed to the low music.

Gods how he wanted to love her again. But he was so afraid of it. Every time he let his guard down, she hurt him. If she would just acknowledge them as friends to the world. Or allow him to know that he really did mean something to her.

Wanting her friendship back, he swallowed. "Artie?"

"Yes?"

"Would you spend tomorrow with me?"

She smiled happily. "I can come get you in the morning."

"Not here. In Didymos."

She pulled away from him. "I don't know, Acheron. Someone could see us."

It always came down to that. "You can take other forms. You don't have to look like you."

She let out a frustrated sigh. "Why is this important to you? Why not stay here with me?"

Don't say it . . .

But he couldn't help it. The drugs wouldn't let him hold his tongue. "I don't feel human here."

She scowled. "What?"

Acheron stepped away from her in indecision. Part of him didn't want to tell her the truth, but the other was sick of hiding it from her. "Being here makes me feel like a pet dog. It's like living in my uncle's home in Atlantis. I'm not allowed to leave your bedroom unless you're with me. I can't go outside without your permission. It's demeaning."

"Demeaning?" She narrowed her eyes on him. "You are in the temple of a goddess on Olympus. How in the name of Zeus could *you* be demeaned by that?"

You. Whore. Given her tone, the words were interchangeable. They struck him like a knife through his heart. "Forgive me, akra. It's not my place to make requests of you."

She curled her lip. "Oh, stop with that sniveling tone. I hate it when you do that. Just get out."

He was immediately thrown back into his room. He looked around the plain furnishings and the dark shadows.

"I'm so sick of this."

Desperate for something to change, he grabbed his cloak and headed out of the palace, into the city. He didn't pause until he reached Merus and Eleni's home. The firelight flickered behind the closed shutters and he imagined the two of them inside, laughing and teasing.

Family.

He knew the word, but he didn't really understand it. What it would be like to be welcomed home. To know that out there was one person who would die for him.

You will never find that here.

Acheron looked around the vacant street and remembered the day his father had thrown him out of Estes's home. He'd wandered for months trying to find someplace to rest. Trying to find work. Everyone refused to hire him. At least for anything other than whoring.

You're such a pretty thing ... Let's put that body to good use ...

He cringed at the bitter memories that always haunted him. *I want out.*

And he'd tried to find that out. He'd gone to city after city, town after town and they'd all been the same. There was nowhere to go and no one who wanted him for a moment longer than it took for them to screw him. The only reason he'd returned here had been the memory of his sister and the one summer when he'd felt like a person and not an object.

Sick to his stomach, he looked up the hill to where the palace twinkled like a magical star.

And still those Atlantean voices whispered to him.

Come to us, Apostolos. Come home ...

Acheron laughed bitterly. "Why? So you can fuck me like everyone else?"

There was nowhere for him to go. No escape from this torment. The only reason he had to live was for the two people in this world who didn't judge him.

Ryssa and Apollodorus. May the gods have mercy on him if he were to lose them. He would never be able to go on should they leave this world without him.

February 18, 9527 BC

"I don't know what it is about you and that baby, but you are the most amazing nurse ever born."

Acheron laughed at Ryssa's comment as she took Apollodorus from his arms. Neither of them could understand why Acheron's presence calmed his nephew, but there was no denying that anytime Apollodorus was fussy, he calmed down immediately for Acheron. In fact, Ryssa had begun bringing the babe to him virtually every night so that she could sleep.

"You know you can leave him with me any time at all. I think we get along so well because we both function on the same level." Acheron ruffled the soft hair on his nephew's head.

Smiling, Ryssa wrapped the blanket around Apollodorus. "Thank the gods I have you. I don't know what I'd do if you weren't here to help out with him."

An instant later the doors to Acheron's room crashed open. Six guards stormed in to tackle him to the floor.

"What is this?" Ryssa demanded.

They didn't respond. Acheron fought them, but in the end they shackled him while the baby screamed in protest.

"He's done nothing!" Ryssa shouted as she followed them out of the room and down the hallway.

They didn't stop until they'd taken him to the throne room and forced him to his knees in front of his father and Styxx who sat smugly on their thrones while they stared at him in disdain.

Acheron glared at them. "Why am I here?"

His father came off his throne with a bellow of rage. "You do not ask questions of me, traitor!"

Stunned, Acheron couldn't even blink for a full minute.

"Father!" Ryssa snapped. "Have you lost your reason?"

His answer was to backhand Acheron. "Where were you last night?"

Acheron panted at the pain that exploded through his cheek and eye. He'd been with Artemis, but he didn't dare tell his father that. "I was in my room."

His father struck him again. "Liar. I have witnesses who saw you in a stew, plotting my murder."

Stunned, he couldn't even respond. All he could do was look at Styxx and the fearful light in the prince's eyes told him exactly who'd been in the stew. "I've done no such thing."

His father hit him again before turned to the guards. "Torture him until he decides to tell us the truth."

Acheron cried out a denial as he fought the guards holding him.

"Father, no!" Ryssa moved forward.

The king turned on her with a feral snarl. "You're not going to save him this time. He's committed treason and I will not allow *that* to go unanswered."

His breathing ragged, Acheron who was being restrained by the guards, met and held Styxx's gaze. How could his brother plot the death of a man who worshiped the ground he walked on? He would sell his soul to have just a portion of the love Styxx spurned.

But there was no need to ask for clemency. His father had already made up his mind. Only the bastard Acheron could be the traitor. Never Styxx. The only person who could exonerate him was Artemis. And she'd rather die than openly admit he'd been with her in her temple last night.

Acheron was hauled out of the throne room and taken to the prison below.

Even though he fought the guards every step of the way, it wasn't enough to prevent them from stripping his clothes off his body and then chaining him down on the interrogation block. The granite stone chilled him to his bones. There were blood stains permanently dried in the stone and there was no doubt that his own blood would soon mix with that of the others who'd been tortured and killed before him.

Closing his eyes, Acheron tried to think of something, anything to protect himself from what was about to happen. But as the interrogator came forward, he knew there was nothing he could do.

Nothing could save him from this.

"The king wants the names of everyone you met with."

Acheron winced in fear of what would come when he told the truth. "I didn't meet with anyone."

He brought a hot steel whip down across Acheron's chest.

Acheron screamed out as he realized just how impossible this was going to be.

Ryssa *was terrified* as she returned to her room and handed her crying son over to his nurse. What was she going to do?

Unlike her father, she knew who the real traitor had to be. If witnesses saw someone tall, blond and looking like Acheron, it was Styxx. Acheron would have nothing to gain by killing the king, other than vengeance and he wasn't the kind of person to go seeking that.

Not to mention Acheron would *never* have been in public uncovered, especially not a stew. Had he done so, he'd still be there, beating people off him.

"What have you done, Styxx?" she whispered through the tight lump in her throat.

Why would he plot against his own father? But then she knew, the history of mankind was written by sons wanting more and willing to do anything to get it. Even so, she'd thought Styxx above such scheming. Who could have poisoned his mind?

"I have to find Artemis." There was no one else who could help save Acheron.

Ryssa headed for her door to leave, but before she took three steps, the doors opened to admit the same guards who'd arrested Acheron.

"Your Highness, you're to be taken for questioning."

Her heart chilled at those words. "Questioning? This can't be."

But it was. Surrounding her, they took her to her father's war room where he waited with Styxx.

She gave them both the coldest look she could muster. "What is this, Father?"

He'd never looked older than he did right then. His handsome features were drawn tight with sadness. "Why would you betray me, Daughter?"

"I've never done anything to betray you, Father, ever."

He shook his head. "I have a witness who came forward and said that you were with Acheron last night."

She leveled a killing glare at Styxx. "Then they are lying as they lied about Acheron. I was with Apollo last night. Summon him and see."

Styxx's face went white.

So, he'd thought to rid himself of her too. She couldn't believe her father's stupidity where Styxx was concerned.

Relief etched itself across her father's brow. "I'm glad they're mistaken, kitten." He laid a gentle hand to her face. "The thought of my beloved daughter turning on me . . ."

What of his beloved son?

She looked past her father to see Styxx staring at the floor. "Acheron is innocent."

"No, child. Not this time. I have too many witnesses who saw him there."

Why couldn't she make him see the truth? "Acheron would never be in a stew."

"Of course he would. He worked in one. Where else would he go?"

Anywhere *but* there. Acheron had hated every minute of being in those places. "Please, Father. You've done enough to him. Let him be."

He shook his head. "There is a nest of vipers coiled around me and until I uncover the name of everyone he spoke to, I won't stop."

Tears filled her eyes as she considered the nightmare they were going to put Acheron through. Again. "The priests say that Hades reserves a special corner of Tartarus for betrayers. I'm sure the name of your real traitor is being carved there even as we speak."

Styxx refused to meet her gaze.

305

So she looked back at her father. "In all these years, Acheron has sought nothing but love from you, Father. One moment of your looking at him with something other than hatred burning in your eyes. Nothing more than a kind word and at every turn you've denied him and hurt him. You have shattered the son who only wanted to love you. Let him go before you do irreparable harm, I beg you."

"He's betrayed me for the last time."

"Betrayed *you*?" she asked, aghast at his reasoning. "Father, you can't believe that? All he's tried to do is stay out of your sight. Away from your notice. He cringes any time your name is brought up. If you'd stop being so blind for one minute, you'd see that he has *never* mixed with people and he has *never* betrayed you."

"He was a prostitute!" he roared.

"He was a boy who had to eat, Father. Thrown away by his own family. Betrayed by the ones who should have protected him from harm. I was there when he was born and I remember how all of you turned away from him. Do you? Do you even recall when you broke his arm? He was only two years old and could barely speak. He reached for you to hug you and you knocked him away so forcefully that you broke his arm like a twig. When he cried out, you slapped him for it and walked away."

"And that's why he plots your murder, Father," Styxx spoke up finally. "Don't let a woman sway you from what needs to be done. Women are our greatest weakness. They prey on our guilt and our love of them. How many times have you told me that? You can't listen to them. They think with their hearts and not their minds."

Her father's face turned to stone. "I will not let him get away with it this time."

Tears flowed freely down her face at her father's blindness. "This time? When have you ever let Acheron get away with anything?"

She blinked away the tears in her eyes as she tried to make him see reason. "Beware the viper in your closet. Isn't that another thing you're always saying, Father?" She cut a meaningful glare at Styxx. "Ambition and jealousy are at the heart of all betrayals. Acheron's only ambition is to stay

306

out of your sight and were he to have jealousy, it wouldn't be directed at you. But I do know of another who would gain immensely in his life were you gone."

Her father backhanded her. "How dare you implicate your brother."

"I told you, Father. She hates me. I wouldn't be surprised if she hasn't bedded the whore too."

Ryssa wiped the blood from her lips. "The only person in this family that I know of who sleeps with whores is you, Styxx. I wonder if Acheron was supposedly seen in your favorite stew . . ." With that she turned and headed out of the room and to the street.

"Leave us!"

Acheron could barely recognize the sound of his father's voice through the throbbing vicious pain. No part of him had been left unviolated or free of abuse. It even hurt to blink.

Once the room was empty, his father approached him where he lay on the stone slab.

To his complete shock, his father brought him a ladle of water to drink.

Acheron cringed, expecting the king to hurt him worse with it.

He didn't. His father actually lifted his head and helped him to drink from it. But for the fact it would kill Styxx, he'd think it poisoned.

"Where were you last night?"

Acheron felt a single tear slide from the corner of his eye at the question that had been asked over and over again. The salt from it stung the open wounds on his cheek as he drew a ragged, agonized breath. "Just tell me what to say, akri. Tell me what will keep me from being hurt anymore."

His father slammed the ladle down on the stone by Acheron's face. "I want the names of the men you met with."

He didn't know the names of the senators. They'd seldom offered one before they'd screwed him.

Acheron shook his head. "I met with no one."

His father buried his hand in his hair and forced him to look at him. "Give me the truth. Damn you!"

Lost to the pain, Acheron struggled to think of some lie that his father would believe, but as with the interrogator, he came back to the one single truth. "I didn't do it. I wasn't there."

"Then where were you? Have you a single witness to your whereabouts?"

Yes, but she'd never come forward. Maybe if he were Styxx . . . But Artemis would never stand up for a worthless whore. "I have only my word."

His father roared in anger. He reached for him, but before he could make contact, he froze.

Acheron held his breath as he tried to understand what was happening. An instant later, Artemis appeared beside him.

Stunned, he couldn't do anything other than stare at her.

"Your sister told me what they'd accused you of. Don't worry, your father will have no memory of this. Nor will your brother."

Acheron swallowed as he tried to understand what she was saying. "You're protecting me?"

She nodded. An instant later, he was back in his room and healed. Acheron lay back on his bed, more grateful than words could express. But even so it didn't erase the pain of what he'd been through. Any more than it concealed the fact that Styxx was planning to overthrow his own father.

What was he going to do?

Artemis materialized beside him. Her expression was sorrowful as she brushed his hair back from his face.

"Will Ryssa remember us?" he asked her.

"No. From this moment forward she won't even remember that you and I know each other. I should have done it sooner perhaps. But she seemed to keep her mouth closed. Now I won't have to worry."

That was for the best.

He stared at Artemis amazed at what she'd done. No, she hadn't stood up for him, but she had saved him. It was a major breakthrough from the last time she'd left him to their "tender" care. "Thank you for coming for me."

She laid her hand to his cheek. "I wish I could take you away from here."

She was the one person who could. But her fear was too great. Maybe she was right. What good would it do for her to be ruined over him?

He wasn't worth it.

Acheron kissed her on the lips even though he was still cold inside. He had nowhere to go and he was tired of being here with people who hated him.

Styxx . . .

In the blink of an eye the simplest answer to his predicament came to him. Why had he never thought of it before?

Pulling back from Artemis, he held her hand. "You should go before someone stumbles in here."

"I'll see you tomorrow."

Not if he had his way. "Tomorrow."

Acheron watched as she faded and the second she was gone, he immediately made plans for what was to come.

His father refused to let him die so long as his life was tied to Styxx's and Styxx was plotting the death of his father.

The answer was so simple. If he killed Styxx, his father would be safe and he'd be free.

Peace. He would finally have peace.

February 19, 9527 BC

Acheron waited until the palace was completely silent. In less than an hour the sun would rise . . .

And both he and Styxx would be dead. The mere thought of it brought more joy to him than anything else he could imagine.

More than eager for it, he held the dagger tight in his hand as he snuck past the guards and crept through the door of Styxx's room. He shut it with only a whisper of a noise. Like a shadow, he made his way across the floor to the large feather-stuffed bed where his brother slept. Heavy curtains hung to shield the heir from a stray breeze.

But they couldn't shield him from Acheron.

His gaze dark, Acheron pulled the curtains back. Naked except for his royal emblem necklace, Styxx was sleeping on his side, completely vulnerable.

All the years of abuse, of Styxx mocking him, went through his mind, as well as the memory of the way his brother had been willing to see him punished for the treason Styxx had committed.

Acheron lifted the dagger. One slash . . . one cut . . .

Peace.

Do it!

He started the downward motion, then stopped before he made contact with the prince's throat.

Silently, he cursed as he realized a horrible truth about himself. He couldn't do this. Not in cold blood. Not this mercilessly.

Disgusted, he stepped back as he realized he was a coward.

No, not a coward. No matter what had happened in their past, they were brothers. Twins. He couldn't kill his own brother. Even if the bastard deserved it.

Your pain won't stop until you do this.

He wouldn't show such mercy to you.

It was true. He'd been willing to see him beaten, gelded and even killed if his father had been able to do it.

Styxx had no mercy for him, no pity or even compassion and if he allowed the man to live, Acheron's abuse would continue. It would most likely worsen once Styxx killed their father. And once their father was gone, Styxx would hurt Ryssa.

He'd already made those threats. Repeatedly.

She Styxx could kill with impunity. Acheron's blood ran cold with the reality of it. If not for himself, he had to protect his sister and her child.

Styxx had to die.

"Forgive me, brother," he whispered an instant before he stabbed Styxx straight through the heart.

Styxx gasped as his eyes flew open. Acheron staggered back, into the shadows while his brother tried to crawl out of bed. Falling onto the floor, Styxx collapsed as blood ran from the wound and pooled onto the stone.

His breathing ragged, Acheron waited for death to claim him too.

It didn't and with every continued heartbeat, panic began to set in.

He felt the same as ever. How could that be?

Maybe Styxx wasn't dead. Terrified he'd only wounded his brother, he went to him and pressed his hand to his neck. There was no pulse at all. No movement or any other sign of life. Rolling Styxx over, he saw that his skin and lips were already turning blue, his eyes were open and glazed.

Styxx was dead.

Yet Acheron lived.

Horrified, he ran for the door and then past the dozing guards, down the hall back to his own room. No! The word echoed through his mind over and over as he tried to make sense of this. If he died, Styxx died. If Styxx died . . .

Nothing happened to *him*. How could this be?

Why would the gods have done that? It didn't make any sense.

You've killed your own brother. Your twin.

Acheron leaned against his closed door as absolute horror filled him. They would kill him if they ever found out the truth. His father wouldn't forgive this. They would tear him apart . . .

Suddenly an alarm sounded through the palace as guards shouted to each other and clamored through the hallway.

They've already discovered his body. Gods help me!

Someone knocked on his door.

"Acheron?"

It was Ryssa. Acheron opened the door to see her there, her face pale and hair mussed. She wore a red wrap around her blue gown. "I wanted to make sure that you were all right. Someone tried to kill Styxx tonight."

Tried? No, he'd fucking succeeded. "What do you mean?"

Before she could answer, he saw Styxx behind Ryssa, his face flushed with anger as he led the guards through a search of the rooms. "Find my attacker! I want him now. Do you hear me? Search every corner until we have him!"

Acheron blinked in disbelief.

Styxx was alive? He was completely unprepared for what this meant. Styxx had been resurrected.

Why?

Ryssa shook her head. "Have you seen anyone?"

"I was in my room," he lied.

As if sensing him, Styxx froze then turned to face him. Though he was covered in blood there was no sign of the wound that had killed him. "Guards!" he roared.

Acheron stepped back in fear.

Styxx pointed to him. "Guard him. My attacker might realize that to kill me all he has to do is kill him first. I want someone guarding his back at all times."

If only his brother knew the truth . . . Thank the gods that he didn't.

"What a horrible night," Ryssa said. "I'd best go to Apollodorus. I know all this commotion will have him scared."

Acheron didn't move as she left him. Through the crack in the door, he watched the guards swarming the hallway and searching rooms. His brother was alive. He couldn't get past that one fact.

So their lives weren't truly bound together. At least not in a traditional sense. If he died, Styxx died. If Styxx died . . . there was no effect on him.

His father was right. He was unnatural.

Why would the gods protect him and not Styxx? It didn't make any sense.

Withdrawing into his room he decided to wait out the search until the house was again quiet. Once he was sure he could leave and not be seen, he wrapped his cloak around himself and headed out into the dark streets.

He remained hidden as he wended his way through the alleys to Apollo's temple. Once there, he knocked on the door.

"We're closed."

"I'm from the royal house," Acheron said forcefully. "It's imperative that I see the oracle."

The door opened a partial degree until the old wizened priest caught sight of his face. His demeanor immediately changed to one of subservience. "Prince Styxx, forgive me. I-I didn't realize it was you."

Acheron didn't bother to correct him. For once, he was grateful they were twins. "Take me to the oracle."

Without further hesitation, the priest led him through the columned walkway to the back where small rooms were set aside for the priests and attendants. The oracle's room was slightly larger than the others. It was bare and stark with only a small drapery-lined bed.

"Mistress?" the priest called as he headed for the bed. "The prince wishes a word with you."

A blond woman who couldn't have been much older than fifteen sat up on the bed and with the priest's help she stood, then walked toward him. By the way she moved, Acheron knew she was drugged. Heavily.

The priest led her to a tall chair that was set over a bowl with vapors. By the scent of it, he'd guess it contained Morpheus Root mixed with Risi Opsi, a compound that created fantastic hallucinations. It was something he'd only taken once after Euclid sang its praises, but that had been enough. It'd left him delirious with nightmares for two days.

"Leave us," she snapped at the priest. "You know the law."

He withdrew instantly.

The girl pulled the cloak up on her head as she added water to the boiling herbs to make them smoke more. "You're not the prince."

He frowned at her. "How do you know?"

"I know all," she said snidely. "I'm the oracle and you're the cursed firstborn son whom the king denies."

That last bit wasn't common knowledge and it made him believe in her abilities. "Then tell me why I'm here."

She breathed in the vapors and writhed on the stool as if she heard the same voices that haunted him. When she opened her eyes, her gaze pierced him like a lance. "You can't kill him. It is forbidden for you to die."

"Why?"

She inhaled again. Her eyes turned a glowing shade of gold. "In the mark of the sun lies a slash of silver. Not once, not twice, but thrice. The mark of the father to the right, the mother to the left and in the center is the one who unites the two. Three lives intertwined. You are what you were though you don't know it yet. You will. The day draws near when your destiny will manifest. Walk with courage and listen. Yours is a birth of pain, but one of necessity. *Akri di diyum.*"

The Lord and Master will rule . . .

She reached out and placed a hand on his shoulder. "Your will will make the laws of the universe."

"What are you saying?"

"He who fights destiny loses. Embrace your fate, Acheron. The harder you fight the more painful your birth." She collapsed.

Acheron barely caught her before she hit the floor. Scooping her up in his arms, he took her to her bed and laid her down. She continued to mumble nonsensical words of birds and demons coming for him.

Even more confused than he'd been before, he left her to the care of the priests and made his way back to the palace.

Her prophecy was gibberish.

It had to be. Why would the gods pick a whore to move through? Why would his will be the will of the universe?

She's drugged . . .

Of all men, he knew how disconcerting that was. It was nothing more than the hallucinations he'd had himself. He was nothing.

Yet in the back of his mind two words whispered over and over again.

What if?

March 3, 9527 BC

Acheron sat in the nursery, spooning strained meat to Apollodorus. The two of them had been alone most of the morning while Ryssa lay with a vicious headache. He didn't know why his nephew appeared to adore him, but the boy would follow him anywhere.

It was the only good thing in his life.

Apollodorus let out a long burp, then giggled.

Acheron lifted his eyebrows. "I think you're done, my lord."

The baby fell over and laughed. Acheron scooped him up and propped him against his shoulder.

He'd just set Apollodorus down for a nap when the doors to the nursery opened. For an instant, he feared it might be his father or Apollo, but luckily it was Ryssa entering with a tiny blond young woman.

It took a moment before he realized who she was.

Maia.

"Acheron! Look who came for a visit with her mother."

Joy filled his entire being as he rose to greet her. "It's so good to see you again." He held her close.

She pulled back to look up at him with a smile. "Acheron . . . it's been far too long. You haven't changed a bit."

But she had. And when she ran her hand down his arm in a disturbing caress, he went cold with dread. Especially when that familiar light came into her eyes. It was as if she couldn't control herself. Damn, his curse.

Not Maia . . .

Stepping back, he put distance between them. "What brings you here?"

316

"I came here with my mother."

Ryssa gave him a wan smile that let him know her head was still paining her. "They'll be staying for a week."

That news should have made him glad, instead he dreaded it. "Really?"

Maia approached him slowly, like a stalking lioness who was hungry to take a bite of him. "You and I should get reacquainted."

Before he could respond, a maid called for Ryssa.

Ryssa grimaced in pain and pressed her hand to her temple, then glanced to them. "I'll be right back."

Maia took another step closer. "I had forgotten how beautiful you were . . ."

He put his hands on her shoulders to keep her back. "I was told you have a husband now."

"He's not with me." She leaned toward him invitingly.

"No," he said firmly. "I won't do this with you."

She licked her lips as she glanced up at him from beneath her lashes. "I'm not a child anymore, Acheron. I'm a woman full grown with a babe of my own."

"And I have no interest in you that way."

She reached for his groin.

Acheron grabbed her hand before she made contact. "Maia, I tended you when you were a child."

"And now I'd have you tend to me as a woman."

"Please, stop this."

"Why? You're younger than my husband is." She tried to pull her hand away from his grip. "Don't you find me attractive?"

Ryssa returned.

Acheron released her and quickly moved away. "I have to go now."

"Is something wrong?" Ryssa asked.

More than he could ever tell her. "No. I'm fine. I just need to go." He practically ran from the room and didn't stop until he was safely locked inside his own chambers.

Leaning his head back against the door, he cursed over what had happened. What was so wrong with him that everyone past the age of puberty wanted to fuck him?

He was so tired of everyone grabbing at him, winking

and looking suggestively. It wasn't normal and now with Maia he realized something terrible.

He would never be able to have a normal relationship with anyone.

Father, sister, even childhood friend.

The moment someone went through puberty, it was over for him. Sick with the thought, he slid down the door and hated whatever curse the gods had given him.

June 22, 9527 BC

Tomorrow Acheron would reach his majority. One and twenty. He should be thrilled and yet the oracle's words haunted him. More than that was the look on Maia's face as she'd attempted to grab him.

"Something has to change," he said with a heavy sigh. His brother was still plotting his father's murder and here he sat doing nothing except trying to stay out of everyone's way, hoping they wouldn't even see him.

"Acheron?"

He leaned his head back to find Ryssa joining him on the balcony. She narrowed her eyes at him. "You're taking that stuff again, aren't you?"

"Only for today and tomorrow," he admitted quietly.

"Why?"

Because Artemis had cut out his heart and he didn't have the stamina to make it through the next two days without it.

It was their old fight. He'd asked the goddess to acknowledge him or at the very least come to him on the anniversary of his birth and she'd laughed in his face. More than that he was tired of watching all the special celebrations that were planned for the anniversary of Styxx's birthday. Celebrations planned by a man whose life would soon be ended by the very son he coveted so zealously. Ironic, yes. But it didn't stop it from hurting.

"Acheron." Ryssa gripped his chin and forced him to look at her. "Can you hear me?"

"Not really."

He saw the frustration in her eyes. "What am I going to do with you?"

"Beat me like everyone else."

She glared at him. "You're not funny."

He wasn't trying to be. It was a simple fact of his life that he moved everyone around him to extreme acts of violence.

She shook her head before she stepped back. "You know I won't let Apollodorus near you when you're like this."

That was the one drawback. "I know. It wouldn't be very motherly of you. Not that I personally would know how mothers behave with their young. I think I saw it once in a play, only then the mother fed her baby to a lion. Too bad my own mother wasn't so merciful, huh?"

She pulled his head against her shoulder and kissed him just behind the ear, then gently ruffled his hair. "Your hair is lighter than before. I think I like it this length. Did you get it cut?"

He shook his head. "Whoever cuts my hair wants to sleep with me afterward. I thought I'd let it grow until it either touches my toes or Father gets angry enough to shear it again. Maybe I ought to go make another offering to the gods. I hear Athena has a feast day coming up."

She let out an agitated breath. "You *are* in a mood today."

It was the drugs combined with his frustration. He'd always hated being like this in Atlantis. His sarcastic brashness had never been rewarded well. And it'd always killed him that they fed him the drugs, then punished him for the effects the drugs had on his mind and body.

Artemis had a strange loving hatred for this mood. At times she liked it and at others she'd punish him for it, too. Problem was, he could never tell how she'd receive it until it was too late.

Ryssa withdrew from him reluctantly. His pain was tangible and there was nothing she could do to alleviate it. She wanted to cry from the weight of her helplessness where he was concerned.

The worst part, something had happened between him and Maia, but he refused to tell her what. Her guess was that Maia had succumbed to the same pull everyone else felt. It must be something to do with puberty. Before sexual maturity, children couldn't discern it. But afterward . . .

Her poor Acheron.

If only there was someone else who could control themselves around him.

I'm the only one.

She didn't consider herself special by any means. But it didn't change the fact that Acheron was alone. He'd always be alone. Their father would never allow him to marry and after the near assassination of Styxx, guards had once again been posted outside Acheron's doors. What little freedom he'd known was now gone.

How she wished she could make it better for him.

After nightfall, Acheron watched the activity below. The moment that caught his attention most was the large procession that heralded the Princess of Thebes. Styxx's new bride. They were to marry two weeks from tomorrow.

This time he planned to keep far away from his brother's woman. As if they understood the danger, his balls ached suddenly at the thought of being cut out again.

Flinching, Acheron damned his brother for the castration. Styxx had known the truth about what his betrothed had done, but the bastard hadn't cared.

So what? What was *his* humiliation anyway? The only thing that mattered was precious Styxx and his dignity.

Sighing, he thought back to the oracle. *Akri di diyum.*

What could that possibly mean?

The Lord and Master would rule. He already ruled the bedroom, what else was left?

It's just a drugged oracle, Acheron, forget it. They were always speaking in nonsensical riddles. And no wonder. The bitch had been higher then than he was now. Maybe he ought to start telling prophecies himself.

Oh wait, he already knew one . . .

Artemis wouldn't come near him today or tomorrow, but on the third day she'd jump on top of him until he was limping.

See . . . prophet. He knew the future even better than the oracle did.

Laughing bitterly, he rolled off the banister and headed to his bed.

The next thing he knew, he was in Artemis's temple, lying on the floor at her feet. "A little warning would be nice, Artemis."

Laughing, she wrapped her arms around his shoulders and nuzzled his neck. "I was feeling peckish."

He should have known. "You told me you wouldn't be able to see me until the day after tomorrow."

She stroked his neck with her nails, causing chills to run up and down his body. "There was a lull so I made space for you. A little gratitude could serve you well."

He leaned his head back to give her a droll stare. "Can't you see the gratitude oozing out of me?"

She nipped at the tip of his nose. "Sarcasm doesn't become you."

"Yet it makes you crave me whenever I am."

She smiled. "How do you manage to read me so well?"

It wasn't hard. She adored the fact he wasn't in awe of her. The fact that her eyes dilated and her breathing increased were clues hard to miss.

She nibbled his lips. "I've missed you."

A sharp gasp intruded on their play.

Acheron froze at the sound that brought Artemis off her chaise in a roar of anger. There in front of them was a tall, slender woman with strawberry blond hair. Her dark eyes were round in terror.

"What are you doing here, Satara?"

"I just . . . I-I-I saw nothing, Aunt Artemis. Forgive me."

Artemis caught her by the hair and jerked her close. "Look at me." Her fangs were out and her eyes were red and tinged by orange. "You speak a word to any being about what you've just seen and there is no power that will save your life or your soul. Do you understand?"

Satara nodded vigorously.

Artemis shoved her away. "Go and don't you dare return until you're summoned."

She vanished instantly.

Artemis then turned on him with a vengeance. "This is all your fault!"

Of course it was. "You're the one who brought me here."

"Silence!" She backhanded him.

Acheron growled at the taste of blood in his mouth. He wanted to strike her back, but he knew the repercussions. He was mortal and she wasn't. Yet it was more than that. As much as that slap hurt him mentally, he wouldn't deal it to her. No one should have to bleed for kindness.

They damn sure shouldn't have to bleed for love.

"Are you through?" he asked.

She set on him then with her fangs.

Acheron hissed as she took her anger at Satara out on him. He felt two tendrils of blood fall from her lips, down the front of his chest. Pain seared him as she fed with no regard for him at all.

When she was finished, she shoved him back.

Weak from the blood loss, he fell to his knees.

She grabbed him by the hair and jerked him back against her. A knife appeared in her hand as she hovered it over his heart.

Acheron met her gaze and waited. "Kill me, Artie. End it."

Her eyes darkened to the point he was sure she'd finish him, but just as the dagger came at his heart, she reversed the direction and flung it against the wall. She wrapped her arms around him and held him close as she wept.

"Why do you make me want you?"

Acheron laughed bitterly. "I'm not the one doing this. Believe me." If he had his way, no one would ever crave him again.

She pushed him out of her arms. "Just go."

As if he had a choice?

At least this time, she put him back in his bed. But he was still bleeding from her dinner. Sighing, he got up to tend the wound.

"You're the only male she's ever had in her temple . . . besides my father."

Acheron spun around to see Satara standing near his bed. "What are you doing here?"

"I wanted to meet the man who would make Artemis risk everything."

He held his breath in sharp panic. "She would destroy us both if she knew you were here."

Satara shrugged nonchalantly. "She doesn't pay attention to the human realm. Trust me."

Acheron didn't move as she crossed the short distance between them.

Frowning, she studied him as if he were some deformed curiosity. "You *are* beautiful. Perhaps I'd risk my godhood for you too." She reached to touch his face.

Acheron caught her hand. "You need to leave."

"I would be a kinder lover to you than Artemis is."

As if he needed that.

"Look," Satara said firmly. "I can tell by your eyes that you're a demigod like me—the fact that your blood sustains her is proof of that. And I saw how Artemis treated you. I promise you, I wouldn't be so callous. Not to mention that with the powers I have, you and I could take hers. Imagine, two demigods with the power of a god. We would be invincible."

"There's no such thing as invincible. There's always something that flaws every being no matter how powerful they are. A weakness . . . You recognize me as Artemis's. Someone will know yours and they'll find mine. Right or wrong, I pledged myself to her and I will not back out on my word."

She sneered at him as if he were mentally defective. "Then you're a fool."

"I've been called worse."

She shook her head. "And you're content to be her lapdog?"

No he wasn't. But what choice did he have? "Again, I gave her my word and I will not be a liar."

She snorted in derision. "Then I'm sorry I misjudged you. However, I find myself in a bit of a quandary. If she ever finds out about this, she'll kill me, niece or not. But since you appear to be a man of your word, do I have your oath that you'll never tell Artemis what I've said today?"

"I don't like plotting another's downfall, not even yours. That being said, if you ever go after Artemis, then I will tell her what you've done. So long as she's safe, you're safe. I swear it."

She cocked her head as if baffled by his threat. "You're bartering with me to protect the same sow who would sooner beat you than treat you with the same loyalty you show her?"

Acheron shrugged. "I'm protecting my best friend. Right or wrong. I will stand by her."

Satara shook her head. "You and I have an accord then. I only hope you find her worth your loyalty."

So did he. But like Satara, he somehow doubted it.

With one last warning glare, Satara left him.

Acheron raked a hand through his hair as he tried to sort this out. So Artemis had as many people plotting her demise as his father. Damn. What was it about power that made everyone covet it so? Why couldn't people be content with what they had? Why must family and friends turn on each other over something so insanely innocuous? Something that in the long run didn't matter at all . . .

When love was shown to someone how could they let greed and selfishness spoil it? He just didn't understand that.

Love was so pure and innocent when given, especially unconditionally. Why couldn't those who received it see it for the beautiful gift it was? Why must they use it as a tool to hurt the one who gave it?

As Artemis did with him.

As Styxx did with his father.

It was why he loved his nephew so. Apollodorus asked for nothing more than attention and when he hugged and gave a sloppy kiss to the cheek it was pure, joyful love. There was no subterfuge. No giving in order to get something back.

Why couldn't the world be like that?

Then again, who was he to ask those questions? His own mother had been incapable of showing even the most basic compassion toward him.

Love, unfortunately, was a weakness squandered on those who didn't deserve it.

Acheron grabbed the wine bottle from his table and uncorked it. There wasn't much solace here, but some was infinitely better than none. The gods knew he couldn't find

325

solace anywhere else. Maybe he should have taken Satara up on her offer.

But what price would she have exacted? There was always a price for everything in life. For that wisdom, he could almost thank Estes.

Nothing in this world ever came freely.

Nothing.

"Acheron?"

He tensed at the sound of Artemis's voice. She was nowhere to be seen. But, he could feel her like a whisper on his soul.

She manifested behind him. "I'm sorry, Acheron. I shouldn't have treated you that way."

"Then why did you?"

Still invisible, she nuzzled his shoulder. "I'm afraid and I let my fear direct me."

"You're a goddess."

"I'm one of many and not as powerful as others. Do you know what they do to a goddess when they strip her of her powers? They cast her to earth to exist among the humans who abuse and mock her. Is that what you'd have for me?"

Why not? It was what she would have for him.

Unfortunately, he wasn't that cruel. "No. I only want what's best for you, Artie. But I'm tired of your taking everything out on me. I'm not a mindless doll you can beat when you're frustrated."

She materialized so that he could see the sincerity in those beautiful green eyes. "I know and I'm trying. I really am. Just be impatient with me."

"Impatient?"

She frowned. "That's the wrong word, isn't it? I don't know why I mix them up sometimes."

These moments when she allowed herself to be vulnerable were the ones that endeared her to him. They were the ones that had allowed him to love her.

Cupping her face in his hands, he gave her a tender kiss.

Artemis sighed as a wave of relief went through her. She loved him so much and yet she was so terrified of what loving him meant. She truly didn't want to hurt him ever. He was the only person she could be herself around. With other gods she had to be fierce and defensive and with mortals she had to be divine and intolerant.

Acheron was the one person who allowed her to laugh. He was the only one who held her and made her feel warm inside. But the problem was, whenever she opened herself up she felt the coldness inside him and knew that even though he was loyal to her, she didn't make him happy. That hurt the most. The pain inside him that she couldn't alleviate made her want to lash out in anger and hurt him for not being as open with her as she was with him.

Why couldn't he feel what she did?

Even now there was a reservation in his touch. A hesitation and she didn't understand why.

How could she make him love her the way he had when they first met?

She wanted to punish him for not loving her like she loved him. To make him beg her for her love. But how?

Pulling back, her gaze went to his neck and she cringed at what she'd done to him while she'd fed—it was something Apollo would have done to her. "I didn't mean to hurt you."

Acheron held his breath at words that had been said to him so many times. Just once couldn't someone think of that *before* they damaged him?

"I'm fine." But the truth was, he wasn't. He'd never been all right with the pain. He'd merely grown used to it.

She brushed the hair back from his face. "You look so tired. I shouldn't have taken so much blood from you." She tugged him toward the bed. "You should rest."

True. There was no telling what horrors would be there for him on the morrow. Another gelding or beating, or just the emotional punching that Artemis excelled at.

He couldn't wait.

"Will you come to me tomorrow?" he asked again, desperate to not be alone while the whole world lavished well wishes on his twin brother.

Artemis hesitated. She wanted to come, but Apollo would be here for Styxx's celebration. She had to be careful. Because they were twins and gods, he could sense whenever she was near. If he felt her, he'd come seeking her and that could very well cost Acheron his life. "You know I have a festival. How can I miss it?"

He looked away and the hurt she felt from him sliced through her own heart.

"I'll visit the next day."

Acheron held his emotions in check. "I'll look forward to it then."

"Are you being sullen with me?"

"No." He was hurt. "I hope you have a good festival."

Artemis raked her hand through his hair. "Will you think of me while I'm gone?"

"I always do."

She leaned down to kiss his cheek. "You always make me feel so special."

And she always made him feel like shit. She tucked her arm under his so that she could take his hand. He held it to his heart and let out a long sigh.

As he did so, a bad feeling went through him. Something was going to happen tomorrow. He could feel it with every part of him. Whatever it was, he was certain it would change him and Artemis forever.

Akri di diyam.

June 23, 9527 BC

Acheron sat on the railing of his balcony completely drunk in the darkness as he watched the elaborately dressed guests arriving for the birthday party in the palace below. His back was pressed against the building while his legs were stretched out before him in a precarious balance. He wasn't sure how much he'd imbibed at this point.

Unfortunately, it wasn't enough to kill him. But if he were lucky, he might yet tumble from his perch to the rocks a hundred feet below and die horribly there.

That would definitely fuck up his brother's birthday celebration. For the first time in weeks, he laughed at the thought of Styxx dropping dead in front of the gathered nobles and dignitaries.

It would serve them right.

"It's my birthday too," he shouted, knowing no one could hear him. Even if they could, they wouldn't care.

Acheron turned his head and flinched as pain cut through him. He hated the fact that Artemis alone could give him so much anguish. He'd been so careful to shield himself from the callousness of others. But Artemis cut him on a level no one else could touch.

And like everyone else, she didn't care how much she hurt him.

Then again, he should be grateful. At least this year he wasn't celebrating the anniversary of his birth in prison . . .

Or a stew.

Ever alone. Even when he was in a crowd, surrounded by people, he was alone.

Truthfully, he was tired of it. No one wanted him. The only reason his so-called family cared whether he lived or died was because if he died, their beloved Styxx died too.

"I've had enough."

Even though he was only one and twenty, he was as tired as an old man. He'd lived beyond his years and wanted no more pain. No more loneliness.

It was time to end it.

The voices he heard in his head were louder now. They were calling him home . . .

Acheron stood up on the railing. The winds from below rushed up over him, fanning his hair out as he stared down at the black sea that beckoned him like a lover. He dropped his goblet and watched as it tumbled down below, vanishing from his sight.

One step.

No pain.

Everything would end.

"It's time," he breathed. There was no one here to stop him now. No Ryssa to pull him back. No father to tie him down and prevent it. No Estes to call for a physician.

Freedom.

Closing his eyes, he let go and stepped off.

Fear and relief whipped through him as he plummeted through the weightless air. In a moment, he'd have his long-sought-after peace.

Suddenly, something hard struck his stomach. Acheron gasped at the pain. He opened his eyes out of reflex.

Instead of falling, he was now rising, away from the sea. The sound of the waves crashing against rocks was replaced by the heavy fluttering of giant wings. He turned to see a female demon holding him. Just as the oracle had said.

"Let me go!" he shouted, trying to free himself.

She didn't. Not until she'd returned him to the balcony where he'd been.

Acheron staggered back as she perched on the railing and watched him closely. She had long straight black hair that fell over skin marbled white and red. Her eyes glowed in the darkness, white irises, surrounded by vivid red. Like her hair, her wings and horns were black.

"What are you doing?" he asked, his voice filled with venom.

"Akri should be more careful," she whispered kindly. "Had Xiamara been a moment later, you would have died."

"I wanted to die."

She cocked her head in a gesture that reminded him of a bird. "But why, akri?" She looked over her shoulder to where the people were still arriving. "So many come to celebrate your human birth."

"They don't come for me."

Xiamara frowned at him. "But you are the prince. Heir."

He laughed bitterly. "I'm heir to shit and prince of nothing."

"Nay. You are Apostolos, son of Apollymi. Revered by all."

"I am Acheron, son of no one. Revered only within the confines of a bedroom."

She stepped slowly down before him. Her wings tucked themselves around her lithe body. "You don't remember your birth. I understand. I was sent here by your mother with her gift for you."

He was trying to follow her words, but his mind was too numbed by drink. The demon was insane. She must have him confused with someone else. "My mother is dead."

"The human queen, yes. But your real mother, the goddess Apollymi, is alive and wishes you all of her love. I am her most faithful servant, Xiamara, and I am here to protect you as I've protected her."

Acheron shook his head. He was drunk. Hallucinating. Maybe he'd already died.

"Get away from me."

The demon didn't. Before he could escape, she placed a small orb to his heart.

Acheron screamed out as pain tore through him. Never in his life had he felt anything like this, and given the tortures they'd put him through, that said much. It was as if there was poisonous fire in his veins, ripping through his entire body.

From the center of his chest where the orb rested, his skin changed from tawny to a marbled blue . . .

331

As the pain and color unfurled through him, images and voices screamed out, piercing his eardrums. Scents assaulted his nostrils. Even his clothes burned against his skin. He fell to the ground and curled up into a ball as every sense he had was assailed.

"You are the god Apostolos. Harbinger and son of Apollymi the Destroyer. Your will is the will of the universe. You are the final fate of all . . ."

Acheron kept shaking his head in denial. No. It couldn't be. "I am nothing. I am nothing."

The demon lifted his head. "Why are you not happy? You are a god now."

Fury rode him hard as he grabbed her. He didn't understand his powers or anything else that was happening to him, but all the years of his life, all the degradations and horrors tore through him. Those he let travel from his mind into hers.

The demon cried out as she slung her head back. "*Ni!* This was not supposed to happen to you, akri. Not this . . ."

He grabbed her and forced her gaze to meet his. "It was bad enough when they thought me the human son of a god. Can you imagine what they'll do to me now? Take these powers away from me."

"I cannot. They are yours by birthright."

Acheron fell back, banging his head against the stone floor. "No!" he shrieked. "No! I don't want this. I only want to be left alone."

Xiamara tried to embrace him.

Acheron pushed her away. "I want nothing from you. You've done enough damage to me."

"Akri—"

"Out of my sight!"

Her eyes glowed with reluctance. "Your will is my own." The orb she'd held against him appeared as a necklace about his neck. "If you need me, akri, call and I will come."

Acheron pressed his hand against his skull that ached and throbbed with new voices and sensations. He felt as if he were going mad and perhaps he was. Perhaps the cruelty had finally shattered his sanity.

He heard the demon leave as unknown voices whispered and shouted through his mind. It was as if he could hear the entire world at once. He knew every thought, every wish, every fear.

His breathing ragged, he wanted an escape from it. He snatched at the necklace, but it wouldn't break. Instead, it glowed in his palm.

Crying out, he wanted to jump again. Unfortunately, he couldn't even stand. He was so dizzy. So ill . . .

What had they done to him now?

Apollymi *paced the* small courtyard in Kalosis, waiting for Xiamara's return.

"Where's the Simi's matera?"

She turned slightly to see a young child in the doorway. Named for her mother, Xiamara, Simi—which was Charonte for baby—was almost three thousand years old and yet she looked no older than a four-year-old human child. Unlike humans and gods, Charonte demons were very slow to mature.

Apollymi knelt down and held her arms out for Simi. "She's not back yet, sweeting. Soon."

Simi pouted before she ran to her and threw her arms around Apollymi's neck. She put one small thumb into her mouth and buried her other hand deep in Apollymi's hair.

Apollymi closed her eyes as she hugged the small demon. How she wished she could have held her own son like this. Just once. Instead, she'd contented herself with lavishing her love on Xiamara's simi while she waited for her son to grow old enough to free her.

Simi laid her head on Apollymi's shoulder while Apollymi sang to her. "Why is akra sad?"

"I'm not sad, Simi. I'm anxious."

"Is anxious like when the Simi eats too much and her stomach hurts?"

Apollymi smiled and kissed the top of her head. "Not exactly. It's when you can't wait for something to happen."

"Ooo like when the Simi is hungry and she's waiting on her matera to feed her."

"Something like that."

Apollymi felt a movement in the air. She looked to the shadows to see the outline of Xiamara's body. For a full minute, she couldn't move as she waited for her best friend to join her.

But there was a hesitancy to Xiamara that made her heart stop. "What is it?"

Xiamara held her hands out for Simi who gratefully went to her mother. The demon held her daughter as tears fell down her cheeks.

Apollymi felt her own eyes mist as fear gripped her. "Xi? Tell me."

She clenched her eyes closed while she continued to rock her daughter. "I don't know how to tell you, akra."

The more she hesitated, the more fraught with worry Apollymi was. "Is he not well? I'm still a prisoner here so I know he lives."

"He lives."

"Does he not . . . love me?"

Xiamara shook her head before she set Simi down. "Go find your sister, Simi. I need to speak with akra alone."

Sucking her thumb, Simi skipped away from them.

When Xiamara faced her, Apollymi felt the blood drain from her cheeks. "What aren't you telling me?"

Xiamara sniffed back her tears before she placed her hand on Apollymi's shoulder and transferred the images Apostolos had given her. Disbelief and horror racked her as Apollymi saw what had been done to her child.

Those emotions gave way to a fury so profound, all she could do was scream. The sound of it echoed through the Palace of the Dead all of the way up to Katoteros where the rest of the gods made their home.

All activity stopped as the other Atlantean gods heard the sound of utmost heartache.

One by one, they turned to face Archon whose features blanched.

"Is she free?" Epithymia, the goddess of desire, asked.

Archon shook his head. "She'd be here already if she were free. No. Something else has happened. For now, we're safe." At least he hoped so . . .

334

Apollymi staggered away from Xiamara as image after image branded itself into her mind. What the humans had done to her son . . .

"I will kill them all," she growled through clenched teeth. "Everyone who laid a hand to him will die in flames, begging for my mercy and I will have none for them. None!" She looked up at Xiamara. "And Archon will know the full weight of my wrath. There is nothing inside me for him now."

Xiamara tucked her black wings around herself. "But Apostolos refuses to accept what's his. He refuses me."

"Go to him anyway, Xi. Comfort him and help him understand what he has to do. Tell him that when he comes to me all will be made right."

"I will try, akra."

Acheron lay in the darkness of his room, trying to breathe as he shook from the pain of his overwhelmed senses. Suddenly, he heard a soft, gentle voice in his head that drowned it all out. It was truly the most beautiful sound he'd ever known.

His breathing eased along with the fading pain.

"I am with you now, Apostolos."

"Who are you?"

"That is the voice of your mother."

He squinted in the dark to see the demon kneeling beside him. He curled into a ball, away from her. "I have no mother. She cast me aside when I was born."

"Ni, akri," the demon said softly. "I was the one who took you from your mother's arms while she wept in fear for you. Your mother, Apollymi, hid you in the human realm to protect you from the gods who wanted you dead. I swear to you on my life. Neither of us ever meant for you to be harmed. You were supposed to be raised as a prince. Pampered. Beloved. None of this should have happened to you."

He found that impossible to believe. "I don't understand. Why do the gods want me dead?"

"It was prophesied that you would be the end of the Atlantean gods. But you have to understand how much your mother loves you. She risked her life and defied the other gods to save you and keep you hidden until you were old enough to use your powers to fight them. Even now she sits imprisoned, wanting you to come to her. Free her, Apostolos and she will make right every wrong ever done to you."

"Make it right how?"

"She will destroy everyone who ever harmed you." The demon stroked his hair like the mother she described. "You are the most loved of any child ever born. Every day I have sat with your mother while she wept for your loss and ached to have you with her. Come home with me, Apostolos. Meet your mother."

He wanted to. And yet . . . "How do I know I can trust you?"

"Why would I lie?"

Everyone lied, especially to him. "For any number of reasons."

Xiamara. They come. Leave him quickly!

The demon shrank back from his bed. "The gods can't find me with you or they'll know who and where you are. Listen to your mother's voice and I'll return as soon as I can. Stay hidden, precious one." She vanished instantly.

Acheron lay alone, listening to the voices that tangled inside him. He heard laughter and tears, curses and screams.

Until his mother's voice soothed him again. He focused on that single tone and closed his eyes as it drove away all the other voices that made his head throb.

Had the demon been telling the truth? Dare he believe for one moment that he was the beloved son of anyone?

Surely it was preposterous.

He cupped the necklace in his hand and studied it. Some kind of stone, it appeared milky and iridescent. Then he glanced to where his slave's mark had been branded into his palm.

It was gone now without a single trace. How could this be?

I'm a god who was a slave . . .

Not just any slave. The lowest of all.

Acheron covered his eyes with his hand as shame overwhelmed him. And as he lay there, images tore through him . . . he saw the past, the present and the future through the experiences of thousands of people. He could hear their hopes and fears. Hear the very essence of the universe.

For the first time, he saw those who had it worse than he did. Those who seemed to have it better. The screams of mothers who'd lost their children. Children who had no parents. Beggars and kings . . .

Now he understood what Artemis had meant when she said she paid no attention to the human world. It was overwhelming. Horrifying. All these people who needed help and as he imagined helping them, he saw numerous outcomes play out in his mind.

But the one thing he couldn't see was his own life.

Or Ryssa's.

Not even Artemis. Why? It made no sense. As if any of this could possibly make sense. Acheron laughed at the absurdity of it all.

Opening his eyes, he realized that he was no longer on the ground. He was hovering over it. He gasped, then fell back to the floor. Pain shot through him as his skin again marbled to blue. His fingernails turned black and grew long . . .

Something wasn't right. His body was now alien to him. He stared at the marbled skin, trying to understand why it would be such a color.

How could he hide *this* from his family? *Do you want to?* A sadistic laugh went through him as he imagined the look on his "father's" face as he told him who and what he was.

"I'm a god."

Not half, but full-blooded. One with a bounty on his head, with an entire pantheon out to kill him. It was ridiculous. It defied belief, yet here he was . . . blue.

Acheron tried to get up, but a wave of dizziness sent him back to his knees. He looked at his bed, wishing he could make it to it. The next thing he knew, he was under the covers.

337

His eyes widened as the full implication of what he was hit him. He was a god with the same powers as Artemis.

Or maybe not. How did god powers work?

"Acheron?"

He tensed at the sound of Ryssa's voice in the room with him. Glancing down, he saw that his skin was again normal and he was grateful that the blanket covered him completely. "Yes?"

"Are you ill?"

Technically no. He wasn't even drunk anymore. "I'm just resting."

He felt her sit beside him on the bed and tug at the blanket. "Will you look at me?"

Terrified of what might happen while she sat there, he uncovered his head.

She smiled. "I haven't seen you all day and wanted to give you this." She held a small box out to him.

Her gift made his throat tight. "Thank you." Returning her smile, he opened it to find a small medallion on a bracelet. It was the symbol of a sun with three lightning bolts piercing it. He frowned at the emblem that seemed eerily familiar.

"I know it's strange, but I saw it in the market and it made me think of you. The jeweler said it was a symbol of strength."

"It's Atlantean." The sun design was that of Apollymi . . . his mother.

I've made him sad. Why did I pick this one? Oh no . . .

He heard Ryssa's thoughts in his head.

"It's beautiful. Thank you."

She reached for it. "I can—"

He covered her hand with his. "I love it, Ryssa."

He's only saying that. I'm so sorry, Acheron. I didn't mean to pick out something Atlantean. How could I have been so stupid?

It was so disconcerting to hear her thoughts so clearly while she held a false smile in place.

"If you're sure . . ."

He nodded. "I'm sure. Thank you," he repeated.

338

I'm such a fool. Here I tried to make sure he had at least one gift and I've ruined it with my stupidity.

The sincere love he felt in those words brought tears to his eyes. His sister really did love him . . . more than he'd ever guessed.

He brought her hand to his lips and kissed it. "You mean everything to me, Ryssa. You know that, don't you?"

"I love you, Acheron." *And I wish I could make this day as special as it should be for you. It's not fair that you're here alone.*

"Ryssa!" Her father's shout was enough to make Acheron glare at the door.

Ryssa frowned at him. *Dear gods, what's wrong with his eyes?*

Acheron averted his gaze, scared of what they might look like now. His body was still normal, but what of his eyes?

His door slammed opened to reveal her father. "What are you doing here? It's time to toast your brother."

She stood up and lifted her chin. "I was giving my brother his gift."

"Don't you dare be impertinent. Your presence is required. Now."

"Go, Ryssa," Acheron breathed. "Your father wants you."

You godless whore.

Acheron laughed at the king's thoughts. If the man only knew . . .

The last word anyone could use to describe him was godless. He had gods coming for him out of the woodwork.

The king didn't move as Ryssa stepped past him. He stood in the doorway, glaring his anger at Acheron. "So you've finally given up calling me your father?"

Acheron shrugged. "Believe me, I know you're not my father. And I'm sure your son is waiting below to hear your most precious ode to him."

He must be drunk. "You're to stay here."

"Don't worry. I have no intention of fucking up your party." Yet . . . Of course had his original plan worked out, the king would be mourning his beloved son right now.

I should have the bastard beaten, except it would cast a pall on Styxx's party. That smug prick . . . The king withdrew and closed his door.

Acheron shook his head, trying to clear it of the king's thoughts. He picked up Ryssa's gift to study it. How ironic that she would give him this tonight. It was as if his mother had somehow guided her to it.

"Apostolos?"

He froze at the hesitant female voice he'd heard so many times in his life and thought himself mad. "Matera?"

"My baby. I swear I will avenge you. But we must be careful. Xiamara will return and show you how to use your powers. Leave them alone for now so that Archon can't find you. Stay hidden and when the others have ceased their machinations, she will lead you to me and I will make sure no one ever hurts you again. I swear it on my life."

He felt the lightest whisper of air against his cheek . . . like a small caress before the air was still again.

Clenching his teeth, he felt the pain overwhelm him. His mother loved him . . . His real mother.

He wanted to see her desperately. To know, just once, what it felt like to have a parent look on him the way the king looked at Styxx or Ryssa. With pride. With love.

I'm wanted.

More than that, Artemis would no longer have to be ashamed of him. While it was unseemly for a goddess to be with a whore, there was nothing shameful about being with another god.

She could love him openly . . .

He wanted to shout in joy. Holding Ryssa's bracelet to his chest, he smiled at the thought of telling Artemis what had happened to him. Surely she'd be thrilled.

How could she not?

Yet he still had a strange sense of foreboding that warned him he should be afraid of what tomorrow would bring.

June 24, 9527 BC

Acheron paced the floor, desperate for Artemis to appear so that he could surprise her with his newfound role. The morning had been interesting as he discovered new things about himself. He could move objects with nothing more than a thought. Like Artemis, he could teleport outside and back in. Granted his mother had told him not to use these powers, but honestly he couldn't help it. They were much more in control of him than the other way around.

And still he heard the voices from the people around him and even off in far lands. Sometimes so loud the pain of it drove him to his knees. Every single thought. The entire world was laid bare at his feet.

The only peace he had was around Apollodorus whose desires were simple. Eat, sleep and be held and loved. There was so much solace in simply holding his nephew that it eased all the other voices screaming at him and allowed Acheron to focus and ground himself.

"Acheron?"

He turned around as Ryssa exploded into his room in a flurry with Apollodorus in her arms. *Apollo is such an ass. I'm so tired of being his plaything or food. He thinks I have no purpose but to come to him the moment he snaps his fingers.* "I have to go for a little bit. Could you please watch Apollodorus? His nurse can't get him to stop fussing and I can't tend him right now." *His father is a selfish pig who thinks I'm his trained bitch.* "I hope you don't mind."

Acheron shook his head in an effort to determine what he heard with his ears versus his mind. It was extremely disconcerting. "I don't mind." He took Apollodorus from her arms.

Mama? Hold me . . .

Acheron tightened his grip on his nephew. "I have him. Don't worry."

"Thank you." *I don't know what I'd do without you, akribos. You're the only one I can depend on. The rest of them are worthless.* "I'll be back as soon as I can." She placed a quick kiss on Apollodorus's head, then ran out of the room, cursing Apollo with every step.

He looked at his nephew who was watching him curiously. "I had no idea your mother knew such language."

Apollodorus laughed as if he understood. *Theo play with me?*

"Absolutely." Acheron knelt on the floor and put him on his feet so that Apollodorus could hold onto him and walk.

Appie love theo.

Acheron smiled at the boy's nickname for himself. *Appie loves his uncle.* He treasured those words. Closing his eyes, he tried to see the man his nephew would grow into, but as with Ryssa, he saw nothing. It was so odd. Everyone who came near him, he saw their future with utmost clarity.

Why not those closest to him?

Apollodorus fell back on his rump to suck his thumb.

"So what shall the two of us do while your mama is away?"

Tickle belly.

Acheron laughed. "All right." He obliged and Apollodorus squealed in delight. He rolled onto his back and kicked his legs while he held Acheron's hand to his stomach.

The pure simplicity of his nephew's joy and love touched him so deep inside that he wanted to hold the child for the rest of eternity and keep him safe. There was nothing he loved more than this one tiny being. He prayed it would always be like this between them. That no hurtful words or actions would drive them apart.

What would the child think when he grew older and Styxx and his father told him what Acheron had been? Would it matter to the child that all of it had been against Acheron's will? That he would never have done it had there been any choice?

Or worse, would he be like Maia . . .

His gut tightened with the thought. Picking up the boy, Acheron held him against his chest as tightly as he could without hurting him. "Please don't ever hate me, Appie. I couldn't take that from you."

Appie loves theo.

Acheron cherished every syllable.

"How touching."

He opened his eyes to find Artemis standing in front of them. "Have you ever seen Apollodorus?"

She shrugged. "Not really. Apollo has bastards aplenty. But he is cute enough I suppose for a smelly small human."

Acheron tried to hear her thoughts. But unlike the humans, it wasn't easy. He had to strain for it and then he could only get pieces of them.

Put the child down. I wanted to be with you. "Where's its mother?"

"With Apollo."

She rolled her eyes and sighed. "Doesn't that thing have a keeper?"

"Yes and at the moment, the keeper would be me."

She put her hands on her hips.

"Sit down, Artie and meet your nephew. His bites don't hurt." *Unlike hers.*

Her entire demeanor showed her agitation as she sat down beside them. "Is it wet?"

"He's not wet."

Apollodorus held one hand in his mouth as he stared curiously at Artemis. *She's not right, theo . . .*

Acheron laughed at the thought.

Artemis glared at them. "What's so funny?"

"Nothing," he said, wondering why she couldn't hear the boy's thoughts too. It made him curious how much the powers of the gods differed from each other—maybe there were a lot of things he could do that she couldn't . . . "As a god, do you ever hear what other people are thinking?"

She rolled her eyes. "I do my best not to. They're always boring. Either they're scheming to hurt someone or begging for something. People are insects."

Her rabid hostility caught him off guard. Although some of the people he'd known in his life were so low, he wouldn't insult an insect by linking them to the cretins who'd abused him. "Including me?"

She brushed her hand through his hair. "No. You're quiet to me. I never hear your thoughts. It's why I like being with you."

He found it disconcerting that he couldn't hear what she was thinking.

Still, as a god, shouldn't she know when she was sitting next to another one? How could she not know what had happened to him last night? "Do you sense anything different about me?"

"Other than the fact you're cuddling a smelly boy, no." She dropped her hand. "I know you humans put a lot of stock in the anniversaries of your birth, but really all it marks is one year closer to death. Who'd want to celebrate that?"

Acheron snorted at her answer. So she couldn't sense his unlocked godhood. Fascinating. "I wasn't talking about my age."

"Then what? You haven't cut your hair and I can tell by the way the small thing is climbing on you and you're not wincing that you haven't been beaten. What else has happened?"

The fact that she could be so cavalier about his beatings set his anger off. The bitch should have to suffer through the pain and humiliation of one to understand it wasn't something to be taken so lightly. "Nothing."

She waved his hostile answer away dismissively. "You're such an odd man."

Apollodorus crawled over to Artemis. They stared at each other for a full minute before he smiled and put his wet hand on her arm.

"Ow! Disgusting." She wiped it away.

Acheron held his arms out and Apollodorus returned to him.

"How do you stand that?" Artemis shivered as he picked the boy up and Apollodorus gave him a wet kiss on his cheek.

344

"I love him, Artie. There's nothing disgusting about him."

She shivered even harder as if it were the most repulsive thing she could imagine. "You want your own child, don't you?" Her accusatory tone amazed him. It was as if she thought him an imbecile for wanting something like that.

Acheron held his nephew close as he considered a question that had never crossed his mind. "Since I can't have any, I've never thought about it really."

"But if you could?"

He looked at his nephew and smiled. He'd give anything to be able to create something so precious. "I can think of no greater gift than to have my own child look at me the way Appie does."

"Then we should find a baby for you."

He scoffed at the thought before he changed the subject to one that really mattered and was a lot more feasible. "Tell me something, Artie. If I were a god, would you acknowledge our friendship to other people?"

She made a sound of utter disgust in the back of her throat. "You're not a god, Acheron."

"But if I were . . ."

"Why do you ponder such ridiculous thoughts?"

"Why do you avoid answering me?"

"Because it doesn't matter. You're not a god. I told you, your eyes are a deformity. Nothing more."

How could a god be so blind as not to see another of its kind? Or was his mother really so powerful that she'd managed to shield him so completely from all gods? "And you've never known a god to have eyes like mine?"

"No."

Maybe it wasn't his godhood . . . maybe it was because they were from different pantheons. "Have you ever met an Atlantean god?"

Exasperated, she flicked her hands at him so hard that her nails actually made a popping sound. "Why are you so inquisitive today?"

"Why are you getting angry over such simple questions?"

"Because I want to spend time with you without that thing attached to you. Could we put him in a cage?"

Acheron was aghast. "Artemis!"

"What? He'd be safe there."

"He'd cry and be scared."

"Fine." She pushed herself to her feet and glared at them. "I'll come back when you're free of him." She vanished instantly.

Apollodorus stared up at him curiously. Acheron patted the boy on the back as he shook his head.

"Well Appie, that was your Aunt Artemis in all her glory."

Art-ee-miss.

He smiled at the boy's attempt to pronounce it in his head. "Close enough. Not that it really matters. I don't think she's going to be around much for you."

Ackee be with Appie.

His smile widened at the way Apollodorus pronounced his name. "Ackee will always be with you."

Giggling, Apollodorus curled up in his lap and laid his head down. Acheron stroked his small back and before he knew it, the baby was asleep.

He picked him up and held him against his shoulder where the sound of the baby's soft snore kept the rest of the world away from his head. He was at peace with the universe right now and wondered if his mother would have held him like this.

For the first time in his life, he thought that she might. At least his real mother.

Apollymi.

Apollymi continued to pace as Xiamara stood, watching her. "That Greek goddess keeps seeing my son. Do you think we could use her to protect him?"

Xiamara hesitated. Perhaps she shouldn't have kept everything from her friend, but if Apollymi knew the full extent of Apostolos's human life there was no telling what she might do. "I don't know, akra. The Greeks aren't like us and Artemis isn't all that powerful within their pantheon. She would be afraid I think to protect him."

Apollymi growled in frustration. "We have to do something."

"I can bring him here, but the moment I do, Archon and the others will descend on us and attack."

"I have no fear. Once I'm free, I can defeat them, plus we have your army. But with Apostolos . . . they would attack him and one of them might kill him while we're occupied with others."

That had been the only reason Apollymi had run from them while pregnant. Fear for the baby had kept her from battling. One stray strike and it could have ended her son's life. It was a risk she'd never take.

"Should I summon a Chthonian?"

Apollymi paused at the question and her heart wrenched. Though the Chthonians were usually human in birth, they possessed the powers of the gods and functioned as a sort of police unit for the various pantheons. They kept order and prevented all-out war between the gods. Even so, they had their own agendas which weren't always in the best interest of the universe and definitely not in *her* best interest. "I don't trust them. They're as likely to kill Apostolos to keep peace as save him. I won't take that chance." Frustration welled inside her. So long as Apostolos was in human form, he was vulnerable. He could be killed so easily right now . . . How could she get her son to her without jeopardizing his life?

Jaden . . .

She turned to look at Xiamara.

"Akra," she said in a chiding tone. "You're not thinking what I think you're thinking, are you?"

"Jaden could be bartered with to bring Apostolos here. But I would need a demon to summon him." She gave Xiamara a knowing look.

Jaden was a broker who made deals between demons and the primary source of the universe. His power equaled if not excelled that of a god. If ever there was a being who could protect and return her son to her, he was it.

"You know there is nothing I wouldn't do for you, Apollymi. But Jaden is unpredictable. Even if he takes the bargain, we'd have to offer him something supreme for this."

Honestly, she didn't care. She'd give anything for her son. "What would he take in exchange for his services?"

"There's no telling."

Apollymi stalked toward her pond where she could spy on the universe through its waters. She could have even used it to check in on Apostolos as he grew to manhood, but her fear for his safety had kept her from it. If Archon knew when she was watching her son, he'd have been able to use the pond to find Apostolos himself. Even now she didn't dare use it to see her son. It was a risk she refused to take.

She raised the water from the pond to form an iridescent ball in the air. There in the center, she focused her powers to find Jaden and see what it was he wanted most.

Dark shadows swirled and twisted. Then they began to take form . . .

Just as it would have been recognizable, it dissolved. Apollymi cursed. The power that owned him wouldn't allow her to see how to control him.

Damn it!

Anger and sorrow mixed inside her. Fine then. "Summon him and offer him my powers and life if he will give me five minutes alone with my son before I die. And if he promises to protect Apostolos for the rest of his life."

Xiamara gaped as she let out a nervous laugh punctuated by disbelief. "Apollymi, you can't."

She met her friend's gaze levelly. "If this were Xedrix, Xirena or Simi?"

Xiamara cursed as she realized she'd do the same exact thing to protect her children. "Are you sure?"

"He's my son, Xi. The only part of me that's worth living. Whatever it takes to save his life, make the bargain. I just want to hold him one time before I die."

Xiamara pulled her into a hug and held her close. "You are the bravest woman I've ever known, akra. I will do as you ask even though I don't want to."

"And will you bond with him when I'm gone?"

"You know I will. After all we've been through together, I'd give my life for you and for your son."

Apollymi choked on her tears. "Then you are the best friend anyone could ever have."

Xiamara tightened her hug before she stepped back. "I will return as quickly as possible."

Despondent and yet hopeful, Apollymi watched as Xiamara left her. She looked at the pond, desperate to check on her son, but knew better than to try. The moment Xiamara had unlocked Apostolos's powers, it had put the others on notice.

The day of reckoning was here. By all the gods of the universe, she would make them pay for what they'd done to her baby and for every day they'd made her live without him.

June 24, 9527 BC

Acheron walked through the center of the city, feeling the power of life moving through his veins. It was as if he were now truly part of the universe. Colors were more vibrant, every sound . . . he could hear heartbeats and blood rushing through veins. Every person he passed, he knew their names instantly. Their past, their present and their futures.

Nothing was hidden from him. He could feel the power of the ages. He felt invincible . . .

Mmmm, I'd love to have a sample of that.

He turned toward the woman whose thoughts were in his mind. She immediately glanced away as if embarrassed by her wantonness.

Acheron stopped dead as he realized something.

With his powers unlocked, the others didn't pounce on him the way they'd done before. Testing his theory since he now knew he could teleport himself away from them with nothing more than a thought, he lowered his cowl. The familiar tremor went through those who saw him, but for the first time in his life, they kept their distance. It was as if they could sense the powers within him and knew better than to approach.

Amazed, he jerked the cloak off and handed it to a beggar as he continued walking through the streets uncovered. Exposed. So this was what it felt like to be normal. It was incredible to live without fear. Without being mauled and hurt.

Wanting to laugh in relief and excitement, he headed toward Artemis's temple and fearlessly strode inside.

The temple was empty this time of day. Emboldened by his powers, he approached her statue.

"What are you doing here?"

He saw Artemis in the shadows. "I wanted to see you."

"You know better than to come here," she growled in a low, fierce tone. "What if someone saw you?"

He tsked at her. "What's the matter, Artie? Why can't I make an offering to a goddess? Am I really that offensive to you?"

Artemis scowled. There was something different about Acheron today. An essence of power rippled . . . like the presence of a god, and yet she knew better. "Are you drunk?"

His grin was actually charming. "I can't get drunk anymore."

"What do you mean?"

"Nothing." He approached her like a feral beast stalking its prey. Slow. Sensual. Seductive. She was mesmerized by the beauty of his fluid movements that oozed an unnatural sexuality. Before she could move, he pulled her forcefully against him and kissed her lips.

Fire spread through her as she forgot all about being in the open with him. He hadn't kissed her like this in a long time. The next thing she knew, they were in her bedroom on Olympus.

Strange, she didn't remember bringing them here . . . But that thought was lost the instant he scooped her up in his arms and carried her to the bed. She loved whenever he carried her. It made her feel so feminine.

Acheron didn't know where his sudden surge of desire came from. It was overwhelming and exhilarating. He couldn't remember ever wanting to be with someone as much as he wanted Artemis just then. It was as if he had to have her right now.

As if something from deep within him was driving him to possess and dominate her.

Her fangs grew in as she made their clothes vanish. "You are so beautiful," she said with the slightest of lisps. "I want you inside me while I feed."

But he wasn't in the mood for that. He pulled her up to meet his lips so that he could kiss her with the fury and strength that boiled deep inside him. It was as if there was no humanity left there. Growling low in his throat, he rolled her over onto her stomach, spread her thighs wide and entered her from behind.

Artemis gasped as unimaginable pleasure tore through her body. Acheron had never been so forceful with her before. But even so, he was gentle. The mixture of the two blinded her with ecstasy. His strokes were so deep and strong. Powerful. It felt as if he were touching a part of her immortal soul.

"Tell me who you hunger for, Artemis," he growled in her ear.

She sucked her breath in sharply as he punctuated each word with a deep thrust. "You."

"And who do you crave?"

"Only you."

"Then say my name. I want you to use it while I'm inside of you. While I possess you."

"Acheron," she cried in pleasure.

He pulled out of her then and rolled her over to face him. His breathing ragged, he stared down at her with a desire so hot, it scalded her. There was nothing subservient about him now. He met her as an equal.

No, he was more than that.

His kiss burned her before he entered her again. Artemis arched her back, drawing him in even deeper.

He pulled back and cupped her face while he rode her deep and hard. His silver eyes flashed red. "Look at me while I'm inside you and say my name again."

"Acheron."

"And who commands you, Goddess? Who is the only man who makes you wet with desire?"

She cried out on the verge of an orgasm.

He froze as if he knew and the frustration of it was almost enough to make her slap him.

"Answer me, Artemis. If you want to come, tell me who you answer to."

She lifted her body and wrapped her legs around his lean hips. "You, Acheron. Only you."

He descended on her lips with another scorching kiss before he returned to thrusting against her. Unable to stand it,

352

she brushed his hair back from his neck and sank her teeth in deep.

The moment she did he drove himself in all the way to his hilt as they both came. Artemis screamed out as she shook in unrivaled bliss.

Acheron felt paralyzed by the spasms in his body. It was so rare for him to actually come inside her that the novelty of it temporarily blinded him. She clamped her body around his before she rolled him over onto his back so that she could feed.

Fully sated, he lay there while she drank her fill of his blood. For once there was no weakness from it.

With a shocked expression on her beautiful face, Artemis pulled back to stare down at him. Her eyes were now silver, her lips coated in his blood. "What are you?"

Before he could answer, he felt that foreign coldness seeping through him with the shiver of electricity that heralded he was turning blue.

Gasping, Artemis shot to the foot of the bed where she crouched naked as if ready to attack him.

Acheron threw his head back as his powers surged out in a wave so powerful, it shattered the windows of her room.

"Get out!" she shrieked. But this time when she tried to flash him back to the human world, he refused to go.

He grabbed her and pulled her against him. True to his suspicions, he saw his blue marbled hand on her pale arm. "What's the matter, Artie? Are you afraid of me now?"

Artemis gulped at the sight of her precious Acheron. Gone was the golden fair man whose every feature was perfect. What held her now was sinisterly beautiful. His skin swirled in a symphony of blue color. His hair was as black as his lips and nails.

And his eyes . . .

They flashed from silver to red and back again.

This was a god of destruction and she knew it. She could feel powers that made a mockery of even the ones Zeus possessed. Acheron could kill her . . .

"You tricked me!" she accused him.

"I've done nothing." His skin flashed back to normal. "I offered my heart to you once, Artemis. You told me I wasn't good enough for you. Am I now?"

No, this was even worse. To bring a more powerful god to Olympus . . .

They would kill her.

"What do you want?" she asked, terrified of his answer. Had he come to destroy all of them?

He reached a marbled blue hand up to cup her cheek. His eyes burned her with their tormented need. "I want you to love me."

"I do love you."

"You say that only because you're afraid of me now. I can feel it."

"No, Acheron. It's the truth. I've loved you since the moment you first kissed me."

His eyes turned vibrant, flaming red. "Then prove it."

"How?"

"Walk with me through the palace at Didymos. By my side. As my equal."

The very thought horrified her. "I can't do that."

"I'm a god. Why can't you walk with a god?"

Artemis shook her head. It wasn't that simple. "You were a whore."

Acheron flinched as those words tore through him with the ferocity of stinging blades.

"I am a *virgin* goddess," she said forcefully. "No one can ever know that I was seduced by a common prostitute. God or not, you cannot be claimed by me. Ever."

He still wasn't good enough. God or not, he was still nothing except unwanted garbage. An embarrassment. Not even his mother could claim him.

His heart shattered, he took a deep breath as he watched her cowering. In that moment, he hated himself for what he'd been and for what he was.

A bully.

He was no better than the ones who'd made him beg and crawl for kindness. The thought sickened him.

Coming off the bed, he pulled Artemis to her feet. She shivered as he leaned down to whisper in her ear. "Don't ever cower before me, Artie. I gave you my word that I would never hurt you and I will always stand by it." He cupped her cheek with his blue hand and laid a gentle kiss on the side of her head.

Artemis didn't breathe until Acheron was gone. Naked and trembling, she stood in the darkness of her room, confused by everything that had happened.

Acheron was a god.

But of what pantheon? She could still taste the power of his blood. That power mixed with hers and gave her just a glimpse of his capabilities.

He was a destroyer. A god-killer. All of her pantheon lived in fear of the dark gods. The ones who could command the primal source of the universe. There weren't many who possessed that ability and none of the Greek gods had it.

None.

But Acheron did . . .

"What have I done?"

Her foolish carelessness could very well cause the death of them all.

June 25, 9527 BC
Midnight

Xiamara stood before an old, gnarled oak tree that grew out of a mountainside, toward the heavens. From the beginning of time, trees had always been associated with the gods. Their roots plunged deep into the heart of the earth, spreading toward its center while their branches soared toward the sky.

It was the life of the earth that they carried in their core and each tree held a piece of the universal spirit that bound all worlds and creatures together.

They were composed of three of the four basic elements. Air, water and earth. When they burned, it united all.

But the most important part of the tree was that, with it and human blood mixed with hers, she could summon one of the most powerful creatures in the universe.

Al Baraka.

Jaden.

No one knew where he came from or when he'd been created, spawned or birthed. If he were human, demon or other. But if a demon needed something, he was the one they bargained with.

Her heart racing, she poured the human blood that one of Apollymi's human priestesses had donated into the roots of the tree. Then she sliced open her own hand and whispered the words to call the demon broker.

"I summon you forth with voice and blood. With weight of the moon and the strength of the sacred wood. Darkness come to me. So say the gods, so let it be . . ."

Lightning flashed as a heavy wind picked up. Xiamara tucked her wings down so that they weren't damaged in the storm.

A swirling black mist rose up from the earth, thick and heavy as it rolled over the tree.

Jaden was ever one for theatrics.

Stepping back, she watched as the mist formed the body of a man. Slowly, it solidified into a pair of inhuman eyes. One was deep, dark brown and the other a vibrant green. From those eyes formed a face as handsome as any man could hope to be. Shoulder-length black hair settled around broad, muscular shoulders. Merciless power and intolerance bled from every fiber of his being.

He stood on a tall branch, looking down at her. His dark brown leather pants and long brown cloak blended in perfectly with the tree.

"Beautiful Charonte," he said in her native tongue, his voice so deep it resonated through her bones. "Tell me why you've come on behalf of your mistress when you know I don't barter for the gods?"

Xiamara let her wings flutter back and open in a sign of trust—even if she kept them clenched to her body, Jaden would still be able to rip them off if he so chose. "Because I love Apollymi and I'm here not as her representative, but to make a bargain with you for me."

He arched a brow at her words. "How so?"

"I know you can't take her life or bargain with her. So I come to you as an unbound demon . . . on my own and of my own free will to bargain with you for what she wants."

He leaned against the tree with one knee cocked forward and folded his arms over his chest. "What do you offer me, demon?"

"My soul. My life. Whatever it takes for you to unite Apollymi with her son . . . at least so long as it's not the life or freedom of one of my own children."

His eyes narrowed as he considered her offer. "You're bonded to Apollymi."

Yes and no. "I'm bonded in friendship and in love, not by slavery. We have been together since childhood and it was before my kind were enslaved to hers."

Jaden let out a long breath. "And what of your Simi? Do you not fear for her without her mother here to protect her?"

Xiamara blinked away her tears at the thought of her youngest growing up without her. "I know Apollymi will see that she has all the best in this world. I have raised two simis to adulthood. Apollymi has only one child. No mother should be without her simi—not even a goddess. I would give her the one thing she wants most."

Jaden jumped down from the tree to land gracefully before her. He was so tall that she had to crane her neck slightly to look up at him. "Do you know how rare it is to be asked for so altruistic a bargain, especially in the name of friendship and not kinship?"

He trailed one icy cold finger down the side of her face. "Are you truly willing to die to give your friend five minutes with her son?"

"If that is what you ask, yes."

He dropped his hand. His soulless eyes betrayed no emotion or any indication of his mood. "I'll have to fully consider this. Give me until tomorrow night to decide. You'll have my answer then."

She sank to one knee before him. "Thank you, akri. Xiamara will await your decision."

He faded into the wind.

Xiamara rose and returned to Apollymi to let her know that Jaden was contemplating the bargain. What she would never tell her were the exact terms they were negotiating.

Acheron tipped his goblet back, drained it, then cursed before he threw it against the wall. He'd drunk enough that he should be blind from intoxication. Yet he was stone sober. Not even his drugs would work on him.

His entire being had been altered.

Damn it all!

He felt the air stirring over his skin. Frowning, he watched as Artemis materialized in front of him.

Acheron lifted a brow in surprise. "I wasn't expecting to see you . . . ever again."

A small smile played at the edges of her lips as she looked at him shyly. "I know. I wanted to apologize for what I said to you earlier. I was wrong."

Every sense in his body went on alert. "You're apologizing to me?"

She nodded as she approached his bed, then climbed on it to rest beside him. "I've even brought you a peace offering."

"A peace offering?"

She handed him a small covered bowl.

Scowling even more, he opened it to find a yellow sticky fruit substance. Never had he seen anything like it. "What's this?"

"Ambrosia. Food of the gods."

He lifted the bowl to smell it. It was sharp and tangy with something else that was invitingly delectable. "Why would you bring this to me?"

"You're a god now. You should eat as we do." Her expression tender, she stroked his thigh and looked up at him from underneath her lashes. "Even I eat it—it's delicious."

Compelled by something he couldn't explain or deny, he picked a portion of it up and sampled it. It was much sweeter than it had smelled. Artemis was right. He'd never tasted anything better.

At least that was his thought until the room started to spin. His eyelids were suddenly heavy and his muscles weak, his breathing labored. In an instant he recognized the biological effects. Rage set fire to his blood as all the years of being drugged against his will rushed to the forefront of his mind.

"You drugged me!"

She bolted from the bed. "Forgive me, Acheron."

Of all the things she'd done to him . . . this betrayal sliced him most fiercely. "What have you done?"

Artemis didn't speak as she watched him turn from human to blue and back again.

He tried to reach her, but she made sure to keep her distance until he'd passed out. There was no telling what he would have done to her had he seized her. As he collapsed on the floor, she finally let out a breath in relief.

Leave it to Hypnos to make the one concoction that not even gods were immune to. She'd been terrified that it wouldn't work on Acheron.

Thank Zeus that it had.

Her hand shaking, she pulled the dagger from its concealed sheath on her thigh. Hephaestus had forged it on Olympus and like the drug, it too would work on a god. She'd even coated the blade with Titan blood just to be sure. One slice and Acheron would be dead.

Biting her lip, she stood over his perfect, naked body that was sprawled sideways and watched as he breathed ever so slightly. His blond hair fell over the handsome features of his face, making him look almost boyish and harmless in his repose.

She remembered the times those full lips had pleasured her. The flash of happiness in his silver eyes when he looked at her. But that was when he'd been human. Now he was a threat not only to her, but to every god on Olympus.

One cut . . .

His throat was exposed, just waiting for her. But as she moved to severe his carotid, an image of him laughing with her went through her mind.

"I love you, Artie."

No one had ever loved her. Not like him. Acheron had never hurt her. He didn't demand. He only asked.

And he gave freely of himself . . .

Kill him, damn you! Do it!

Artemis gripped the knife tightly. She lifted it with every intention of stabbing him. But she couldn't. Over and over, images of him played through her mind.

Acheron loved her and she loved him.

Sobbing, she dropped the knife and placed her head on his chest. As a man, he'd exposed her and threatened her in a way no one else ever had. As a god, he threatened the very existence of her pantheon. She needed to be rid of him.

But she couldn't.

Furious over her own weakness, she put him back in bed. She traced the line of his jaw and wanted to weep. She would have to do something.

Maybe she could find one of the other gods to kill him . . .

*

360

Acheron heard someone scream out. The sound was horrifying and gut wrenching. It echoed through his room. Rolling over in bed, he tried to get up, but couldn't. The drug Artemis had given him was still pressing down on him. He had no control over his body at all.

Then he heard Apollodorus crying.

"Theo! Appie need theo! Mama! Mama come to Appie. Mama!"

Acheron wanted to go to the baby, but he couldn't. His head was swimming viciously and even the subtlest movement made him queasy.

"I'll be there tomorrow, akribos," he whispered to his nephew before he passed out again.

And still the screams echoed in his drugged stupor.

June 25, 9527 BC
Noon

Acheron came awake to the sound of ultimate grief. Someone was wailing as if their heart was splintered. Blinking open his eyes, he found the sun bright, streaming through his open windows.

His head pounding in agony, he pushed himself up in bed, but almost fell as his stomach lurched sharply. He hadn't awakened this sick since he'd left Estes's home. It felt as if he'd overdosed on something.

Artemis.

There in the blinding light, he remembered her "gift." More than that, he remembered her holding a knife over him as she debated whether or not she should kill him.

"You fucking bitch," he snarled.

An instant later, his doors were thrown open. The sound echoed so sharply in his head that it made him flinch and made his head pound even more. "Not so loud," he whispered.

The next thing he knew, Styxx had him by the throat. He shoved him back on the bed to straddle him. "Are you drunk?"

Acheron shook his head.

Styxx backhanded him. He pulled the arc of herbs from the table next to the bed and flung it into Acheron's face. "You worthless whore. You lie in here on your drugs and drink while my sister was murdered!" Styxx punched him again and again.

Acheron tried to block the hits, but his muscles and reactions were still sluggish from Artemis's drugs. It took a full minute for those words to permeate the fog in his mind. "What did you say?"

362

"Ryssa's dead, you bastard!"

No! The denial echoed in his head. It wasn't right. Styxx was being an ass.

Surely not even the gods who hated him would do this to him.

Shoving Styxx away, Acheron forced himself out of bed and staggered down the hallway to Ryssa's rooms. Oblivious to the fact he was naked, he walked in to find the king holding Ryssa in his arms. She looked like a doll. Her face was blue, and her body . . .

He choked on what he saw. She'd been ripped to pieces. Her face and body ravaged by something that looked like large claws. There was blood all over the bed and floor. Falling to his knees, Acheron couldn't breathe or even think past the agony of what he saw.

Ryssa was dead.

And it was then, there on the floor before him that he saw Apollodorus and the nurse. Both bloody. Both dead.

Acheron banged his head against the stone floor, trying his best to clear the fog in his mind. To feel something other than the shattering of his heart.

"I heard them . . ." he whispered as the reality of last night slammed into him with fists more powerful than any that had hit him before.

Damn you, Artemis! He had the powers of a god, but not the power to come and save the only two people who'd ever loved him. And why? Because that whore had drugged him!

He screamed out in anguish.

At that instant, in his mind, he saw the entire event unfold. Saw the ones who'd come into the room from the windows and slaughtered them. He heard Ryssa screaming out for his help.

Heard Apollodorus again begging for his uncle . . .

Suddenly, something slammed into his ribs. The force of the blow knocked him to his side. Looking up, he saw Styxx's furious face as he kicked him in the stomach. Then his twin was on the ground, slamming his head against the stone floor over and over again.

"Why wasn't it you, you worthless maggot!"

Acheron couldn't even think to protect himself. In that moment, he wanted to die too. There was no reason for him to live. Ryssa and Apollodorus were gone.

Even Artemis had tried to kill him.

Impotent rage roiled through him. Roaring from the force of it, he shoved Styxx away from him, but before he could regain his feet a bright light exploded through the room. Acheron lifted his arm to shield his eyes as Apollo manifested.

There was complete silence as the god looked slowly around the room taking in every detail. Even the king had stopped crying in expectation of the god's reaction.

Apollo didn't speak as he saw Ryssa lying dead in her father's arms and his son's lifeless body still in the arms of his savaged nurse.

"Who did this?" Apollo demanded through clenched teeth.

Styxx pointed to Acheron. "He let them die."

Before Acheron could think to deny those words, Apollo spun on him and hit him with his fist so hard that it lifted him from the ground and slammed him into the wall ten feet above the floor.

Acheron fell to the ground, his body aching. Apollo grabbed him by the hair and wrenched his head. Acheron tried to push him away, but his muscles were still too weak.

The god backhanded him. Blood and pain exploded as his nose was broken and his lips split. The god set on him with such fury that Acheron couldn't even recover from one blow before two more were delivered to him.

"Artemis!" Acheron shouted, needing her to help calm her brother.

"Don't you dare say my sister's name, you filthy whore!" Apollo grabbed a dagger from his waist and snatched at Acheron's tongue. He sliced it off.

Acheron choked on the blood that poured through his mouth. Unimaginable pain throbbed to the point all he could think was to try and crawl away from Apollo.

But Apollo grabbed him by the throat in a grip so searing it burned the god's handprint into his skin.

"Akri! Ni!" Xiamara's cries filled the room as she appeared above him and dove for Apollo. She knocked the god back from him and put herself between them.

"Out of my way, demon," Apollo demanded.

Her response was to launch herself at the god. The two of them tangled in a flurry of light and feathers as they pounded each other.

Tears filled Acheron's eyes as he fought against the pain that was trying to drag him into unconsciousness. His only thought to kill Apollo, he crawled to where the god's knife had fallen. His own blood coated the blade. With a fury born of grief and all the years where he'd been abused, Acheron seized it and spun on the combatants.

Ryssa had meant nothing to Apollo. No more than he meant to Artemis. His sister had loathed the god and now the bastard acted as if her death meant something to him.

It wasn't right and by the gods who'd birthed him, he wasn't going to let the god get away with attacking his mother's demon. His fury set fire to the blade, causing it to glow as he raced toward them.

Acheron set his gaze on Apollo and was oblivious to the fight. All he could focus on was stabbing the god through his callous heart. But just as he reached Apollo, the god knocked Xiamara back, into Acheron. She turned into him with eyes wide as his stomach shrank in the realization that Apollo had slammed the demon into the knife . . .

Acheron felt her blood coating his hand. Looking down at the wound, she staggered back with a small cry of pain. He wanted to say something to her, but without his tongue, it was impossible.

He grabbed her against him as she struggled to breathe.

She lifted a bloodied hand to place it to his cheek. "Apollymi loves you," she whispered in Charonte—a language he somehow understood even though he'd never heard it before. "Protect your mother, Apostolos. Be strong for her and for me . . ." Then the light faded from her eyes as her final breath left her body.

Acheron threw his head back and tried to vent the fury inside him. But it came out as a strangled cry. Grabbing the knife, he spun on Apollo.

Apollo caught his hand and wrested the knife from him. The god seized him again by the throat and threw him down to the ground. Acheron kicked him back and rolled to his side.

A shadow in the corner caught his eye. He froze as he saw Artemis standing there, watching the fight with her hands over her mouth. Her eyes were filled with horror.

Needing her, he reached a hand out toward her.

She shook her head no and took a step back, out of her brother's sight.

In that instant, something inside him died. Coldness filled every raw inch of his body.

Artemis refused to intervene. Even now when he was wounded and hurt more than any human should ever be hurt, his love wasn't enough. He didn't matter to her.

Tired, grief-stricken and defeated, he rolled over onto his back at the same time Apollo appeared before him. He met the god's angry glare. Growling in rage, Apollo sank his dagger deep inside Acheron's heart and sliced him open all the way to his navel.

Unmitigated agony burned through him as the god slowly gutted him on the floor, no more than three feet from Ryssa's body, and right there, before Artemis.

Tears fell from his eyes as the light and pain began to fade . . .

Artemis remained in the shadows, silently weeping as she watched her brother kick Acheron's dead body aside. It wasn't until Apollo approached the king on the bed that the king realized Styxx was also lying dead in the doorway.

Not that Artemis cared about the prince.

Her heart aching, she slid down the wall to crouch in the corner as her teary gaze remained on Acheron and what was left of him.

She'd thought his death would bring her relief. Instead agony over his loss tore through her with a finality that left her bereft of any thought. Only raw emotion.

It hurt on a level she'd never known existed.

The king's cry of pain matched the one in her soul as Apollo took Ryssa from his arms and he realized that his heir was dead.

For all his dignity and power, the king crawled on the floor to Styxx and screamed as he rocked his son against him.

No one mourned Acheron.

No one save her.

Unable to stand the sight, she returned to her temple where she shattered every mirror, every piece of glass and pottery. Her rage roiled through the room, laying waste to everything around her.

What had she done?

"I let him die."

No, she'd tried to kill him. Last night, she'd wanted him dead. But never had she dreamed just how much he meant to her.

His touch, his friendship . . .

Now he was gone. Forever.

"I love you, Acheron," she sobbed, tearing at her hair.

It's over. No one will ever know about the two of you now. You're safe.

It seemed so petty a concern compared to the fact that she'd live out eternity without ever seeing his face again . . .

Apollymi *gasped as* she felt the weight in her chest lift. Without being told, she knew that she now had the ability to leave Kalosis.

Leave . . .

"No!" she screamed as she realized the significance of that. There was only one way for her to gain her release.

Apostolos was dead.

Those three words chased themselves around in her head until she was sick from them.

Unwilling to believe it, she ran to her pond and summoned the universal eye. There in the water, she saw Xiamara lying dead on the palace floor and Apostolos . . .

No!

From the deepest part of her being, a scream of rage and grief swelled and when she gave vent to it, it shattered the pool and rocked the garden around her.

"I am Apollymia Thanata Deia Fonia!" she screamed until her throat was raw and bleeding.

She was ultimate destruction.

And she was going to bring her son home . . .

May the gods have mercy on each other because she was going to have none for them.

June 25, 9527 BC
Tartarus

Hades, the Greek god of death and the Underworld, stood in the center of his throne room, staring in disbelief at their newest arrival who lay in one of the darkest cells of Tartarus.

And he hadn't put him there . . .

He looked down at the timepiece on his wrist and ground his teeth. It was still three months before his wife would be returned to the Underworld to be with him. But honestly, he had to speak with her.

It couldn't wait.

"Persephone?" he called, hoping her mother wasn't close enough to hear him. The old bitch would have a stroke if she caught them together. Not that it would be a bad thing . . . if only it would kill her.

An image of his wife flickered in the darkness by his side. "Butterbean!" Persephone breathed. "I was just missing you something terrible."

He really hated the nicknames she came up with for him. Thank the gods that she only used them when the two of them were alone. Otherwise, he'd be the most mocked of all gods. But he could forgive his beautiful wife anything. "Where's your mother?"

"Off with Zeus looking over some fields, why?"

Good. The last thing he needed was for Demeter to come in and catch them talking.

But that brought him back to his current "dilemma." Anger swept through him as he gestured toward the wall that showed the cells where his prisoners were kept. "Because I'm getting really sick of cleaning up the messes of

369

the other gods and right now I'd love to know whose ass I need to bust over this latest fiasco."

She solidified before him. "What's happened?"

Taking her hand, he led her to the cell where they could see inside, but its occupant was completely unable to see them.

At least that was the normal case. In this one, who knew what the occupant could and couldn't see?

He pointed to the blue-fleshed god who lay cuddled into a ball on the floor. "Any idea who killed that and sent it here?"

Eyes wide, Persephone shook her head. "What is it?"

"Well, I'm not completely sure. I think he's a god . . . Atlantean . . . maybe. But I've never seen anything like him before. He came in a short time ago and hasn't moved. I'd try to destroy his soul and send him into complete oblivion, but I don't think I have the powers to do it. In fact, I'm pretty sure that just by trying, all I'd do is piss him off."

Persephone nodded. "Well, sweetie, my advice to you is if you can't defeat it, befriend it."

"Befriend it how?"

Persephone smiled at her husband who was far from a sociable entity. Tall and muscular with black hair and eyes, he was gorgeous, even when befuddled and angry. "Wait here." She opened the door to the cell and made her way slowly to the unknown god.

The closer she moved toward him, the more she understood Hades's concern. There was so much power emanating from the god that the air was rife with it. She'd been around the gods her whole life, but this one was different. His marbled blue skin was strangely attractive as it covered a body of perfect proportions. Long black hair fanned out. He had two black horns on top of his head and black lips and claws.

And more than that, he wasn't a god of creation. He was one of ultimate destruction.

Seph, get out of there.

She held her hand up to signal her husband that she was fine. Her legs trembling in trepidation, she reached out to touch the god.

He opened his eyes that were a yellow orange encircled by red. They flashed from that to a swirling silver color. And they were filled with raw anguish.

"Am I dead?" he asked, his voice demonic.

"You want to be dead?" She actually dreaded his answer because if he didn't want to be dead, there could be serious consequences.

"Please tell me I've finally made it."

Those desperate words tugged at her heart. Reaching up to comfort him, she brushed the black hair back from his blue cheek. "You're dead, but as a god you live."

"I don't understand. I don't want to be any different than anyone else. I just want to be left alone."

Persephone smiled at him. "You can stay here as long as you want." She summoned a pillow for him and tucked it under his head. Then she covered him with a blanket.

"Why are you being so nice to me?"

"Because you seem to need it." She patted him on the arm before she got up. "If you need anything, I'm Persephone. My husband, Hades, is the one in charge here. You call for us and we'll come."

He gave a subtle nod before he closed his eyes and returned to lying quietly in the darkness.

Mystified by him, she returned to her husband. "He's harmless."

"Harmless, my ass. Seph? Are you insane? Can you not feel the powers he holds?"

"Oh I feel them. Go near him and you'll have nightmares. But he doesn't want anything. He's hurt, Hades. Badly. All he wants is to be left alone."

"Yeah, right. Left alone here in *my* Underworld? Another god whose powers rival mine? Fuck that. They trump mine. How stupid would I have to be? You know there's a reason pantheons don't mix."

"You can ally him," she said, trying to calm him down. "Having a friend is never a bad thing."

"Until the friend turns on you."

She shook her head. "Hades . . ."

"I'm a lot older than you, Seph. I've seen what can happen when one god turns on another."

"And I think he poses no harm to either of us." She lifted herself up on her toes to kiss his cheek. "I have to go before my mother finds me missing. You know how she gets when I see you during her time with me."

"Yeah and a pox on the—"

She pinched his lips together before he could let fly the insult. "I love you both. Now behave and take care of your guest."

Only his wife could get away with treating him like this and being so cavalier with his body. But then she held his heart and he'd give her anything.

He kissed her finger. "I miss you."

"I miss you too. I'll be home soon."

Soon, yeah . . . right.

But there was nothing to be done about that.

He nodded glumly, then cursed as she faded away from him. Damn the bitch, Demeter, for cursing them to live apart half the year. But right now he had bigger problems than his wife's mother.

And at about six foot eight, that god-killer was definitely one *big* problem.

June 25, 9527 BC
Didymos

With the icy wind twisting her ghostly pale hair around her and plastering her black gown to her limbs, Apollymi staggered on the rocks of the sea where Apostolos's body rested in a broken heap. Her precious son had been dumped here as if he were nothing.

Nothing . . .

Unshed tears racked her. She was so cold inside. So defeated. So . . . There were no words to describe the anguish of her seeing her son's body lying face down in the water, abandoned and forgotten.

Thrown away.

After all they'd done to him, they couldn't even provide a decent funeral.

Weak from her grief, she sank to her knees in a pool of water and pulled him from the rocks to the beach. Unable to stand it, she screamed out, sending birds into flight.

"Apostolos!"

But he couldn't hear her. His body was as cold as her heart. His silver eyes were open and glazed, and even now, they swirled like a stormy sky. Yet for all the horror of his death, his features were serene.

And they were beautiful. More so than any mother could have hoped for. She saw in his face, herself. Saw her hopes for him made real. He was so perfectly formed. So tall and strong . . .

And they had butchered him. Tortured him. Defiled and humiliated *her* son. Her precious baby.

Choking on a sob, she ran her hand over the long gash in his chest to seal it closed. Only then, when he was perfect again did her tears break as she laid her lips to his cheek to kiss him and cry.

This was the first time she'd held him since the moment she'd cut him from her womb. Gathering him close, she rocked him on the beach and let all the horror inside her free. "I tried to protect you, Apostolos," she breathed against his ear. "I tried so hard."

She'd failed miserably and in her attempt, had made his life an unbearable one.

Wanting to comfort him and knowing it was too late, she futilely rubbed his cold arms to warm them.

If only he could look at her. Hear her voice. But he never would.

And she would never hear him call her matera.

It was more than she could stand. "Please," she breathed. "Please come back to me, Apostolos. I swear I'll keep you safe this time. I won't let anyone hurt you. Please, baby, I can't live knowing I killed you. I can't. Look at me, please!"

But he couldn't and she knew it.

If only she had the power to restore his life. But unlike his father, she was born of destruction. Death. Pestilence. War. Those were her gifts to the world. There was nothing she could do to bring back the one she loved most.

"Why!" she screamed at the sky. Where were the Chthonians now to demand blood over the death of her precious child? Why weren't they here on Apostolos's behalf?

They didn't care. No one cared, but her.

And Xiamara who'd tried so hard to save him. Xiamara, her closest friend. The only one she'd ever been able to confide in. Closer than sisters, closer than mother and daughter. Now she, too, was gone.

Apollymi was alone. Bitterly alone.

She cradled her son's head to her breasts and screamed out so loud that the sound was carried on the wind all the way to the halls of Atlantis. "Damn you, Archon! Damn you!"

How could he have ever claimed he loved her? How could he have allowed Apostolos to die like this? To suffer so much pain?

Her heart broken, she buried her face in her son's wet blond hair and cried until her sobs were spent.

Then her fury mounted and took a vicious root into her heart. They'd both been betrayed by the very ones who were supposed to love and honor them.

Now there would be Kalosis to pay.

It was time to take her son home where he belonged. Time to make her so called family bleed for their betrayal.

Her course set, Apollymi clothed her son in the black formesta robes of his station. This was his birthright. As the son of the Destroyer, his symbol was that of the sun that represented her, pierced by the three lightning bolts of his power.

He wasn't garbage. He was an Atlantean god.

And he was the son of the Destroyer.

Picking him up from the surf and cradling him in her arms, she took them both home to Katoteros.

It was an island surrounded by islands. Breathtakingly beautiful, there was no place in the human realm that could compare with it. Standing at the highest point, where her mother the North Wind shrieked on her behalf, Apollymi looked out over the landscape that should have been owned by Apostolos.

The islands sparkled in the perfect light under the sun that attempted to warm her cold skin. It was futile.

The island to her right housed the paradise lands where the souls of their Atlantean people went to rest until reincarnation. The one on her left had been held by the Charontes before her banishment—unlike her family, her demons had been loyal to her. They had all followed her into Kalosis.

And the island before her had been intended as the home of her son.

But it was the one that possessed the second highest point in Katoteros that held her attention now. The one that ruled and united all the islands. It was the one where the hall of the gods had been built.

Archon's.

Her vision darkening, she took them there, outside the grand marble hall that stood so tall and proud as it looked

375

down upon their world. Music and laughter drifted out to her.

Music and laughter.

Oblivious to what had come to pass and to what they faced, the gods were having a party. *A fucking party*. She could feel the presence of every god inside. All of them. Celebrating. Laughing. Cheering. Having fun.

And her beloved son was dead . . .

Dead!

Her world was shattered. And still they laughed.

Holding Apostolos close, she ascended the stairs with a deceptive calm and flung the doors wide with her powers. The white marble foyer was circular with statues of the gods taking up station every four feet against the pristine walls.

Her heart hammering with vindictive fury, she walked through the center of the foyer where her emblem of the sun had been etched into the floor. As she crossed over it, she changed it to that of Apostolos. One by one, his bolts of power pierced her symbol.

The colors now red and black to represent her grief and his spilled blood.

Without hesitating, she walked straight for the set of gold doors that led to Archon's throne room. To the room where the gods made merry while her son lay dead from their treachery.

By all the dark powers of the universe, they wouldn't be laughing for much longer.

She opened those doors with the full force of her fury. The clattering sound rang out as the doors slammed against the marble walls and broke from their hinges to fall to the shiny, perfect floor.

The music stopped instantly.

Every god in the hall turned to look at her and one by one, their faces blanched white.

Without a word, Apollymi held her son in her arms and walked with a calmness she didn't feel toward the dais where her black throne sat beside her husband's gold one. Archon stood up at her approach and moved to the side as if to speak to her.

She ignored him as she placed Apostolos on Archon's throne, where he belonged. Her hands shaking, she sat him up and carefully placed each of his hands on the arms. She lifted his head and brushed the blond hair back from his bluish face until he looked as if he would blink and move at any moment.

Only he would never blink again.

He was dead.

And so were they . . .

Apollymi's heart beat with fury as her powers mounted. A feral wind exploded through the hall, sweeping her hair up as her eyes glowed red. She turned on the gods then and leveled a malevolent glare at each of them as they held a united breath in expectation of her wrath.

Until she came to Archon.

Only then did she speak in a voice that was laced with her hatred. "Look at my son."

He refused.

"Look, damn you!" she snarled. "I want you to see what *you've* done."

Archon winced before he complied and the relief in his eyes notched her wrath to an even higher level. How could she have ever allowed something so callous and putrid into her bed?

Into her body?

Apollymi growled. "Your bastard daughters deprived my son of his life. Those little whores damned him. And *you*," she sneered the word, "dared to protect them instead of my child!"

"Apollymi—"

"Don't you ever speak my name again." She sealed his mouth shut with her powers. "You had every right to be afraid. But your bastard bitches were wrong. It won't be my son who destroys this pantheon. It is I. Apollymia Katastrafia Megola. Pantokrataria. Thanatia Atlantia deia oly!"

Apollymi the Great Destroyer. All powerful. Death to the gods of Atlantis!

It was then they scrambled for the doors or to teleport out, but Apollymi would have none of it. Drawing from the darkest part of her soul, she sealed the hall closed. No one was going to leave here until she was appeased.

No one.

If the Chthonians killed her for this, so be it. She felt dead inside anyway. She didn't care about anything except making them all pay for their part in her son's suffering.

Archon fell to his knees, trying to plead for her mercy. But there was nothing left inside her except a hatred so potent and bitter that she could actually taste it.

She kicked him back and blasted him until he was nothing more than a statue remnant of a god.

Basi screamed out as Apollymi turned toward her. "I helped you. I did! I put him where you told me to."

"You didn't do shit, except whine and piss me off." Apollymi blasted her into oblivion.

One by one, she faced the gods she'd once considered family and turned them into stone as her relentless fury demanded appeasement. They tried in vain to subdue her, but once her wrath was unleashed, there was no power in the universe to stop her.

Except for the child they'd stupidly killed. Only Apostolos could have saved them.

The only one she hesitated at was her beloved stepgrandson, Dikastis—the god of justice. Unlike the others, he didn't cower or beg. Nor did he fight her. He stood with one hand braced on the back of a chair, calmly meeting her gaze as an equal.

But then he understood justice. He understood her wrath. Inclining his head respectfully, he didn't move as she blasted him.

And then there was Epithymia. Her half-sister. The goddess of wealth and desire. She was the bitch Apollymi had so foolishly trusted more than the others.

With tears of crystal ice in her eyes, Apollymi confronted her. "How could you?"

Tiny and frail in her angelic appearance, Epithymia stared up at her from where she cowered on the floor. "I did what you asked. I delivered him into the world of man and made sure he was born into a royal family. I even tried

378

to hand him to the queen to suckle him. Why would you destroy me?"

Apollymi wanted to claw her eyes out for what she'd done. "You touched him, you slut! You knew what that would do to him. To be touched by the hand of desire and to have no god powers to countermand it . . . You made it so that every human who saw him was driven mad with their lust to have him. How could you be so careless?"

It was then she saw the truth in her sister's eyes.

"You did it on purpose!"

Epithymia swallowed. "What was I supposed to do? You heard the Fates when they spoke. They proclaimed him to be the death of us all. He would have destroyed us."

"You thought the humans would kill him in their efforts to possess him?"

A tear slid down Epithymia's cheek. "I was only trying to protect us."

"He was your nephew," Apollymi spat.

"I know and I'm sorry."

Not as sorry as she was going to be.

Apollymi curled her lip. "So am I. I'm sorry I ever trusted you with the one thing you knew I loved above all others. You ungrateful bitch. I hope your actions haunt you into eternity." Apollymi blasted her sister.

And yet she was unappeased. Even with all of them dead and gone . . .

The hole inside her was still there and it hurt so much that all she could do was scream. She screamed until her throat was raw. Throwing her arms out, she splintered the hall until there was nothing left but rubble. Nothing left but her memories of her hope for a son now dead.

Still it hurt.

Apollymi wiped the tears from her face as she stood, looking at what she'd done. There was no satisfaction to be felt.

There was only justice to be done.

"One down . . ."

She turned then and headed to the island kingdom Archon had created for her.

Atlantis.

Those poor fools had thought to strike out at Apollo by killing his son and mistress. Today they were cowering in fear of being discovered by him and punished for their actions. But it wasn't the Greek god who wanted them dead.

It was she. Their patroness.

It would be by her hand and for the acts they'd committed against her son that they would suffer and die.

No mercy. It was what they'd given Apostolos and it was what she'd return to them.

With one swipe of her arm, she sank the entire island into the sea and listened to the beauty of their terrified screams and pleas for clemency and deliverance as the elements struck and ended their putrid lives. It was the sweetest music she'd ever heard. Let them beg . . .

If only Apostolos and Xiamara could be here.

Wincing in pain, she pushed her grief aside as she struck out on their behalf.

The last of the island kingdom faded into the sea just as the sun was setting. Apollymi turned then and looked to the land of Greece.

They were the last to suffer. Not just the humans who'd hurt her child, but those fucking gods who thought they were so smart and smug.

Most of all, Archon's bastard daughters would pay. They thought themselves safe on Olympus under the care of their mother. But the three Fates were nothing in comparison to the daughter of Chaos.

To the mother of absolute destruction.

Their dying screams would be the ones she'd relish most.

June 25, 9527 BC
Mount Olympus

Small and thin in stature with dark hair and eyes, Hermes flew through the hall of Zeus until he stood before his father who only looked a few years older than he. Hermes wasn't sure what was going on, but most of the gods were gathered here and lounging about.

They ignored Hermes until he spoke. "You know the saying, don't kill the messenger? Hold that thought, really, really close to your hearts."

Zeus scowled at him as he stood up from the chair where he'd been playing chess with Poseidon. Dressed in a flowing white robe, Zeus had short blond hair and vividly blue eyes. "What's going on?"

Hermes gestured toward the wall of windows that looked down onto the human realm. "Have any of you taken a look out at Greece in the last, say, hour or so?"

Artemis held her breath as a bad feeling went through her while she sat at a banquet table across from Aphrodite, Athena and Apollo.

Apollo rolled his eyes and waved his hand in arrogant dismissal. "What? Are they reacting to the fact I cursed the Apollites?"

Hermes shook his head in a gesture of sarcastic denial. "I don't think that bothers them nearly as much as the fact that the island of Atlantis is now gone and the Atlantean goddess Apollymi is cutting a swathe through our country, laying waste to everyone and everything she comes into contact with." Hermes gave Apollo a smug look. "And in case you're curious, she's headed straight for us. I could be really wrong here, but I'm guessing the woman's extremely pissed."

Artemis shrank back at those words.

Zeus turned on Apollo. "What have you done?"

All arrogance now gone, Apollo blanched as fear tinted his eyes. "I cursed my people, not hers. I didn't do anything to the Atlanteans, Papa. Unless their blood was mixed with my Apollites, they were unharmed by my curse. This is not *my* fault."

Her stomach drawing tight, Artemis covered her mouth as she realized what pantheon Acheron must have belonged to. Terrified of what she and Apollo had set in motion, she left the hall where the gods prepared for war and went to her temple so that she could think without their angry shouts in her ears.

"What can I do?"

She was just about to summon her koris to her when the three Fates appeared in her room: As triplets in the height of youthful beauty, their faces perfect duplicates of each other. But that was the only thing that united them. The eldest, Atropos, had red hair while Clotho was blond, and the youngest, Lachesis, had dark hair. They were the daughters of the goddess of justice. No one was sure who their father was, but many suspected Zeus.

The one thing every god on Olympus knew was that these three girls were the most powerful of the entire pantheon. Even Zeus didn't try to circumvent them.

Since the moment of their arrival a decade ago, everyone had given them a wide berth. When the three of them held hands and made a statement, it became the law of the universe and no one was immune to it.

No one.

Artemis couldn't imagine why they'd be here in her temple. "If you don't mind, I'm a little busy right now."

Lachesis grabbed her arm. "Artemis, you must listen to us. We've done something terrible."

That was why the gods lived in fear of them. They were always doing something terrible to someone. "Whatever it is, it'll wait."

382

"No," Atropos said grimly, "it won't. Apollymi is coming here to kill us."

Stunned by that proclamation, Artemis scowled at them. "What?"

Atropos swallowed. "You must never tell anyone what we're about to tell you. Do you understand? Our mother made us swear to keep it a secret."

"Keep what secret?"

"Swear to us, Artemis," Clotho demanded.

"I swear. Now tell me what's going on." And most important, why it involved her.

Atropos spoke in a whisper as if afraid someone outside the temple might hear her. "Our father is Archon—the king of the Atlantean gods. He had an affair with our mother, Themis, and we were born of it. Our mother sent us to Atlantis to live and our father took us in. Apollymi is our stepmother and we unknowingly cursed our half-brother when we learned of his coming birth."

"It was an accident," Clotho blurted out. "We didn't mean to curse him."

Lachesis nodded. "We were just children and didn't understand our powers yet. We never meant to curse our brother. We didn't, we swear!"

Artemis went cold inside. "Acheron? Acheron is your brother?"

Clotho nodded. "Apollymi barely tolerated us while we lived with them. We were a reminder of our father's infidelity and she hated us for it."

That didn't make sense, any more than their fear did. Artemis tried to sort through what they were telling her. "But everyone knows that Archon has never been unfaithful to his wife."

Lachesis snorted. "That's a lie the Atlantean gods keep so that Apollymi won't harm them. You don't understand just how powerful she is. She can kill us without even blinking. All the gods fear her power. Even Archon. He's as faithless as most men and so here we are."

"She wants us dead," Clotho interjected.

Still Artemis was piecing the story together. "How exactly did you curse Acheron?"

"We were so stupid," Atropos said. "When Apollymi began to show her pregnancy, we spoke out of turn and gave Apostolos the power of final fate. We said he'd be the death of us all and it seems today we are about to see our demise met."

Artemis was even more confused. "But it's not him who threatens us. It's his mother."

Clotho nodded. "And she will kill all of us for our part in his curse. Including you."

"I did nothing!"

Atropos scoffed at her as the young women encircled her. "We know what you've done, Artemis. We see all. You hurt him even more than we did. You turned your back on him while Apollo gutted him on the floor and Apollymi knows it."

Fear tore through her. If what they said was correct, there would be no mercy from Apollymi. Truthfully, she didn't deserve any, but on the other hand, Artemis really didn't want to die. "What can we do? How do we defeat her?"

Atropos sighed heavily. "*You* can't. She's all-powerful. The only one who can check her powers is her son."

In that case, they were in serious trouble since Acheron was now dead. Couldn't someone have told her this *before* she'd left him to Apollo? This information was just a little late in coming and would have been much more beneficial earlier in the day.

"We're dead," Artemis breathed as images of her being gutted by Acheron's mother went through her head.

"No," Clotho said firmly, shaking her arm. "You can bring him back."

Artemis scowled at the woman. "Are you insane? I can't bring him back from the dead."

"Yes, you can. You're the only one who has the power."

"No, I don't."

Atropos growled at her. "You drank of his blood, Artemis. You absorbed some of his powers."

Clotho nodded. "He's the final fate. He can resurrect the dead, which means you can too."

Artemis swallowed. "Are you sure?"

They nodded in unison.

Still, Artemis was uncertain. Granted she'd tasted Acheron's powers, but that particular one was reserved for only a very select group of gods and if they failed to bring him back . . .

It could only get worse.

Atropos took her by the arm. "The Atlantean gods used their combined powers to bind Apollymi. So long as Apostolos is alive in the human realm, she's locked in Kalosis."

Lachesis took her other arm and nodded. "We bring him back and she's interred again."

"We'll be safe," Clotho offered. "All of us."

"You will be the savior of the pantheon!" they said in unison.

Did she really have a choice? Drawing in a deep breath for courage, Artemis nodded. "What do I have to do?"

"You will have to get him to drink your blood," Atropos said as if it would be the easiest thing in the world to accomplish.

"And just how do I do that?"

"With our help."

A*cheron lay on* the floor in calm serenity, finally numb to everything from his past and present. He was at peace in a way he'd never been before. The walls of his cave shielded him from the voices of others. Not even the gods were in his head.

For the first time in his life, he had total silence.

There was no aching in his body, no grief. Nothing. And he loved this feeling of tranquility.

"Acheron?"

He tensed at Artemis's voice. Of course the bitch was going to disturb his haven. She could never leave him in peace.

Damn her.

He tried to tell her to go away, but nothing other than a hoarse croak left his lips. Coughing, he tried to clear his throat to speak.

Still no words would come. What was going on? What had taken his voice?

Artemis gave him a tender, concerned look as she appeared before him. "We need to talk."

He shoved her back, but she refused to go.

"Please," she begged with a look that would have weakened his resolve only a few days ago. But that concern for her was now long gone. "Just a few words and I'll leave you. Forever if you wish."

How could they talk when he couldn't speak?

She held a cup out to him. "Drink this and I'll be able to talk to you."

Furious with her and wanting to vent his anger at her, he grabbed the cup and downed the contents without tasting them. "Go to Tartarus and rot," he snarled at her, grateful that this time she could hear the venom in his voice.

Then something happened. Pain and fire ripped through his body as if something was setting his internal organs aflame. Panting, he looked up at Artemis. "What have you done to me now?"

There was no mercy or remorse in her gaze. "What I had to do."

One moment he was in the quiet darkness of Hades's domain and in the next, he was standing on the shores of Didymos, not far from the palace.

Or rather what was left of it.

Confused, he looked around, trying to understand what had happened to him and the land. But before he could figure it out a searing pain tore through him with such ferocity that it drove him to his knees in the surf.

Acheron cried out, wanting it to stop.

Suddenly, Artemis was there before him. Gathering him into her arms, she held him close as the waves crashed against them. "I had to bring you back."

He shoved her away from him as he looked around at the smoldering remains of Didymos. "What have you done?"

"I didn't do this. Your mother did. She's destroyed everything and everyone who ever went near you. And she was coming to kill us on Olympus. It's why I had to bring you back. She would have killed us all had I not."

He glared so hard at her, he was sure his eyes were red. "You think I give a damn about that?" He started away from her, only to be frozen in place by the pain tearing at his stomach. The agony caused him to double over as he struggled to breathe.

Artemis approached him slowly. She stood above him, looking down. "I'm the one in control here, Acheron. I've bound you to me with my blood. I own you."

Those three words set fire to his wrath. He felt the familiar heat ripple over him as his human appearance gave way to that of his god form. Rising against the pain, he held his hand out and brought Artemis into his grasp. "You seriously underestimate my powers, bitch."

She clutched at his hand, trying to loosen his feral grip. "Kill me and you'll become the worst sort of monster imaginable. You need my blood to maintain any sort of sanity. Without it, you will become a mindless killer, seeking only to destroy any and everyone you come into contact with . . . just like your mother."

Acheron roared with frustration. The bitch had thought of everything. Even as a god, he was still a slave. "I hate you."

"I know."

He shoved her away from him and turned his back on her.

"Acheron, did you not hear what I said? You will have to feed from me."

He ignored her as he made the long trek from the beach to the hill where the royal palace had once stood. Now there was nothing left but smoldering ashes and busted stones. There were bodies of servants and merchants everywhere.

Tears filled his eyes as he ran through the debris, seeking a sign of Ryssa or Apollodorus. Aching and broken, he used his powers to move stone and marble until he uncovered the room that had been hers.

There in the wreckage he found three of the diaries she'd so meticulously kept. They were a little scarred by fire, but miraculously, they'd somehow survived intact. He opened the first one and stared at her childish writing as she described the very day he'd been born and the joy she'd felt at having twin brothers. Wiping his tears, he closed it and held it close to his heart as he heard her voice in her words.

His precious sister was gone and it was all his fault.

Aching from the truth of that, he saw one of the silver hair combs he'd given her . . .

He crawled over to it and placed it against his lips. "I'm so sorry I failed you, Ryssa. I'm so sorry."

As he sat there, it hit him how pathetic it was that all he had to show for a life so vibrant, a soul so beautiful, were such minuscule things. Three diaries and a broken hair comb. That was all that was left of his precious sister. Leaning his head back, he sobbed from the pain of it all.

"Apostolos . . . please don't cry."

He felt his mother's presence. "What have you done, Matera?"

"I wanted them to pay for hurting you."

Did it even matter? What they'd done to him was nothing compared to what had been done this day. "And now Artemis owns me."

His mother's scream mirrored his own. "How?"

"She's bound me to her with her blood."

He could feel his own anger through his mother's voice. "Come to me, Apostolos. Free me and I will destroy that bitch and those bastards who cursed you."

Acheron shook his head. He should do it. He should. They all deserved nothing better and yet he couldn't bring himself to destroy the world. To kill innocent people . . .

His mother appeared before him as a translucent shade. Acheron sucked his breath in sharply as he saw her for the very first time. She was the most beautiful woman he'd ever seen. Hair as white as newfallen snow fell from a crown that shimmered with diamonds. Her pale, silver eyes swirled just as his did. Her black dress flowed over her body as she held one hand out to him.

He tried to touch her, but his hand passed through hers.

"You are my son, Apostolos. The only thing in my life that I've ever truly loved. I would give my life for yours. Come to me, child. I want to hold you."

He treasured every word she spoke. "I can't, Matera.

Not if that means sacrificing the world. I refuse to be so selfish."

"Why would you protect a world that turned its back on you?"

"Because I know what it's like to be punished for things not my fault. I know what it's like to have things forced on me that were wrong and against my will. Why would I ever serve that to someone else?"

"Because it would be justice!"

He glanced around at the scattered bodies. "No. It would only be cruel. Justice to the humans has been more than served."

Her eyes flashed angrily. "What of Apollo and Artemis?"

He ground his teeth at the mere mention of their names. "They hold the power of the sun and the moon. I can't destroy them."

"*I* can."

Thus she'd destroy the entire earth and all who lived here. It was why he couldn't free her. "I'm not worth the end of the world, Matera."

Her eyes burned him with her sincerity. "To me you are."

In that moment, he would have sold his soul to be able to hold her. "I love you, Mama."

"Nowhere near as much as I love you, m'gios."

M'gios. My son. He'd waited his entire life for someone to claim him. But as much as he wanted his mother, he wouldn't end the world for it.

Suddenly a cold wind whipped around him, tearing at his clothes and hair, yet not hurting him. The world around him faded as he found himself on unfamiliar ground. His mother's image flickered by his side. "This is Katoteros. Your birthright."

He frowned at the pile of rubble. "It's in ruins."

She cast a sheepish look toward him. "I was a little upset when I came here."

A little?

"Close your eyes, Apostolos."

Trusting her completely, he did.

"Breathe in."

He took a deep breath and then he felt his mother inside him. Her powers merged with his and in the blink of an eye, the ruins reunited to form a beautiful palace of gold and black marble. His mother's presence pulled out of him.

"Welcome home, palatimos." *Precious one.*

The doors opened and as Acheron passed through them, his clothing changed. His hair grew long and black and a flowing robe fanned out behind him as he walked over the white marble floor. He paused at the sign of the sun that was pierced by three bolts of lightning.

His mother slowed as she noted him studying it. "The golden sun is my symbol and it represents the day. The silver of the lightning bolts is for the night. The bolt to the left is for me and the past, and the one on the right is your father and the future. Yours is the bolt in the middle that unites and binds the three of us together and stands for the present. That is the sign of the Talimosin and represents your dominion of the past, the present and the future."

He frowned at the Atlantean word. "The Harbinger?"

She nodded. "You, Apostolos. You are the Talimosin. The final fate of all. Your words are law and your wrath absolute. Be careful as you speak for whatever you will, even in carelessness, will determine the fate of the person you're speaking to. It's a burden I would never have wished upon you. And it's one I hate those bitches for. But I can't undo what they've given you. No one can."

"What exactly are my powers?"

"I don't know. I took them from you and never looked at them for fear of exposing you to the others. I only know what Archon's daughters cursed you to. But you will learn your powers in time. I only wish you'd come to me so that I could help you until you grow stronger."

"Matera—"

"I know." She held her hand up. "I respect you for being the man you are and I'm proud of you. However, should you change your mind, you know where I am."

He smiled at her.

"In the meantime, this is all yours."

Acheron looked around at the statues and somehow he knew who each and every one of them were. As he approached the set of gold doors, he saw the image of his mother to the left and Archon to the right.

The doors opened and there he saw the remains of the gods where his mother had attacked them. They were frozen in the horror of their last moments.

His mother didn't show the tiniest bit of remorse for what she'd done to them. "If the sight of them bothers you, there is a room below the throne room where you can store them. While I'm locked in Kalosis, my powers won't let me put them there, but you shouldn't have that problem."

Closing his eyes, he wished the statues gone. In an instant, they were. He had no desire to see the images of people who'd wanted him dead.

His mother smiled approvingly. "You should have the ability to come and go from the human realm to this one at will. You'll find that Katoteros is a large place with areas unexplored. The mountaintops are windy . . . and it's on the northernmost point that you can hear the sound of your grandmother, the North Wind. Zenobi will whisper to you and succor you in my absence. Any time you need to be comforted, go there and let her hold you."

"Thank you, Matera."

"I will go now and give you time to adjust. If you need me, call and I will appear."

He inclined his head to her as she faded away and left him alone in this unfamiliar place.

It was so strange to be here and it would take some getting used to. Closing his eyes, he could see the gods as they'd been. Hear their voices echoing in the faintest of whispers. And when he opened them, they were all gone and he heard nothing.

As he moved around the room, he realized he wore some kind of leather leggings.

Pants.

How very odd to know the names of everything and everyone without even trying. Whatever information he needed was there instantly.

Crossing the room, he approached the single black and gold throne . . . Archon's. An image of Acheron's dead body in it appeared in his mind. And in the next, Acheron was sitting in it, looking out on the gleaming, empty room. Though ornate and gilded, it was sterile.

There was no life to the palace. No comfort here.

He stood, and as he did so a large staff appeared by his side. Over seven feet in length, it held his emblem in gold and silver on the top. Atlantean words were inscribed down the smooth wood.

By this, the Talimosin will be known. He will fight for himself and for others. Be strong.

Be strong. He clenched his teeth as Xiamara's words whispered through his mind. Gripping the staff tightly, he teleported himself to the top of the northernmost mountain. The sun was just beginning to set as the winds whipped his formesta out behind him. He gripped his staff tight, looking back over his shoulder to see where the palace stood below.

Then he heard it.

Apostolos . . . feel my strength. It will be yours when you need it.

He smiled sinisterly as he felt his grandmother's caress against his skin. Closing his eyes, he took comfort and strength.

When he opened his eyes, he could tell they glowed red now. His vision saw so much more than it had as a human. He felt the pulse of the universe in his veins. Felt the power of the primal source and for the first time realized his place in the cosmos.

I am the god, Apostolos. I am death, destruction and suffering. And I will be the one who brings forth Telikos— the end of the world.

That was if he could ever figure out how to use his powers. Acheron laughed at the truth of it.

Turning, he headed down the mountain and back to the throne room in Archon's palace. No, it was his now. Sadness hung deep inside him as he realized that though he had his grandmother and mother with him in spirit, he was still alone in the world.

Completely alone.

He froze as he heard something moving behind his throne. It was a soft scurrying sound . . . like a large rodent. Frowning, he teleported toward it, prepared to kill whatever dared defile his new home.

What he found there stunned him completely.

It was a small demon with marbled red and white skin and long black hair. Small red horns poked through the tangles of her curls as she looked up at him with red eyes that were rimmed in orange.

"Are you my akri?" she asked in a childish lilt.

"I'm no one's akri."

"Oh . . ." She looked about. "But akra sent me here. She said my akri would be waiting. The Simi is confused. I lost my mama and now the Simi needs her akri." She sat down and started crying.

Acheron laid down the staff to pick the toddler up. "Don't cry. It'll be all right. We'll find your mother."

She shook her head. "Akra said the Simi's mama is dead. Them evil Greek people killed the Simi's mama. Now the Simi needs her akri to love her."

Acheron rocked her gently in his arms as his mother's shade appeared before him.

Simi stopped crying. "Akra, he says the Simi's akri isn't here."

His mother smiled at them. "He is your akri, Simi."

Acheron scowled at her declaration. "What?"

"Her mother was your protector, Xiamara. Like you, Simi is all alone in the world with no one to care for her. She needs you, Apostolos."

He looked down at those large eyes that swallowed the demon's small round face. Blinking, she stared up at him with the same trust and innocence as Apollodorus. And he was lost to that loving gaze that didn't judge or condemn him.

"Bond with him, Simi, protect my son as your mother protected me."

The thought of tying someone to him terrified Acheron. He didn't want anyone enslaved to him. "I don't want a demon."

"Would you cast her out alone in the world?"

"No."

"Then she's yours."

393

Before he could protest again, his mother faded away.

Simi snuggled against him and laid her head against his shoulder. "I miss my mama, akri."

Guilt slammed into him at her whispered words as he held her close to him. But for him, her mother would still be alive to love her. "Where's your father, Simi?"

"He died before the Simi was born."

"Then I will be your father."

"Really?" she asked hopefully.

He nodded, smiling at her. "I swear to you that you'll never want for anything."

Her innocent smile warmed his heart. "Then the Simi has the best akri-papa in the world." She hugged him tightly. "Simi loves her akri." As soon as the words were spoken, she faded as his mother had done. But as she faded, his skin, just above his heart, burned.

Hissing, Acheron jerked up his tunic to find a small colorful dragon emblazoned on his skin. He touched it gingerly, and heard Simi's laughter in his head. The tattoo inched its way up, toward his neck. Her motion on his skin tickled until she settled over his collarbone.

"Simi is a part of you now, Apostolos. While on your body, she won't be able to hear you unless you call for her. But she will be able to monitor your vital signs. Should she sense you're in danger, she will appear to you in demon form to protect you."

"But she's only a baby."

"Even as a baby, she's deadly. Never mistake that. The Charonte are by their very nature killers. She will be hungry and you'll have to feed her often. If you fail to, she'll eat whatever is near her ... even you. Make sure she doesn't get overly hungry. And the last thing you should know is that her kind age very slowly. Roughly one year of a human's development equals a thousand years of theirs."

That did not sound good. "What are you saying?"

"The Simi you have is over three thousand years old."

Acheron gaped at the information. "Shouldn't she be with another demon who can train her?"

You are all she has in this world, m'gios. Take care of

394

her. As you have said, you are her father now. You'll be the one to teach her everything she knows."

Acheron placed his hand over the tattoo on his shoulder. He was a father . . .

But how could he train and protect a demon daughter when he didn't even know how to use his own powers?

June 30, 9527 BC
Athens, Greece

Acheron was desperate to find food for Simi. He'd awakened to her this morning after she'd bitten into his hand. Luckily, he'd stopped her before she did anything other than break his skin.

"You're not supposed to bite your father, Simi," he'd told her kindly, but firmly.

"But the Simi's hungry and akri was lying there all still and yummy looking."

And he'd thought the worst that could happen was to look yummy to horny humans . . .

But now as they wandered through the streets of a once great city, he realized just how much damage his mother had done in the brief time she'd been released. The world he knew was gone. Roads and buildings had been leveled. People lay dead all over Greece . . .

Apollymia Katastrafia Megola.

Apollymi the Great Destroyer. While a small part of him was flattered by her love, the other part was horrified by what she'd done. So many lives gone. The entire world scattered into debris. All of Atlantis was now lost. Mankind had been thrown back into the Stone Age. All their technology and tools had been lost.

The survivors wailed in the streets that the gods had abandoned them when the truth was, they'd have been better off if they had. All of them were unfortunate victims of a war they didn't even know had been fought.

He gripped Simi's hand as they walked around, searching for a marketplace. In human form, she'd taken on an appearance very similar to his. They both had long black hair and while his eyes were the same swirling silver, hers were a light blue. She looked like any small girl out with her father.

"Hey, Simi. I have something for you to eat."

Acheron jerked around at the deep masculine voice that called out to them. There was a tall, dark-haired man whose beard was thick. His skin was dark like a Sumerian and yet he spoke flawless Greek. Acheron held Simi back to keep her from running to him. "Who are you?"

The man stepped around a fallen column to kneel before Simi. He set a basket down at her feet and uncovered loaves of bread, fish and cheese. "I know you're hungry, sweet. Dig in."

Simi let out a squeal of delight before she set on the food with a vengeance.

The man stood up and offered his arm to Acheron. "My name is Savitar."

Acheron frowned at the tattoo of a bird that marked his forearm before he shook it. "How do you know Simi?"

One corner of his mouth lifted. "I know lots of things, Acheron. And I've come to help you learn your powers and to understand your simi demon. She's too young still to be left to callous care and the last thing I want is to see either one of you hurt because of it."

"I would never hurt her."

"I know, but the Charonte have special needs you must understand. Otherwise she could die . . . as could you."

Acheron felt the brush of hackles rise and he wasn't sure why. There was something about this being that rubbed against his godhood and made him wary. "Are you threatening me?"

Savitar laughed. "I never threaten. I just kill whatever annoys me. Stand down, Atlantean. I'm here as your friend."

Once Simi had devoured every crumb, Savitar picked her up in his arms to carry her while he walked through the crumbled streets. "She's impressive, isn't she?"

"My mother or Simi?"

Savitar laughed. "Both, but I was speaking of your mother."

Acheron looked around and sighed at the destruction his mother had wrought. "Yes, she is." And as they walked Acheron realized something. "I can't hear your thoughts."

"No, you can't. And you never will. You'll find that many of the higher beings of the universe will be silent to you. Some gods, demons, and other special creatures. We all have our secrets, but the comfort to you is that most won't be able to hear yours either."

That *was* comforting. "Can you hear them?"

"The answer you seek is no, but the truth is, I hear you, Acheron, and yes, I know all about your past."

He cursed at what he didn't want to hear. "What of the others? Will they know my past too?"

"Some will." Savitar shifted Simi in his arms, then paused to look at him. "I don't care about your past, Acheron. It's your future that matters to me. I want to make sure that you have one and that you comprehend how important you are to the balance of power."

Balance of power? "I don't understand."

"Apollo cursed his Apollites."

"And my mother killed them all."

Savitar shook his head. "Many died with Atlantis, but there are thousands of them who have spread over the Mediterranean and who live in many other countries now, including Apollo's own son, Strykerius. All of them have been cursed to die on their twenty-seventh birthday. *All* of them."

"Then how are they a problem? If they all die in a few years, they'll be extinct."

Savitar stroked Simi's head before he started walking again. "They're not going to die, Acheron. They will live and they will procreate many times over."

"How?"

Savitar sighed before he answered. "A goddess will lead them and show them how to prey on human souls to circumvent Apollo's curse."

Acheron was appalled. "I don't understand. Why would anyone do such a thing?"

"Because the universe is complicated and there's a delicate balance in all things that must be maintained."

"Yes, but if you know these people will die, can't you stop the goddess from teaching them?"

"I could. But it could unravel the very essence of the universe."

Frustration ran deep through Acheron. He didn't understand. Why would someone fail to help another if they had the power to?

Savitar picked up a random stone from the ground and held it in his hand. "Tell me what happens if I throw this with all my power."

Acheron frowned until he saw an image in his head. It was the stone traveling through the air . . . it sped until it hit a man in his shoulder, wounding him. No, not any man. A soldier. His arm now lame, the stone's wound forced him to become a beggar . . .

Eight score people would then die because the soldier could no longer protect them in battles that wouldn't even be fought for years to come. But out of those people who died . . .

"It goes on and on and on," Savitar said. "One tiny decision: Do I throw the rock or do I drop it? And a thousand lives are changed by one innocuous decision." He let the rock fall to the ground.

Now it was harmless again and history wrote itself forward the way it was supposed to.

Savitar smiled down at Simi who'd fallen asleep in his arms. "You and I are cursed to understand how the tiniest decision made by every being can go onward to affect the rest of the universe. I know what should happen . . . what needs to happen. And if I stop something as simple as a rock throw, it could cause catastrophic consequences. However, unlike you, I don't see the future until *after* I act. The moment I do something, I then see everything unfold from that point on. You are lucky. You will always see the future *before* you act."

"But I didn't see my sister's death."

"No. The Greek Fates, when they cursed you, blinded you to the fate of those closest to you. Anyone you care about will be your blind spot."

"That's not right."

"Well, kid, brace yourself. This one's even worse. You also will never be able to see your own future or the future of anyone who seriously impacts your future."

Acheron ground his teeth at the injustice. "Can you see it?"

"It's why I'm here."

"Then tell me what you see."

Savitar shook his head. "Just because you can, doesn't mean you should. If you knew what was ahead of you, you'd avoid doing the very things you must do in order to have it unfold properly. One small innocuous decision and your destiny will be altered forever."

"But you can see your future."

"Only after I've set it into motion and can't change it."

Acheron shook his head as he pondered which of them was the most cursed. The one who was blind or the one who saw it instantly and was powerless to stop it.

Savitar clapped him on the back. "I know how confusing it is for you to have all this power and knowledge and not know how to channel it. Or tap it."

Acheron nodded. "It is hard."

Savitar smiled. "That's why the first thing I want to teach you is fighting."

"Why fighting?"

Savitar laughed as they walked. "Because you're going to need it. There's a war coming, Acheron, and you have to be prepared for it."

"A war? What kind of war?"

Savitar refused to answer. Instead, he shook Simi awake. "Little one, I need you to return to your akri and stay on him while he fights. Don't worry though, it's only pretend fighting. No need for you to come off him to protect him."

Simi nodded sleepily before she obeyed. She drifted onto Acheron's arm.

"Move up, Simi," Savitar said to her. "Go to his neck where you won't be hit."

Acheron frowned at his orders. "Can she feel a blow when she's on my skin?"

"Yes, she can. And if she's stabbed while she's there and

it wounds you, it will wound her too. Guard your demon, boy."

The next thing Acheron knew, they were alone on a beach. "Takeshi!" Savitar shouted.

Black smoke roiled out of the earth.

Acheron stepped back as the smoke cleared to reveal a man in armor the likes of which he'd never seen before. Blood red, it was made of shining metal. Wickedly carved blades curved up over his shoulders while a neck piece came up to cover the lower part of his face. All that could be seen were his eyes and the red scrollwork tattoo that was drawn across his forehead.

His black hair was tinged with red tips. His eyes slanted exotically like a feral cat and they were a deep, blood red. But the moment those eyes fastened on Savitar, they lightened with friendship. The metal around his neck folded down from his handsome face to show a man no more than a year or two older than Acheron.

"Savitar-san," he greeted with a crooked grin. "It's been a long time."

Savitar inclined his head to him. "And I'm calling in a favor."

With one hand resting on the hilt of his sword, Takeshi tsked as he looked about the beach. "Sav, you can't keep doing this. I'm running out of places to put the bodies."

Savitar laughed. "Nothing like that." He stepped back to allow the two of them to size each other up. "Takeshi, meet Acheron. Acheron this is Takeshi-sensei. Listen to him and he'll teach you to fight in ways you can't imagine."

Takeshi narrowed his gaze on Acheron. "You would have me train a new god?"

Savitar leaned in and whispered something to Takeshi that he couldn't hear.

Takeshi nodded. "As you wish, brother." Stepping toward Acheron, Takeshi smiled and knocked the staff out of Acheron's hands. He let out a long sigh of disappointment. "I have much to teach you. Come and learn the art of war from the one who invented it."

Cocky, Acheron went with him—after all, he was a god now, surely he could fight. At least that's what he thought until Takeshi pinned him to the ground with a move so fast, he hadn't even realized the man had gone into motion until Acheron was face down in the sand.

"Never take your eyes off your opponent," Takeshi said before he moved back and allowed Acheron to rise. "And never think you don't have to work for a victory. Even now, you could surprise me."

Acheron frowned.

Takeshi rolled his eyes. "Surprise me, Atlantean. Attack. This isn't a dance party."

Acheron went for him and again, he landed face down in the sand. "You know, this isn't building my confidence. In fact, I think I'm just going to lie here for a bit and take in some sun."

Takeshi laughed, then patted him on the back. "Get up, Acheron." He looked over to where Savitar was now sitting on a rock watching them. "He doesn't anger easily. This is good."

Acheron laughed bitterly. "Yes, I'm more of a simmer slowly until it boils over and ruins everything kind of man."

Takeshi turned back to Acheron and handed him his staff. "Just remember, anger is always your enemy. You must keep your emotions in check. The moment you lose control of them, you lose the fight every time."

Acheron twirled the staff around and brought it into a defensive block.

Takeshi tsked at him. "Always be the attacker. A defender never wins."

"Defenders get their asses kicked," Savitar said. "Trust me. I've got crack impressions on every pair of shoes I own."

Takeshi arched a brow at Savitar. "Do you want to teach him?"

"Not really."

"Then shut up or grab a sword and come help."

The humor fled Savitar's face. "Is that a challenge?"

"It would be if I didn't know for a fact that you're too lazy to rise to one."

"Lazy? Mesoula?"

"Eqou," Takeshi taunted.

Savitar flashed from the rock, to stand before Takeshi with a sword the likes of which Acheron had never seen before. He brought it down across Takeshi's vambrace. The next thing he knew, the two of them were at war.

Takeshi scoffed. "Ah, you fight like a sissy demon."

"Sissy demon? Have you ever met a sissy demon?"

"I killed three this morning."

Savitar swung at his throat. The blade whistled through the air, narrowly missing the man's adam's apple.

Feeling neglected, but grateful he wasn't in the middle of this titanic brawl, Acheron went to sit on the rock Savitar had vacated.

Savitar shoved Takeshi back. "Your mother was a goatherder."

"It's an honorable profession."

"Yeah for a goat."

Takeshi swung around and kicked Savitar away. Savitar flipped over and came back with an upstroke that barely missed gutting him.

Takeshi shook his head. "Have you been drinking this morning? How did you miss me? I swear I've fought old women with better reflexes."

"The fact you fight old women tells me just how rusty you've become. What? Your ego needed the boost and they were the only ones you could find you could beat?"

"Savitar, Savitar, Savitar. At least I won. Wasn't it you who had to cry to the counsel to come save your ass from an attack of a four-year-old?"

Savitar gaped in feigned anger. "Four-year-old . . . tarranine demon. Don't forget the most important part. Those bastards are hatched full grown and it wasn't just one. It was a swarm of them."

"So you admit you had help?"

"Oh that's it, sensei. You're tasting sand . . ."

Acheron shook his head at their bantering. While they were being harsh to each other, there was a good-natured spirit that let him know they didn't mean a word of it. It was as if they were sparring with words the same way they were sparring with their swords.

403

Honestly, they amazed him. He'd never had a friend he could do that with. He envied them that.

Savitar twisted out of a nasty-looking headlock. "Hey, aren't we forgetting something?"

"Your dignity?"

Savitar rolled his eyes. "No, you have me confused with you again." He pointed to where Acheron sat. "Aren't you supposed to be training *him*?"

Takeshi let out a taunting breath. "So you admit my superiority by deflecting my attention to the neophyte . . ."

"I'm not admitting shit. I'm merely pointing out the fact that you and I know how to fight and he doesn't. Might be a good idea for him to learn."

"True." Takeshi put his sword across his shoulders where he held it with both hands and smiled at Acheron. "Are you ready to begin again?"

"Sure. My ego's had enough time to recover a modicum of dignity. Let's make sure we crush it again before I mistake myself for a god."

Takeshi laughed. "I like him, Savitar. He fits with us."

"That's why I called you." Savitar handed his sword to Acheron. "Good luck, kid."

"Thanks."

Acheron spent the rest of the day training with Takeshi who had to be the worst taskmaster ever born. He worked him until Acheron was sure he'd drop from sheer exhaustion. By the time the sun set and he was free to rest, his entire body ached.

Even so, he felt more confident in his skills than he'd ever felt before.

Savitar handed him his staff. "Go home to Katoteros and we'll begin again in the morning."

Still unsure why Savitar was helping him, he wished the older . . . being . . . good-night and returned home.

Acheron pulled up short as he saw Artemis waiting in the throne room for him. "What do you want?"

"I haven't seen you in days."

"And what a beautiful thing they have been."

She narrowed her gaze. "I told you that you'd have to feed from me."

Acheron looked at her coldly. "I think I'd rather be a sadistic monster . . . like you."

She curled her lip at him. "So that's it then. You're just going to be mean to me."

"Mean to you? Mean?" He repeated angrily. "Fuck you, Artemis!" His words were punctuated by a blast of wind so strong, it knocked her onto her ass on the floor. He stalked toward her and saw the fear in her eyes. There was a time when that fear would have ignited guilt and compassion within him. Today it just pissed him off. "I was butchered on the floor by your brother while you watched it happen. Then, when I was finally happy someplace, gods forbid, you tricked me into drinking your blood to bind me to you. And you think I'm mean? Bitch, please, you haven't seen mean yet."

She covered her ears with her hands and cringed on the floor.

That actually succeeded in turning his anger away from her to him since he had a twinge of pity for her and he hated himself for it. She didn't deserve his pity. Only his contempt.

"I loved you, Acheron."

He scoffed. "If what you've shown me is love, I'd rather you hate my guts and be done with me."

She burst into tears.

Acheron leaned his head back and cursed at the fact that those tears affected him. Why did he care? What the fuck was so wrong with him that he actually wanted to comfort her?

I'm even more defective than she is.

He slammed his staff down on the floor, making her cry even harder. "What do you want from me, Artie?"

"I want my friend back."

"No," he said bitterly. "You want your pet back. I was never your friend. Friends aren't ashamed of each other. They don't live in fear of other people seeing them together."

She looked up at him with her green eyes swimming in tears. "I'm sorry. There, I said it. I wish I could go back and repair everything that's happened. But I can't. I wish I could save our nephew. I wish that I'd been more decent to you. I wish . . ." She paused, but it was too late. He'd heard it loud and clear.

"That I'd never been a whore. Trust me, what you feel about that is a pittance compared to my sentiments. You were never the one they degraded and used. I'm the one who has to live with that past. Not you. You should be grateful those nightmares don't haunt your sleep."

"I have my own nightmares, thank you."

Perhaps she did. After all, she was the pitiful child who had to tolerate Apollo.

She looked up at him. "Food can't sustain you anymore, Acheron. You don't even have to eat human food again. But you do have to feed from me or you will revert to the Destroyer's Harbinger. You will have no compassion for the world and you will destroy it."

A muscle worked in his jaw. He wanted to call her a liar, but he knew the truth. He already felt those violent urges inside him. And he hated her for this "gift."

Cursing, he held his hand out to her.

She took his hand and he jerked her to her feet and into his arms. Then, just as he started to ravage her throat, he pulled back and bit into her gently.

At the end of the day, he wasn't a monster. He wouldn't brutalize her even if she did deserve it.

He'd made her a promise and though he may have been a thief and a whore, he wasn't a liar. He wouldn't serve to her what she'd served to him. He would always be better than that.

Artemis sighed as she felt Acheron's powers surging around her. His skin marbled to blue while he drank. The heat of his breath on her flesh ignited her desire, but when she tried to remove his clothes, he stopped her.

"I'm in no mood to play with my food, Artemis."

She closed her eyes as she heard his voice in her head.

When he'd taken his fill, he stepped away from her. His eyes were blazing red as he wiped the blood from his lips. "I need time away from you."

Those words sliced through her. "What are you saying?"

"Send a kori to me with your blood."

"No."

This time, he turned on her with all his powers ignited.

Artemis shrank away at the sight of his true god form. He was massive and terrifying.

"You will do as *I* command," he snarled through his fangs. "You brought me back against my will and you will not tell me how to live this new life. Do you understand?"

She nodded slowly as her heart broke again over what she'd lost. "While you're telling me what to do, you should know that when I brought you back, Styxx came with you. And he's filled with even more fury and hatred than you are."

Acheron cursed at the mention of his twin. "Where is he?"

"He's on the Vanishing Isle, under the care of a god who owes me a favor. He can't harm anyone where he is and he's in a good place with his every desire fulfilled."

"Then leave him there. I have no wish to ever see his face again."

"Rather difficult, isn't it?"

He curled his lip at her reminder. "Don't push me, Artie. I'm one step away from the edge and it wouldn't take much to step over it. Trust me, you don't want me there. Now get out of my sight. I don't ever want to see you here in my domain again."

Her tears started falling again, but this time they didn't affect him. He refused to allow that. She'd changed him from the man he'd been.

The whore was dead and a god of destruction had been born. Cursed. Hated. Powerful. Lethal.

His hatred for the world was carved into his heart. His past was a weight he carried on his back and his future was uncertain.

He had enemies aplenty who wanted him dead, an angry mother out to end the world, a baby demon who needed to be fed every few hours, two lunatics training him for a coming war neither would explain, and a horny goddess who only wanted him chained to her bedpost.

Yeah . . . it was "good" to be back in the mortal realm. He couldn't wait to see what tomorrow would bring. Too bad he had no warning for his place in it.

Damn the Fates—his sisters who'd betrayed and condemned him to this existence.

One day, he'd pay those bitches back too.

April 10, 9526 BC
Mount Olympus

Acheron didn't know why he'd agreed to meet Artemis. The mere thought of looking at her right now was enough to make him physically sick—if he could get sick. For almost a year, he'd been cleaning up Apollo's mess. There were remnant Apollites turning into soul-sucking Daimons on a daily basis.

Not that he blamed them, really. It'd been a small group of men that the Atlantean queen had sent out to assassinate his sister and nephew. Jealous over the fact that Apollo no longer came to her bed, the Atlantean queen had turned her venom to Ryssa. In the middle of the night, the queen's men had snuck into Ryssa's bedroom and killed her while she was feeding Apollodorus.

Then after Apollo had finished killing Acheron, the god had turned on the very race of people he'd created. Since the assassins had made it appear as if an animal had torn into Ryssa and Apollodorus, Apollo cursed them to feed on each other. Only Apollite blood could sustain them. What was it with Apollo and Artemis and blood?

If that wasn't enough of a curse, Apollo had banished them from the sun so that he'd never have to see them again and be reminded of their treachery. And not to be outdone, he'd then condemned their entire race to die slowly and painfully on their twenty-seventh birthday—the same age Ryssa had been.

Given the severity of the punishment, Acheron might have thought the god loved his sister. But he knew better. Apollo was no more capable of love than Artemis was. It was nothing more than a show of power. A warning to others who might think of turning on Apollo who was now telling everyone that he'd destroyed Atlantis to get back at the Apollites.

Stupid bastard. And stupid people for believing his lies.

Acheron kept his silence, not to protect the god, but only because Apollo's pathetic arrogance amused him.

By his own stupidity the god was going to be undone. Even now Acheron's mother sat in her prison, plotting the god's death . . . along with Artemis's. No sooner had Apollo damned his people than Apollymi had gone to Strykerius, Apollo's condemned son, and showed him how to circumvent death by taking human souls into Apollite bodies and thus elongating their lives.

No wonder Savitar had failed to tell Acheron the name of the goddess Acheron would be fighting.

It was his own mother. She was the one leading the Daimon army that was set on its own vengeance. He should have known.

But then his revenge had been more direct. He'd hunted down the ones who'd killed his sister and nephew—those who'd survived his mother's attack, and he'd made them wish they'd never been born with nerve-endings.

Now he was at war with his mother.

Acheron sighed heavily. "One day, I'm going to kill those damned Fates."

But it wouldn't be today. Today he was meeting with Artemis to see why she'd been shrieking and threatening to kill him these past months. Between her and his mother ranting at him, this was the first time since he'd died that his head had been clear of their incessant nagging.

He felt the ripple of power down his spine that signified her arrival. He stiffened in expectation of her shrewish voice. When she didn't start yelling at him, he turned his head to find her hesitating.

"Why so nervous, Artemis?"

"You're very different now."

He laughed at her acute sense of perception. He *was* different. No longer a subservient slave, he was a pissed off god who wanted the entire world to leave him alone.

"I don't like your hair black."

He gave her a droll stare. "And I don't like your head attached to your shoulders. Guess we can't all have what we want, huh?" He narrowed his gaze on her. "I don't have time for this shit. If all you want is to gawk at me, then you can admire my back as I walk away from you."

He turned his back to her.

"Wait!"

Against his better judgment, he hesitated. "For what?"

She had approached him cautiously as if terrified of him. "Please don't be angry at me, Acheron."

He laughed bitterly at her words. "Oh, anger doesn't even begin to describe what I am at you. How dare you bring me back."

She gulped as her features drew taut. "I had no choice."

"We all have choices."

"No, Acheron. We don't."

As if he believed that. She'd always been selfish and vain and no doubt that was the only reason he'd been brought back when he should have been left dead. "Is this why you've been summoning me? You want to apologize?"

She shook her head. "I'm not sorry for what I've done. I would do it over again in a heart pound."

"Beat," he snarled, correcting her.

She waved the word away with her hand. "I want there to be peace between us."

Peace? Was she insane? She was lucky he didn't kill her right now. If it wasn't for fear of what could happen, he would have.

"There will never be peace between us. Ever. You shattered any hope of it when you watched your brother kill me and refused to speak up on my behalf."

"I was afraid."

"And I was butchered and gutted on the floor like an animal sacrifice. Excuse me if I don't feel your pain. I'm too busy with my own." He turned to leave her then, but she stopped him again.

It was then he heard the muffled whimpering of a baby. Scowling, he watched in horror as she withdrew an infant from the folds of her peplos.

"I have a baby for you, Acheron."

He jerked his arm away from her as fury singed every part of him. "You bitch! Do you honestly think that could *ever* replace my nephew whom you let die? I hate you. I will always hate you. For once in your life, do the right thing and return that to its mother."

She slapped him then with enough force to split his lips. "Go and rot, you worthless bastard."

Laughing, he wiped the blood away with the back of his hand while he stared venomously at her. "I may be a worthless bastard, but better that than a frigid whore who sacrificed the only man to ever love her because she was too self-absorbed to save him."

The look on her face scorched him. "I'm not the whore here, Acheron. You are. Bought and sold to anyone who could pay your fee. How dare you think for one minute you were ever worthy of a goddess."

The pain of those words seared a permanent place in his heart and soul. "You're right, my lady. I'm not worthy of you or anyone else. I'm just a piece of shit to be dumped naked in the street. Forgive me for ever sullying you."

Then he vanished from her.

Their relationship was now over. There was no power in the universe that would ever make him speak to her again.

You need her blood.

So what? Let the world die for all he cared. Better everyone should perish than he spend five more minutes enslaved to that bitch. He was tired of being everyone's scapegoat. For once he was going to think of himself and screw the rest of them.

"I'm through, Artemis. Completely through."

Greece, 7382 BC

Acheron felt a presence behind him. He spun around, staff ready to strike, expecting it to be another Daimon attacking him.

It wasn't.

Instead, he found Simi hanging upside down in a tree, her long, burgundy bat-like wings folded in against her child-like body. She wore a loose black chiton and himation that rippled gently with the night's breeze. Her blood red eyes glowed eerily in the darkness while her long black braid dangled from her head, down to the ground.

Acheron relaxed and set one end of his staff against the damp grass as he watched her.

"Where have you been, Simi?" he asked sharply. He'd been calling for the Charonte demon for the last half hour.

"Oh just hanging about, akri," she said, smiling as she swung herself back and forth on the limb. "Did akri miss me?"

Acheron sighed. He loved Simi more than his life, but he wished he had a mature demon as his companion. Not one that even at five thousand years old functioned on the level of a five-year-old child.

It would be centuries before Simi was fully grown.

"Did you deliver my message?" he asked.

"Yes, akri," she said, using the Atlantean term for my lord and master. "I delivered it just as you said, akri."

The skin on the back of Acheron's neck crawled. There was something in her tone that concerned him. "What did you do, Simi?"

"The Simi did nothing, akri. But . . ."

He waited as she looked about nervously.

"But?" he prompted.

413

"The Simi was hungry on her way back."

He went cold with dread. "Who did you eat this time?"

"It wasn't a who, akri. It was something that had hornies on its head like me. There were a bunch of them actually. All of them had hornies and they made a strange moo-moo sound."

He frowned at her description. "Do you mean cows? You ate cattle?"

She beamed. "That's it, akri. I ate cattle."

Then why was she so worried? "That's not so bad."

"No, it was actually rather good, akri. Why didn't you tell the Simi about cows? They are very tasty when roasted. The Simi liked them a lot. We need to get us some of them moo-moos. I think they'd fit in the house."

He ignored her side commentary. "Then why are you worried?"

"Because this really tall man with only one eyeball came out of a cave and was screaming at the Simi. He say the Simi was evil for eating the cows and that I would have to pay for them. What does that mean, akri? Pay? The Simi know nothing about pay."

Acheron wished he could say the same for himself. "This really big man, was he a cyclops?"

"What's a cyclops?"

"A son of Poseidon."

"Oh see, that's what he said. Only he had no hornies. He had a big, bald head instead."

Acheron didn't want to discuss the cyclops' big bald head with his demon. What he needed to know was what to do to make amends for her voracious appetite. "So what did the cyclops say to you?"

"That he be mad at the Simi for eating the cattle. He said the horny cows belonged to Poseidon. Who is Poseidon, akri?"

"A Greek god."

"Oh see then, the Simi is not in trouble. I just kill the Greek god and all's fine."

He had to hide his smile from her. "You can't kill a Greek god, Simi. It's not allowed."

"There you go again, akri, saying no to the Simi. Don't eat that, Simi. Don't kill that, Simi. Stay here, Simi. Go to

Katoteros, Simi, and wait for me to call you." She crossed her arms over her chest and gave him a stern frown. "I don't like being told no, akri."

Acheron grimaced at the ache that was starting in the back of his skull. He wished he'd been given a pet parrot for his twenty-first birthday. The Charonte demon was going to be the death of him . . . again.

"So why were you calling the Simi, akri?"

"I wanted your help with the Daimons."

She relaxed and went back to swinging on her limb. "You didn't seem to need any help, akri. The Simi thinks you did quite well with them on your own. I particularly liked the way that one Daimon flew up into the air before you killed him. Very nice. I did not know they were so colorful when they exploded."

She flipped off the limb and came to stand by his side. "Where we go now, akri? Will you take Simi somewhere cold again? I liked that last place we went. The mountain was very nice."

Acheron?

He paused as he felt Artemis summoning him. He let out another long-suffering sigh.

For two thousand years, he'd been ignoring her.

Still she insisted on calling out to him.

There was a time when she'd sought him out in the "flesh," but he'd blocked her from that ability.

Her mental telepathy to him was the only contact he couldn't sever entirely.

"Come, Simi," he said, starting his journey that would take him back to Therakos. The Daimons there had set up a colony where they were preying on the poor Greeks who lived in a small village.

Acheron. I need your help. My new Dark-Hunters need a trainer.

He froze at Artemis's words.

New Dark-Hunters? What the hell was that?

"What have you done, Artemis?" his voice whispered along the wind, traveling to Olympus where she waited in her temple.

So, you do speak to me. He heard the relief in her tone. *I*

*had begun to wonder if I would ever hear the sound of
your voice again.*

Acheron curled his lip. He didn't have time for this.

Acheron?

He ignored her.

She didn't take the hint.

*The Daimon menace is spreading faster than you can
contain it. You needed help and so I've given it to you.*

He scoffed at the idea of her help. The Greek goddess
had never done anything for anyone other than herself since
the dawn of time.

"Leave me alone, Artemis. We're through, you and I. I
have a job to do and no time to be bothered with you."

*Fine then. I shall send them out to face the Daimons un-
prepared. If they die, well, who cares for a human? I can
just make more of them to fight.*

It was a trick.

Yet in his gut, Acheron knew it wasn't. She probably had
made these Dark-Hunters and if she truly had, then she
would definitely do it again.

Especially if it would make him feel guilty.

Damn her. He would have to go to her temple. Personally, he would rather be disemboweled.

His gut tightened at the memory and it didn't appreciate
his jest.

He looked to his demon. "Simi, I need to see Artemis
now. You return to Katoteros and stay out of trouble until I
summon you."

The demon grimaced. "The Simi don't like Artemis, akri.
I wish you'd let the Simi kill that goddess. The Simi want to
pull out her long, red hair."

He knew the feeling.

"I know, Simi, which is why I want you to stay at Katoteros." He stepped away, then turned back to face her.
"And for my sake, please don't eat anything until I get
back. Especially not a human."

"But—"

"No, Simi. No food."

"No, Simi. No food," she mocked. "The Simi don't
like this, akri. Katoteros is boring. There's nothing fun

416

there. Only old dead people who want to come back here. Bleh!"

"Simi . . ." he said, his voice thick with warning.

"I hear and obey, akri. The Simi just never said she would do so quietly."

He shook his head at the incorrigible demon, then willed himself from earth to Artemis's temple on Olympus.

Acheron stood on top of the golden bridge that traversed a winding river. The sound of the water echoed off the sheer sides of the mountain that rose up all around him.

In the last two thousand years, nothing had changed.

The entire area at the top of the mountain was made up of sparkling bridges and walkways, covered by a rainbow fog, that led to the various temples of the gods.

The halls of Mount Olympus were opulent and massive. Perfect homes for the egos of the gods who lived inside them.

Artemis's was made of gold, with a domed top and white marble columns. The view of the sky and world below was breathtaking from her throne room.

Or so he had thought in his youth.

But that was before time and experience had jaundiced his appreciation. To him there was nothing spectacular or beautiful here now. He saw only the selfish vanity and coldness of the Olympians.

These new gods were very different from the gods Acheron had learned about since his days as a human. All but one of the Atlantean gods had been full of compassion. Love. Kindness. Forgiveness.

His pending birth had been the only time the Atlanteans let their fear lead them—that mistake had cost all of them their immortal lives and had allowed the Olympian gods to replace them.

It'd been a sad day for the human world in more ways than one.

Acheron forced himself across the bridge that led to Artemis's temple. Two thousand years ago, he'd left this place and hoped that he would never return to it.

He should have known that sooner or later she would devise a scheme to bring him back.

His gut tight with anger, Acheron used his telekinesis to

open the oversized, gilded doors. He was instantly assailed with the sound of ear-piercing screams from Artemis's female attendants. They were wholly unaccustomed to a man entering their goddess's private domain.

Artemis hissed at the shrill sound, then zapped every one of the women around her.

"Did you just kill all eight of them?" Acheron asked.

Artemis rubbed her ears. "I should have, but no, I merely tossed them into the river outside."

Surprised, he stared at her. How unusual for the goddess he remembered. Perhaps she'd learned a degree of compassion and mercy over the last two thousand years.

Knowing her, it was highly unlikely.

Now that they were alone, she unfolded herself from her cushioned ivory throne and approached him. She wore a sheer, white himation that hugged the curves of her voluptuous body and her dark auburn curls glistened in the light.

Her green eyes glowed warmly in welcome.

The look went through him like a lance. Hot. Piercing. Painful. He'd known seeing her again would be hard on him—it was one of the reasons why he'd always ignored her summons.

But knowing something and experiencing it were two entirely different things.

He'd been unprepared for the emotions that threatened to overwhelm him now that he saw her again. The hatred. The betrayal. Worst of all was the need.

The hunger.

The desire.

There was still a part of him that loved her. A part of him that was willing to forgive her anything.

Even his death . . .

"You look good, Acheron. Every bit as handsome as you were the last time I saw you." She reached to touch him.

He stepped back, out of her reach. "I didn't come here to chat, Artemis, I—"

"You used to call me Artie."

"I used to do a lot of things I can't do anymore." He gave her a hard stare to remind her of everything she had taken from him.

"You're still angry at me."

"You think so?"

Her eyes snapped emerald fire, reminding him of the demon who resided in her divine body. "I could have forced you to come to me, you know. I've been very tolerant of your defiance. More than I should have been."

He looked away, knowing she was right. She, alone, held possession of the food source he needed to function. When he went too long without her blood, he became an uncontrollable killer. A danger to anyone who came near him.

Only Artemis held the key that kept him as he was. Sane. Whole.

Compassionate.

"Why didn't you force me to your side?" he asked.

"Because I know you. Had I tried, you would have made us both pay for it."

Again, she was right. His days of subjugation were long over. He'd had more than his share of it in his childhood and youth. Having tasted freedom and power, he'd decided he liked it too much to go back to being what he'd been before.

"Tell me of these new Dark-Hunters," he said. "Why did you create them?"

"I told you, you need help."

He curled his lip in anger. "I need no such thing."

"I and the other Greek gods disagree."

"Artemis . . ." he growled her name, knowing she was lying about this. He was more than able to control and kill the Daimons who preyed on the humans. "I swear . . ."

He clenched his teeth as he thought about the first days of his new life. He'd had no one to show him the way. No one to explain to him what he needed to do.

How to live.

The new ones would be lost without a teacher. Confused. Worst of all, they were vulnerable until they learned to use their powers and there was no way Savitar would teach them.

Damn her.

"Where are they?"

419

"Waiting in Falossos. They hide in a cave that keeps them from the sunlight. But they're not sure what they should do or how to find the Daimons. They are men in need of leadership."

Acheron didn't want to do this. He didn't want to lead anyone any more than he wanted to follow someone else's orders. He didn't want to deal with other people at all.

He'd never wanted anything in his life except to be left alone.

The thought of interacting with others . . .

It made his blood run cold.

Half tempted to go his own way, Acheron knew he couldn't. If he didn't train the men how to fight and kill the Daimons, they would end up dead. Dead without a soul was a very bad existence. He, of all men, knew that one.

"Fine," he said. "I'll train them."

She smiled.

Acheron flashed from her temple back to Simi and ordered her to stay put a little longer. The demon would only complicate an already complicated matter.

Once he was sure she would stay, he teleported to Falossos.

He found the three men huddled in the darkness just as Artemis had said. They were talking quietly among themselves, grouped around a small fire for warmth and yet their eyes watered from the brightness of the flames.

Their eyes were no longer human and could no longer take the brightness that came from any source of light.

He had much to teach them.

Acheron moved forward, out of the shadows.

"Who are you?" the tallest one asked as soon as he saw him.

The man was no doubt a Dorian with long black hair. He was tall, powerfully built, and still dressed in battle armor that was in bad need of care and repair.

The men with him were blond Greeks. Their armor was no better than the first man's. The youngest of them had a hole in the center of his breastplate where he'd been stabbed through his heart with a javelin.

These men could never go out and mix with living people dressed like this. Each of them needed care. Rest.

Instruction.

Acheron lowered the cowl to his black chiton and eyed each man in turn.

As they noted the swirling silver color of his eyes, the men paled.

"Are you a god?" the tallest one asked. "We were told a god would kill us if we were in their presence."

"I'm Acheron Parthenopaeus," he said quietly. "Artemis sent me to train you."

"I am Callabrax of Likonos," the tallest said. He indicated the man to his right. "Kyros of Seklos." Then the youngest of their group, "And Ias of Groesia."

Ias stood back, his dark eyes hollow. Acheron could hear the man's thoughts as clearly as if they were in his own mind. The man's pain reached out to him, making his own stomach tighten in sympathy.

"How long has it been since you men were created?" Acheron asked them.

"A few weeks for me," Kyros said.

Callabrax nodded. "I was created about the same time."

Acheron looked to Ias.

"Two days ago," he said, his voice empty.

"He's still sick from the conversion," Kyros supplied. "It was almost a week before I could . . . adjust."

Acheron stifled the urge to laugh bitterly. It was a good word for it.

"Have you killed any Daimons yet?" he asked them.

"We tried," Callabrax said, "but they are very different from killing soldiers. Stronger. Faster. They don't die easily. We already lost two men to them."

Acheron winced at the thought of two unprepared men going up against the Daimons and the horrific existence that awaited them when they'd died without souls.

It was followed by the memory of his first fight . . .

He blocked the thought out of his mind. Though Takeshi had been a great teacher, he'd never fought a Daimon. And the one thing Acheron had learned was that both he and Savitar had failed to tell him *everything*. Those first years had been hard and brutal.

"Have the three of you eaten tonight?"

They nodded.

"Then follow me outside and I'll teach what you need to know to kill the Daimons."

Acheron worked with them until it was almost dawn. He shared with them everything he could for one night. Taught them new tactics. Where and how the Daimons were most vulnerable.

At the end of the night, he left them to their cave.

"I shall find you a better place to hide in daylight," he promised them.

"I'm a Dorian," Callabrax said proudly. "I require nothing more than what I have."

"But we're not," Kyros said. "A bed would be most welcomed to me and Ias. A bath even more so."

Acheron inclined his head, then motioned for Ias to join him outside.

He stood back as Ias left the cave first, then directed him away from the others' hearing.

"You want to see your wife again," Acheron said quietly.

He looked up, startled. "How do you know that?"

Acheron didn't answer. Even as a human, he'd hated personal questions as they most often led him into conversations he didn't want to have. Pricked at memories he wanted to keep buried.

Closing his eyes, Acheron let his mind wander out, through the cosmos until he found the woman who haunted Ias's mind.

Liora.

She was a beautiful woman, with hair as black as a raven's wing. Eyes as clear and blue as the open sea.

No wonder Ias missed her.

The woman was currently on her knees, weeping. "Please," she begged to the gods. "Please return my love to me. Please let my children have their father home."

Acheron felt sympathy for her at the sight and sound of her fears. No one had told her yet what'd happened. She was praying for the welfare of a man who was no longer with her.

It haunted him.

"I understand your sadness," he said to Ias. "But you

422

can't let them know you live now in this form. Humans will fear you if you return home. Try to kill you."

Ias's eyes welled with tears and when he spoke, his fangs cut his lips. "Liora has no one else to care for her. She was an orphan and my brother was killed the day before I was. There is no one to provide for my children."

"You can't go back."

"Why not?" Ias asked angrily. "Artemis said that I could have my vengeance on the man who killed me and then I would be alive to serve her. She said nothing about my not being able to go home."

Acheron tightened his grip on his staff. "Ias, think for a moment. You are no longer human. How do you think your village would react if you returned home with fangs and black eyes? You can't venture out into daylight. Your allegiance is to all mankind, not just to your family. No one can meet the obligations of both. You can't ever go back."

The man's lips quivered, but he nodded in understanding. "I save the humans while my innocent family is cast out to starve with no one to protect them. So, that was my bargain."

Acheron looked away as his heart ached for the man and his family.

"Go inside with the others," Acheron said.

He watched Ias return while he thought over the man's words. He couldn't leave it like this.

Acheron could function alone, but the others . . .

Closing his eyes, he willed himself back to Artemis.

This time when her women opened their mouths to scream, Artemis froze their vocal cords. "Leave us," she commanded them.

The women rushed for the door as fast as they could, then slammed it shut behind them.

As soon as they were alone, Artemis smiled at him. "You are back. I didn't expect to see you so soon."

"Don't, Artemis," he said, curbing her playfulness before she started with it. "I'm basically back to yell at you."

"For what?"

"How dare you lie to those men to get them into your service."

423

"I never lie."

He arched a brow.

Looking instantly uncomfortable, she cleared her throat and leaned back into her throne. "You were different and I didn't lie. I merely forgot to mention a few things."

"That is semantics, Artemis, and this isn't about me. This is about what you've done to them. You can't leave those poor bastards out there like you have."

"Why not? You've survived quite well on your own."

"I was never the same as they and well you know it. I had nothing in my life to go back to. No family, no friends."

"I take exception to that. What was I?"

"A mistake that I've been lamenting for the last two thousand years."

Her face flushed. She came off her throne and descended two stairs to stand before him. "How dare you speak to me that way!"

Acheron whipped his cloak off and tossed it and his staff angrily into a corner. "Kill me for it, Artemis. Go right ahead. Do us both a favor and put me out of my misery."

She tried to slap him, but he caught her hand in his and stared down into her eyes.

Artemis saw the hatred in Acheron's gaze, the scathing condemnation. Their angry breaths mingled and the air around them snapped furiously as their powers clashed.

But it wasn't his fury she wanted.

No, never his fury . . .

Her gaze drifted over him. Over the perfect sculpted planes of his face, his high cheekbones, his long, aquiline nose. The blackness of his hair.

The eerie mercury of his eyes.

There had never been a god or mortal born who could equal his physical perfection.

It wasn't just his beauty that drew people to him. It wasn't his beauty that drew her to him.

He possessed a raw, rare kind of masculine charisma. Power. Strength. Charm. Intelligence. Determination.

To look at him was to want him.

To see him was to ache to touch him.

He had been built to please, and trained to pleasure. Everything about him from the sleek muscles that rippled to the deep, erotic timbre in his voice seduced anyone who came into contact with him. Like a lethal wild animal, he moved with a primal promise of danger and masculine power. With the promise of supreme sexual fulfillment.

They were promises he delivered well on.

In all eternity, he was the only man who had made her weak. The only man she'd ever loved.

He had the power in him to kill her. They both knew it. And she found the fact that he didn't intriguing and provocative.

Seductive and erotic.

Swallowing, she remembered him as he had been when they first met. The strength of him. The passion. Defiantly, he'd stood in her temple and laughed when she threatened to kill him.

There before her statue, he had dared do what no man before or since had ever dared . . .

She could still taste that kiss.

Unlike other men, he had never feared her. Now, the heat of his hand on her flesh seared her, but then his touch always had. There was nothing more she craved than the taste of his lips. The fire of his passion.

And with one mistake, she'd lost him.

Artemis wanted to weep with the hopelessness of it all. She'd tried once, long ago, to turn back the hands of time and redo that morning.

To win back Acheron's love and trust.

The Fates had punished her severely for the audacity.

For the last two thousand years, she'd tried everything to bring him back to her side. Nothing had worked. Nothing had ever come close to making him forgive her or to journey back to her temple.

Not until she thought of the one thing he could never say no to—a mortal soul in jeopardy.

Acheron would do anything to save the humans. Her plan to make him responsible for the Dark-Hunters she'd created with his resurrection powers had worked and now he was back.

If she could just keep him.

"You want me to release them?" she asked.

For him, she would do anything.

"Yes."

For her, he would do nothing. Not unless she forced him to it.

"What will you do for me, Acheron? You know the rules of the gods. A favor requires a favor."

He released her with an angry curse and stepped back from her. "I've learned better than to play this game with you."

Artemis shrugged with a nonchalance she didn't feel. At this moment everything she cared about was on the line.

If he said no, it would destroy her.

"Fine, they will continue on as Dark-Hunters then. Alone with no one to teach them what they need to know. No one to care what becomes of them."

He released a long, tired breath.

She wanted to comfort him, but knew he would reject her touch. He'd always rejected comfort or solace. He was stronger than anyone had a right to be.

When he met her gaze, it sent a raw, sensual shiver over her." If they are to serve you and the gods, Artemis, they have things they need."

"Such as?"

"Armor for one. You can't send them out to fight without weapons. They need money to procure food, clothes, horses and even servants to watch over them in the daylight while they rest."

"You ask too much for them."

"I ask only for what they need to survive."

She shook her head. "You never asked any of that for yourself." She was hurt now at that fact.

He never asked for anything.

"I don't need food and my powers allow me to procure everything else I need. As for protection, I have Simi. They won't last alone."

No one lasts alone, Acheron.

No one.

Not even you.

426

And especially not me.

Artemis lifted her chin, determined to have him by her side no matter the consequences. "And again I say to you, what will you give me for what they need?"

Acheron looked away, his gut tight. He knew what she wanted and the last thing he wanted was to give it to her. "This is for them, not me."

She shrugged. "Fine then, they can do without since they have nothing to barter with."

His fury ignited deep at her casual dismissal of their lives and well-being. She hadn't changed at all.

"Damn you, Artemis."

She approached him slowly. "I want you, Acheron. I want you back the way you were before."

She wanted him as a whore. *Her* whore. He inwardly cringed as she cupped his face in her hand. They could never go back as they'd been. He'd learned too much about her since then.

He'd been betrayed one time too many.

Acheron would say he was a slow learner, but that wasn't true. What he'd been was so desperate for someone to care about him that he'd ignored the darker side of her nature.

Ignored it until she'd turned her back on him and left him to die. Some crimes were even above his ability to forgive.

His thoughts turned from himself, to the innocent men who were living in a cave. Men who knew nothing of their new existence or enemies. He couldn't leave them there like that.

He'd cost enough people their lives, their futures.

There was no way he could let them lose their souls and life too. "All right, Artemis. I will give you what you want, if you give them what they need to survive."

She beamed.

"But," he continued, "my terms are these: you are going to pay them every month a wage that will allow them to buy whatever they need or desire. As stated earlier, they will need shieldbearers to care for them personally so that they won't have to worry about scrounging for food,

427

clothes or arms. I don't want them to be distracted from their work."

"Fine, I will find humans who will serve them."

"Living humans, Artemis. I want them to serve of their own free will. No more Dark-Hunters."

She gaped at him. "Three of them are not enough. We need more to keep the Daimons in check."

Acheron closed his eyes as he felt the endlessness of this relationship. All too easily he could see into the future and where this was headed.

The more Dark-Hunters, the more he would be locked to her. There was no way to keep her from tying him to her forever.

Or was there?

"All right," he said. "I'll give on this, if you will agree to provide them a way out of your service."

"What do you mean?"

"I want you to establish a way for the Dark-Hunters to regain their souls so that they are no longer bound to you if they so choose it."

Artemis stepped back. This wasn't something she'd foreseen. If she gave him this, then even he would be bound by it.

He could leave her.

She'd forgotten just how devious Acheron could be. How well he knew the rules of the game and how to manipulate them and her.

He was truly her equal.

Yet if she failed to give him this, he would leave her anyway. She had no choice and well he knew it.

However, there were still things that could keep him by her side. One way she knew that would ensure his presence in her life for all eternity.

"Very well. Let us make the rules to govern them, then." She felt his thoughts drift back toward Ias. He pitied the poor Greek soldier who loved his wife. Pity, mercy and compassion would always be his downfall.

"Number one, is that they must die to reclaim their souls."

"Why?" he asked.

"A soul can only be released from a body at the moment of death. Likewise, it can only return to a body that is no longer functioning. So long as they 'live' as a Dark-Hunter, they can never have their souls again. That's not my rule, Acheron, that is simply the nature of souls . . . ask your mother if you doubt me."

He frowned at that. "How do you kill an immortal Dark-Hunter?"

"Well, we could cut off their heads or expose them to daylight, but since that damages their body beyond repair, it rather defeats the purpose."

"You're not funny."

Neither was he. She didn't want to release them from her service.

Most of all, she didn't want to release him.

"You have to drain their Dark-Hunter powers," she told him. "Make their immortal bodies vulnerable to attack, then stop their hearts from beating. Only then do they die in a manner that will enable them to return to life."

"Fine, I can do that."

"Actually, you can't."

"What do you mean?"

She fought the urge to smile. Here was where she had him.

"There are a few laws you need to know about souls, Acheron. One is the owner must freely give it up. Since I own their souls . . ."

Acheron cursed. "I will have to barter with you for every soul."

She nodded.

He looked less than pleased by the knowledge. But he would come around in time. Yes, he would definitely come around . . .

"What else?" he asked.

Now for her one rule that would bind him to her forever. "Only a true, pure heart can release the soul back into a body. The one who returns the soul must be the one person who loves them above all others. A person they love and trust in return."

"Why?"

"Because the soul needs something to motivate it to movement, otherwise it stays where it is. I use vengeance to motivate the soul into my possession. Only an equal and as powerful an emotion will motivate the soul back into its body. Since I can choose that emotion, I choose it to be love. The most beautiful and noble of all emotions. The only one worth returning for."

Acheron stared at the marble floor as her words whispered around him.

Love.

Trust.

Such simple words to say. Such powerful words to feel. He envied those who knew their true meaning. He'd never really known either one. Betrayal, pain, degradation, suspicion, hatred. That was his existence. That was all he'd ever been shown.

Part of him wanted to turn about and leave Artemis forever.

"Return my beloved to me. Please, I will do anything to have him home . . ." Liora's words rang in his head. He could hear her tears even now. Feel her pain.

Feel the pain of Ias as he thought of his children and wife. His worry over their welfare.

Acheron had never known that kind of unselfish love. Neither before nor after his death.

"Give me Ias's soul."

Artemis arched a brow. "Are you willing to pay the price I ask for it, and to the terms for their release?"

His heart shrank at her words. He remembered the youth he'd been long ago.

Everything has a price, Acheron. Nothing ever comes to anyone for free. His uncle had taught him well the price of survival.

Acheron had paid dearly for everything he'd ever had or wanted. Food. Shelter. Clothes. Paid with flesh and blood.

Some things never changed. Once a whore, always a whore.

"Yes," he said, his throat tight. "I agree. I'll pay."

Artemis smiled. "Don't look so unhappy, Acheron. I promise you, you'll enjoy it."

430

His stomach tightened even more. He'd heard those words before, too.

It was dusk when Acheron returned to the cave.

He wasn't alone as he walked up the small rise. He led two men and four horses.

"What is all this?" Callabrax asked.

"These are to be the shieldbearers for you and Kyros. They've come to show you both to the villas where you'll live. They will see to anything you need and I will come by later to finish our training."

A twinge of fear darkened Ias's eyes. "What of me?"

"You're coming with me."

Acheron waited until the other two had mounted their horses and left before he turned back to Ias. "Are you ready to go home?"

Ias looked surprised. "But you said—"

"I was wrong. You can go back."

"What of my oath to Artemis?"

"It's been taken care of."

Ias embraced him like a brother.

Acheron cringed at the contact, especially since it aggravated the deep welts on his back where Artemis had beaten him in exchange for Ias's soul—at least that was the lie she told herself. But he knew the truth. She beat him to punish him for the fact that she loved him.

And those marks were nothing compared to the even deeper welts that resided in his soul.

He'd always hated anyone to touch him.

Gently, he pushed Ias away. "Come, let us see you home."

Acheron flashed them back to Ias's small farm where his wife had just sent their two children to bed.

Her beautiful face paled as she saw them by her hearth.

"Ias?" She blinked. "They told me this morning that you were dead."

Ias shook his head, his eyes bright. "Nay, my love. I'm here. I've come home to you."

Acheron took a deep breath as Ias rushed to her and hugged her close. It went a long way in ebbing the pain of his back.

"There's still a couple of things, Ias," Acheron said quietly.

Ias pulled back with a frown.

"Your wife will have to release your soul back into your body."

Liora scowled. "What?"

Ias kissed her hand. "I swore myself to serve Artemis, but she's going to let me go so that I can come back to you."

She looked baffled by his words.

Ias looked at Acheron. "What must we do?"

Acheron hesitated, but there was no way to avoid telling him what had to be done. "You'll have to die again."

He paled a bit. "Are you sure?"

Acheron nodded, then handed his dagger to Liora. "You'll have to stab him through his heart."

She looked horrified and appalled by his suggestion. "What?"

"It's the only way."

"It's murder. I'll be hanged."

"No, I swear it."

"Do it, Liora," Ias urged. "I want to be with you again."

Her face skeptical, she took the dagger in her hand and tried to press it into his chest.

It didn't work. All the blade did was prick the skin.

Acheron grimaced as he remembered what Artemis had said about Dark-Hunter powers. An average human wouldn't be able to hurt a Dark-Hunter with a dagger.

But he could.

Taking the dagger from Liora, he drove it straight through Ias's heart. Ias stumbled back, panting.

"Don't panic," Acheron said, laying him down on the floor before his hearth. "I've got you."

Acheron reached up and pulled Liora down by his side. He took the stone medallion that contained Ias's soul from his satchel. "You have to take this into your hand when he dies and release his soul back into his body."

She gulped. "How?"

"Press the stone over his bow and arrow brand mark."

Acheron waited until the moment right before Ias died. He handed the medallion to Liora.

She screamed as soon as it touched her hand, then dropped it to the floor. "It's on fire!" she shrieked.

Ias gasped as he struggled to live.

"Pick it up," Acheron ordered Liora.

She blew cool air across her palm as she shook her head no.

Acheron was aghast at her actions. "What is wrong with you, woman? He's going to die if you don't save him. Pick up his soul."

"No." There was a determined light in her eyes that he didn't understand.

"No? How can you not? I heard you praying for him to return to you. You said you would give anything for your beloved to return."

She dropped her hand and eyed him coldly. "Ias is not my beloved. Lycantes is. It was he whom I prayed for and he is dead now. I was told the ghost of Ias murdered him because he killed Ias in battle so that the two of us could be together to raise our children."

Acheron was dumbstruck by her words. How could he not have seen that? He was a god. Why would that have been hidden from him?

He looked at Ias and saw the pain in his eyes before they turned blank and Ias died.

His heart hammering, Acheron picked up the medallion and tried to release the soul himself.

It didn't work.

Furious, he froze Liora into place before he killed her for her actions.

"Artemis!" he shouted at the ceiling.

The goddess flashed into the hut.

"Save him."

"I can't change the rules, Acheron. I told you the conditions and you agreed to them."

He motioned to the woman who was now a human statue. "Why didn't you tell me she didn't love him?"

"I had no way of knowing that any more than you did."
Her eyes turned dull. "Even gods can make mistakes."

"Then why didn't you at least tell me the medallion
would burn her?"

"That I didn't know. It doesn't burn me and it didn't
burn you. I've never had a human hold one before."

Acheron's head buzzed with guilt and grief. With hatred
for both himself and her. "What happens to him now?"

"He's a Shade. Without a body or soul, his essence is
trapped in Katoteros."

Acheron roared with the pain of what she was telling
him. He had just killed a man and sentenced him to a fate
far worse than death.

And for what?

For love?

For mercy?

Gods, he was such a fool.

Better than anyone, he should have known to ask the
right questions. He should have known better than to trust
in the love of another person.

Damn it, when would he learn?

Artemis reached down to him and lifted his chin with her
hand until he looked up at her. "Tell me, Acheron, is there
anyone you will ever trust enough to release your soul?"

He shook his head. "You know better. You've tutored me
too well on how vicious women are. On how much love
ruins and destroys. Thank you for the lesson, Artemis. It
was just what I needed. And I assure you, it's one I'll never
forget."

Part II
ACHERON
Present Day

You'll never see the moments coming that will forever mutilate your life—at least not until *after* they've mowed you down.

—SAVITAR

CHAPTER ONE

October 21, 2008
The Parthenon
Nashville, Tennessee
6:30 p.m., Tuesday

Acheron teleported himself into the main room where the statue of Athena stood, covered in gold. Because of the lecture that was going to start in a few minutes in another part of the Parthenon, the statue area had been closed off.

He should probably obey the rules, but why? It was one of the few perks he had from being a god.

Casts of the original Elgin marbles stood at stations that lined the walls on both sides. Even though the interior of the Parthenon wasn't exactly the way it'd been in ancient Greece, he'd always loved to come here. Something about it comforted him. And any time he was in Nashville, he made sure to stop in and visit.

He moved to the center of the room so that he could look up at the artist's rendition of the goddess Athena. It looked nothing like her. Raven-haired and pale, Athena was as frail in appearance as she was striking. But those looks were definitely deceiving. As a war goddess, Athena could pack a punch as hefty as any man.

"Acheron . . ." the statue said, coming to life before him. "Tell me what it is you seek."

He rolled his eyes. "A night away from you, Artemis. It's not like you don't know that."

She came out of the statue to stand in front of him at her natural height. "Oh, you're no fun."

"Yeah, right. Sorry. The statue thing lost its humor eleven thousand years ago. It hasn't become any more appealing over time."

Crossing her arms over her chest, she pouted. "You just blow all the fun out of everything."

Ash let out a slow, impatient breath. "Suck, Artemis. The phrase is 'suck all the fun.'"

"Blowing, sucking. Same difference."

He scoffed as he walked past her to look at the casts against the wall. "No, it isn't. Take it from someone with intimate knowledge of the two."

She screwed her face up at him. "I hate it when you're crude."

Which was exactly why he did it. Unfortunately, all the crudity in the world wasn't enough to drive her away from him. "Why are you here?" he asked over his shoulder.

"Why are *you* here?" She dogged his every step.

Again, he moved away from his least favorite stalker. "There's some archaeologist who thinks she's found Atlantis. I was curious so here I am."

Her eyes lit up. "Oh this I have to see. I love it when you go for the vernacular."

"Jugular," he corrected between clenched teeth. Too bad he didn't have the same enthusiasm. He hated to take anyone's credibility from them, or worse, publicly embarrass them. But the last thing he needed was for the world to find Atlantis and then expose what he'd been there. For the first time in his existence he had people who looked at him with respect and who allowed him dignity.

If they ever knew . . .

He'd rather die again. No, better a sting to the professor's ego than to his. While he had moments of altruism, in this he didn't. No one would ever expose him again.

Artemis blinked in happy expectation. "Where is this lecture going to be?"

"Room down the hall."

She vanished.

Acheron shook his head. He took a few minutes to walk around the exhibit and smile at the modern world's interpretation of the past. How could humanity be so strangely astute and at the same time dense? Their perceptions swung from being unerringly accurate to downright ridiculous.

Then again, didn't all creatures suffer from that same dilemma?

"Dr. Kafieri?"

Soteria looked up at the docent who was watching her with a perplexed expression. *Oh, please don't tell me I was talking out loud to myself.* By the woman's face she knew the answer and hated having been caught . . . again. "Yes?"

"You've got a good crowd gathering. I just wanted to know if you needed some water for your presentation?"

Her gut knotted at those words. Good crowd. Yeesh. She hated crowds and public speaking. If not for the fact they needed funding for new equipment in Greece, she'd have never agreed to this. "Yes, please, but make sure it has a screw cap. I'm always spilling drinks when they don't."

The woman turned and left. Tory looked down at the notes she was reviewing, but the woman's words hung in her mind.

Good crowd. What an oxymoron for a woman who hated crowds. Her throat tight, she went to spy on the room.

Yeah, it was definitely a crowd. At least sixty people were there. She felt sick.

As she started to withdraw into the shadows, the door opened and in walked a man who took her breath away.

Unbelievably tall, he strode into the room as if he owned it. No, he didn't stride, he loped in like a seductive predator. Every woman in the room turned to stare at him. You couldn't help it. It was like he was a magnet for the eyes.

His long black hair held a streak of bright red in the front and framed a face so incredibly handsome that he'd be pretty if he didn't have such a rugged aura. It also made her want to know exactly what his eyes looked like, but since he wore a pair of opaque black Oakley sunglasses, she couldn't tell. Dressed in a long black distressed coat, he wore a dark gray hoodie underneath that was opened to show a Misfits T-shirt. His black pants were tucked into a pair of dark cherry red Doc Martens boots with skull and crossbone buckles going up each side.

Ignoring the women who ogled him, he shrugged a black leather backpack off his broad shoulder and set it on the floor by an aisle seat before he sat down. The leather was as worn as his coat and the backpack was marred with a white anarchy symbol and one of a sun pierced by three lightning bolts.

She didn't know what it was about those long legs stretching out in front of him that made her heartbeat speed up, but it did. He looked so masculine sitting there like that. With his large hands covered by black fingerless gloves, he pushed the sleeves of his coat up on his forearms, then leaned back in the chair, completely at ease. She caught a glimpse of a red and black dragon tattoo on his left arm. He also had a small silver stud pierced through his right nostril, as well as a tiny silver hoop in his left ear.

He took a deep breath and hung one arm over the back of the chair. Dang, the man moved like water. Slow, graceful and yet he gave the impression that at any minute he could explode into action to take down anyone who threatened him.

Yeah . . .

"Dr. Kafieri?"

It wasn't until the third time her name was repeated that she realized the docent had returned. "I'm sorry. I was having a bit of stage fright." And a long minute of lust-filled fantasies about wrapping herself around Mr. Goth.

"Oh you'll be fine." The woman handed her the water.

Tory wasn't so sure. Crowds terrified her and unlike the Goth man outside, she hated to stand out. She would try picturing him in his underwear, but that was even more disturbing since all it did was make her hot and even more nervous . . .

He had to be the only man alive who could pull off intimidating in his tighty-whities.

God, what if all that massive hotness was commando?

Forcing herself to stop those thoughts, she checked her watch and saw that it was almost time to begin.

Tory gulped.

She glanced back at the crowd to see a tall, extremely voluptuous red-headed woman approach the Goth man. The woman was as beautiful as the man was gorgeous, but she didn't look like the type who would normally associate with his. Where he was dressed in black, FU clothes, she wore an all-white suit, right down to the dainty Jimmy Choo shoes. Immaculately coifed, the woman reminded her of a runway model. And when she sat down by the Goth man, he actually grimaced at her even though she was smiling and offering him some of the drink she'd brought with her.

The woman spoke to him and he turned his head to respond with a very harsh, "Fuck off."

She looked completely stricken by his coldness. Tory clenched her teeth. It was obvious they knew each other and while the woman was enamored of the man, he couldn't care less about her.

Typical jerk. Tory hated to judge people, but she'd seen his type over and over again in the classes she'd taught and had made the mistake of thinking herself in love with someone just like him once upon a time. Users who took advantage of the women who loved them. No doubt the redhead had bought every piece of the expensive clothes he so proudly wore.

But their relationship was none of her business. She just hoped the woman came to her senses soon and dumped the asshole.

"I'll go introduce you."

Tory jumped at the sound of Dr. Allen's voice as he moved past her. Just over fifty, he was fit and trim with gray hair and a small moustache. He'd been the professor who invited her to speak about Atlantis as part of the Parthenon's classic civilization series. Now if she could only use this as a way to help finance her next excavation, she'd kill two birds with one presentation.

Just don't let me fall down and stutter . . .

She crossed herself three times, spit and quickly prayed.

"I *know many* of you are familiar with the Kafieri name and the dubiousness of Soteria's father's and uncle's research and their claims. But in all fairness, Dr. Kafieri has taken her scholarship extremely seriously and I have to say that her findings have impressed me enough that I wanted to bring her here. Not to mention, being one of the few people who received a doctorate by age twenty shows exactly her level of commitment. I've yet to meet anyone who can flaw her theories or her dedication to the field of ancient study. Now if you'll all help welcome Dr. Kafieri."

Ash withheld his applause as he waited to see the professor he was about to roast.

"Shoot!"

The embarrassed word wouldn't be audible to anyone other than Artemis and him, but the stress in her voice evoked a wave of pity in him. He arched a brow as he heard papers being pushed together as if the presenter had dropped them.

An instant later, she popped out of the door behind the podium. Very tall and slender to the point of waifishness, she was pretty with plain brown hair she'd pulled back into a severe bun. A pair of small round bronze-rimmed glasses covered her deep, intriguing brown eyes. The beige box-cut suit did little to complement her body and it was obvious she wasn't comfortable wearing it. In fact, she looked really itchy.

She set her papers down on the podium and cleared her throat before she offered all of them a sheepishly charming grin he was sure had gotten her out of much trouble growing up. "I know we're not supposed to open a speech with an apology, but I dropped my pages on the way out here so if you can bear with me for a moment as I realign them I'd appreciate it."

Ash hid his smile.

Dr. Allen looked perturbed, but graciously nodded. "Take your time."

And she did.

People around him were getting agitated by her delay as she tried to put the speech together again.

Dr. Allen leaned forward. "Aren't they numbered?"

Her face turned bright red. "No. I forgot to do that."

Several people in the audience laughed while a couple more cursed.

"Sorry," she said, looking up hastily as she patted the pages together. "Really. I'm very sorry. Let me just go ahead and get started."

With one last wistful look at her abandoned speech, she clicked a photo onto the overhead projector that showed an image of the Parthenon in Greece. "Many of you know that it was my father's and uncle's lifelong obsession to find Atlantis—they both gave up their lives to that quest, as did my mother. And like them, I've made it my mission in life to solve this mystery. Since I was in diapers, my family and I've been excavating in Greece, trying to find Atlantis's true location. In 1995, my cousin Dr. Megeara Kafieri found what I believe to be the correct site and though she abandoned her quest, I never did. This past summer I was finally able to find definitive proof that Atlantis is real and that Megeara's research finally uncovered it."

Ash rolled his eyes at the claim so many had made. If he had a nickel, he'd be even richer than he already was.

Soteria pressed the button and switched the photo to one that made him sit up straight in his chair as he recognized it. It was the broken bust of his mother, Apollymi. And there was only one place the good doctor could have found it.

Atlantis.

She pushed her glasses up on her nose with her knuckle. "This is one of many artifacts my team and I have brought

443

up from the bottom of the Aegean." She used a red laser pointer to show the Atlantean writing on the bottom that spelled his mother's name. "I've been looking for someone who can translate what appears to be a form of early Greek writing. Yet no one has been able to decipher the words or even all the letters. It's as if this alphabet has characters that are missing from the traditional Greek."

Artemis hit him on the arm. "Looks like you're broken, Acheron."

"Busted," he corrected under his breath.

"Whatever," Artemis huffed.

Soteria looked out at the audience and then centered her attention on Dr. Allen. "Because no one can read this or even identify all the ancient letters, I'm convinced it's Atlantean. After all, if Atlantis was in the Aegean Sea, as my family and I believe, it's possible their language had a Greek basis or maybe it was their language that shaped what we know as Greek. The island's location would have firmly put it in the center of where Greek sailors traded, making it a power to be reckoned with and allowing it to shape the culture, traditions and language of ancient Greece."

She clicked to the next photo which showed a fragment of wall from the royal Atlantean palace. "This is from a building I uncovered . . ."

"Aren't you going to say something?" Artemis whispered.

Ash couldn't. He was too stunned as he stared at images he hadn't seen in over eleven thousand years. How could this one young woman have found it?

How could he have not known?

Then again, there was an easy answer. Damn his mother. She would have known they were pilfering the island's site, but rather than let him in on it, she'd be sitting back hoping one of the archaeologists released her from her captivity.

"My partner thinks it's from a temple," Soteria continued, "but given its location I'm convinced it was a government building. You can see here where there's more of the writing we saw on the bust, but again I can't decipher it."

She flipped to another photo of underwater columns. "Now here is a sister site we found that we believe to be a Greek island which traded frequently with Atlantis. I found a piece of stone with the name Didymos etched into it."

Ash couldn't breathe. She'd found it. Dear gods, the woman had found Didymos . . .

She went to another picture that literally made him break into a cold sweat. "This is a journal we uncovered in the Didymos ruins of what appeared to be a royal palace. A bound journal," she repeated excitedly. "I know what all of you are thinking—they didn't bind books at this period in time. They shouldn't even have had paper. But again, we have the same writing and the dating on it shows it to predate anything we've ever found in Greece. What we have here is the Holy Grail of Atlantis. I know it with every part of me. These two sites are integral to each other and the main site is in fact Atlantis."

"Acheron?" Artemis snapped again.

He couldn't speak as he stared at one of Ryssa's carefully made journals—at her handwriting that was as clear as if it'd been written yesterday. That page documented nothing in particular, but what scared him most was what else it might contain and, unlike the other writings, it was Greek. There weren't many people in the world who could translate it. But there were enough that it could ruin his life if they did and it held something incriminating.

"Oh this is boring," Artemis huffed. "I'm out of here." She got up and left.

The next picture was a bust with a crushed-in head. It had been one of many in Didymos that had lined the streets and it was an image of his twin brother Styxx. Ash almost came out of his seat.

It was time to stop this before she exposed him.

He forced himself to appear nonchalant even though inside he was terrified and angry. "How do you know the carbon dating on the journal isn't contaminated?"

Tory looked up at the calm masculine voice that was so deep it commanded attention. It took her a second to realize who it belonged to.

Mr. Goth Asshole.

Pushing her glasses back on the bridge of her nose in a nervous habit, she cleared her throat. "We were meticulous with it."

He gave her a cocky grin that seriously annoyed her. "How meticulous? I mean let's face it, you're an archaeologist with an agenda who's out to prove her father and uncle weren't treasure-hunting crackpots. We all know how data can be corrupted. What was the time span of the journal?"

She cringed at the question. *Lie, Tory, lie.* But it wasn't in her. "Well some of the initial tests showed a much younger date."

"How much younger?"

"First century BC"

One finely arched brow peeked up over the rim of his black sunglasses, mocking her. "First century BC?"

"Still too early for a book and yet we have a book," she said firmly, flipping back to the picture of the journal. "Hard empirical evidence that no one can refute."

He actually tsked at her. "No, Dr. Kafieri, what we have is an archaeologist with a preconceived agenda looking to wow us into financing another vacation for her in the Mediterranean. Isn't that right?"

Several people in the audience laughed.

Tory felt her anger rising at his accusations. "I'm a serious scholar! Even if you discount the journal, look at the other pieces of evidence."

He scoffed. "A woman's bust? A building? Some pottery fragments? Greece is littered with that."

"But the writing—"

"Just because *you* can't read it doesn't mean it can't be read by someone else. It could be nothing more than an undocumented provincial dialect."

"He's right," a man in the front row said.

A man behind the Goth dick laughed. "Her father was a lunatic."

"Nothing compared to her uncle. Must run in the family."

Tory gripped her pointer in her hand, wanting to hurl it at the jerk who'd started this session of ridicule. Worse, she

446

felt the prick of tears behind her eyes. She'd never cried in public, but then she'd never been so humiliated either.

Determined to succeed, she went to the next photo and cleared her throat. "This—"

"Is a small household statue of Artemis," the Goth prick said in a sarcastic tone she could swear resonated throughout the entire building. "Where did you find it? A giousouroum in Athens?"

Laughter rang out.

"Thanks for wasting my time, Dr. Allen." The older man in the front row got up and walked out.

Tory panicked at the way the crowd was turning on her. At the look of disgust on Dr. Allen's face.

"Wait! I have more." She went to a picture of an Atlantean necklace that held the symbol of a sun. "This is the first time we've seen anything so stylized."

The Goth dick held up a komboloi that had the same exact image on it. "I picked mine up in a store at Delphi three years ago."

Laughter rang out as the rest of the room got up and left.

Tory stood there in complete embarrassment and rage.

"Whatever committee was dumb enough to approve her dissertation should be ashamed of itself."

Dr. Allen shook his head before he abandoned her, too. Tory gripped the pages so tight in her hands that she was amazed the edges didn't turn into diamonds.

The Goth man got up and retrieved his backpack from the floor. He loped down the stairs, over to her. "Look, I'm really sorry."

"Fuck off," she snarled, using the phrase he'd delivered to the other woman.

She started to leave, then stopped and reversed course before she raked him with a scathing glare that was only a pittance of the hatred she felt stinging her every molecule for this man. "You punk asshole. What was this? A game for you? This is my life's work you just annihilated and for what? Shits and giggles? Or was this nothing more than a fraternity prank? Please tell me that you didn't just ruin my integrity to get some kind of drinking points. This is something I've been working for since before you were born.

How dare you make a mockery of me. I hope to God that one day someone degrades you like this so that you'll know, just once in your spoiled pompous life, what humiliation feels like."

Ash was going to respond until he realized something.

He couldn't hear her thoughts. Nor could he see her future. She was a complete blank slate for him.

"You better hope that I never see you walking down the street while I'm driving my car!" She whirled about and stalked off in anger.

He didn't even know where she was going. Everything about her was a complete blank for him. Everything.

What the hell?

Not wanting to even contemplate what that might mean, Ash teleported himself from the room to his condo in New Orleans. He didn't like not being in control or being blind to anything.

Until he figured out what was going on, retreat was the best answer.

Tory *threw her* pages into a garbage can on her way out the door. It wasn't until she'd reached her car outside that she finally let her tears fall.

The laughter still rang in her ears. Her cousin Megeara had been right, she should have let Atlantis go.

But both of her parents had given their lives in pursuit of it. Unlike Geary, she wasn't going to stop until she restored honor and dignity to her family name.

Well you certainly did a good job of it tonight.

She snatched the rental car door open and threw her purse inside. "You freaking, flippin', moronic frat boy!" she shouted, wishing she'd pulled that stud out of his nose and made him eat it.

Disgusted, she pulled her phone out and started the car. She called her best friend, Pam Gardner, as she left the parking lot for Centennial Park and headed for her hotel room.

"How'd it go?"

Tory wiped at the tears as she stopped at a light. "Awful! I've never been more embarrassed in my life."

"You didn't drop your pages again?"

She cringed at how well her girlfriend knew her—the two of them had been best friends since they'd met in her aunt's deli up in New York when they'd both been small kids. "Yes, but that's nothing compared to this."

"What?"

Tory pulled out into traffic as she snarled. "There was this . . . this . . . I can't even think of a word strong enough to convey what he was, there, and he made them all laugh at me!"

"Oh no, Tory." She could hear the tears in Pam's voice for her. "Are you serious?"

"Do I sound like I'm kidding?"

"No, you sound really pissed."

And she was. God, how she wished she could find him walking back to his dorm room so that she could mow him down. "I can't believe this night. I was supposed to be applauded and instead, I'm ruined. I swear to God in heaven if I ever see that man again, I will commit murder."

"Well if you need help moving the body, you know where Kim and I live."

She smiled at her friends. She could always depend on them in any crisis. Kim and Pam were living proof that while a good friend would bail you out of jail, a best friend would be in jail alongside you. "Thank you."

"Any time, sweetie. So when are you coming back?"

"I'll be back in New Orleans tomorrow." She couldn't wait to be home again where everything was familiar.

"Well look on that bright side, Tory. Whoever the dickhead was, you'll never have to worry about seeing him here."

That was true. Tomorrow she'd be home and she'd never see that asshole again.

CHAPTER TWO

Tory's dignity was still stinging two days later as she knocked on the office door of Dr. Julian Alexander. He was supposed to be the leading expert in the world on ancient Greece. She'd been told that if anyone in the world could read her journal, he was the man.

She prayed it was so.

A deep masculine voice told her to enter.

She pushed the door open to find an exceptionally handsome man in his early thirties sitting behind a beat-up wooden desk. He had short blond hair and beautiful blue eyes that seemed to gleam in the dim light. His office was littered with ancient Greek artifacts, including a Bronze Age sword hanging on the wall behind him. Bookshelves lined the walls and were filled past brimming with additional artifacts and textbooks.

Man, she could easily call this place home and was grateful to be with a kindred spirit. Even though she didn't know him, she liked him already.

"Dr. Alexander?"

Looking up, he frowned at her as he closed his leather-bound agenda. "You're not one of my students. Are you considering taking one of my classes?"

She hated how young she looked at times, not that she was any older than an average grad student, but still . . . she had a hard enough time with her credibility that she didn't need that strike, too. "No. I'm Dr. Kafieri. We spoke over the phone."

He stood up immediately and offered her his hand. "Sorry for the confusion," he said graciously as she shook it. "I'm really glad to finally meet you. I've heard a lot of . . ."

"Mixed things I'm sure."

He laughed good-naturedly. "Well, you know how our circles go."

"Not broad enough most days."

He laughed again. "True. Do you have the book with you?"

She set her briefcase down on the small chair in front of his desk and opened it. She'd very carefully wrapped the book in acid free paper to protect its delicate condition. "It's extremely brittle."

"I'll be careful."

She watched as he unwrapped it and frowned. "Is something wrong?"

"No," he said with a note of awed reverence in his voice, "it's just amazing. I've never seen a bound book this old."

By his face she'd say it also brought back some kind of painful memories for him. "Can you read it?"

He opened the cover carefully before he studied the brittle pages. "It looks Greek."

"Yes, but can you read it?" she repeated, hoping that he could at least recognize some part of it.

He looked up and sighed. "Honestly? I can make out some of the words from basic root meanings, but this particular dialect is something I've never seen before. It definitely predates my area of expertise . . . probably by several hundred years or more."

She wanted to curse in frustration. She was so tired of hearing that. "Do you know of anyone who might be able to translate it?"

451

"Yeah, actually, I do."

It took a full minute for that unexpected answer to seep in. Dare she even hope so? "Are you serious?"

He nodded. "He's the historian I always go to whenever I need information. There's no one in the universe who knows more about ancient civilizations than he does. In fact, he knows so much about them you'd think he lived through them."

This was even better than she'd hoped for.

"Where does he teach?"

Julian closed the book and wrapped it back up. "Ironically, he doesn't. But you're in luck, he's here in town for a few weeks helping with Project Home Again and Habitat for Humanity."

Her heart was racing with the prospect of having someone corroborate that the book was as old as Atlantis—to have them verify it was Atlantean in nature . . .

It would be a dream come true if he could actually read some of it.

"Is there any chance we could meet with him?" she asked breathlessly.

"Hold on a second and let me see." He pulled a cell phone out of his pocket and dialed it.

Tory chewed her thumbnail and silently prayed to talk to the one man who held the key to her book. She'd give anything to meet him . . .

Julian smiled at her. "Hi Acheron, it's Julian Alexander. How you doing?"

She could faintly hear the voice at the other end of the phone.

Julian laughed at something the man said. "Leave it to you . . . look the reason I'm calling is I have a colleague here in my office who has something we need you to take a look at—I personally have never seen anything like it, and I think from a historic point of view you'd be very interested in it, too. Any chance we can stop by?" He shook his head. "Yeah, it's some really old shit—nice phraseology, by the way." He paused as he listened. "Yeah, okay."

Julian looked at her. "Can you leave right now to see him?"

"Absolutely." She'd crawl over broken glass to meet the man!

He returned to his call. "She can do it. We'll see you in a few." He hung up and smiled. "He's a little busy at present, but he's more than happy to look at it."

"Oh bless you both!"

Julian returned the book to her. "Would you like to follow me over?"

"Sure. Where are we going?"

He picked his jacket up off the back of his chair and shrugged it on. "Acheron's doing volunteer work for Habitat for Humanity. He's over on Esplanade on a rooftop."

Tory frowned at the image in her mind of a stodgy classics professor on top of a roof. "So his name is Acheron . . . ?"

"Parthenopaeus."

She laughed. "Good grief, I never thought I'd meet someone more Greek than me." With a name like that, he had to be old. No modern parent would be so cruel.

With a strange twinkle in his eye, Julian grinned. "Yeah, he's amazing when it comes to historical facts. Like I said he knows ancient Greece better than anyone I've ever known or heard of." He led her out of his office.

"How long has he been studying it?" she asked as he locked his office door.

"Since the moment he was born."

She cradled her briefcase to her chest. "Poor thing, he sounds like me. I swear my father was reading the *Iliad* to me the instant I was conceived."

Laughing, Julian led her out to the parking lot. She got into her white Mustang GT and followed his black Range Rover over to Esplanade. There were still a lot of homes in New Orleans that hadn't been repaired from Katrina. It did her heart good to know that Julian's friend would be kind enough to help out with the rebuilding. It said a lot for the man, especially given how old he must be.

She parked on the street behind Julian and grabbed her briefcase. As they neared the house that was teeming with volunteers, she tried to pick out who this incredible historian was that the leading expert in the world would consult.

There was a handsome older man handing a piece of lumber off to a younger man. He looked like he might be a historian.

Julian headed toward him. "Hey, Karl, could you tell Ash that I'm here to see him?"

"Sure." He headed away from them and rounded a corner, out of sight.

Julian held his hand out for the book. Tory pulled it out and gave it over to him.

She scanned the area and looked up at the roof where five people were sitting. Two were women and three were young men. But it was the one off by himself who captured her attention. Wearing a black tank top, he had the best set of arms she'd ever seen. Tanned and gorgeous, every muscle was honed to perfection . . . and it wasn't just his arms. The sweat from his hammering made the shirt cling to a muscled back that had been custom made for licking.

He wore a black ball cap turned backwards and even from where she stood she could see the black earbuds that led to an iPod in the back pocket of his ragged jeans. His left foot kept time to the beat while he worked.

She sucked her breath in sharply at the sight he made. Mama, if that man had a face even remotely cute, he'd be a god among men.

Her phone started ringing. Distracted, Tory glanced at it to see her friend Kim calling. She shut it off and then looked back at the roof.

Dang, Mr. Hottie was gone. It was just as well . . . she didn't have time for men anyway and a guy like that would never look at a woman like her. She glanced around again for the man they'd come to find.

She saw the one who'd gone for Acheron. He headed off to the other side of the house without saying a word. A couple of people came from around the corner and then she saw the guy from the roof . . .

Holy gods of Olympus. He was unbelievably tall, lean and ripped. His shirt clung to that perfect body and didn't quite reach the waistband of his pants. Instead, it exposed a mouth-watering glimpse of a hard tanned washboard stomach. His jeans rode low on his narrow hips, dipping down

454

so much that it made her wonder if he had on underwear. He wore a pair of dark sunglasses and was chewing gum in the sexiest manner she'd ever seen. Sweaty and gorgeous, he reached up to pull the ball cap off . . . and set free a mane of coal black hair with a red stripe in the front.

No . . . surely this wasn't . . .

Of course it was. She'd know that meticulous, sexual lope anywhere.

He slowly pulled the earbuds out as he approached them. "Hey Julian."

And when he looked at her, she wanted to scream.

"You fucking asshole!" she snarled, shocked at the fact that such language actually left her lips in front of Dr. Alexander. She'd very seldom in her life used such, but then she'd never hated anyone as much as she hated this guy.

She looked at Julian. "You go to him for advice? He's only what? Five years old? I swear I own older sweaters." She whirled around to go back to her car.

"Didn't you want me to look at something?" the man taunted with a hint of laughter in his voice.

Those words put her into a realm of pissed off the likes of which she'd never known before. Raw, unmitigated fury blinded her and before she knew what she was doing, she'd jerked a hammer off the sawhorse beside her and thrown it at his head.

Unfortunately, he ducked it . . . then laughed. Laughed!

Unable to stand his mockery, she rushed to her car, hoping she didn't give into the urge she had to run them both down.

Julian turned a wide-eyed stare at Ash. "Damn, Atlantean, what did you do?"

"I apparently made a new friend."

Laughing nervously, Julian shook his head. "I made a friend like that once. The bastard almost gutted me."

"Yeah." Ash felt a wave of guilt that he'd hurt her so badly. But it was nothing compared to what would be done to him if she'd succeeded in her quest. "Guess I'll get back to my roof."

Julian inclined his head to the street. "I have to go and find her so I can return this."

Ash went cold as he saw the small square package in Julian's hand. "Return what?"

"It's a journal she found on some dig in Greece."

"Can I see it?"

"Sure." Julian pulled it out and handed it to him.

Ash's hand shook as he made himself betray no emotions. But inside . . . inside he was raw with grief. He opened the cover and saw the handwriting he knew so well.

Today is the eighteenth anniversary of my birth. Father woke me up with a new necklace and Mother and I spent the morning in our garden. Father was always kind enough to let her visit for the anniversary of my birth.

Ash clenched his teeth as he pictured the garden that Ryssa had kept so meticulously groomed. He'd never known that she'd shared it with her mother.

"You can read it, can't you?"

Ash nodded. "It's an old dialect. Provincial."

"Well, I'd say it would make her happy to know that, but after her reaction to you, I'm not so sure."

Neither was he. Then again, he deserved her anger. "Mind if I hang on to this?"

Julian hedged. "It's not really mine. However, I trust you to do what's right with it."

"Believe me, I will."

Julian inclined his head to him, then turned to leave.

Ash stood there, holding his sister's journal. He couldn't believe it'd survived so well. It'd been buried under the sea since the day he'd sunk Didymos. But unlike his mother, he'd made sure that all the living people were gone before he'd obliterated it.

Now he had a piece of his past returned to him like a haunting ghost. The question was what was he going to do with it?

CHAPTER THREE

Three days later as she walked across campus, toward her office, Tory was mad enough to spit out iron nails. How dare Dr. Alexander give her journal to that . . . that . . .

One day she was going to think of a word that would adequately describe Acheron's particular breed of low, gutter, nasty, vile . . . ness.

"Dr. Kafieri?"

She turned to see Kyle Peltier, one of her students, running up to her. He was a typical junior, with blond hair and a sweet face. He'd just transferred from another school this semester and was one of her better students. "Yes?"

"A friend of mine asked me to give you this." He held out a box wrapped in kraft paper.

She stared at the unexpected gift. "I don't understand."

"Me either, but when he asks for a favor, you do the favor without asking why."

Tory frowned at his cryptic words as she took the box. Kyle immediately rushed off before she could ask him anything more. "Well that was interesting." The box was heavy. She shook it, but couldn't figure out what it might contain.

Her current luck, a bomb.

Pushing the thought aside, she made her way to her small office, grabbed a cup of coffee and then set about opening it which was easier said than done. It was like the giver had hermetically sealed it shut with tape. "I hate when people do this!"

Finally, after no less than five minutes, she was able to detach the lid from the box and pull it free. Opening it up, she froze. It contained a hammer, a handful of olive leaves, a note attached to a single red rose, and a leather pouch the same size as a small book. Her heart pounding, she picked up the brown leather pouch and opened it to find her journal.

A smile curled her lips. So the little monster had done the right thing. Now she was able to laugh about the hammer and the olive "branches" he'd put inside. She picked up his note and opened it to find a beautiful masculine script.

> I'm really not the asshole you think I am. The journal's from a young woman in an isolated part of Greece and documents her life for about eighteen months. It's pretty much boring reading, but if you want more details, call me. 555-602-1938.
>
> Eirini,
Ash

Eirini—Greek for peace. Tory shook her head. Not the asshole she thought, yeah right. But it was kind of a sweet gesture and he had returned her journal.

With a rose.

Holding it up, she inhaled the sweet scent and debated whether or not she ever wanted to lay eyes on the troll again.

With his arms crossed over his chest, Urian frowned at Ash while Ash sat on his throne in Katoteros and played the guitar. Almost as tall as Ash, Urian had long white blond hair that he wore pulled back into a ponytail. A former Daimon, Urian had been saved by Ash after Urian's father viciously cut his throat. And like his father, Urian had a most acerbic personality that he was more than proud of.

Not willing to deal with Urian's ill mood swings or explain himself, Ash ignored the man while he continued to sing Matchbox 20's "Push" under his breath.

Simi lay on her stomach, watching QVC as she devoured a tub of barbecue-flavored popcorn. She was dressed in black tights and a short plaid skirt with a pink and black peasant top and corset.

Urian moved to where Alexion stood off to the side, also staring at Ash as if Ash were a science experiment that had gone seriously wrong. For thousands of years, Alexion had been the only person Ash allowed in his home besides Simi. Of course that was out of profound guilt since Alexion had been Ias—one of the first Dark-Hunters Artemis created. Ash had managed to bring him back to a quasi-ghost existence by using his blood to keep Ias from being a Shade.

Too bad Savitar hadn't explained those powers to Ash sooner. It would have saved both him and Ias a lot of grief. But at least Ias wasn't in constant pain and misery.

"What's the deal with the bossman?" Urian asked him.

Alexion shrugged. "I don't know. He came in last night with a book, went to his room to read, I suppose, and then he came out here this morning and has been playing . . . *those* songs ever since."

Those songs were ballads, which Acheron never played. Godsmack, Sex Pistols, TSOL, Judas Priest, but not . . .

"Is that . . ." Urian physically cringed before he spat out the name, "Julio Iglesias?"

"Enrique."

Urian grimaced in horror. "I didn't even know he knew any mellow shit. Dear gods . . . is he ill?"

"I don't know. In nine thousand years, I've never seen him like this before."

Urian shuddered. "I'm beginning to get scared. This has to be a sign of the Apocalypse. If he breaks out into Air Supply, I say we sneak up on him, drag him outside and beat the holy shit out of him."

"I'll let you and the demons do that. I personally like my semi-living state too much to jeopardize it."

459

Ash looked up and pierced them both with a malevolent glare. "Don't you two girls have something better to do like pick out toe lint?"

Urian grinned. "Not really."

Ash growled a low warning, but before he could really threaten them, his phone rang. Leaning his head back, he sighed in frustration. Damn phone was always going off. This time it better not be Artemis screwing with him or he'd hunt her down and—

His thoughts scattered as he saw a New Orleans area code. He didn't recognize the number and it didn't register a name. How weird. Flipping it open, he answered.

"Is this Ash?"

"Soteria?"

Tory's throat went dry at the way he said her name. Because she was Greek, she'd never really thought Greek was a pretty language, but when he spoke it . . .

She could barely form a coherent thought. "Um, Tory. I go by Tory."

"Oh, I didn't know. Can I do something for you?"

Yeah baby, get naked and . . .

She shook her head. She never had thoughts like that and she didn't know why she had them now when she had business to discuss with someone she absolutely hated. "Uh, yeah, I was wondering about the journal. Is there any chance you could meet me later and tell me more about it?"

"What time?"

Grateful he wasn't hanging up on her after she'd tossed a hammer at him, she smiled. "I'll be home in about an hour."

"I'll be there." He hung up.

It wasn't until Tory closed the phone that she realized something. She hadn't told him where she lived. "Oh my God, he's a stalker."

Her phone rang.

She answered it to find Ash there with that deep, mesmerizing voice. "I just realized I don't have your address."

Laughing, she shook her head at her overactive imagination. "I'm not hard to find. I'm at 982 St. Anne down in the Quarter."

"I shall see you later then."

The archaic way he said that actually sent a shiver down her spine. Hanging up, she couldn't help but smile and she didn't even know why.

He's a jerk. A complete and utter ass.

Who'd sent her a rose and who appeared to know how to read a language no one else could. A language she desperately needed to understand. This was business. It wasn't a date. She could stand his pushy arrogance long enough to get what she needed and then she was going to toss him out on his butt.

A*sh hesitated as* he flashed himself a few houses down from Tory's. Like the woman who owned it, it blended in with the rest of the houses on the street. Really nothing about it stood out, yet it was plainly beautiful. Painted a very pale pink and trimmed in antique white, it was a typical New Orleans turn-of-the-century shotgun rowhouse. The shutters were drawn tightly closed and as he tried to see inside to find her, he saw nothing.

Nothing.

You should probably run.

But why? All it meant was that they'd be friends of some sort. This wasn't the first time this had happened to him.

Bullshit. Even when you were destined to be friends with someone you caught glimpses of them.

With her there was nothing . . .

That actually scared him and yet he found himself walking up to the door and knocking on it.

He heard what sounded like something getting knocked over inside followed by a low whispered, "Shoot!" He bit back a smile at her obvious distress. There was more scrambling about before she opened the door.

Her brown hair was down today. Thick, shiny and wavy, that hair beckoned to be touched . . . no, it beckoned a man to bury his face in it and breathe her in. How could he have ever thought it plain? No wonder she'd worn it up the other night. Not to mention, it made her look a lot younger

461

when it was down around her face. Her cheeks were flushed which made her sharp, intelligent eyes glow.

And those lips . . .

Plump and full, they were made for a night of kissing.

But the best part had to be her glasses which were ever so slightly askew. As if sensing it, she straightened them and blew a stray piece of hair out of her eyes. "Sorry. I have technical difficulties making it through a room without bumping into something. Thank God my clumsiness is only restricted to the ground. I'd probably kill myself diving if I was this bad under water."

"No problem." Ash ducked down to enter the doorway.

Tory's eyes widened as she watched him walk into her living room. While she knew her place wasn't large, his presence in it seemed to shrink it down to nothing. He literally filled the room with his commanding presence. "You are freakishly tall, aren't you?"

He arched a black brow over the rim of those sunglasses that seemed to be permanently attached to his head. "For a woman wanting my help you are ever determined to insult me. Should I make this as painless as possible and leave now before the die-painfully-you-asshole-prick stuff starts again?"

She shut the door. "I would say I'm sorry about that, but you have to admit you *were* an asshole. What would you do if someone had done that to you?"

Ash didn't answer. It depended on if it'd been before or after his godhood had been unlocked. Before he'd have taken it. Now . . . oh they'd regret it for eternity.

He scanned the small house that was littered with ancient artifacts from Greece and Rome, as well as tons of framed photos of their ruins. Then he saw the small trash can she'd stumbled into. The contents were still half on the floor. She was a walking disaster that he found oddly charming.

"Interesting place you have here."

"Yeah, I love old things."

A wave of amusement went through him as he considered his own age. "How old?"

"Oh, the older the better. You can never be old enough where I'm concerned."

Then she should worship the ground he walked on.

"Can I get you something to drink?" she asked, pushing her glasses up on her nose.

"You got a beer?"

She scowled at him. "Isn't it a little early in the day for that?"

"Wine?"

Rolling her eyes, she made a sound of supreme disgust. "I swear you are such a frat boy. Are you even old enough to drink?"

The insult amused him. "Yeah. Trust me, I'm a lot older than I look."

"I've heard that before. I'd ask for your license, but it's probably fake."

Actually, it was, but only because no one would ever believe his real birth date and if they did, they'd be trying to lock him in a cage to study his longevity.

"Don't you want something else? Tea? Coffee?"

Ash shook his head. "I'm good, really. I don't want any more insults. I'd like to experience three whole minutes in your presence before you lay into me again . . . and we really should make sure the tools are all locked up." He pulled the sleeve of his jacket back to look at his watch. "Let me start timing . . ."

She opened her mouth to respond, but he held his hand up. "Wait for it. We got two minutes and fifty-five seconds to go."

"I'm not that bad."

"Yeah . . . you're not standing in my shoes."

She looked down at his huge feet which had to be a size fourteen or fifteen—if they even made such a thing. "And judging by the ungodly size of them, I don't think there are many people who could."

He tsked. "We almost made it to thirty seconds without an insult. I think we just set a new record."

She hated the fact he was actually charming. Worse, he was charming her. "All right, I'll behave. If you don't mind following me, the kitchen's back here."

Ash adjusted the backpack on his shoulder before he followed her through the house. As they neared the kitchen he paused at one of the pictures on the wall. It was a family photo with Tory standing front and center, but there were three people in it he knew intimately.

Geary, Arikos and Theodoros Kafieri.

No wonder he couldn't see her thoughts or future. "Is this your family?"

She glanced back. "Yes. My papou's the one next to me."

Theo. Ash smiled at his old friend. Theo had been only seven years old when he'd been blinded during a World War II attack on his village that had killed his whole family. Ash had been the one who'd brought the child to America where he could start a new life and be safe. He'd been watching over Theo ever since.

So it wasn't that Tory had anything to do with him, it was the fact she was tied to Theo and to Arik who was married to Geary. Arik had once been a Greek god of sleep. Those connections to Tory explained so much.

Ash relaxed immediately. "You've got a great looking family."

She smiled. "Typical Greek. There's a million relatives, but then with a name like Acheron, I'm sure you know all about it." She cocked her head as if she thought of something. "You know, my grandfather has a dear friend named Acheron."

"Really?"

"Yeah, they met in Greece and came to America together. But that was a long time ago." She went back to the kitchen and pulled open a drawer that held small brown packets of coffee and tea. Pulling one out, she started her Flavia coffee pot, then pointed to the kitchen table where she had a bunch of books, maps and notes littered.

Ash made his way over to it and was impressed by it. She'd been a very busy woman.

"Cop a seat," she said, pulling her mug out before she opened the door to her fridge.

Ash widened his eyes at the sight of her extremely organized refrigerator. The shelves were lined with neatly stacked clear plastic containers that had white labels with their contents carefully catalogued. "Got enough Rubbermaid there?"

"I have a little problem with Obsessive Compulsive Disorder. Ignore it." She grabbed a container from the B section. Seriously.

"That's really beyond slightly OCD. You've got a major problem, don't you?"

"Shut up, sit down and read."

With the exception of his demon Simi, no one since his rebirth as a god had ever been so dismissive with him. "Please?"

"You need something?"

He cocked a brow at her. "You to be polite to me, Ms. I Own The World—Now Do What I Say You Pathetic Pleb."

She scoffed at him. "You don't strike me as the kind of guy who takes orders anyway."

"Yes, but a simple please goes a long way. I'm the one doing you a favor here."

She set her container of baklava on the table. "Fine. Please sit down, shut up and read."

Ash lifted his hands up in surrender. Honestly he should be appalled by her treatment of him and yet he was strangely amused by her. Shrugging his backpack off, he sat down and pulled Ryssa's journal over to him. "What do you want to know?"

"You claim you can read it. Read it."

Tory sipped her coffee while she watched him and noted that his long legs barely fit beneath her table.

He turned to a random page and then started speaking in what had to be the most beautiful and fluent pronunciation of ancient Greek she'd ever heard. She could only recognize random words, but the ease with which he read and the inflections in his voice led her to believe he might actually be telling the truth about understanding the words.

"Could you try that in English?"

He didn't even pause. "It's raining today. I don't know why the sound of it bothers me so, but it always has. Before it began storming, I went to see Styxx out in the covered atrium. He was with Father as usual and the two of them were learning war tactics. Even at eleven, Styxx shows a lot of promise to be a leader and warrior of great renown. I

465

couldn't be prouder of my brother. His blond hair has grown lighter this summer since he's spent so much time outdoors. I tried to get him—"

"Stop," she interrupted. "You're really translating that, aren't you?"

He looked perplexed by her question. "Is that not what you wanted?"

Tory didn't even know how to respond to his question. Yes, it was what she'd wanted more than anything. But no one knew this language.

Except a Goth, punk alcoholic frat boy with a stud in his nose . . . and a body made for sin.

How in the world was this possible?

"Where did you learn Greek?" she asked.

"In Greece."

She couldn't accept that. "No, *ancient* Greek. Who taught this to you?"

"I grew up with it."

"You're lying. I know you're lying. No one on this planet speaks ancient Greek the way you do. I've consulted experts all over the world and not one of them could do what you just did."

He shrugged nonchalantly as if her concerns were nothing. "What do you want me to say?"

She shook her head, not really sure herself. "I want you to tell me how you know ancient Greek like that."

"My family spoke it and I learned it from the cradle. In many ways, it was my native tongue."

She would have called him a liar but for the fact that her own parents had been that way with her. Even so, she couldn't do what he'd done. It was simply amazing. "Tell me about your accent when you speak. It's not a typical Greek accent."

He answered her in flawless Greek. "I was born in a place called Kalosis. It's so small that it's not on a map. It's an island province and my accent is a cross between my mother's and old Athenian."

"When did you come to the U.S.?"

"After my twenty-first birthday."

"And yet you speak English like a native?"

466

He switched back to his mainstream American English. "I'm exceptionally good with languages. As for my native accent, it comes and goes depending on my mood and the word I'm speaking."

Such simple explanations really, and they made her suddenly feel like Torquemada during the Inquisition. "I'm sorry, Acheron. I just realized how shrewish I must sound while you're trying to help me." She let out a tired sigh. "You and I have gotten off to a really bad start, haven't we?"

He shrugged. "I've gotten off to many worse ones during my lifetime."

She appreciated his graciousness. "Yeah but not from someone you were trying to help, I'd wager."

Ash had to bite back a sarcastic laugh at that. If she only knew . . .

She smiled at him and strangely everything seemed to be forgiven. "Again, I'm sorry that I attacked you. It's just Atlantis has been my whole life. You can't imagine how important the history and my research are to me."

Probably as important as keeping it hidden was to him. "Look, I was a shithead in Nashville. I admit it and for that I apologize completely. I don't normally embarrass people like that. It's just I know for a fact that Atlantis is only a myth. You found some really interesting artifacts, but that's all they are. It's apparent to me that you're a brilliant and sincere scholar and I can appreciate the dedication. However you're wasting valuable time on a moot topic."

She narrowed her eyes at him. "How do you *know* it's a myth?"

"How do you know it's not?"

She leaned forward, so close that they were almost nose to nose. "Because the man who brought my grandfather over as a child told him stories of Atlantis and the ancient island of Didymos to entertain him and to take his mind off the severe burns he'd received from the Nazis. My papou said that the way this man described Atlantis and its marvels was as if he'd lived there. The man described the same exact buildings that I've found buried in the Aegean."

467

Ash went cold as she pricked memories he'd buried. Why had he ever told Theo those stories?

Because he'd been a terrified child and Ash had wanted to comfort him. Reassure him. Damn. How could he have known that that one act would come back to burn him so badly sixty years later?

"But the most important is this." She reached into the wooden box on the table and pulled out a coin he hadn't seen since he'd placed it in Theo's tiny hand when he'd left the boy with an adoptive family in New York with the promise that he'd be back to visit. It held the image of Ash's mother on one side and her sun symbol on the other.

Fuck.

Tory tapped the coin. "The writing on one side is something I'd never seen anywhere else until our discovery last summer. On the other side, it's Greek and though I don't know all of it, I can make out the name Apollymi. Now tell me this isn't from Atlantis."

"It's not from Atlantis," he said, his voice sounding hollow to his own ears. It had actually been from his pocket. "It could be anything. Might not even be a coin. It could be a necklace. Maybe she was someone's wife." Or *his* mother.

"I never said it was a coin. They wouldn't have had money at the time, would they?" Her gaze pierced him. "You know the truth, don't you?"

Ash made his phone ring. "Hold that thought." He pretended to answer it and got up as he tried to think of a plausible answer.

Damn her for being so quick.

Tory watched as Ash walked out of the room to take his call. He came back a few minutes later.

"I have to go."

"But you can't. I've got more questions for you."

He seemed frustrated about something. "I really don't have time to answer them."

"Can you come back?"

He shook his head at her. "I doubt it. I travel a lot for work and I won't be in town much longer." He grabbed his backpack from the floor and headed for the front.

She followed him. "I can pay you for your time."

"It's not about the money."

She pulled him to a stop. "Please, Acheron . . . please."

Ash wanted to shove her away and frighten her. The god in him didn't like to be grilled.

The man in him wanted to taste those lips that beckoned for a kiss. "I can't, Tory." *I can't.* . . . His resolve set, he gently took her hand from his arm and left.

Tory wanted to scream as she watched him descend the stairs in front of her house that led to the street. He turned right and headed toward Bourbon Street.

There had to be some way to get him to help her. He was the only one who could read that book and by all the conviction inside her, she wasn't going to take no for an answer.

At the end of the day, she was a Kafieri and no one told a Kafieri no. "You can run from me all you want, Mr. Parthenopaeus, but you won't be able to hide. You *will* give me what I want." She was going to make sure of it.

CHAPTER FOUR

Ash did his best to get Tory out of his mind, but it was impossible. There was just something about her that beckoned him.

He hated that.

But not half as much as he hated the way he'd bailed on her like a coward the day before. He kept telling himself it was for the best and yet he couldn't quite convince himself of it. There was something about being around her that was comforting which given her normal hostility toward him made no sense whatsoever.

Now he sat up on the roof of the house he was helping to build, trying to clear his head and get back to business.

Someone touched his foot. He glanced up to see Karl in front of him. Ash pulled one of the earbuds out. "Yeah?"

"Visitor."

Assuming it was one of his associates in New Orleans, Ash set down his hammer and headed for the ladder. It wasn't until he was halfway down that he saw Tory waiting for him. Her hair was pulled forward into wavy pigtails. She wore a long beige skirt and brown blazer.

But it was her large brown eyes that seared him.

Looking at them and not at what he was doing, he missed a step and went slamming down the ladder, straight to the ground where he landed in a most embarrassing lump that wasn't helped when the ladder then fell across him, drawing all eyes to his clumsy stupidity. Pain hit him hard in his back, hip and shoulder as he struggled to find some semblance of dignity.

Given the way he was sprawled, it was actually hopeless. Sighing, he moved the ladder off his legs.

Tory came running over to kneel beside him. "Are you all right?"

The answer had been yes until she placed her hand on his chest. In this position, all he could think of was pulling her across him and making use of her hand for something much more pleasurable.

"Yeah, I'm fine." Then he glanced around at the other people staring at him in concern. His face heated in embarrassment. "I'm fine, everyone," he said louder. "Just a small slip."

They went back to work while he wanted to make himself invisible. He *never* did stuff like this.

"You should be more careful," Tory said in a chiding tone. What happened to her concern for him? Obviously it'd gone the way of his last vestige of dignity. "You could have broken your neck or as big as you are landed on someone and killed them."

Okay . . . the woman was nuts.

"What are you doing here, Tory?" He rolled over and pushed himself up, then realized he'd done some real damage to his leg as it throbbed painfully in protest at being used again. It was all he could do not to grunt or limp.

Her smile dazzled him. "I've come to tempt you."

It was too late, she already had and he knew she didn't mean it the way he did. "I can't be tempted."

"Yes, you can. All people can be tempted."

But he wasn't a person. He picked the ladder up and returned it to its previous position. Then he went to pick up the nails that had spilled out of his tool belt. When he

471

started back toward the ladder, she planted herself firmly in his way.

"Tory . . ." he growled.

"Look, I'll be honest, there has never in the whole history of mankind been a more stubborn human being born than me."

"Yes, there has. Me."

When he started around her, she ran around him to the ladder and put herself on the first rung. He should be pissed as hell and yet she was so adorable standing there in her long skirt and flats with one arm wrapped around the rung over her head that it was all he could do not to smile at her. "Fine, you don't have to translate it. Just teach me how and I'll leave you alone. If it helps, I'm a really quick learner."

He ground his teeth in frustration. "I don't like arguing. I don't like conflicts. I basically like to be left alone to do my thing and that doesn't include teaching you anything. Now do you mind?"

"Please . . ." Her expression was the hottest mixture of cute pleading and raw seduction that he'd ever seen. "I'll be your baklava slave until I die."

He scowled. "My what?"

"Baklava slave. I make the best you've ever tasted and I'll keep you supplied in it until you're fat and old."

"I don't eat baklava."

"That's because you've never had mine. Unless you're allergic to nuts, you'll love it."

He tried to pry her loose from the ladder, but true to her words, she wouldn't be moved. His anger snapped. How could he be one of the most powerful beings in the universe and not be able to move a single frail women out of his way?

She made her eyes look like a sad puppy. "Please, Acheron," she said in Greek. Then she switched to English. "Three days and then you'll never have to see me again. Tell me what you want in exchange and I'll do it."

Karl laughed as he overheard them. "Why don't you ask her to be your sex slave? For that I'd teach her whatever she wants."

Her jaw dropped as if that was the most nauseating thought she'd ever had. "Ew!"

That one single sound caught him off guard. "Ew?" Ash repeated. "You can't be serious?"

"Yeah, ew! I don't even know you really and here the two of you think I'm just going to jump in bed with you. No thanks! God, you're such an arrogant man pig."

Arrogant man pig?

She screwed her face up in distaste and left the ladder. "Fine, I'll research without you." She shivered. "Sleep with him for a translation, disgusting," she said under her breath as she walked off.

Ash hung his arm on the ladder while watching her head for her car. He was completely stunned.

She didn't want to sleep with him . . .

She thought sleeping with him was disgusting.

Everybody over puberty wanted in his bed. *Everybody.*

Except Tory. A burst of hope went through him as he realized that she might be one of the exceptionally rare people who was immune to his Aunt Epithymia's curse. Even women who didn't find men attractive looked at him.

There had only been a handful of them throughout history and up until now they'd always been men who were immune . . . or those who were blind.

To find a human female who didn't want him . . .

He could be normal around her. Let his guard down and not have to be worried that she was going to start grabbing at his crotch. The novelty of that alone made him crave being around her.

Before he could stop himself, he went to her car and stopped her. "I'll teach you."

She turned angrily and pressed her index finger into his chest. "I'm not sleeping with you, buddy."

He smiled at her. "I'm not asking you to. I swear it. I would never ask that of you."

Her jaw fell open before she raked him with an offended snarl. "What? You think sleeping with me would be repugnant? Oh you're such a jerk!"

Ash held his hands up in frustration. "Why can't I ever

win with you? If I want to sleep with you I'm a pig and if I don't I'm a jerk. What do you want from me?"

She stood in the open door of her car and stared up at him with those soulful eyes that seared him all the way to his gut. "I want you to translate the journal and to keep your hands to yourself."

"And yet still be attracted to you?"

She let out an evil laugh. "Exactly. Now you're getting the hang of it." She clapped him on the arm. "I'll see you tonight at seven."

He couldn't wait, he thought sarcastically. Maybe he ought to have Simi come with him. Every time he was around Tory, he felt the deep need for protection. At the very least he should make sure he wore a cup tonight so she couldn't cold-cock him when he wasn't looking.

What kind of masochistic bastard was he that he kept getting involved with women who loathed him?

You should forget about teaching her anything.

Yeah, but she held a part of his past and if he didn't get her away from Atlantis and Didymos, there was going to be even bigger problems. May the primal source take mercy on him if she happened on another of Ryssa's journals. He had what he thought were the most damning of them. But he didn't know what else his sister had written about. Tory and her obssesive quest had to be dealt with.

The last thing he needed was for the Dark-Hunters to find out that his mother was the one who'd created the Daimons they spent eternity fighting against and that they were being led by a tsoulos who was still selling himself to protect them. It would be disastrous for him.

No, he had to help her enough to get her sidetracked off this quest. Maybe he should find something Lemurian and get her on that topic. After all, its past had nothing to do with his.

You could just kill her.

That would be Savitar's answer. But Ash couldn't do that either. Theo had buried most of his family already and if he knew anything about his old friend it was how much Theo loved his family.

No, he'd have to find another way to move the inert mass that was Tory's obstinacy before it was too late . . .

Scylla and Charybdis. Like Odysseus, he was stuck between a rock and a hard place.

Tory had everything laid out perfectly. Her notebook, the journal and a beer on ice for her prickly tall guest. She was on the couch, nibbling on a cheese cube when there was a knock on the door at the precise minute the clock struck seven.

Dang . . . how punctual could one person be?

Getting up, she went to the door and opened it to find Mr. Goth all decked out in a long pirate-styled leather jacket, black pants and a pair of black boots with neon green skulls painted on them. His hair was damp as if he'd recently bathed and he smelled like strawberries. He was also still in those dark sunglasses.

"Come in," she said, stepping back to let him enter.

He bent his head down so as not to bump her doorframe and went to the armchair where he dropped his backpack on the floor and then took his coat off. He laid it over the backpack and kept the fingerless black gloves on his hands.

She frowned at the tattoo on his muscled biceps that peeked out from under his black T-shirt. "I thought that was on your forearm."

He glanced down at the tattoo and shrugged. "Should we get started?"

Before she could shut the door, his cell phone rang.

He let out a tired sigh before he flipped it open. "It's Ash. Go."

She went to open the beer and handed it to him while he listened.

He gave her a grateful smile as he took the beer. "Uh, no. That would be really unwise. Trust me, she has no known sense of humor about anything male . . . Okay I'll see what I can do." He hung up and dialed the phone at the same time he took a swig of beer.

"I'll be right with you," he told her, then he spoke to someone else on the phone. "Hey, Urian, I need you to ride herd on Zoe in Seattle. She's one step away from running afoul of Ravyn who's threatening to behead her . . . No, I won't be able to get up there for a few days." He took another swig. "Thanks." Hanging up, he put the phone in his back pocket.

Tory frowned at him. "So what exactly is it that you do?"

"I'm a wrangler."

"A wrangler?" she asked, amused by the mere thought of him on horseback with a black cowboy hat decked out with skulls. "Like a cowhand?"

He laughed. "Yeah, only I wrangle people with nasty attitudes. You'd like them. Most are real jerks."

"Ah, a true meeting of the minds then."

"Something like that." His phone rang again. Growling, he pulled it out and looked at the number before he opened it. "No . . . You don't have to ask it, I know what you want. The answer is no. Hell, no, since it's coming from Dominic." He hung up and then dialed another number. "Hey, Alexion. I'm forwarding some calls to you for the next hour or so. I'm not in the mood to deal with it right now." He flipped the phone closed again, then dropped it into the pocket of his coat on the floor.

Raking one insanely large hand through his black and red hair, he sat down in her armchair and looked up at her. "I'm ready when you are."

"You sure? You look a little tense and I don't want to make any sudden moves in case you've had a lot of caffeine or something."

One corner of his mouth quirked up into a charming half smile. "I'm fine."

Tory went to the coffee table and picked up her journal so that she could hand it to him. "What's the best way to do this?"

He took the journal and carefully opened it before he balanced it on his thigh. "How much ancient, ancient Greek do you know?"

"Extremely fluent."

He spoke to her again and she recognized it as Greek, but had no idea what he was saying. It was beautiful gibberish.

She frowned. "Is that the same dialect as the journal?"

"No . . ." he said in English before he switched back to Greek, "Can you understand what I'm saying to you now?"

"That Greek I fully comprehended."

"Okay," he said in English. "You're good with the Iron Age language. That'll help."

Tory crossed her arms as she tried to understand the time period the journal covered. "So the diary is from the Bronze Age."

He rubbed his thumb over his brow. "What did your dating tell you?"

Her cheeks heated as she was forced to admit the fact he'd pegged her correctly in Nashville. The troll. "It was basically inconclusive."

"I'll bet," he mumbled, then louder he said, "Brace yourself. The journal is from the Stone Age. The Mesolithic period to be precise."

Tory sputtered in disbelief. There was no way it was that old. Not even slightly possible. "You're screwing with me."

He shook his head slowly.

Tory stared at it. "No. You're wrong. Completely and utterly. It's just not possible. Do you understand what you're saying?"

"I understand totally."

Still she refused to believe him. "They didn't have books then. They weren't civilized. They didn't have writing . . . they didn't even have houses! People were still living in caves. They barely had fire."

He remained completely stoic under her tirade. "And you know this how? 'Cause you lived during that period?"

"Well no, but the archaeological record tells us that writing isn't that old."

"And the archaeological record is only as sound as the latest find." He held the journal up. "Congratulations, Dr. Kafieri, you just extended it."

Stunned, Tory couldn't do anything other than stare at the book in his hand. "It's too well preserved to be that old."

He shrugged nonchalantly. "It is what it is."

"Yeah, but if it is that old, how do you know the language when we've never had anything from that period in written form before now?"

"I told you, it's basically the same language I was raised with. I lived in a pocket community where our Greek isn't the same as what you were raised speaking." He inclined his head to the book. "This is my language."

Tory shook her head as she tried to fully comprehend the importance of her discovery. Of what he was telling her. It was so mammoth. So much more than she'd ever hoped to discover. "Do you understand the significance of finding a diary this old?"

"More than you do."

"No one's ever going to believe it. No one." They'd laugh her out of the profession if she even tried to present this.

Ash took another drink of beer. "You're probably right about that." Because he was going to make damn sure of it.

Her eyes bright, she cradled the diary against her like a precious infant. "I'm holding something that someone once cherished . . . eleven thousand years ago. Eleven *thousand* years ago," she repeated. "My God, Ash, do you understand how old that is?"

Better than she could imagine.

"This book could tell me everything. What they ate, how they lived . . ." Tears filled her eyes. "With this book, we've unlocked a world that no one alive has ever glimpsed before. I can't believe this discovery. No wonder no one knew the languages or that the equipment couldn't get the right date. It was coming up with dates, but no one believed it so we kept testing and retesting. Oh my God," she breathed. "Eleven thousand years ago. Just imagine how beautiful the world must have been."

Not from his perspective. Personally, he'd like to be able to purge most of those years out of his memory. "You're getting your skin oil all over the journal. You might not want to do that given its age."

She immediately set it down. "Thanks. I tend to get carried away sometimes." She sat next to him on the floor and captured his gaze as she braced her hands on the arm of his chair. "What else can you tell me about it?"

Again, more than she'd ever believe. He could tell her who every person in it was and introduce her to two of them who were currently living and breathing. That was scariest part of all. But the contents of it were harmless. All it showed was how sheltered and naive Ryssa had been as a girl. How precious she'd been. "What else do you want to know?"

Before she could answer, her phone rang out with Ozzy Osborne's "Bark at the Moon." "Hold on a sec. That's David."

Ash leaned back in his chair while she went to answer it. *You know you shouldn't have told her what the journal was.* But then it didn't really matter. There were only a handful of beings who could read it and one of them was human. Besides, better he look at it and read the book first. Now he knew he had nothing to fear from it. But he needed to keep Tory near him and distract her from this quest before she found a journal that was damning.

It could have raised questions he didn't want answered.

"That's terrible! Was anyone hurt?"

Ash frowned at the stress in Tory's voice before he turned his attention to her call.

"Okay, just keep me posted. Thanks, sweetie." Her features were pale as she returned to him.

"Is everything all right?"

"No, someone attacked a member of my crew in Greece yesterday."

Ash frowned. "What do you mean?"

"Oh it was awful. We lost some research and a couple of artifacts that'd just been brought up. David said Nikolas tried to stop the muggers, but he couldn't. He'll be all right, but he's really banged up from it." She shook her head. "I swear we're cursed. Every time we get close to bringing up large chunks of the find, something bad happens."

"Maybe it's the ancient gods telling you to leave it be."

She snorted. "Maybe, but I can't. Both of my parents gave their lives to prove the existence of Atlantis. My uncle sacrificed his life and his sanity to it. My cousin may have given up the search, but I swore on my parents' graves that I wouldn't. Not until my father's reputation is restored. I'm tired of him being the punchline at parties whenever someone brings up Atlantis." She looked at him. "I'm sure you have no idea what it's like to be mocked and ridiculed—"

"You don't know me well enough to make that assertion."

"Sorry," she said quietly. "You're right. Who was that redhead by the way?"

Her constant shift in thoughts baffled him. "What on earth are you talking about now?"

"In Nashville, you were with a beautiful redheaded woman who got up and left in a pique. Who was she?"

Damn, she'd been attentive. "An old friend."

"You were really nasty to her. By the way she was acting, I assumed you two were hooked up."

It was his turn to snort at the very idea. "Oh I can guarantee you we're not an item." That would involve Artemis admitting openly that she was intimate with him. So what if they had a daughter together and half her pantheon knew they slept together, she still couldn't bring herself to admit he was anything other than her platonic pet.

"You were still mean to her," Tory chided.

He had to bury the ire he felt at her condemnation when she had no idea how much shit he'd taken from Artemis over the centuries—including the fact that she'd kept his daughter's birth a secret from him for over eleven thousand years. The goddess was lucky he hadn't killed her over that little stunt. "Look, my private life is private. If that's the only topic you're interested in, I'm leaving."

She slapped lightly at his knee. "Don't be so testy all the time."

"Yeah well, I don't like talking about myself and I despise personal questions."

"Fine. All I want is that brain of yours for a few." She handed him a shallow Rubbermaid container of baklava.

Ash frowned. "What's this?"

"I told you. Baklava."

"And I really don't eat it, but thanks for the thought." He returned it to her.

"Your loss." She grabbed a triangle of it before she set it back on the table. "Now teach me how to read this."

Ash opened the journal again. "There are a few additional characters and diphthongs that aren't in the classical

Greek you're used to. The endings and conjugations are also different."

She nodded, then pointed to a word. "Adelphianosis. Is that 'brother'?"

He was impressed by how quickly she identified the unfamiliar language. "Yes."

She frowned. "So if I'm reading this correctly, it says that her brother . . ." she pointed to the word before it. "Styxx?"

"Yes."

She shook her head in confusion. "Why is he named Styxx? That was a female goddess name."

He'd always thought it an odd choice for his brother's name too, but what the hell? No one had asked him and Ryssa's parents had never been right in the head. "And how many men are named Artemis?"

"Good point. It just seems strange to me."

"Well that's why it has the additional X at the end. It's to differentiate the masculine from the feminine forms."

"Ah, that makes sense." She looked back at the book in his lap and he felt a strange dipping sensation in his stomach. Like a punch only it was more sexual than that and it took him completely by surprise.

He didn't react to people like that.

Yet he had this sudden compulsion to lean forward and just breathe in her scent. To touch her cheek and see if it was really as soft as it appeared. Or better yet to take her hand and press it against the sudden bulge in his pants that cried out for her body. His cock tightened at the mere thought of her unzipping his pants and touching him.

Unaware of his sudden mood, she trailed her finger down the page, trying to decipher Ryssa's neatly written words. "So this is her talking about a fight with her brother?"

It took a full three seconds for those words to descend past the desire he had to kiss her. "Uh . . . yeah. Her brother was angry because she was planning to visit her aunt in Athens and she didn't want her brother to go with her because he was annoying to travel with."

Tory glanced up as she heard the deepening of Ash's voice. She couldn't tell where he was looking since he still wore those dark sunglasses. "Can you see all right?"

481

"Fine."

"Why don't you take the sunglasses off?"

"I see better with them on."

"Oh," she dragged the word out as she had sudden clarity. "You're one of *those*, aren't you?"

"Those what?"

"Vain guy who needs glasses, but doesn't want anyone to know it and you can't stand contacts so you wear prescription sunglasses instead." She rolled her eyes. "I've had several of you in my classes. Really, no one will think less of your manhood for needing glasses—that alone does not a geek make." She indicated hers by tapping a fingernail on the lens. "Look at me. I'd rather be able to see than be vain about it."

Ash hid a smile at her latest wrong conclusion about him. Without commenting, he reached for his beer and took a drink while she returned to the journal.

They sat there for over two hours as she learned his native tongue. It was so strange to hear someone else speaking it after all this time that he couldn't help but be warmed by it. There was even a part of him made homesick from the sound. It was a feeling he didn't get often since he'd had a less than desirable existence there, but then home was home.

Even a bad one.

And honestly, he liked having this connection to someone. He'd been alone for so long. Had taught himself to trust no one. Yet he found himself wanting to trust her and he didn't know why. Perhaps it was her fierce loyalty. He craved someone to be that loyal to him. If only they would . . .

"What do *you* mean the journal wasn't there," Costas Venduras asked as he narrowed his gaze on his underling. As members of the Atlantikoinonia—a society founded to serve the goddess Artemis—it was their sacred duty to protect anything relating to Atlantis.

George swallowed nervously before he answered. "We took all the artifacts the man had with him, but the journal wasn't in with them."

"You know what the oracle told us. Atlantis can never be uncovered. Use whatever means necessary to ensure that all the artifacts are returned to the sea or destroyed."

George nodded. "Yes, sir. As the goddess wills it, it will be done." He started to leave, then hesitated. "By the way, we think the young professor might have the journal with her in New Orleans."

Costas felt his temper rising at the mere mention of that nosy little trifle who'd been a source of aggravation for him for over a decade. "Then send a team to recover it. In fact, our little professor has become too much of a liability for us and our cause. I'm tired of dealing with her. Signal the others with a TOS for Dr. Kafieri."

"Termination on sight. Yes, sir. It will be done."

CHAPTER FIVE

Ash was still in bed, not quite awake, but no longer sleeping when his phone rang. Assuming it was another Dark-Hunter in need of something stupid, he answered it without even looking at the number.

"Hey, Ash, it's Tory. I'm at the grocery store. What do you want tonight?"

You on a platter . . . He forced himself away from that uncharacteristic line of thought. "I really don't eat much, Tory. There's nothing I need."

"Oh come on. You didn't grow to the height of a mountain without eating someone out of house and home."

Actually he had.

"There has to be something you live on besides beer and if you say wine, I will hurt you."

He smiled in spite of himself. "I swear to you, there's nothing I want."

"You like frustrating me, don't you? Fine, I'll make falafel and humus—you're Greek. You'll live with it, like it, and you're going to eat some whether you want to or not. I'll see you tonight."

What was it with Tory and food? She was almost as bad as Simi. How could a woman *that* skinny eat all the time? He tossed his phone down, then rolled onto his back and covered his eyes with his arm, not wanting to get up yet. He'd been out late the night before hunting Daimons after he'd left Tory's house. Something was brewing here in New Orleans, but he couldn't figure it out.

Stryker was plotting something. He could feel it.

But he didn't want to think about Stryker right now either. Letting his thoughts drift, they came back to a pair of beautiful brown eyes circled by small glasses and set into the face of the most frustrating human being on the planet.

Soteria.

Before he could stop himself, he imagined her naked in bed with him. Her hair falling forward over her face as she leaned over him for a kiss . . . His cock hardened instantly.

Unable to stand it, he reached down to move himself so that it didn't hurt.

"You want a hand with that?"

Moving his arm, his eyes flew open to find Artemis in bed with him which instantly killed his peaceful mood. "No."

She pouted. "Oh c'mon, Acheron. You're not really going to let all that go to waste, are you?"

He rolled over to give her his back. "I'd rather masturbate."

She punched at his shoulder. "You're in one of those moods again, aren't you? I hate when you get so sullen with me."

Then why did she keep coming around him when it was his natural state in her presence? Well that, and severely pissed off.

"What do you want, Artie? It's not like you to pop into my bed and you know better than to come to Katoteros. How the hell did you get past Alexion anyway?"

"He's too preoccupied with his wife to notice me these days."

Note to self, kill Alexion again later. At least make the bastard wander around the shores of the Isle of the Dead for a while.

"So why are you here, Artie?"

"You want me here."

Yeah, like an alien rectal probe up my sphincter. "How you figure that?"

"Since you can't see it because it would impact your future, you told me to always let you know whenever something happened involving the Atlantean remains."

And she'd already failed to tell him about the diary which could have been disastrous for him if it'd been one from Ryssa's twenties. "And?"

"Well I just had those people arrested in Greece for excavating without a license. Say thank you, Artemis."

Ash turned his head to look at her. She was literally simpering with pride over what she'd done. "What people?"

"You know, that pathetic-looking archaeologist that we saw? Her people. They'd uncovered the site and were pulling things out of the water yesterday by the handfuls. Found all kinds of things. I know how upset you get when people do that, so I had the authorities go arrest them and confiscate the artifacts."

"Did you happen to have anyone beaten up while you were at it?"

"Why would I do that?"

He scoffed as he rubbed his forehead. "You seem to get off on seeing someone beaten."

She narrowed those evil green eyes on him. "You are in such a foul mood. I don't like to see you beaten either."

He'd seen the gleam of sexual satisfaction one time too many in her eyes while he was being punished to believe that. She loved making him bleed. It was the only time she felt more powerful than he and it made her even hornier than she was right now.

"Whatever you say, Artie."

"Then roll over and satisfy me."

"I have a headache."

She brushed her hand through his black hair, turning it blond. "You can't get a headache."

"Sure I can. I have a hundred twenty pound one rubbing on me even as I speak."

486

She slapped at his bare back. "You're such an asshole." She bit him hard on the arm before she vanished.

Grimacing, Ash rubbed at the spot. At least she hadn't torn his skin out. This time.

"I had them arrested."

He sighed as he realized those would be friends of Tory's. He better get up and go deal with it. Tory would be furious and scared for them.

"Greetings, brother."

Stryker glanced up to see his half-sister, Satara, standing in the doorway of his office. Because they'd had different mothers Satara had been spared the Apollite curse of death that Stryker bore, but then again, since their father had given her to Artemis to be a permanent servant to the bitch, he wasn't sure which of them had the worse life.

Today, Satara's hair was coal black like his and she wore a tight, red leather dress that clung to every deep curve of her body.

"What brings you here, sister?"

"Auntie Artemis, of course. You said to always tell you when she was in a tizzy over something. She went off on a big one last night."

"Over what?"

"It seems a team of archaeologists stumbled onto Atlantis. The real one. And some of the artifacts, including a pristine journal, were recovered."

Stryker sat back in his chair. "One of Ryssa's journals?"

"Given the way Artemis reacted, my guess is yes."

Oh this was good. The humans had no idea that Apollites and Daimons lived among them and they'd gone to quite a bit of effort to make sure it stayed that way. But if one of Ryssa's journals was uncovered . . .

It could tell everything about them.

It was bad enough he and his Daimon brethren had the Dark-Hunters after them. The last thing they needed was for their food source to get scared and start hiding from them at night. They only had a few hours each night to hunt or die. This could be bad.

"I need you to find that journal."

Satara walked forward to lean on his desk. "Artemis is already one step ahead of you."

He pondered that. Artemis seldom ever bothered herself with anything other than chasing after Acheron. "Why does she want it so badly?"

Satara shrugged. "I guess her fear is someone will learn that it wasn't Apollo who sank Atlantis. Or maybe Ryssa knew about Artemis's relationship with Acheron and wrote about it."

Stryker's mind whirled with other possibilities. "Or maybe there's something in that book that tells Acheron's weakness. Maybe even a way to kill him or Apollo and Auntie too."

Satara's eyes sparked with new interest. "I'll find that book."

"You do that. And if anyone gets in your way—"

"They're lunch."

"*Forget Jake Gyllenhaal* and Shia LaBeouf, have you ever seen a better looking man in your life?"

Tory frowned as she walked past a group of female students who were giggling and agog over who knew what.

"I don't think he goes here. I've never seen him before, but I'd kill to have him in at least one class."

"I'd kill to have him under me!"

"I've seen him around. He's been at the bar Sanctuary on Ursulines a couple of times when I was there partying with friends. I think he's hooked up with that tall blond waitress who has such a nasty attitude."

"Are you serious? How on earth did I miss *that*? I must have been good and drunk."

Their comments faded out as Tory made her way to her office. But as she neared it, the female student body count got higher and higher or more to the point thicker and thicker. She actually had to push her way through them.

Yeah . . . this wasn't right. She'd never seen so many people this interested in the Anthropology department before.

It wasn't until she neared her door that she realized why.

Ash was there. Dressed in a long black duster that made her wonder just how many ankle length coats he had, he leaned against the wall with his arms folded over his chest. His was a powerful nonchalance that was riveting. She looked down and smiled at his crossed booted feet and the ever present black backpack resting behind them.

Those dark sunglasses were in place and today his long hair was pulled back into a ponytail. And his silver nose stud had been exchanged for one that looked like a small red ruby.

"What are you doing here?" she asked, reaching her door.

"Waiting for you."

She glanced around at the traffic jam he'd caused. "Really, you should have called. I think the Fire Marshal would have issues with this."

A slow grin broke across his face. "Sorry."

She opened the door and stood back. "You better get inside while I hold them off."

Picking up his backpack, he laughed before he complied.

Tory turned toward the collection of students. "See how exciting Anthropology is? He's a leading expert in ancient Greece. Now you should all change your majors so that you can ogle men like him all day long. Or better yet, uncover naked male statues."

She closed the door to find Ash smirking at her. "Was that necessary?"

"Hey, I live to recruit students for the department. If I can make you good for something, then by golly I'm going to do it."

"By golly?"

She shrugged as she put her armload of books down on her desk. "Yeah, like you don't have weird things you say, too. So what can I do for you?"

"I want to go back to that 'make you good for something' statement for a minute . . . Why do you hate me so much?"

Tory squirmed a bit under his hidden scrutiny and pointed question. "I wouldn't say I hate you. The hatred has fallen down to a mild distaste."

"Why?"

She sighed as she returned some of her books to the shelves behind her desk. "Because everything seems so easy for you. Have you ever had a day in your life where people weren't lining up to take care of you?"

"Yes, Soteria. I have. I assure you, my life has never been an easy one and you should be grateful every day you live that you can't imagine what kind of childhood I had."

Tory paused at the note in his voice and the deadly sincerity of his words. "I'm sorry, Ash. I didn't know."

He set the backpack down on the floor. "It's easy to look at people and make quick judgments about them, their present and their pasts, but you'd be amazed at the pain and tears a single smile hides. What a person shows to the world is only one tiny facet of the iceberg hidden from sight. And more often than not, it's lined with cracks and scars that go all the way to the foundation of their soul."

He was right and it made her feel guilty that she was so quick to assess people. It'd always been a fault of hers that she tried not to give in to. "You are amazingly astute for someone your age."

He snorted. "I told you, I'm older than I look and I've never had anything in my life that I didn't pay for one way or another."

She shuffled a stack of papers into her inbox. "Now that I think about it, you'd have to be a glutton for punishment to keep coming near me given my acerbic personality where you're concerned."

Ash offered her his hand. "Truce?"

"Peace, my brother," she said shaking his hand. "Now why are you here?"

Sighing, he stepped back and crossed his arms over his chest. "Well, I heard from a friend that some archaeologists in Greece had been arrested for excavating without a permit. I wanted to see if they happened to be your team."

She waved her hand dismissively. "Why would they be my team?"

"They were excavating a site they claimed to be Atlantis. Sounded like your guys to me."

"But we have all of our paperwork."

"If you're sure . . ." he let his voice trail off meaning-fully.

She screwed her face up as if she realized her luck would have them in trouble. "Wait. Let me call."

Ash sat down in the chair in front of her desk and stretched his legs out while she dug her phone out of her purse.

Tory frowned at his backpack on the floor and the way he kept it within easy reach. "What's in that backpack, by the way? You're always guarding it like it holds national se-curity secrets or something."

"Dirty underwear."

She rolled her eyes. "Thanks so much for that image."

"You asked."

Shaking her head, she dialed David's number. When he didn't answer, she rang Justina. Again, no answer. Her panic set in as she tried for Bruce.

"Tory?"

She breathed in relief as he answered. "Hey sweetie, I can't get—"

"They've all been arrested."

Disgusted and afraid, she glanced to Ash whose hand-some face was completely stoic. "What?"

"The whole team. I stayed on land to wait and sign for the new diving gear that was coming in and the next thing I knew, the boat was impounded and everyone was taken into custody."

Tory let out a frustrated breath. "How is this possible?"

"They say our paperwork is forged."

"Bullshit! It's not forged. Solin helped us to get it re-newed just last spring."

"Yeah and as usual Solin has fled the scene. We can't find him either. For all I know he's in jail alongside them."

"Oh good grief. Okay, you sit tight and I'll see what I can do." Hanging up, she looked at Ash who sat as still as a statue. "You were right. My whole crew. Gone. Arrested. Perfect. Shoot me now and save me the expense of a bullet later."

He let out a tired breath as he rubbed one large hand down his thigh. "Don't worry. I'll make a call and get them out."

"You can do that?"

"I can do it." He pulled his phone out and flipped it open with a stern flick of his wrist.

Hoping he wasn't lying, Tory sat behind her desk and held her breath while she leaned her head against her hands. How had this happened? Her poor team. They had to be terrified over this.

Ash spoke in that deep, rhythmic flawless Greek of his that sent a shiver down her spine. "Hi Gus, it's Acheron Parthenopaeus. I need to pull in a favor from you. There's a group of anthropologists who were arrested for excavating in the Aegean, this morning I think. Can you get them out and clear them of all charges?"

He laughed. "I know they think it's Atlantis. Everyone wants to find a treasure. But I don't want to see them hurt for a pipe dream. They're harmless friends of a friend if you know what I mean. Get them out of trouble for me."

He tapped his thumb on his thigh while he listened. "No . . . I don't think they need a lesson. I'm sure they're rattled enough as it is. Give Olympia my best and let me know the minute the baby's born. I'll see the two of you next time I'm in Greece."

She straightened as he closed the phone. "Well?"

"He can get them out without a problem, but the artifacts are confiscated and there's nothing he can do about that. If you guys go digging down there again, they're going to execute you."

"You're joking."

"Not really. The authorities are extremely hot over this."

"But we had the right permits."

Ash held the closed phone against his chin. "According to them you didn't and they were one step away from issuing a warrant out for you because you took part of their national heritage out of their country without permission."

"What I have isn't Greek, it's Atlantean."

"The diary *is* Greek and they're not stupid. Even if it was Atlantean, they'd claim it since it came out of the Aegean which is their territory."

Tory hung her head in her hands. "I can't believe this. I was going to hand it over to them once I got a translation for it—I always give them whatever we find . . . just not necessarily as soon as we find it."

"Well Gus can get it smoothed over. Your guys'll be out of jail shortly and it would probably be in your best interest if you get that book back to the Greek government before they reconsider their decision and issue a warrant for you."

She looked at him. "Thank you for all your help, Ash. Really. Thank you. I don't know what we'd have done had you not heard about this and been here."

"I would say no problem but actually it is, so please don't do this again. Calling in favors is something I try really hard not to do. It usually bites me on my ass somehow."

Tory gave him a wan smile, knowing that she'd put him in a bad position. "Tell me what I can do to make this up to you?"

"Just stay out of trouble."

"I plan to." She growled before she pushed herself away from her desk. "Okay, enough pity party, I—" Her words were interrupted by her cell phone ringing. "I'm holding that thought." She picked up the phone. "Yes? No, I'm not at home. Yes, please dispatch the police. I'm on my way."

Ash frowned. "What's wrong?"

"That's the alarm company. There was a three-alarm burglary at my house." She grabbed her purse and keys.

"I'll drive."

"What?"

"You're too rattled to drive and you don't need to go alone to confront burglars. I'll go with you."

Tory was so grateful to him just then. She handed him her keys and followed as he led the way out of the building to the parking lot where she'd left her Mustang.

"What a day . . ." she breathed as she buckled herself in. "No, what a crappy week. I'm almost afraid to get up tomorrow."

Ash started the engine. "I know, first you met me—perish the thought—then your team got attacked. Now your house. Where's a hammer when you really need one?"

She smiled in spite of herself.

"It'll be all right," he said reassuringly.

493

She hoped so. But in the back of her mind, she was telling herself that it was a false alarm. That there was nothing bad at her house.

Please don't let there be anything bad at my house. She couldn't stand the thought of a stranger touching her things. Of her life being scrambled.

The moment Acheron parked out front, she knew better. Her front door was wide open and there was no sign of the police. She started to open the car door, but Ash stopped her.

"Wait for the police."

"Why?"

"You don't want to contaminate any evidence before they get here."

He was right, but she hated it.

It was another fifteen minutes before the police arrived. They went in first and then motioned to let them know it was safe.

Tory felt her tears starting even before she entered the living room. Her entire house had been ransacked. "Oh my God . . ." The OCD in her was horrified by what had been done. Everything was out of order.

The police, a man and woman officer, looked at her sympathetically. "We'll need a list of everything that's missing."

Tory barely understood what they were saying. Covering her mouth with her hand, she stared at pictures of her parents and family that had been thrown on the ground. Her drawers had been opened and their contents dumped all over her floor. She hadn't seen this much damage since she'd helped friends clean up after Katrina. "I can't believe one human being could do this to another."

Suddenly Ash was there, holding her against his chest. "It's all right, Soteria. Just breathe."

She held on to him, grateful he was with her. Grateful that he was holding her while her whole world was turned upside down. First Nikolas's attack, then her team arrested and their equipment confiscated, now this . . .

The female officer frowned as she scanned the damage. "Is it just me or does it look like they were searching for something?"

494

Tory pulled back at her question. "What do you mean?"

The male officer indicated the drawers on the floor. "In most burglaries, especially when you have houses this close together and it's daylight, they usually grab some big ticket items and run." He shined his flashlight at her television, still on its stand in the corner in front of her tall windows. "They didn't even grab your TV."

The female officer nodded in agreement. "Not to mention, it appears the alarm was tripped on their way out of here. Like they were trying to draw you out or something."

Tory scowled at them. "Why would they want to draw me here? That doesn't make any sense."

"No, it doesn't," the male officer said, turning his light off and returning it to his belt. "Unless they were looking for something."

The woman offered her a kind smile. "We've got the CSI unit coming over to take some prints. There's really nothing else we can do. Make a list of whatever's missing and we'll put it in your file and run it through the local pawn stores. Other than that, you'll have to file a report with your insurance company."

The male officer concurred. "And you might want to have your boyfriend stay with you tonight."

A wave of fear went through her. "You think they'll come back?"

The male officer shook his head. "We don't know. Besides most burglary vics have trouble sleeping for a night or two after a break-in."

Tory sat on the arm of her couch as she surveyed the destruction around her. She was grateful she kept her precious artifacts either with her or locked in a vault on campus. "I can't believe this." Ash took her hand in his and didn't speak while the police questioned her about possible suspects and their people came in to dust various areas and pieces for fingerprints.

They found nothing. Not a single smudge. Either the burglars were wearing gloves or they were mutants.

Personally she voted for mutants. She preferred to think that than deal with the fact that a normal, everyday person could do something like this to another.

When the police were finally gone, she turned to Ash. "I'm sure you have something better to do than baby-sit me."

"It's all right. I don't mind. There are some things you shouldn't be alone for."

There was a slight note in his tone that made her think he'd been alone through a lot of them.

He stooped down to pick up the pictures of her parents before he returned them to her mantel. She didn't know why, but the way he handled them made her heart clench with tenderness at his consideration for her.

"Do you have any family, Ash?"

He put the pictures right back where they'd been, as if he remembered the exact spot from his previous visit. "We all have people we love."

She didn't miss the fact that he avoided answering her question. Without looking at her, he went to the items that'd been knocked off her end table.

Kneeling on the ground, Ash frowned as he picked up a shadow box that had a small black rock in it. A tiny bronze plaque on the bottom read SOTERIA'S FIRST EXCAVATION 1985.

"What's this?"

Her eyes misted as she moved to take it out of his hand. "It's from the first time my parents allowed me to dig with them. I was so proud when I found this. I thought I'd discovered a rare spear point. My father didn't have the heart to tell me it was only a rock. So they framed it for me and put it in my room by my bed with a light that used to shine on it." She sobbed as a tear escaped past her control. "Those bastards touched my parents' belongings!"

Ash came to his feet to hold her as she cried. She clung to him as if her entire world had been shattered. He'd learned to bury his tears so deep inside that he couldn't fathom the passion and hurt it took for her to cry like this. All he knew was that the few times in his life when he'd cried this way the one thing he'd craved had been comfort.

And not once had there ever been any.

So he offered to her what no one had ever given to him. He let her sob until she was spent and the shirt over his chest was damp from her tears.

Tory pulled back, wiping at the wet spot she'd made. "I'm so sorry, Ash. I'm not an emotional person. I'm not." She cleared her throat and gave him the most determined look he'd ever seen. "I will not let them do this to me. I'm stronger than this."

"Everyone cries sometimes, Tory. There are some pains that run too deep for even the strongest to take without breaking. I don't think any less of you for it."

She laughed nervously. "You really aren't the asshole I thought you were, are you?"

He offered her a kind smile. "Actually, I have moments of great assholishness. Unfortunately, you seem to have been witness to most of the recent ones."

Tory patted his muscular arm in gratitude for his understanding. He was so easy to talk to at times. Sniffing back her tears, she looked around at the mess. "I'll never get all of this cleaned up."

Her house phone rang. She left Ash in her living room as she went to the kitchen to answer it.

Ash returned to gathering up the photographs as he tried to understand what had happened here. He should be able to replay the entire scene in his head, but like trying to see Tory's future, it was blank. This just wasn't normal for him.

He was a god of fate . . .

Glancing over his shoulder, he watched as she returned to his side and picked up one of the drawers that had been tossed upside down next to the couch.

"That was my friend Pam. She panicked when I didn't answer my cell and called the house. She and Kim are going to come over and help clean the mess."

"You want me to leave then?"

She hesitated. "Only if you want to. It's actually comforting to have you here with me." She looked away from him as if admitting that embarrassed her and put the drawer back in place. She stepped back and froze. "How weird."

"What?"

"They didn't steal my stereo either." She moved a sweater that had been tossed over it by the burglars to show him her white Bose wave system.

That was an odd thing for a burglar to miss. "Maybe they didn't see it."

"Maybe." She pushed it back on the shelf, then turned it on.

Ash frowned as the Bee Gees blared. "Night Fever?" He shuddered. "Disco?"

"Shush," she said, waving at him before she picked up another drawer. "It comforts me when I feel bad."

"How on earth can disco comfort you?"

She picked up a picture of her parents and turned it toward him. Her mother, who looked a lot like Tory, was in a white halter top dress with feathered brown hair while her father was in a yellow paisley polyester shirt and brown leisure suit with curly black hair and a mustache. They were leaning together in front of what appeared to be a New York disco club that Ash vaguely remembered from the late 1970s.

Tory stroked the photo lovingly. "My mother's best friend, Sheri, who is a major shutterbug, took this the night my parents first met. My father thought my mother was the most beautiful woman he'd ever seen. So he sheepishly went over and asked her to dance, expecting her to say no. She didn't. She thought his bashful hesitancy was so sweet that she said yes. They went out onto the dance floor right as Donna Summer's 'Last Dance' began playing. The extended dance version. By the time it ended, my father went down on his knee right there in the club and proposed to her. They married a year later and were never parted again until the day my mother died."

She swallowed as if the memories were hard for her to handle. Her bottom lip quivered as she swayed to the song. "When I was little, my parents used to break out their disco albums and we'd dance to them until we were too tired to move. Hearing disco is like having them with me again. I swear every time I hear Thelma Houston's 'Don't Leave Me This Way,' I hear my mother's voice singing to me while she holds me in her arms and dances around the room with me laughing."

He envied her those memories of being loved and cherished. He wished for her sake that her parents were still here to comfort her. "How old were you when they died?"

"I was seven with my mother and ten when my father died. He was never the same after she left us."

"She didn't leave you by choice."

"I know." Tory placed the photo back on her bookshelves on top of an old, worn copy of Homer's *Odyssey*. "It's just easier to say she left than to say she died." She looked at him. "What about you? Do you have any memories like that?"

He tried not to think about it. "Not really. I grew up without my parents."

"Did they die?"

He turned away and focused on cleaning the mess in her floor. "It's more complicated than that which is why I don't talk about it."

Tory scowled at the coldness in his voice that she was sure he was only using to shield himself. "I'm sorry, Ash. Did you know them at all?"

He didn't answer, but she could feel the sadness in him which led her to believe that he hadn't really known anything about them at all.

She watched as he quietly made order out of the chaos the burglars had left. There was an Old World air about him. A really old soul trapped inside a young body. More than that, there was something soothing. As if being with him calmed her deep inside in a way nothing else ever had. It was almost like being home . . . It didn't make any sense, but there was no denying what she felt when she was around him.

All of a sudden, there was a sharp knock on her door.

She went to find Pam and Kim standing outside with two boxes of extra large pizza and a twelve-pack of beer. The two of them looked a lot alike in many ways. Pam was taller and had her spiked hair bleached blond in front and dyed jet black in back. Kim's hair was the same style but the exact opposite in color. Decked out in their uniquely

Goth fashion, they looked like they belonged with Ash a lot more than Tory.

Pam indicated the road behind her with her thumb. "Hey, is that a cop in the car across the street?"

Tory saw a brown sedan. "I don't think so. Why?"

"Cause the two guys in it had a pair of binoculars trained on this place when we pulled up."

Ash was at the door before Tory could even blink. He brushed past her, but before he could make it to the first step the car peeled out.

Ash almost summoned Simi to follow the car, but caught himself the moment the words gathered to this tongue. Damn, that had been close. The women would have been shocked to find a demon coming to life off his arm . . .

"Why would they be watching the house?" Tory asked.

Ash turned to face her. "I think you need to tell me everything you found on that dig."

"What do you mean?"

"I think something was uncovered that a lot of people are suddenly interested in."

Tory scoffed. "They're museum pieces. Nothing of any real value to anyone other than a collector."

Yeah and the small sfora necklace Ash had given to his daughter also had the capabilities of ending the entire world. The problem with the most powerful amulets and talismans was that mortals couldn't identify their significance.

But in the right or wrong hands, rather, they could have cataclysmic consequences. "Humor me and show me what you've found."

CHAPTER SIX

"Good tuna fish sandwiches; he's the tallest man I've ever seen."

Tory laughed at Pam, who was gawking at Ash.

Ash shook his head at what had to be Pam's most commonly uttered phrase since she'd walked into the house with him. She'd said it four times already.

"Pam," Kim chided as she set the pizza on the coffee table. "You're going to make him self-conscious."

Pam set the beer next to the boxes. "Well it's not like he doesn't know. I mean at five nine, I know how tall I am. Tory's six one so we're allowed to gawk. It's not every day we meet a man who actually makes us feel like we're short, right, Tory?" Pam stood up on her tiptoes next to Ash. "Kim, you're tiny and barely crack five feet. You have no idea what it's like to be tall in a world of average height men. I could finally wear heels!"

Ash laughed before he scooped her up in his arms and moved her over by the couch.

"Oh, good grief!" she said as he set her down. "I've never had a man pick me up before and not grunt like he's dying. I'm in heaven. Marry me, Ash, please!"

"I would say yes, but I come with more baggage than even Samsonite can cover."

Tory ignored them as she entered the room with her dig journals. She pushed the pizza boxes aside on her coffee table, then set them down. "All right, this is everything over the last year."

Ash knelt down and started flipping pages.

Tory leaned over his shoulder as she reviewed what he was looking at. "See, mostly pottery shards and fragments. A few friezes and some bottles."

Ash paused as he found one familiar piece that made his breath catch . . . it was Ryssa's hair comb that matched the one he'd found centuries ago. His heart clenched as he ran his hand over the photograph, remembering how beautiful she'd been with them in her blond hair.

"It's incredibly well preserved, isn't it?" Tory said, unaware of how much this one piece meant to him. "The pearls are even still set where they'd been. It looks like something you could buy today. The workmanship on it's incredible."

"Yeah." He forced himself to turn the page to see more pottery before he betrayed himself with misty eyes.

Then he found it . . .

"Where's this piece?"

Tory frowned at the deep, firm tone from Acheron. Looking over his shoulder, she saw an ornate gold dagger that Bruce had excavated. "That one is still being tested in the lab, why?"

"We need it."

Wow, his tone was more commanding than a general calling for war. "Is it that valuable?"

Ash hesitated. Not from her standpoint, but since it was a weapon that could kill anything that breathed it was extremely valuable to him and to other nonhuman entities who'd do anything to possess it. "Yes."

Pam rolled her eyes. "I don't understand you people and your old stuff."

Kim patted her shoulder. "It's okay, sweetie. We don't understand you and your BeGoth doll obsession either." She looked at Tory. "You should have been with us on our Leda

Swanson quest. She dragged me to three states until we finally found the doll in a boutique in Alabama."

Ignoring them, Ash finished looking through the book, but he couldn't find anything other than the Atlantean dagger that could be important. But given that, why would a human in a car be after it?

No human would understand its significance . . .

And no nonhuman would have made this kind of mess and left it. They'd have simply attacked and tortured Tory until she told them where to find it.

It was baffling. But what else could they want?

More importantly, how far were they willing to go to get it? It was one thing to break into a house. Would they kill for it as well?

Ash stood up. "I'm going to walk around outside for a bit and check things out. I'll be back."

Tory nodded. "We'll save you some pizza."

Ash didn't comment as he left the house and used his powers to leave New Orleans and venture to Savitar's island where the sun literally never set. Magical in nature, the island constantly moved around the world as Savitar searched out the "perfect" wave.

As expected, Savitar was lying on his back on a surfboard out in the water, staring up at the clear bright sky as the waves rocked him.

Unlike the omniscient Chthonian, Ash wasn't a water baby. He hated surfing and lying under the sun. But he also knew that when in Rome . . .

He popped himself onto a board beside Savitar who laughed when he saw him sitting on the longboard. "You look so out of your element."

"I am out of my element. Much like you in a Seattle Goth club."

Savitar gave him a wry grin. "I'm *never* out of my element, Atlantean. And it must be dire indeed to get you in shorties and on a board. One day I'm actually going to get you to say 'Rad four-mill steamer, dude!' "

Crossing his arms over his chest, Ash laughed. "Not likely."

Savitar tsked at him before he returned to staring at the sky. "I've heard that before. So what brings you here, Grom?"

Ash ignored the surfing term that was usually reserved for kids under fifteen. Only Savitar could get away with calling him a youngster. "There's a woman—"

"Isn't there always?"

Ash chose to ignore the sarcastic comment. "She's being pursued by someone and I don't know who."

Savitar arched a brow as he floated one heavily tattooed arm in the ocean. "Then you know I can't tell you anything."

Those words and his condescending tone set Ash's temper on fire. "Dammit, Savitar, don't play this game with me. Her life is in danger . . . maybe."

Savitar grabbed Ash's board and snatched him closer. "Like you, I won't tamper with fate."

"Bullshit. You tamper with fate all the time."

He shoved Ash's board away from him. "But I won't tamper with yours. Ever."

Ash cursed as he paddled back to Savitar's side. "Have you any idea how frustrating it is to be the final fate of the world and to have no control over your own?"

"Sure you do, little brother. Every decision you make causes your fate to unfold or to change. Have I taught you nothing?"

Savitar was right, but it wasn't that simple. Especially not when there was another person's life involved.

What would it take to make the Chthonian care?

Ash narrowed his eyes. "They've uncovered an Atlantean dagger."

Savitar sat up on the board to glare at him. "I hope you're planning to destroy it."

"I have to get it first. But that's the plan." Ash returned his hostile glare tit for tat. "Can you please, just this once, give me some insight into the future?"

Savitar shook his head. "You know what the Fates decreed for you. Through your own actions you will be saved."

"That could mean anything."

Savitar was silent for several heartbeats before he pierced Ash with a sinister look. "All right. I'm screwing with things here, but I'll tell you this much. It's not the dagger the thieves were after in her house. There's another journal her people found."

Ash cringed over that bomb. "Ryssa's?"

He nodded. "It's not the one Soteria showed you. This one was found yesterday by one of her buddies. And it was written after Ryssa became Apollo's mistress. In it is the truth about him and Artemis and their need for blood. It also tells how to kill them."

Ash felt sick. Yeah, that would cause a global annihilation that would impress even his bloodthirsty mother. "And me? Am I in it too?"

Savitar sighed. "Trust me, you don't want that in the hands of anyone else."

Ash's gut tightened. "Where is it now?"

"I can't tell you that."

Ash flashed himself to Savitar's board so that he could tackle him. Unfortunately, Savitar popped himself and the board out from under him and appeared on the other side of Ash's abandoned board before Ash could grab him.

"Hitting me changes nothing."

Ash swam to his board and glared at Savitar. "Why didn't you tell me?"

"You of all beings know how fate works. What happened to you as a human happened because everyone from your parents on down tried to circumvent what was supposed to be—which ultimately was the destruction of the Atlantean pantheon. There was no changing that prophecy. But the way you suffered was completely unnecessary. Had your parents embraced their true destiny, you would have been saved years of torment. Fate will not be denied. We can sculpt it, but in the end we're all pawns to our final destinies. Good, bad or indifferent."

Those words offered him about as much comfort as one of Artemis's beatings. "I'm going to be exposed, aren't I?"

"I don't know. You planning on dropping your pants around me? If so, warn me first. I don't want to go blind."

Ash pulled himself up on his board. "You know what I mean. After all the battles I've fought to save the world and all the sacrifices in dignity and blood I've paid to set free so many Dark-Hunters, they're all going to know that I'm nothing but a pathetic whore, aren't they?"

Savitar's look was sharp and angry. "You have never been pathetic."

But they both knew he'd been a whore. That at the end of the day he was still one. Ash wanted to scream at the injustice of it all.

You can't outrun your past.

His own words were coming back to bite him. "How long do I have before I'm found out?"

Savitar let out a long, tired breath. "There are three outcomes for your journey, Apostolos. In one you're exposed and you lose everything, even your life, and your mother destroys the entire world in a fit of anger. In the other, you're exposed and the Dark-Hunters turn on you and Apollo's enemies destroy the god, then they wreak untold horrors on mankind as they enslave and abuse them . . ."

Ash hesitated to even ask for more. "And the third?"

"In one word, grisly."

Ash cursed. "So no matter what I do, the world is fucked?"

"I didn't say that. There's always hope, Apostolos. Of all men, you know that. It's only when you stop trying to affect the outcome of your life that you're truly defeated. What will come will come. It's how we deal with the shit in between that shapes us."

Ash snorted at his words. "You don't deal with anything, Savitar. You sit out here in the sun, catching waves, spewing bullshit philosophy you don't follow."

"You're right. I gave up trying to affect my destiny a long time ago. But that's because every time I tried to change the future, I fucked it up worse. Eventually the rat gets tired of pulling the lever and sits down in his corner to lick his wounds. So if you're ready to hang it up and come sit on the beach with me—"

"I'm stuck fighting."

"You're stuck fighting." Savitar lay back down on his board. "But you're welcome to come share my beach any time you get tired of the brawl."

506

Ash let out a long sigh as he considered it seriously. "Save me a spot. If this blows up in my face, I'll be back with my tail forever tucked between my legs." Because deep inside he knew the truth—he'd been through enough ridicule. He couldn't stand to see the people he loved look at him the way Ryssa had when she'd found him in the stew in Didymos. Even though she'd loved him and had forgiven him, the disappointment in her eyes was still seared into his soul.

He couldn't take that again.

"Wave's coming," Ash warned his mentor.

He didn't move as Savitar popped up on his board with one perfect flip.

The moment the wave struck, Ash returned to New Orleans. Water sports had never been his thing. He preferred freefalling through the air or speeding on the ground.

And he hadn't been a spectator in over eleven thousand years. If he'd learned anything in his godhood, it'd been to fight until they dragged him down.

Even then, he didn't know how to not keep battling.

There was another journal out there. Fine. He was going to find it and make sure no living human or other being ever read it.

CHAPTER SEVEN

Ash paused as he entered the house to find the three women lined up and . . . singing to . . . dear gods, anything but this.

"Fergilicious."

All he needed was for Simi to be here and off-key with them since it was her favorite song and he'd spent the better part of the last year cursing whoever was dumb enough to introduce that song to a hormonal teenaged demon. Worst part? Simi wanted him to call her Similicious.

Yeah, like that would ever happen. He'd sooner become a Calvin Klein underwear model.

"C'mon, Ash," Kim called. "Join us."

He looked at her with horror filling his soul. "Oh hell no. Not enough beer in the world to make me sing 'I'll put your boy on rock, rock.' "

The women laughed so hard, Kim collapsed on the couch while Pam and Tory roared.

"So did you find anything?" Tory asked after she finally sobered.

"A broken headlight on the car across the street and two streetlights that are out." Ash picked up Tory's cell phone and held it out to her. "I actually need you to call your people and ask them if they found another journal."

Tory gave him a droll stare. "Believe me, if they'd found something as monumental as that they would have told me immediately."

"Even if they'd done it right before they were taken into custody?"

"Then the government would have it."

"Tory, please, just humor me. I've got a bad feeling."

As she reached for the phone in his hand, it started ringing. By the tone and the look on her face, he could tell she knew who it was before she answered.

"Hey Bruce, what's . . . "Her voice trailed off as her face lost color.

Ash put his hand on her shoulder to steady her.

"Oh my God. No . . ."

He exchanged a confused look with Pam until he listened to the other end of the conversation.

"It was awful, Tory. We'd just been released maybe an hour when I got the call that he'd been mugged—just like Nikolas—on his way into his flat and was in surgery."

"What are the doctors saying?"

"They don't know. It's not looking good. But what's scariest is that the guys who ran him down rifled through his bag and pockets . . . like they were looking for something in particular. They didn't take any money or his watch. Nothing . . . Harry said they were asking him questions as they beat on him, but since his Greek isn't fluent he couldn't understand what they wanted. They just kept beating the shit out of him until he lost consciousness."

Tory glanced up at Acheron, becoming suspicious about all of his "feelings." They were so unerringly accurate that she wondered if he might not be a part of them. "Did any of you happen to find another journal during the dig?"

"Earlier in the morning, just before the police arrived, we'd hit the mother lode of artifacts."

"But was there another journal?"

"It wasn't as well preserved as the one you have, but yeah, there was another book and get this . . . it wasn't wet. It'd been sealed in an airtight container that was inside a

509

wood chest inlaid with gold. It looked like someone had stashed it there out of fear or something."

"Where is it now?"

"I don't know. Last I heard, Dimitri had it."

"I need you to find Dimitri and get that book to me."

"Why? It's not like anyone can read it."

"Yes, they can."

"Who?"

She looked up at Ash and wished that she could see the eyes he kept hidden from the world. "A man here in the States."

"Are you serious?"

"Yes. He's the one who told me that there were probably more of them to be found and he's the one who got you guys out of jail. Now listen, my house was broken into and it appears they were looking for something, too. My friend says it's the journal. I don't know the truth, but until we do, you guys be really, really careful and keep me posted on Harry and Niko."

"Will do, Doc."

She turned off the phone and looked up at those dark sunglasses that she suspected hid a lot more than just his eye color. "What's going on, Ash?"

He rubbed his thumb over his bottom lip. "You've found a crucial piece of history and there are factions out there who are willing to kill for it."

No, it had to be more than that. It had to be. "Look, this isn't the Mummy. It's not like a teenaged girl's diary could resurrect the dead or anything. It's just the story of her innocuous life. What on earth could an ancient girl have known that would be worth killing someone over?"

He scoffed at her. "You're asking me that question? People kill each other over a pair of shoes or for wearing the same jacket."

Pam nodded. "He has a point there."

"I still don't understand it. I don't."

Ash shook his head. "There's a lot of things about this world, and people in particular, that I don't understand." And considering the fact he was an eleven-thousand-year-old god, that pretty much said it all.

510

He looked at Tory, wishing he could trust her enough to tell her why that book was so important, but for all he knew the reason he couldn't see her future was because she'd end up being the one to destroy him or the world.

I'm the Harbinger. Only I can bring about Telikos.

Or maybe not . . . His prophecy was to bring it about. By teaching her to translate his native language, he might have already set it in motion. If only he'd known about the second diary. It'd all seemed so harmless—a way to make amends for embarrassing the granddaughter of an old friend. Now it could be a disaster.

Feeling suddenly ill, he sat down on the arm of her couch. What had he done?

"Are you all right?" Tory asked. "You look really pale all of a sudden."

No, he wasn't all right. He was sick to his stomach at the thought of what he might have inadvertently done. Just like with Nick Gautier. In the heat of anger, he'd cursed his best friend to kill himself. Unfortunately, Artemis had then brought Nick back from the dead and created a nasty situation for Ash. Now his best friend was out to kill him in revenge.

Be careful what you say even in passing. Your word is law. His mother's warning rang in his ears and now that he thought about it, his mother had been eerily quiet for the past week.

Matera? he called out to her with his mind.

Apostolos? He was grateful for her quick response. By that he knew she wasn't hiding from him in fear of making him angry at her.

What is going on with the discovery of Atlantis?

Nothing. Stupid humans. Even when I tell them how to open the seal to my prison, they can't follow the simplest of directions. Where's an Atlantean when I need one?

Dead, courtesy of you, Mom.

Oh don't remind me . . . Did you need something, m'gios? You've been very quiet lately.

I've been busy and I have a problem. Someone's found one of Ryssa's diaries. Do you know where it is?

She paused before she answered hesitantly. *Yes.*

And?

She didn't answer.

Matera?

Yes? Her voice was sharp with impatience.

Don't play this game with me. I need to know where it is. Now.

I'm your mother, don't you dare take that tone with me.

He softened his voice before he spoke again. *Please, Matera, where's the journal?*

I can't tell you.

"Dammit to hell, Matera, answer me!" Ash shot off the couch in anger only to realize all three women were staring at him curiously.

Pam cleared her throat. "Any idea what he just said?"

Tory frowned. "Um . . . not really."

"Wow," Kim said with a light laugh, "some Greek the Greek princess can't understand. I'm impressed."

Pam arched one brow. "Must be the voices in his head that he was responding to. I just hope they're not telling him to kill us."

Ash felt heat scalding his cheeks.

"Ooo," Pam cooed. "That's nice. I like the way his cheeks mottle with red when we embarrass him."

"They do that when he's angry or sweating too," Tory said, eating a bite of cold pizza.

"Really?" Pam asked. "I have to say it makes him even hotter in my opinion."

Ash growled at them. "Women, please, could you not discuss this while I'm standing here?"

Pam cocked her other brow. "Are you back with us or still talking to the people in your head?" She reached into her pocket and pulled out a Bluetooth headset. "Tell ya what . . . Son of Sam. Why don't you put that on so that I have some peace of mind and can at least pretend that you're on the phone with someone else and not taking orders from dogs or something."

Ash laughed at her halfhearted truth. "It's okay, I was just thinking of how bad things could have gotten had Tory been here when the house was broken into."

The women exchanged nervous looks of doubt.

Pam glanced toward the door. "You know, Tory, he has a point. What with the others being mugged . . ."

"Maybe you shouldn't stay here," Kim added. "Why don't you come stay with us?"

Tory shook her head. "I can't put you guys at risk and I don't want to live in fear. I can load Henry and take care of myself."

"Henry?" Ash asked curiously.

Kim answered, "Her Baretta baby-sitter."

He was surprised that Tory would have a gun. She didn't seem the type. "Can you use that thing?"

Pam laughed as she gestured to Tory who appeared extremely unassuming as she ate more pizza. "Look at her. She looks so harmless and meek, but inside she's a lion. Tory is an adrenaline junkie the likes of which you've probably never seen . . . everything from deep sea diving to base jumping. Hell, she even jumps out of perfectly good airplanes for fun."

Ash was surprised and impressed by that. "Really?"

Tory shrugged. "I do like to live dangerously."

"No," Pam said, her voice filled with pride for her friend, "she lives fearlessly."

He inclined his head respectfully. "Fearless is a most desirable trait in any human being. Stupidity isn't. I'll stay with you until this blows over." The statement surprised him, but then again it made complete sense. Her team would get the journal to her and if he stayed close to her, he'd be the first one to find it. Then he could destroy it before anyone else had a chance to read it.

He hoped.

Pam hooked her arm into Tory's. "I'd go with his offer. You've been to our place before which means you know about Kim and her 'underwear on the floor' problem."

"That's not my underwear! That's yours."

Pam waved her ire away with one hand. "Let's not bicker over the small things in life such as who owns the underwear. Point being, I'd hang with the big guy. He's a lot more intimidating than us."

"He's cuter too," Kim grinned. "If she passes on his offer, can I beg protection? I think I have a neighbor who's been giving me the evil moti. He could hurt me, you know?"

Ash laughed. "I don't know . . . that underwear problem of yours . . ."

Pam burst out laughing.

Kim pouted. "Like you've never done it."

Actually he hadn't. He didn't wear underwear to drop on the floor. But the women didn't need to know that. "Switching topics again. Did you hear back from Dimitri about the journal?"

"Not yet."

"He's in Greece?" Ash asked.

Tory nodded.

"Okay." Ash swung his backpack up on his shoulder. "I hate to leave you guys, but I'm going to my place to grab some clothes. You have my cell phone number. If you so much as see a shadow out the window, call me and I'll be right back. I only live a few blocks away."

Tory smiled. "We'll be fine."

Ash hoped so. Heading for the door, he left them and went out to the street. As soon as he was sure no one could see him, he flashed himself to Greece outside the door of Augustus Tsigas's house.

Gus's father had been a Squire, one of the human servants who helped Dark-Hunters. As an adult, Gus had gone to work for the Greek government, thus helping not only Ash, but other Greek Dark-Hunters when they needed it.

He knocked lightly on the door so as not to scare Gus's wife Olympia who had no idea about the paranormal world her husband was involved with. Not to mention the fact it was two o'clock in the morning here.

He heard footsteps on the other side of the door before a light came on.

Gus opened the door with a scowl on his face. "This better be important, Acheron."

"Would I wake you for any other reason?"

"Yes."

Ash laughed at his surliness when they both knew he would never bother Gus needlessly. "This is important. Remember the group of people you helped out?"

"The archaeologists?"

"Yes. There was one named Dimitri. I need his address."

Gus looked extremely irritated. "I thought you were omniscient. Can't you get it yourself?"

"I come with some restrictions and unfortunately Dimitri is one of those exceptions."

Rubbing his eyes, Gus yawned. "Come in and I'll pull the record for you."

"Gus? Is something wrong?"

Ash closed the door as Olympia came into the room. Tiny and petite, she had long black hair and big brown eyes. "Sorry I woke you."

She smiled as she saw him. "It's all right, Acheron. I know you two probably need me to leave you alone. I'll go back to bed."

"Good night." He followed Gus into his office. "It's a boy, by the way."

Gus grinned proudly. "Thanks for letting me know."

"No problem." He waited quietly while Gus signed onto his work account on the computer.

After Gus jotted down the address, he handed it off to Ash. "I hope this helps."

"It does. Thanks."

Grateful that at least one person was being helpful to him, Ash flashed himself from Gus's house to Dimitri's apartment across town. He took a deep breath as he tried to think of the best way to handle this. He could either teleport into the house and search it while the man slept or he could wake him and ask him where it was . . .

Better to find it while he slept.

Ash entered the small, cluttered flat and paused. At first he thought Dimitri was asleep on the bed, but he didn't hear a heartbeat. Walking closer, he saw the man lying dead, face down in a pool of blood.

"Not good," he breathed, looking around at the chaos that had been left behind as someone tore the place apart during a search.

Ash took a deep breath and closed his eyes, hoping this time his powers worked. Just as it should have done at Tory's house, he saw everything in sudden crystal clarity.

Three large men dressed in black had barged in on Dimitri, wanting the book. Dimitri had fought and told them nothing, even while they tortured him.

His loyalty to Tory had ended with a silenced gunshot two hours ago.

Ash knelt down beside the body and closed the man's eyes. "Sleep in peace, little brother. The ones who did this will pay. I promise."

The men had left here in frustration after tearing the flat apart. But if they didn't have the journal, who did?

"Matera?"

Are you going to yell at me again, Apostolos?

I'm sorry. A wave of guilt sliced through him as he regretted being short with her. In all his life, his mother and Simi had been the only ones who'd really loved him. Because of that, he hated losing patience with them. *I didn't mean to take my anger out on you, but will you please answer me one question?*

The book isn't here, pratio. Dimitri gave it to someone else.
Who?

An image of his mother appeared before him. Her swirling silver eyes held sadness and regret. "I would give my life for you and you know that. But I can't answer that question. Its existence is tied too tightly to your own. You are a father yourself. You know that you can't always give your children what they want. I'm sorry, Apostolos."

He wanted so badly to take her hand in his. To feel her touch, just once in his life. "I understand. I don't like it, but I understand."

She took a deep breath before she spoke again in a voice that was filled with conviction. "I know what Savitar told you. But he was wrong about one of those outcomes. I won't let anyone kill you. Not again. If anyone comes near you, I will schism the realms and unleash my army for your protection. I am the goddess of destruction and I don't care what happens to this world of man. You are the only thing I love, and I will kill whatever and whoever I have to to save your life."

That wasn't overly comforting. Honestly, he'd rather be dead than suffer any more humiliation. But her love and devotion meant everything to him.

"I love you, Matera."

"Then release me."

He shook his head at the one request he could never fulfill. And it broke his heart. "You will destroy the world if I do."

To her credit, she didn't bother to lie to him. She would omit things and keep vital secrets such as the existence of his daughter from him and the fact that while Simi was the last of her line from Xiamara and the last of the Charontes in the human realm, she wasn't the last Charonte left alive, but his mother had never outright lied.

His mother swallowed. "In anger, I swore to kill Artemis and Apollo for what they did to you should I ever be free of Kalosis again. We both know that if I fail to keep my word, I would perish. So you're right. I would have no choice except to end the world on my release."

"And I have no choice except to keep you there."

She shook her head. "I'll never understand how you can bring me so much pride and pain at the same time. I don't agree with your loyalty to a race that betrayed you . . . no, they did worse than that—they tortured and abused you in a way that deserves no compassion or leniency. But I respect your convictions even when they violently collide with my own. No mother could be prouder of her son, Apostolos. Go find your book and know that I'm here to help you in any way I can."

He held his hand up to her so that she could place hers against his. It was the closest they could come to touching. Part of him wanted to release her at any cost.

But having suffered the way he had, he couldn't live knowing he'd hurt someone else like that. At least not unless they deserved it.

"Go with my love, Apostolos. Do us both proud."

Fading back to New Orleans, he stood on the balcony of his apartment at 622 Pirates Alley that overlooked the courtyard of the St. Louis Cathedral. It was dark, but he could hear the music drifting up from the Old Absinthe House below, as well as laughter and chattering from people on the street. There were Daimons in the alley stalking victims, but before he could even worry about it,

517

Janice was there. He watched the Trini Dark-Hunter follow them toward Royal Street where he knew she'd dispose of them.

Tonight he had bigger concerns than the Daimons who trolled for victims. Someone had a journal Ryssa should never have written. He could go back in time and seize it, but he didn't know how that would disrupt the present. What changes it could incur. It could all work out well.

Or the earth could end.

He leaned against the railing, considering his options. Had he already sown his own destruction? He'd given Tory a key that had seemed harmless and now she was the greatest threat he could think of.

Protect the girl, Apostolos. Keep her safe . . .

He cocked his head at his mother's voice inside his head. "What are you saying, Matera?"

I shouldn't tell you this, but the survival of the world hinges on hers. Keep her safe.

Ash laughed as he was struck by a line from the TV show *Heroes. Save the cheerleader. Save the world.*

"Why are you telling me this?" he asked.

Because I love you. Now go.

Ash hesitated, but at the end of the day he knew the truth. His mother wouldn't have told him that unless it was truly important.

Fine, he'd protect Soteria.

And he would protect himself.

"What are you doing, Apollymi?"

Apollymi turned away from her fountain to find Savitar standing in her garden looking angry at her. "Get out, you bastard."

He refused to move. "You shouldn't have told him that."

She lifted her chin in defiance of the Chthonian. For all his power, he was no match for her and he knew it. "Who are you to lecture me on what should and shouldn't be done?"

His eyes flashed from lavender to silver and then turned a dark vibrant blue. "You are tampering with fate."

She snarled at him. "I am protecting my son. If that's a crime, then punish me. Oh wait, I'm already being punished for protecting him. So be it."

Savitar narrowed his eyes on her. "This isn't a game."

"No, it isn't. I don't play those. I never have." She started past him, but he caught her arm and stopped her.

"I didn't have to contain the powers of the gods you destroyed on Atlantis the way I did when you went wild on them. But for me, the other Chthonians would have torn you apart for that."

Apollymi refused to be intimidated by him or anyone else. "So what? You want me to thank you?" She snatched her arm free of his grip. "The only thanks I owe you is for helping Apostolos learn his powers. For that, I will always be grateful to you. But that's as far as my gratitude goes. If you really think I fear you or those other mortal gods you run with, think again. In this universe, only the primal source outpowers me. There is nothing I fear."

His expression turned cold, brutal. "Not true. You fear the loss of your son and so long as you fear that, you're as controllable as the rest of us."

She hated the fact he was right. "Don't push me, Savitar."

"And don't push me. You may be a goddess by birth, but I'm a lot more than just a Chthonian and you know that. I survived a hell you can't even imagine and its fires forged a core of steel within me. You want a battle, pick your sword. But remember the number of gods before you who sought to kill me and failed."

She raked him with a heated glower. "In turn, you'd do well to remember that I destroyed not only my entire pantheon, but my very family to protect my child. Don't get in my way, or we will find out once and for all which of us wields the most powerful sword."

Savitar wanted to choke her for her obstinacy. But then she'd always been this way. Stubborn to the core of her being. "Fine, but consider what happened the last time you tried to protect him. The suffering your tampering caused Apostolos. Is that really what you want?"

Her eyes teared up and he hated himself for giving her that pain. "Damn you."

He scoffed. "I was damned long before this. Let fate unfold as it should, Apollymi. I beg you to stay out of this. For all our sakes."

Her crystal tears glittered like diamonds on her dark blond lashes. "Keep him alive for me, Savitar. Otherwise you know what will happen."

He inclined his head. "I will do what I can but in the end we both know that only Apostolos can make the fate we want for him."

Because if Acheron screwed this up, he wouldn't be alone in his suffering.

The entire world would be destroyed.

CHAPTER EIGHT

Ash knocked on Tory's front door. He heard the women giggling like girls in the living room before Kim snatched the door open and gave him a devilish grin that made him nervous.

"You like black, don't you, Ash?"

Not sure if he should answer, he frowned. "It's okay."

"But what's your favorite color?" she asked, stepping back so that he could enter the house.

He walked in and wondered if maybe he shouldn't be running in the other direction. What were they up to? "I've never thought about it."

Pam cleared her throat. "But if you had to pick one, what would it be?"

He flexed his hand on the strap of his backpack. "Anything not white." That was Artemis's favorite color and the thought of it made him sick to his stomach.

Tory huffed at his evasive answer. "Could you narrow that down a bit?"

Pam tsked. "She's not going to let you have peace until you answer."

Still apprehensive over what they had planned, he shrugged. "Uh, okay. Red I guess. Why?"

Something came flying at his head. Without flinching Ash caught it and it squeaked. Scowling, he opened his hand to find a small red demon duck that had black horns . . . it strangely reminded him of Simi in her demon form.

He scowled at the women. "Uh . . . thank you?"

They burst out laughing.

Ash glanced around at them as Kim moved to sit beside Pam. "You ever feel like you've just walked into the middle of a movie and they forgot to tell you what it's about?"

Kim waved her hand in dismissal. "Happens to me all the time at work. I just go with it."

Pam laughed. "Which is really bad when you consider she's a labor and delivery nurse."

"Oh shush," Kim said, playfully hitting at her friend on the arm.

Pam and Kim grabbed their jackets from the couch. Pam shrugged hers on. "Well since Ash is back, we'll leave the two of you alone. Ash, if she throws another hammer at you, let us know and we'll take her to task for you."

Baffled, he didn't move or speak again until after they'd left. "You have interesting friends."

Tory locked the door as she smiled in pride. "No, I have the best friends in the world. I don't know what I'd do without them."

Ash felt his heart sink as he thought of Nick. "Yeah I had one of those once."

She turned to him with a frown. "What happened?"

He slept with Simi and I killed him for it. Well, not in actuality. He'd only cursed Nick to die which was the same thing as having pulled the trigger that ended Nick's life. "We don't talk anymore."

They only fought and tried to kill each other. And it was all *his* fault. In one fit of anger, Ash had destroyed their friendship.

She placed a comforting hand on his arm. He was sure she thought nothing of it and yet it touched him deep inside that she would even bother to reach out to him at all. "I'm so sorry, Ash. I can't imagine what I'd do without my girls.

It's so comforting to know that I can call on them anytime of day or night and they'd be here as soon as they could. Everyone should have friends like that."

"Yes, they should."

Tory picked up the pizza remains as she remembered Ash telling her that he had no family either. "So who do you call whenever you're down?"

He shrugged off his backpack. "I don't."

She paused. "You don't ever get down or you don't call anyone?"

He looked around the room. "So am I sleeping on the couch?"

She didn't miss the fact he was changing the subject away from the personal topic. "No, I have a spare bedroom upstairs. You can even leave your backpack there and have no fear that I'll touch it."

He nodded slowly.

The silence was a bit awkward as she tossed the pizza boxes in a garbage can. "We finally got everything the burglars screwed up put back in place. OCD reigns supreme once again."

"Good. Did you figure out what was missing?"

She ground her teeth at the innocent question. "Nothing."

"Nothing?"

"Obviously they were looking for something that wasn't here—like you and the police thought. Which makes me wonder when they'll come back."

"You want to go to a hotel to sleep then? I'd offer you my place, but I only have a one-bedroom efficiency. At four hundred square feet, there's not a lot of room for two people."

Wow, that was a small place to call home and it told her a lot about his solitary nature. "Do a lot of entertaining, do you?"

He smiled. "I told you, I like to be alone. But I do have some friends we could crash with if that would make you feel more comfortable. Their places are huge and you'd have plenty of room to get away from me. I'm sure some of them even have toolboxes should you need them."

523

She patted his arm again as she laughed at his gentle jibe. "If it makes you feel any better, I missed you on purpose with the hammer. I'm a championship hatchet and ax thrower. Believe me, if I'd really wanted to hurt you, I would have."

He snorted. "Not really comforting from my perspective. You don't date much, do you?"

Tory laughed again as she thought about that. "I try, but it never goes well for me."

"Really?"

"Yeah. It's like I'm cursed or something. Any time I get really close to a guy, he either discovers he's gay or he has a freak accident and decides to break up with me."

"Freak accidents that include hammers?"

She rolled her eyes. "No, but one guy did break his leg while trying to climb into bed with me. Kind of put a major kibosh on my love life. Not to mention a serious blow to the ego. Oh well . . . you haven't eaten. Would you like some food?"

He shook his head. "No thanks. I grabbed a sandwich at my place."

She looked at him suspiciously as she tossed away the last of the beer bottles. "You know we're Greek. We're supposed to eat and eat a lot."

"That's a bad stereotype."

"Not in my family, it isn't. In fact, it's more like an Olympic sport. My aunt Del is a twig of a woman who has been thrown out of all-you-can-eat buffets because she plows through food like a linebacker in training camp. In my family, we women cook and you men eat. That's just the natural order."

Ash crossed his arms over his chest as he noticed the curve of her ass as she bent over to pick up a small napkin that had fallen on the floor. Damn, that position went through him like fire as an image of her doing that naked tortured him. He could make some serious use out of her like that . . .

His breathing suddenly ragged, it was all he could do not to reach out and cup her in a place that was guaranteed to get him slapped hard. Then again, it might be worth it.

"Well I truly don't eat much so don't worry about feeding me."

She straightened to scowl at him. "Are you like some sort of weird vampire? You never take off your sunglasses and you only subsist on beer . . . then again, that also sounds like a frat boy and I have seen you out in daylight . . . So ends my vampire fantasy."

If only his fantasy of her naked would end as easily. "And on that note," which was a little close to home for his tastes, "I'm going to take my stuff upstairs. Which way do I go?"

"Second door."

Ash headed for the stairs and as he ascended them, the family photos on the wall struck him again. Tory was so completely normal. He'd spent so little time around people like her that he couldn't help but smile.

But more than that, he wondered what it would be like to have grown up in such a large family environment, loved. Everyone looked so happy in all the photos. Tory was standing with cousins in Greece as they hugged each other. There were more photos of them in Theo's deli in New York.

His favorite was one of Tory around the age of fourteen on a boat with Geary. The two of them were wearing brown wide-brimmed hats with white sunblock on their noses while they were locked in an embrace and laughing. Before he could stop himself, he reached out to touch her face. And against his will, he tried to imagine someone holding on to him like that, someone who was that happy to be with him.

What did that feel like?

You are tired.

The only person who loved him like that who could ever touch him was Simi. She thought the world of him and it was why he was so protective of her.

He touched the tattoo of her on his chest, grateful she was with him. He needed to let her loose soon, but honestly he hated whenever they were apart. There was such comfort from having her with him . . .

It was selfish, but he couldn't help himself.

Gripping the strap of his backpack, he continued up the stairs, to his room. Like the rest of the house, it was small and cozy. The curtains and comforter were beige with pink flowers.

Someone had come in and turned the sheets down for him. He didn't know why, but it made him feel welcome.

He set his backpack down and reached for an acoustic guitar that was set in a rocking chair. He felt a presence behind him. Turning, he saw Tory in the doorway, watching him.

"Do you play?" he asked.

"I torture it from time to time. What about you?"

"I do sometimes."

"You any good?"

"I do all right."

She entered the room with a small stack of towels and washcloths that she set on the dresser. "The bathroom's across the hall. You need anything else?"

You to touch me like I matter . . . He shook his head at the forbidden thought. "I'm a man of few needs."

She sighed. "I've noticed that about you."

Before Ash could stop himself, he took a step closer to her. Close enough that he could smell the precious scent of Tory mixed with peaches from her shampoo. He savored it. Just as he savored the sight of those inquisitive brown eyes that questioned everything about him.

Gods, how he wanted a piece of this woman . . .

Tory couldn't breathe as Ash stood so near her, she could feel his body heat. He was so incredibly sexy. So beautiful.

He's going to kiss you . . .

She could already taste those masculine lips. Feel his arms around her.

But that wasn't reality. The moment he would have touched her skin, she leapt away. "All righty then. I'll just leave you alone."

Ash wanted to whimper as she shot out of the room so fast she left a vapor trail. How could she not want him? All his life he'd been fighting people off. Fending away unwanted gropes and touches. Now he finally found someone he wanted to touch him and she treated him like a leper.

What the hell was this?

Aggravated, he raked his hand through his hair and cursed under his breath. It was going to be a long night with her sleeping so close to him and yet so far away.

Too *early the* next morning, Tory was awake and still bleary-eyed as she staggered downstairs to her kitchen. The moment she entered the room, she froze in her tracks.

Ash was there. Dressed only in jeans, he stood with his back to her.

Holy saints! The expanse of flawless tawny skin was more than a mere mortal woman could see and not salivate over. Wide muscled shoulders tapered down to narrow hips and a perfectly formed butt. His hair still mussed from sleep, he popped the top off a beer.

Tory made a sound of disgust over his actions. "You have got to be kidding me."

He turned and what little sanity she had fled. Yes, he still had those annoying sunglasses on, but the top button of his jeans hadn't been fastened. They rode low on his hips, and the dark trail of hair that ran south of his navel was slightly thicker at the opening.

He was commando . . .

And that long, hard body was made for sin. Really, no man should look like that and definitely not one who was standing in her kitchen . . . In her bed was another story. Man, how she wanted to take a bite out of him.

"Is something wrong?" he asked innocently.

It took her three heartbeats before she could remember her objection to his near naked state. "You're drinking a beer first thing in the morning. What kind of alcoholic are you?"

He flashed a taunting grin at her before he took a deep swig. "I'm not an alcoholic."

Yeah, right. "That's what they all say. At least put something on your stomach before you drink that."

His features hardened. "I don't need a mother, Tory."

She didn't believe that for one minute. Angry at what he was doing, she tried to take the bottle from him, but he refused to let her.

She glared at him. "You need someone to take care of you. Jeez! How can you do this to yourself?"

"It's just a beer."

"And hell is just a sauna." She went to the fridge and grabbed eggs and some cheese. "Sit down and I'll make you something to eat."

"I'm not hungry."

"And I'm about to be wielding a frying pan and a knife so if you know what's good for you, you'll stop arguing with me and sit down."

"I don't eat breakfast," he mumbled under his breath as he moved out of her way.

"I really don't care," she mocked in a sing-song voice that was as close to his thick accent as she could manage.

He moved to the other side of her breakfast counter. "You are so bossy."

"Yes I am. Now sit."

"Yes, Your Majesty. Is there anything else I can do for you?"

"Put a shirt on like a civilized human. Do you know how unsanitary it is to be in a kitchen with no shirt?"

Ash laughed even though he wanted to strangle her. She had to be the only person he'd ever met who wanted him to wear *more* clothing. He started to get up, but she made a squeal of disapproval.

"What now?" he asked, truly baffled by her mood swings.

She pointed threateningly at him with her knife. "Don't you dare move until *after* I see you eat something."

He let out a frustrated breath. "You told me to go put on a shirt."

"Since when do you listen to a single thing I say? Never. I know what you're planning to do. You'll go upstairs and not come back. So sit."

He held his hands up in surrender while he watched her crack open two eggs and put them in a bowl so that she could beat them with a fervor that would have scared him

528

if he wasn't a god with protective powers. "You're not a morning person, are you?"

She put a handful of cheese on top of them. "No and I haven't had my caffeine IV either which means it would be wise of you to humor me."

Ash hid his smile. Why did she amuse him so? He didn't understand it and unless he wanted to tell her the truth about what he really fed on, he had no choice except to sit here while she made him an omelette, bacon and toast.

She plopped the plate down in front of him. "Fie!"—Eat in Greek.

He stared at the delicious smelling food as buried emotions surged. *You want to eat, whore? Please me . . .*

In the back of his mind, he saw himself in Estes's office, on his knees on the floor, naked and chained to the desk while his uncle read late into the evening. Starving because he'd been allowed nothing to eat all day while he'd worked until he was bleeding and sore from it to make his uncle rich, Ash had stared at the bowl of dried sugared figs Estes had left in front of him. His stomach cramped from hunger, his mouth had watered for a single taste. For over an hour he'd stared at the food, biting his lips in desperate agony. Convinced Estes was so engrossed in his reading that he wouldn't see him, Ash had reached for one.

He could still feel the sting of that vicious slap. See the anger in Estes's eyes as he snatched at his hair and held Ash at his feet. *"Did I give you permission to eat, whore? You don't ever take from me without earning . . ."*

Even Artemis withheld her blood from him in an effort to control him. If he didn't please her, he starved. More than that were the memories of being force-fed by his father's guards. *Shovel it down his throat. Hold his mouth and nose shut until he swallows.* And when he'd choked on what they were brutally pouring into his mouth, they'd punched and slapped him, too.

He *hated* to eat.

Tory reached for the cheese and froze as she caught the strange look on Ash's face. If she didn't know better, she'd swear he was afraid of the food in front of him. "What's wrong?"

"I really don't eat breakfast."

This time she heard the underlying note in his voice that reminded her of a small, fearful child. Before she could stop herself, she walked over to him and stood by his side. He continued to look at the plate.

Gently, she took his whiskered chin in her hand and turned his head so that he was looking at her. "I won't force you to eat against your will, Ash. But I don't want to see you starve. Please, eat something."

Ash stared at the vein on her neck that throbbed with the vitality of her life. He could hear her heart beating . . . that was the food he craved.

His incisors elongated at the surge of hunger that went through him. His senses sharpened as he felt his eyes turning red.

Eat . . .

But he couldn't bring himself to feed from her the way Artemis had done him when he'd been human. Even though he could make it pleasurable for her, he couldn't do it. It was such a feeling of being violated to have someone drain the blood out of your body. Have them rip through your flesh with their teeth while you were powerless to stop them . . .

I won't do it.

She reached down and cut a small bit of the eggs off before she brought the fork up to his lips. "Would you please take one bite?"

His instincts were to shove her away from him as his teeth receded. Instead, he found his lips parting so that she could place the eggs on his tongue. The taste stunned him. He hadn't tasted food since before he'd died.

But even better than the food was the satisfied smile on Tory's face. She reached out and stroked his jaw with the backs of her fingers.

Closing his eyes, he savored the tenderness of that touch as his cock hardened forcefully. In that moment, it took every ounce of strength he had not to pull her to him and kiss her. Or more to the point, strip her naked and sate the hollow ache inside him.

Never in all of his existence had he tasted lust like this.

It was more than a mere craving, it was a raw, demanding need.

She broke off a piece of toast and held it up to his mouth. Dutifully, he parted his lips and let her feed him again.

Tory couldn't explain the peculiar sense of satisfaction she had from feeding him, but there was no denying it. She felt as if she were taming a feral lion. And when she fed him a piece of bacon, he gently nipped her fingers.

A shiver went over her.

"It's not so bad, is it?"

He shook his head.

She gave him another bite of the eggs. He swallowed them, then took a swig of beer. She couldn't see his eyes, but she could feel the weight of his gaze on her and it made her entire body hot.

"Now that I've placated *you* . . ." He pulled her against him and captured her lips.

Tory moaned as his tongue touched hers. Never in her life had a man kissed her like this—as if he were breathing her in. Possessing her. His kiss was hot and demanding as he cupped her face in his hands.

Ash was on fire from the taste of her, of the feeling of her tongue against his. Over and over, he could imagine himself buried deep inside her. Feel her hands on his back, stroking him with the same tenderness she'd used to touch his cheek.

Unable to stand it, he trailed one hand down her arm, and around her hips to press her closer to him.

Tory's body throbbed with an unbelievable demand. She wanted to strip those jeans off and taste every inch of his body until she was blind from ecstasy, but at the end of the day, she wasn't stupid.

A man like this didn't date a woman like her. It just didn't happen.

"Whoa, boy," she said, pulling back. "Down. We just met. For that matter, I don't even know what your eye color is."

Ash wanted to whimper as she stepped away from him. His gaze dropped to her nipples that were plainly visible beneath the tank top she wore. All he wanted was to shove her shirt up and take one of them into his mouth.

531

Would she hold him like he mattered?

Or would she slap him after he'd pleased her and kick him out her bed?

That last thought went over him like ice water. He didn't want to feel used anymore. Not to mention he had one large, red-headed problem who would beat him until he had no skin left on his body if she ever found out he'd kissed another woman.

Damn it. His life had never been his own.

"I'm sorry," he breathed. "You're just extremely irresistible."

"Strange, men have been resisting me for years."

"Yeah well, they were idiots."

Smiling, she reached up for his glasses. "Can I take these off?"

Ash swallowed as fear tore through him. "I wish you wouldn't."

"Why?"

"Because they'll make you uncomfortable. No one likes to look at my eyes."

She scowled at him. "What are you? Rosemary's baby?"

"Kind of."

She shook her head at his fear. "Well in case you haven't noticed, I'm not most people."

No, she wasn't. But not even the gods could look at his eyes without curling their lips in disgust. "Just remember, when you do this, there's no going back."

Tory froze at those dire words. Now she had to know what they looked like. Reaching up slowly, she pulled the sunglasses off his eyes.

Ash looked down at the floor, preventing her from seeing their color. But dayam, the man was even more gorgeous without the sunglasses on. Never had she seen a more perfect set of features.

"Look at me, Ash."

Ash ground his teeth as he remembered Artemis telling him the same thing. Back then, he'd been afraid of her hurting him over them. Now there was no fear of Tory doing him harm, but even after all these centuries he knew how seldom people met his gaze without curling their lips or cringing. He hated for anyone to see the evidence of his godhood.

Tory stroked his brow with a light, gentle touch. "Please, Ash?"

Bracing himself for her horror and fear, he looked up and met her gaze levelly.

Tory stared in shock at the swirling silver color. Never in her life had she seen anything like them. The color was so pale and pure. They reminded her of mercury. "Are you blind?" Even as the question left her lips, she knew it was absurd. He could see plainly.

His features were stoic. "No, I'm not blind. It's just an unfortunate birth defect."

She saw the shame in his eyes as he spoke and it made her chest tight that something so beautiful would hurt him so much. "It's not a defect. Your eyes are beautiful. Unique . . . like you. I think they're very cool."

He glanced away.

She caught his chin and forced him to look at her again. "Who hurt you?"

His gaze was guarded. "What?"

Tory stroked his jaw as she realized how shrewish that must have sounded. "I'm so sorry, that was so nosy of me. It's just, you're so guarded and private about even the most innocuous thing. Like you're afraid to let anything out for fear of it being turned against you. And it's everything, right down to your eye color. I'll bet black isn't even your natural hair color, is it?"

Ash swallowed at her question. She was eerily perceptive. "Like you said, we barely know each other."

She brushed his hair back from his face. "Have you ever been intimate with anyone?"

"Of course I have."

"I don't mean sexually intimate. I've no doubt you've been with countless women, even at your age. What I'm talking about is having someone who knows your most intimate thoughts. Someone you can be yourself with without fear of them judging you or thinking less of you?"

Ash laughed bitterly at the mere thought of being so open with another person. "It's in the nature of people to hurt each other. No one really cares about your thoughts or your feelings."

Tory ached for him. He was so closed off that it made her want to weep. "I care about your thoughts, Ash."

"You? You've misjudged everything about me from the very beginning. I'm nothing but another asshole you have to deal with."

"Because you haven't given me anything other than your worst to judge you by. Why did you come to Nashville? Huh? Why was ruining my reputation so important to you?"

She saw the light fade from his eyes as he withdrew further into himself. But it was the pain in them that made her ache for him and in that moment she knew he'd had a very personal reason for what he'd done.

"Why, Ash?"

Her hall clock chimed.

He pulled back. "It's nine o'clock. I have a date."

Bemused, she frowned as he left the kitchen with his beer and headed to her living room where he'd set up an Xbox 360 to her TV. At least that's what she thought it was, but instead of being white it was covered with black hacker/pwn3d stickers.

Ignoring her, he pulled a T-shirt out of his backpack, put it on, then sat on her sofa and attached an earpiece to his head.

She sat on the arm of the couch. "What does pwn3d mean? I see that all over the Internet."

"It's a gamer's term that means you've been owned or defeated badly." He turned everything on.

"You do this a lot?"

"Every Saturday morning."

She rolled her eyes, waiting to see something like Halo or Gears of War or some other macho male game come up. So when it started out with pink dancing animals, she scowled. "Viva Piñata?" It looked like a young kid's game.

"Yeah," he said as he signed in under his own name. "Hey Tobe."

She realized he was talking to someone on the earpiece.

"Yeah, I know I'm a little late. Sorry."

534

Confused, she saw Ash pick a fox character while someone named Tobinator was a bear. Then JadeNX joined in and Toki-san.

Ash glanced at her, then turned all his attention to the game. "Toby, watch Jaden. I heard he had a bad night and is in the mood for annihilation." He laughed. "End of the world's not on me today, bud. Hey Takeshi, get your fat butt off me. You're squishing the fox." He skidded his character sideways in the race. "There is no honor in sacrificing the fox, you ugly hedgehog."

Completely baffled by the fact a grown man was playing a small kid's game, she went to bathe and dress.

She came back thirty minutes later to find him still at war with his opponents.

"Where's a friggin' rocket when you need it? Ah crap, Jaden, stop with the pollen. I hate that." Screwing his face up, he hit a button. "Yeah taste honey, you punk."

She heard the sound of a little boy's loud laughter through the earpiece.

Ash's phone rang. He glanced at it before he muted his earpiece and answered. "Hey, Trish. Yeah, I understand." He hung up the phone and returned to the game. "Guys, I think we have to declare Toby the de facto winner. His mom says he has to get out of his pajamas and get cleaned up to meet the world." There was an audible cry of protest. "I know, Tobe. PT sucks, but I'll see you later, right?"

Ash smiled sadly. "Listen to Takeshi, buddy. He's right." He paused to listen. "Good game, gentlemen. Thanks for the competition. Jade, me and you are going to rematch on this later. Peace, my brothers." He hung up and turned the game off.

Tory watched as he packed everything up. "Toby is how old?"

"Eight."

"And the other two?"

"Older than eight."

"So you grown men get online to beat an eight-year-old kid every Saturday morning?"

He laughed. "Nah, Toby always wins."

Tory let out an irritated sigh. "You see, you're doing it again. Telling me nothing."

Ash turned to look at her. "You know trust is always a good idea . . . for someone else. Every time I've ever made the mistake of trusting someone . . . it was a mistake that I regretted and paid for dearly. I'm really happy that no one has ever hurt you badly. I haven't been so lucky, okay?"

"I would never betray you, Ash."

He shook his head bitterly. "I've had people I've known a lot better than you tell me that. In the end, they lied and I was screwed over by them. No offense, but I don't want a repeat."

Tory wanted to weep at that. How badly had he been burned that he couldn't even tell her if the people on the other end of the game were friends, family or other?

"I'm going to go grab a shower." He picked up his backpack and took it with him.

Damn, she'd never seen anyone so mistrusting. He probably didn't have anything in that backpack except for dirty underwear. But God forbid someone should ever see his undies—they might learn something personal about him like his clothing size. Call the feds! Such a thing could jeopardize national security.

Sighing, she picked up the black controller from the coffee table and paused as another thought occurred to her.

Don't do it.

She couldn't help herself. Turning the system back on, she signed in under Ash's profile. JadeNX was offline, but Toki-san was still there.

She messaged him. "Are you a friend of Acheron's?"

He came back with, "Are you?"

Dang, was everyone Ash knew defensive like that? "Yes. My name is Tory, would you please call me? 204-555-9862."

Her phone rang a few seconds later. Tory turned the game and TV off before she answered it. "This is Tory."

"Takeshi," he answered in a voice thick with a Japanese accent. "What do you want with me?"

She suddenly felt ridiculous and prying. "I'm sorry, I shouldn't have bothered you. Forgive me." She started to hang up.

"Wait. You wouldn't have contacted me without it being important. Is Acheron in trouble?"

"No. I'm an archaeologist and he's staying with me because we think someone might be trying to steal some Atlantean artifacts my team has found." She had no idea why she was telling him all this. "Ash is so quiet about everything that I just . . . I don't know."

"I wouldn't tell him that you spoke to me. He's very closed about such things and would take this angrily."

"I know. I shouldn't have contacted you. I just needed to know that he's . . . not insane or something."

Takeshi laughed. "You're safer with him than with your own family. He holds his honor above all things, even his own life."

That made her feel better. "Thank you."

"You are very welcome." He paused before he spoke again. "Take care of him, Soteria. And remember it takes great courage and heart for a man who knows no kindness to show it to another. Even the wildest of beasts can be tamed by a patient and gentle hand." He hung up.

Tory stood there, digesting that last bit when it hit her . . . he'd called her Soteria.

How on earth had he known her real name when she hadn't given it to him?

CHAPTER NINE

"What did you do?"

Tory jumped at the sound of Ash's deep, accented voice behind her. Guilty about contacting his friend, she turned around to face him and froze. Dressed in black pants and boots, he'd left his damp hair to hang freely around his broad shoulders. Good night, the man was unbelievably delectable. But it was the faded gray T-shirt that had a pile of skeletons on it that really caught her off-guard and made her wonder if his propensity for that wouldn't have him kill her over what she'd done behind his back.

She cleared her throat and tried her best not to look too nervous. "What?"

"You turned something on while I was in the shower and froze the crap out of me."

Relieved that was all that had him ticked off, she laughed. "Sorry. Dishwasher. I won't do it again."

"Please don't. One minute it was scalding. The next freezing."

She scowled as she saw the dragon tattoo back on his forearm—where it'd been originally. "Is that like some sort of temporary thing you do to screw with people's heads? I swear it keeps moving to different parts of your body."

Before he could answer, her phone rang. Tory groaned at the sound. "You know, between the two of us, we can't have a minute's peace from these stupid phones." She picked up the phone, surprised to find Bruce there. "Hey, sweetie. Did you get the journal for me?"

"No. Someone killed Dimitri last night and ransacked his place. They must have taken the book."

Staggering back at the unexpected news, Tory dropped the phone as horror and grief enveloped her.

Ash barely caught Tory before she fell to the floor, sobbing. "Breathe," he whispered.

But she didn't appear to hear him as she kept saying, "No, no, no," in a low tone.

He picked up the phone from the floor. "Hello?"

"Where's Tory?" a man demanded.

Ash looked at her. She'd gathered her legs to her chest and was sobbing against them while she covered her head with her arm. "She's really upset. What happened?"

"One of our friends was killed last night."

Ash ground his teeth as he remembered the horror of Dimitri's final hours—no one deserved that. "Okay. I'll have her call you back when she calms down." He hung up the phone and pulled her against him.

Tory buried her face against his shoulder and wrapped her arms around his neck in a stranglehold that somehow didn't manage to hurt him. "How can he be dead? Why?"

He held her close. "I don't know, Tory. Shit happens to the best of us."

"No. Not over a fucking book." Her language shocked him and let him know exactly how upset she was. "Please, Acheron, tell me a book isn't worth a man's life." She launched herself from the floor and grabbed the phone.

"What are you doing?"

Lifting her glasses up, she wiped at her eyes as her cheeks flushed red with anger. "I'm calling everyone on my team and telling them to hide immediately. I won't have another person hurt. I won't!"

He didn't try to stop her as he rose to his feet. Instead, he attempted to sense something about this with his powers. It was so frustrating to have no insight or clues about what was going on. He hadn't felt this vulnerable since the day he'd died.

After calling everyone she could think of, Tory hung up and sighed. "Everyone else is accounted for and safe. Let's hope they stay that way." Sniffing, she pulled her glasses off and used her shirttail to wipe the lenses. Ash admired the way she'd pulled herself together.

She put her glasses back on and pierced him with an angry, hurt look. "What do you think is in that book that makes it so important?"

"The end of the world."

She scoffed at him. "Be serious."

"What if I was?" he asked, wanting to feel her out and see what she'd do if she had it. "What if there was something in that book totally apocalyptic?"

She didn't hesitate with her answer. "Then it would have to be destroyed."

"Even if it contained proof of Atlantis?"

She pushed her glasses up with the back of her hand. "Well since we're being hypothetical, yes. Proof of Atlantis wouldn't be worth the destruction of the world. I mean, really, what good would it do to save my father's reputation when there's no one left who cares?"

He smiled at her indignation. "You think quickly on your feet."

"So they tell me." Tory paused and closed her eyes. "I can't believe Dimitri. God, I hope he didn't suffer."

Ash didn't comment. He didn't want to lie to her and the truth . . .

Sucked.

Instead, he tried to get her mind off it. "What do you normally do on a Saturday?"

She sighed as she put away her dishtowel. It was obvious she was still torn up over Dimitri, but trying to be brave. "Depends on the Saturday. Here, lately, I've been sky-diving, but my pilot canceled day before yesterday due to illness. So I was planning on grading papers and watching bad movies. What about you? Other than stomping a young boy's ego first thing in the morning, what do you do?"

Smiling at the mock sarcasm in her voice, he pulled a pocket watch out of his jeans. "In about two hours, you'll know."

"What's in two hours?"

"Basketball game."

She made a sound of supreme disgust. "Oh no. I don't do spectator sports. They bore me to tears."

Ash tsked at her. In this one thing, he was the mighty mountain who wouldn't be moved. He'd made a promise and he was going to be there no matter what. "You might as well reconcile yourself to the fact that you will be sitting on the bench today since I can't leave you here alone."

She actually hissed at him like a cat. "Dream on, buddy. Not going to happen."

"Yes it will."

"No," she said firmly. "It won't." Tory couldn't believe his obstinacy. Why was he being so unreasonable? What difference would it make if he missed a stupid game with his friends?

But the more she protested, the more he ignored her. They literally fought over it up until Ash came downstairs wearing a black and white polyester referee shirt. He even had on basketball shoes instead of his requisite boots.

The sight of him dressed like that stunned her until the ludicrousness of it struck her.

It was all she could do not to laugh at the sight he made with his long red and black hair pulled back in a ponytail and nose ring . . . not a stud. A small silver hoop to match the two he now wore in his left earlobe. "They let you referee, huh?"

"No one argues with my calls."

"I'll bet."

He shrugged his coat on and picked up the backpack of death. "You want to ride with me over to the game?"

His offer surprised her since she hadn't seen him do anything other than walk or ride with her. "You have your car?"

Ash smiled. "Motorcycle. I brought it over last night when I went to get my clothes." It was a small lie. He'd actually manifested it this morning when he'd decided he wanted to ride for a bit and he was hoping she wouldn't balk over it.

"I don't have a helmet."

He pulled a black one out of the backpack. "You do now. What do you say? You up for some adventure?"

Tory wrinkled her nose at the helmet and folded her arms over her chest. She would love to join him, but she wasn't stupid either. "I have no gear to wear and the last thing I want to be is SQUID."

He laughed at her use of a biker's term to describe anyone dumb enough to ride without the proper safety gear on.

He pulled a worn, black Stitch Brazilian leather jacket out of his backpack. The shoulders, elbows and waist of it were heavily stitched and the armor in it extremely lightweight, but it was the dark gray skull and crossbones on the back with a gold Hayabusa symbol over it that made her laugh. "You have a thing for skulls don't you?"

"They're all right."

His attention to detail was admirable and the truth was, she hadn't been on a bike since the summer.

"You game?" he asked.

She took the jacket and shrugged it on. As she did so, the scent of leather and Acheron struck her hard. He must have worn this jacket a lot. Completely broken in, it felt warm and soft as she tightened it up with laces and Velcro. It fit her surprisingly well. It was also extremely expensive. She wouldn't be surprised if he hadn't paid at least a grand for it given the way it was made.

What on earth did he do for a living that he could afford toys like this? And just how did he fit everything in that Mary Poppins backpack of his?

Grateful that it was obviously bigger than it looked, she took the helmet from him and smiled. "Lead the way."

Ash's throat went dry at the sight of her in his favorite riding jacket. It looked alien and adorable on her. Definitely not her usual style and at the same time it made him feel as if she'd somehow claimed him by wearing his clothes. She reminded him of a kid in her big brother's jacket as she pushed her glasses up on her nose, then braided her hair to fall down her back so that the wind wouldn't tangle it. He waited for her to put her boots on before she was ready to leave.

Damn, the woman was strangely beautiful. Those brown eyes seared his soul and made him hard every time she met his gaze. And if he didn't get her out of this house soon, he was going to scoop her up in his arms, take her upstairs to her bed and show her exactly where his true talents lay . . .

Pushing that thought away before it got him into trouble, he took her down to the street where his sleek black and gold motorcycle gleamed in the sunlight. It looked like a nasty predator that tore up the road and made him feel a freedom he only had when he dreamed. There was nothing he loved more than climbing on the back of it and flying down the interstate like a bullet.

On that bike, his soul felt free and no matter how bad he felt, it made everything okay.

"What in the world is that?" she asked as she cocked her head to look it over.

"Custom built Hayabusa-Turbo," he said as he pulled his helmet off the handlebars and put it on over his head.

Tory hesitated as she realized that the bike had been built for only one rider. But truthfully, the thing was gorgeous. "I don't think we're both going to fit."

"Sure we will." He flipped the tail of it up to show her the customized passenger seat before he secured his back-pack over the gas tank with custom-made clips to hold it into place. Then he straddled the bike with an undeniable male grace that said he was more at home here than any-where else she'd ever seen him. He closed the shield on his helmet and pulled a key out of his pocket. Then he secured his long coat around him.

Oh good grief, there was something innately masculine about him on that motorcycle. Commanding. Fierce.

Most of all, he was hotter than hell and made her want to strip him naked and throw him down on her lawn in front of God and everyone as she made love to him until they were both begging for mercy.

"Hop on, *koukla*."

Her heart warmed at the Greek endearment that meant doll. Tory was a little more hesitant than normal as she approached the huge bike that had been built for obvious speed. She slung her leg over and wrapped her arms around his lean waist as he started it.

Oh yeah baby. She could stay like this for eternity. Snuggled up against his hot body as the clean scent of him filled her nostrils . . . surely there was nothing better to be found.

"Hold tight." His voice came through an intercom in her helmet.

She did and he squealed out, into the street. Her heart sped up at the way he rode as if hellbent for Lucifer. But honestly, she loved it. There were two truths about her—Things could never be old enough to please her and nothing could ever go fast enough to scare her. She loved history and she loved speed.

"You do this a lot?" she asked.

"Every chance I get. I live to ride."

Wow, he'd actually admitted to something. That was a first. Maybe she should mark the date to remember it by. But that thought left her as he flew over a bump that made them airborne for a minute.

She whooped and laughed at the feeling.

Ash smiled at the sound of her laughter in his ears. He'd been afraid at first that doing that would scare her. But as Pam had noted, she was fearless, and it softened his heart for her even more.

So did the sensation of her arms wrapped around him as she leaned against his back. Now if she'd only drop one of those hands a few inches down to the sudden bulge he had for her, he'd be open for business. Unfortunately, he wasn't that lucky.

He growled at the thought and urged the bike faster.

Tory didn't say anything else as they sped over to Kenner, to a grade school gym in what had to be record time—thank God she didn't have to pay his insurance bill if he went this fast all the time. She couldn't even begin to fathom the number of tickets he must have collected—it was a wonder the man still had a license.

"What are we doing here?" she asked as he put the side stand down.

"Game." He held the bike upright as she climbed off. He grabbed his sunglasses out of his backpack before he removed his helmet.

Tory didn't miss the fact that he kept his eyes closed while he exchanged the helmet for the sunglasses. For some reason she couldn't name, it bothered her that he was so self-conscious over his eyes. And yet at the same time, that one vulnerable self-doubt made him seem more human and actually adorable. How could a man so gorgeous and confident be that shy over something she found extremely seductive?

Tossing his backpack over one shoulder, he carried his helmet under his arm as he led her through a back door into the gym where a group of small boys were practicing. The kids had to be between seven and nine in age.

Tory's heart melted at the sight of them. Oh they were so cute and as they saw Ash, they came running to high five him—only he had to stoop over to accommodate their heights. She knew he was tall, but right then, he really looked like a giant. They surrounded him as they all chattered and vied for his attention.

Ash laughed. "All right, guys, you need to practice while you can. I don't want to see any traveling today or fouls. Got it?"

They nodded and shouted before they went back to their ends of the court.

Tory shook her head as she closed the distance between them. "You're just full of surprises, aren't you?"

He frowned. "I'm not sure what you mean."

She gestured toward the kids. "I'm truly amazed. This is the last thing I would have ever imagined you doing on a Saturday afternoon."

"Ash is one of the best refs we got. He's always fair and the kids love him."

Tory turned to see an average height, older African-American man with graying hair and a well-groomed mustache.

Ash held his hand out to him and smiled. "Hey Perry, how's it going?"

545

Perry shook his hand and patted him on the arm. "Glad you could make it. We had two refs call in sick and was afraid we'd have to cancel the games. I really appreciate you and your friend helping us out."

"Anytime. You know how much I love watching the kids dribble."

Perry laughed as he playfully elbowed Tory in the side. "And he doesn't mean the balls either."

Tory smiled.

Ash pulled his coat off and slung it over his shoulder. "Perry Stallings meet Tory Kafieri."

Perry winked at her. "So Ash has a girl finally. I was beginning to wonder if he'd ever settle down on one female."

Ash snorted. "Ah, you think too much."

"And T-Rex doesn't think enough."

Ash shook his head as a tall, well-built blond man approached them. "Good to see you, Talon. Even if you are nothing but a pain in my ass."

"You too." Talon hitched a thumb over his shoulder. "Was that your Busa outside?"

"Yeah."

"Sweet. Anytime you're ready to let it go, call me."

"Don't hold your breath," Ash said teasingly before he introduced them. "Talon this is Perry and Tory."

Talon shook their hands in turn and held onto Tory's as he saw the helmet she held by its strap in her left hand. He arched an inquisitive brow. "Matching Busa helmets?"

"I came with Ash," Tory explained.

He turned a curious eye to Ash.

Ash wiped the corner of his mouth with his thumb. "Friends, Celt. Don't make anything more out of it than that."

"Whatever you say, T-Rex. Whatever you say . . ." there was enough doubt in that tone to fill the Superdome.

Perry clapped his hands together. "Well, now that the two of you are here, I'll let the coaches know. You get settled and we'll be underway in just a few."

Ash looked past Talon to the bleachers behind him. "Sunshine with you?"

"Parking the car."

"Cool." Ash gently took Tory's arm and led her toward the small crowd of parents. "Let me get you situated."

Tory looked at his shoulder where his ever-present backpack was snuggled close. "You going to trust me to guard the magic backpack?"

He smiled. "Sure. I know where you live and I've seen where you sleep." He sat her down on the bleachers just as an exuberant, voluptuous brunette came in with a flurry of excitement.

Dressed in a flowing pink skirt and tunic that was covered with a painted denim jacket trimmed in pink lace, the woman headed straight for Ash and placed a quick kiss on this cheek. "How have you been, baby?"

"Decent." He indicated Tory with a tilt of his head. "Sunshine meet my friend Tory. Sunshine's Talon's wife."

Tory smiled as she shook Sunshine's hand. "The tall blond who can't shoot hoops?"

Sunshine's laugh was infectious as she looked at Talon proudly. "That's my baby. Ain't he beautiful?" She raised her hand at her husband. "Go Talon, show them how it's done," she shouted.

Ash turned and laughed as Talon made a shot that fell far from its mark.

"Well, maybe next time," Sunshine whispered under her breath before she shouted. "Good try, baby, good try! Next time you'll make a home run!"

Ash exchanged an amused grin with Tory. "Yeah and on that note let me go stop him from embarrassing himself further." He dropped his coat, helmet and backpack at her feet.

Tory smiled as he ran across the court, pulling a silver whistle out of his back pocket before he put it on over his head and blew it. Talon turned toward him and Ash made an ancient Celtic obscene gesture at him that luckily only Talon, Tory and possibly Sunshine would recognize as extremely offensive.

Talon glared at him. "You're lucky there are kids here, buddy."

Ash gave him an evil grin before he wrangled the kids toward their starting places.

547

Sunshine sat down beside her and pulled a bottle of water out of her giant organic wicker bag. "So how long have you known Ash?"

Tory watched the grace Ash showed as he moved fluidly around the kids who were so tiny compared to him. She didn't know why, but he reminded her of some ancient warrior trying to train them for battle. "Not very. About a week."

"And he brought you here?"

Tory shrugged, not really understanding his compassion herself. "My house was broken into and a good friend of mine killed last night. Ash was afraid to leave me alone."

Horror filled Sunshine's dark brown eyes as she reached out to touch Tory's arm. "Oh my God, sweetie . . . are you okay?"

Tory swallowed as she thought about Dimitri and grief overwhelmed her. He'd always been the jokester of their crew. Full of life and preciously sweet. She was really going to miss seeing him on the boat and hearing his good-natured taunts. "Not really. But I'm holding it together. One step at a time, right?"

Sunshine took her hand into hers and offered her a kind smile. "Absolutely. And if you need anything, you call us. Talon and I live outside of town and can be anywhere pretty quickly because he drives like a lunatic. Night or day, you need something, you call."

The warmth from this woman touched her deeply. They were strangers and yet Sunshine didn't care in the least. "Thank you. Ash is lucky to have you guys as friends."

Sunshine waved her words away as Ash blew the whistle and separated two of the boys who were trying to bite each other. Smiling a smile that warmed her heart, he tucked one of the boys under his arm as he moved him away from the other one before he set him on his feet.

"I don't know," Sunshine said wistfully. "I think we're more lucky to have him."

Yeah, Tory was beginning to feel lucky that she'd met Ash too. Though to be honest, she wished they'd met under a better set of circumstances than his embarrassing her. "How long have you guys known him?"

"A few years for me. A lifetime for Talon. The two of them go way back."

Tory looked at the tall blond who was probably no more than two or three years older than Ash. His short curly hair was sweaty and he had two tiny braids that fell from one temple. She was glad to meet someone Ash knew really well. "No kidding? Ash never really talks about the people he knows."

"Yeah, he's brutally evasive."

Tory nodded in agreement. "Good description."

Sunshine offered her a bottle of water. "But even so, you have to love Ash. He's one of the few truly reliable people you'll ever meet."

Taking the water from her hand, Tory watched as Ash showed Talon how to shoot a basket during a time-out, then he laughed and shook his head when Talon screwed it up again. This was the first time she'd seen him really having fun. Most of the time, he was so reserved and closed off—as if afraid of allowing anyone to have any kind of power over him. There was only one reason she could think of that he'd be like that.

"Ash had a hard childhood, didn't he?"

Sunshine frowned. "I don't know. I've heard mixed things from different people. Some say he was very privileged and rich."

Yeah there was something very wealthy and Old World about him. Dignified as if he were accustomed to only the best things in the world . . . like the handsewn jacket she wore. "He does seem to have a lot of money."

Sunshine snorted. "Oh no, hon. What he has now, he earns. Believe me. But no one I know—and I know a lot of people who've known him for many years—really knows anything about his past or his family. He just refuses to talk about it."

Which meant it had to be brutal. Why else would someone hide it? Thoughts of family should be comforting. She was forever thinking about hers and smiling. The fact that Ash had closed himself off entirely from the subject said it all.

They were sources of pain for him.

Her heart heavy, she watched as the game picked up again. Ash was actually adorable as he ran alongside the kids who could barely play. They bumped into each other and tripped onto the court. Ash would run to make sure they were okay before he picked them up and set them back on their feet.

She'd never seen anything quite like it. But they were all cute. Especially Ash in all his Goth glory.

Sunshine dug out a bag of cinnamon flavored oatcakes. "Want some?"

"Thanks," she said, taking one from the small bag.

As they snacked, a mother and a small boy in a wheelchair came in and parked beside them so that the boy could watch the game. The boy who had short black hair and bright blue eyes grimaced as if he were in pain while his mother gently stroked his back. He was an almost exact physical duplicate of his mother, except the boy had a smattering of freckles over the bridge of his nose.

Tory scooted down to sit closer to him. "Hi," she said, holding her hand out to him. "My name's Tory."

He looked at his mother to make sure it was okay to talk to her.

"His name's Toby."

"Toby?" Tory grinned at him. "Really? My friend Ash was playing a boy named Toby this morning on the Xbox."

Toby smiled through his tears. "That was me! I kicked his butt!"

"Toby," his mother chided, "such language. What have I told you about that?"

He sat taller in his chair. "Well, I did."

Tory introduced herself and Sunshine to Toby's mother. "So are you two here to watch Ash?"

Toby shook his head. "My brother Zack is number seven on the blue team."

"Oh," she said, spotting the boy with brown hair, "he's the best player on his team."

The buzzer sounded for halftime. Ash came running over. His cheeks were mottled with red from his exertion. He held his hand out for Toby to high five him. "Hey Tobinator. How you doing?"

Toby squealed in glee. "Can we play?" he asked Ash.

Ash looked at Trish. "Is it okay?"

She frowned in apprehension. "Be gentle. He had a hard session with his therapist today."

"Will do." Ash picked him up and cradled him against his chest before he returned to the court where the teams were practicing again.

Zack passed his brother the ball. Laughing, Toby caught it and Ash ran him at the basket so that he could slam dunk it in to the basket that had been lowered to accommodate their smaller size. He held Toby over his head and twisted him back and forth, making the boy squeal in delight.

Trish's eyes misted at the sight of Ash with her son. "I don't know what I'd do without that man."

Tory frowned. "What do you mean?"

Trish wiped at her eyes. "Toby and my husband were in a bad car wreck a year ago. Barry was killed instantly and Toby was partially paralyzed. For weeks in the hospital, Toby was unresponsive to everyone. He wouldn't eat or speak. And then one day Ash and a friend of his came in and were singing with the kids on Toby's floor, handing out gifts. When he saw Toby, he went over and the next thing I knew, he had Toby laughing again." She sniffed. "Just look at them out there . . . God love that man."

Ash was holding Toby low to the ground so he could dribble the ball while his brother tried to block him. Lifting him up, Ash feigned to the right and ran at the basket so Toby could slam dunk it again. The boy lifted his arms up and whooped in triumph. Ash tickled him before he cradled him in his arms and ran him back over to his mother.

He set Toby back in his wheelchair and wiped his arm over his sweaty face. "All right, Tobe, we have to get back to the game. But Zack wants a rematch afterwards."

"He's on!"

Ash ruffled his hair before he glanced to Tory. "You doing okay?"

"Fine."

"Cool. But stay away from Sunshine's oatcakes. Talon says they're disgusting."

"Hey!" Sunshine shouted indignantly. "I'll get you for that, Ash."

Laughing, he stood up and returned to the center of the court.

"How are you doing, Toby?" Trish asked, her voice full of concern. "Did that make you hurt more?"

He beamed. "Nope. I feel great. Ash says I'll be walking again this time next year."

His mother winced as if the thought made her ache. "Oh baby . . . you know what the doctors think."

Toby lifted his chin. "I believe Ash. He says I'll be walking and I will. Just watch and see."

Tory smiled at the little guy. "That's the spirit."

Toby took her hand while they watched the rest of the game and cheered for his brother Zack.

When the game ended, Talon grabbed a ball to shoot again.

Ash scoffed at him. "Stop embarrassing the gene pool, Celt."

"Shut-up, T-Rex." He shot and missed.

Ash came to stand in front of Toby, arms akimbo. "Ready, squirt?"

"Ready."

Ash picked him up and looked at Tory. "You know how to play?"

"It's been a while, but yeah."

His grin taunted her. "Want to join us for a game?"

"Love to."

Talon handed her the ball as he came to sit beside Sunshine and drink some water. "I'm tired of being laughed at. Go avenge me."

Tory took her jacket off before she bounced the ball on the floor. Ash held Toby to his chest. "All right, Toby, let's annihilate the kyria."

Toby frowned. "Kyria?"

"Lady."

"Oh. Okay."

Tory feigned left and twisted around them as she ran at a basket. She was almost to it when Toby grabbed the ball and Ash put him up on his shoulders. Shouting in glory, Toby shot it at the basket and scored.

"And the crowd goes wild. Ahhhhh," Ash mocked the sound of cheering fans.

"Hey Ash?" Zack asked, running up to them. "Can I dunk one too?"

"Sure." He held Toby out to Tory who took the boy. He wrapped his little arms around her neck and made her melt while Ash grabbed his brother and put him up on his shoulders.

Zack dunked the ball and held his hands up in triumph while he bounced on Ash's shoulders.

Trish came forward, shaking her head at them. "Okay boys, tell Ash thank you, but it's time for us to go and let the next team have the court."

Toby pouted like a pro.

"Aw, mom," Zack whined as Ash set him on his feet.

Then Ash took Toby from her arms and carried him back to his wheelchair. "Don't worry, squirt. We'll beat Zack in a couple of weeks when I'm back in town."

"Okay and don't forget next Saturday! Nine a.m. sharp!"

Ash gave him a staunch Roman salute. "Ever at your service, my lord and tormentor." He brushed his hand over Zack's hair. "You played unbelievably well today. Keep practicing, kiddo."

"Will do. Bye Ash."

"Bye guys."

Tory walked up to him as they left. "You are so not an asshole."

He glanced down at her, making her wish she could see his eyes through his dark sunglasses. "Trust me, I can be. But I have a height requirement before I break ass on someone."

Talon snorted as he walked past them. "Yeah, take it from someone who's had his ass broken by him. Ash ain't all fun and games."

Without thinking, Tory put her hands on Ash's hips and leaned against his back. The moment she did, she realized she'd made a mistake as a wave of desire hit her so forcefully, it was all she could do not to pull his lips down to hers. Oh dear heaven, the man was sweaty, but he didn't stink at all. Instead, he smelled so good she wanted to take a bite out of him.

And all she wanted to do was run her hands down that hard chest and nibble him until he begged her for more.

Ash couldn't breathe as he hardened to the point of pain. Thank the gods he wasn't wearing tight pants. And the thought of her hands only being a few inches away from his cock only made him ache more.

Clearing her throat, she stepped back. "How many more games do you have to referee?"

"Two."

"Okay, I'm going back to my seat to eat some oatcakes. Good luck with the kids . . . oh and my favorite has to be the little guy over there, picking his nose."

Ash didn't speak as she went to sit by Sunshine. It took every bit of his willpower not to pull her back to him.

Talon handed a ball to him. "You all right, T-Rex?"

"I'm fine, why?"

"Cause in all the centuries I've known you, I've *never* seen you do that with a woman before."

"Do what?"

Talon laughed. "Boy, I don't think you need me to tell you what *that* is." He cast an incredibly quick glance down to Ash's groin.

Ash went ramrod stiff as he discreetly looked down to make sure he wasn't standing at attention. Well, he was, he just wanted to make sure it wasn't obvious.

Thankfully, it wasn't.

Which begged the question . . . how did Talon know?

Out of nowhere a ball came at his head. Ash caught it. Picking up his whistle, he blew it to call the players to start the game.

Tory was still rattled by what had happened. By how badly she wanted a piece of that man . . .

Sunshine wiped at the crumbs on her skirt. "Are you sure the two of you are just friends?"

Tory tried to appear nonchalant. "What do you mean?"

"I have never seen Ash allow someone to touch him from behind before. He normally bolts across the room if someone even comes near his back. The fact he didn't even twitch . . . highly suspicious."

Tory frowned at that new disclosure. "I didn't know that bothered him. He rode me on the back of his motorcycle over here."

Sunshine gave her a wide-eyed stare. "Touch you, girl. You are special."

"You think?"

"Honey, trust me. What you just did was a freaking miracle and I really wish you could appreciate how amazing it was."

Tory took a sip of water as she watched Ash with a set of older kids. And as she watched him and pieced together what little she knew about his past, she had a really bad feeling about his childhood.

There was only one reason she could think of that it would bother him that much for someone to stand behind him. And the thought of it made her sick to her stomach.

"Every time I've ever made the mistake of trusting someone . . . it was a mistake that I regretted and paid for dearly. I'm really happy that no one has hurt you, but I haven't been so lucky, okay?"

His words rang ominously in her ears as she watched him calling a foul.

Please let me be wrong . . .

But the more she thought about it, the more sense it made. Someone had hurt him badly in the past. So much so that he couldn't even deal with it.

It was why he hid his eyes from the world. Why he pierced a face that was so perfectly handsome it beckoned to be touched . . . Why he dressed in those FU clothes. It was to keep everyone away from him.

Closing her eyes, it was all she could do not to go to him and just hold him. To promise him that he was safe. How stupid a thought was that? The man was huge and he was fierce. The last thing he needed was *her* protection.

But he hadn't always been a man . . .

Tory winced as she remembered what he'd said about his parents. What had they done to him?

She didn't speak much until the last game was over. Ash and Talon stayed on the opposite side to talk to Perry for a few minutes.

Sunshine was packing up as Talon came over. "Did you have fun, baby?" she asked her husband.

Talon grinned at her. "I'm thinking we ought to make a few of those small things for ourselves."

Sunshine laughed. "Anytime you're ready. My mother is more than willing to be a grandma."

Talon kissed her passionately. "Yeah, we definitely need to get home and practice . . ."

Sunshine pulled back with a smile before she handed him her purse. "Lead the way."

Talon sucked his breath in before he turned to Tory. "It was nice meeting you."

"You too."

Sunshine hooked her arm in his. "Don't forget what I told you. If you need us . . ."

"Will do."

Ash pulled the whistle over his head as he approached her and tucked it back into his pocket. "I hope you weren't too bored on the sidelines."

"No, it was actually fun. You have great friends."

"Yeah, I do."

He bent over to pick up his coat. The moment he did, she decided to test her theory. She reached down and lightly brushed her hand under the band that held his ponytail over his neck. Her ring caught in his hair and pulled it.

Hissing in anger, he grabbed her hand and snatched it away from his hair. "Don't you ever touch me like that again." His growl was so feral, she actually thought he might hit her.

She swallowed against the severe lump in her throat. "I would never hurt you, Ash."

He didn't respond as he jerked his backpack and helmet up from the floor and stalked toward the doors.

Grabbing the jacket and helmet she'd worn, Tory followed him, wanting to cry. "Ash?"

He didn't stop until he reached his bike. He put his keys between his teeth before he shrugged his coat on.

"Ash?" she repeated. "I'm sorry. I didn't mean to make you angry."

Ash tried to calm down. She'd done nothing wrong and he knew it. It was just . . .

He ground his teeth at the memories. He'd shave his hair off except the only thing he hated more than having his hair grabbed was feeling something, especially a breath or breeze against the nape of his neck. He hated people breathing in his ears or standing close to him, especially at his back. Even after all this time, one touch, one breath could make him feel worthless all over again. Make him feel . . .

Like a whore.

But Tory wasn't a part of that past. She wasn't Artemis who used those tactics to remind him of his place in her world. To remind him that he should be grateful he was allowed any kind of dignity.

Tory was simply a woman who'd touched a man not knowing the scars that lined his soul.

He let out a long breath as he calmed down. "I'm sorry I overreacted. I just don't like people grabbing my hair."

"Duly noted. Will never happen again."

He nodded.

Tory lifted her helmet as she again watched him close his eyes, remove his sunglasses and put his helmet on. Was he aware of what he did or was it so habitual that he didn't even realize his actions?

"Ash?"

He turned toward her as he fastened his chin strap.

"I think you have the most beautiful eyes I've ever seen."

Ash froze as those words touched him. But then Artemis had said that to him once . . . and then cursed him for them later. *Don't be suckered in.*

"Thanks," he said, his voice hollow as he slung his leg over to straddle the bike. Then he set his backpack over the gas tank while she climbed on behind him.

She slid up against his back, her thighs intimately pressed against his buttocks.

He waited for that familiar disgust to fill him, but it didn't. And when she wrapped her arms around his waist and leaned against his back, he actually savored it. Starting the engine, he looked down at her tiny hands that she had laced together over his stomach.

He'd never allowed another soul to ride on his bike with him . . . not even Simi.

She squeezed him in a tight hug and it was all he could do not to haul her off this bike and screw her like an animal in the parking lot until the fire he felt was quenched. But he'd never do that to her. He wasn't an animal and she was . . .

There were no words to describe her. She was infuriating, stubborn.

And wonderful. Absolutely wonderful.

Touching her hands with his, he gave a light squeeze before he took the handlebars. "Hold tight."

"Will do, Achimou."

He laughed and cringed simultaneously at the Greek endearment of his name. Since the true pronunciation was Ack-uh-rahn the shortened form of it was Ack-ee-moo. Something he'd always feared someone using. So he'd learned to Anglicize his name to Asheron and then later to Ash to keep anyone from doing what she'd just done.

Yet, for reasons that were totally beyond him, he didn't mind her doing it.

Amazed by that, he headed out of the parking lot, back toward her side of town. They hadn't gone far when he felt a weird sensation go down his spine . . .

They were being followed.

Looking around, he saw a gray sedan closing in on them while the car in front of them was slowing down. Ash wanted to pass the car ahead, but there was too much traffic in the other lane.

Suddenly the car in front of him stopped.

He slammed on brakes at the same time a man sat up in the back seat of the car in front of them with a gun and opened fire. "Hold on!" he roared as the bullets slammed into him. Had he been human, he'd be dead. As it was, he put a shield around them to keep Tory from being hit and him from taking any more damage.

Gearing the bike down, he gunned it full throttle and shot around the car to the right, onto the sidewalk to get away from them.

Tory was terrified as she clung to Ash with everything she

had. She wasn't sure how the gunshots had missed them, but she was grateful they had.

Now she saw the two cars racing behind them.

Ash took a corner so low to the ground he was amazed Tory stayed with him even with the shield around her. She hadn't been kidding. She had to be an experienced rider to take the corner and not fall off.

He considered using his powers to get them out of this, but that would tip her off big time that he wasn't human and she would lose her mind over the fact that they literally popped back into her yard. No, he was a god. He could surely outrun them.

At least until a third car cut them off. He swung to the left at the same time a fourth car drove straight for them. That car clipped his back tire.

Cursing, he felt the bike slipping out from under him. Before he could react, they went flying off the bike. Making sure to keep Tory shielded as she slid, Ash hit the ground hard as he skidded on the road.

Damn the consequences.

He was about to teleport them out of this right when the car that had hit them ran him over. Ash bellowed in pain as the front then rear tires crushed his legs. Unable to focus on anything but the agony, he dropped the shield around Tory at the same time she went slamming into a set of garbage cans that were lined around a pole.

Tears of pain filled his eyes as he struggled to breathe. He replaced the shield around Tory to protect her from any more harm and to knock her out as he rose to his feet.

Pain hit him hard. He might be a god, but he wasn't immune to damage. It wouldn't kill him. It just hurt like hell.

The men opened fire on him.

Ash slung his hand out and turned the bullets back on them. Fury rode him hard as he killed them as mercilessly as they'd tried to kill Tory.

All except one . . .

A small, wiry man, he was cowering beside the brown Audi sedan that had run him over.

"Who the fuck are you?" Ash snarled angrily.

The man didn't answer.

Ash grabbed him up by his throat and slammed him against the trunk of the car. "Answer me!"

But then he didn't have to . . . In that instant, Ash saw everything about him and the organization he served. *Don't kill me please . . .*

He heard the voices from the man's past. Voices of people who'd begged for their lives and this prick had killed them without caring.

So be it.

Ash crushed his windpipe and left him sprawled dead on the trunk of the car not caring who saw what he was doing. Still not satisfied, he looked at Tory who lay unmoving.

As he started toward her, he realized his legs were torn open and most of his body was covered with road rash because she'd been wearing his protective jacket. But none of that mattered as he knelt down on the ground beside her. Carefully, he pulled her helmet off to see the bruises on the side of her pale face and the blood on her lips.

He threw his own helmet aside. Fear and grief racked him as he felt for her pulse. She had to be okay. She had to be . . . His stomach knotted until he touched the faint beat.

He wanted to cry in relief. She was still alive, but she was weak from internal injuries.

Ash held his hand out for his backpack which flashed into his grip. Slinging it over his back, he picked Tory up and teleported them to Tulane Hospital. He cradled her against him as he limped painfully into the emergency room entrance.

Luckily it was someone he knew, Wanda, at the front desk.

A heavyset African-American woman, she gaped as she saw him walking toward her. His leg buckled from the pain and he almost fell. But he wouldn't do that. Not while he held Tory. He had to get her help.

"Oh my God, Ash! What happened?"

He couldn't speak as he felt Tory expel one last shallow breath before she died in his arms.

CHAPTER TEN

Ash sank to his knees in the middle of the ER as the pain from his injuries and an overwhelming, unbelievable wave of grief and anger assailed him. He didn't understand why, but he couldn't even breathe at the thought of Tory not being here.

"Tory," he snarled, holding her against his shoulder as he cupped her cold face in his hand and gently shook her body. "Don't you dare fucking die on me. Tory!"

Wanda was there with a doctor and orderlies. Standing behind him, she took his shoulders as the doctor pulled Tory out of his arms.

Ash wanted to fight them and yet he knew he couldn't. They had to save her. *Don't interfere. Don't. Interfere.*

Wanda's touch was gentle, but it wasn't the touch he wanted to feel. "Ash?" she said, her voice breaking.

He couldn't respond as he heard them calling for a Code Blue. They ripped Tory out of his arms and put her on a gurney before they whisked her away.

Ash knelt there on the floor, his bloodied coat fanned out, watching them run with her through the hallway while his soul screamed out for vengeance against those who'd hurt her.

"I think he's in shock."

Someone touched him. Ash growled, shoving the intern back as he came to his feet and stood there with his legs wide apart. "I'm not in shock. I'm fine."

The intern passed a wide-eyed stare to Wanda.

"Sweetie," Wanda said, touching him lightly on the arm. "You're not all right." Her gaze skimmed down his ravaged body. "You are very hurt and you need to let the nice doctor look at you."

Ash wiped at something warm that was running down his face. Thinking it was sweat, he glanced down to see his hand covered in blood that was pouring out of his temple. How could he explain to them that he'd heal? If they weren't staring at him, he'd make all the injuries vanish . . .

The one who couldn't heal herself was Tory. She was the one who was dead.

"I'm fine. I swear. I just need to go to the bathroom."

The intern was still suspicious but no one stopped him as he left them and entered the small room. Rage so raw he could taste it scorched him. He wanted blood and he could feel his eyes turning red. He manifested a pair of sunglasses over them before someone came out of a stall and caught sight of him in all his immortal glory.

His fury was so great that it arced a burst of power so strong, it shorted out the lights over him. Sparks rained down and sizzled while he struggled for control.

Save her . . .

With a mere thought he could heal her back to normal. No cuts. No wounds.

One stone throw and everything changes . . . He heard Savitar's voice in his head and he hated that part of his conscience. His entire human life had been ruined because of gods playing with his destiny. Of people bringing him back from the dead.

Falling to his knees, he screamed out in raw, unmitigated pain as he buried his face against his arm and struggled for sanity. He couldn't do it to Tory. He couldn't risk what

562

saving her might do to the world. If she was supposed to die, she'd have to die. He refused to tamper with fate.

Fuck fate! You're a god, damn you, Apostolos. Seize your destiny! Save her!

Just because you can, doesn't mean you should. It was the one code he lived his entire life by.

"Don't die, Tory," he whispered, knowing he wouldn't forsake his oath. He wouldn't be like the ones who'd screwed him over by tampering with what should have been left alone.

Disgusted with his cowardice, he glanced at the mirror and flinched. No wonder they'd been so freaked out. He looked like walking death. His face was battered, his clothes torn and bloodied. He would change them, but then the staff would get suspicious if he walked out totally repaired. So he cleaned up his face and went back outside where Wanda was waiting. His heart stopped as he saw her holding the leather jacket that Tory had been wearing.

Wanda offered him a kind smile. "Your friend was resuscitated. They've taken her into surgery."

He took the jacket as a wave of relief washed over him. "Thank you, Wanda."

She nodded. "You sure you don't want to see a doctor?"

"Positive."

She shook her head as if disappointed by his decision. "Well I'll take you up to the waiting room. Do you have any of her information to fill out the paperwork?"

"No, not really. But you know I'm good for the bill. You do whatever it takes, damn the cost."

"I know, baby." She patted his arm as she led him toward the elevators. "We do need the names of her next of kin though."

"Megeara and Theo Kafieri. Theo is her grandfather who lives in New York and her cousin Geary lives in Greece."

"All right. I'll show you up and then come back with the forms."

Ash didn't say anything as she led him into the elevators where he'd been a thousand times while coming in here with Simi to do volunteer work. That was how he'd met Wanda. Her father had been on one of the wards where they'd brought presents at Christmas a couple of years ago after her father had had bypass surgery. They'd been friends ever since.

She took him to a small room that was sterile and cold . . . just like him.

"You need anything?"

He shook his head. What he needed was to know how Tory was doing. But his powers told him nothing.

"Okay. I'll be back."

He sat down to rest his legs that were still throbbing from the car having crushed them. As he moved, he caught a whiff of Tory's scent clinging to his jacket. Holding it to his nose, he inhaled her and wanted to cry. The fear of losing her actually made his hands shake and he didn't understand why. They barely knew each other.

Yet he wanted to storm upstairs and heal her.

All things go rotten. His mind roared at him for allowing himself to care about a mere human. Look at how great Artemis had treated him in the beginning. She'd bought him gifts and made sure he was comfortable, and then she'd turned on him the first time he hadn't pleased her. It was progressive entrapment that always turned against him.

Tory hated you first and then liked you . . .

He smiled at the memory of her throwing the hammer at his head. She was prickly. And smart. And funny. Most of all, she treated him like he was normal. Of course she didn't know he wasn't, but unlike other people she didn't grope him or make him nervous that she was a hair's breadth from trying to screw him.

She treated him like he was just another guy on the street.

"Ash?"

He looked up to see Tory's friend Kim in front of him. Her face was lined with fear and concern as she looked at him and the bloodied jacket he held.

"What are you doing here?" he asked her.

"I work here. Remember? I'm an L&D nurse. I was told by an ER friend that Tory had come in. What happened? Are you okay? Shouldn't you be downstairs being treated?"

He shook his head. "We wrecked on my bike."

Kim swallowed as her eyes filled with tears. "Is she okay?"

"They said she was in surgery. I'm waiting to hear."

She sat down beside him. "No offense, but you look pretty torn up too."

"I'll live."

She gave him a look of supreme doubt. "Why don't you give me your cell number and I'll call you the minute I hear something about Tory. You know I won't leave and you need to see a doctor and get cleaned up." She narrowed her gaze on the hole in his jeans that revealed his ravaged skin. "By the way, that wasn't a request."

Ash nodded as he realized that she was right. He wasn't doing anyone any good like this and he had another matter to attend to. Giving her his number, he left and headed for the elevator. The instant he was alone, he flashed himself to Artemis's temple on Olympus.

His anger mounting, he flung open the doors to her temple with such force, they clamored against the walls. Her koris shrieked before they ran out to leave Artemis alone with him.

Artemis sat up in a huff as she raked him with a feral glare. "What is your wreckage?"

"Damage," he corrected as he stalked toward her. "Can't you tell?"

"What? That you look like crap? You're filthy and you smell. Why didn't you bathe before you came to me?"

"Because a car ran over me, after I was chased by a group of men shooting at me, Artie."

"And that's my fault? How?"

He took a deep breath and counted to ten before he killed the mother of his daughter. Though to be honest, Katra was a grown woman who didn't really need her mother anymore . . . "Does the Atlantikoinonia ring any bells for you?"

"Yes, they do. So what?" That unrepentant stare went through him like an exploding grenade.

When he spoke it was through his clenched teeth as he fought for the strength not to lash out and hurt her. "They tried to kill me, Artemis. And as you can plainly see, I'm not really thrilled over it."

Her face paled. "They weren't supposed to touch you. Ever."

"No," he said, his voice dropping to the low cadence of a demon's, "their orders were to terminate an innocent human on sight. I just happened to be with her when they struck."

She gave him a droll look as she dismissed his concern and anger. "Why do you even care about the human? I was only trying to protect you."

"No you weren't. I know what's in the missing journal. You don't give a shit about my dignity. It's your own ass you're trying to save."

She scooted back on the couch, trying to escape him. "Does this mean you're the one who took the book?"

He paused. "I thought your people had it."

She curled her lip at him. "If we had it, why would we be after the bitch?"

The insult to Tory pissed him off even more. "She's not a bitch, Artemis. Now call your dogs off. I mean it."

She rose to her knees to meet him without cowering. "What if I don't do what you want? They're innocent humans too. Are you going to kill *them*?"

His hands itched to wrap themselves around that perfect, swan neck of hers and wring it until he had satisfaction. "I am not playing with you."

"And neither am I," she shrieked. "That journal threatens everything and I won't stop until I have it."

He hissed in anger, but she didn't retreat.

She tossed her head back, proud in her defiance. "You won't hurt me and I know it. You love Katra too much. She would be devastated to know her father killed her mother. I should have introduced you two a long time ago. So long as I have her love, I know I'm completely safe from your wrath."

He held his hand up as if he'd choke her anyway, but in the end, they both knew the truth. She was right. As angry as he was, he couldn't hurt her because it would tear his daughter apart.

Artemis smiled seductively. "I've missed you." She slid her arm around his waist.

Ash shoved her away from him. "If you value your worthless life, stay away from me."

He flashed himself from Olympus to Katoteros.

Urian was on his way out the door of the main hall as Ash entered it. "What the hell happened to you? You have a bad run-in with Artemis?"

Ash curled his lip at the ex-Daimon. "One day, Urian, I'm going to bitch-slap you so hard your ears will ring for eternity."

Urian laughed. "But it won't be today, mostly because you don't look like you could do much of anything to hurt someone. Seriously what happened?"

"I wrecked my bike."

Urian rolled his eyes in disbelief. "Fine, don't tell me. Whatever."

Ash let out a bitter laugh as he realized how preposterous that sounded. He'd never laid a bike down before in his life. Upset, angry at Artemis and worried over Tory, he paused to look at the Daimon. "You know, Uri, there's something seriously wrong with me."

"And you're just now figuring this out? Damn, you're the poster child for slow learning."

Curling his lip, Ash started past him.

Urian pulled him to a stop. "That was a joke, Acheron. You were supposed to laugh."

"I'm not in a laughing mood."

Urian nodded in understanding. "So what really happened?"

Ash hesitated. It wasn't in his nature to talk to anyone about anything. And yet he had one burning question that wouldn't go away. "What is so wrong with me that I'm only turned on by women who hate my guts?"

Urian snorted at his question. "You're right. That's sick." He clapped his hand on Ash's shoulder. "One word for you, my brother. Therapy. Get some."

"That's three words."

"It needed expanding . . . and speaking of expanding things, you have a visitor inside who wants to be your new best friend."

Ash cursed as he realized who was waiting for him. "Who the fuck let him out?"

"The girl ghost who wants the two of you to kiss and make up."

Ash ground his teeth together. "I'd rather be hit in the head with the tack hammer Tory threw at me."

"Tory?"

"Long story." Ash let out a tired sigh. "Thanks for the warning. I'll go deal with him."

Ash headed for the doors that led to his throne room. As he passed over the seal in the floor, his clothes changed to his Atlantean formesta and black leather pants. He threw open the doors to find Styxx waiting on the other side.

He paused at the sight of his twin who always caught him off-guard. Every time he looked at Styxx he was reminded of his past. Of the brutality. Of the injustice of their lives.

And against his will, he heard Estes growling drunk in his ear as he held him down by his hair and violated him. *"How dare you make me want you like you do. I hate you for what you do to me, you disgusting whore. I. Hate. You."* The only thing his uncle had ever freely given him had been blows and insults.

Now Styxx stood before him, a perfect replica with short blond hair and normal blue eyes that Ash would have killed to possess.

Ash looked away as he reminded himself that he was a god and not a worthless whore at the mercy of his brother's cruelty. "I'm really not in the mood to deal with you today, Styxx. What little patience I have was eaten alive about two minutes ago."

"I know. I can sense your moods."

Ash narrowed his gaze threateningly.

"It was a gift," Styxx said sarcastically, "from Artemis when she threw me into Tartarus and gave me your memories. I'm only here to ask you one favor."

Ash felt his skin flash to blue as anger pierced him fervently. "You would dare ask a favor of me?"

Styxx stepped back and nodded before he went down on one knee. "I ask as your brother and as a supplicant to a god."

Ash would have laughed had he not been so angry. What game was Styxx playing with him now? "As a supplicant, what sacrifice do you offer for this favor?"

"My heart."

Ash scowled. "I don't understand."

Styxx looked up with a sincere gaze that scalded him. "I offered you my loyalty and it wasn't enough. So in this, I offer my heart to you. If I lie or betray you, you can rip it out over and over again. Chain me next to Prometheus on his rock."

If he ever betrayed him again, he would. "And what favor do you ask?"

Styxx's eyes were haunted before he whispered. "Let me go. I can't live here anymore, isolated from people. Alone. Banished. I just want the chance to live a life that neither of us ever had a chance to live."

Any other time, Ash would have laughed in his face. But today he was weak with understanding and sympathy for the very thing he wanted himself. What had been done to them hadn't been fair. Styxx's life shouldn't have been tied to his and because of Acheron, Styxx had lost his family, his life and his home.

Maybe a fresh start would do them both good. "Fine, brother. You'll have everything you need to start over."

Throwing his hand out, he flashed Styxx to New York where the prince would blend in best with the population. It was also an area where he would hopefully never lay eyes on his brother again.

Besides, Styxx was right. He could kill him at any time. Let the man have a life if he could find it. Honestly, he wished him luck.

Most of all he wished Styxx a peace that seemed to forever elude them both.

"Simi?" He'd been holding her on his body, against her will.

She pulled off his arm and manifested beside him. Yawning, she glared at him in aggravation. "Akri done left his Simi on his arm for far too long. She done got tired and cranky. Why you treat the Simi like that, akri?"

He cupped her cheek in his hand before he kissed her

forehead. "I'm sorry, baby. It's why I brought you here. You should stay for a bit with your sister and Alexion."

She frowned up at him. "But what about you, akri? You've been so sad, but you wouldn't let the Simi come off you . . ."

"I know. I have things I have to deal with and I don't want you hurt. You stay here, Simykee."

She beamed at the endearment he hadn't used since she was a baby demon. "Only if akri promises he will call for his Simi if he needs her."

"I promise."

She held her finger up to him. "Good, cause the Simi knows akri can't break his word."

He smiled and pulled out his black American Express card for her. "Go shop."

She squeed before she ran to the TV and turned it on.

Wanting to be alone, Ash walked through the palace even though he could teleport. There were some times when walking and just being normal meant more to him than all of his god powers combined.

Just because you can, doesn't mean you should. There were some things that didn't need to be done. It was why none of the beings he'd consulted with would tell him shit about his future. Why he didn't heal Tory. There were some lessons, even hard ones, that everyone had to learn. Even the gods.

But right now, he didn't want to learn anything else. He wanted solace and comfort and there was no one for him to turn to to get it. So he entered his bedroom and picked up his guitar from its floor stand. He had a couple of dozen guitars spread throughout the palace here and the various apartments that he kept all over the world, but this one . . .

This was his baby. A Fender James Burton Telecaster with a maple neck and black body covered with red paisley flames, it had the fullest sound he'd ever heard. Sure he had more expensive guitars, but to him nothing played sweeter or smoother than this one.

Simi had even carved a message for him into the back of it. *Allagapi akri, Simi*. Charonte for "Simi loves her akri."

Ash smiled every time he saw that and his heart swelled with love for her. She could make him smile no matter how upset or sad he was, but she couldn't comfort him today.

He sat down on the bed and just started strumming. Before he knew it, he was playing Pink Floyd's "Wish You Were Here." It was a song that had haunted him since the first time he'd heard it. It was like the writer had known exactly what was in his heart. It was all about the decisions that changed a life and how perceptions could change any and all situations and feelings.

The problem was right now his feelings were so twisted and conflicting that he didn't even know how to begin to sort through them. Torn between what he should do and what he wanted to do.

Torn between three women who were at odds with each other and with him. His mother who wanted to destroy the world, Artemis who wanted to kill Tory, and Tory who wanted to expose him to save her father's reputation.

Unable to stand it, he got up and tossed the guitar on his bed.

"I am a god."

But what good did it really do him? He was still ensnared by Artemis, controlled by her. He was no less afraid now than he'd been as a human. In fact he was more so because now his powers were absolute. With one whispered word, he could end the world. His decisions didn't affect just his life, they could affect everyone's.

Look what he'd done to Nick. Had Ash still been human, he'd have only beat Nick up for sleeping with Simi. As a god, he'd not only caused Nick to kill himself, but in order to bring that commanded fate into being, Nick's mother had been murdered as well as the sister of his friends Tabitha and Amanda.

He hated these powers. Most of all, he hated the responsibility. "I just want to be alone . . ."

A knock on his door intruded on his thoughts.

Ash let out a tired breath as he dreaded what was happening now. "Yeah?"

The door opened to show Urian standing there, looking at him with a guarded expression. "You're really not right, are you?"

Ash narrowed his gaze. "I hope you mean that the way I'm going to take it. Otherwise, in the mood I'm in, you might get your ass kicked."

Urian laughed. "Yeah I do." He entered the room and shut the door. "Look, I heard you when you came in. Not what you said, but what was underneath it. I know it's in my best interest to stay out of it. However, you saved my life once, even though I didn't want you to at the time, and I feel like maybe I should return the favor."

Ash frowned at him as those words pricked at the times in his life when he'd been brought back from death against his will. "I shouldn't have interfered with that, Urian, and I'm sorry for the pain you live with because of it."

Urian's eyes were full of bittersweet torment. "You know, it's all right. If I'd died, Phoebe would have followed me to the grave anyway." Phoebe had been Urian's wife. They'd met when Stryker had sent Urian after her to kill her. Instead he'd fallen in love with her and turned her into a Daimon like him so that they could be together. That forbidden love that had cost him his life and Stryker had killed Phoebe in a fit of anger.

Urian cleared his throat. "Unlike me, she wasn't capable of taking a human life, even if the human deserved to die. The only way she could have continued living would have been to feed from another Daimon and that she wouldn't have done either. So you didn't really change her fate by saving me. My father was going to kill her regardless."

But if Urian had stayed dead, he wouldn't have witnessed Phoebe's death and he wouldn't live with the constant pain of it.

"Besides, if I'd died, my niece and nephews wouldn't have someone to threaten their dad when he's overprotective of them." Urian smiled sadly. "I'm the only uncle they have. Kids need an uncle, you know?"

Not from Ash's point of view, but that was a different wound. "So why the sudden girlspeak, Urian? Neither one of us is really into discussing our feelings . . . and no offense, I like the fact we don't."

Urian's gaze burned him with its passion. "I do too most times and I'm truly grateful you don't pry, but as a man who defied everything he once valued in this world and one who sacrificed the love of a father he worshiped . . . even though it ended badly, the days I had with Phoebe were worth *every* wound I've suffered."

He moved closer to Ash. "I know what it's like to be torn between a love so pure it burns you deep down in a place you didn't know someone could touch you and between your oath and duties. Between the love of a father you've always known and one you know you can depend on forever versus a love that's new and untested. But you know what I learned? It's a lot easier to live without my father's love than it is to live without Phoebe's. I just thought you ought to know that."

Ash didn't speak as Urian left him alone. But he did feel the fissure of power in the air behind him. It was a sensation he knew well.

Jaden.

"That just makes you want to vomit doesn't it?"

Ash arched a brow at the caustic words.

Jaden folded his arms over his chest as he leaned against the wall so that his long brown coat fell open. "Lovey-dovey bullshit. Now let me tell you about what happens when you betray everything you hold dear and the bitch doesn't return the favor. Oh wait, you know that lesson already. The problem is you take the leap and you don't know until it's too late to pull back if you're going to land on a foam-covered mattress or jagged rocks where you lie impaled, slowly bleeding and wishing you'd just die already."

Ash scoffed at the vivid imagery. "You are such a bitter shit."

Jaden shrugged. "My bitterness comes with good company which is normally you."

It was true. They both knew betrayal and they both knew ultimate suffering and the scars it left on the soul and heart. "Why are you here?"

Jaden rolled his eyes. "Your demon is calling me to barter with for a new bag. Thought her daddy might want to take her shopping before she makes me an offer I can't refuse and I make you one really unhappy god—not that I'd care, but since we've been known to help each other out from time to time . . ."

"I appreciate the warning."

"Yeah well, it's what happens when we spoil the things we love. They don't always understand the boundaries and their ridiculous wants can get us killed if we're not careful."

Ash inclined his head in understanding. Though to be honest, he didn't know what had caused Jaden to become the demon broker. If there was ever a being who was less communicative about his past than Ash, it was Jaden. And in all these centuries, Ash had never met a creature yet who knew exactly how Jaden had come to be what he was.

Jaden offered him a sinister smirk. "Bed the woman until neither of you can walk, and get her out of your system. Remember, no matter what they are or where they come from, all women have one simple birth defect. BPD."

"BPD?"

"Bitch Personality Disorder."

Ash laughed bitterly. "Are you sure they didn't misspell your name on your birth certificate? I'll bet if you check, your real name is Jaded."

Instead of answering, Jaden grimaced as he rubbed at his neck as if it were burning. "You know what? I'll trade you my demons for your Dark-Hunters any day. You haven't seen crybabies until you deal with a freakin' demon who is pissed he sold his soul or something else and things didn't turn out just the way he or she envisioned it." He curled his lips. "Demons without backbones should be shot. I'll catch you on-line Saturday." Jaden vanished.

Ash shook his head. He didn't envy the man his role as go between. As bad as the gods were, he'd hate to have to deal with the primary source and while immortals were annoying, they didn't carry the kind of power a demon did and as a rule, they weren't quite so . . . impulsive.

Not that any of this mattered to him at present. The only thing really on his mind was Tory and the bastards out to kill her.

They were still out there. Damn it, he'd gotten so tangled in other matters that he forgot about the fact that the Atlantikoinonia was still gunning for her. He had to get back to the hospital and protect her.

He started to flash out, then remembered he needed to speak with Simi first. She lay on the floor alone, cell phone in hand, ready to shop. "Sim?"

She didn't look at him. "Not now, akri. *Kirk's Folly* is about to come on."

He turned the TV off with his powers, making her shriek in protest. "Don't bother Jaden again."

She looked up at him and pouted. "But Xirena say he can get the Simi anything she wants. All the Simi has to do is tell him what she will exchange for it so it won't cost akri money so I offered him my boots, but he say no, Simi. I don't like no, Simi."

Ash rubbed his head. "Don't listen to Xirena, Sim. Listen to your akri. Just put it on my card like always and don't barter with Jaden for anything. Ever."

She gave him a childlike smile. "Fine. Can we have TV now?"

He turned it back on.

She went back to ignoring him.

Hoping she could stay out of trouble for the next few days, he returned to the hospital. Pam was now in the waiting room where he'd been earlier.

"Any word?" he asked.

"Not yet. Kim went to check." She skimmed his body which was now covered with his long duster, a gray hoodie and black shirt and jeans. "You don't look as near to death as Kim said you did."

He shrugged as he pushed his sleeves up on his arms. "A shower does wonders for a body."

"So they tell me."

Ash sat down beside her, his heart heavy as they waited and waited with no word. Kim joined them and after what seemed like forever a doctor came out to talk to them.

575

"How is she?" Kim asked before he had a chance.

"Amazingly resilient and very lucky she got here as fast as she did. Her spleen was damaged, but we've got it put back together. Barring a bizarre infection, she'll be good as new."

Ash let out a deep breath in relief.

"Can we see her?" Pam asked.

"She's still in recovery, but we'll have her out within the hour. You'll be able to see her then."

Kim shook the man's hand. "Thanks, Phil."

"No problem."

As the doctor walked away, Ash turned to Kim. "Since she's going to be here for a couple of days, I have something you need to know."

Kim's face blanched. "Oh God, you're a serial killer aren't you?"

Her logic baffled him. "What?"

"See this is what happens," Kim said to Pam before she looked back at Ash. "You're too perfect which means you're probably Dexter right? Hiding bodies someplace weird. You probably have your mom's body stashed away in your closet."

Ash shook his head. "No, at least not this week." He paused as he hoped he was doing the right thing by telling them what'd really happened this afternoon. "We didn't just wreck. We were run off the road."

Pam narrowed her eyes. "What do you mean?"

"Someone was trying to kill us. Last night, her friend Dimitri was murdered in Greece and his house searched. One of her team must have found something significant and someone wants it bad enough to kill for it. I don't think Tory should be left alone until we know more about it. The guys who came after us today, could very easily show up here."

Pam paled. "Can we get security on her?"

Kim shook her head. "The police won't do anything without concrete proof."

"I can guard her," Ash told them, "but I wanted you guys to know why if I'm not here, another guard needs to be. She can't be left alone."

Pam nodded in agreement. "Don't worry, I'm a major conspiracist anyway."

"And on that note," Kim said, stepping back, "I'm going to cruise by the recovery room and check in on her just to make us all happy."

"Thanks."

Kim patted him on the arm. "No problem. I'll be in touch."

But even so, Ash didn't breathe comfortably again until Tory was in a private room with him by her side.

She was hooked to several monitors and an IV. Her face was so pale that it scared him and he hated that sensation. It was also strange to see her without her glasses on.

Brushing her hair back from her forehead, he smiled at how beautiful she was. Not in a classic way—she honestly had nothing on Artemis in terms of looks, but there was something about her that even while she was unconscious shined through. Her spirit and her impishness. He could already hear her insulting him.

I thought you knew how to ride a bike. Gah, I can't believe you wimped out and lost control like that.

He could almost laugh at her imagined barbed comments as she took him to task for letting her get hurt.

His gaze dropped to her hand. Picking it up, he studied the daintiness of it. Her fingers were long, thin and graceful. The kind of hands that were made to stroke and to soothe. Fingers made to suckle and nibble. Before he could think better of it, he held her hand to his cheek and savored the soft feel of her skin. All his life, he'd craved a loving touch. One that wasn't selfish or hurting.

The only one to touch him like that had been Ryssa, but even she'd been stingy with them. Part of it had been his own fault. So many years of being slapped, pinched and hurt had preconditioned him to tense whenever someone came at his face. Even now he didn't really like anyone to touch him and yet he craved it.

I'm psychotic.

No, not really. He wanted what he didn't know and he didn't know how to get what he wanted. It was that simple and that difficult.

But as he held her hand against his cheek, he imagined her awake, touching him. His cock hardened with need and his heart broke over the reality that he could never be with someone like her.

He was forever tied to Artemis. Forever tied to a destiny he'd wanted no part in. Trapped between his mother and a goddess who claimed ownership of him. What he wanted was one single day of freedom to be a normal man who could make decisions that would only affect his own life. A day to laugh and to relax.

And people in hell want ice water.

Wishes weren't magical and his life was what it was. All the wishing in the world wouldn't change that. Sighing, he led her hand back to the bed and placed it beside her.

What he was about to do was wrong and he knew it. He tried to rationalize it by saying that she was going to heal anyway . . . barring infection and what were the odds she'd get an infection? She was young and healthy. He was just speeding the process up so that she wouldn't be tied to the hospital in case the men hunting her came here.

If she's supposed to die, she's supposed to die.

Then she would die and his healing her wouldn't matter at all.

"I'm not messing with her fate. I'm only healing her." As he reached to touch her chest, he remembered the times he'd wanted to die and had been prevented from it. The time when he'd been dead and Artemis had tricked him into taking her blood to bring him back.

But this was different.

Yeah it was real different. Artemis had saved the world by bringing him back. By waking Tory, he might end it.

Still he couldn't stop himself from doing this.

Taking a chance he knew better than to risk, he touched the valley between her breasts and let the energy of life flow from his body into hers. The monitors popped ever so slightly before Tory gasped.

Ash moved his hand away the exact instant she opened her eyes to look up at him.

Tory lay confused as she saw Ash standing over her. With his sunglasses on, she couldn't gauge his mood. Her entire body was sore and she couldn't quite figure out where she was. "Did you hit me?"

Ash gave her a crooked smile. "Why would I hit you?"

He had a point. And as she tried to get her bearings, a faint image went through her mind . . . it was Ash holding her. *"Don't you dare fucking die on me. Tory!"* Those angry words brought back an immediate flood of memories as she remembered the guys chasing them.

"You were shot!" she said, looking for his wounds.

"No. They missed."

Tory frowned. The one guy had shot them at almost point blank range. How could he have missed? And then she saw the bike going down in her mind and remembered sliding over the street. "Where did you learn to ride anyway? Disasters-R-Us?"

Ash laughed. "I knew you were going to insult me when you woke up."

She wasn't amused by it. "What happened to wreck us?"

"One of the cars clipped our tire."

"And we lived?"

He nodded. "We lived."

"You sure?"

"I think so."

"Yeah, I think you're right." She looked around the hospital room that wasn't much more than a blur of lights and shadows without her glasses. "I don't think I'd be in this much pain if I were dead. Not to mention, if I'm this blind after death, I have a bone to pick with the higher powers."

Ash stared at her in disbelief. How could she be making jokes about what had happened? "I think we left your glasses under the car that hit us."

"Figures. I'm just glad you didn't leave me there too, though to be honest, my ribs feel like the car is still parked on top of me."

Ash didn't say anything since his legs weren't quite the same either.

"Oh my God, you're awake?"

Ash stepped back as Kim squealed and then ran to the bed to embrace her friend. He was always amazed by such friendship and love. Throughout history, he'd witnessed it, but he'd never really felt it. He had people he could rely on. People he called friend, but none of them—not even Alexion—was ever privy to the real him. None of them knew his thoughts and though they might know some of his past, they certainly didn't know all of it.

He was a ghost who walked through life observing it, wanting to take part, but too afraid to risk being hurt to reach out. No wonder he and Jaden got along so well. They were armored to the point they were hollow inside.

And as he'd learned when he'd been human, nothing could ever fill that vast hole. It was endless and it was ever consuming whatever he attempted to put there.

Tory had a strange sensation go through her as she remembered something else from the wreck.

Ash had been hit by the car . . .

Releasing Kim, she looked at him and saw no injuries on his body. Not even a bruise. Yet she remembered clearly the last thing she'd seen before she blacked out.

Ash being run over. Completely run over. It stood out because until then, she'd felt no pain, sliding on the street. Then the instant the car hit him, her pain had set in and her last thought had been that she'd just watched him die . . .

You're imagining things. It's shock from the accident.

Or was it?

What are you saying, Tor? The man's immortal?

How stupid could one woman be? He wasn't immortal by any means. She had an overactive imagination and it was playing with her again.

"Ash said someone intentionally ran you guys off the road."

She blinked at Kim's chatter. "Yeah, they did."

"So what are you guys going to do?"

She looked to Ash who appeared to be watching her. "What *are* we going to do?"

"I don't know about you, but my plan is simple. Find the bastards and kill them."

CHAPTER ELEVEN

Kim's eyes widened at Ash's harsh words. "A little blood-thirsty isn't it?"

Not to him and not when they so richly deserved it. He flashed her a taunting grin. "Given what they did to Tory, I'm thinking a quick death is merciful. Not to mention they ruined one of my favorite jackets and totaled my bike."

Pam snorted. "Well let's just torture then bomb the bastards. How dare they!"

Ash ignored the sarcasm as he crossed his arms over his chest. "Now you're thinking like me. A little eye-gouging, some slit nostrils . . . I could seriously get into that."

Kim shuddered as she spoke to Tory. "I think your new friend is a *little* bloodthirsty."

Ash stifled a smile at her words. If she only knew that was his primary nourishment. And yes, he could definitely use some blood since it'd been over a week since he last ate.

Kim's phone rang. "Work calls. I'll be back soon."

Ash stepped back toward the bed to check in with Tory. "How are you feeling?"

She smiled up at him. "Amazingly whole. How about you? I thought the car ran you over."

"I rolled out of the way."

Her eyes narrowed suspiciously. "It didn't look like that from my perspective. I could have sworn it plowed right over both of your legs."

He looked down at them before he shrugged. "Obviously not."

Tory's expression turned sweet and adoring, and it hit him like a blow to his stomach. She placed her hand gently on his arm in the most loving touch he'd probably ever experienced. "Thank you for getting me here. Kim said they told her you were bleeding like crazy when you carried me in through the ER doors."

He felt his face flush at her gratitude. "Don't worry about it. Next time I'm hurt, you can carry me."

She laughed at his humor. "I think it would take at least a team of people to carry you."

"Back to the insults, huh?"

She shook her head at him. "That's not an insult. You are a *big* man."

Ash opened his mouth to speak, but before he had a chance, the doctor came in to examine her. He moved away while the doctor chatted with Tory.

"You are one very lucky woman. But for your friend getting you here as quickly as he did, you wouldn't have made it. Your spleen was severely damaged in your wreck."

Tory was still amazed by what Ash had done for her. Kim had told her that he'd been in bad shape himself and that he'd been overwrought when she'd died in his arms. Tenderness for him overwhelmed her.

When the bike had gone down, she remembered him reaching to protect her. He'd tried to keep her near him, but the force of the crash had separated them.

She grimaced as the doctor touched a tender spot on her abdomen.

He pulled back with an incredulous look. "You're healing unbelievably fast."

"Good genes and lots of vitamins."

He laughed at her. "You keep this up and we'll have you out of here in about three days."

Ash cleared his throat. "Is there any chance she can leave sooner?"

Tory caught Ash's meaning. "Yeah, I can't really afford to be out of commission too long."

"Honey," the doctor said in a strained tone, "you died. You might want to think about that for a minute and let it digest. You're really lucky you're still with us so let me watch over you for a few days before we turn you loose, okay?"

It was hard to argue when he put it like that. "All right. Thanks, doctor."

He inclined his head before he left them alone.

Tory looked over at Ash who was standing back with that stoicism he wore like a force field to keep the rest of the world away. She knew how hard she'd hit the ground and it wouldn't have been a bit softer for him. Yet he'd dragged himself to his feet and then carried her. His strength mystified her. "How did you get me here?"

"I have my evil Jedi ways," he said in a flat, even tone. "The Force is strong with this one."

She laughed again. He could be so charming when he wanted to. And so sweet. "Well if the doc won't release me, what do we do?"

He shrugged while keeping his arms crossed. "We keep an eye out for our new friends and make sure they don't decide to finish the job they started."

She nodded. "They think I have the journal, don't they?"

"Would be my guess. Either that or they're just really bored and thought knocking us around would alleviate it."

"Speaking of boredom . . . what am I going to do while I'm locked in here?"

"Wanna read some manga?"

She grimaced at him. "Are you serious?"

He nodded. "It's like crack. Once you start, you have to keep reading. I have some *Priest*, *Hellsing* and *Trinity Blood* issues handy. Interested?"

"Actually, I'd like to read the journal we found. Someone who's really tall and male hasn't finished teaching me Atlantean."

"It's not in Atlantean. It's Greek."

"So say you."

Groaning, Ash shrugged his backpack off his shoulder and manifested the journal inside it. One of the reasons he always kept a backpack with him was so that he could teleport things that he needed without arousing mortal suspicions. Since no one knew what was in his pack, they didn't know when he used his powers to get something he needed or wanted.

It also held the things that meant the most to him and kept them from harm. Ryssa's three journals that he'd found after Didymos had been destroyed, her hair comb and Simi's teething toy that Savitar had given him for her when she'd been a toddler. Her baby fang marks were forever etched into the wood. The backpack also held his mother's medallion wrapped in one of the black scarves that Simi had brought back from one of her many visits to Kalosis.

And Nick's soul that he'd traded to Artemis, that Artemis had then given to Acheron.

He pulled out Ryssa's journal and handed it to Tory. "Can you read it without your glasses?"

She sighed irritably. "Not a single word. I hate being blind. Any chance I can talk you into going to my house and getting my spare pair?"

"I can't leave you unattended. You know that."

"Then will you read it to me?"

Ash looked down at the leather as a sharp pain pierced his chest. It was hard to read Ryssa's words because with each one, he saw her clearly in his mind and heard her sweet, calm voice speaking to him.

And it cut him deep in his heart.

Tory touched his arm again. "Please, Achimou?"

A muscle worked in his jaw as her tender voice worked magic on his resolve. "You are the only being who's ever called me that."

"Well I'd call you babycakes, but I think that might offend you even more."

He smiled. "All right, stop the torture. I'll read."

Tory watched the blurry shadow that was Ash as he took a seat near her bed and opened the book. When he started reading, she closed her eyes and listened to the deep resonant tone of his voice. From the ease with which he translated as he read, one would have thought it was written in English. He didn't even hesitate with the words.

"Today I spoke to my father about visiting Atlantis."

Tory straightened up in the bed. "Atlantis?"

Ash cringed as he realized what he'd said. He'd actually forgotten he was reading to an outsider. Tory had become such a part of him that he actually wanted to confide in her. "Yeah, that's what it says."

"See! I told you it was real!"

He had to calm her down. "It doesn't mean anything. For all you know this is an ancient *Bridget Jones's Diary*."

She scoffed. "They didn't have novels back then."

"History says they didn't have books, yet what's this thing in my hand? It's square, bound paper that's been written on. Looks like a book to me."

"Thank you, Captain Sarcasm. How nice of you to join us again. Can we get back to the story?"

"Just don't throw another hammer at me," he mumbled under his breath before he returned to the book. "Today I spoke to my father about visiting Atlantis and as usual it made him angry. Our negotiations with them aren't going well. Uncle sent word that war could break out again at any moment. But I don't understand why it's too dangerous for me to visit there while my brother and uncle live there. Surely it's not safe for . . ." Ash paused as he saw his name mentioned, "my brother. I can't stand not seeing him. The letters he sends aren't enough for me. I want—" Ash choked on the words on the page as pain hit him hard in his chest. —*my brother home with me. Someone needs to make sure Acheron is kept safe from harm and though Uncle swears he's fine, I wish I could make sure of it for myself.*

"She wants what?" Tory prompted.

"My eyes are hurting," he lied. "I think it's the lighting. Can we pick this up later?"

Tory frowned at the odd note in his voice. It sounded like he was choking on tears, but that didn't make sense. "If you wish."

585

"Cool. I'll just return it to my backpack." He got up and rustled around in it.

"Ash?" she asked after a couple of seconds.

"What?"

"Did anyone call my family?"

"I don't know. You want me to ask?"

"Please. I don't want my family invading when I feel fine. Especially not while we have insane people chasing us. I would die if one of them got caught in the crossfire."

"Okay. I'll go get Kim and find out. If you need anyone . . ." He put the hospital buzzer in her hand. "I know you can't see well so if you get scared at all, buzz the nurse and I'll be right back."

His concern touched her. "Got it."

Tory sat in the silence, processing everything that'd happened today. The things she'd learned and those she still only suspected about Ash. Not to mention the fact that she now knew she had people out to end her life any way they could over something she didn't even possess.

What was she going to do?

Ash returned a few minutes later. "Kim spoke to your grandfather and Aunt Del. She said they want you to call them as soon as you can." Ash stepped close enough that she could see him.

"Thank you, Ash."

"You're welcome. Kim also said she'd have Pam bring your spare glasses over to you just as soon as she can."

She put her hand over the one Ash had resting on her railing and gave a light squeeze. "Thank you for remembering to ask about them, too." She picked his hand up and placed hers against it. She'd always thought of her hands as mannish since they were so much bigger than most women's, but compared to his hand, hers were dainty. His fingers were long and graceful with calluses that also marred his palms. They were manly hands and she couldn't help wondering what they'd feel like skimming her body . . .

"Your hands are so huge."

"Yours are soft and little." She didn't miss the catch in his voice before he moved his hand away. "Mine are also really rough." He said it as if it embarrassed him.

"I like your hands. I think they're beautiful."

"I don't know about that, but they do what they're supposed to most times I guess."

She shook her head. "You hate compliments, don't you?"

Ash's gut tightened at the unwanted memories her question provoked. As a human, compliments had been followed by either unwanted gropings or all-out beatings from the people who didn't want to be attracted to him. As a god they'd become extinct which, given his former experiences, was fine by him.

"You want me to get you something to eat?"

Tory nodded. "I'm always hungry."

"I'll be back."

She didn't move as she watched him leave again. He was so strange and so seductive. Protective, arrogant and at same time unsure of himself. Which really made no sense to her. How could he ever be uncertain?

She lay there for several minutes as she pondered the dichotomy.

"Hey girl."

She smiled at the blur that was Pam. "Hey hon."

Pam came forward and put Tory's glasses on her face. Tory breathed a sigh of relief as the world came into focus again. "Bless you."

"Anytime. How are you feeling?"

"Pretty good considering I just got hit by a car and died."

Pam growled at her. "You're not funny. And where's your delectable bodyguard?"

"He went to find food for me."

"Ooo, good looking *and* he quests for food when you're hungry. He's a keeper. So when are you going to sleep with him?"

Ash paused outside the door as he heard Pam's question to Tory.

Tory made a very undignified snort. "Sleep with him . . . pah-lease. Like I don't have better things to do with my day. I swear the way you have sex on the brain, you should have been born a guy."

"Oh yeah right, Tor, look at the man. They don't make a finer model than that one. Trust me. Unlike you, I look a

587

lot. He's without a doubt the finest thing on two legs, or three if you play your cards right."

Tory let out a sound of utter shock. "Stop talking about him like that. He'd die of embarrassment if he heard you."

Pam tsked at her. "I'm telling you right now, Tory, if you let that one get away without sleeping with him, you'll regret it for the rest of your life."

"And given my history with men, if I tried to sleep with him I'd kill him. The last guy I tried to sleep with ended up in a body cast."

Pam laughed. "Look at me and tell me honestly you haven't thought about it."

"I'm not *that* blind, but I don't think of Ash that way. I'm much more interested in him for his brains than his body. Now move on to the next topic before I push the button and tell the nurses I'm being harassed by an insane stalker friend."

"You would, too."

Deciding it was now safe to make an appearance, Ash walked in. Pam's face turned instantly red as she moved to the other side of the bed.

He set his bag down on Tory's tray table and moved it closer to her. "I wasn't sure what you'd like, so I got some of everything."

Tory smiled. "There's not much I don't eat. Curse of my Aunt Del always telling me about the poor children who have to eat dirt just to keep from going hungry."

Ash adjusted the tray for her, then opened her soda.

"Um guys," Pam said as Tory unwrapped a hamburger. "I don't think you're supposed to eat that right after surgery. Don't they put patients on clear liquid diets or something?" She looked uneasily out the door. "Where's Kim when I need her?"

Tory waved her words away. "I feel fine."

Ash pulled the fries out for her and set them down. "I wouldn't have gotten anything for her that would cause her more pain."

Tory held the burger up toward him. "You want a bite?"

"No, thanks."

Looking at Pam, she gestured at him with the burger. "I swear he's living proof that air has calories. Otherwise he'd shrivel up to nothing."

"Oh like you have room to talk. If there was any justice in this world, you'd be bigger than my house. You eat like a man and you're skinny as a rail." Pam smirked at Ash. "My mother used to call her Jack Sprat when we were kids. Thank God her aunt owned a deli, though I swear Tory ate up all the profits whenever she worked there."

Ash laughed.

"Only 'cause Del makes the best koulourakias, kourabiethes and melomacarinas ever."

Pam smirked at Ash. "Did you understand a single word of what she just said?"

"Of course he does, he's Greek. Even if he doesn't eat, he knows the cookies. I'll bet his mother stuffed him full as a kid."

Ash snorted at the image of his mother cooking anything, other than world destruction. "Not really. My mom wasn't the Betty Crocker kind." Not unless it involved napalm or plagues.

A sharp gasp at the door made them all look to see Kim in the doorway. "What are you doing eating that!"

Tory and Pam pointed at him. "He brought it."

Making a sound of distress, Kim rushed to the bed to take the burger from Tory's hands.

Tory pulled it away. "Not on your life, Kim, and I mean that literally."

"You can't eat that right after surgery. It'll make you sick."

"Better the cow than your hand which I'm going to take a chunk of if you reach for it again. I'm hungry. You of all people know better than to come between me and food."

Kim whirled on Ash with a malevolent glare. "How could you bring this to her?"

"She said she was hungry."

Kim popped him hard on his butt. "Don't do it again! You clear her diet through her doctor or a nurse. You don't just bring food to someone in a hospital. Are you out of your mind?"

Ash was too stunned to even react as Kim went back to the sack on the tray and rifled through it.

"You two are awful, just awful." Kim started to roll the top down.

Tory glared at her like a feral lion. "You take that bag, Kim, and I'll make you regret it."

"Tory, be reasonable."

"My stomach wants food."

Kim held her hand up. "And when you're being attacked by vicious gastric pain later, remember I tried to stop you." She turned back to Ash who made sure his ass was covered. Literally. "If you two weren't being chased by homicidal loons, I'd order you out of here."

Ash backed up another step. "You're not going to hit me again, are you?"

"I ought to. If you were a couple of feet shorter, I'd take you over my knee." Kim made one last sound of disgust before she left them alone again.

Pam shook her head as she met Ash's gaze. "Want me to kiss your boo-boo and make it better?"

"Pam!" Tory snapped.

"Oh like you didn't have that thought, too. Relax both of you, I'm only kidding. Let me go calm down Nursezilla before she gets you two in trouble with your doctor."

Tory sighed as Pam left. "I am so sorry about my friends, Ash. I really did attempt to give them some home training growing up, but obviously it didn't take."

Ash laughed at her words. Truthfully, he found the ease they had in his company refreshing. Most people were either intimidated or frightened by him. Only kids seemed indifferent and treated him like anyone else on the street. "It's okay. I like them."

She took one last bite of her burger before she wrapped it up. "I better stop before I hurt myself. But it is good. Thank you so much for getting this for me."

"There's a ham sandwich, pickles, chips and yogurt also in the bag."

"What a sweetie you are. You really did get some of everything. You sure you don't want a bite?"

"I'm fine."

She handed him the bag. "All right then. How about I swap you the food for the journal?"

Ash hesitated. Since his name was all over it . . . *I could tell her it's another name.* True. She didn't know what the letters were. If he could convince her it was something like Archon and not Acheron, that would work.

Shrugging his backpack off, he unzipped the top and pulled the journal out. "Here."

She opened it where they'd left off. "Now where were we?"

"Ryssa was talking about her brother in Atlantis."

She drew her brow together in confusion. "Ryssa? How do you know her name was Ryssa?"

Ash tensed as he realized that his sister hadn't written her name anywhere in it. "Uh . . . I don't. I just gave her a name. It seemed more polite than calling her 'hey you, ancient chick.'"

She wrinkled her nose up at him. "FYI, I hate the word chick."

"Then I shall delete it from my vocabulary."

Smiling she put her hand on his arm and leaned against him. "You're so accommodating. Was this the spot?"

It took him a full second to catch his breath at the casual way she touched him. At the way her lips looked so inviting and sweet.

"Yeah," he said, forcing himself to look at the page.

She pointed to a line a few down from where he'd been reading. "I miss him?"

"Yes."

Her finger went to the next sentence. "He was sent away?"

"You're an incredibly fast learner."

"That's what my father used to say. His nickname for me was Athena."

Ash was surprised by that. She was nothing like the Greek goddess. "Athena?"

"You know, she sprang fully formed out of the head of Zeus. My dad used to say that I did the same thing and, like Athena, I gave my father a splitting headache." She smiled widely. "Show me a little of anything and bam, instant

591

expertise. But this language is hard to learn. Beautiful, but difficult. Could you read in it for a moment so I can hear the way it lilts?"

Ash nodded before he obliged the request.

Tory listened to the inflections in his voice, mesmerized not only by how sexy it was, but by his intelligence. Before she could stop herself, she placed her hand to his jaw to feel the way his muscles worked while he spoke.

Ash paused at the tenderness of her touch and met her gaze.

"Don't stop speaking it," she whispered. "I love to hear your accent."

Little did she know he'd do anything she wanted so long as she touched him like this. He swallowed before he spoke again. *"I wish Soteria. I wish I could make love to you like a human man. With no pasts to get in our way and no regrets. I would sell my soul for it."*

Tory frowned at the words that seemed to come from his heart. "What did you say?"

"That you are an inquisitive imp."

She snorted. "No you didn't."

"Maybe, but you don't know for sure, now do you?"

She growled at him even though she enjoyed the fact that when he spoke in English, his accent was thick and lilting. "You know when you use that accent of yours, you could get away with murder." She pulled his sunglasses off, then folded them and put them in his pocket. "I like looking at your eyes."

"You're a very strange woman."

Perhaps, but there was something about him that made her feel warm and safe. She brushed the pad of her thumb over his lips. "Why do you hide from the world?"

"I don't hide from anything."

"Yes you do. The clothes you wear . . . they're your armor that you use to keep everyone away. You like to look dangerous and rebellious . . . it's like there's a part of you that thinks if you give people a cause not to like you, then, when they don't it's okay because you were the one who decided they weren't allowed to like you anyway."

He started to pull away, but she stopped him.

592

"I would be a friend to you, Ash. A good one, if you'd let me."

Ash looked away as he remembered Artemis offering her friendship to him. "No offense, Tory, people say that with all good intentions. Unfortunately when the test comes, we inevitably fail it."

"Have you ever failed it?"

"Yes, I have." His sister had trusted him to protect her and he'd let Artemis get in the way of that. Nick had been the closest thing to a real friend and he'd cursed him to die.

As a friend, he sucked and he wouldn't wish his friendship on anyone.

"Well I haven't failed," Tory said firmly. "Not once. But the only way for you to know that is to trust me. And since I know you can't give me your trust, I'll forget we had this discussion." She looked back at the book. "What's this word?"

Ash hesitated as he saw his name in Ryssa's handwriting. He started to lie to her, but it caught in his throat. He wanted to trust her. He didn't understand it. But he couldn't help himself. With a deep breath, he did what he hadn't done in centuries. He trusted. "It's Acheron."

Tory looked at him intently. "It's your name?"

"Yes," he said, making sure he kept all emotion out of his voice. "She had two brothers. Acheron and Styxx."

"Named for the rivers of woe and hate? How morbid of their parents."

"More apropos perhaps."

"That would be worse, I think." She turned the page. "It's so weird reading this. She seems like anyone you'd meet today walking down the street. Her main concerns are pleasing her father and she misses her brother. She has the same fears as modern women— being taken seriously. Being listened to." She let out a wistful sigh. "Can you imagine the world she lived in? I wonder what kind of clothes she wore. What kind of bed she slept in . . ."

"I imagine she was a lot like you. Gentle and unassuming. Determined and protective of those she loved. And she probably annoyed both of her brothers from time to time."

His words touched her. "Is that what you see when you look at me?"

"No. I see a homicidal maniac who hates my guts."

She laughed. "Seriously?"

His teasing look sobered. "Yes, Soteria. That is what I see when I look at you."

She laced her fingers with his.

Ash stared at their hands entwined. It was the most incredible sight he'd ever witnessed.

Pam rejoined them. He expected Tory to let go of him and stiffen uncomfortably as everyone else did. She didn't. She kept her hand in his.

"Did you save our skin for the burger?" she asked Pam.

"You're off the hook for the moment. What can I say? Super Pam to the rescue."

Ash put his sunglasses back on as Pam moved to the other side of the bed. She saw their hands and smiled. "I'm glad you two made up."

"Hey, the man saved my life. That ought to be worth a bump or two on my ego."

Pam arched both brows. "Who are you and what have you done to my best friend?"

Tory looked up at Ash. "Dying tends to put a few things into perspective."

She had no idea.

"Have you ever had a near-death experience, Ash?" Pam asked.

"You could say that."

Pam snorted. "What? You get caught sneaking out of the house by your dad, too?"

If the woman only knew. "That one definitely left a lasting impression on me."

"Yeah. I ended up grounded for a month."

Tory was watching Ash. There was a note in his voice that told her there was a lot more to his story than he was letting on. But if he wouldn't tell her anything in private there was no chance he'd say anything in front of Pam.

His phone started ringing. Releasing her hand, he stepped back to check the ID. "I have to take this. Excuse me."

Tory watched as he walked into the hallway.

Pam let out a low, appreciative whistle. "Jiminy Cricket, that man has the finest ass I've ever seen. No wonder he wears long coats. We should swathe him head to foot just to save human sanity."

Tory playfully slapped at her friend's arm. "Would you stop."

Pam gestured toward the door. "You have your glasses on. Do you not see how fine an ass that is? And he's Goth too." She made a purring sound deep in her throat.

"We've got to get you hooked up with someone soon. The extra hormones are eating away your brain."

"I know. It's so sad, isn't it?"

Tory laughed as she returned to staring after Acheron and wondered what was going on with his call.

"Are you sure about this, Urian?"

"Absolutely— it pays to have friends on the dark side. Stryker is sending out scouts even as I speak to find the journal. He wants to take down Artemis and Apollo and absorb their powers. He's also hoping there's something in the journal to hurt you, which now has your mom going ape shit and sending out her demons to look for it too." Urian laughed evilly. "Welcome to Armageddon, buddy. Looks like they're starting without you."

CHAPTER TWELVE

Ash had just stepped back into Tory's room when his phone rang again. Looking at the ID, he sighed. "Excuse me. I'm having to answer another round of 'Help me, Mr. Wizard' calls."

Tory shook her head at the poor man whose phone seemed to be a constant source of irritation for him.

Pam sat down in the chair where Ash had been earlier. "How many friends does he have?"

"I think they're work-related calls."

"Ah, so what does he do?"

"He's a wrangler."

"Uh-huh . . ." Pam's voice was filled with doubt.

"I know. He hasn't told me exactly what he does either, but apparently they're always calling him for it."

Pam's eyes sparked with interest. "Maybe he's an international assassin. Oooo wouldn't that be cool?"

"We have got to get you away from movies."

*

Ash *paused mid-sentence* as a unique fissure of power went down his spine. The sensation was unmistakable . . . there were demons in the hospital. And he would pretty much stake his life on who they were after.

Hanging up, he backed into Tory's room. "We have to go."

"Uh, hello?" Tory said sarcastically. "Hooked to an IV here. Not going anyplace in the near future."

He moved to the bed and pulled it out of her arm before she could even blink.

Tory was aghast at his actions and was stunned when her arm stopped bleeding. "What's going on?"

"People who want us dead are closing in. And if we don't get moving, it's going to get ugly."

Her heart hammered at the thought of someone coming after them. "There's only one other problem—clothes. I don't have any."

Pam stepped forward. "Yes, you do. Ash guard the door and give us a minute."

"You have twenty seconds." He hit the door and closed it tight.

"Can you move?" Pam asked.

"Surprisingly yes."

"Okay, switch clothes with me and let's be quick."

Tory was out of her gown in an instant. She was a little sore from the wreck, but not nearly as much as she should be for someone who'd just been operated on. It didn't make a bit of sense.

But before she could think anything else about that, Ash was in the doorway again.

"We're out of time." He held his hand out to her.

"I don't have any shoes."

"We'll cope. Come on."

She took his hand.

Without another word, he hauled her into the hallway, toward the elevators. When the doors opened, he pulled her into a room and motioned for her to be quiet. His actions terrified her. Who was out there?

"Wait here," he mouthed to her before he opened the door and vanished into the hallway.

Tory wasn't sure what was happening. She only hoped Ash knew what he was doing.

A few seconds later he came back and motioned for her to move quickly. He practically shoved her into the open elevator. But as the doors closed, she looked back toward her room where two very tall men were headed. Dressed all in black, they appeared sinister.

"What about Pam?"

Ash pulled her back so that the doors could close. "She'll be fine. They know who they're after."

"Who are they?"

Ash cringed at the question he couldn't really answer. Demons out to torture her just seemed a bit farfetched, especially since he wasn't sure how Stryker had known to send them here. "I don't know their names. But I for one don't want to introduce myself to them right now."

"Are you sure they won't hurt Pam?"

He handed his phone to her. "When we get in the car, you can call her."

"What car?"

He didn't answer since he was focusing all of his power on masking their presence from the demons and on locating the rest of their crew. There were at least ten of them crawling through the hospital. He could shield his powers from them and mask Tory's looks.

At least from everything except an archdemon. Born of a demon's union with a god, they were a unique and highly unpredictable breed. And one of them was in the hospital leading the others.

Ash led her to the parking lot and over to his silver metallic Porsche 911 GT2. He opened the passenger door while he scanned the lot.

She paused in the opening. "Please tell me we're not stealing this."

"It's mine." He dangled the fat Porsche key in front of her.

Tory was still suspicious. Having done the Porsche driving school a few years ago just for fun, she'd learned the various models and their price tags. This was the creme de la creme of Porsche—and it drove like a badass dream.

She'd wanted one so badly she could taste it, but the price tag was way out of her reach. "You own a quarter-million-dollar car?"

"Give or take a few ten thousand, yeah. Now get in."

Tory wasn't completely convinced. How on earth could he afford a car like this? But as she looked over at the driver's seat and realized that it was definitely designed for a very tall human, she couldn't deny the obvious. It had to be his. She got in as he slid into the driver's side.

Yeah, the car fit him like a glove and the fact that he knew the key went in on the left hand side said he'd been in the car enough not to hesitate with it.

"Acheron!"

As Ash shut his door, she looked up at the shout to see a large brown-haired man running toward them.

"Buckle up." Ash slammed the gearshift into reverse.

The man ran up onto the back of Ash's car.

"Oh you fucker," Ash snarled angrily. "Getting paw prints on my car . . . I swear, you scratch it, you die." He slammed on the brakes and sent the man flying onto a parked blue sedan.

Ash turned the steering wheel sharply and headed straight for the man who had rolled to the ground.

Tory cringed as she expected them to plow straight into him. Just as they reached him, he jumped out of the way with an astounding agility.

"You're crazy, aren't you?"

Ash didn't answer her as he took a corner so fast, she swore she felt a 2G pull. There on the street was a white BMW that fell in behind them.

"We're being followed."

Ash cursed at the sight of them in his mirror. More demons. But he was grateful they were at least attempting to blend in. Stryker must have had a talk with them about keeping anonymity in the human realm. Their inhibition to blast him leveled the playing field since he couldn't use his powers outright either.

Downshifting, he cut through traffic, heading toward the interstate. He needed to get them out of the populated areas before an innocent was hurt. Something easier said than done as two more cars appeared and then opened fire on them.

Ash threw a shield up to protect the car. He tried to use his powers to flip over the cars chasing them or at the very least stall the engines, but because they were demons inside and not humans, they countered his abilities with their own.

Damn them!

"My God," Tory gasped. "Do they suck at shooting or what?"

He didn't comment as he caught sight of four sleek black Honda Blackbirds closing in on them. Two of the bikes had double riders and the rider on the back was loaded for bear with KAC 6x35mm PDWs that they pulled out from under their jackets.

Ash cursed. "Looks like they're opening for business."

At least that was what he thought until one of the motorcycles opened fire on the cars after them.

Tory scowled at the sight of the bikers helping them. "Friends of yours?"

"Not that I know of." If not for the fact they were using guns, he'd suspect Were-Hunters since many of them used motorcycles to travel by while in human form. But Were-Hunters would be fighting with magic.

The bikes fell into formation, forcing the BMW to drive into the retaining wall. Then they moved on to the other Beamer before they made short work of it, too.

Ash gunned the engine as they approached. At least until he realized they were definitely on his side. He swerved to the shoulder, then slammed on the brakes.

"Wait here," he said as he got out to confront the riders.

They stopped a few feet behind his car. The two who were armed swung off first and turned their backs to him as they scanned the road for more demons. But what caught his attention most was the gold sun symbol emblazoned on the back of their Brazilian leather Stitch suits.

His mother's symbol.

The drivers got off the bikes in unison and approached him like a single trained unit. They stopped before him and stood wide legged until they each brought their right fist to their left shoulder and bowed their heads. Then they sank down to one knee right there in the street.

What the hell was this?

The one who was the leader got up and removed her helmet. She was breathtakingly beautiful with long blond hair that fell in waves around her shoulders. In the leathers, her broad shoulders would make her easily mistaken for a man, but there was nothing masculine about her. "Sorry we couldn't arrange a better introduction. I'm Katherine Zanakis, head priestess of the Apollymachi."

Ash looked over them as he realized they were all human women in service to his mother. "What are you doing here?"

Katherine moved to the side as the others rose and another one came forward and removed her helmet. Very cute and probably a good ten years older than Katherine, she had short black hair and warm eyes.

"Justina?"

He turned at Tory's confused call to scowl at her and then the imp who was running to join them. "I thought I told you to stay in the car."

"I don't listen," Tory said dismissively as she joined him.

Justina came forward and pulled the messenger bag off her shoulder. "I was told to deliver this to you." She handed the bag to Tory.

Tory looked as confused by the gift as he felt. "What is it?"

"It's what Dimitri died for," Justina explained. "I was there when the Atlantikoinonia stormed in and I managed to escape out the back door with the journal and seal while he held them off." Justina crossed herself three times as her eyes filled with tears over their lost friend.

Ash cursed as he remembered seeing Justina in his vision. Only then he hadn't realized whose side she'd been on. He'd assumed she'd been working for their enemies.

"The Atlantikoinonia?" Tory asked Justina.

"A group of lunatics," Justina spat. "They've chased us all the way from Greece to New Orleans. Every time we turn around, there they are trying to nab the journal."

Katherine nodded. "They're a group of men who are sworn to protect the secrets of Atlantis and they're ruthless."

"They destroyed our boat," Justina told Tory. "I killed one of them as he fled and that's what made me run to Dimitiri to get the journal. I didn't realize how important our research was until then."

Tory shook her head as if all this was making her dizzy. "I am so confused."

Ash put an arm around her to hold her steady. "She also just had surgery and was almost killed earlier today. Not to mention, our friends might find us again and when they do, I don't want to be in the open where they can get her or take a clear shot at us. Do you guys know where Sanctuary is on Ursulines?"

"I do," one of the women with the PDWs said.

"Then we'll meet you there." Ash went to open the door for Tory who gave him a hard stare.

"What exactly is going on here, Ash?"

"I'm not sure, but I think we're about to get a few answers."

"Good. 'Cause I'm tired of being in the dark." Tory got in and started to open the bag in her lap, but Ash put his hand on hers.

"I'd rather you not do that."

She looked up with a frown. "Why?"

Because you'll expose me. "Let's wait until we get to Sanctuary." *And I can safely get it away from you.*

"All right." Her blind trust sent a wave of guilt through him. She folded her arms around the bag and held it tight, not knowing it was his life and dignity she held so close to her heart. Every secret he'd worked so damn hard to keep was right there . . .

He wanted to curse. His stomach knotted, he went to the other side and slid in before he led the way back to the Quarter.

Tory ran her hand over the sand beige leather interior of his car as if she admired the German styling. "You know what I think is so off about these cars?"

He had no idea. There was nothing he found off about them. He loved his Porsche. "What?"

"The cupholders."

He laughed. They were tucked into the trim which had to be flipped down so that they could swing out and unfold.

"Yeah. Transformers. Cupholders in disguise. But that's not really what's on your mind, is it?"

"No. I'm trying to distract myself from the fact that I'm holding something in my lap that someone is ready to kill for. That one of my dearest friends paid for this discovery with his life and that if I'd just left Atlantis alone, Dimitri would be alive now. His wife wouldn't be a widow and his poor mother wouldn't be burying her only son." She winced. "I can't believe my selfish stupidity killed someone. What have I done?"

Ash's heart lurched as he thought about Nick. "It's easy to make mistakes. It's living with the consequences of them that's the hardest."

"Tell me about it. Do you have any secret spy ring that helps with the pain?"

"I wish, but no. There are some pains that run too deep for anything to absolve them. The best we can do is pick up the pieces and hope for the strength we need to keep going."

"Is that what you do?"

"No, I beat shit up—that helps even more."

She gave a light laugh. "I can't see you being that harsh."

She had no idea, but he was glad she didn't know the part of him that was capable of complete destruction.

Tory leaned her head against the glass and stared out the window.

They didn't say anything more until Ash pulled into the small driveway behind Sanctuary. The priestesses parked on the street while he led Tory toward the front door.

Dev Peltier was guarding it in human form . . . while it was still daylight. There were two kinds of Were-Hunters. Those born as humans who could become animals and those who were animals who could become human. During the daylight hours, Were-Hunters preferred their native form which for Dev would be a bear. The fact he was human made Ash extremely curious since only the most powerful of their breed could do that.

As a man, Dev wasn't much shorter than Ash. He had long curly blond hair and a dimple that only flashed when he talked since the bear didn't smile often. Dressed in jeans and a black Sanctuary staff T-shirt, he sat with a deceptive nonchalance. Even in human form, he could launch into action fast enough to give Ash a run for his money. But what amused Ash most was the Dark-Hunter bow and arrow Dev had on his biceps. He wasn't sure why the bear thought it was funny to wear the mark of Artemis, but Dev wore it proudly.

And as soon as Dev saw him, he reached to the small remote on his belt to cue the song "Sweet Home Alabama" to play inside the bar, alerting the rest of the inhuman inhabitants that Ash was about to enter the building. It was a game they played. Since the Were-Hunters were cousins to the Apollites, they often sheltered Apollites and Daimons. Ash, being a Dark-Hunter, would be obliged to kill any Daimons he found which meant the Daimons would be running for cover right about now.

The Apollites preferred to not see a Dark-Hunter so they made themselves just as scarce whenever he was around.

"How you doing, Dev?" Ash asked.

"Good." Dev arched a brow at Tory and the other women who were approaching. "Nice of you to beautify the bar for us. Appreciate it greatly."

Ash shook his head. "We need a quiet corner."

"Upstairs to the right. The whole area's cordoned off this time of day. I'll have Aimee head up to bring drinks."

"Thanks."

Tory smiled at the blond man who winked at her as she followed Ash. She'd walked past this place dozens of times, but since heavy metal wasn't her shtick, she'd never gone inside. It was huge—much bigger than it appeared from the street.

There were three levels with sections set aside for a bar area, a billiards section, a stage and dancing floor, and a restaurant. It was rustic and at the same time rather homey—except for the coffin in a corner by the bar that had a small plaque on it reading THE LAST GUY WHO ASKED AIMEE OUT—it had a dismembered skeleton in it.

Obviously Aimee was someone visitors were meant to keep their hands away from.

Tory followed Ash upstairs to a large round table in the rear, against a wall. He walked to the back so that he would be against the wall and waited for all of them to be seated before he sat down.

Once everyone was situated, he inclined his head to them. "All right, ladies, let's piece this puzzle together."

"It's not hard," Katherine said. "Since Tory's family first started poking close to the Atlantean ruins, we were assigned by the goddess to watch over them and make sure that the humans didn't offend her with their actions."

"Your goddess?" Tory asked.

Katherine smiled. "Apollymi the Great Destroyer. Our Order goes back to the days when Atlantis was the ruling power on earth. After Atlantis was destroyed, under the protection of our goddess who saved us from the great fall, we went to Greece and set up our Order where it's been maintained in secret ever since."

"We were one of the great Amazon tribes," Justina said. "Only where the others were Greek, we kept to the Atlantean ways."

Katherine smiled with pride. "And we were the strongest of them. But since the moment our foremothers escaped to Greece, we've been hunted by the Atlantikoinonia. A group founded by the goddess Artemis. Their mandate is to eradicate all evidence that Atlantis and Apollymi ever existed."

"Which means killing all of you," Tory whispered.

Katherine nodded. "Another reason we've been in hiding for centuries."

Justina pulled her jacket off and put it on the back of her chair. "But for Apollymi's protection, we wouldn't have survived so long."

Tory admired the way they spoke—the loyalty they showed to their goddess. "You speak as if she's real."

Justina smiled. "To us, she is."

"Did anyone read the journal?" Ash asked, changing subjects.

"No," Katherine said quickly. "To our knowledge, no one knows the language it's written in. Our oracle told us to bring it to Tory and that's what we're doing. It's foretold that she, like the ancient Atlantean Soteria, will be its guardian."

Tory was caught off guard by the use of her formal name. "Excuse me?"

"It's an old legend," Ash said. "When Atlantis was being destroyed, the head librarian of the national archives tried to save as much of their work as she could. It's said that her Shade now oversees the treasures of Atlantis and keeps them safe from plunder."

Katherine indicated the entire group with a wave of her hand. "The Apollymachi are her Shades. We are the guardians and the Atlantikoinonia are the destroyers."

Ash looked at the bag that Tory still held against her chest. "Perhaps in this *we* should be the destroyers."

Tory shook her head. "I want to know what the book says before we destroy it."

"No one can read it," Katherine repeated.

Tory shook her head. "Ash can."

The women looked at him with surprise etched on their faces.

Justina exchanged a glance with Katherine before she spoke. "Is that why the oracle said to deliver it to the Elekti?"

"Elekti?" Tory asked, not understanding the word.

"It means chosen one," Justina explained.

Tory scowled—that could be rather ominous. "Chosen for what?"

Katherine pushed the sleeve of her jacket back. "Our Order speaks of a man in every generation who bears the Destroyer's grace. He's known by her ring that he bears on his right thumb."

Tory looked down to see a thick gold band on Ash's thumb. It bore the same sun symbol that marked the women's jackets and his backpack. "What are you not telling me?" she asked Acheron.

"Lots." He turned back to Katherine. "So what are your orders now that you've delivered the book?"

"We are to guard Soteria and to follow the orders of the Elekti."

"Why?" he persisted.

"Because it's the will of the goddess."

Ash scoffed at her words. "You should never blindly obey anyone. Take it from someone who knows. Your goddess isn't infallible."

Katherine sucked her breath in sharply. "That is blasphemy."

Ash didn't respond but something in his features led Tory to believe that he knew a lot more about their goddess than he was letting on. "These Atlantikoinonia. They're human?"

Katherine nodded.

Tory was confused by his strange question. "What else would they be? Turnips?"

Ash shook his head at her sarcasm. Though to be honest, it amused him. However, that didn't change the predicament they were in. "Does anyone else know you have the journal?"

"No," Justina said assuredly. "Dimitri wouldn't have broken his word."

He hadn't detected that either. "Then for now, we need to get Tory back to bed to rest."

"I feel fine."

He arched a brow at her protest. "You just had surgery. You need to be in bed, resting."

Tory hated to admit he was right. "Fine. Take me home."

He looked down at the bag and shook his head. "I don't think that's wise given today's adventures. Whoever is after you knows where you live and I for one don't think we ought to make it easy on them. Let the bastards have to search to kill you." He stood up as an attractive blond woman reached them. Dressed in a skimpy black Sanctuary T-shirt with a howling wolf on the front, she was carrying a serving tray.

Pulling her off to the side, Ash talked to her in a low tone.

"No problem," the blonde said. "Follow me."

Ash took the bag from Tory. "C'mon."

Irritated by his highhanded demeanor and the fact he hadn't asked her opinion on this, Tory followed him to a door not far away. Aimee, whose name was on the back of her T-shirt, pulled out a set of keys and unlocked it. It led to a small room with another door that was locked with a palm scanner.

Tory was impressed by the security. "Get out of town . . ."

607

Smiling, Aimee opened it to show a large bedroom with no windows. "There's a bathroom through the other door. It's steel reinforced, so nothing's going to pop through it uninvited . . . heavy emphasis on the uninvited part."

Ash inclined his head to her. "Thanks, Aim."

"Anytime." She handed him the key to the outside door. "You can leave this door open so you don't have to use the scanner."

Ash gestured toward Tory. "You want anything to drink?"

"Apple juice would be a godsend."

Aimee nodded. "I'll bring some right up."

Tory headed for the bed as Aimee left them alone. "Can I read now?"

Ash made a low sound of irritation. "Do you mind if I look at it first?"

"Yes, I do." She held her hand out, wanting it immediately. She was desperate to see what all the hoopla was over.

"I read faster than you do," he reminded her.

She made a strong sound of her irritation to compete with his.

Ash paused. In that moment, he wanted to tell her the truth about what was happening and why. Wanted her to know that the beautiful waitress Aimee was Dev's younger sister . . . and a bear in her other form. He had a fantasy in his mind of Tory welcoming him in spite of it all. Of her taking it in stride without freaking out and shrieking. Of her not minding the fact that he was a cursed god.

But he knew better. He wasn't some kid with his first crush. He'd lived long enough to know people and their reactions to things that were radically different was seldom positive.

No matter how much he might want her to smile at him and tell him none of it mattered, he knew better. How many centuries had he waited for it not to matter to Artemis? And she was a goddess who couldn't accept him.

How could a mere mortal take him in stride? Besides, it was a dangerous world he lived in and she didn't have the power to survive in it.

608

He cleared his throat. "You'll get over your disappointment."

"Ash . . ." she said, with a note of warning in her voice, "don't make me get out of this bed."

He grabbed the bag and was out of the room before she could reach him. Shutting the door, he sealed her in.

"Hey!" Her muffled outrage made him cringe as he felt her anger inside him. He'd been held prisoner enough to hate himself for what he'd just done.

But he had to protect himself . . . and her.

He paused inside the outer room to open the bag. There was an Atlantean seal that had his mother's sun symbol with Archon's hammer and lightning bolt forming an X over it. There were three priestess necklaces that could be used to summon his mother's powers into a human body and the Atlantean dagger.

Ash cursed as he realized this was more destructive than a nuclear bomb. With this, anyone on the planet could end the world in the blink of an eye.

"Is there a reason she's locked up?"

Aimee's voice distracted him. "Yeah," he said, putting the items into his own backpack before he stood up. "I need her to stay there for a bit."

She gave him a sheepish frown. "You like to live dangerously, don't you?"

He ignored the question. "Tell her I'll be back shortly with some of her clothes."

Aimee shook her head as he she reached to open the door and confront a human who looked ready to take on a bear. Literally.

"Shouldn't you be in bed?" Aimee asked.

Tory glared at the woman. "Are you going to make me?"

"Hopefully, I won't have to. Ash wants you protected and I would think you'd agree with that."

Tory lifted her chin in defiance. "You always do what he wants?"

"No, but I know what it's like to protect someone when you care about them, even when they're being pigheadedly suicidal. So don't make me do something you'll hate me for later."

That took some of the steam out of Tory's anger. That and the fact that Aimee looked pretty stout and not much shorter than her. "I don't like being told what to do and I hate being locked in a room."

"Well if you promise to stay here and behave, I'll leave it open. But don't make me have to chase you down. I assure you, I'm a lot faster than I look."

Even angry, Tory understood why she couldn't go chasing out the door after Ash. There were still people looking for her and she was recovering. So she headed to the bed and got back into it.

Smiling, Aimee handed her the juice. She opened the drawer in the nightstand and pulled out a remote. An instant later a panel opened in the wall to show a large plasma TV. "It's not a prison. Hit the yellow button on the bottom and it'll call for me if you need anything."

"Thank you."

"You're welcome, and try not to kill the tall guy in black. He might be an asshole at times, but he's basically a good man and there are so few of them in the world that we don't need to start weeding them out."

Tory laughed at her perfect description of Ash. Aimee was right. There really wasn't a plethora of good people in general. "Have you known Ash a long time?"

She tucked her tray under her arm before she answered. "Since I was a kid . . . he actually saved my life."

Tory didn't know why, but that surprised her. "He saved your life?"

She nodded. "My older brothers were killed in front of me. The men who did it were drunk on bloodlust and when they found where I was hiding, they dragged me out to kill me too. The next thing I knew, Ash was there and they were dead. He picked me up and returned me to my family. If he hadn't found me, I know they'd have killed me, too."

Tory frowned at the conflicting images in her mind that didn't make sense. "But you're older than him."

"No, I'm not."

Her frown deepened. Aimee looked at least a decade older than Ash's early twenties. "How old is Ash?"

"I don't know exactly. I've never met anyone who knows his precise birthday—but I know he's older than me. He doesn't offer and we don't ask. By the way, he said to tell you he'd be back with some clothes for you." Before Tory could say another word, Aimee was gone.

Tory lay in bed with those words running through her head. There was a lot more going on here than she knew and it bothered her that they all thought she was so stupid that she didn't know it.

What was the deal with Acheron? Who was he really?

And how old was he?

She looked up as a shadow fell over her bed. Her heart missed a beat until she realized the shadow was Justina. "You scared me!"

"Sorry. There was something I forgot to give you. It was so small, I didn't put it in the bag with the rest." She pulled a small sandwich baggie out of her pocket. "I think you'll find it really interesting."

Scowling, Tory took it from her and pulled the coin out. They'd found a lot of coins so that wasn't surprising. The back of it was the same as other Didymos coins.

But when she turned it over, she gasped.

The face on the coin was Acheron's.

CHAPTER THIRTEEN

It wasn't Ash who brought Tory's clothes to her later. He sent them up via Aimee which was a bit disappointing, but if he wanted to be a coward after locking her in, so be it. Besides, she liked Aimee who had a biting sense of humor and a very keen wit.

It also gave her time to plot revenge on the tall Goth who irritated her to distraction.

With nothing better to do, Tory took a shower in the small bathroom, careful not to get her sutures wet. She was extremely bored with her bed rest. She didn't understand how she could feel so good given what had happened to her. Honestly, she was only a little sore from the almost fatal wreck.

It was so strange.

Not wanting to be alone where thoughts of Dimitri and worry for her team made her ache, she left the room and headed into the bar area, seeking distraction. As she came out, Justina and Katherine got up from a small round table where they'd been sitting—Justina facing Tory's door and Katherine scanning the bar around them.

She didn't know where the other priestesses were, but the fact that those two were still here made her arch an eyebrow.

"What are you doing?" she asked them, curious about their nervous twitching.

Katherine looked away sheepishly. "We were watching you to make sure no one disturbed you."

Well at least the man hadn't made them keep her locked in the room. She should be grateful for some small liberty. "Ash's orders?"

Justina smiled. "I finally found someone even bossier than you. Who knew? Not to mention he's a lot more fierce."

Ha, ha, Tory thought sarcastically. She didn't really find that particularly funny—most likely because she was on the receiving end of his bossiness. "So where is he?"

Probably out chasing the redhead or some other woman.

Katherine pointed over the banister down to the stage area. Tory looked below, then gaped as she saw the one man at the back of the stage who didn't have a spotlight on him. There was no mistaking the giant dressed only in black as he played a black guitar emblazoned with red flames.

Justina joined her at the banister. "The band's guitarist jammed two fingers right before they were supposed to play so they begged Ash to cover for him."

Tory was absolutely stunned as she watched his long fingers fly over the neck into perfect chords. "Get out."

Justina grinned. "Yeah, I know, he's impressive isn't he?"

No, he careened past impressive and went straight into the realm of guitar god. Because she played herself, she could easily appreciate the talent it took to make what he did look and sound so effortless. He didn't make a single mistake.

And when he broke into a screaming solo that rivaled Hendrix, Rhodes or Van Halen, the crowd went wild.

Before Tory even realized what she was doing, she was heading down the stairs to watch him play at closer range.

Ash didn't normally look at the crowd what few times he'd filled in with the Howlers—which was only during practice sessions or when the bar was closed to anything not preternatural, but for some reason he felt an uncharacteristic compulsion to do so now. He immediately saw Tory in front with Justina and Katherine behind her.

Time seemed suspended as he met those beautiful brown eyes that always seemed to see through him, straight into his soul. As he stared at her, he forgot everything else, especially when he finally heard her thoughts above those of the people around him.

Why do you live in the shadows away from everyone else? You should be out front and shining with that talent. I've never heard a better guitarist. How do you do that? Were you born with a guitar in your hands?

She looked at him in awe. *You are so beautiful, Acheron. All of you. Why do you hide from the world and from me in particular? I would never hurt you . . .*

The sincerity of those words reached out to him in a way nothing had before. But more than that were the other glimpses he finally had into her. Some of them he would never have guessed. Her soul was beautiful. Her heart unbelievably kind. He was used to dealing with those who, like him, were jaded. Those who expected only the worst from other people and the world.

But not her. She saw even the evil around her with a child-like hope.

Gods, how he wanted to touch that purity. To feel the magical way she saw the best in people, even when they didn't deserve it. Most of all, he wanted to see himself the way she did. To be the person she thought he was, instead of the animal he knew himself to be.

Just for one minute.

This had to be the greatest gift anyone had ever given him and she hadn't even realized she'd done it. It was just who and what she was. That was what made it perfect.

And he wanted to return the favor to her as they ended the Godsmack cover they were playing. He went over to the lead singer of the band, Angel Santiago, who had long brown hair and a cocky grin, and whispered to him.

Angel shook his head, laughing. "For you, man, anything." Angel went to the others while Ash adjusted the mike in front of him to accommodate his height.

An instant later, Ash cringed as a spotlight was turned straight on him. He'd never craved this kind of attention and every part of him wanted to run for cover.

But Tory had a stupid fantasy and the part of him that she'd unknowingly touched wanted to give it to her.

His throat dry from embarrassment and fear, he met her gaze. "This is for Soteria." He went into the opening strands of Nickelback's "Savin' Me." The moment he did, he wanted to die as he realized how badly he'd just screwed up—in public. The club was filled with people and animals in human form who knew who and what he was. Beings who would be dying to know who Soteria was and why he'd dedicate a song to her when he *never* did such a thing.

More than that, he'd most likely angered Tory by linking her name to his. Damn it. He knew better. No one wanted to be seen with him. Ever.

When was he going to learn that one basic fact? Decent people only wanted to interact with him in private. He was an embarrassment. A freak.

But it was too late now. All he could do was see this through and hope she didn't publicly bitch-slap him for the affront when it was over.

I'm such an idiot.

Tory couldn't breathe as she heard Ash sing. He had the most amazing voice. Low and deep, it sent shivers over her.

Good gods of Olympus . . .

She'd never heard this song before but the lyrics were beautiful . . .

> *Heaven's gates won't open up for me.*
> *With these broken wings I'm fallin'*
> *And all I see is you.*

Those lyrics brought tears to her eyes. All her life, she'd had a fantasy about a great-looking guy in a band singing to her. She knew how stupid it was, but to be here right now having Ash of all men sing to her.

It was surreal and it was wonderful. Most of all, it made her want to cry.

And when the song ended, the spotlight was turned off. Ash set his guitar on the stand by the drum set and jumped down from the stage.

"We'll be taking a twenty-minute break," the lead singer said.

Tory barely heard him as Ash approached her slowly and for the first time she saw hesitancy in his powerful gait. Unsure, he stopped in front of her.

Ash cringed, dreading her reaction. "I'm sorry if I—" He was going to say embarrassed you, but before he could get the rest of the sentence out, she pulled the sunglasses off his face and grabbed him into the fiercest kiss he'd ever known.

Everything around him receded as her lips set fire to his entire body. It wasn't demanding or painful. It was a kiss of commitment. Of caring.

One that made him growl with need as she cupped his face with her hands, then trailed them down his body to hold him so close to her that his head spun with disbelief.

And in that moment, all he wanted was to be inside her. To have her hold him like this while there was nothing between them. Just bare skin to bare skin.

Tory couldn't breathe as she tasted Acheron. His body was so incredibly hard. She doubted there was a single molecule not muscled and ripped. Except for his lips. They were as soft as a whisper and tasted of raw masculine power.

"Damn Ash, get a room."

Ash tensed at the sound of Dev's voice as the bear walked past him. But he was still incredulous that Tory had grabbed him like this in public. No woman had ever done that before. He'd always been relegated to the shadows—to places where no one could see them together.

The fact that she'd kissed him openly . . .

It was heaven.

Biting her lip, Tory pulled back to see his face mottled with red. Whether from anger, exertion or embarrassment she couldn't tell for sure. "I'm sorry. I hope I didn't offend you."

Ash shook his head as he laid his hand to her cheek. Pulling her against him, he buried his face in her hair and

616

inhaled the sweetness of her scent. It was a scent he wanted to bathe in until it coated every inch of his flesh and branded him as hers.

Tory closed her eyes at the tightest embrace she'd ever had. She hugged him back and just held him while people walked around them. She'd never really been one for public displays of affection, yet with him it was different.

Nothing seemed to matter except being with him right here and right now.

Ash squeezed his eyes shut as raw emotions tore through him. *Let her go. Shove her away.* It was the sanest thing to do. The safest thing to do.

But he couldn't. He'd lived his entire life for other people, trying to please them and failing with every attempt. First it'd been his human father, then his uncle. The clients he'd taken.

And then Artemis.

He'd never been good enough to earn their love. Never good enough for them to make him feel the way Tory did. To her he was neither whore nor god. Neither property nor a source of shame.

He was just a man.

And that man wanted to make love to her.

Don't be stupid. Don't. You'll only get hurt, Ash. You know better. Artemis will make you suffer until you beg for death . . . and then she'll torture you even more.

Yet when he looked into those deep brown eyes that saw him as a human with feelings, he was lost. Most of all, he was tired of taking nothing for himself. Of sacrificing himself for other people's happiness while he had no one who made him feel like *he* mattered.

Surely he deserved to have someone hold him close and soothe him. Would that be selfish?

His resolve bucked under the weight of conscience. Fuck it if it was.

If he had to pay for this later, he would. He'd suffered unbearably for a lot less than Tory. And she'd be worth every scar.

Stepping back, he took her hand and led her to the stairs and up to her room. He closed the door, isolating them from the sounds and people downstairs, then turned to face her.

Tory was unprepared for the ferocity of his kiss as he pinned her to the wall. He'd always been so reserved and cool that she'd never suspected how sexy it would be for him to lose control like this.

The fact that she was the one who drove him to it only made her hotter. His lips tormented her as his hands began unbuttoning her blouse. She swallowed at the heat pounding through her. She'd never been with a man before.

And she barely knew him.

Yet she realized Pam was right. If she didn't sleep with Ash, she'd regret it for the rest of her life. There was something about him that made her restless and calm. Something that touched her heart in a way no one ever had before.

She wanted to be with him. To hold him close and never let him go.

Ash pulled back from her lips as he opened the last button of her blouse. Her breasts, covered by purple lace, were small and inviting. Adorable and perfect. He kept waiting for her to push him away and reject him.

She didn't.

Taking a deep breath, he reached to the gold clasp between her breasts. He met her gaze and the raw hunger there set fire to him as he opened her bra and spilled her breasts to his gaze. He cupped the right one in his hand, amazed by the softness of her skin as her taut nipple teased his palm. Dying for a taste, he dipped his head down to gently suckle her.

Tory gasped as he flicked his tongue over her nipple. With every lick, her stomach contracted sharply. His mouth was so hot as he sucked and played. His breath scorched her skin. She cupped his head to her, unable to believe how much pleasure he gave her.

He moved to her other breast as he unzipped her pants. Tory felt herself getting wet already. "Touch me, please," she begged, dying for something to sate the fire inside her.

Ash obliged her as he slid his hand under the waistband of her panties. He let the small hairs tease his fingers as he sank his hand down further until he could separate the tender folds of her body and run his finger down her cleft.

She made a strangled cry of pleasure. Smiling in satisfaction, he dipped his hand down lower to let her moisture coat his fingers before he moved his hand up to massage her.

Tory cried out as she felt her body exploding with pleasure. She'd never had an orgasm before. It was raw and it was unbelievable and even a little frightening. Words couldn't describe what she felt. She clung to Ash as he continued to heighten the ecstasy. He sank to his knees in front of her.

Still shaking and weak, she looked down to meet that hungry silver gaze. He reached up to pull her jeans down her legs with a feral intent that made her even more breathless. She lifted one leg and then the other so that she was completely bare from the waist down. Her shirt was open.

Ash couldn't breathe as he took in the sight of her like that. She was so beautiful and all he wanted to do was please her—to have her hands on his body, not hurting him or demanding he submit to her to make her feel more powerful. Just simply pleasing him. Soothing him. He brought her delicate hand to his lips so that he could taste her fingertips. The scent and sweet taste made his cock so hard it was all he could do not to attack her where she stood. But he wanted to savor her slowly.

The one thing in the universe that he excelled at was this and he wanted her to know the height of his skills.

She reached down to brush his hair back from his forehead. Ash buried his face against her thigh and nipped the tender flesh there as her hand touched his cheek.

"Please don't pull my hair," he breathed in a ragged whisper, not wanting anything to spoil this moment.

"I would never hurt you, Ash."

And that was why he was willing to risk the wrath of a goddess to be with her. For once in his life, he wanted to make love to someone who didn't make him feel like shit for it. Covering her hand with his, he turned his face so that he could kiss her soft palm.

Tory was stunned by his tenderness. He reminded her of a skittish fawn as he suckled her fingers. And when he looked up at her, she saw the unadulterated pain and torment inside him. His soul was as naked to her as her body was to him.

He licked her palm in one sensual swipe before he rose up to bury his lips against the center of her body.

Tory cried out as pleasure blinded her. She reached for his hair, only to catch herself. Instead, she clasped the door knob with one hand and bit her knuckle on the other one.

Her body took on a life of its own as he licked and teased her with his tongue. He lifted his hands to spread her wider so that his tongue could flick and delve deep inside her.

Ash reveled in the taste of the most private part of her body. The remnants of her last orgasm made him hungry for his own, but more than that, it made him want to hear her scream out his name.

Dying to be inside her, he slid his finger in, then froze as he found the last thing he expected.

He went cold inside.

"You're a virgin?"

Tory scowled at the venom in his voice as he spat the word out as if it were disgusting to him. "Is that a problem?"

He jerked away from her as if he'd discovered leprosy. "Why didn't you tell me?"

"I didn't think it would matter."

He cast her a feral look that made her pull her blouse closed. "It matters. Damn it, woman!"

She was completely baffled by his unexpected response. Why would he be so angry over the fact that she'd never been with another man? "I thought men liked having virgins."

Ash raked his hand through his hair as he struggled to keep his temper in check. But it wasn't just anger he felt. There was shock, guilt and a hunger for her so profound he wasn't sure how he kept himself from her.

"I'm not most men." He picked her jeans up from the floor and handed them to her.

She gaped at him. "So that's it? You're just going to leave because I've never been with anyone else?"

"That's exactly what I'm going to do." He tried to reach the door, but she put herself in front of it as she raked him with her own furious glower.

"Oh the horror of this situation," she said, her tone so thick with sarcasm he'd need a chainsaw to cut through it. "So what you're telling me is if I go downstairs and get laid by some other man first, I'll then be good enough for you?"

Jealousy ripped through him at the mere thought.

She narrowed her gaze suspiciously. "You don't like that idea either, do you?"

Ash struggled to breathe as images of her with someone else tore through him. No, he didn't want her with anyone else, but at the same time he didn't want to be her first. He didn't want to hurt her and honestly, he didn't want her to remember him or have any regrets. She deserved better than that. Someone better than him to sleep with her. "How can you be a virgin at your age?"

"I'm not ninety, Acheron. Good grief. I told you, I have a bad history with men. Every time I ever tried to sleep with one, something happened. Either someone came in on us or . . . in one case the guy fell off the bed as he climbed in and broke his collar bone."

She took his head in her hands and forced him to look at her. "I want to be with you, Ash. No strings. No commitments. I'm a big girl and I'm not going to turn into a stalker. I just want to love you for a little while."

Those words seared him and at the same time he wanted to curse because they made it impossible for him to walk away from her. "You don't deserve to be laid in a room in a bar for your first time."

"And that right there is why I want to be with you. You're the only man I've ever met who would even think about that."

Because he knew what it was like to be ruthlessly violated and to be haunted by it. For some reason, the first encounter lingered in everyone's memory. It was why he'd always made sure to take special care with virgins and why he'd been so good at what he did. No one deserved to be humiliated the way he had been. To cry from the pain of it and be laughed at while he begged for mercy.

Stop your damn blubbering, whore. It'll be over when I'm finished with you. He'd then been backhanded so hard, it'd broken his nose. *There now. That pain'll get the other off your mind.*

Why with all the powers that he had could he not purge his own memories? Why was eleven thousand years not enough to make the pain turn dull?

All he wanted was one moment free of those memories. One safe place where no one reminded him of what they'd made him. Of what he'd done to himself.

Tory frowned at the shadows she saw in Ash's eyes as if some painful memory tortured him. She wanted to soothe that ache more than anything. Why wouldn't he let her? "Ash?"

He reached down to put his hand on the scar where they'd operated on her. "You shouldn't be out of bed."

"I'm not in pain. I don't understand it, but I'm not. And I don't want to go to bed alone. Are you going to make me beg?"

Anger curled his lips. "You don't ever beg for anything."

She pulled his head down so that she could kiss him.

Ash growled as she stirred inside him an animal part that scared him. But he refused to give in to it. "I won't tup you like a whore in a backroom, Soteria. Let me finish playing with the Howlers."

She eyed him suspiciously. "Then you'll be back?"

The hesitation in his eyes made her hurt for him. He drew a deep breath before he spoke. "I'll be back."

"Promise?"

"I promise."

She kissed the tip of his nose, hoping he was being honest with her. "I'm going to hold you to that."

Ash swallowed. She didn't have to. Once he made a promise, he was bound by the laws of the universe to see it through or die. "Rest until I get back." He gave her a deep kiss.

Tory melted at the feeling of his arm around her while he cupped her cheek with his other hand and ravaged her mouth.

He pulled back and drew another deep breath as if fighting for the strength to leave her.

622

She smiled at him. "Don't make me wait too long."

He nodded as he left her to dress.

Tory pulled her clothes on before she went outside again to find Justina and Katherine back at their chairs. Heat rushed over her cheeks until she remembered that the room was completely insulated from noise. "Can I borrow your cell phone?"

Justina pulled it out and handed it to her.

She called Pam. "Hey, sweetie . . . no I'm fine. I'm at the Sanctuary Bar over on Ursulines. Any chance I can get you two over here?"

"Sure. We'll be right there."

Tory hung up the phone and returned it to Justina. "Just FYI, I'm going to head out for a few minutes, but I'll be right back."

Katherine's expression turned stern and immovable. "You're not going anywhere without us. We're under strictest orders to keep you safe at all costs."

Ash . . . she could almost beat him for it, but then again that protectiveness was part of what she adored about him the most. At least sometimes.

Unwilling to fight, Tory held her hands up. "Fine. Just don't tell Ash. We'll slip out and be back before he finishes the next set."

Katherine didn't look convinced. "I'm not so sure about this."

"Oh, come on. It's just around the block a bit. We'll be fine. Besides forewarned is forearmed. We know to watch for them."

Katherine was still resisting.

"I trust her," Justina said. "She's stubborn, but not stupid. Tory wouldn't do this if she really thought there was a problem."

Katherine finally relented. "All right. So where are we going?"

Tory grinned. "It's a surprise."

Tory *hesitated in* the doorway of the overly bright store. Maybe this wasn't such a good idea after all . . . She looked over her shoulder at Pam who was proudly sporting her most prized possession, her vintage 1984 Duran Duran tour T-shirt.

"I don't know about this place. Isn't there another, less . . . um, extreme place to shop?"

Pam pushed her forward, into the store. "Oh shush, get inside. This is one of my favorite places and it's perfect for what you want."

Which didn't really endear it to Tory since Pam's fashion sense was the polar opposite of her own. While she was sedate, Pam was outrageous.

Kim pushed her from behind while Justina and Katherine opted to stay outside on Bourbon Street. "Come on, people, we're blocking the exit. Fire hazard here."

Tory's eyes widened as she went deeper into Pandora's Box, which was covered with spiked black leather corsets and teddys. All kinds of sex toys and pasties. *Oh my word*! She might be adventurous, but really, some of this stuff was just too much for her . . . like the men's bikini briefs that held an elephant's trunk where a certain piece of male anatomy would be. "I thought we were going to the little lingerie store on the corner."

"This is so much better." Pam pulled her to a display of edible panties.

Tory cringed at the thought of putting something like that on—would Ash even like it? "I'm not ready for all of this. Can't we ease me in slowly?"

Pam scoffed. "You're such a prude! How can a woman who lives to base jump cringe over edible panties?"

"Cause no one sees my panties when I base jump and they certainly don't eat them off me."

Pam gave an evil laugh. "Believe me, the panties are a lot more fun than base jumping. And given Ash's height, think of it more like pole vaulting." She wagged her eyebrows playfully.

Tory rolled her eyes.

"How about this?" Kim held up a pair of pink fuzzy handcuffs. "These could be fun . . . ooo and look at the sex dice. You get to roll for positions and acts."

"Hi, can I help you guys?"

Tory turned around to find a woman not much shorter than her with long auburn hair and a very round, pregnant body. Dressed all in black, she had a spiked purple collar that was decorated with chains and amethysts. She smiled as Pam turned to greet her. "Hey girl, how did those whips work out for you?"

Pam beamed with pride. "Like a charm, until we broke up. Men suck."

The woman winked evilly. "Yes, but that's when we love them best."

Pam laughed. "Tabitha Magnus, meet my best friend Tory Kafieri."

Tabitha sucked her breath in sharply as she wrinkled her face up and waved her hand in a kill gesture at her throat. "Ex-nay on the Greek ame-nay. Hubby's in the backroom doing taxes and he has a mental problem with all things Greek."

Kim looked shocked. "Really? I thought he was Italian."

"He is. It's that whole Rome versus Greece thing that he never really got over. He's a nutcase, but I love him."

Pam gestured to Tabitha's belly. "Obviously, and considering your condition and the store you own, I'd say you love him often."

Tabitha laughed insidiously as she placed a protective hand over her distended belly. "Honey, if you ever saw that man naked, you would, too." She grinned. "So what can I do for you guys?"

"Tory is planning on having sex."

"Pam!" Tory would have crawled under the nearest rack except for the fact it contained sex swings and other items she didn't want to think about.

Pam gave her an innocent blink. "Well you are, aren't you? It's not like Tabby can't tell from the mere fact that we're here. Not to mention you can see that she's had some herself." She pointed to Tabitha's stomach again.

Tory growled at her as she shook her head, then spoke to Tabitha. "I apologize for Pam. I accidentally hit her in the head with a baseball when we were in fifth grade and knocked her out cold. She's never been right since."

Tabitha laughed. "You can't embarrass me. Believe me. Pam and I are cut from the same cloth. So tell me a little bit about this guy and I'll find you the perfect thing for him."

Tory smiled at the mere thought of Ash. She didn't know why but it made her giddy and warm. "Well he's tall and dark-haired."

"Tall, please," Pam scoffed while Kim laughed. "The man is a giant. She found the only six-foot-eight guy I've ever seen. Ooo and Tab you ought to meet him. He's Goth and gorgeous."

"And Greek," Kim whispered.

Tabitha frowned as she looked at them suspiciously. "Really? He sounds just like a friend of mine . . ." Wrinkling her nose, she shook her head, "But no, it couldn't be him."

"Him who?" Tory asked.

"Ash Parthenopaeus."

Tory's eyes widened.

Then so did Tabitha's. "NO!" she breathed in total disbelief. "You're getting a piece of Ash? Oh my God, girl, you go!" Tabitha started waving her hands and cackling excitedly. "If you want to make some real money, make pictures. I know women the world over who would pay big to see him naked, myself included!"

Pam high fived her.

Tory buried her face against Kim's shoulder while Kim patted her on the head. "There, there, baby. We'll hide her body in the trunk later."

Tabitha began running around the store, pulling things down from racks and shelves. "Ash definitely requires something black . . . no wait. Red. *Racy* red." She held a red furry teddy up, made a face and shook her head before Tory could even comment. "Not really your color. Oh wait!" She ran to the back room, then came out with a sheer black babydoll that had small skull and crossbones with tiny pink bows on their heads. "Perfect for Ash. He'll love it."

Tory had to agree. But it made her wonder just how well Tabitha knew him. "Tabitha have you and Ash ever . . . ?"

"Please, no. Don't I wish." She leaned over to whisper in Tory's ear. "And don't tell my hubby I said that cause it would just make him mental. But before I met my baby, I dreamed many a dream of taking a bite out of that man if you know what I mean and since you're here I know that you do."

Tabitha went to a bookshelf at the back of the store and grabbed two books down. "You'll want these too."

Tory frowned at the one on top that featured a woman in a corset holding a cucumber. "*How To Tickle His Pickle?*"

Tabitha nodded proudly. "My personal fave. It's all you'll ever need to know to make a man go crazy."

The next book was even stranger. This one was even shrink-wrapped. Tory looked at it suspiciously. "*Manga Sutra?*"

"Ash loves manga." Tabitha patted the book and grinned. "He'll be very interested in that one, not that I think he doesn't know everything in it. But . . . could come in handy." Tabitha went to the front of the store and opened the glass cabinet near the register before she started pulling other things out.

Tory's face flamed at the items Tabitha piled on the counter. "They make flavored nipple cream?"

"Oh yeah, great stuff. It's not only flavored, but tinted to make you a bit rosier *and* best of all, it has a dab of menthol to make your nipples really hard so they're extra sensitive and men go wild for it. They just love stiffened nipples."

Kim and Pam laughed.

Tory covered her face with her hands and wanted to die of embarrassment. It was bad enough to have this stuff, but the fact that Tabitha knew Ash just made it all the more horrifying.

She was sure he'd be mortified to know that a friend of his had helped her pick this stuff out. And by the time she was being rung up, Tory was almost too embarrassed to go back to Sanctuary and face him.

As she dug out her credit card to pay for it, a tall extremely good looking man came out of the backroom. Dressed in a black turtleneck and slacks, he frowned at Tabitha who was still chattering away with Pam.

"You okay, baby?" he asked Tabitha, his eyes dark with concern as he came up to place a hand against her cheek. "You're extremely flushed."

Tabitha turned to him with an impish squeal. "Oh brace yourself, Val. Ash is getting laid tonight!" She pointed with both hands at Tory who wanted to crawl inside her purse and hide until old age claimed her.

To Val's credit, he didn't so much as blink. He offered Tory a commiserate smile. "It helps if you don't react to her comments. Tabitha lives to get a rise out of people. Just go with it and don't encourage her."

Tabitha snorted. "Be that way." She handed Tory the bag and thanked her.

"Thank you," Tory said.

"Good luck, hon, and remember . . . pictures!" Tabitha waited until they were gone before she whirled on Valerius. "Can you believe our Ash is getting laid?"

Val snorted. "Call me provincial, but I don't really consider him mine. And yes, I can believe the man has sex. What I find surprising is that this is the first time we've met the woman involved." He reached for his phone. "Maybe I should call and warn him."

"Oh put that away." She pushed it toward his pocket. "Our baby is growing up. I'm so proud!"

Tory *had barely* put the bag in the room before the band took another break. She'd just lain back down in bed when Ash opened the door with a tray in his hands.

"What's that?"

"I thought you might be hungry. I ran the options past Kim and she picked out what you should be eating." He set it down on the table beside her.

Tory smiled at his thoughtfulness. "*Efharisto.*"

"*Parakalo.*"

She melted at his unique accent as he said "you're welcome" in Greek. "I love the way you speak. I could listen to your Greek all day long."

He handed her another bottle of apple juice while he took a swig of his beer. "Are you completely bored?"

She reached up and pulled his sunglasses off so she could see his eyes. "Not entirely. How's the set going?"

"It's all right. I could kill Colt for hurting his hand. I don't really like playing in public."

"But you play so well."

"Yeah, but I'd rather play with myself." There was an evil glint in his eyes at the double entendre.

Laughing, Tory shook her head at him. "You and Pam, always trying to embarrass me."

"In my defense, it's because you're adorable when you blush."

She wrinkled her nose at him as she swallowed her bite of applesauce. "You want some?"

"*Ochi.*" No, in Greek.

"You sure?" She tried to tempt him again.

"Positive." Ash remembered the last time he'd eaten an apple. It'd been that day in the orchard with Ryssa when he'd begged his father not to send him back to Atlantis. Ever since then, he'd despised the fruit. The mere thought of it turned his stomach.

"So how many more sets do you have to play?"

"One more."

She bit her lip in a way that made him harden for want of her. "Then I get to play with you . . ."

His cock jerked, ready for action even while his brain knew better. "You should reconsider."

She reached out and took his hand in hers. Her thumb swept against his palm in the gentlest of caresses. "When was the last time you made love to someone, Ash?"

Ash looked away as painful memories surged. Honestly, he couldn't remember. Had he ever really made love to Artemis? Maybe in the very beginning. But it was so long ago and it hadn't lasted.

All he could remember was the pain of her criticisms. The sheer agony of being nothing more than her boy-toy, there only to please her while he wasn't allowed to have any feelings or opinions of his own. Only she could show her pain and displeasure while he was permitted nothing. Not even his dignity.

What they had was sex. Basic and primitive. There was no emotion involved really, unless it was anger.

Like all the others before her, she hated the fact that she

629

craved him and she sought to punish him for the fact that she slept with him. They merely used each other. If there had ever been any real tender feelings, they'd been shredded centuries ago. Nothing was left now except tattered remains of a yesterday neither could recapture.

"Can't you remember?" Tory asked.

"Not really," he answered truthfully.

Tory's heart tugged at the way he said those words. She touched his whiskered chin and turned his head until he was looking at her. "I'm going to make love to you, Ash. Tonight, I will rock your world."

Ash pressed her hand to his lips and nibbled her fingertips as fear and trepidation filled him. This night would cost him dearly.

No one should pay for love with blood and bone.

Yet he knew no other way. He'd always paid for every caress and every kindness. Nothing was ever freely given. The only question that ever mattered was, was it worth it?

Would Tory be worth the cost?

He hoped so. He returned the sunglasses to his face. "I'll be back."

Tory watched as he left and her heart was heavy for him. What were the secrets that tortured him so? Why did he look so afraid of touching her?

Finishing up her food, she went downstairs to watch him again. Pam and Kim were standing in the front, smiling. She came up behind them and goosed them on the bottom.

Pam goosed her back. "He's amazing, isn't he?"

"Yes, he is." Tory waved as Ash looked at her.

His answer was a sincere yet shy smile that warmed her heart and made her hot all over. The man was so choice . . .

She stayed there for several songs to watch and listen to Ash. When they started their final song, she went back upstairs so that she could get ready.

A*sh frowned as* he watched Tory leave the stage. *Is she all right?* he mouthed to Pam.

Pam nodded reassuringly.

Relieved, he couldn't wait until the song was done. The instant it was, he slung his Fender over his back, unplugged it, and jumped off the stage.

"You guys have fun," Pam said to him while Kim giggled. "We'll see you two later. Tell Tory to call me tomorrow."

"Will do." Ash cut through the crowd as he made his way back upstairs.

Justina and Katherine also took their leave with a promise to return in the morning.

Ash closed the outside door and locked it before he opened the one with a scanner. The moment he saw Tory, he froze. Dressed in a sheer black teddy that showed every curve of her body, she was dazzling. She'd brushed her hands through her hair, making it look rumpled.

Making her look delectable.

"Let me go shave real quick."

She frowned at him. "Shave?"

He ran the back of his fingers down his jaw, feeling how rough it was. "I don't want to give you whisker burn."

Tory was touched by his thoughtfulness. Until he tried to walk into the bathroom with the guitar on his back. He cursed as it caught sideways in the doorway. His face mottled with color from his embarrassment. "Guess I should take this off." He shrugged it over his head before he leaned it against the wall.

She covered her smile with her hand as she struggled not to laugh. He could be so adorable at times.

While he was in the bathroom, she thumbed through the quick notes she'd made in Tabitha's book. When he turned the water off, she put the book in the nightstand and tried to pose seductively on the bed.

Ash paused the towel against his chin as he caught sight of Tory on the bed with her legs tucked under her. She was trying to look seductive, but with her glasses on, it was a strange combination of the serious Tory and vixen.

And it made his cock hard. Tossing the towel aside, he dropped his coat in the doorway, then pulled his shirt off over his head.

Tory was stunned by that body and the muscles that rippled with every move. He knelt on the bed and crawled toward her on all fours like some lumbering, hungry predator.

He paused over her as his long black hair fell forward to frame his face. Their bodies weren't touching, but his swirling silver eyes seared her with heat. The muscles of his arms bulged from supporting his weight as he met her gaze. It was open, honest and at the same time she saw the fear in the back of those eyes and wondered what caused it.

The scent of leather and masculine skin made her instantly wet. He dipped his head down to hers and she shivered as only his lips made contact with hers. Then ever so slowly as he deepened that kiss to one of extreme potency, he lowered himself down on top of her until his weight pressed against her.

Tory sighed at the incredible sensation of his body on hers, of his lean hips resting between her legs. Her heart pounded at the bulge in his pants pressing against the center of her body. There was just so much of him. She reveled in the way he surrounded her with warmth and strength.

She ran her hands over his perfect back, feeling his muscles contract and tense as his mouth plundered hers. Wrapping her body around his, she rolled him over until he was pinned under her.

Ash didn't move as she pulled back to kiss her way down his chest toward his navel. The sight of her so hungry for him made him ache not just from lust but from some inner part of him that wanted, just once, to have someone really love him. She cupped him through his pants, making him growl in pleasure. Looking up, she smiled at him as she nipped his stomach. Her playfulness was so charming and sweet. So very precious.

He cupped her face in his hands and returned her smile as he sought to burn this memory into his heart so that he'd always have it close.

She moved to take his boots off. He held himself perfectly still as she unzipped his left one and removed it. She tossed his boot to the floor.

She pulled the other boot off and tossed it over her shoulder before she moved toward his pants. Ash sucked his breath in and held it as she reached for his zipper. The sight of her head poised over his fly . . . It was almost enough to make him come.

She pushed her glasses back up on her nose. Smiling at him, she unbuttoned his pants. Ash waited, his heart pounding as she slowly slid the zipper down to expose him.

Tory bit her lip in satisfaction as she freed him from his pants. The man was completely commando and he was huge. Not that she was surprised. Her earlier encounters with that bulge had given her some idea of its size, but this . . .

She pulled his pants off and took a minute to just soak in the beauty of his naked body. Tabitha was right, she could be rich if she took pictures of him and posted them online. He was flawless. Absolutely flawless. From his wide shoulders to the narrow hips all the way down those long, muscled legs that were dappled with black hairs.

And she wanted to please every bit of him.

Taking her glasses off, she placed them on the nightstand, then returned to stroke his hardness.

Ash leaned his head back as pleasure assaulted him. He watched through hooded eyes while she studied his cock. Opening her lips, she started to take the tip into her mouth then pulled back and frowned. She tilted her head and opened her lips as if trying to think of the best way to taste him.

She moved toward his cock again, then pulled back . . . again.

"You're killing me, Soteria."

"I'm sorry." She scurried away from him, and put her glasses back on before she opened the drawer and pulled out a book.

Ash scowled while she thumbed through the pages to a section that had a small makeshift bookmark and notes in the margin. "What are you doing?"

She ran her finger down the notes. "I just want to make sure that I do this right."

Leaning up on one elbow, he nipped her shoulder then gaped at the graphic drawings of a woman going down on

633

a man. He pulled the book out of her hands and frowned at the title. "*How to Tickle His Pickle?*"

She shrugged adorably. "You know I don't know what I'm doing. I wanted to make sure that I pleased you, too."

Those words struck a chord so deep inside him that for a solid minute he couldn't breathe past the swell of emotion he felt for her. "There's nothing you could do that wouldn't please me." He kissed her gently as he dropped the book to the floor. "You don't need that, Tory." He took her glasses off and put them away before he returned to her lips. "All you have to do is touch me and I promise you I'm in ecstasy."

Tory swallowed as he led her hand to his cock and showed her how to stroke him. Wanting to make him happy, she dipped her head down to taste the moisture that was leaking from his tip.

Ash stopped moving the moment her lips closed around his cock. Not wanting to hurt her, he didn't so much as breathe while she explored him with her mouth. "You have the sweetest tongue," he growled.

She ran her hands over his thighs until she cupped his sac while she tasted him. Ash was blind from the pleasure of her touch. Unable to stand it, he pulled himself away from her. "I have a lot of control, Tory, but not with you doing that and I want to be inside you too badly to spoil it."

"Okay." She leaned to her side and pulled her sheer black panties off. Ash watched as she slid them down those long, graceful legs. His mouth literally watered as his body turned so hard he could drive a nail in with it.

She dropped her panties to the floor before she pulled a condom from the nightstand. "So how do we do this?"

As he unwrapped it and put it on, a thousand different positions played through his mind of how he'd like to take her. And just the thought of being inside her was enough to make him whimper.

But sex always hurt the first time and he was big enough to make it excruciating for her. That was the last thing he wanted.

"First, we have to get your body ready for me."

"I'm ready."

He laughed at her eagerness. His body burning, he sank his thumb inside her. She bit her lip and jerked in response. "You are wet." He dipped his head so that he could tongue her and make her even more slick.

Tory spread her legs wider wanting to feel as much of him as was possible. "You're killing me, Acheron."

"Patience, love, patience." He slid one long finger deep inside her. She shivered in response as his tongue swirled and teased. That finger was followed by another. He slid his chin against her. "Come for me, Soteria. I want to taste you."

When he returned to her, she had no choice except to obey. Her orgasm split through her until she was sure she'd die from it. Wave after wave cascaded over her and still he didn't enter her.

Instead, he rolled her over, onto her stomach. Before she could ask him what he intended, he began massaging her. Not just a regular massage, but one that loosened every muscle in her body.

"I don't want you to tense," he explained, his voice thick with his melodic accent.

"Oh trust me, I'm putty."

His deep laughter filled her ears before he slid his fingers into her again.

Ash bit his lip as his body ached, wanting inside hers. She was even wetter now. One more orgasm and he'd be able to enter her without too much pain.

Leaning down, he nipped at her buttocks.

Tory yelped at the pleasant pain that was followed by his hands delving even deeper inside her as Ash moved his mouth to kiss her at the base of her spine. He pushed her sheer gown up to her shoulders with his face while his hands worked magic on her body. Then he moved his hand so that he could rub his cock against her without entering her. She gasped at the sensation while he moved his hands to cup her breasts.

It was more than she could stand. Before she could draw another breath, her body climaxed again.

This time, he drove himself deep inside her body as her orgasm mounted. Tory groaned at the foreign sensation of his body inside hers. The thickness only made her orgasm all the more intense.

She cried out from the blind pleasure of it.

His throat dry, Ash didn't move as he felt her body clutching his. It took all of his strength not to thrust, but it wasn't time yet. Her body was still stretching to accommodate him. "Are you all right?"

"Are you kidding?" She slid herself further down his shaft.

He gasped as pleasure almost overrode his control.

"Is this right?"

"Yes," he breathed, squeezing his eyes tightly shut as his entire body shivered.

She rocked herself against him even harder.

"Stop!" Ash cried.

Tory froze, afraid she'd hurt him. "What's wrong?"

He pulled out of her and rolled over onto his back to look up at her. He brushed the hair back from her face before he ran the pad of his thumb over her bottom lip. "I want to come while looking at you."

She kissed him as he pulled her over his body. She straddled his hips while they kissed.

Ash trailed his hand down her back until he touched himself so that he could guide his shaft back inside her. They gasped in unison as she sank herself down on him.

As she did so, her thoughts whispered through his head. *Am I doing this right? I hope he's not disappointed. Why can't I do this with my glasses on so that I can see him better? Please don't be disappointed, Ash.*

Those doubts tore through him. Most of all the sincerity of them, the concern for him brought tears to his eyes. "You're wonderful, Tory. Perfect."

She paused to squint at him. "Really?"

"Yes," he breathed, reaching down so that he could stroke her while she rode him slow and easy. His throat tight, her gentleness succeeded in breaking him where the beatings never had.

One small tear slid from the corner of his right eye. Slamming them shut, he surrendered himself to her. Right now, this moment, she owned him in a way no one ever had before.

No, she didn't own him.

He gave himself to her and for the first time, he understood the difference. He understood what it meant to make love. To share his body with someone not out of obligation or fear, but because it made them closer.

In this one heartbeat, he was hers and she was his.

Tory burned at the sensation of Ash deep inside her. All her life she'd wondered what this would feel like. But her imagination had nothing on this reality. Nothing on the beauty of feeling the restrained strength of Ash lying under her.

He was so hard and fierce and yet so gentle. She wished that she could crawl inside him or more to the point that she could wrap herself around him and keep him from harm forever.

If only he'd let her.

Ash cupped her face in his hands and kissed her passionately an instant before he came with a force so strong it rendered him temporarily senseless. Growling, he pulled back to stare in her eyes as he tasted the first real bliss he'd ever known.

And it was followed by a fear so profound that his heart stilled. Now that they were finished, how would she react?

Would she shove him away? Would she cry? Hit him? Curse him?

He held his breath, waiting.

Smiling, she leaned herself against his chest and cuddled there like a kitten while their bodies were still joined. She let out a deep sigh as she stroked his shoulder and arm. "That was even better than I'd ever dreamed."

Ash flinched, still expecting the worst. "You're not mad at me?"

"Why would I be?" She took his hand in hers and brought it to her lips so that she could nibble his knuckles.

Ash relaxed as he realized that she wasn't angry or upset at him for what they'd done. And the more he relaxed, the more he enjoyed the sensation of her naked body lying against his. "I could stay like this forever."

"Wouldn't it be nice?"

He nodded as he leaned his head against hers and inhaled the scent of her hair. Unfortunately, he felt himself sliding out of her. Damn.

"I better take care of this." He reluctantly moved her to her side so that he could pull the condom off.

Tory watched as he left the bed. Hating to not see him, she reached over to get her glasses. After they were in place, she opened the Sprite that she'd left there and took a sip.

Ash returned with a wet cloth for her. "Sorry it's so messy."

She fingered his lips. "I like your mess. I think you taste wonderful." She exchanged her drink for his cloth.

Ash had never tasted a soda before. Curious, he took a drink of it and was surprised by the sharp tartness. "Wow, this is actually good."

"Haven't you ever had a Sprite before?"

"No."

She rolled her eyes as she cleaned herself. "I know, you stick to beer."

Ash didn't answer as he took a deep draft of it again. He frowned as a strange wave of dizziness went through his head. If he didn't know better, he'd think he was getting a buzz from it. But that was impossible. As a god, he didn't get drunk. And even if he did, there was nothing in soda that would intoxicate him.

Tory frowned as she watched Ash down the whole twenty ounces of Sprite in one gulp. "Ash?"

"Is there more of this?"

He was acting peculiar. Like he was drunk.

"There should be another bottle in the fridge."

He licked his lips as he cupped her chin in his hand. "You know, you are beautiful for a human."

"What else would I be?"

He laughed before he kissed her. "You could be a goddess, but you're not bitch enough for that. Then again, Katra isn't a bitch. She's beautiful like you." He cocked his head as if another random thought occurred to him. "I need to see my daughter soon. She's going to have a baby. A girl like her only not like her. It'll be a baby her with a lot more power. I just hope she has enough of her father in her not to be a goddess of destruction. There are already too many of us. We need more who are innately good."

Tory was baffled by his rambling tone that was half Greek and half English. "What in the world are you talking about?" There was no way he was old enough to have a daughter old enough to give birth to a baby. "Are you screwing with me, Ash?"

He nipped her breast. "I've already done that, Soteria, and I enjoyed it like nothing I've ever enjoyed ever. Where's that drink?"

She handed him another bottle. "Are you drunk?"

"I feel drunk." He looked up at her and smiled brightly. "I'm drunk on your beauty. Look what you've done to me, human." He took a drink of Sprite, then set it aside and reached for her. "Touch me, Soteria. I feel so clean and whole when you touch me." He rubbed her hand against his chest, raking her nails against his nipple and as he did so, she saw a scar appear that ran from his throat all the way down past his navel. Another scar, a hand print, appeared around his throat as the hair on his entire body changed from black to blond.

"Ash?"

His eyes turned a dark, fiery red.

Terrified, Tory got up to run for the door.

Somehow Ash appeared in front of her. "Where are you going?"

Terrified and unsure of him, she gulped. "What are you?"

"I'm a god, Soteria. The last of the Atlantean pantheon."

CHAPTER FOURTEEN

Terrified, Tory backed away from Ash as those words went through her. He was insane . . . and she was in a sound-proof room, naked with a lunatic.

Oh dear God!

"Okay," she said slowly, stretching the word out until she could think of some way to get to the door behind him and safely out of the room before he killed her. "Let's calm down. Can I get the normal, brooding Ash back?"

He looked as if her words hurt him. "Don't be afraid of me, Tory. I wanted to tell you that I was a god, but I didn't know how." Closing his eyes, he slid down the door to sit on the floor with his legs gathered tight to his chest. That gesture reminded her of a little boy who was upset that he'd been banished to his room for something he hadn't meant to do. "I knew you wouldn't like me if you found out the truth. No one ever likes me when they find out."

He looked up at her and his eyes returned to that swirling silver color. "He will be called Acheron for the river of woe. Like the river of the underworld, his journey shall be dark, long and enduring. He will be able to give life and to take it. He will walk through his life alone and abandoned—ever seeking kindness and ever finding cruelty. May the gods have mercy on you, little one. No one else ever will."

Tory frowned as he recited something that obviously caused him a great deal of pain. "What is that from?"

A tic worked in his jaw as his cheeks mottled with color. How could a lunatic be so handsome?

"It's what the priestess said over me when I was born into the mortal realm as a cursed god because my father wanted my mother to kill me to prevent our pantheon from falling." He looked away. "I wish she had . . . You don't know what it's like to walk through the world always alone in every crowd. Everyone sees me, but no one knows me." He hung his head in his hands. "I should never have touched you. What have I done? I will pay for this night for the rest of eternity." The anguish in his tone tore through her.

Tory approached him slowly. "If you're really an ancient god, prove it to me. Make me see clearly without my glasses."

He kept his face buried on top of his arms. "Okay."

The word had barely left his lips before her vision clouded. She sucked her breath in sharply at the pain. Removing her glasses, she blinked and then gasped as everything came into focus. Everything.

Her sheer babydoll then turned into a flowing silk gown that clung to her body and covered her completely.

Unable to believe it, she ran her hands over the cool, slick material and looked around the room at things that had always been shadows to her. It was all sharp and crisp now.

All of it.

Which meant she had a choice to make. Either he was telling her the truth or he was a very hot-looking faith-healer or they were both nuts.

She opted for the truth, which explained a lot more than just her sudden ability to see. It explained those strange eyes of his and his ability to read a language no one else could even identify.

Kneeling on the floor by his side, she approached him warily, ready to bolt if she needed to. "You kept me from dying, didn't you?"

He lifted his head and reached out to put one hand over the small scar on her forearm that she'd had there since a childhood accident from a broken bottle mishap. As he touched it, it glowed and then vanished. "I know better than to interfere with the natural order, but I couldn't let you die. I didn't want to watch you suffer."

"Why would you do that?"

He led her hand to his face so that she was touching his cheek as he stared at her. His eyes and the pain in them burned her soul deep. "Because I don't feel broken when you look at me."

Those words brought tears to her eyes. "How could you feel broken?"

He rubbed his face against her palm and when he spoke, his breath scorched her skin. But it was his words that branded her heart. "I was shattered as a child and thrown away, like a piece of trash no one wanted. But *you* don't treat me like that. You see in me the human bit and you touch that part of me. You make me feel whole and wanted."

Tory pulled him against her and held him close as her tears finally fell.

"I love when you hold me," he whispered against her shoulder.

Tory laid her cheek against the top of his head. "Why did you come to Nashville?"

He went rigid in her arms, then spoke in a language she couldn't understand.

"I don't know what you're saying, Ash."

He pulled back and cupped her face so that she could see the fury in his eyes as red tinged the outer line of them. "No one can know about Atlantis. They can't know about me, Soteria. No one can ever know what I was there or what I am now. I didn't mean to hurt you, but I can't let you expose me. *Ever.*" He growled that word through clenched teeth.

A tremor of fear went through her along with a jolt of anger. "Are you the one who killed my parents when they got too close?"

He shook his head in denial. "I don't like taking human lives. They're too short. Daimons, demons, immortals and gods . . . they're fair game. But I don't tamper with humans if I can help it. I won't do to them what was done to me."

"What was done to you?"

He grimaced and pulled away. He tried to stand, then staggered and fell back to the floor. His expression baffled, he reminded her of a boy and not a powerful god. "What is wrong with me?"

"I think you're drunk." He sounded extremely intoxicated.

"I am drunk, but I don't know why." He started to lie down on the floor.

Tory caught him. "We need to get you into bed. C'mon, sweetie, help me get you there."

His hair turned black, then a very dark green laced with black streaks through it as they staggered toward the bed. The stud in his nose vanished, along with the scars of it ever having been pierced. She helped him lie down and covered him with a blanket. As he closed his eyes, she realized something.

For the first time, she was looking at the real him. He was completely naked and exposed to her. And she wasn't talking about his body. He had no defenses against her. No sunglasses or piercings to hide behind. He was completely vulnerable to her and something told her that he'd never been like this with anyone else.

She ran her hand over his chest as another thought tore through her mind. Acheron was Atlantean.

Atlantean . . . He knew every secret she'd spent her lifetime trying to learn. *Dear Lord, I'm touching someone who's lived thousands and thousands of years*. She could barely fathom it. He'd seen every culture that had ever fascinated her. "Ash?"

"Mmm?"

"What was Atlantis like?"

He let out a tired sigh. "It was ugly and beautiful."

"Can you show me?"

Ash came awake to the worst imaginable pain throbbing in his head. For the merest instant, he thought he was human again, waking up after a night of binge drinking and drugs.

But that was thousands of lifetimes ago.

Blinking open his eyes, he found himself naked in bed with Tory sitting on the floor, staring at him as if she were in shock while an odd noise kept an off beat rhythm in the background.

"Is something wrong?" he asked, his voice thick and scratchy.

She screwed her face up as she scowled at him. "Define something wrong."

Ash rubbed a hand over his face. "Did you beat me with a hammer while I was sleeping?"

"No."

"Then why do I feel like this?"

She still hadn't moved from her spot on the floor. "Apparently you can't hold your Sprite, buddy."

"Wha . . . ?"

She pointed at the two empty green plastic bottles on the nightstand. "Did you know that when you get drunk, *she* gets drunk too."

"She?"

Tory gestured toward the strange sound Ash had been hearing, but ignoring. He looked to see Simi lying on the floor, under the TV with her legs propped against the wall while she slept on her back and snored. That would have been bad enough, but the fact that she was in her demon form, complete with horns, tail and wings made his stomach shrink.

What had he done?

And then his gaze fell to the three-dimensional hologram on the floor that was a perfect replica of Atlantis. It even had tiny people moving around like some glowing white movie . . .

Oh shit.

Shit, shit, shit. It was all he could think to say as disbelief overwhelmed him.

Tory rose slowly and folded her arms over her chest. Narrowing her gaze on him, she approached the bed. "You don't remember anything about last night, do you?"

"I remember us . . ." He looked down to see the blood on the sheets that substantiated that part of his memory. They had slept together. The memory of her touch was branded in his mind and on his skin.

"But you don't remember the Sprite?"

He shook his head.

"Interesting."

He didn't know why that one word frightened him, but it did. "Interesting?"

She nodded. "You're a very cuddly drunk and quite the chatterbox too."

He felt the blood leave his face. "How chattery?"

"Very . . . Apostolos."

Ash sat up, mortified by what he might have said to her. *Please gods, please . . .* surely he hadn't told her what he was. Surely he wouldn't have been so stupid as to lose the only person he'd ever found who didn't see him as a whore. And it was then he realized she didn't have her glasses on. "Did I—"

"Fix my eyes? Yes. Then you summoned your demon and the two of you fought over taking me to Atlantis. Simi's the one who made the map on the floor so that we could all stay here because she said going there while you two were drunk might be bad since you'd probably destroy it before your mother had a chance. And then you shrank me down to toy size and took me through the city street by street, telling me about every piece of it, until you both passed out. Thankfully when you did so, I got bigger."

Still his stomach churned. "Did either of us physically take you to the real Atlantis?"

"I should tell you yes, to make you sweat. But Simi won the battle and we stayed here."

He let out a long relieved breath that he'd listened to his demon. Thank the gods for small favors there.

But it still didn't change the fact that he'd exposed himself to Tory. Completely. Utterly.

Damn.

He swallowed as he met her unflinching gaze. "Are you mad at me?"

"Furious. Truly. But I understand the lies. I mean, really, who's going to believe that this hot twenty-one-year-old buff stud Goth guy sporting a black backpack is an eleven-thousand-year-old omnipotent god who travels with a demon companion? Right? It's ludicrous."

Ash cringed as all of his secrets poured out of her mouth.

"By the way, you do know that you and I have met before."

He paused as he tried to recall the event and couldn't. "When?"

She sat down on the bed beside him. "1988. You were playing chess with my grandfather in the park when he had his heart attack. I was seven."

Now *that* Ash remembered vividly. Theo had just moved his bishop to take down Ash's queen when the old man grabbed at his chest and started groaning.

His tiny granddaughter with big brown eyes and a flurry of brown pigtails had come running. "Papou! Papou!"

Not wanting the child to see her grandfather die—if that was to be Theo's fate that day—Ash had summoned Simi to watch over the girl while he called an ambulance. *"Watch her, Simi. Keep her happy and make sure she has everything she needs and wants."*

Then he'd gone with Theo while Simi took Soteria back to Theo's condo to wait.

How had he forgotten that?

He shook his head as he looked at her and finally saw the little girl's sweet features in the face of the woman before him. "I remember."

"You know, I thought you were Billy Idol."

Now *that* he couldn't understand at all. "Billy Idol? I don't look anything like him and I've never had spiked hair."

She shrugged. "He was the only rock star I knew who wore leather and chains and sunglasses—like you had on

646

that day. You also had long purple hair and an earring. Later, I kept telling everyone about this punk guy who saved my papou. My idolizing you is a big part of the reason Kim and Pam ended up Goth . . . ironic really."

She glanced over to where Simi was still sleeping against the wall. "It wasn't until I saw Simi again last night that it all clicked into place for me." When her gaze locked onto his, the intelligence and accusation in it actually made him cringe. "You're the one who dug my grandfather out of his burning house when he was seven years old and brought him over from Greece. The man who watched over him the whole way here and told him the stories about Atlantis that he told to my father and uncle."

Ash wanted to deny it, but how could he? She now knew everything. "Yes."

She nodded. "That alone is why I'm controlling my anger at you for lying to me and humiliating me in public after I was doing nothing more than telling the stories you, yourself, told my grandfather. How can I be mad at a man who braved a Nazi attack to pull a seven-year-old boy out of the wreckage of his house and save his life? My grandfather said that you bandaged his eyes and then carried him in your arms for days until you reached the docks where you had to bribe the snot out of everyone to get him out of the country. He was so scared and griefstricken from the loss of his family. The only thing that kept him sane was the deep voice of Acheron telling him that he'd be all right. That he wouldn't let anything else bad happen to him while the man held him and soothed his tears . . . that was *you*. You were the one who found the American family who adopted him, who helped him finance his first deli, and all his life you were the man he met in the park on Sunday afternoon to play chess with." She sniffed back tears that made his own eyes water. "How could I ever hate you?"

Ash looked away as his own emotions tangled. Everyone else had hated him. How could he expect her to be any different?

Tory swallowed and looked at Simi. "I've spoken to her so many times on the phone and through e-mails. My cousin Geary and I even named our expedition the Simi Project because Simi was the one who helped us find the location of Atlantis."

Ash's eyes widened at something he'd had no knowledge of. Anger snapped to the forefront of his emotions as he wanted to choke the demon. "Simi did what?"

"You told me to, akri," Simi said from her place on the floor before she yawned loudly. When she spoke again, her voice was a perfect duplication of his. "Watch her, Simi. Keep her happy and make sure she has everything she needs and wants." Her voice returned to normal. "So that's what the Simi did, akri. Just what you told me to do."

"That was for one afternoon."

"Akri didn't say that to the Simi. You say make her happy so the Simi did. If you wanted me to stop, akri, you should have said so."

Ash raked his hands through his hair as he realized how much pain he'd brought to Theo when all he'd ever wanted to do was help the boy—that he'd exposed himself and revealed the location of Atlantis without meaning to. Damn it. "I know better than to interact with humans. How could I have been so stupid?"

Tory leaned over him, her face so sweet and inviting even though to him, right now, she was the greatest threat. "You can't live alone all the time, Ash . . . or is it Asheron, Acheron or Apostolos? I don't even know what to call you."

Call me yours . . .

It was such a stupid thought. And he knew better than to ever let that one out. He was owned body and soul by Artemis. "I don't care which one you use. I answer to all of them."

"You must have a preference."

"Only his mama, Akra-Apollymi, call him Apostolos. Ooo and sometimes that Jaden demon man and Savitar who is always so nice to the Simi. He always brings the Simi good things to eat. But I think akri likes Ash best cause that's what he tells most people when he meets them nowadays."

Ash gave her a dry stare. "Thanks, Sim."

648

"You're welcome, akri," she said, oblivious to his sarcasm. "Now the Simi's head hurts. Can I sleep on you where it's comfortable until it stops aching so much? I don't like the floor anymore. It hurts the Simi's wings."

He held his arms out. "Of course you can, Simykey."

Smiling, she transformed and flew as a black mist onto his body to form a small dragon tattoo on his shoulder.

Tory narrowed her gaze on Simi's form. "Now I know the secret of the ever-changing tattoo. You got anymore surprises for me?"

"I suppose that depends on what else I said last night. Damn. At what point did I pass out?"

"From your point of view, not soon enough I would imagine."

If he were able to get the sick lump of dread out of his stomach, he would have laughed at that. As it was, the best he could muster was a grimace. "You are taking all of this remarkably well."

She crossed her legs under herself before she shrugged nonchalantly. "What am I supposed to do? I mean it's not like I have some precedent for dealing with this. I don't know anyone who's ever met a guy who turned out to be a god with his own personal demon. Inner demons, yes, but a tattoo that becomes a demon . . . no. Definitely off the grid."

"Actually that's not entirely true."

She blinked. "What do you mean?"

"You should talk to your cousin Geary. Her husband, Arik, used to be an Oneroi."

Tory sat perfectly still as if she couldn't believe what he'd just told her. Kind of funny to him given the way she seemed to be accepting everything else. After a brief pause, she asked a single question. "Arik was the Greek dream god?"

He nodded.

Tory covered her mouth with her hand. "So that's why Geary gave up the hunt for Atlantis. That weenie! It was right after she'd met Arik in Greece." Her expression angry, she slapped at his thigh.

"Ow!" Ash rubbed the spot, grateful she hadn't hit him any higher on his leg. "What's that for?"

649

"Why didn't one of you tell me?"

"It's not exactly something we're supposed to talk about with humans. Most of them aren't as reasonable as you're being."

"Yeah well, you do know this changes nothing." Her gaze showed every ounce of her determination. "I still intend to be the one who discovers Atlantis."

Ash froze as his own resolve set itself. In this battle, he was going to win no matter what. "Don't be stubborn, Tory. Let it go."

"That's easy for you to say. You don't know the mockery my family has lived with because you told my grandfather stories that enchanted the imagination of his sons. Both my father and uncle gave their lives to find Atlantis and prove it's there. I can do no less than to revive their reputations."

He cupped her face in his hand and tried to make her understand why she couldn't do this. "They're dead, Tory. Their reputations mean nothing to them."

Ash felt her clench her teeth as anger and grief flickered in her brown eyes. "They mean *everything* to me."

How could he make her see his point of view?

"You want to salvage your father's reputation and I want to preserve mine. You and I are at war with this. No one can know ever about the Atlantis that was destroyed."

"You're a god. Why would its location hurt *your* reputation?"

A twinge of hope went through him. "Did I tell you why I was in Atlantis as a human?"

"No."

Oh thank the gods that even drunk he'd had at least an ounce of self-preservation. Relief and joy poured through him. No wonder she was still giving him some respect.

And that was why he couldn't let anyone know about Atlantis. "Why can't you let this go?"

"Because I loved my father. I owe this to him."

Ash narrowed his gaze. "Would you destroy me in the process?"

Tory shook her head, trying to understand why he was so insistent. "You're not making any sense. How could this possibly hurt you?"

650

Tell her the truth, Apostolos. Ash flinched at the sound of his mother's voice in his head.

He looked up at the ceiling as he sensed her presence. *You've been remarkably quiet throughout this, Matera. Why didn't you tell me about your priestesses?*

Why should I? Besides you knew I had to have worshipers to maintain my god powers at their current strength. Did you think the Daimons were the only ones who paid homage to me?

Yeah, stupidly he had.

Show her the journal, m'gios.

And if she betrays me?

She's a human. I will kill her if she hurts you.

But he wouldn't allow that and he knew it. *I can't, Matera. I don't want to see her look at me like that too.*

What if she doesn't? What if she's being honest and to her you are nothing more than a friend? Your past doesn't matter to me. It doesn't matter to Savitar or Simi. You must learn to trust sometime, Apostolos. Don't you think that maybe she's the one person who won't judge you over something that was done to you against your will? Give her a reason to abandon Atlantis. Let her understand.

He looked back at Tory, terrified of the thought of seeing the same pity in her eyes that Ryssa had held in hers. He liked the fact that Tory saw him as a normal human.

Then again, she now knew him to be a god and her treatment hadn't changed. Maybe his mother was right. Maybe he could trust her.

"You can't live in darkness all the time, kid"—Savitar's words haunted him. "Sooner or later, everyone puts their ass in a sling. But you know what, most of the time you're still laughing about it, grateful you had the fun that caused the injury."

It was true. Yet the one thing Ash understood to the depth of his soul was that a physical pain healed a lot cleaner and sooner than a mental one.

"Please don't hurt me, Soteria," he whispered in Atlantean. Feeling sick with dread, he decided to trust in his mother. He held his hand out and used his powers to bring his backpack into his grasp.

651

Tory let out a nervous laugh. "You weren't joking about those evil Jedi tricks, were you?"

"Not really." He reached to the bottom and pulled out the last journal. His stomach knotted to the point he feared he'd actually be sick, he handed to her. "I grant you the ability to read this fluently. But know that I'm doing this against my better judgment and I'm trusting you with something about me that no one else has ever known. No one. This is the secret I'm willing to kill to protect. Do you understand?"

Tory swallowed at the ominous note in his voice. What could it contain that was so appalling to a god? "I understand."

He put the backpack down on the floor. "I'm going to shower while you read."

She didn't move until after he'd left the bed. Curious, she opened the book and gasped as she realized that she was able to read it as if it were English. She knew every letter, every definition. It was incredible and as she read, she saw the scenes as clearly in her mind as if she were watching a movie unfold.

At first it was just the intimate and innocuous details of a princess's life until it started talking about her brother . . .

The whore.

Ash let the water slide over his skin as he fought the pain and anger inside him. Tory would never look at him the same way again. Ever.

Why the hell had he listened to his mother? He should have destroyed every one of his sister's journals.

I'm such an asshole.

There was no denying the truth of him. He was forever tainted by a past he'd never wanted. In this moment he hated Estes more than he'd ever hated him before. That one foul bastard had deprived him of everything.

Even Tory's respect.

Turning the water off, he stepped outside the shower to find her standing in the doorway, staring at him. Shame and embarrassment filled him at her silence as he reached for a towel to dry himself. He braced himself for her insults and anger. "I'm sorry I tainted you, Soteria. I had no right."

A single tear slid down her face as she approached him.

Ash tensed in expectation of her slap or insults. He deserved no less and he expected nothing more. So when she pulled him into her arms and kissed him, he was stunned completely.

Tory pulled away from his lips and wrapped her arms around his neck to hold him close as the true horror of his human life tore through her. And to think she'd dared to accuse *him* of not understanding what it was like to be mocked or humiliated. Thank God she had no idea of the depth of his sorrow that made a mockery of hers.

She couldn't speak for the tangle of emotions that gathered in her throat to choke her. She was angry for him and heartbroken.

And in that moment, she realized how much she loved this man. Now Takeshi's words made complete sense to her.

"Take care of him, Soteria. And remember it takes great courage and heart for a man who knows no kindness to show it to another. Even the wildest of beasts can be tamed by a patient and gentle hand."

She ran her hand down his smooth, perfect back as she remembered the stories of his beatings. They hadn't even allowed his back to scar so that the thicker, scarred skin would help to shield him from the pain of new lashes. What had been done to him was so wrong . . . "I'm so sorry for what they did to you, Acheron. I'm so sorry."

Ash closed his eyes as he held her against him and breathed her in. "You don't condemn me for it?"

"For what?"

"I'm . . ." He couldn't bring himself to say the word whore to her.

Tory tightened her hold as she remembered his words about being broken the night before. This was what he'd meant by them. Pulling back, she cupped his face in her hands so that he could see her sincerity. "Nothing has changed between us. I don't care about your past, Ash. I don't. All that matters to me is the man in front of me right now."

"I'm not a man, Soteria."

No, he wasn't. He was a god. Powerful. Humble. Kind and deadly. For the first time, she understood all the glimpses of him that she'd seen. "I know. But if you think your godhood excuses you from putting the toilet seat down, think again."

Ash laughed, amazed by her strength and humor no matter the situation. "I'm not used to anyone standing with me."

"I know. I was always lucky. My family would fight back the devil himself to keep me safe. I can't imagine the strength it took for you to be alone in the world. To have no shelter from those out to hurt you. But I won't abandon you. If I'm nothing else in my life, I'm loyal to those I call friend. And I'll be more than honored to be your friend, Acheron, if you'll let me."

Pain ravaged his heart at her offer and at a single truth he couldn't deny. "I've never had a friend who knew all about me before." He didn't count Artemis as a friend and that lack of knowledge was how Nick had ended up dead. Had he trusted Nick enough, just once, to introduce him to Simi, Nick wouldn't have slept with her because he'd have known she belonged to Ash. It was a mistake that had cost them both everything.

"I know what you're thinking, Ash," she said, stepping back to look up at him. "You have trusted me and I will never forsake you."

Time would tell.

She looked down and smiled warmly. "By the way, you're very cute naked. Now get dressed. I have some questions for you."

He was instantly clothed.

Tory's eyes widened at his powers. "You know that could come in handy. I'll bet you're never late, huh?"

"I try. Now what questions do you have?"

She led him back into the room where the journal was lying on the bed. "You told me last night that you have a pregnant daughter. Now from the journal's date, I know how old you are. How old is she?"

"I was twenty-one when she was born." It was the easiest explanation for Kat's age.

Tory picked the journal up and opened to the scrap of paper where she'd left off reading. "Okay so she's a great-great-great-grandmother. Messes with my head, but I can deal with that." She made a note in the margin of the journal. "Who's her mother?"

"I'd rather not say."

"Artemis. Understood. We never talk about that."

He frowned at her ability to guess and to be so accommodating about his redheaded problem. "How—"

She put her hand to his lips to keep him from speaking. "I got it from the journal that you protect her even when she refuses to return the favor. But my next question to you is what is she going to do when she finds out about me?"

Satara stayed back in the shadows of Sanctuary, pretending to be a patron at a table sipping her longneck beer—a rather nasty concoction—as she waited for Acheron to leave the room where he was holed up with his newfound pet. The only real gift her father, Apollo, had ever given her was the ability to pass undetected by other gods. He'd done that so she could spy for him. Little did he know that she used her gift against him more than for him—for a god of prophecy, her father could be unbelievably dense. Then again, his ego was such that he couldn't conceive of anyone not absolutely adoring the very ground he stood upon.

And because of her gift, to Acheron, even with all the powers he possessed, she blended into the background. How nice to have an anti-Atlantean cloaking device.

Which had been very helpful last night while she'd been in the club trying to gather information for Stryker and instead had learned about Acheron's current female obsession. Or should she say, weakness.

The journal she sought was here—she could feel its pull but the Atlantean god protected it and as long as he did she couldn't touch it without risking his wrath.

So she was waiting for him to let down his guard and leave either the bag or the bimbo unguarded. And if her demons would do their job correctly, she'd have a shot at Ryssa's book and the secrets it contained.

Satara gasped as she felt the pain in her chest that signified Ash had left the building. Smiling, she got up and headed upstairs to steal his most guarded possession.

CHAPTER FIFTEEN

Satara pulled back as she caught sight of Aimee Peltier with Ash's new pet standing outside the room where the two of them were staying. Damn! She couldn't touch the little slut so long as the bear was with her. She'd attempted to violate the sanctity of a Were-Hunter safe zone once in Seattle and had almost been killed over it.

Savitar had made his point loud and clear. The Weres were off her menu.

Bastard.

But if nothing else, she learned from experience. Which meant she couldn't grab the journal until either the bear was gone or they left the opening of that room so that she could sneak inside. Not to mention the fact that two of Apollymi's high priestesses were near them too. The last thing she needed was for one of them to summon their goddess's powers—Apollymi was a lethal bitch who made Artemis appear a whipped puppy in comparison.

She'd have to bide her time.

Stepping back, she returned to the shadows to wait until either she had a moment to pounce, or her demons arrived—if they would just get here. Those demons were turning out to be more trouble than they were worth most days. Unlike the Daimons they had a god complex and didn't like answering to anyone they didn't have to obey.

But the demons were handy at times. If they violated sanctuary laws, oh well. Who cared if they died?

Or better yet . . .

Auntie Artie might prove to be the better ally in this. If nothing else, Artemis would get Acheron out of the way for a while . . . especially if Auntie were to learn that Acheron had been playing in another woman's garden.

Tory *was desperate* to keep reading, but on the off chance that Aimee might know the ancient language, she refrained and put the journal in her backpack purse to keep it safe.

She looked around the small round table where Aimee, Justina and Katherine were hanging out and exchanging bad date stories.

Not exactly Tory's favorite way to waste her life. "Guys," she said, smiling at them. "No offense, but I'm getting stir crazy. Can we please go downstairs and hang in the bar or do anything that keeps me from sitting here bored out of my mind while the three of you watch me grow eyebrow hair? I mean really, I am fine. I'm not going to spontaneously combust or do anything else freaky. Promise."

Aimee laughed. "Yeah, but if I go down there and the guys see me, they'll put me to work."

Tory grinned. "Put me to work, I beg you!" Anything was better than growing inert.

Aimee cocked her head suspiciously. "Do you know how to wait tables?"

"Absolutely. My family owns three delis and two restaurants in New York. I'm slave labor anytime I go near them."

Justina held her hands up and grimaced. "I don't do tables, dishes, windows or anything else that involves other people's germs or saliva."

The three of them looked at her curiously at the un-solicited confession that really was more information about her than any of them needed to know.

"Okay, sex and kissing notwithstanding. That's completely different. Eating food is another matter. People are gross."

Tory laughed.

"I'll help out too," Katherine said. "Tina can follow Tory around and make sure no one grabs her while we're goofing off—that should keep Tina safe from saliva germs and Tory safe from boredom."

Aimee scoffed at Katherine. "Ladies, have you not seen the muscle we have downstairs? Anyone or anything comes in here with a nasty intent and my family will mop the floor, ceiling and walls with them. Why do you think Ash brought Tory here in the first place?"

Katherine smiled. "Okay, we're sold. Plus I have my priestesses dispersed in the crowd so that we can watch too. We should be pretty well covered."

"Cool beans." Tory followed Aimee downstairs so that she could get her a Sanctuary T-shirt and a white half apron to wear around her jeans. Tucking the journal into the apron pocket, Tory set about waiting tables while Justina tried to follow her around and remain inconspicuous.

Yeah . . .

It was hard to miss the tall brunette with an FO attitude so thick it could wall in an ancient city, who eyed everyone like they were the next victim. But that was okay. Tory loved the woman, attitude and all.

Smiling at her friend, she went over to a table where an extremely good-looking man sat alone, wearing a pair of sunglasses that reminded her of Ash's. Dressed all in black, he also had the same FU attitude that she'd noted on Ash the night they met. His brown hair was brushed back from his face which bore the same double bow and arrow mark that Dev had on his arm. Ash had told her those were used by Artemis to mark her Dark-Hunters, but it was still daylight outside so maybe he was like Dev and wore it because he thought it was cool.

As she drew closer, Tory assumed he was another Were-Animal. "Hey sweetie," she said in greeting. "What can I get for you?"

She couldn't tell he was looking at her for the sunglasses, but she could feel the weight of his gaze like a tangible touch. Before she could blink, he was on his feet, standing behind her with one hand across her waist. He leaned his head down to her hair and took a deep breath.

"You stink of Acheron." His voice was deep and laced with a thick Cajun accent.

Tory put her hand on the journal, ready to fight to the death over it. "You might want to take your hand off me and step back."

"Or what?"

"Or I'm going to ruin your day."

He laughed bitterly in her ear. "You think so?"

As quick as she could, she moved her hand from the journal to his crotch. Grinding her teeth, she took hold of him with a grip made strong from her years of archaeology and twisted until he was doubled over in pain. She let go as his face turned bright red and he cursed her.

"There's no thinking to it, buddy. Given the fact that I'm six foot one, you had to know I wasn't a wimpy female."

Justina moved in behind her.

He started for her, but before he could make contact, Dev was there, pushing him back. "Nick, you know better."

Nick shoved Dev away from him. When Dev started for him again, Nick held his hand up and with an unseen force, he slammed Dev against the wall. "I'm not your bitch, Dev. Don't ever put your hands on me again." Straightening his jacket with a tug at the lapels, Nick sauntered over to her. He lifted one piece of her hair off her shoulder. "Give Ash my best and make sure you tell him that you met Nick Gautier." He tossed her hair away from him as if she disgusted him before he walked out.

Dev went slamming to the floor.

Tory ran to him to make sure he was all right as he cursed at being defeated. "What was that about?" she asked him.

Sighing, he pushed himself to his feet. "Nick has issues. Unfortunately, Ash seems to be his biggest one."

"How so?"

"They used to be best friends and now they're mortal enemies. I didn't know Nick would be able to tell you were with Ash or I wouldn't have let him in here. Sorry."

Tory waved his apology away. "You didn't do anything wrong. I'm just stunned by the animosity." She thought Ash only elicited that kind of anger from her. "What happened to make them enemies?"

"I honestly don't know. But given how close they were a few years ago, it must have been one hell of a fight."

Tory shook her head at the disclosure. Poor Ash. Couldn't he depend on anyone to keep faith with him? No wonder he was so skittish of everyone. It seemed he collected enemies the way some people collected trading cards.

It made her want to protect him all the more.

Ash stopped right before he entered Liza's store. He didn't know why, but he had a bad feeling about Tory. Unable to explain it, he flashed himself back to Sanctuary where he found her standing behind the bar, making beers.

Relief the likes of which he'd never known filled him. Without thinking, he dodged behind the bar and pulled her back against him so that he could feel her there, safe and whole.

She reached up and cupped his cheek with her hand. "Are you all right?"

"Yeah, I just . . ." He snorted at his own stupidity. "Never mind."

Aimee paused beside them. "If you were about to say that you had a bad feeling, you weren't being ridiculous. Nick was here a few minutes ago."

His stomach hit the floor as fear filled his entire being. "What happened?"

Tory turned to face him. "He told me to give you his regards."

Ash cursed at the veiled threat. "I can't believe that sack of shit. If he so much as breathes on you, I swear I'll rip his throat out."

Dev laughed as he leaned against the bar from the other side. "No fear there. Tory took him out on her own."

"What do you mean?"

"I mean I'd be really nice to her if I were you, Ash. She dropped his ass like a trained combat SEAL with one well planted squeeze in a highly sensitive area. It was entertaining as hell for those of us not on the receiving end of it. Nick, however, will probably be a limping falsetto for at least a week." He shuddered. "I for one plan to keep at least three feet between me and her arm's reach for the rest of my lifetime."

Tory's face turned bright pink. "I don't like being manhandled by strangers."

He didn't like her to be manhandled either and it snapped his fury to the forefront. "Nick really didn't hurt you?"

"Not a bit. But I hate that I had to hurt him. Poor guy."

Ash closed his eyes behind his sunglasses as those words touched him. That was why she meant so much to him. She could see the best in even the worst of creatures—well, except for him when they first met. But even that he was beginning to find charming. "Why are you down here and not upstairs resting?"

"Boredom. It's not in me to sit around and do nothing all day. I'm Greek. We must work. To quote my Aunt Del there is no lean when you can clean."

Aimee laughed. "Don't worry, we're not letting her out of our sight . . . and after the Nick incident, we're not letting her out from behind this bar."

"Yeah," Tory said wistfully, "Prisoners R Us."

Ash arched a brow. She said that like it was a bad thing. Truthfully, he was grateful for it. "Good. Since all of you have it under control, I'm going to return to my errands and I'll be back shortly."

"Be careful."

He inclined his head to Tory and the words that touched him before he returned to Liza's store. Just as he reached for the knob, he heard Artemis's shrill scream in his head echoing like barbed wire against his brain.

"*Acheron! Here! Now!*"

"*I'm not your dog, Artemis.*"

She appeared in front of him on the street, her eyes flaming red. "Then if you won't heel, let's see if I can make your bitch beg." She started to fade.

Ash grabbed her arm and held her beside him. "What are you talking about?"

She wrenched her arm out of his grasp. "You didn't really think you could go off and fuck another woman and I wouldn't find out about it, did you? You faithless pig! I'm going to make her scream like no mortal has ever screamed before."

This time when she started to leave, Ash launched himself at her and took them to her temple on Olympus. He held her pinned between him and her bedroom wall. Artemis let out a shriek so severe he was amazed he still had his hearing.

"Let me go!"

He shook his head. "Not until we settle this."

"Settle what? That you're a lying, faithless bastard? How could you!" She tried to scratch at his face.

Ash held her hands and kept her pinned between him and the wall.

"I will have her life, her soul, everything!"

"You won't touch her."

"You don't command me!"

Those words set his wrath off to such a height that he immediately shifted into his true destroyer's form. He saw his blue hands and could only imagine what the rest of him must look like. "Don't push me, Artemis. I haven't fed in weeks and in this matter, I will kill you. Do you understand?"

She snarled at him. "I hate you!"

"You've always hated me. Since the moment I first kissed you in your temple, you've despised me and I know it."

With a furious scream, Artemis started sobbing as if her heart was being ripped into shreds. She fought against him. "That's not true. We were friends. I loved you!"

He scoffed at the lies she still believed. "You loved me so much that you watched as I was butchered on the floor at your feet. That's not love, Artie. I felt your relief when I was dead."

She shook her head in denial. "I brought you back because I loved you."

"That's the lie you tell yourself, but I know the truth. You brought me back because you were afraid of my mother."

"I am a goddess!"

"And I'm a god. One whose powers mock yours and you know it."

She shrieked again as she tried to buck him off. "You've betrayed me and I want vengeance for it."

"Then take it out on me."

She froze at his words and for the first time since she'd attacked him, there was a semblance of sanity there. "What are you saying?"

Ash took a small step back, prepared to seize her again if he needed to. "I'm the one who betrayed you. If you want to make someone bleed, then I offer myself to you as your victim. But you have to swear to me that you'll never lay a hand on Soteria. Ever."

The flame of sexual heat in her eyes sickened him. She could deny it all she wanted to, but she got off on making him bleed and suffer. She always had. "Only if you swear not to use your powers to heal yourself. You will take the punishment you have earned and you will suffer for what you've done to me."

Because it was always about Artemis.

Of course he wouldn't have been with Tory because Tory was kind to him. The only reason he could ever be with someone else was to hurt Artemis and for that he'd bleed.

Yeah . . .

"I swear it."

She lifted her chin. "Release me."

"Not until I have your word."

"Oh I promise you, I won't touch your slut."

He cringed at her words and their unspoken threat against Tory. "And that you won't send anyone else after her either."

She balked.

"Artemis?"

She pouted like a toddler who'd just broken her favorite doll. It wasn't until she realized that he wouldn't give in on this that she crossed her arms over her chest and spat, "Fine. I swear your whore will never be hurt by me or any of my minions."

He wrapped his hand around her neck. "And I swear if you ever call her whore or slut or any other insult again, I will kill you. Do *you* understand *me*? Her name is Soteria and you will call her nothing else."

Fear replaced the anger in her eyes. She knew he had no choice except to fulfill whatever oath he took. And right now the thought of killing her ranked right up there on his list of things he'd most like to do.

"I understand," Artemis said coldly. "Now prepare yourself for me, whore."

Ash winced at words she knew hit him on a level no one should ever be hit on, and he hated her for that. In one heartbeat, they destroyed all the centuries of dignity he'd tried so desperately to build and reduced him to the little boy who'd pathetically begged his father not to hurt him.

Damn her for it. He didn't want to do this, but he knew he had no choice. His stomach was so tight with anger and disgust, he was amazed he wasn't vomiting from the sensation.

Last night was worth it.

No . . . Soteria is worth it. When she held him, he wasn't a whore. He wasn't pathetic or unwanted. For that moment of peace that he'd had in her arms, this was nothing.

He only hoped that once Artemis finished with him, he was still able to feel that way.

Sick with dread, he stepped back from her and dropped his long coat to the floor then pulled his shirt off over his head. Gods, it felt just like selling himself in his uncle's house all over again. All he needed was to have those gold bands back in place on his wrists and ankles and his tongue pierced. To have her grab his hair and tell him how to please her best.

He ran his hand over his chest where Simi slept. "Simi? I need you to take human form." If she were still on his skin when Artemis began beating him, she'd come off and attack the goddess. Since he'd promised total submission, he couldn't allow his girl to do that.

Simi appeared with a precious smile on her face until she realized where she was. Then her lips curled in repugnance. "Why we here with that old heifer-goddess, akri? The Simi thought we were going to have fun again."

"I know, Sim. I need you to leave me for a little while."

Her nostrils flared angrily as her eyes turned dark red. She knew what happened to him whenever he made her leave here. "Akri—"

"Just do it, Simi." He looked past her to see Artemis glaring at them. "I want you to go to Sanctuary and protect Soteria for me. Make sure no one hurts her."

Simi turned and hissed at Artemis. "I'll go protect Akra-Tory, akri. But the Simi don't want to leave you. I wish you'd let the Simi eat the heifer instead."

Ash cupped her face and placed a quick kiss on her cheek. "Go, Simi, and don't eat the humans or Weres."

Simi nodded before she vanished.

Ash swallowed as he met Artemis's glower. An instant later his wrists were encircled by chains. They were pulled up and spread wide as a whip appeared in Artemis's hand. He let out a long breath as centuries of this went through him and he fought the anger that swelled inside his heart.

How could she do this and still claim to have feelings for him?

"You have betrayed me for the last time, Acheron."

He laughed bitterly. "I've betrayed *you*? When have you ever kept faith with me?"

She answered his question with a stinging backhand across his face that split his lip. Only now that he was secure could she strike him. She grabbed his hair, turning it instantly blond, and jerked his head back as hard as she could. "I wish I'd never met you."

"I assure you the feeling's more than mutual."

Then she did the cruelest thing of all. She manifested a mirror before him and dressed him in the same chiton he'd worn when they met. Brushing the hair back from his neck, she blew her breath on his skin, knowing how much he hated it.

"This is what you're afraid of, isn't it? The entire world knowing what a whore you really are. Eleven thousand years later, you're still crawling into the bed of whoever can pay your fee. Tell me, Acheron, what did Soteria give you to sleep with her?"

He glared at her in the mirror and answered her with the truth. "She bought me with the one thing you've never been able to manage, Artemis. Kindness. Warmth."

She wrenched his hair so hard he was sure she pulled a full handful of it out. "You bastard whore! I would have given you the world had you asked it of me, but instead you'd rather be in the bed of a common human."

He licked the blood from the corner of his mouth. "You've never given me anything, Artemis, without making me pay dearly for it. Not even your heart."

"That's not true. I bore your daughter for you!"

"No. You bore *your* daughter. You didn't keep Katra because of me. You kept her out of total selfishness and you know it. You never really intended for me to know I had her because you didn't want to share her with me or anyone else. You could have told me the truth at any time, yet you hid her from me for more than eleven thousand years." He shook his head at a truth that scalded his soul. "You're selfish and you're cold, and I'm tired of getting frostbite when I touch you."

She brought the whip down across his back. Ash hissed as pain tore through him.

"I own you!" she shrieked.

Ash tightened his grip on the chains that held him in place. "I won't be owned by you, Artemis. Not anymore. I shouldn't have to barter myself to you for kindness and I'm through with it."

She hit him again. "You would rather sell yourself to a human who can't understand you? She knows nothing of our powers. Nothing of what it means to be a god. The responsibility. The sacrifice."

His breathing ragged, he stared at her in the mirror. "And neither do you. Soteria doesn't ask me for anything.

She gives, Artemis. No strings. No hidden agenda. She takes my hand in public and she holds it. She's not embarrassed to be seen with me."

She jerked his head back and snarled in his ear. "Because it costs her nothing to be seen with you! You ask too much of me. You always have."

"Did it never occur to you that you ask the same of me? I've given to you for eleven thousand years and I'm tired of it. I'm tired of being ridiculed by you and your brother. I'm tired of taking your shit and dealing with your moods while you refuse to allow me the same courtesy. I want my freedom."

After releasing his hair, she hit him three more times before she raked her nails painfully down his back. "There is no freedom for you, whore. Ever."

Tory *smiled as* she saw Simi walking up to the bar. She still remembered the first time she'd seen the demon, though at the time she'd thought Simi an average college age girl who'd made a great babysitter for her. It was hard to believe after all the phone and e-mail conversations they'd shared that Simi had failed to mention the one basic fact that she was a demon.

Then again . . .

But as Simi approached, she could tell something was wrong with her. "What's wrong, Simi?"

"That old heifer bitch goddess is hurting akri again and akri won't let the Simi do anything to help him, but the Simi isn't supposed to say anything about what the bitch-goddess does so forget the Simi said anything." She huffed as she sat down on a bar stool and propped her chin in her hand. "Hook the Simi up with some ice cream, Akra-Tory. I need double scoops."

Aimee went to accommodate Simi while Tory walked around to sit beside the demon.

"What do you mean the heifer goddess is hurting Ash? You mean Hera?" She was the goddess most often referred to as cow-eyed in mythology.

"Not that one. The redheaded mean one that the Simi

wants to eat, but akri say 'No Simi. You can't eat Artemis.' The Simi hates that heifer.''

Tory went cold as she remembered what Ash had told her about Artemis and their relationship. "Where's Ash?"

"On Olympus. He told the Simi to come stay with you and make sure no one hurts you."

This couldn't be good and Tory felt ill that she couldn't help him. "What does Artemis do to Ash?"

"The Simi isn't supposed to say." She looked around the bar like an impish child before she lowered her voice. "But akri didn't say the Simi couldn't show you . . ." She reached out and touched Tory's arm. The moment she did, Tory saw Ash being beaten.

Unable to stand it, she shot to her feet and tried to focus. But she couldn't. Her heart pounding, she was hyperventilating at the thought of causing him that kind of pain. "We have to do something!"

"We can't. Artemis hurt akri worse if we try. Believe me, I know. He promised her she could hurt him if she didn't hurt you and she say okay, so now . . . the Simi hates the heifer goddess."

So did Tory. If she could turn back time, she'd beat the snot out of her in Nashville.

Aimee brought Simi the ice cream while Tory tried to think of something, anything, she could do. She looked at Aimee, then Katherine and Justina, but decided not to ask their opinions. Ash would die of shame if he knew they knew what was being done to him.

You now have the secrets that I would kill to protect.

No doubt this was one of the secrets he held dearest. No wonder he'd been so harsh to Artemis in Nashville.

"If I ever get my hands on her . . ."

She'd do what? Bleed on her expensive shoes? Artemis was a goddess and Tory was human.

Wait . . . there had been something in the journal about Artemis and her weaknesses. Her heart hammering with hope, Tory headed toward the kitchen behind the bar where it was light enough for her to read.

But before she could make it to the room, she saw a tall, black-haired woman at a table off to the side.

You want to hurt Artemis? Come talk to me.

Tory looked around at the voice in her head until her gaze returned to the unknown woman.

Yes, it's me talking to you, Soteria. The woman motioned for her to join her at the table.

Reversing course from the kitchen, she patted Aimee on the arm. "I'll be right back." Before Aimee could respond, she went straight to the woman who was unbelievably attractive and probably as tall as she was.

"Hi," the woman said, her voice thick with its Greek accent. "I'm Satara. You should consider me a friend."

Yeah, right. Tory would wait and make up her own mind about that. "How did you do that thing where you talked to me in my mind?"

She smiled before her voice was in Tory's head again. *I'm the daughter of Apollo and if you want to help me, I'll be more than willing to help you kill Artemis.*

CHAPTER SIXTEEN

Tory was instantly suspicious of the unknown woman and her motives. "Why would the daughter of Apollo help me hurt her aunt?"

Satara twisted her lips up into a seductive, yet impressed smirk. It was as if she begrudged giving Tory any kind of respect. "You're a smart little human. Most don't know their mythology. But that's neither here nor there, is it? Let's just say that like you I'm a friend of Acheron's. I'm tired of seeing him hurt."

Knowing Ash as well as she did, she knew Satara wouldn't have gotten that tidbit from him. Which meant the woman was in league with Artemis and was now trying to turn on her own aunt. Yeah, that really lent itself to Tory trusting her . . . not even a bit. "Strange, he never mentioned you to me." Tory started to leave.

Satara leapt at her and grabbed her painfully by one wrist. "Give me Ryssa's journal if you want to live."

Biting Satara's hand, Tory twisted away and ran for the bar. Simi was across the room, hissing at Satara who vanished the moment she saw the demon.

"That the heifer-goddess's mean niece. The Simi don't like her neither."

Agreeing with her, Tory rubbed her bruised wrist. What else was in that book that she had yet to read? It had to contain a lot more than she'd seen so far. "Simi, grab your ice cream and come upstairs with me. I think you and I need to do some research."

As they headed up, Tory considered calling her cousin Geary, but decided against it given how secretive Ash was. He went out of his way to make sure no one knew his business and since she'd promised him that he could trust her, she wouldn't do anything to violate that oath.

But it was hard . . .

Once Simi was settled in with her in the small room, she pulled out a notebook and pen, and attacked her reading with a renewed vengeance. Though to be honest that was easier said than done. Every time Ryssa wrote about Ash, it broke her heart. The senseless abuse and cruelty was unimaginable and when she saw what they'd done to him during Artemis's feast day she wanted blood for it.

No wonder Simi hated the goddess the way she did.

How could Artemis turn her back on Ash and leave him there to suffer? Truly, she didn't understand this need to save face that Artemis had. But then Tory didn't care what other people thought of her. She never had. Yes, they'd mocked her incessantly in school for being too smart, blowing the bell curve and for being a tall, skinny nerd. Her hair was frizzy, she'd had braces and glasses so thick they'd melt plastic army men.

But then she remembered clearly that day when she'd come home crying to her father over the words Shelly Thornton had assaulted her with at school—*your father's a crackpot that everyone laughs at, your mom's an idiot and you're a pathetic geek who'll never have a boyfriend outside of the one you make up in your head and your dress looks like you found it in a dumpster*. If that wasn't bad enough, all the girls who were afraid of Shelly being mean to them had laughed at her too. Then they'd joined in on attacking her clothes.

The worst part was, Tory had loved her dress dearly. It'd been one her Aunt Del had made for her out of Greek lace and a bright purple satin material they'd found in the fabric store that Tory had fallen in love with.

Her heart had been splintered that day by their cruelty until her father put her on his knee and kissed her tears away. *"No one can ever make you feel inferior without your permission, Tory. Don't give it to them. Realize that it's their own insecurities that make them attack you and others. They're so unhappy with themselves that the only way they can feel better is by making everyone as unhappy as they are. Don't let those people steal your day, baby. You hold your head high and know that you have the one thing they can never take away from you."*

"What's that, Papa?"

"My love. Your mother's love and the love of your family and true friends. Your own self-respect and sense of purpose. Look at me, Torimou, people laugh at me all the time and say that I'm chasing rainbows. They told George Lucas that he was a fool for making Star Wars—*they used to even call it Lucas's Folly. Did he listen? No. And if he'd listened to them you wouldn't have had your favorite movie made and think of how many people would never have heard the phrase 'May the Force be With You.' "*

He'd brushed her hair back from her wet cheeks. *"I want you to always hold your head up and follow your dreams wherever they take you. Don't you ever listen to the people out to hurt you or make you cry. Listen to your heart and be better than them. No one gets ahead by hurting others. The only real peace anyone will ever have is the one that comes from within. Live your life on your own terms and make it a happy life. Always. That's what's important, Torimou."*

It wasn't always easy to listen to those sage words and the sad truth was that she'd never worn her purple dress again, or purple period. But over time, she'd learned to care less and less what others thought about her as she made her own way in the world. The only thing she couldn't stand was to have her beloved father and uncle mocked.

The world could laugh at her if they must, but she couldn't stand anyone to make fun of those she loved.

But as she read the insecurities of Artemis, she realized how lucky she'd been to have her father. Poor Artemis for not having anyone to love her like that.

And poor goddess for hurting the only one who would have . . .

Tory looked over to see Simi watching QVC. She was lying on her back with her head hanging over the edge of the bed as she watched it upside down.

Okay . . .

"Simi?"

The demon looked at her curiously.

"Do you think Artemis is sad?"

"I think she's just plain mean."

"Yes, but people aren't mean just to be mean. There has to be a reason for it."

Simi let out a forlorn sigh. "Well, akri say that the heifer-goddess doesn't have anyone to love her and that's why we have to be nice to her. But the Simi say so what? There's a reason she gots no one to love her. She's mean."

There it was in a succinct, if not semi-humorous, nutshell. And it made her wonder if Ash had been recognized as a prince how much different their relationship would have been.

But the point was moot really. And as the hours went by, Tory learned a lot more about ancient Greece, Atlantis and Acheron than she'd ever dreamed possible.

Aimee brought food for them and somewhere around midnight, Simi fell asleep on the floor with her feet rising up at a ninety degree angle against the wall.

Shaking her head at the strange position, Tory pulled one of the blankets from the bed and draped it over her. Just as she tucked it around Simi, a small fissure went through the air.

Unsure of what caused it, Tory looked to her right to find Ash standing outside the bathroom with one arm braced against the wall. His face pale, he appeared to be in severe pain. But most shocking was the fact that his hair was golden blond and he wasn't wearing a long coat. Only a long-sleeved black shirt that had been left untucked.

"Ash?" she whispered.

He didn't respond.

Concerned, she closed the distance between them and saw that he was sweating profusely. "Baby, what's wrong?"

He looked at her with a confused frown. "I didn't know where else to go. I . . . I didn't want to be alone."

"Do you need to lie down?"

His eyes empty, he nodded.

Tory waited for him to move. When he didn't, her concern tripled. "Ash?"

"I need a minute."

She stood there waiting. After a long pause, he pushed himself away from the wall and started for the bed. He'd only taken a single step when he sank to his knees. Without thinking, she reached to touch his back.

He hissed and recoiled as he tried to crawl away from her. Pulling her hand back, she gasped as she saw the blood coating her palm.

She knelt beside him. "What can I do?"

His breathing ragged, he ground his teeth as if fighting an unbearable agony. "My powers are unstable. I'm in too much pain to direct them accurately."

"Okay. You can lean on me and I'll get you to the bed." She stood up and held her hand out for him.

Ash couldn't speak as he saw her there with her outstretched hand. He shouldn't be here and he knew it. Yet that was what had made him seek her out when he would never have sought out anyone else. She wouldn't hurt him or mock him. She would help. The only other person he allowed to tend him when he was weak was Liza. But not even Liza had ever seen him when he was this vulnerable.

He damn sure didn't want Alexion or Urian to know.

Taking her hand, he allowed her to pull him up. He ground his teeth as another wave of pain ripped through him. She wrapped his arm over her shoulders and carefully placed her arm around his hips where he wasn't hurting so much.

Together, they walked him to the bed and helped him to lie down.

"Don't tell Simi," he whispered. "I don't want her upset."

Tory nodded as she watched him pass out. Angry and aching for what had been done to him, she very carefully cut his shirt from his back. And with every inch of bleeding skin she uncovered, her fury mounted at the horrific mutilation. This was unbelievable.

She didn't care how much Artemis was unloved. If she had the bitch here right now, she'd tear every strand of red hair out of her selfish head!

"This is going to stop," she whispered to him. "One way or another, Ash, I'm going to find a way to put that goddess in her place."

Ash *came awake* to the odd sensation of something cold on his back. For a moment, he thought himself at Artemis's temple until he opened his eyes and saw Tory in a chair a few feet away from him, reading.

Everything came flooding back and when he took a deep breath, the pain in his back reminded him of how real his visit with Artemis had been.

Tory immediately set the book aside. "Try not to move."

"Believe me I am."

She knelt on the floor in front of him. "I put one of my Aunt Del's concoctions on your back. It's aloe, cucumbers and potatoes mixed with Vaseline and lanolin. I know it sounds gross, but it's really good to take the sting out of cuts and burns."

"Thank you."

She smiled as she rested her chin on the hand she had on his mattress. "I've got you covered with a sheet and I told Simi that you were sleeping. She went downstairs to eat so she has no idea that you're hurt. No one does."

He took her hand in his and kissed her fingers. "Thank you."

"Anytime, sweetie."

He treasured that endearment. Most of all, he treasured her.

She cocked her head while she toyed with his fingers. "Can you not use your god powers to heal yourself?"

"I could, but I promised not to."

"Why?"

Because I'm an idiot. No, he'd done it to protect her and if this was the price for her safety, so be it. "I'd rather not say."

She patted his hand. "Then I'll keep running cover with you and Simi—who was asleep when I tended your back. And speaking of, I think I finally met someone who eats more than I do. Geary would be impressed."

How did she do that? He was lying here with a ravaged back and she was blithely ignoring it and treating him like he was recovering from nothing more than a common cold. How was she able to take things like this in stride and not make him feel like a freak over it? "You're not going to ask me anything more than that?"

She shook her head. "I trust you, Ash. Completely." She held the book up. "You've trusted me with a lot of your secrets already. If you want to keep a few to yourself, I understand and I won't pry."

"You're too good to be real."

She smiled. "Not really. Remember, I'm the one who tried to hammer you."

He laughed, then grimaced at the pain.

She scowled in sympathy before she brushed his hair back from his cheek. "Is there anything I can get for you?"

Make me human, like you . . . But that was a stupid thought. "Please don't tell anyone I'm down. I should be better in a couple of hours. I just need a little more rest."

She rubbed his jawbone with the pad of her thumb. "You got it. By the way, your backpack is right here." She took his hand and led it to where it was set on the floor by the bed. "I haven't touched it except to put it there."

"Thank you."

"No problem." She stood up slowly. "Are you hungry or thirsty?"

He was starving, but there was nothing here that would satiate him. "I'm fine."

Tory cocked her head as he closed his eyes and let out one long breath. Even with his ravaged cheek and the bruise on his lip, he was still one of the most handsome men she'd ever seen. The fact that he'd have any interest in

677

her at all amazed her. Honestly, she was no Artemis. The goddess was stunningly beautiful.

What human could compare to that?

Yet Ash was here with her. He trusted her when he trusted no one else. That alone touched her heart. And the more she read about his past, the more she wished she could wrap her arms around him and just hold him until all the bad memories were wiped away.

She looked down at the journal in her hand. There was so much sadness in it. Not only with Acheron, but with his sister too. Ryssa had tried so hard to help him while Apollo had been every bit as cruel to her as Artemis was to Ash.

And while she was fascinated by the history and glimpses of daily life she'd seen through Ryssa's words, she'd read enough. Ash's past was tragic and it said a lot for him that he could have any compassion at all.

She was through spying on him.

Tucking the journal into his backpack, she made sure it was completely zipped before she went downstairs to check on Simi.

Ash felt Tory's absence like an ache in his soul. There was something about her presence that lifted his spirits and made him happy just to be near her, which, given how much pain he was in, said much.

You should leave her.

He'd bought her a reprieve from Artemis's wrath, but for how long? The longer he stayed with Tory, the greater the danger to her. Not to mention Artemis wasn't the only one he had to deal with.

Stryker would kill Tory in an instant and by now Nick had most likely told the Daimon overlord about her. She was a human who didn't fit into his world of viciousness. Of beings who held no regard for anyone or anything.

But the mere thought of not seeing her was enough to bring him to his knees. Why couldn't he have something for himself?

You're a worthless whore. You deserve nothing but scorn and ridicule.

How could anyone ever love him?

Simi was blind to his faults because he'd raised her. He'd protected her. His mother loved him, but again, it was a parent-child bond. And Katra . . .

They were still learning each other.

"Stop it," he growled at himself. He wasn't a child. He wasn't the same pathetic creature who'd begged his father for a mercy that had never come to him.

He was a god.

She was human.

It was that simple and that impossible. He'd survived for eleven thousand years alone. By comparison, she was an embryo. What did she know about life? How to survive in the world he knew?

This would have to end. He was old enough to know better. There was no way for a happy ending for him. He'd willingly sold himself to Artemis when he'd been nothing more than a boy and there was no way out. His existence was too complicated. Once he healed, he'd end this and send her on her way. It was the best for all of them.

Tory *laughed as* she watched Simi pour hot sauce over her ice cream. More than that, she was grateful *she* didn't have to eat it—even if Simi did keep taunting her "wimpy" taste-buds. Better that than the stomach ache she was sure the demon would have later.

She was just about to tease Simi over that when there was a sudden rush of air around her.

Not sure what the sensation was, she stopped speaking mid-sentence and saw the color fade from Aimee's face as she stared in horror of what was behind Tory's back.

Dev and Katherine rushed forward.

Tory turned to see a group of extremely tall, handsome men there. The leader had eyes as black as space . . . and just as vast and empty.

He laughed at the bear clan before he seized her and everything went dark.

CHAPTER SEVENTEEN

Ash heard the door to the room open again. Expecting Tory, he didn't move until he felt Dev's presence near him. He opened his eyes to find the bear looking down, his expression a mixture of dread, fear and anger.

"What?" Ash asked, half afraid of the answer.

"A group of demons just seized Tory."

It took a full minute for those words to penetrate the denial inside him. When they did, a rage so volatile Ash could taste it, rose up. Grinding his teeth against the pain, he clothed himself before he threw the covers back and stood against the injuries that made every molecule of his body throb. "Where did they go?"

"Kalosis."

He let out an expletive so crude, Dev actually blushed. It took every ounce of willpower not to lash out at the bear for allowing them to take her out of here. Lucky for Dev, he knew it wasn't the bear's fault. Sanctuaries only protected Apollites, Daimons and Were-Hunters.

Demons existed outside their rules.

And they'd gone to the one place Ash couldn't follow.

The plan had been carefully thought out and executed. He'd congratulate them except for the fact he wanted their blood.

Simi popped in directly behind Dev. "I can go to Kalosis, akri. The Simi will get Akra-Tory back for you."

"No!" his voice came out completely demonic at the thought of what they might do to her. The gallu demons and the Charonte were natural enemies and while Simi could hold her own against virtually anyone, she couldn't fight all the gallu by herself. She was still a very young demon in terms of power and strength. "I won't risk you."

If they'd taken Tory to use against him, they'd take Simi in an instant. Honestly, he was amazed they hadn't tried. Of course even young, Simi had the powers to put up a strong fight and though they would have taken her, they would have paid for her abduction.

Tory on the other hand was completely at their mercy.

"Simi, return to me."

Her eyes large, she obeyed and placed herself back on his forearm. Ash turned back to Dev. "How many were there?"

"Six. They popped into the bar, right behind her and homed in as if she'd been marked by something. Before I could reach her, she was gone through a bolt hole. I'm really sorry. We did our best."

"I know you did." It was why the bear was still breathing. "Now it's between me and them." Ash flashed himself to Katoteros. His body throbbing, he walked through the main foyer and allowed his human clothes to melt away into the flowing silk formesta that was easier to bear on his bruised body.

He walked out onto the balcony that overlooked a tranquil sea. Even so, he wasn't overly fond of this spot. It reminded him too much of the balcony to the room where his adopted father had kept him in Didymos. But he needed the clarity of the balcony right now.

"Matera?" he called, summoning her from the depths of the hell realm where she lived.

"*Apostolos?*"

He counted to ten to get his temper under control so that he could talk to his mother without the fury he felt offending her. Even though they fought against each other over mankind, she was still his mother and he loved her enough to keep his tone respectful. "I forgave you for sending Stryker after Marissa Hunter in an effort to lure me into Kalosis to free you, but this . . ." He paused before he exploded in anger. "How could you?" he asked from between clenched teeth.

"How could I what?" Her tone showed genuine surprise. *"What are you talking about?"*

"Demons entered Sanctuary and took Soteria into Kalosis. Are you telling me that you have no knowledge of this?"

"That's exactly what I'm saying." The angry denial in her tone was too sincere to be feigned. Her shade appeared beside him and there he saw for himself her anger on his behalf. "I will take care of them, Apostolos. Have no fear. I'll be right back."

Ash inclined his head to her shade respectfully, but something inside him warned him that it wouldn't be that easy.

Apollymi *left her* dark garden with a swirl of fury as she teleported from her area of the palace to the hall where Stryker held court over his Daimons. He was sitting there, nonchalantly, as a group of them were feeding on some hapless human at his feet that they'd no doubt kidnaped and brought here.

Stryker looked up with a frown at her approach. "To what do I owe this honor?"

She ignored his sarcasm as she looked around at the Daimon horde. "I want them out of here. Now."

Stryker made a noise of irritation before he nodded. "You heard the goddess. Out."

They obeyed instantly, taking the human with them. Apollymi felt badly for the person they'd killed, but it was the state of nature that one life form invariably fed on another. While it wasn't fair the human had been prematurely killed, the Daimons had it even worse. They were cursed to watch themselves and everyone they loved decay over a twenty-four hour period because eleven thousand years ago a god had been angry over the actions of only a dozen Apollites.

No, life wasn't a balance sheet of fairness. It was survival of the fittest, smartest and swiftest.

And right now, that was her.

As soon as she was alone with Stryker, she narrowed her eyes on him. "Where is she?"

Stryker gave her a blank stare. "*She* would be?"

"Soteria Kafieri. Your demons took her out of Sanctuary in New Orleans. Where are they holding her?"

Stryker scowled as if he had no idea what she was talking about. "What do you mean *my* demons took her?"

Why was he playing this game with her? "The Sumerian gallus you welcomed here. Surely, not even you can miss their stench. They violated the Chthonian laws of Sanctuary and they took her hostage to hold against Apostolos. Don't you dare feign ignorance in this."

"I'm not feigning anything." He stood up indignantly. "Kessar!" He shouted, summoning the gallu leader who was as evil as any being Apollymi had ever met.

The demon appeared before him with an arrogance that was commendable given the fact Kessar would have been dead had Strykerius not taken him in. Tall and lean with brown hair and red eyes, he looked more like a fashion model than a demon and he used those good looks to his advantage whenever he sought humans to eat.

He curled his lip in repugnance as he faced Stryker. "I despise whenever you do that, Daimon. I'm not one of your pathetic minions to come when you call my name."

Stryker wasn't intimidated in the least. "So long as you reside here and benefit from my protection, you'll come when I call."

Kessar's eyes narrowed dangerously. "What can I do for you, my lord?"

His sarcasm made a mockery of the tone Stryker had used on him.

"I want to know about this woman you've taken hostage. How dare you move into the human realm without my knowledge."

Kessar shrugged. "We did what your sister asked us to do. I assumed she had your ear. If you have issue with what's happened, perhaps you should have a family meeting." He vanished.

Stryker cursed. "I hate that sonofabitch."

"Then why did you offer him refuge?" Apollymi asked.

He looked at her with a coldness she could feel all the way through her. "You have your demons for protection, it seemed only fair I should have mine. We both know I no longer have your favor, Apollymi. Even though I killed my own son to make you happy. Even though I've spent a million lifetimes in blind service to you, I'm only a means to an end. You want to hurt my father for what he did to your son and I'm the chosen tool for it. Honestly, I didn't mind your using me so long as I thought of you as a mother. But you declared war on me and so here we are. Neither of us happy. Both of us alienated from our children." He let out a bitter laugh. "We're a pair, aren't we?"

Apollymi approached him slowly as her restrained emotions roiled through her. It wasn't as simple as he made it sound. "In spite of what you think, Strykerius, I did love you. But I'm a goddess of vengeance and you made the mistake of forgetting that. The moment you went after Apostolos to harm him, you drew the battle declaration, not I. Where my son is concerned, I have no reason or loyalty to anyone above him. He is what I cherish most and he and his daughter and grandchild are the only things in this world I would die to protect. Now you hold what is sacred to him. Release her immediately, or not even your demons will be able to save you from me."

Stryker eyed her angrily as he realized this was no bluff. "Satara!"

His sister appeared instantly in a pique. "Don't take that tone with me."

Apollymi glared at her. "Where's Soteria?"

The stupid child didn't even have the sense to fear her. Instead, she shrugged. "She's safe for the moment."

"Release her," Apollymi demanded.

"Hardly."

Apollymi threw her arm out and brought Satara into her grasp so that she could choke her with one hand. "I'm not into games, little one. Release her or I *will* kill you."

Satara sputtered and choked as she tried to pull Apollymi's hand from her throat. It was useless. No one outpowered Apollymi. "You kill me and she dies, too."

Apollymi squeezed her neck tighter.

"Apollymi, wait!" Stryker snapped. "She's not lying. Look at her wrist. She's wearing the Atlantean cuffs. And I'm willing to bet the other one is on Soteria. You kill her and Soteria dies with her."

Satara smiled evilly. "And you would be correct, brother."

Cursing, Apollymi threw her against Strykerius. "I want Soteria freed."

Satara straightened and met her anger with a smugness that made her want to blast the chit into oblivion. "When I have my journal from Acheron, she will be freed. Trust me, I don't want her harmed any more than you do." The taunt in her voice didn't fail to register with Apollymi, who also recognized the fact the bitch was lying. "I merely want what Acheron has."

Apollymi scoffed. "Do you think he would ever trust you to make a trade for her?"

"No. That's why I've had my demons summon Jaden. Jaden will broker the deal. That way I know Acheron won't use his powers against me and I won't use my demons or powers against him."

Apollymi rolled her eyes at the ridiculous boast. She was ever amazed by the arrogance of people who seriously overestimated their abilities. "Little girl, you have no powers."

Satara laughed evilly. "Oh Apollymi, for all yours, you greatly underestimate me if you think that." She faded out.

If she rolled her eyes any further back, she'd go blind from it. Apollymi turned to Strykerius. "I understand the need for family, but if I were you, I'd let that one go before she drags you down to a depth so low you drown in it." Then she too faded back to her garden where she could speak to Apostolos alone.

As a mother, she hated delivering bad news to him and that made her hate Satara all the more. "There's nothing I can do, m'gios. They've gone to Jaden who will contact you with the terms to get her back."

She could feel Apostolos's impotent fury. "Matera—"

"They have the bracelets on Soteria. If I try anything, Satara will kill her."

He sighed wearily. "What do they want?"

"Ryssa's journal."

"Which one?"

"They didn't say, but I'm sure Jaden will tell you all you need to get her back." And once Satara was free of that bracelet, she was going to wish she'd never dared to cross Apollymi or her son.

Ash *pulled away* from his mother and wished her well. Right now he had bigger things to concern himself with. If Satara wanted one of the journals, there was only one reason.

She wanted to kill Artemis and Apollo.

"Damn it, Ryssa." Why had she always felt the need to journal her every thought? Yet those words had comforted him over the centuries.

Now they were the greatest threat he'd ever known.

He grimaced as a severe pain cut through his back. For that alone, he should let Satara have at Artemis.

But unfortunately, her death would end the world.

There was nothing to be done for it. He'd deal with Satara, but for now he had to secure Soteria.

Closing his eyes, he took himself back to their room in Sanctuary. He walked to the other side of the bed and froze.

There was no backpack.

What the hell? He looked around for it, but as he couldn't even sense the items it contained, apprehension shrank his stomach tight. This wasn't good. No one should have had access to this room or his backpack.

Leaving the room, he went outside to find Aimee who was waiting tables. She pulled aside into a quiet corner at his approach.

"Hey," he said in a low tone. "Have you seen anyone in our room upstairs?"

"No, why?"

"My backpack's missing."

Unaware of how important it was, she frowned. "Let me go ask and see if someone knows something."

Ash tapped his thumb against his thigh as he struggled to locate the pack with his powers. Nothing came to him. It was as if it'd been sucked out of existence.

When Aimee returned shaking her head, he knew something had gone seriously wrong.

Since the backpack didn't appear to be in the human realm and it wasn't in Katoteros or Kalosis, there was only one more likely place.

Olympus.

Pissed to a level only Artemis could elevate him to, he went to her temple and found her sitting on her white chaise as if she hadn't a care in the world. As if she hadn't beaten every fragment of skin from his back. And when she looked at him with a cold, simpering smile of pride he knew she'd fucked him over yet again.

"What did you do?" he demanded.

"I've done nothing."

"Don't lie to me, Artemis. I'm not in the mood."

At least that succeeded in wiping the stupid smile off her face. "I'm not lying to you. You haven't asked me any real questions."

He hated playing the literal game with her. "Fine. My backpack's missing. Have you seen it?"

It appeared instantly at his feet.

Artemis let out a slow breath of disgust. "I don't know why you love that matted out rag."

"Ratted out."

"Whatever. You should think about getting a new one."

Ash didn't respond as he knelt down to search it. The moment he opened it, his fury ripped through him with a renewed vigor. "Where are Ryssa's journals?"

"Safe."

Yeah and she so wasn't at the moment. "That is not an acceptable answer."

She rose slowly from the chaise in a swirl of red hair and white cloth. She was regal and cold as she raked him with a snarl. "It's the only answer you're going to get. Those books posed a risk to me and I've now illuminated it."

"Eliminated, Artemis. Damn, learn to speak." He jerked the backpack closed before he stood to confront her eye to eye. "Those journals are my property. I want them returned to me, right now, along with my mother's medallions and the Atlantean dagger."

She didn't even have the sense to look scared. "No."

Ash roared at her as she continued to taunt him with her nonchalance. "Don't test me!"

"Or what?" she snapped. "We both know you'd never hurt me. You've sworn it. I'm safe from your wrath." She actually smiled at him as if his anger amused her. "Forget your human and I'll forgive you for what you've done." She reached to touch his face where she'd slapped him earlier.

Ash grabbed her hand to prevent it. "I want my property back."

Her nostrils flared. "And I want mine. Shall we make an even exchange? You for the journals."

"I'm not your property, Artemis."

"Then I don't know what you're talking about with the journals and other matters."

He tightened his grip on her wrist, wanting to slap her so badly that he was amazed he kept himself in check. "Did you ever really love me? Even a little?"

"Of course I did."

He knew better. She wasn't capable of it. Disgusted, he shoved her hand away from him. "But only because I belonged to you and you alone. Even as a god, you don't think of me as your equal. To you I've never been anything more than a toy to be discarded when you're bored or through with me." He stepped back from her. He picked his backpack up and slung it over his shoulder, intending to leave.

She followed him. "If you want to save the life of your human, Acheron, you have to give me what I want. Swear to me that you'll never touch or see her again and you can have your stupid journals and toys."

Ash looked at her as desolate pain tore through him. In all his life, he'd wanted only one thing. Someone to make him feel the way Tory did whenever she looked at him.

And now Artemis was demanding he give that up.

To save Tory's life.

His back burned from Artemis's anger, reminding him of how broken their relationship was. How could he go back to her when he'd found something so much better?

Then again what good would standing his ground do if Tory were dead? Could he live with the thought that she'd died because of him?

There has to be a way out of this. You're a god, not some worthless pawn.

No, he was through playing this game. "I won't pay your price, Artemis. And you should know that by asking it, you've severed the last vestige of me that ever cared for you."

She laughed bitterly. "You'll be back, begging for me to help you. Begging for the life of your pitiful human. I know you, Acheron."

He shook his head in denial. "No, you don't. And that's the most pathetic part of the sum of us. In all these centuries, you've never bothered to learn the most basic thing about me at all."

His heart sick with worry for Tory and hatred for Artemis, Ash returned to Sanctuary to page Jaden. Unlike many of the gods, Jaden refused to embrace modern technology. He'd banned all cell phones from working anywhere near him, but Ash had managed to talk him into a beeper so that he could at least page the broker so that they could partake of the one thing Jaden did like about the modern age.

Video games.

He'd barely dialed the number before Jaden appeared beside him looking as ill as Ash felt.

"Is Tory all right?"

Jaden crossed his arms over his chest and nodded. "She's angry and indignant—not that I blame her in the least—but she hasn't been hurt."

Thank the gods for that. But it was only an extremely temporary relief. "I don't have the journal they want."

Jaden let out a low whistle. "That is going to be a problem. Can you get it?"

The answer would have made him laugh if it wasn't so sickening. "If I swear myself to eternal slavery to Artemis. Yes."

Jaden snorted. "I'd rather trade places with Prometheus and have my innards ripped out every day."

"So would I."

"Then what are you going to do?"

That seemed to be the question of the day. If only he had some solution. "Can you buy me some time?"

Jaden hedged. "Demons aren't exactly patient as a rule and particularly in this case. They seem to think that the journal will somehow free them."

"Free them from what?"

"Being servants. Living underground. Having to suffer the presence of Daimons and their stench—can't really blame them there. Escaping death-matches with you and Sin every time they pop out of the ground—again can't blame them for that. But still . . ." Jaden shook his head in bitter amusement. "You have to remember that what we're dealing with here are Sumerian gallu demons. The next to the lowest form of demon on the demon food chain. They're simple demons really. Lowly. You know . . . morons."

Ash snorted. "They were bright enough to take her out of a Were sanctuary without getting caught."

Jaden arched a single brow over that. "That could probably bring Savitar over."

He wished. But their laws didn't work that way. "Humans aren't a protected class."

"Really?"

"Yeah. Savitar shares your 'all humans are vermin' mind set."

One corner of Jaden's mouth twisted into an evil smirk. "I wouldn't say *all* humans are vermin. They do have their uses—especially the females for brief periods of time. They're just so . . . pathetically human."

"Which is why you deal with demons."

"Who are even more pathetic than humans when you think about it. Personally, I'd rather play video games.

Wouldn't it be great if we could suck the souls of the people we hated into the box, shoot them down and then dance in their entrails?"

Acheron rolled his eyes at the glee in Jaden's voice. "You woke up on the wrong side of the oak tree, didn't you?"

"Yeah. I have my own issues to deal with and, right now, the primary issue appears to be fucking over one of my only friends. I'll do my damnedest to buy you some time with the demons, but you need to come up with a miracle quickly." He started to fade out.

"Hey, Jaden?" Ash waited until he'd rematerialized before he spoke again. "Thank you. I know you don't have to do what you're doing for me and I just wanted to let you know how much I appreciate it."

"It's okay. I'm sure one day I'm going to need help bending some rules backwards. And when I ask for your help I don't want to hear any shit from you."

"Anytime, agriato."

Jaden inclined his head respectfully to him as Ash spoke in Jaden's native tongue and called him brother. It wasn't a language the demon broker heard often. He gave Ash a slight imperial bow before he vanished.

Ash stood alone in the room that seemed so empty without Tory here to fill it. Though she was tall, she was very slight of frame, almost frail in appearance and yet her spirit was so enormous that it filled the emptiness inside him in a way nothing had before.

Just trade yourself to Artemis for her and be done with it.

"You are not a whore to be bartered and sold!" He swore he could hear Tory's indignant voice in his head. And for the first time in his existence, he didn't feel like one.

Ash lifted his chin as a surge of pride and power swept away the pain of his beating. The pain that had lived inside him for so long that he'd almost forgotten anything else.

Taking a deep breath, he let his true voice out and spoke the words that now burned inside him. "I am the god Apostolos. The Harbinger of Telikos. The Final Fate of all. Beloved son of Apollymi the Great Destroyer. My will makes the will of the universe. I am not your whore, Artemis, and I will never be your slave."

He was through bartering and playing. Tory had done something no one else ever had. She'd given him self worth and a resolve he'd never known before. A woman like Soteria Kafieri wouldn't love a piece of shit. She wouldn't love a whore who crawled at the command of a goddess he despised.

No, Tory deserved more than that. And the love he felt for her made him better than his past. He loved her not only for who and what she was, but for the way she made him feel every time she looked at him.

No one was ever going to hurt her so long as there was breath in his body.

If Satara wanted a fight for Soteria, the bitch was going to get one.

CHAPTER EIGHTEEN

Tory ground her teeth at the indignity of her stance. Her hands were chained over her head to a board. Her legs had a degree more freedom, but they too were chained into a wide stance and she hated it. It was so degrading to be held like this and to not be able to get free. She couldn't even scratch the itch on her nose and it was making her crazy.

More than that, this gave her an understanding of Acheron that made her want to kill over the way he'd been treated. How many times had he been tied like this? Savagely beaten while those around him cheered and jeered? Or worse, took sexual pleasure from his degradation?

Today they finally carried out Acheron's castration for a crime I know he'd never commit. I can still hear his screams of unbearable pain. His cries for mercy and for death. The way he sobbed like I'd never heard him cry before. I don't think he knows how the sound of his misery echoed through the halls. How those screams scarred my soul. And I doubt if I will ever be able to silence them from my heart.

Ryssa's words spoke to her. Now she fully understood what Ash had endured as a human being. A pawn to his enemies. A pawn to the brutal machinations of people who had no regard for his life or feelings. Assaulted, betrayed and abused. It was a wonder the man was even sane. That he wasn't as merciless and callous toward the world that had been that way to him. The fact that he could find even a modicum of compassion astounded her. And she wasn't going to let these assholes use her to hurt him.

Growling in rage and determination, she pulled at the chains on her hands as hard as she could.

Laughter rang out. "You might as well stop that. All you're going to do is hurt yourself. Even if you get free, you'll never survive the Daimons and demons who'll eat you the minute you leave this room."

Tory paused to see Satara standing a few feet from her dressed in a black pantsuit, her hair a deep burgundy color this time—what was it with these god people that they constantly played with their hair?

She narrowed her gaze on Satara. "You know, my whole life I've taken pride in the fact that I'm Greek. But I have to say that after you and Artemis, I'm seriously beginning to hate some of my heritage. Is it congenital or is there something else that has made you such a bitch?"

Satara hissed at her like a cat who'd just had its tail crushed. "Don't insult me, human. I'm not supposed to harm you. At least in theory. Though now that I think about it, a little ruffling of your feathers might not be such a bad thing."

Maybe that should scare her, but for some reason she couldn't fathom, it didn't. "Seriously, why do you want to kill your aunt so badly?"

Satara scoffed. "You serve her spoiled rotten ass for eleven thousand years and let's see to what extremes you'd go to free yourself. I offered a deal to Acheron centuries ago to free us both and the bastard refused. He deserves the hell she gives him and then some. But I don't. Unlike him, I didn't bind myself willingly to her. I was forced into this and one way or another, I'm going to get free."

"And when Ash comes for me—"

She laughed, cutting off Tory's words. "He won't come here, sweetie. He can't. You're in the Atlantean hell realm. If your lover sets one foot down here after you, his mother goes free and the world ends. He thinks too much of humanity to let that happen. So you are mine for a bit. And personally, I think we should have some play time."

Ash *summoned Simi* off his body.

Cocking her head, she studied him like a small child. "What's the matter, akri? You look very sad."

He didn't answer her question since it would most likely upset her and that was the last thing he wanted. "I'm leaving you here at Sanctuary while I do something."

"What are you doing?"

Going to commit suicide most likely, but that didn't matter. Only Tory's welfare did. However if he was to enter a fight, which he was about to, Simi would come off his body to battle by his side and he couldn't let her be hurt because of him.

"Humor me, Simykee. I'm going where you can't."

She wrinkled her nose in distaste. "You going to see that heifer, aren't you? Fine. The Simi will stay so she don't gots to hear no huffing and puffing or anything else that turns a demon's stomach. Akri, have you any idea what it's like to be sick as a tattoo? It's not fun, believe your Simi when she tells you that."

He shook his head at her, amazed that she could make him smile while he felt so bad. "I believe you, Sim. Now stay put." He took her downstairs to where Dev, Angel, Kyle and the rest of the bears were having a powwow of some sort. Some customer must have made a pass at Aimee and they were contemplating making him tomorrow's daily special.

"I'm going to leave Simi here for a bit," he told Dev. "Will you guys watch her?" It was a rhetorical question.

At least that's what he thought until Dev shook his head. "We're going with you."

Ash scowled. "What are you talking about?"

"We know what you're planning," Angel said, "and we're going with you."

He was completely stunned. And when he saw Valerius, Talon, Kyrian, Julian, Zarek, Sin, Vane, Kyl, Katra, Fang,

Tabitha and Fury walking in, all he could do was scowl in confusion.

Why would all of them be here?

"What's going on?" Ash asked them.

Kyrian gave him a droll stare. "There's not one of us here that you haven't put your ass on the line for—most of us more than once. Alexion told us what happened with Tory and we're here to watch your back no matter what you have planned."

Talon nodded. "Wulf is on his way, too. He'll be here as soon as the plane lands and Otto can speed him over. And Otto plans to stand with us too."

Valerius pulled Tabitha back. "Tabitha won't be fighting. She'll be going home very shortly, but she wanted to let you know she's here in spirit."

Tabitha made a face. "But for the baby, I'd be busting balls for you, Ash. You know that."

He smiled at her. "I know, Tabby."

"The other Dark-Hunters wanted to be here," Talon said, "but since the sun hasn't quite set yet, they couldn't. However, once the blazing ball goes down, they're here if we need them."

Ash was amazed by their willingness to bleed for him. It touched him on a level he hadn't realized existed. It was why he wanted to keep his past a secret so much. Would they be this willing to stand by him if they knew the truth of his past? Or would they be like everyone else and step on him?

Just like Merus . . .

But even so, this meant everything to him.

He looked at Kat. "I don't want you in this fight."

She growled at him. "Dad—"

"No arguments," he said, cutting her off. "If Simi stays out of the fight, so do you."

Sin gave a low, evil laugh. "I'm so glad he's your father. And that for once we see eye to eye."

Kat held her finger up to Sin. "You are out of my bedroom tonight. And you . . ." She turned to Ash. "Just irritate me. Tory is a good friend of mine. If anything goes wrong and you need me, you guys better call. Otherwise, you're all in the dog house." She looked back at her husband. "And you're in it regardless."

Sin shrugged her ire off good-naturedly.

Zarek ignored them with his habitual sneer. "This still doesn't mean I like you, Acheron. But I owe you for my wife and son. I would lay my life down for yours because without you, I wouldn't have shit and I know it."

That was probably the closest thing to a declaration of love the man could muster and it honestly touched him.

"I wasn't expecting any of you to stand with me. We're not fighting just the Daimons in this. We're fighting demons too."

Sin snorted. "I live to tear demons apart. Bring the bastards on."

Zarek nodded. "Agreed . . . bring on the rain. The one thing I learned from Astrid is that life isn't about finding shelter in a storm. It's about learning to dance in the rain. I don't care what I kill as long as I get bloody while doing it."

Talon smiled. "We're here for you, T-Rex. Just like you've always been here for us."

And to think he'd always thought of himself as alone. While he'd trained the Dark-Hunters and had fought with the Were-Hunters to help them, he'd never expected them to return the favor. "Thanks, guys. I'm not used to people standing at my back." They'd always handed him over to his enemies or screwed him hard. It felt good to know he wasn't alone. "I know you all have families who love you so if you want to leave—"

Vane scoffed. "We wouldn't be here if we didn't want to. You and Val fought to save my sister when no one else would have bothered. I haven't forgotten it."

"And I haven't forgotten what the Dark-Hunters did for me and Maggie," Wren said sternly.

Fury nodded. "Yeah, we're family. Psychotic, bizarre and a hodgepodge of personalities that should probably never be blended, but here we are. Now let's go kick some ass."

Satara smiled cruelly at Nick as she faced him toward Tory. "Think about it, love. It's the perfect revenge, isn't it?"

Tory glared at the woman who had to be the most heartless of creatures. Someone really needed to give her a beating.

Satara left him to return to Tory's side. "I know she's not much to look at. But you can pretend you're screwing me." She stood directly behind Tory and reached around her to cup Tory's breasts for Nick's inspection. "Think of how much it'll kill Acheron to know you raped his woman while he was powerless to stop you. Think of the guilt and agony he'll live with every day, thinking of her crying and begging for mercy while there was no one to help her. Of her calling out for him when he couldn't be with her. It's the perfect revenge."

Tory shoved herself back against Satara and slammed her head into the woman's face. "You better be glad I'm tied up, you bitch."

Satara buried her hand in Tory's hair and snatched her head back. "It's time to gag you."

A cloth tie appeared around Tory's face.

Satara cut her shirt open with a gold-handled dagger. She trailed it against Tory's skin until she hooked the blade underneath Tory's bra. "C'mon, Nick. The little whore humiliated you in Sanctuary. Take your revenge on her and on Acheron."

He approached them slowly. Methodically.

Tory tried to scream through her gag, but no sound came. Terrified, she jerked on the chains and hated that she was so powerless to defend herself.

Satara sliced open her bra, spilling her breasts out. "She's all yours."

Nick took the knife from her hand.

Tory felt the tears of frustration stinging her eyes. How could any man worthy of the name do this to a woman? She would never hurt another being like this. The fact that Satara as a woman would orchestrate the rape of another made her the most repugnant of creatures.

And they better kill her after this, because once she had her freedom, she *would* kill them.

His features completely stoic, Nick fingered the edge of blade.

Satara was all but glowing with satisfaction. "Go on, love. Make me proud."

Nick paused his hand and looked up at her. "You know what, Satara? There's only one person I've ever given a shit about making proud." He gripped the knife tight in his fist. Pulling his sunglasses off, Tory gasped as she realized he had the same silver eyes as Acheron.

He met her gaze before he looked back at Satara who was smirking in pride.

"And that person was never you." The moment those words left his lips, he buried the dagger deep in Satara's stomach.

Satara stumbled back, gasping as she covered the wound. Blood flowed between her fingers. Her face was a mask of pain and disbelief. "What are you doing?"

"I'm embracing my fate." He snatched the keys from her pocket. Spinning around, he removed the thick silver bracelet from Tory's arm and let it fall to the floor where it landed with a loud thud.

Satara let out a shout for her brother as she ran for the door.

Nick threw the dagger at her fleeing form with a lethal aim. It slammed into her lower back and sent her straight to the ground.

Tory was too stunned to move as Nick opened the chains that held her arms in place. "Why would you help me?"

When he straightened up from freeing her feet, he pulled her shirt closed over her chest. Then he shrugged his jacket off and handed it to her. "Don't get me wrong, I hate Ash with every part of me and I will kill him one day, mark my words. But I don't have to imagine the pain he would feel if I tortured you. I live with that pain every fucking day because of him. I hear my mother's voice crying out for me to help her. To save her life while she was tortured and killed. And because of her, I'm a better man than Ash is. I won't let an innocent die to get back at him. You don't deserve to die any more than my mother did."

Tory shook her head, trying to understand him. "But you threatened me at Sanctuary."

"No, I only wanted to rattle him. I would never hurt a woman. My mama raised me better."

She looked to Satara's lifeless body.

Nick scoffed at the pity on her face. "She wasn't a woman, trust me. She more than deserved what I did and she's done a lot worse to others, including me. I ain't ever going to be a pawn to no one else again." He left her to pull the dagger out of Satara's back.

Tory followed him. "That's Atlantean, isn't it?"

He smiled evilly. "You make sure you tell Ash I have it." Then he took her arm and hauled her toward the door.

The instant he cracked it open, she realized that they were in a room that led out into a great hall filled with demons and Daimons.

She shrank back as Nick gave a low curse.

"We can't go that way, can we?"

He shook his head. "Not unless you want to be eaten." He was just about to pull back when the impossible happened. The bolt hole in the center of the room opened.

It flared bright and gold.

And when it dulled Acheron and Urian stood there, defiantly facing the Daimons.

CHAPTER NINETEEN

Still hidden behind the door with Nick, Tory blinked, then smiled at the sight of Ash standing tough and large in the middle of the Daimons. His stance said it all: *I'm here to clean your house and I won't be merciful while doing it. Fuck with me and you'll be nothing more than your mama's bad memory.*

His black hair was streaked through with dark red. The hem of his long, pirate style double breasted coat swung around those cherry red Doc Martens that he'd worn the night they first met. The ruby stud was back in his nose and for once she adored the sight of the sunglasses perched on his face.

Man, Acheron was hot and her heart raced in gratitude that he'd come for her.

The tall, blond man beside him was much more sedate in appearance. With a black button down shirt that was rolled back at his wrists and jeans, his clothes were plain in comparison. But he was almost as handsome with perfect features and white blond hair that he wore pulled back into a ponytail. She also didn't miss the fact that but for the blond hair, the man bore a remarkable resemblance to Stryker.

Like Stryker, he had a deadly air that was only surpassed by the one enveloping Ash.

"I thought Ash couldn't come here," she whispered to Nick.

"Apparently he's willing to end the world for you. You should be impressed. I am."

Her eyes widening, she definitely was. Why would Ash take such a risk?

And every demon and Daimon was frozen into place by his presence. Not a single word was said by the crowd outside. It was as if they were all holding a collective breath as they waited for Armageddon to begin.

All except Stryker who glared at the blond man beside Ash with an expression that was best defined as pained hatred. "You dare to stand with my enemy?"

"Against you, Father, I'd stand with Mickey Mouse."

Stryker curled his lip. "You worthless sonofabitch. You should never have been anything more than a cum stain."

The blond scoffed. "I could definitely say the same thing about you. It would have saved the world and all of us a lot of misery now, wouldn't it?"

The Daimons started forward, but they were thrown back by an unseen force.

Ash turned to Stryker and growled. "Enough of the family reunion bullshit. Where is Soteria?"

Tory frowned at Ash's words. Though the voice was his, it had a thick Greek accent and not the more fluid Atlantean one he used whenever he wasn't speaking colloquial American. How odd. Even when he spoke flawless Greek, his accent wasn't that throaty and traditional.

"She's over there." A tall blond woman appeared a few feet from Ash and indicated the door where Tory stood with an imperious jerk of her chin.

Tory gasped at her beauty as the woman crossed the short distance to embrace Ash. "At last, m'gios. You've come to set me free." She placed a kiss on his cheek and whispered something in his ear.

Tory was stunned as she realized this was the goddess Apollymi. Ash's mother.

The goddess of utter destruction.

Ash hugged her close and nodded before he stepped back. With a sneer thrown at Stryker, he turned and headed for her room.

Before Nick could stop her, Tory shoved open the door and ran for Ash. She threw herself into his arms and held him close from her giddy relief. And when their lips met . . .

She went cold in confused shock.

This wasn't Ash. In looks he was completely identical, but he neither smelled nor felt like Acheron. And he definitely didn't kiss like him.

Nick ran at the Ash imposter, but before he could reach him, Urian grabbed Nick and shoved him back into the room where they'd been.

"We have to go," Urian said to her and the fake Ash as he slammed the door shut behind them. He looked at Nick. "And you need to come with us."

Nick curled his lip in obvious hatred. "I'm not going anywhere with him. I'd rather be dead."

Urian forced Nick to look down at Satara's body. "I'm going to make the wildly unfounded assumption that Satara's dead by your hand and not Tory's." Gripping Nick's chin, he forced him to meet his gaze. "Now, stay with me on this, Cajun. My father slit my throat and murdered my wife because he thought I'd betrayed him by getting married. Before that, he loved me more than his life and I was his last surviving child. His second in command. Now what do you think he's going to do to you once he sees her body? I can assure you, it won't be a fun-filled trip to Chuck E. Cheese. For all their animosity toward each other, Satara is his sister and she's served him well over the centuries. If you really want to stay here and have some fun with Stryker, I won't stop you. But I really wouldn't recommend it."

That seemed to get through to Nick. Sanity returned to his eyes. "Fine. I'll go with you."

"Urian," the fake Ash said between his clenched teeth. "I think they're catching on."

"Catching on to what?" Nick asked.

Tory rolled her eyes at the dense question. "That this isn't Ash."

The words had barely left her lips before they faded out of the room.

Zolan, Stryker's third in command and the leader of his personal Illuminati attack force, cleared his throat in the still silent room. "Um . . . boss, I don't mean this disrespectfully, but why are we still here? I mean, if Acheron has come to free Apollymi, shouldn't there be an explosion or something?"

The Daimons and demons looked around as if waiting for an opening to the outer world to appear or for Apollymi to burst into song and dance, or for something else unnatural to happen. Meanwhile, Apollymi just stood there completely stoic, appearing almost angelic and sweet, as she watched Stryker closely.

His second in command, Davyn, scratched the back of his neck nervously. "I agree, kyrios," he said to Stryker, using the Atlantean term for lord. "It doesn't feel like the end of the world."

Stryker turned a cold sneer to Apollymi. "No, it doesn't . . ."

Apollymi arched a taunting brow. "How does the song go, 'It's the end of the world as we know it and I feel fine'?"

Something was wrong and in an instant he realized what it was. Launching himself from his throne, he ran to the room just as Urian, Tory, Nick and what had to be Ash's twin brother Styxx vanished.

His anger over the obvious trick mounted until he saw Satara lying on the floor in a pool of blood. Fear washed away his rage as he ran to find her dead. Her eyes were glazed and her skin tinged blue.

His heart shattered as he pulled her into his arms and held her close, fighting against the tears of grief and pain. "You stupid psychotic bitch," he growled against her cold cheek, fighting the sobs that demanded release. "What have you done now?"

Apollymi stood in the doorway, aching for Strykerius as he rocked his sister's body in his arms, reminding her of the day she'd found her son's body dumped on the cliffs. Sympathy and a newfound respect for him tore through her.

The fact that he could love someone as broken as Satara said much for him. Yes, he could be cold-blooded, but he wasn't heartless. Closing her eyes, she remembered him the day they'd first met. Stryker had been young and bitter over his father's curse.

"I gave up everything I ever cared about for him and this is how he repays my loyalty? I'm to die in agony in only six years? My young children are now banished from the sun and are cursed to drink blood from each other instead of eating food, and to die in pain at only twenty-seven? For what? For the death of a Greek whore killed by soldiers I've never even seen? Where's the justice in that?"

So she'd pulled him to her ranks and taught him how to circumvent his father's curse by absorbing human souls into his body to elongate his life. She'd given him and his children shelter in a realm where the humans couldn't harm them and where there was no danger of his children accidentally dying by sunlight. Then she'd allowed him to convert others and bring them here to live.

In the beginning, she'd pitied him and she'd even loved him as a son.

But he wasn't her Apostolos and the more he was around her, the more she wanted to have her own child with her no matter the cost. She admitted it was her own fault that she'd put a wall between her and Strykerius. And the two of them had used each other to get back at the people they hated.

Now it had all come to this . . .

"I'm so sorry, Strykerius."

He looked up at her, his silver eyes swirling in pain. "Are you? Or are you gloating?"

"I never gloat over death. I may relish it from time to time when it's justified. But I never gloat."

"And I don't let challenges like this go unanswered."

Tory didn't have time to even orient herself to her new location before someone seized her in a hug so tight, she feared her ribs might break. It wasn't until the scent of Acheron hit her and he kissed her deeply that she smiled and laughed in relief. She was safe.

She started to wrap her arms around his back, but remembered his injuries. Instead, she hugged his neck and held him close.

This was the real Acheron and he felt great in her arms.

He cupped her face in his hands. "Are you all right?" he asked, his eyes darkening as he saw her torn shirt and Nick's buttoned up jacket.

"I'm fine. Really."

"But we're not," Urian said drily. "Nick killed Satara while they held Tory."

"He did it to protect me," Tory interjected.

Urian snorted. "We'll put that on the headstone for you. In the meantime Stryker's going to want blood for this. A lot of blood."

Nick scoffed at his dire tone. "No offense, your father doesn't scare me, especially given how bad I want a piece of his hide. Come get some."

Urian looked less than impressed. "I know you think you share powers with him, but trust me he didn't give you anything but the leftovers. Not to mention one small thing. No one gets a piece of him until after I do."

Ash let out a shrill whistle. "Down, children. We have more important things to do than just save your machismo."

Tory hid a smile as she finally understood exactly what Ash's job was and why he described himself as a wrangler. He really was.

Ash leveled a determined look at Nick. "We have a battle to prepare for. I'm not letting Stryker take Nick."

Nick laughed bitterly. "I don't need your fucking help. I can fight on my own."

Ash didn't respond to the hatred in his tone. "I know why you hate me, Nick. I get it. But your mother wouldn't want you to kill yourself again. Hate me tomorrow. Tonight tolerate me as a necessary evil."

Nick shoved him back. "This doesn't make us friends."

Ash held his hands up. "I know." He turned back to Tory. "Styxx, take her out of here. Keep her safe."

706

Tory gaped as she realized that this was the same Styxx she'd read about in the journal—the same one who'd tortured and castrated Acheron.

A wave of rage so bitter she could taste it washed over her. She was going to tell Ash that she had no intention of going anywhere with the man who'd gone out of his way to hurt him, but before she could even open her mouth a bright flash of light blinded her.

A nanosecond later a herd of mean, blond men stepped out. They looked deadly serious as they took up formation.

Stryker came through and his gaze went straight to Urian. "You've betrayed me for the last time." He threw something at Urian.

Tory had no idea what it was until Ash caught it in his hand. It was a strangely shaped dagger that reminded her of an ancient Greek design and yet it bore the same sun symbol on the pommel that Ash had on his backpack.

Ash narrowed his gaze on the Daimons. "Take your girls, scream and run away now, Stryker. It'll save you time later. Believe me, you don't want a taste of me in the mood I'm in."

Stryker ran his tongue over his fangs as if he was savoring the idea of feeding on Acheron. "There's nothing I crave more than the taste of blood. Your Dark-Hunters aren't here." He looked around at the men who stood with Ash and laughed in derision. "Tonight we feast, Spathi. Attack!"

Tory was snatched behind the group that stood with Acheron. She wanted to tell them that she could hold her own, but as the men attacked and the Daimons fought back with punches and lightning bolt strikes, she realized that she wasn't as proficient as she needed to be.

They weren't just fighting with their fists and weapons, they were fighting with preternatural powers she could never compete with. And the thought had barely finished before a group of demons joined ranks with the Daimons to fight them.

Stryker went for Nick, but Ash caught him and the two of them went to the ground, slugging. Urian stabbed a demon between the eyes before he turned and ducked the fangs of a Daimon.

Tory stumbled back, looking for a weapon of some kind.

A demon launched itself at her. She tried to kick him back, but he didn't even flinch. Just as he would have reached her, Julian was there with a sword. He severed the demon's head with one well-placed swing.

Balancing the blade of his ancient Greek sword on his shoulder, he turned to face her. "Can you handle a sword?"

"Yes."

"Kyrian!" Julian shouted to the other tall blond man on their team. "Give me a sword."

Kyrian tossed what appeared to be only a hilt. In one fluid move, Julian caught it and pressed a button on the cross hilt. The blade shot out to just under three feet in length. He handed it over to her. "Daimons have to be stabbed through their hearts. Demons between their eyes and if you cut the heads off any of us, we all die."

"How do I tell the difference?"

"Most of the Daimons are blond and they explode into dust when you pierce their hearts. Hit the heart and if that doesn't work, try the eyes. If you stab someone who whimpers, then hits the ground, you attacked a good guy. Just FYI."

She inclined her head. "Thanks for the tutorial."

He laughed before he put his battle face on and went back to the fight.

Tory swung the blade around her body, getting a feel for the balance. Out of nowhere a female Daimon came at her and manifested a staff. She swung it at Tory's head.

Parrying the blow with her sword, Tory pulled the blade back and went on the offensive. The woman met her stroke for stroke and she made every blow count. The ferocity of it rattled all the way to Tory's bones.

She hated to admit it, but the Daimon was actually winning. With a feral growl, she tried to shove the Daimon back.

Suddenly, Nick was there. He swung the Daimon away from her and into another one. "No one hurts a human on my watch," he snarled before he stabbed the Daimon through the heart. As Julian had noted, the Daimon screamed, then turned into a golden powder.

Nick moved away from Tory before she could thank him.

Another flash of light heralded an even larger group of demons and Daimons.

Tory stepped back, her jaw dropping. They were so outnumbered . . .

The guys on her team were brilliant fighters, but they were being overrun by the sheer number of enemies. "This is bad . . ."

Ash froze as he saw one of the Daimons sink his fangs deep into Vane's arm at the same time more demons joined them.

He couldn't let his friends be hurt. Closing his eyes, he summoned his staff from Katoteros. He'd just tightened his hand around it when he felt someone stumble into him.

He opened his eyes to see Styxx there with an Atlantean dagger stuck completely through his stomach. Stryker cursed as he jerked it free, then went for Ash again.

Ash caught the Daimon overlord with the blunt end of his staff and shoved him back. "Flee or die," he growled.

"Fuck you."

Narrowing his gaze on Stryker, Ash shoved him back, then slammed the staff to the pavement. A wave of raw, unfettered power shot out from it to the demons and Daimons around him. Every one of them turned to dust.

Except for Stryker. He hovered above the ground in his dragon form, snarling and flapping. Bellowing, Stryker spewed fire.

Ash lifted his arm, barely in time to keep it from burning him. He shot another god bolt at Stryker who dodged it.

"This isn't over, Acheron. Next time you won't be able to use your powers." With another blast of fire, Stryker vanished.

Vane shook his bleeding arm in an obvious effort to alleviate the pain of the Daimon's bite. "Why were we fighting if you had that kind of power?"

In unison, every ex-Dark-Hunter and Nick said, "Just because you can doesn't mean you should."

"And sometimes things have to go wrong in order to go right," Wulf said. When the other guys looked confused by

709

his solo outburst, he added, "I guess I'm the only one he ever said that one to."

Fury made a strange wolf-like noise. "I still don't see why we were fighting when you could have just kicked their asses without us."

"Because I believe in giving everyone a fighting chance . . . until they piss me off." Ash cast Vane a quick stoic glance. "Bringing in reinforcements was Stryker's mistake."

"And be glad it wasn't yours," Fury said with a nervous laugh to Vane. "I know I'm thrilled it wasn't mine." The wolf looked around at the Daimon and demon remains, or rather what little of it there was. "Acheron. When it absolutely, positively must be destroyed overnight."

Ash knelt by Styxx's side to inspect the damage done. He wasn't overly worried since Styxx couldn't die unless he did. But that didn't mean it didn't hurt like hell. The dagger Stryker had held would have killed him had Styxx not stopped the attack.

His brother, who had wanted to die as much as he had, had saved his life.

He could barely even fathom that.

Styxx met his gaze levelly, even though he was shaking from the pain of his wound. "You know, brother, you're never supposed to close your eyes in battle."

Ash laughed at his ill-placed humor. "I wasn't the one training to be a general."

Styxx glanced around at the men surrounding them. "Perhaps. But you do a much better job of leading than I ever did. I definitely think Father trained the wrong one of us."

That was the kindest thing Styxx had ever said to him. Ash didn't speak as he placed his hand over Styxx's wound.

Styxx's gaze didn't leave his. But when Ash sealed the wound closed, Styxx let out an expletive about Ash's "kind" touch that would have made Stryker proud.

"Am I dead yet?" Styxx asked sarcastically.

"Not yet. You still have a few years left to seriously piss me off."

Styxx smiled. "I look forward to it."

For once, so did Ash. "You did a good job for me. Thank you."

"Yeah well, next time you need someone to descend into a Daimon sanctuary, pick one of your other assholes to do it. I don't have the powers of a god when they come at me and it puts me at a definite disadvantage."

Still, he'd thrown himself in front of Ash to protect him . . . It went a long way in allowing him to put the past to rest and to accept his brother. Grinning, Ash helped Styxx to his feet.

Talon scratched his head as he watched them. "Hey T-Rex? Remind me next time I want to get smartass with you that it's a really stupid move on my part."

Wulf gaped. "Oh no you don't, you wuss. You told me the next time you saw Ash you were going to ask him if he'd seen the movie *10,000 BC* and if it'd made him homesick."

Talon made a cut-off gesture at Wulf. "Do you mind not getting me fried tonight? I'd like to use some of my body parts later if you know what I mean and since you're married with a brood of kids I know that you do."

Ash looked at Tory and any semblance of agitation he might have felt evaporated. She was safe and that was all that mattered to him.

He looked around at the group who'd come to help him and marveled at it. "Thank you, guys."

Kyrian offered him his hand. "Anytime you need us, Acheron, we're here for you."

And one by one, they shook his hand and made a like declaration.

Until he got to Talon. "One day, you've got to tell me how you did that stick thing. That could come in handy not only with Daimons, but stray alligators and annoying neighbors."

Ash laughed. "One day I might."

At least until Nick walked past him and shoved his shoulder into Ash's. It was such a juvenile thing to do. Ash glared at him as he stalked away, into the darkness. "For the record, Nick, I loved Cherise too."

Nick flipped him off and kept walking.

Zarek was the last man to leave. He sauntered over and cocked his head. His gaze went to Tory before he returned it to Ash and spoke to him in Greek. "You know, it's amazing to me the wounds we can carry for eternity. But what has fascinated me most these last few years is how the right person can heal them. I remember a wise man once said to me that everyone deserves to be loved. Even you."

Ash snorted at the advice he'd given to Zarek after the man had almost let his wife go. "And as I recall, you told me to shut up."

Zarek shrugged, taking it in stride. "I'm an asshole. I admit it. I've been going to weekly Assholes Anonymous meetings, but it takes a long time to undo a few thousand years of habit. And to think you have even more years to undo than me."

"So how's Bob doing?" Ash asked, changing the subject to Zarek's young son. "Has Astrid won the battle yet?"

"On calling him Menoeceus? Hell no. I still say it's too close to Menopause for my taste and there's not even a good nickname for it. Can you imagine being stuck with that name at school? Call me ridiculous, but I'd like the kid to grow up without a stigma."

Ash laughed at a tirade Zarek had delivered on more than one occasion. Yet his wife Astrid completely ignored it and continued to call the poor child Menoeceus while his father called him Bob.

Zarek shook his head. "But I tell you this, there's nothing better than looking at a kid and seeing you mixed in with the one person you know you can trust to never screw you over. And I owe you for that, Acheron. Every time I look at them, I never forget what I owe you." He stepped away and switched to English, not knowing that Tory understood Greek as well as he did. "You two take care. And for the sake of the gods, stay out of trouble. At least until it warms up. You know how much I hate being in cold places." He vanished instantly.

Ash sent his staff back to Katoteros as Tory walked over to him. He repaired her shirt.

She tried to peer over his back. "How are you feeling?"

"Right now I could fly." He held his hand out for her.

The instant she took it, he teleported them back to his small flat on Pirate's Alley.

She looked around with an arched brow. "Wow, you weren't kidding. This place is itty-bitty."

He shrugged his backpack off his shoulder. "I don't need much."

"You know, me either. But there is one thing I need."

"And that is?"

The heated, sincere look in her eyes scorched him. "You."

He savored that word and the surge of love that went through his heart. But in the end, he knew the truth. "I can't stay with you, Tory. There can never be an us."

"Why not?"

Was she insane? Had she wiped the whole event they'd just lived through out of her mind? "You saw what I deal with on a daily basis. My enemies aren't human and I have a lot more than just Stryker to deal with, and while Nick might have set you free tonight, he might not tomorrow. Not to mention the large redheaded problem. I can't put you in that kind of danger. Ever."

"And if I disagree?"

"I won't let you. I'm a god, Tory. If I have to, I'll erase myself from your memories."

"You ever monkey with my brain and I swear, Acheron, you will be hurt."

And now that he thought about it, she was probably just like Nick—too flippin' stubborn for his powers to work on her. "Be reasonable, Tory. My life is very complicated and it's dangerous."

Tory wanted to cry over his obstinacy. "Everyone deserves love, Acheron," she said, repeating Zarek's words. "Look me in the eye and tell me you really want me to leave. Tell me you never want to see me again."

Ash swallowed as his emotions roiled through him. He didn't want her to go. He wanted to hold her and keep her by his side for the rest of his unnatural life.

But so long as she was human, she made him vulnerable. And as long as he had enemies determined to hurt him, he couldn't allow her near him. "I want you to leave, Tory."

"Yeah, well, people in hell want ice water. Now take your clothes off and let me see to your back. It has to be killing you right now."

"So you're going to completely disregard me?"

"Not completely. I hear what you're saying and I respect the fact that I was outgunned and outfought tonight—that those demon things came in and snatched me up from where I was sitting. I'm not a stupid woman, but that being said, I don't give up when I set my sights on something either. I love you, Acheron, and I intend to stand by your side even when you're trying to push me away."

Ash closed his eyes as he savored every word out of her mouth. "I don't know how to love someone, Tory. I don't."

"The crowd of people I saw who were willing to lay down their lives for you says you're full of more manure than a cow pasture, buddy."

"Artemis isn't going to let us live in peace. You do understand that?"

"I understand that I told you to take your clothes off and you're just standing here arguing with me. Give in to me, Ash. Trust me, it's easier that way."

Holding his hands up in surrender, he used his powers to remove his shirt.

Tory sucked her breath in as she saw the reopened wounds that lacerated his back. "How can you stand it?"

The blank look he gave her tore through her. "I'm used to it."

"Get in bed. That back needs to be tended and you need to rest."

"Yes, ma'am." Ash headed the short distance to his bedroom while Tory went to the kitchen. He paused in the doorway to watch her. Oblivious to him, she pulled a bowl out and ran water in it.

A wave of desire hit him so hard that it literally took his breath away. If he didn't hurt so badly, he wouldn't be going to bed alone. But the pain in his back was infinitely more demanding than the one in his groin.

Yet neither of them could compare to the one in his heart which told him that this couldn't last. In spite of her stubbornness, she was going to have to go before Artemis killed her.

And Artemis was right. He was about to have to go crawling back to her to beg for food. Between the fighting and the wounds on his back, he was starving and if he didn't feed very soon, he would start killing.

Wincing, he wondered what Tory would think if she ever saw that side of him. The sad thing was, he never wanted her to deal with him like that. Never wanted her to see the demon beast that lived inside him.

No, Artemis had created that monster. It was only fair that she should be the one who fed it.

He sighed and went to bed to wait on Tory, knowing that come morning, he'd have to let her go.

CHAPTER TWENTY

Tory paused as she entered the room where Ash was sleeping. His breathing was so strange. Not like a human, it reminded her more of a dog panting. Worried about him, she put her bowl and cloth down on the nightstand and sat down by his side.

She placed a hand on his feverish cheek. The moment she made contact, his entire body turned a vivid blue. Gasping, she watched as his skin marbled and swirled with varying shades of blue color. His nails turned black and two small horns emerged from the top of his head.

Shooting off the bed, she scowled as Artemis's bow and arrow mark appeared over the wounds on his back.

Ash growled even in sleep. And when he opened his eyes to look at her, it was all she could do not to run. No longer silver, they were glowing red and shot through with yellow streaks. He opened his mouth and hissed, showing her a set of serrated fangs.

"Baby?" she whispered, searching for some sign of the man she loved in the creature who terrified her.

He blinked as if seeing her for the first time and crouched on the bed.

Tory approached him slowly. Holding her hand out, she gently laid her palm against his blue cheek. He closed his eyes and nuzzled her hand while he took a sniff of her wrist. That seemed to calm him. He said something to her in a language she couldn't even begin to translate. "I don't understand," she said in Atlantean.

"Akee-kara, akra."

She brushed his black hair back from his face. "Do you need something, sweetie?"

Ash was trying to focus, but it was impossible. Everything was so hazy. He wasn't even sure if he was awake or dreaming. The pain in his back seemed to be gone now. And he was around fresh blood—he could smell it and hear the heart beating.

That sound made his mouth water.

Licking his lips, he inhaled the scent of feminine flesh that covered the veins he wanted to puncture . . .

Eat.

He wasn't supposed to. Even in this state, he remembered the rule that he'd taught himself. He wasn't allowed to taste humans. It was wrong. But right now while he was starving, he couldn't remember why.

All he could think of was sating his demanding ache.

He pulled the human closer so that he could inhale her neck. Licking the tender flesh there, he grazed her skin with his fangs, wanting to sink them in deep. He felt the chills sweep over her as she sighed in pleasure.

She spoke to him, but he couldn't understand her words. At least not until her lips touched his. The sweetness of her mouth touched the man inside him and it sent the beast back into submission.

Tory shivered as Ash returned to normal. His skin was once again tawny, his eyes that calm beautiful silver. Even so, there was a ferocity to him that reminded her of a barely leashed tiger.

And when he led her hand to touch him, she hesitated. "You're hurt, Ash. You should rest."

He shook his head as if trying to clear it. Her clothes vanished. And this time when he took possession of her mouth, she couldn't remember her argument. He laced his fingers

717

with hers and pressed her hand against his hardened cock. She felt his shiver in her own body as he rubbed himself against her palm.

He left her hand there so that he could touch her. One moment, she was standing beside the bed and in the next, she was pinned beneath him. She sighed at the wonderful sensation of his naked body lying against hers.

Careful not to touch his back, she cupped his face as he deepened his kiss.

Ash still wasn't sure if this was a dream or not. All he knew was that the scent of Soteria filled his head and he had to be inside her. His heart hammering, he spread her legs and slid himself deep. The moment he did, he gasped at the pleasure he felt. But it didn't last long before the beast inside him was back, wanting to feed as her blood rushed through her veins. It was all he could hear. All he could focus on.

It overrode his pleasure and left him salivating.

Tory whimpered as Ash pulled back. At least until she saw his face. The torment there branded itself on her heart. "What's wrong, Ash?"

Ash wanted to stay with her. He wanted to be inside her again . . .

No, he wanted to feed. The urge to rip her throat out was fierce.

He was losing control. It slipped and broke free until he was no longer able to remember anything other than the misery of hunger. Every second with her brought him closer to the edge.

Unable to handle it without killing her, he left the human realm.

Tory blinked as she realized she was alone. "Ash?" she called, wondering where he'd gone off to.

Completely naked, Ash threw open the doors to Artemis's bathing chamber. No longer human in any way, he was the beast he despised. Nothing mattered to him but feeding. Destroying.

Killing.

Acheron was gone. Only Apostolos was here. And the Harbinger Apostolos wanted blood and there was only one person he wanted it from.

Artemis . . .

Artemis gasped at the intrusion on her bath until she realized it was Acheron. She smiled at his blue skin and black hair. "I told you you'd return to me."

He flew from the doors to the pool where she bathed. Landing in a crouch on the ledge near her, he reminded her more of a bird than a man.

He grabbed her and pulled her close.

She put her hand on his jaw and pushed him away from her neck before he could sink his fangs into her. "You haven't earned your food. I'm angry at you and you're not going to eat until you please me."

Incapable of language in his destroyer's form, he hissed at her and tightened his grip.

Artemis blasted him away. He tumbled back to land on his side. In one fluid move, he flipped to his feet and snarled.

He bared his teeth in anger before he launched himself at her.

She teleported out of his way, knowing that if he laid hands, or in the current case, claws, on her, she'd be killed.

He stalked her like prey. She should probably be afraid, but her anger overrode that. Normally neither one of them allowed him to go this long without eating. But he'd betrayed her and honestly she didn't care right now if he died.

Refusing to give in to him, she ran for her backroom.

He tried to cut off her retreat, but she shot through him and entered her safe room. Stupidly, he followed. The moment he was inside, she flashed herself to the door and slammed it shut, leaving him trapped inside.

He threw himself repeatedly against the clear door like an animal gone insane. But honestly, as hard as he struck it, she was amazed he didn't break through.

"You can't escape here, Acheron. You're powers are useless in that room and until I let you out, you're mine."

He slammed one clawed hand against the door and let out a howl so feral it made the hair on the back of her neck stand up. Oh, he would definitely kill her right now if he got free.

Narrowing her gaze, she crossed her arms over her chest and gave him a smug glare. "As I said, I own you. Now sit in there and starve until *I'm* ready to feed you."

Ash could barely understand those words past the hunger gnawing at him. In this state, he was like the Shades of Dark-Hunters who'd died while Artemis held their souls in thrall. Forever hungry and thirsty. Unreasonable and unable to make himself understood. It was the most wretched of existences.

The door solidified and left him alone in a small, dark room. There was no furniture, no windows . . .

No light whatsoever.

For an instant, his sanity returned and he felt like a boy in prison again. He twisted around, looking for the rats that used to bite him. Listening for the telltale sound of their scurrying feet.

"Artemis!" he shouted. "Let me out!"

I'm afraid. Those words caught in his throat.

"Acheron? Are you there?"

He heard Ryssa's voice in his head.

And then his hunger returned, driving all semblance of humanity away from him. He slashed at the doors with his claws. The pain of his hunger was excruciating. Unable to stand it, he slammed himself against the door, again and again, determined to break through it.

Four *days went* by while Artemis pondered what she should do about Acheron. His incessant slamming against the wall and snarling howls were beginning to wear on her.

But he needed to be taught a lesson. He needed to be punished and until he learned to come to heel, she wasn't about to let him out.

Not to mention, at this point, she was honestly afraid of him. He'd never gone this long without feeding. And past experience told her that a small gobbet of blood would only whet his appetite for more.

She considered feeding one of her maidens to him, but that would be cruel.

And on the tail end of that thought came another one. "Not a Kori . . ."

No. Something that rhymed with it rather. She smiled at her ingeniousness. She'd sworn to Acheron that Soteria wouldn't be harmed by her or one of her minions.

But she hadn't promised to keep Acheron away from her.

He'd told her that Soteria soothed him. Fine, let the bitch soothe him now. Let her feed him.

Preening with satisfaction, Artemis flashed herself to New Orleans where the little slut was teaching a class. Aggravated at having to wait, she stood in the hallway until it was over.

Tory *was heartsick* as she dismissed her students. She hadn't seen or heard from Ash in days and the fact that he'd left her in sole possession of his prized backpack made her wonder if something bad hadn't happened to him.

Putting her books into her own backpack, she pulled it off the table and headed for the door. But before she reached it, a tall gorgeous redhead stepped inside. Dressed in an expensively tailored white suit and Prada shoes, she was stunning.

Tory wanted to rip every strand of hair out of her head.

"Why are you here, Artemis?" she asked coldly.

Artemis curled her lip as if she hated to be around Tory even more than Tory hated being around her.

Nah, it wasn't possible.

"Acheron needs you, human. He's hurt and he can't come."

Tory scowled. "Why would you come to get me?"

"He wants you. Believe me, there's no other reason I'd be here."

Still suspicious, Tory gripped the strap of her backpack. "Are you lying to me?"

Artemis made an ancient Greek gesture of loyalty and truth. "I swear to you, he's in ultimate suffering and he needs you. Are you really so selfish that you won't help him?"

She was selfish? Tory would have laughed if she hadn't been so worried about him. "Take me to him, then."

Artemis flashed her out of her classroom and into what appeared to be an ancient Greek temple. The room was surrounded by columns and above her head was an amazing hunt scene stamped into gold. It was exquisite.

"Where am I?"

"Olympus." Artemis led her into a bathing room that had an ancient styled bathing pond. She didn't stop until she reached a door on the other side of it. As she lifted her hand, the door lightened to transparency.

Tory gasped as she saw Ash lying naked on the floor. His black hair was matted, his breathing shallow. His skin was marbled blue again and two black horns jutted out from his head. His lean muscles were starkly outlined by the dual blue skin tone. His hands ended in long black claws and when he saw them looking at him, he bared a pair of sharp fangs in their direction.

Pushing himself up, he kept one arm around his stomach as if he were about to be ill. He took one step and collapsed on the floor again in obvious pain. He roared a bellow of frustration and agony.

"He's disgusting in his god form, isn't he?"

Tory raked the goddess with a repugnant stare. "He's never disgusting. What's wrong with him?"

"He needs to eat. This is what always happens to him if he ever goes too long between feedings."

"Why haven't you fed him then?"

A slow, evil smile curved Artemis's lips. "Sweetie, why do you think you're here?" She reached out and opened the door.

The next thing Tory knew, Artemis had shoved her inside the room and shut the door, locking her in with Ash. "Bon appetit."

Tory turned to the door, trying to open it. But it was hopeless. There was no latch or key or anything on this side. All she could do was see Artemis's gloating face.

Oh if she ever had three minutes alone with her . . . It would be a death match worthy of pay-per-view.

With no other choice, Tory approached Ash slowly.

Warily. Could he even tell if it was her? By the way he was acting, she didn't think so. "Baby?"

He looked up at her with blood red eyes that held no semblance of understanding. They were feral and cold. The eyes of a predator.

With a speed she couldn't even see with her naked eye, Ash was off the floor. He grabbed her by the throat, threw her down on the ground and sank his fangs deep into her neck.

Ash's *head buzzed* and his shoulder ached as he finally slaked some of the hunger that had been tearing at him for days. The blood was so good. So warm and satisfying. He licked and sucked, drinking it in until he was normal again.

But as he returned to himself, his anger mounted that she'd let him go so long without nourishment. Even though he hadn't been able to speak, he remembered her watching him through the door.

"You'll eat when you please me . . ." She knew what those words did to him and he was tired of her abuse.

"Artemis, you . . ." His words trailed off as he pulled away from her throat and realized it wasn't Artemis he was holding.

It was Tory and she was extremely pale from the blood loss.

Horror filled him. Her neck was savagely torn from his teeth, her brown eyes half-hooded as she struggled to breathe. No! His soul screamed out. How could he have hurt her?

How could he be so far gone that he hadn't even realized it was Tory he tasted?

Because Artemis had kept him without food for too long. And then she'd thrown a human in with him, knowing a human couldn't survive his feeding.

"Oh gods," he breathed, choking. "Stay with me, baby. I'll get you help."

She coughed as she reached up to touch his lips that were covered in her blood from his feeding. He saw the fear in her eyes and the pain that he'd caused her. The guilt was more than he could bear.

"Soteria?" he whispered her name like a prayer. "Akribos?"

She expelled one last breath before her eyes glazed over and her hand fell limply to the ground where it landed palm up.

Unimaginable grief tore through him as he realized he'd just killed her. Throwing his head back, Ash bellowed from the weight of guilt and pain that assaulted him.

He would never have hurt her. Never!

Then he saw Artemis at the door, safely tucked on the other side of it, watching. The satisfaction in her eyes made him want to gouge them out.

He carefully laid Tory down before he charged at the door, determined to get to the bitch who'd taken everything from him. Again. "Why!" he roared.

She narrowed her eyes in pitiless fury. "You know why." Then the door darkened and left him alone with the body of the only woman he'd ever really loved.

The woman he'd just killed. And in this room where his powers were negated, he couldn't heal her or bring her back. Tory was dead and he'd killed her. Throwing his head back, he roared with pain.

Tory *was wandering* through a thick, oppressive fog. She felt lost and disoriented. The last thing she remembered was seeing Ash. Seeing the look of horror and fear on his beautiful face while her neck throbbed in pain.

Now there was no pain. There was nothing. No light. No sound. No smell.

The deprivation was terrifying.

"Ash?" she called, trying to get her bearings.

"He's not here, little one."

She turned at the thickly accented, kind voice behind her to find Apollymi standing there in the darkness. "What are you doing here?"

Apollymi held her hand out to her. "I stole your soul the moment you died and brought it to Kalosis, but I can't keep it unless you allow me to. I wouldn't allow it if I were you. Souls are too precious to squander and yours in particular has great value to me."

"I don't understand." She put her hand into Apollymi's and the moment their skin touched, she had total clarity of everything that Apollymi knew about her and Acheron—more than that, she saw the memories of Ash and how he died. Of Artemis turning her back on him and leaving him while he reached out for her to help him.

How could she have done such a thing?

Tears welled up in her eyes and then when she saw her own death and the satisfied look on Artemis's face as Ash cried out, she wanted blood.

"Artemis killed me?"

Apollymi nodded. "She's still punishing my son and there's nothing I can do to stop it . . . but you, Soteria, *you* can."

"How?"

"I can send your soul back to your body for a brief moment of time. Once I do, the only way you can return to the living is to drink the blood of Apostolos before your soul flees your body again."

Tory had a hard time believing that. "What?"

Apollymi patted her hand. The dim light reflected in her crystal tears as those swirling eyes glowed warmly. "I am a goddess of destruction. His father was a god of creation. Inside Apostolos, our powers are joined and he is one of the rare gods who can both create and destroy life. It's his creative powers that Artemis uses to bring her Dark-Hunters back to life. Without feeding from him, she'd never have that ability. And like Artemis, if you feed from my son, you will share his powers with him. You will have the ability to cure yourself and to return to your life. More than that, you'll have the powers to protect yourself and I will send my priestesses to serve as your guardians to make sure that no one ever harms you again."

It all sounded too good to be true. She could return to Ash and the world with the powers of a god . . . Surely it couldn't be that simple. "What's the catch?"

"It's the same catch Artemis used on Apostolos. Once you feed from him, you will always have to feed from him."

Tory cringed as she remembered the pain of Ash biting her. "Blood?"

Reluctantly, she nodded. "Please, Soteria. Do what I can't. Save my son from that monster who willfully hurts him. Apostolos will never willingly take the blood of another and bind that person to him. Not after the violent way Artemis tricked him into bondage. But if you return and you feed him and he feeds you, he will be free from that bitch forever."

She looked away as she considered what would come. "I can stay with Ash?"

"Yes and I will give you enough of my powers to make sure that neither Artemis nor any other enemy of Apostolos will ever be able to harm you again."

The depths to which Apollymi would go for Ash touched her and it reminded her of her own mother—a mother she missed every day of her life. "But what about you? Won't that weaken you?"

"It will, but I don't care. I want my son free and I want him happy, no matter the cost to me. I'm tired of seeing the weariness in his eyes when we speak. Of seeing the pain that I can't soothe. Will you help him? Please?"

Tory tightened her grip on the goddess's hand, wanting her to know how sincere she was. "I would do anything for that man."

Apollymi smiled. "I thought your cousin Geary would be the one to free my baby. But the moment I first saw you when you were only ten, poking around the ruins of my temple under the Aegean, I knew you were the one. It was why I never allowed any other man to touch you."

She covered Tory's hand with her other and held it tight. "Soteria. The keeper of Atlantis who stood at her post even against my anger, and who went down fighting to protect what she loved most. You do your namesake proud."

Apollymi pulled the necklace from around her neck and then folded it into Tory's palm. "When are you are ready to

726

fight for him, press that to your heart and you'll have the powers of a goddess. Forever."

Tory held the necklace in her hand and studied the red swirling mist inside a translucent stone. Grateful for the gift, she embraced Apollymi.

Apollymi was stunned by the hug—no one had touched her with so much affection since the night she'd conceived Apostolos. Closing her eyes, she held the girl close. "So long as you're kind to him, you will always be my daughter. If you ever need anything, call for me and I will answer."

"I won't let anything happen to him again. I promise."

Apollymi kissed her cheek before she pulled back. "Then go to him, Soteria. He needs you."

Nodding, Tory stepped back and pressed the stone to her heart. The moment she did, a searing pain ripped through her. "Ow! You didn't tell me it'd hurt."

Apollymi shrugged. "Birth is never painless and especially not a rebirth."

She wasn't kidding. Tory felt like something was shredding her from the inside out. Nauseated and dizzy, she blinked at the darkness that was so oppressive it was blinding.

The next thing she knew, she was in Ash's arms again. He sat on the floor, holding her to him, cheek to cheek, as he rocked her and whispered to her, "Please, Tory, please don't be dead. Please don't leave me alone. I don't want to live without you . . ."

Those heartfelt words choked her, but what stunned her the most was the wetness of his cheeks.

He was crying.

For her.

Lifting her hand, she brushed her fingers against the whiskers of his jaw. He pulled back with a startled gasp. "Soteria?"

She nodded, then she felt the hunger his mother had mentioned. It burned through her with an unbelievable ferocity that lengthened her incisors. Determined, she met his gaze. "Let me stay with you, Ash."

Ash couldn't breathe as he understood what she was asking. What she needed. And for the first time in eternity, he was willing to bleed in order to give her life. "Are you sure?"

She nodded.

He brushed his hair aside and tilted his neck for her. Closing his eyes, he braced himself for the pain of her bite. For the hated sensation of her breath on his neck while she fed.

Tory paused as she felt him go rigid. It took her a second to realize why. Ash couldn't stand to have anyone breathe on his neck and yet there he sat, offering himself to her without complaint or comment. In that moment she loved him all the more.

And with her newfound senses, she knew his neck wasn't the only place she could feed from . . .

Ash opened his eyes as she moved away from him. Frowning, he watched as she dipped down and bit into his inner thigh. He sucked his breath in sharply as a wave of desire blinded him and hardened his cock which was only a few inches from her mouth. But greater than that was the shock that she hadn't grabbed his hair and hurt him while she fed from his neck. She was being gentle and considerate, and when she looked up at him, her eyes matched his.

That deep swirling silver that he hated so much was beautiful on her. They were bound together now. His powers. His blood. They were hers too. But even so, he wanted her as she'd been. Kissing her lips, he turned her eyes back to the brown color that had stolen his heart the first time she'd looked around the room in nervous panic.

This was the woman he loved. The one he couldn't live without.

Tory felt a raw unimagined power deep inside her. She could hear everything now. See the most minute color changes in every object. "Is this how you see the world?"

"Yes."

It was all so vivid. Overwhelming. At the same time her body was hot and needy. She looked at him and he actually blushed before he clothed himself.

Clearing his throat, he indicated the door with a tilt of his head. "We can't do that here."

"Artemis," she growled the name.

He nodded. "We're still locked in her temple."

"Not for long." Rising to her feet, she went to the door.

Ash scowled as Tory closed her eyes and held her hands out by her sides. He felt the wind of his grandmother stirring around them. His jaw went slack as he realized what was happening—his mother had surrendered part of her powers to Tory. She didn't just have his inside her.

And the combination of his powers with his mother's . . .

Scary stuff that.

The thought had barely finished before the door splintered into a thousand fragments.

Artemis shrieked from the other side, then ran to her throne room.

Ash stood up and went to Tory. "Let's go home."

She shook her head. "You go on ahead. I'll be there in a minute."

He paused at the odd note in her voice. "Tory . . ."

She gave him an impish smile, cutting his words off. "I'm just going to talk with her. Don't worry."

Yeah, right. Don't worry? Was she insane? And for once, he wasn't sure which of them was in the most danger.

Ash hesitated, but ultimately he trusted Tory. "Remind her that I'll know if she hurts you and if she does, there's not enough power on Olympus to protect her."

She kissed the tip of her finger and pressed it to the tip of his nose. "Don't be such a worrywart. We're just having girl talk."

Ash somehow doubted that. Knowing Tory, it would be more like a cat fight. But he wouldn't interfere. It was time someone took the goddess down. "All right, baby. I'll be waiting at my apartment."

Tory didn't move until Ash was gone. The moment she sensed his powers safely back in the human realm, she headed in the direction Artemis had run off to.

Her new powers surging, she went to have a long overdue Come-to-Jesus talk with the goddess.

CHAPTER TWENTY-ONE

Artemis kept waiting for all of the powers to fade from her temple.

They didn't. She felt Acheron's primary ones leave, but there was more still here. Powerful. Cold. Calculating.

That wasn't Acheron.

And when Soteria came through the doors of her bathing chamber and into her throne room with a deadly lope, the blood completely drained from Artemis's face. There was no denying the woman wanted a piece of her and was ready to fight for it.

Still she refused to let the girl see her panic. "You're nothing to me, human."

Tory scoffed, and spoke to her in perfect Greek. "Oh you're wrong about that, Artemis. I'm not nothing. I'm the one who's going to kick your butt if you ever go near Acheron again."

Artemis flung her hand out and sent Tory flying across the room. "You don't threaten me."

Tory lifted her hands and just as she would have hit the wall, she stopped moving. Opening her eyes, she was stunned to find herself floating over the ground a few inches from the stone that Artemis had intended to slam her into.

Artemis shrieked in outrage while Tory laughed in relief. These powers were very cool.

Holding her hands out, she centered herself back on the ground.

Artemis ran at her and caught her about the neck. Tory slid out of her grasp, then shoved her away. "Oh, bitch, please." She threw her hand out and pinned Artemis to the wall.

"Let me go!"

Tory tightened the hold on her. "For all the times you've hurt Ash, you're lucky I'm not ripping the heart out of your chest right now. How could you?"

Tears formed in Artemis's green eyes as she struggled to free herself. "I love him."

Tory shook her head. "How can you say that? You don't even understand what love means. Love isn't being ashamed to be seen with the one you care about. It isn't about punishment or hurt."

Feeling sorry for the goddess, Tory let her go. "Love is what gives you the strength you need to face anything no matter how brutal or frightening. It's what allowed Ash to be beaten rather than tell his father about you. It's what allowed him to be gutted on the floor at your feet rather than publicly shame you. And you spat on him for that love and tore him apart. For a goddess, you're pathetic."

Artemis sneered at her. "You're human. No one cares if *you* sleep with a whore."

Tory did something she'd never in her life done before. She slapped another person.

Artemis shrieked and tried to claw her, but Tory caught her wrists in her hands and pushed her back. She leveled a murderous look on the goddess to let her know she meant business. "You ever insult Acheron again and so help me, I'll do to you what you allowed your brother to do to him. I'll cut your tongue out for it. Acheron is the man I love and no one, ever, takes issue with him without having issues with me."

Artemis snatched one hand free and tried to backhand her, but Tory caught her wrist again. "You're no better than I am," Artemis snarled. "You would sacrifice him in an instant to save yourself and I know it."

Tory shook her head in denial. "You're wrong. There is nothing on this earth, above or below, that I value more than Acheron. And we're both done with you. Have a great eternity and if you want to continue having an eternity, stay out of my way and leave Acheron alone."

Artemis curled her lip. "You're not done with me entirely, human. I'm the mother of his daughter."

That turned her stomach. "You're right. You are Katra's mother, poor her. But you're wrong about one thing."

"And that is?"

Tory let the Destroyer's power unite with Ash's inside her. One minute, she was normal and in the next, she felt her hair turn white blond and fan out around her as lightning engulfed her and flew out of her fingertips. "I'm no longer human," she said in a demonic voice. "I'm the Atlantia Kedemonia Theony—the guardian of the Atlantean gods. And right now there's only one of them walking about and to save him from one more bad memory created by you, I'd bathe in your entrails, bitch. As for Kat, she's a big girl—I know, I used to live with her. She'll survive the death of her mother. Trust me, I have firsthand experience with the subject."

Artemis gaped at her. "You would destroy the entire world for him?"

"Yes, I would. Would you?"

Artemis looked away.

"And that is why you're going to wish him well and get out of our lives. The next time I see you, Goddess, you better be bringing presents that make me smile, otherwise the Greek pantheon will be looking around for a new goddess of the hunt. Do you understand me?"

"I understand." But her eyes said she was already plotting some way to get back at them.

So be it. Enemies were an unfortunate part of life. There was nothing Tory could do about that except make good her promise should Artemis ever discover enough backbone to come after her again.

No one took from her without a fight, and for Ash she'd lay down her life.

"Good-bye, Artemis, and for your own sake, should you ever find someone who loves you the way Ash once did, take better care of him."

With those words spoken, Tory returned to New Orleans where she found Ash waiting on the couch of his apartment. He shot to his feet before he inspected her body for damage—it was actually quite adorable. "Are you all right?"

"I told you I'd be fine."

His gaze was filled with doubt. "She didn't hurt you?"

"Nope." She held her hands up to show him exactly how undamaged she was. "I'm all hunky-dory."

The relief in his eyes touched her deeply as he bent down to place a light kiss on her lips. Oh how she loved this man.

"I'm so sorry for what I did to you," he breathed. "I never meant to hurt you."

"I know, sweetie." She smiled up at him. "What was it Wulf quoted from you? Sometimes things have to go wrong in order to go right? Had you not fed on me, I wouldn't have the powers I need to be with you. So don't be sorry, Ash. I'm not."

He winced as if she'd struck him and that made her ache for him. "I never wanted you to see me like that."

"See you like what?"

"A monster. I despise my true form."

She shook her head at him as he put his arms around her waist. "I can't imagine why. Other than killing me, you were actually cute in a very Papa Smurf kind of way."

"Papa Smurf?" He made a sound of ultimate suffering and scowled at her. "I don't look like Papa Smurf."

"No, baby," she said in a feigned patronizing tone as she playfully patted his cheek, "you don't at all. You look like sex on a stick. Now is your ego all better?"

One eyebrow shot up at her words. At least until she reached down to cup him in her hand. Then he sucked his breath in sharply as she slowly unzipped his pants. "What are you doing?"

She licked her lips at the heat that pounded through her veins. "I'm still feeling rather . . . perky from that feeding. And honestly, Papa Smurf, you look good enough to eat."

Ash could barely breathe as she sank to the floor in front of him and opened his fly. She looked up at him, her eyes bright with love an instant before she took him into her mouth.

All reason flew out of his head as he watched her tease and lick. "You've been reading your book again, haven't you?"

She laughed and the sensation of her throat vibrating around him was more than he could stand. Before he could stop himself, his body released. Ash leaned back against the wall as his body spasmed. Honestly, it was one of the best he'd ever had and the fact that she didn't pull away from him only made it sweeter.

Until he realized what he'd done. Then he cursed at his stupidity while he waited for her to let him have it. "I didn't mean to, Tory. I should have warned you."

She scowled up at him as she zipped his pants. "Warned me about what?"

He looked away, unable to meet her gaze. "I normally have more control. I promise I'll give you time to pull away in the future."

Tory rose up and turned his chin until he met her gaze. "Ash, there is nothing about you that I find disgusting. Nothing. Not your eyes. Not your funky blue body. And especially not something that I initiated. In fact, I love the way you taste and I like it that you lost control. It means I'm doing it right."

Cupping her cheek, he nuzzled her cheek, delighting in the smoothness of her skin against his. "You're too good to be true."

"You only say that 'cause there's no hammer around."

He laughed and dipped his head to nuzzle her neck. "I'm so grateful you don't find me repulsive anymore."

She teased his ear with her fingers. "Just remember to always warn me before you drop fang on me again."

He looked at her with a frown. "Drop fang?"

She smiled playfully. "Yeah, it's a term from the vampire series L.A. Banks writes. You should read her books sometime. They're great."

"With an endorsement like that, how could I refuse? But

first, I think we need to read more of this Tickle Pickle book of yours."

She laughed until pickles made her think of food. "Hey, does the blood thing mean I can't eat anymore?"

"No, Tory," he teased. "You just don't *have* to eat real food. You can taste it, but it won't quench the blood hunger. That you'll have to feed every couple of weeks."

"Or I turn into Mrs. Smurf?"

He laughed. "No. Only I do that. You'll just turn into . . ."

"What?"

"I was thinking of Simi's term. A bitch-goddess."

She punched playfully at his stomach. "Don't you ever call me that! You evil man."

Ash sobered as he realized the way they were playing and bantering. Not once in all of his life had he been so at ease with anyone. She knew everything about him.

Everything.

And none of it mattered to her. His past was nothing.

But she was his future.

Taking her hand, he led her to his bed where he intended to make love to her for the rest of the day. He kissed her as he dissolved their clothes and placed her in the bed. "I love you, Soteria."

Tory rolled him over, wrapped her long, lean body against his and held him close. "*Sagapo*, Achimou. *Sagapo*."

Her Greek warmed him as the hairs at the juncture of her thighs teased his stomach and made his body start to harden again. "*Agapay*, Sota."

Tory frowned up at him. "*Agapay*?"

He nodded. "Atlantean for I love you. Sota is the Atlantean endearment for your name."

Tory loved the sound of that, especially the way it rolled off his tongue in that sexy, lilting accent of his, and she loved most that he was sharing his language with her. "What would an endearment of your name be?"

"Acho."

"*Agapay*, Acho."

He toyed with her hair as he smiled down at her. "I always hated Atlantean, but not when you speak it."

She couldn't imagine why, given how beautiful it was. She could listen to him speak it all day and when he did— watch out. It made her extremely hot.

Nipping his shoulder made her wonder something else. "Out of curiosity, how many languages do you know?"

"I'm a god, Tory. I know all of them. And when you come into contact with them, you will too."

"Now that's impressive." She bit her lip in glee and then her eyes widened. "Ooo and I have another thought. You're omniscient, right?"

"For the most part, yes."

"Then you have to tell me this 'cause I have to know. What's at the end of everything?"

He shrugged. "That's easy enough."

"Then tell me."

"The letter G."

Groaning, Tory hit him in the head with a pillow. "You're rotten, Achimou. For that, you get a tongue lashing." She rolled him over until he was under her.

Ash sucked his breath in as she encircled his nipple with her tongue. Now this was the kind of tongue lashing a man could look forward to. "What else can I do to piss you off?"

She nipped at his ribs. "You can leave me."

He sobered with the thought. "I would never do that, Tory. No one can live without their heart and that's what you are to me."

Tory lay down over him and held him close. Until another horrible thought occurred to her. She tensed and pushed herself up so that she could meet his gaze. "Wait, Ash . . . doesn't Artemis own your soul?"

"No. I'm not really a Dark-Hunter. Unlike them, I didn't willingly give my soul to her. She used my powers to trick me and brought me back against my will. But because I'm a god, she couldn't take my soul from me. I've always had it"

"But you had the bow and arrow mark." Which wasn't on his body at present.

"Only because I didn't want the other Dark-Hunters to know I wasn't one of them. I just wanted them to treat me like I was normal. It's the same reason I have fangs whenever they're around even though they recede unless I'm about to feed."

She propped her head up in her hand and made circles over his chest. "You know you don't have to be normal around me, right?"

"I know."

"Good."

And for the rest of the night, Ash took his time making love to her. Showing her exactly how much she meant to him and how much he treasured her.

It was just after midnight when she finally fell asleep from sheer exhaustion. His body fully sated, Ash covered her with a blanket before he left the bed and dressed himself in black leather pants and a long VG Cat Rat Flail T-shirt. Pulling his long coat over it, he flashed himself from New Orleans to Mount Olympus.

For once he didn't go to see Artemis. Instead he made his way over to the temple of the Fates. The moment he set foot in the foyer, Atropos, Clotho and Lachesis appeared to block him from the rest of their domain. Not that they could. As the Final Fate, he ruled them and they knew it.

"What are you doing here?" Clotho asked, her voice high-pitched from her nervousness.

"I wanted to speak to you."

"About what?"

He looked at Atropos who was tall and blond and who absolutely hated him with a passion he'd never understood. In that moment, he allowed her to see every ounce of fury inside him. "You *ever* sever the thread for Soteria's life again and there's no power in existence that will keep me from tearing your throat out. The three of you have screwed me over for the last time. In all these centuries, I've left you alone. Now, I'm warning you to return the favor because the next time you tamper with my fate, I will end yours."

The fear on their faces told him that they understood and had taken his point to heart. Good.

He was through playing games. When it came to Soteria, he had no sense of humor whatsoever. Anyone who threatened her, ended their own life.

It was that simple.

She'd taught him to finally embrace who and what he was. Woe to the rest of them. Because he was now the Harbinger not just for his mother, but for a slip of a woman who held his heart.

For her, he'd do anything.

Even end the world.

CHAPTER TWENTY-TWO

Two weeks later
New Orleans

Even though Ash trusted Tory, his gut was in a knot as he followed her toward the lecture hall at Tulane where she was going to give another speech on Atlantis. "Why won't you tell me what you're planning to say?"

The obvious answer was she wanted to torture him, which she'd been doing for days.

Damn, she could give Artemis lessons on it.

She gave him that same, warm smile that only served to scare him more. "It's none of your business. But if you start in on me and my reputation like you did in Nashville, you're going to be living in your own apartment again. Alone. Remember, I get Simi custody. Right, Sim?"

"That's right." Simi grinned proudly as she skipped along beside him. "Relax, akri. Akra-Tory won't do nothing to make you angry. Only the Simi does that."

He laughed even though the knot in his stomach drew tighter with every step they took closer to the room.

"You still haven't answered my question," Tory said, returning to the topic she'd started on their way over here. "What was Julius Caesar really like?"

He shrugged nonchalantly. "The man was brilliant, but he cheated at dice."

She let out an impressed breath as she tightened her shoulders dreamily. "I can't believe you met him *and* Alexander the Great."

"Well, Alex was an accident. I was chasing a Daimon who ran into the town where he was staying and after I killed it, he tried to get me to join his army. I told him I was leading my own and didn't have time to unite."

Tory never grew tired of hearing the memories of Ash's past. He'd done so many fascinating things and had witnessed the history that she'd only read about. He'd been there during the first sack of Rome. Had stood on the Wall of China just days after it'd been finished. He'd debated philosophy with Confucius and had eaten dinner with Kublai Khan and attended a feast with Buddha when he'd been just a young boy. He'd walked in Egypt when the Giza necropolis was being built. He'd played games with the dauphin when the boy had been a toddler and eaten dinner with the real King Arthur . . . it was just incredible the life he'd lived.

And he made her wonder what future historical events the two of them would share together.

"What about Jesus?" she asked, dying to know. "Did you ever meet him?"

"I heard him speak on several occasions. Again, he was brilliant and fascinating. There was just something about him that made you pay attention."

"But you didn't meet him?"

He shook his head.

"Why not?"

"For the same reason I never officially met Gandhi. I didn't feel worthy enough. I just liked to listen to them speak." Ash opened the door to the lecture hall.

Tory froze as she saw the gathered crowd.

Ash put his hand on her arm to steady her. "It'll be all right. Simi and I will eat anyone who so much as blinks at you in the wrong way."

Still she wasn't comforted. "I don't know about this."

"Then let's leave. My bike's outside, fully fueled."

She glared at him before she shook her head. "At least my pages are numbered this time." Taking a deep breath for courage, she forced herself to enter the room where the people looked more like sharks to her than historians, students and archaeologists.

But at least this time she had Ash with her. And Simi.

Ash stayed by her side until he reached the first row. He set his backpack down then took a seat. Simi flounced down beside him and smiled encouragingly.

Tory felt like her heart was going to leap out of her chest as she approached the podium. The crowd here was almost as large as the one in Nashville.

God, how she hated speaking in public.

As she readied her pages, the door opened to admit Kim and Pam who waved at her before they came forward to sit beside Simi. Grateful for their support, Tory adjusted the microphone. And just as she was about to start her speech, Artemis opened the door.

She went cold at the sight and what it might mean. Not to mention, she saw the way Ash visibly tensed as if waiting for Armageddon to start.

Without a word to anyone or a glance to Ash, Artemis moved to sit in the back row, away from Ash and the crowd.

What the devil did she want?

Clearing her throat, Tory forced herself to ignore her. Artemis wasn't the important one here.

"Um, hi everyone," she said, speaking lightly into the mike. "I wanted to say thank you for coming today. I know some of you were there in Nashville to witness the debacle of my extreme humiliation . . ." she narrowed her gaze at Ash who had the good grace and sense to look sheepish and contrite, "but as you know, my team, a couple of weeks ago, excavated a large section of the underwater ruins we believed to be Atlantis."

A hand went up from a man she recognized as a historian, but she couldn't recall his name. She pointed at him.

"I heard that among the things found were conclusive artifacts that date back to 9,000 BC. If you can confirm this, you do know that you will have totally rewritten the historical record?"

Before she could respond the doors opened one more time to show her a UPS delivery man. Oblivious to the fact that he was interrupting her lecture, he headed straight for her. "Dr. Kafieri?"

"That would be me."

He handed her an electronic pad to sign.

Confused, she nervously looked around. "Please excuse me," she told the room as she signed her name, then took the small package from his hands. Frowning, she opened it to find Ryssa's final journal, the one that Artemis had had her men steal along with Ash's backpack.

It was the conclusive proof that would rewrite history and make not only her name but that of her father and uncle legends in their field.

This was the moment she'd always dreamed of. Ever since they'd laid her father to rest, her sole goal in life had been redeeming his name.

Her heart hammering, she looked at Ash whose face was now pale. He met her gaze and she saw his fear fade.

"Go ahead, baby. I know how much it means to you. Give your father back his reputation." Only she could hear Ash's deep voice in her head.

Those words brought tears to her eyes. She knew what that would do to Ash. The men and women he called friends would know exactly how ugly his past had been. While she was sure many of them wouldn't care, she knew enough about people to know that not all of them would feel that way. Some of them would never see him the same way again. They would laugh and they would mock.

Most of all, they would never forgive him for a truth that hadn't been his fault. They would make him feel the same way Artemis had for all these centuries.

And that would crush him.

"I'm sorry, Dad," she whispered under her breath before she put the book back into its envelope and returned to her speech. She cleared her throat. "Yes, we found quite a few items that are quite old. Unfortunately, none of them date back to what I believe to be the time of Atlantis. More than that, the ruins we found appear to be nothing more than a small Greek shipping village. I fear that the experts are correct. There is no Atlantis in the Aegean. After all these years, I've come to understand that my family and I have been on the wrong path.

"That being said, my team is currently heading to the Bahamas to rendezvous so that we can look more closely at the Bimini Road find. If there is an Atlantis, which I now doubt completely, that might be the key to it."

She swallowed as she looked around the room and saw the scowls on the faces of her peers. "I wish I had better news for everyone and you can all read my report on our findings in my upcoming paper, as well as on my Web site once I get it finished. In the end though, my quest for Atlantis did teach me something. In all our pasts lie our futures. By our own hands and decisions we will be damned and we will be saved. Whatever you do, put forth your best effort even if all you're doing is chasing a never-ending rainbow. You might never reach the end of it, but along the way you'll meet people who will mean the world to you and make memories that will keep you warm on even the coldest nights. Thank you all for coming."

Pushing her pages together, she met Ash's incredulous stare and smiled at him.

There were murmurs and whispers as the crowd quietly dispersed, including a few derogatory ones about her and her father. But for once, she didn't care. Words were nothing. It was the people in her life who mattered most.

As they left, Simi punched Ash in the arm. "See, akri. The Simi don't raise no fools. I told you my girl was a good one. Akra-Tory never do anything to hurt her Achimou."

Ash laughed.

Artemis, however, looked less than pleased as she made her way down to Tory.

Tory tightened her grip on the package that Artemis had sent to her, ready to fight to the end of time to keep the journal out of Artemis's hands again.

"I thought for sure you'd use that to save face."

Tory shrugged. "I loved my father more than anything. But as much as it pains me to admit it, I know he's dead. Ash isn't. Better everyone laugh at me than they laugh at him."

Artemis looked incredulous that she'd say such a thing. "You really do love him, don't you?"

"More than my life."

"And more than your dignity." There was a note of respect in her voice. Artemis turned to glance at Ash. When she looked back at Tory, there were tears in her eyes. "Take care of him, Soteria. Give him what I couldn't." She gave one light squeeze to her hand before she turned away.

Ash stood up as Artemis approached him. He saw the longing in her eyes as she started to touch him, but even now she couldn't bring herself to do so in public.

"I want you and your human to have a good life. But I do want you to remember one thing."

"And that is?"

"There will never be another Dark-Hunter who goes free. Your happiness comes at the expense of their freedom because there's no one else I want to barter with. No one else to pay the fee you set up centuries ago. Knowing that, I hope you sleep well at night."

Ash ground his teeth in rage of her coldness as she walked away. He started after her, but Tory stopped him.

"Let her go, Ash. We have the journal. Her Azlantikoinonia have been neutralized and my team is none the wiser about our search. They just think we've changed directions. All in all, we've done well."

"But what about the Dark-Hunters?"

She smiled with a newfound optimism. "The one thing I've learned most out of all this is that it's not over until all the cards are played. She laid down her ace, thinking we can't beat it. But there are fifty-one other cards in the deck and the game isn't over yet. We'll figure something out. Her little fit right now just shows that she's played her best hand. That was all she's capable of doing to hurt you which is exactly why she did it. Don't let her ruin your day, baby, and don't let her take from us what we have. We've gotten this far together. What's another bitter goddess to us? Like my papou always says, over, under, around or through. There's always a way and we'll find it."

By his features she could tell he was impressed. "How can a woman so young be so wise?"

"I'm an old soul."

"And I'm a lucky man to have you."

She smiled as she handed him Ryssa's journal. "Yes, you are. But that's okay. I'm a lucky woman to have you."

"I still say one of you people like people should let the Simi eat the heifer-goddess. She be good eats. The Simi would even share her with her sister."

Laughing, Ash took Tory's hand and once the room was cleared, he flashed her to Katoteros. Simi flounced off to watch TV.

Without a word, he pulled Tory through the throne room toward the ballroom that hadn't been used since his mother destroyed the Atlantean pantheon.

Tory frowned as Ash turned around and walked backwards while smiling at her. The doors opened at his approach and the minute he was inside the huge dark room his clothes changed to vintage 1978 punk, complete with black combat boots, ripped jeans, a torn Union Jack T-shirt and a black motorcycle jacket with chains and an anarchy symbol emblazoned on the back.

"What are you doing?" The words had barely left her lips before her own clothes changed to the same exact dress her mother had worn the night she'd met her father.

The doors closed, sealing them into darkness. An instant later a light came on to showcase a silver mirrored ball at the same time Donna Summer's "Last Dance" started playing. The floor under her feet lit up like a 1970s disco as Ash twirled her under his arm.

Smiling at her, he began to sing, "I need you. By me. Beside me . . . to guide me. To hold me. To scold me . . ."

She laughed even as tears of happiness stung her eyes. As the beat picked up, he danced with her until she was outright crying and laughing to the point she was sure she must look insane.

The fact that he'd recreate this memory for her even though he hated her music with a passion . . .

He was the best ever.

She laughed as he moved flawlessly around the dance floor with her. "You would give John Travolta a run for his money."

"Yeah and I'm sorry about my clothes. I tried, but I just couldn't bring myself to wear that. Hell, I couldn't do the disco look even when it was popular. I swear I'm allergic to polyester. Thank God for the punk movement. Otherwise I'd have been naked for a decade."

She laughed as she tried to imagine him in a green leisure suit. No, it definitely didn't work.

She much preferred thinking of him naked. But only when they were alone.

"So what would you have worn back in the days when you were human?"

"A bedsheet."

Tory nodded as she thought about it. "See I knew that's what they made chitons out of. Geary said I was crazy, but I always suspected as much."

Ash froze as he realized that she hadn't understood his reference to being a whore. She merely thought he was describing the fabric of his clothes. To her, he was a man. Nothing more and definitely nothing less.

Lifting her up and twirling around with her, he held her close, savoring the way that she never reminded him of his past.

And when he set her down, she was dressed as an Atlantean princess.

Tory gasped at her long, flowing gown. Bright blue, it fell in pleats from a deeper blue underbust bodice that was covered with pearls and sapphires. But what made her face flame bright was the sheer material that barely covered her breasts. Her nipples were plainly visible. "Oh no! Tell me they didn't wear this."

Nodding, he turned her to face a mirror that appeared out of nowhere so that she could see the entire outfit as they swayed together. Gold chains draped from her bare shoulders to her elbows and her hair, which was curled into ringlets, was covered with a gorgeous gold headpiece. Tory stared at herself, adoring the clothes but hating that she was too tall, too skinny and too plain to do them justice.

And as she looked at Ash over her shoulder, still dressed as a punk rocker, she wanted to weep. He was gorgeous and she looked like the booby prize.

"Ash," she said, her voice catching, "can you do one thing for me?"

"Anything, Sota. You name it and it's yours."

"Make me beautiful."

He turned her to face him and he laid a kiss on her lips that set fire to her blood. Pulling back, he smiled down at her. "There you go. You're the most beautiful woman in the world."

Tory spun back to the mirror, dying to see what she looked like.

As she saw herself, she scowled.

She hadn't changed. "Ash!"

"What?" he asked innocently, pulling her back against his front so that he could stare at her in the mirror.

"You didn't do anything."

His gaze met hers and the sincerity in those swirling silver eyes scorched her. "You are the most beautiful woman in the world, Soteria. This is the woman I fell in love with and there's nothing about you I'd ever change."

Leaning back against him, she reached up to touch his cheek. "Really?"

"Absolutely. And I hope that one day, we have a houseful of kids who look just like you."

747

EPILOGUE

Three months later
New Orleans

Ash stood in the doorway, looking out in the church that was teeming with people. For the first time in his immortal life, he was actually scared. He didn't want to mess this up or worse, embarrass or shame her in front of her family. This was Tory's dream wedding and he wanted everything to go off exactly as she wanted it.

Her side of the church was packed to capacity from her family. The only one missing was her grandfather who was waiting to walk her down the aisle.

On his arrival in New Orleans, they'd taken Theo aside and told him the truth about Ash.

At first Theo had refused to believe it, but in the end, as Ash told him every detail about their journey across the Atlantic together when Theo had been a boy and about their chess games in the park over the years since, Theo had had no choice except to accept the truth. Then he'd been thrilled to have Tory marrying the man who'd saved his life.

The rest of her family, with the exception of Geary, who knew the truth about Ash, were told that he was the grandson of the man who'd saved Theo. It was a small lie, but so long as it kept peace and the secret of the world Ash lived in, it was a necessary one.

"You ready, T-Rex?"

Ash nodded at Talon who was one of the groomsmen. Since Tory had eleven bridesmaids, Ash had been grateful for all the Dark-Hunters. Her friend Pam, as the maid of honor, was paired with Ash's best man . . . Savitar. Kim was with Vane, Geary with her husband Arik, Katra with her husband Sin, Danger with Alexion—both of whom were in temporary human bodies. Simi was with Zarek, Justina with Kyrian, Katherine with Styxx and Aimee was there with Dev. Sunshine was with Talon and Tory's cousin Cyn, who bore an uncanny resemblance to Artemis, was with Urian—something that had irritated the woman who hated being stuck with a Greek grooms-man.

For some reason only Tory seemed to get, that amused her and so Ash had accommodated her request to give Cyn the most Greek of all his groomsmen.

Talon vanished as Savitar came forward. "You nervous, Grom?"

Maybe he should be and yet he couldn't wait. He pulled the three-carat canary yellow diamond wedding ring out of his pocket and watched as it flashed in the dim light of the church. The center stone was flanked by smaller white diamonds in a very antique and unique setting—Tory had decided to go with the more traditional ancient custom of having a single wedding ring with a stone—just as they would have done in Ash's lifetime.

It would be beautiful on her.

"Not a bit," he said to Savitar. "But you look rather ill."

"It's all the clothes I'm wearing. Tuxedos make me itch. I told you the third outcome would be grisly. Marriage." He shuddered.

Ash shook his head, especially as he noted the fact that Savitar was wearing sandals. "You're barely one step up from the Australopithecines, aren't you?"

He cocked one condescending brow. "Hey, be respectful when you say that, snot nose. Haven't you seen the commercials? Us cavemen are very sensitive people."

Ash laughed, relieved that for once he wasn't the oldest person here.

They left the room to stand by the altar and wait as the long procession of bridesmaids and groomsmen began.

Jaden and Takeshi sat in the first row with Tabitha, Xirena, Grace and Amanda—the latter two were riding herd on their hyperactive children as well as Kat's daughter.

Ash was actually stunned by the number of current and former Dark-Hunters who were here. His side of the church rivaled Tory's. Of course that was probably more from the shock value of Ash getting married than anything else. Last he'd heard they were betting on the Dark-Hunter.com Web site that he'd get cold feet and bolt.

Still, it was good to see them for whatever reason and their presence here was why they'd held the wedding after dark.

As Simi came down the aisle, she lifted her bouquet to her lips and started nibbling the flowers. Ash shook his head, grateful she didn't pull the barbecue sauce out of her purse and pour it over the gardenias. When she drew near her sister, she mouthed the words, "Good eats. We'll get you one later."

Then Kyrian's daughter Marissa and Geary's daughter Kalliope came down the aisle, sprinkling red and pink rose petals on the floor.

Ash looked at the door as they started playing the wedding march. For the first time, he was actually anxious. *Please don't let her be the one to get cold feet . . .*

Then he saw her.

His breath caught in his throat as Tory came down the aisle not in white but wearing black. She'd explained her choice of color to her family by saying that since white was the traditional color of Greek mourning, she wanted no part of it in her wedding. But the truth was, she knew how much he hated it because of Artemis.

She even carried a bouquet of mavyllos—the sacred black roses that had been created by Ash's mother. The bouquet had been a gift from Apollymi and to receive them was considered the highest honor one Atlantean could give to another.

Ash smiled in pride. But what still amazed him most was that she was willing to stand up before all these people and claim him. He'd even offered to elope with her, but she'd refused.

"*Boy,*" she'd said, angry over the fact he'd even suggested it, "*you are mine and I want the entire world to know it.*" For his wedding present, she'd even tattooed his sun emblem on her shoulder with his name underneath it.

Nothing in the world had ever pleased him more.

Tory almost stumbled as she caught sight of Ash in his tuxedo. His black hair was slicked back into a sophisticated ponytail. And for once his eyes were plainly visible to all. There were no piercings—he'd forgone them by saying that he wanted nothing to embarrass her before her family.

"*You could never embarrass me, Ash,*" she'd told him. "*Besides you are my family now.*" Even so, he'd toned his appearance down.

Theo released her to Ash with a gentle pat on Ash's hand and a kiss on Tory's. Hand in hand, they stood before the Greek priest and took their vows in ancient Greek.

When it was over, Ash pulled her to the back of the church and held her close. He placed a kiss on her bare shoulder where his emblem was plainly visible. "I guess it's too late for you to back out now, huh?"

Tory scoffed at him. "Honey, it was too late for me to back out the first time you opened the door and sauntered into my lecture. I was a goner and didn't even know it."

He laced his hand with hers. "I have no idea what our future will hold and it makes me ill. But I promise you that no matter what, you won't ever regret being with me. I swear it."

She looked up at him. "You know what amazes me? I went searching for Atlantis and found an Atlantean god. How could I ever regret that?"

N*ick stood outside* the garden of Kyrian's house, staring in at Ash's wedding reception. Everyone was laughing and celebrating as Ash and Tory danced to the Bee Gees' "To Love Somebody." Hatred scalded his tongue as he watched

Ash laughing with Tory. And yet the part of him he hated most was glad to see Ash so open and happy. There had always been an air of hopelessness around Ash.

Now that was gone. He only wished he could have been so happy.

"It's not fair, is it?"

He turned his head to see Artemis standing behind him. Dressed all in white, she was unbelievably beautiful. "What are you doing here?"

"The same thing you are. Spying." She let out a long breath as she closed the distance between them. "He turned us both, didn't he?"

Nick frowned at her nonsensical words. "Turned us?"

"You know, missed us up."

Missed? What the—Suddenly, he understood what she was trying to say. "You mean screwed?"

"Yes, he screwed us both."

She had no idea. "And what did he do to you?"

"He abandoned me. He took my daughter and what do I have left? Nothing."

Nick scoffed at her self-pity. "Yeah, well, at least you're not on the Daimons' most wanted list. I swear I haven't had a single moment's peace. And the last thing I heard, Stryker's getting ready to break badass all over us."

She rolled her eyes. "You think Stryker doesn't want me dead? My brother's the one who turned on him. It's a cold world where I live."

"It could be worse. You could be friendless."

She gave him an arch glare. "You think I'm not?"

Nick disregarded her question. She had no idea how miserable his life was. How lonely and heartbreaking. "How can a goddess be friendless?"

"The same way a human can."

Yeah, she was insane. "You have the power to make your life better. I don't."

"That's not true. I've lost my only friend."

Honestly that's how Nick felt. He'd loved Ash like his brother and missed the friendship they'd had. Even though Ash had screwed him over, they had been so incredibly close.

Now, because Stryker could see everything Nick could whenever the demigod chose to look, he was completely isolated from the world he'd known before. No friends. No family.

He was alone and he hated it.

Artemis turned a speculative look toward him. "Would you be my friend, Nicholas? I promise you, you won't regret it."

A *burst of* wind blew through the party, lifting the hem of Tory's dress.

Ash looked up at the sky and frowned as he heard the sound of far-off thunder.

"Is something wrong?" Tory asked.

"There's a storm brewing."

"You mean the weather, right?"

Ash shook his head slowly as his senses tingled. No, there was something coming for them. He could feel it. Dark and deadly, it wanted a piece of him.

"Don't worry, Sota. I'll keep you dry." But even as he said the words, he knew the truth. He wasn't her haven. She was his, and so long as he had her by his side, he could face anything. "Bring the rain," he whispered, "bring the rain."

These are two scenes that I wanted to work into other books, but they really didn't have a place in them. The first one was originally in *Seize the Night*, but the length of the book was such that my editor at the time thought we should cut it, especially since it didn't really relate to the story at hand. Our thinking then was that it might fit into another book, but it never did. So here it is now, in its entirety.

SEIZE THE NIGHT OUT-TAKE

Ash listened quietly as the priest spoke words of comfort outside the tomb in the St. Louis cemetery where Cherise Gautier had been laid to rest. Julian, Grace, Kyrian, Amanda, Tabitha and Valerius stood to his right while Talon, Sunshine and the Peltiers were lined up on his left to pay respect to one of the finest women Ash had ever been privileged to know. He was dressed in the same clothes he'd had on the day he'd first met the woman: a pair of slouchy black pants, an oversized black sweater and a long leather coat. Cherise had taken one look at him and clucked her tongue.

"When was the last time you ate?" she'd asked him.

"An hour ago."

His words hadn't fooled her at all. Convinced he was lying to save his pride, she'd promptly sat him down in a chair and proceeded to make him a plate of Cajun hashbrowns while Nick had tried not to laugh at them.

In the last eleven thousand years, Cherise had been one of the rare people who'd treated Ash like a human being. She hadn't seen him as anything more than a young man who needed a mother's love and a friend.

And he missed her more than anything.

As he stood with the cold wind cutting through him, he could hear his own soul screaming out in rage that he'd caused this. That he had no one to blame for her death but himself. How could one sentence uttered in anger cause so much damage? But then words were the most powerful thing in the universe. Cuts and bruises always healed, but words spoken in anger were most often permanent. They didn't damage the body, they destroyed the spirit.

"I first met Cherise the day her mother bore her," the old priest said to them. "And I was there the evening she brought her own child into this world. Nick was her pride and all of you who knew her know that if you'd ever asked her what her most prized possession was, she would have answered with Nick's name."

Kyrian slid a sideways look at Ash who heard the former Greek general's thoughts. Since Nick's body hadn't been found after the vicious murder of Cherise, the consensus among the New Orleans Dark-Hunters and Squires, both former and current, was that Nick had become a Dark-Hunter himself.

They all knew better than to ask Ash for the truth. The humans who didn't know of their world all assumed that Nick had been another casualty to whatever fate had befallen his mother, while the authorities believed Nick had killed her.

That latter was why Ash knew he couldn't bring Nick back to New Orleans. Not for a long time at least. The police were looking for him and they would convict him in a heartbeat.

Not to mention he didn't really want anyone to know about Nick. At least not until Nick was ready to deal with the world. Right now the man was too hurt and too angry.

Not that Ash blamed him in the slightest.

After the priest finished, Amanda and Tabitha placed the roses they held in their hands at the door of Cherise's tomb while the priest and the Peltiers left.

Amanda paused beside Ash. "We're having a memorial service later for Nick at our house. Just the Dark-Hunters and Squires. We'd like for you to be there."

755

Ash nodded, but refused to meet her eyes. If he did, he was sure she'd know the truth.

He didn't move until he was alone. Sighing, he glanced at the stone monuments around him that made up the cemetery. There were so many people here whom he'd personally known. So many he'd seen live and die.

He could hear the sound of their voices on the wind, remember their faces, their lives.

Just like Cherise, they were now nothing more than memories to haunt him.

"I'm sorry, Cherise," he whispered.

Stepping forward, he created a mavyllo, a sacred black rose that had been created by his mother, and laid it beside the red ones. Unlike the red ones, it would take root here and grow in memory of her.

It was the highest honor his kind could bestow on anyone.

"Don't worry, Cherise. I won't let anything else bad happen to your son . . . I promise."

This scene is the one I'd thought to put in the back of *Dream Chaser*, but again, it didn't really fit. For those who've followed the Dark-Hunter and Dream-Hunter series, you'll recall that in Talon's book, *Night Embrace*, the Charonte escape from Kalosis and vanish. They're all assumed dead.

In *Dream Chaser*, we find out that they did survive. In fact, a large group of them have taken refuge in New Orleans. And for those of you curious, the demons will return in Fang and Aimee's book which will be out summer 2009.

In the meantime, here's the reunion scene between Simi and her brother.

DREAM CHASER OUT-TAKE

"Why we coming to an old stupid club, akri? The Simi wants to shop."

Ash looked hid his smile as she led Simi and Xirena toward the building at the corner of the block. "Well, it's a special club."

"Special how?" Xirena asked irritably. Like Simi, she wanted to shop and eat. "Is there food there?"

Ash nodded. "Pretty sure since the name of it's Club Charonte."

Simi stopped in the middle of the sidewalk. "Did akri buy his Simi a club?"

"No, I didn't."

"Then how did it get named that?"

"You'll see." Ash tugged her gently forward.

The demons picked up their pace as they neared the club that wasn't open for business yet. A screaming pink neon sign flashed above it.

Ash used his powers to unlock the door before he led them inside. The moment he did, Xirena let out an ear-piercing shriek. "Xedrix!" She ran across the room to tackle her brother to the floor.

Simi scowled. "Is that the Simi's Xedrix, akri?"

"Yes, Sim, it's your brother."

Simi bit her lip, but was more cautious as she went toward her siblings. Xedrix was trying to push Xirena off, but the moment he saw Simi, he froze.

"Xiamara?" he breathed. There was no way to mistake Simi since she was the exact image of the mother she'd been named after.

"Rik-rik?"

His human body changed immediately to his demon form as he shot out from under Xirena to embrace the little sister he hadn't seen in centuries. "You're alive!"

Simi wrapped her arms around him and squealed. "Rik-rik! I've missed you so much."

Ash stepped back, his heart pounding at the sight of her happiness. He knew he made the other Charonte demons in the bar nervous, including Xedrix. Since they were in thrall to the Atlantean gods, he technically owned them, and they still had a hard time believing that he wasn't interested in putting them back into chains.

"That was very decent of you."

He turned to find Xedrix's wife, Kerryna behind him. Tiny and blond, she was beautiful. The Dimme demon was also on the run from those who would harm her if they had a chance. But Ash didn't have a problem with demons.

Hell, he owed his sanity to one. And as he watched Simi he was grateful that he hadn't sent her packing when his mother had given her to him.

"Simi's my family. What makes her happy, makes me happy."

"I keep telling Xedrix that you're not like the other gods. He doesn't believe me yet. But I think he will eventually."

Ash offered her a smile. "Thanks. In the meantime, I'm going to wait outside. If Simi realizes I'm gone, tell her not to worry and to take her time."

Kerryna laughed. "Yeah, it's not like we don't have all the time in the world, right?"

"True." He looked down at her belly. She and Xedrix were expecting their own baby. "Congratulations."

"Thank you."

He started away.

"Acheron?"

He paused to look back at her. "Yes?"

"To answer your unasked question; yes, we are deliriously happy. The most beautiful thing about love is that it's blind to who and what we are. One day I hope you find it too."

Ash inclined his head to her before he left. How he wished he could believe that, but he knew better.

Happy endings were for other people. Never for him. But that was okay. He could take pleasure from other people's happiness. And looking back at Simi's, he was thrilled. He could live his life through her and that would always be enough for him.

Do you love fiction with a supernatural twist?

Want the chance to hear news about your favourite authors (and the chance to win free books)?

Keri Arthur
S. G. Browne
P.C. Cast
Christine Feehan
Jacquelyn Frank
Larissa Ione
Darynda Jones
Sherrilyn Kenyon
Jackie Kessler
Jayne Ann Krentz and Jayne Castle
Martin Millar
Kat Richardson
J.R. Ward
David Wellington
Laura Wright

Then visit the Piatkus website and blog
www.piatkus.co.uk | www.piatkusbooks.net

And follow us on Facebook and Twitter
www.facebook.com/piatkusfiction | www.twitter.com/piatkusbooks

piatkus